trouble

NYLA K.

Paperback ISBN: 979-8-9869189-6-9

Cover by Mel D. Designs

Interior Formatting by Andi Jaxon

Proofreading by Nice Girl Naughty Edits

To all the troublemakers out there...

Raise hell, and plenty of eyebrows.
Life is too short to be the good guy ;)

Blurb

From the world of *Push* and *Pull* comes a new emotional, forbidden romance...

My name is Tate Eckhart, and I love my life.

I have a great job, a sick wardrobe. I drive a fancy car and sip scotch old enough to be my *Daddy*. I'm fine with being known as the bad guy, the troublemaker, and the unattached harlot out of all my friends. *Hey, if the Burberry loafer fits, right?*

Money, control... Sex, no strings attached. It's how I've been living since that one night, back in college... When I stepped over a line with one of my closest friends, only to discover the truth. *Love is for suckers.*

Who *cares* if he's abnormally beautiful and built like a Norse god? He ran out of my life after an incident that was very ungodly. But that's all in the past... Or at least, it *was*.

Bumping into each other in the most unexpected of places has to be a coincidence; a humorous joke from the big guy upstairs. Because my old pal is now a *pastor*. And he's married... to a woman.

Doesn't matter. I don't have time for relationships, feelings, or thinking about what could have been...

But when we're alone, it seems like neither of us can practice what we preach. And what we do in secret feels *damningly* good.

Keeping it going is asking for trouble...

But I suppose if I'm already on my knees, I might as well beg for forgiveness.

Foreword

For a long time before writing this book, I could hear Tate Eckhart in my mind, sighing, "Always a side-character, never an MC."

Well, guess what, Trouble??

Message received.

Let me start by saying you **do not** have to have read *Push* or *Pull* to fully enjoy this book. I'm not even classifying it as part of the Love Is Love *series*, because this book is a total spinoff with its own storyline, completely separate from that of *Push/Pull*. I don't want anyone to worry about needing to read in order or anything, because it's not necessary in the slightest.

Just know that this book does take place *post-Push*, if you will, so there are definitely references to some events from there, of which those who have read it will have a deeper understanding and appreciation for. The *Push* characters make appearances and play a sort of pivotal role in the found family vibes of this book, which will be very satisfying to *Push* fans. Also, in this book, there are two scenes from *Pull* (the *Push* continuation novella) that you get to see from Tate's point of view.

Nonetheless, you still don't need to read either of them before reading this book. If anything, it would simply introduce you to Tate as the pot-stirring bachelor he is.

This story is not dark at all. Like *Push*, it's a ***forbidden*** romance with a decent amount of angst for what's technically a fast-burn (*I'm talking first chapter action*). But despite it not being *dark*, it does contains a few subjects that could potentially make some readers uncomfortable. And for that reason, I'm listing the **content warnings on my website here**, or via the QR code below for paperback readers.

Here's the thing... There's a plot twist in this book that *really* should be experienced organically. Now, I know I can't prevent readers from sharing spoilers or looking them up before reading, but as I have with some of my books in the past, I'm going to strongly suggest you don't read or post them, mainly out of respect for readers who don't want to be spoiled.

I *promise* that the plot twist isn't anything triggering. ***Trust me.***

That's all I'll say for now, other than putting myself out there as a story-teller and assuring you that reading this book—*in full*—will be a million times better if you don't know the outcome going in. If you have triggers, the CW's are on my website, but as far as the plot twist goes, *I promise it's best to go in blind.*

Honestly, when it comes to plot twists, this is nowhere near as shocking as I've taken you in the past—*hello, Dash*—though it does have the potential to make you gasp. So with that, I'll just say trust the author and enjoy the ride.

You have my word it'll all work out in the end. Tate and Lance get their HEA, and it's very swoony and beautiful, and *fully* deserved.

So, on that note, prepare for the drama, the secrets, the lies, the filthy, *deliciously* sacrilegious sexy times and deeply yearning love of Tate and his naughty preacher.

Hold onto your butts, kids. It's Trouble's turn to fall.

Foreword

PLAYLIST

Unhold – Sam Smith, Kim Petras
The Edge Of Glory – Lady Gaga
Piece Of Your Heart – MEDUZA, Goodboys
King – Years & Years
Alejandro – Lady Gaga
Ex Lover Syndrome – Jet B
ack Alley Cat
Champagne & Sunshine – PLVTINUM, Tarro
Levels – Avicii
Teenage Dream – Katy Perry
Dancing on My Own – The Regrettes
Pink – Two Feet
Save Your Tears (Remix) – The Weekend, Ariana Grande
7 rings – Ariana Grande
bad guy – Billie Eilish, Justin Bieber
Trouble Is a Friend – Lenka
Sunsetz – Cigarettes After Sex
Love Me Harder – Ariana Grande, The Weekend
Lips of an Angel – Starletta
MONST3R IN A MAS3RATI – Emerald Royce
Hit My Spot – ur pretty
You're All I Want – Cigarettes After Sex
Heat Waves (Slowed) – Glass Animals
Ur Perfect I Hate It – Mickey Valen, Emilia Ali
Take Me to Church – Hozier
Kiss Me More – Doja Cat, SZA
Heavenly – Cigarettes After Sex
Lucky Strike – Troye Sivan
PILLOWTALK – ZAYN
Moonlight – Chase Atlantic
Broken In All The Right Places – Lost Kings, MOD SUN
Daddy Issues (Remix) – The Neighbourhood, Syd
Adore You – Harry Styles
Sunflower – Post Malone, Swae Lee
Falling In Love – Cigarettes After Sex
Vibes – Chase Atlantic
All 4 Nothing (I'm So In Love) – Lauv
God Must Have Spent – Boyce Avenue
Born This Way (Acoustic) – Michelle Treacy
Teenage Dream – MITCH DB, Emilio, Renato S
You Are My Sunshine – Johnny Cash

ix

"Friends love all the time, and kinsfolk are born for times of trouble."
Proverbs 17:17

Prologue
Lance

That night...

Sin's of the father...
Chest heaving, heart leaping, *thwack thwack thwack.* I slam the door shut behind me.

I'm spinning. This haze of confusion, lust, *need* is overpowering; so heavy, I can barely keep my feet moving fast enough to run away.

But I *have* to.

I need to *leave*, because this isn't right.

So bad...

God, what have I done??

Pressure builds inside my skull as I force myself to keep walking. Staggering up the hall and away from that room... The place where I just made a *huge* mistake.

But it didn't feel like one.

In the moment, it was dazzling. A high unlike any I could have prepared for. The single most perfect sensation of bliss I always knew I wanted.

Divinity happening in a small bed in Dalton Residence Hall.

I can still feel him... lingering on me. In my puffy lips, tender skin, and the way my body still tingles from the wicked gratification. I hear his voice in my head, hushed and throaty...

You feel so good, Sunshine...

Squeezing my eyes shut, I shake it away, sniffling and picking up to a hearty jog.

I had to leave. I *have* to.

Because it isn't right, no matter how badly I want it to be.

It's wrong.

Bad. *Sick.*

As much as it's *killing* me inside, this wrenching, awful pain that seems to be growing stronger with each step I take away from where I really want to be, I know I can't turn around. Ever.

This is all my fault.

Don't look back... Lest the sins of the father become your own.

Chapter One
Tate

Now...

Pride.

It's funny, having pride in oneself, like in terms of where I am right now, and what we're celebrating... It's supposed to be a good thing. Gay pride. Lesbian pride. Trans pride.

Bi, Pan, Demi, Omni, Ace... Queer, overall, in all its many shapes, colors and considerations. Non-binary and gender fluid... Truth and acceptance.

Pride is good.

But then, isn't the old saying, *pride cometh before the fall?*

Is that from the Bible? I think it is... I've read the thing, but it was a while ago, and it's hard to wade through what I was actually able to retain. I mean, the book is ninety percent meaningless info dumping and run-on sentences. Not to mention the hypocrisy...

But I digress.

That quote kind of makes sense. Because it's well-known counsel to avoid being overly prideful. No one likes a cocky show-off, right?

I realize, coming from me, this might sound disingenuous. Because I *am* an inherently proud person. I'm proud of myself and what I've become, all on my own.

I made seven figures last year. I drive a Maserati. I've traveled to many exotic places, and I've been fucked in half by some of the hottest dudes you could ever imagine.

Should I be *proud* of that?

It remains to be seen, I suppose, but I've always enjoyed living the way I do. I'm *proud* of the way my life looks from the outside...

Still, I'm not saying it won't be my ultimate downfall.

I guess we'll just have to wait and see.

In this moment, pride is pretty fucking great. Because it's *Pride* the event, as opposed to pride the action. I've been to many Prides all over the world, but coming home for the celebration in Albuquerque is a top fave. Most of my real friends are here. I say *real* in italics because yea, I've known them for a long time, and yes, we're theoretically there for each other. But then how *real* is anyone or anything, anyway?

How real am I?

Sipping away those thoughts with a glass raised to my lips, my eyes scan the crowded room. I like this club—Xquisite. I know a few of the bartenders, and I come here a lot when I'm in town. It's usually always pretty packed on weekends, but because of what specific weekend it is, the place is damn near overflowing with bodies, all scantily clothed, draped in rainbows and sparkles, grinding on each other like they're trying to rub genies out of one another's lamps.

The mood in this room is top-notch. Sex, if *sex* was a mood.

I like that. Sex *is* my favorite thing, after all.

Some might call me a *slut*... But to those people, I would smirk and murmur, *"Jealous?"* And regardless of their response, I would know the answer to my rhetorical question.

Of course they're fucking jealous. Anyone who's not having sex is jealous of those who are, whether they admit it or not. Because sex is the ultimate act of everything we all want.

Freedom, connection, intimacy, pleasure, control... power.

Sex is all of it and then some. And it doesn't hurt that I'm fucking *great* at it.

Finishing off my drink, I clunk the glass down on the bar, peering over my shoulder at the bartender—this dude Nick. Nick winks at me, and I give him a sultry smile.

We've fucked. *Duh.*

Nick and his great dick. Long and thick... uncut. The perfect thing to slurp on when you're bored.

Trouble

Hey, it's better than snacking on empty calories. How do you think I stay in such great shape?

Pulling my phone out of my pocket, like a reflex, I open Grindr first. It's almost hilarious how many people are in my area right now. The sheer volume of available dick is staggering. And I'm not usually someone who has trouble deciding on things, but even *my* head is spinning from all the available cock in my immediate area.

Not that I would need Grindr to find a hook-up. I could just turn to my left—or right—and choose. A quick smirk and a nod toward the bathroom, and I could be bent over, getting exactly what I want in seconds. What I *need*.

But because I'm me, that seems a little too easy. I've always enjoyed a challenge... Maybe we could call *that* my downfall. I'm forever more attracted to the guys I can't have, which becomes a problem I refuse to address.

I'm not opposed to meeting up with the dudes who hit me up on Grindr. In fact, I thoroughly enjoy the interactions. They're always fun, and they always get me off—*well, most of the time*—the way I need it. Still, I know that swinging a dick in any direction right now, in a gay bar at Pride, is only going to get me so far.

Maybe we'll try something else. It's Pride...

I'd like to get on my knees and work for it a little.

Waving off Nick when he gives me the silent nod about another drink, I leave the bar, weaving through muscle, toward the back of the crowded dance floor. I reach the restroom and slink around the corner, not at all surprised to find many guys, doing everything from pissing—which is what you're supposed to do in here—to making out, to bickering and laughing and fixing their faces in the mirror.

My eyes land on an empty stall, and I push my way inside it, closing the door behind me. No lock... *Why am I not surprised?*

I don't have to use the bathroom, but I'm in here, and I still don't really know why. So my instincts take over again, and I lift the phone I'm clutching in front of my face, checking Grindr once more. I think a lot of these guys are actually *in* this bathroom, which has me chuckling.

Trevvie P... In your area. Quite literally. He's within a few feet.

The walls of the rickety stalls shift a bit when someone hastily enters the stall next to mine and whips the door closed. I glance away from my phone screen, raising a brow at the sound of a long sigh. It's almost jittery.

Ragged. Like this person shuffled into the bathroom stall to escape from something, and now he's finally able to breathe.

The wall separating us moves again, as if he just slumped his body against it. It must be a *big* body... Not that a majority of the dudes in this club aren't huge. It's pretty common. There's a ton of beefcake around.

But something has me intrigued by the form on the other side of this wall. The way I can hear him breathing over the noise. The way I feel like I *know* he's hiding in there.

What are you hiding from, mystery man?

Inching closer to the wall, my hand slips my phone into my pocket as I lean in, listening. I can feel him in there, only an inch of hollow metal separating us. I feel him moving, breathing and maybe... running his fingers through his hair.

What does he look like? Is he really as big as it feels like he might be? Tall, built...

Is he tan? Dark or light-skinned? Is his hair dark like mine, or light... or some other color? Does he even have hair?

Tattoos, piercings, big hands, straight teeth, full lips...

The man on the other side of this wall could look *any* type of way, and that brand of enigma has my spine tingling with excitement. My fingers lift tentatively, brushing on the solid surface. I hear him mutter a hushed, "Fuck," and my balls thump.

I need...

My lips part, like maybe I'm going to ask him a question, but I'm not really sure what it would be. Then my eyes fall, and my head tilts, a slow, sly smirk washing over my mouth.

Well, now I know it's meant to be. Kismet.

There's a hole in the bottom of the wall. A glory hole.

Fucking kismet at Pride.

Crouching down, I assess the hole. I can see into his stall through it, making his legs visible. He's wearing shorts, but not the skimpy ones a lot of the guys are wearing today. They're regular men's shorts. In fact, they're khakis. Longer and a bit too baggy. Not something I, or any of my gay friends, would ever be caught dead wearing.

Straight guy shorts.

My gaze narrows as I peer through the hole at the stranger's legs. They're long, from what I can gather with a limited view. Muscular calves dusted in light hair. He's white, but with a bit of a glow to his complexion...

Trouble

Hm.

Suddenly, the stranger starts to move. He's kind of pacing in there, like he's stressed out about something.

Aw. Poor thing. You should never be stressed when there's a glory hole nearby.

"Hey," I whisper through the hole.

The guy freezes.

I chuckle to myself, imagining him looking around like he's wondering where the voice is coming from. I guess he wasn't aware of the glory hole either. Truthfully, I never knew there were glory holes in this bathroom. *Maybe it's a new addition for Pride.*

"Down here," I hum, poking a finger through the hole to get his attention.

"What the..." he starts to say, then trails off. It's a deep brogue. *Sexy...*

So sexy I'm buzzing.

"Need help?" I sink onto the floor, ignoring the fact that I don't really want my expensive clothes touching whatever is down here. I barely even care. I'm thrumming with need already, from the voice and overall secrecy of the stranger in the next stall. Bracing my hands flat on either side of the hole, I inch up closer and whisper, "Show me what you got."

"I... I don't..." the deep voice rumbles. And the hesitance in his tone is killing me even more.

I love it. I hate that I do, but it's something that just turns me the fuck on. It always has...

Straight guys. *Curiosity.*

It's a thread I can't help pulling, no matter how badly I know it'll eventually unravel.

"I'm really good," I hum. "Don't you wanna find out?"

I can feel this random dude debating, warring inside against the tiny flicker of intrigue, which has me wondering what such a hesitant person is doing in a gay club at Pride.

None of the other guys out there would be nervous about this. The second they saw that hole and realized there were waiting lips on the other side, their dicks would be shoved through the wall and into my mouth so fast, it'd be like getting stabbed in the throat.

But not my mystery man. He's weighing his options, wondering if this is something he wants. *God, I fucking love that.*

Maybe he's not straight... Maybe he's just in a relationship, and he's trying to fight the temptation, which isn't exactly a deal breaker for me, either. I know, it's fucked up. I shouldn't fuck around with someone else's man... But my problem is that I've never had enough fucks to give.

We're all adults here. If someone wants to step out on their partner to get with some stranger, who am I to be the morality police?

I probably have less morals than I have fucks.

Watching the legs of the strange man, now standing before the hole, I decide to give him a little push. Leaning down, I urge my mouth up to the hole and stick my tongue out. Just real quick, so he can see that I'm serious.

"Who are you?" I hear the guy whisper, and something about his voice settles into my mind, like it's getting cozy in a warm, safe place.

His voice feels like it's *supposed* to be in my head, and the sensation has me momentarily trembling.

It's just exciting. That's it.

He's a stranger, with a new, special dick.

And I wanna taste it.

"You must be new here," I mumble. "The point of the glory hole is anonymity, stranger."

He huffs a sound. But then his legs inch closer, until all I can see through the hole are khaki shorts. And the outline of an erection pushing against their front material.

I feel him brace himself on the wall. Then I see fingers working on his button and his zipper. Reaching down, I adjust my aching cock in my pants, biting my lip. I'm fidgeting in anticipation as the zipper slides. A large hand slips inside his pants, and pulls out a purely *fantastic* dick.

I can't help but gulp. It's huge—*and not even fully hard yet!* Decorated with veins, leading up to a plump, pink head, shining at the tip.

That is one of the best dicks I've ever seen. Pants down.

I'm too busy ogling it, I'm surprised when the head comes jutting through the hole in the wall. My head moves back, eyes wide as I admire the inches. Only a few of them are on my side now, but I'm sure this means there are at least a few more on his side.

Damn. Damn damn God-fucking-damn. Prepare your jaw.

Licking my lips, I slowly move my face in closer. I part them, tongue waiting as I pop the fat head into my mouth.

Simultaneously, my lashes flutter as I exhale through my nose, while my stranger lets out an audible, shivering grunt.

Then he backs up. Pulling it away from me... My snack.

I gulp down the saliva filling my mouth. "Don't tease me like that." My voice is hushed and desperate. But I don't even care. I want more.

"I-I'm sorry..." the stranger says, sounding like he might want to bolt, though he doesn't.

"Come back," I whisper.

It takes him a few seconds, but he does. The dick sneaks through the hole once more, and this time I don't give him any space for doubt. I wrap my lips around his cock, sliding my tongue along the underside while my mouth advances, right up to the goddamn wall.

Something bangs on his side. Maybe a fist or his palm. He hisses, and I groan on his thick, solid, *oh-so* warm flesh, sucking gently, but hard enough that I get a sweet pulse of salt.

Fuck yea.

My right hand is rubbing viciously on my cock while I suck up and down on the stranger's inches, teasing him with my tongue and giving him my best moves. And I think he likes it. Because only a few seconds later, I feel his hips flicking, feeding me his perfectly delicious dick through the glory hole.

"Fuck fuck fuck..." he growls, and just as I'm working up a nice rhythm, eyes closed and desperately chasing more of his flavor, he yanks it away again.

"Jesus..." I breathe, sucking air into my lungs. My head is spinning, and I'm actually confused by this need for more.

It really is like he's teasing me with it, and I honestly don't think he's doing it on purpose. But whatever he's doing, it's working. I'm *salivating*.

"This is... crazy," I hear him murmur, and it sticks in my mind.

Something about it feels familiar to a part of my thoughts I never let myself access.

"Don't be scared," I rasp, standing up on shaky legs and going for my belt. "We can go tit-for-tat."

"What?" he gasps.

But I ignore him, taking my dick out and aiming it up to the hole. "Here ya go. See? Mine is nice too."

I stuff my cock into the hole, and I feel the stalls rattle again, like maybe he just crashed against the opposite wall. It makes me chuckle.

"What the fuck, man?!" he rumbles.

"Come here, stranger." I smirk to myself, pushing my hips into the wall. "It's waiting for you."

"Are you nuts??" he breathes. "I'm not... I can't just..."

"Just *try* it," I croon, petting the wall with my fingers. "For me?"

"I don't even know you," he grunts.

"Even better." I give the wall a little tap with my knuckles. "Knock knock."

He's quite for a moment before he murmurs, "Who's there?"

"Richard." I grin.

"Richard... who?"

"Richard, but you can call me *Dick*."

He's silent again for only a second before I hear him snort a laugh. It has me beaming.

By myself, in a bathroom stall, with my cock sticking through the wall.

Already the most entertaining Pride I've had in a while.

"You're funny..." he whispers.

Obviously, I can't see anything anymore, but I can feel him getting closer to me. I feel his proximity on my rock-hard, aching flesh, and I'm crumbling inside with the need to be touched.

And much to my own shock, I get my wish.

Fingers brush along my length, and I slump into the wall.

Jesus, something so simple and I'm falling apart.

"More," I plead on a bated breath.

The stranger touches me again, this time curling his fist around my erection. I bite my lip to keep in a sound that's *way* too needy. He strokes me slowly, timidly, and I can tell in this one action that he's definitely never done this before. Or if he has, it's still very new.

But in my mind, I'm choosing to imagine that I'm his first. The fantasy of it gives my balls a heavy thump.

He's touching me like he has no idea what to do, and I can't believe it, but it's really winding me up. My forehead drops to the wall as I hump gently into his hand, completely forgetting where I am.

I wish I was naked. I wish this stupid wall wasn't in the way.

Then the stranger pushes his erection up to mine.

"Fffuck," he sighs, his head fighting to get through the hole, onto my side. But there isn't enough room for both of us. "I shouldn't be doing this..."

"Who gives a fuck about *should*," I whisper, writing against his hand, chasing the feel of his big, thick cock on mine.

But he freezes again. I feel him stop, his fingers slipping away from my cock as he backs up.

He goes quiet, and the sounds of both of our breathing are drowning out the noise of all the people coming and going outside of this little world we've somehow created inside our adjacent bathroom stalls.

Trouble

I'm about to playfully scold him again when he whispers, "You're trouble."

My heart stops.

It falls into my gut so fast, if I weren't holding myself up on this wall, I'd be crashing to my knees.

Those words... That voice.

It's... *so* fucking familiar.

Whipping my dick out of the hole, I quickly stuff it away and open the door to my stall. Just as he's doing the same.

And I'm met with deep chocolate brown eyes, sandy blonde hair, a square jaw, and perfectly pillowed lips. Features I remember all too well, even though I've spent *years* trying to forget them.

I blink up at him over the inches in height that separate us... *I forgot how tall he is.*

"Tate..." he mutters, the quaver in his voice distracting me from the horrified look on his face.

My mouth opens, but I have no words. I can't speak... I'm fucking *stunned*.

It's really him.

It's Lance fucking Hardy.

One of my closest friends from college... who I haven't seen or spoken to in a very long time, for a *very* good reason.

Shaking myself out of it, I croak, "What are you doing here?"

His deer-in-the-headlights look somehow turns even more terrified. He covers his face with his hands. "I... I'm not sure, honestly."

Naturally, the first thing I notice is the ring on his finger.

There are so many questions, *so many* thoughts suddenly rushing up to the forefront of my mind. Things I've been forcing away and stuffing down for years are flood my brain and it's almost too much.

I scoff and shake my head. "I can't believe that was you..."

"Me neither." He rubs his eyes.

Just seeing how visibly distraught he is brings up way too many old wounds; so many memories and feelings, I just can't deal with it.

I need to leave.

"Well... great reunion, Hardy, but I should be going." I push past him to stalk out of the restroom.

He rushes after me, grabbing my arm. *Very different from the last time I saw him.*

"Wait... hang on, T. Let's just... talk for a second."

Whipping around, I glare at him. "Blast from the past, huh?"

He gawks at me, eyes wide and filled with shame. *That's* a look I remember well.

Fuck all of this.

I fold my arms over my chest. "So I see you're still married," I hiss accusingly.

He says nothing, simply looks around, as if anyone here is going to care what we're talking about. It's like we're back in the dorms, fifteen years ago. Not standing in a gay club during Pride.

I mean, seriously. What the fuck is happening right now?!

"What the hell are you *doing* here, Lance?" I ask again, through gritted teeth.

This is all so fucked up. I swore up and down that when he walked—or rather *ran*—out of my life all those years ago, it would be the last time I'd ever see him. And now here he is, standing, *fluttering*, in front of me... Still as huge and beautiful as he always was. Giving me that straight guy act. Only this time, it makes no fucking sense, and is enraging me much more than when we were in college.

Lance's eyes fall to our feet between us. "I... I don't know."

I roll my eyes. "Okay, well, now it's my turn to leave you standing around like an idiot."

I spin away from him again, pausing at the sound of his voice. "Tate... don't go."

Closing my eyes, I push down the hostility. The anger and the vulnerability I've been fighting so hard to overcome since the last time I saw him... I swallow it down and take a breath, forcing a casual, unaffected twist of my lips as I peek at him over my shoulder.

"Good to see you, Hardy. I hope you eventually figure out what you're doing here."

And I leave him standing there, mouth agape, as I rush out of the club.

I leave him in the past, where he belongs, and go to find another bar. One with less... emotional damage.

Chapter Two
Lance

Tate probably thinks I'm lying.

It's always been like this with him. No matter how sincere the words are coming out of my mouth, I always have this feeling creeping around inside me; this sensation of dishonesty. A thick, hearty mass that lodges in my throat until, even though I swear I'm telling the truth, I *feel* like I'm lying to him.

I don't understand it. I never have.

Even back in college, when I considered him one of my best and closest friends. Before what happened between us... *happened*, and I turned my back on him, I still always had this feeling that what I was saying to him wasn't true. And more to the point, I felt like he could *tell*.

It used to stress me out as much as it's stressing me out right now. Because I don't want him to think I'm being dishonest. But maybe I am... and I just don't know it?

Confusing. This is all so confusing.

Welcome back into my life, Tate Eckhart. Apparently, I'm still just as uncertain as I was fifteen years ago.

My eyes follow Tate as he disappears out of the club, and I release a breath it feels like I've been holding since college. Peering left, then right, I take in the sight of half-naked guys dancing all around me. My heart bunches up so tightly in my chest I actually cough.

The thing is, I *wasn't* lying when I told Tate I didn't know what I'm doing here. I don't.

13

Nyla K.

A week ago, I got a Facebook invite from Kennan, a friend of our mutual friend, to attend a Pride party at his place here in ABQ. I haven't seen a lot of these guys since college, but of course the general rule is that we're all still acting like we're actively part of each other's lives through social media. And while I'm sure there are many internal reasons why I decided to accept the invitation this year, for the first time since we all parted ways, I don't think I can deal with acknowledging any of them.

The surface reason is a simple desire to reconnect with people I'd been close to in college. That would be the short answer as to why I, a married straight man, am here at Pride.

Unfortunately, the invite to Kennan's party doesn't quite explain why I'm in a gay club... Or why I went into the bathroom and touched a stranger's dick through a hole in the wall.

I rub my eyes hard enough that there are spots in my vision.

Not a stranger... Tate. It was Tate's dick I was touching... Tate's mouth on me, sucking out little pulses, accompanied by noises from my lips that only he's ever dragged out of me.

"Fuck my life," I mumble to myself, shaking my head at the sheer insanity that is my existence.

The first time I let another guy near my dick, and it just so happens to be the same guy who handled it the last time. The first time... The *only* time.

Tate. *Fucking Tate...*

"You alright there, Daddy?" A guy in skimpy shorts runs a hand up my arm, startling me out of the trance brought on by this bizarre cosmic rigamarole. "Maybe a dance will take your mind off your troubles..."

Trouble...

Trust me, friend. Apparently, nothing *can get me away from this kind of trouble.*

My lips twist into a curt, yet polite smile. "Thanks, but I'm taken." I hold up my left hand to display the wedding band.

The creep kryptonite.

The guy smiles back wistfully. "That dude who just walked out on you?" He lifts a brow.

My mouth opens to correct him, but when my eyes flick back in the direction Tate just went, for some strange reason, I find myself nodding. It's fucked up, but I can't help it.

"Well... your husband's a lucky guy," the man says, then elbows me.

"You should go get him." He begins walking away, turning to holler over the noise, "He's hot."

The guy winks at me, then wanders off. And I'm just standing there like an idiot, feeling out of place and uncomfortable in my own skin. It reminds me so much of the last time I was in a gay club...

Another thing that only happened with Tate.

Dammit, Tate...

The random stranger is right. I need to go after him. At the very least, to apologize and turn this awkward mess of a reunion around.

I always assumed I'd run into Tate again one day, but I didn't want it to be like this.

Okay... Maybe I had no idea how I wanted it to happen, but accidentally fooling around through a hole in a bathroom stall, then watching him storm off definitely wasn't a top contender.

For years, I've felt awful about how I left things with Tate. How I selfishly and immaturely ended our friendship, abruptly, after a stupid, drunken mistake that cost us years of closeness. This could be a sign that I need to make things right.

A rather aggressive way of doing so, but whatever.

Could God be giving me this opportunity? Would God even do such a thing...?

Or is this more like a temptation I'm meant to overcome?

Should I just turn around and go home, back to my wife, to the life I've been building for years; a stoic carpenter, constructing walls around myself to keep the memories out?

My chest tightens, and I blink hard. This *has* to mean something. And regardless of all the rest of the bullshit, I need to do the right thing and apologize to my friend, whom I wronged.

Stalking toward the door, I slink in between the mass of bodies dancing and celebrating, exiting the club into a wall of even hotter, even stickier air. June in ABQ is the summer you'd expect. Sun beating down, sizzling everything. And the sheer crowdedness of the streets during the city's annual Pride parade celebration isn't helping to cool things off at all.

What it *is* doing, however, is burying me in the midst of experiences I've never actively sought out before, for *myself*.

I've had gay friends all my life, and it's never something I gave a second thought to. I interact with people based on who they are inside, not their sexuality, skin color, or factors like that. And it's this sort of perpetual love and acceptance that makes me one of the more celebrated, and sometimes controversial, pastors in our area.

Yes, that's right. I'm a man of God...

Who just had his dick inside the mouth of another man.

Putting the blurriness of my current state aside, I trudge around the corner, face flinging about in search of Tate. I'm not sure if he's going to another bar, or if he's going to Kennan's party, but I suppose the safest bet would just be to go straight to Ken's house and wait for him to potentially show up, rather than searching the streets like a manic weirdo.

While I'm walking, my mind begins to wander, dazzled by where I am. I didn't necessarily come here to invite people to our church, though I think maybe next year I should. Church—and religion as a whole—gets a bad rep within the queer community, and I don't blame them. A majority of hate for LGBTQ+ people seems to stem from confused heretics and Bible thumpers. Truthfully, it couldn't be more misguided.

I've been spiritual all my life, and I've never once found that God *hates queers*. In fact, He doesn't hate anyone, not even sinners. Of course, there's a lot of *man and woman* jargon in the Bible, but that's just because it was written by straight men, a very long time ago. Humanity has always been made to grow, adapt, evolve. To assume that God *hates gay people* just because of a few wayward words in the Bible seems beyond ridiculous. But unfortunately, a lot of people interpret it that way, which is why I've made a point to correct that way of thinking in my church.

I became a pastor at the South Valley Pentecostal Church four years ago, following in my father's footsteps. I grew up in the church, but my parents raised my sister and me openly spiritual, more or less. We've always believed more in having faith than the strict rigidity of other organized religions. Still, when I took over as the pastor at South Valley, I chose to bring on some subtle changes.

For the most part, our congregation has been welcoming of the modern inclusions. Some haven't, but all I can do is respect their choices and pray for their minds to open up a little.

But regardless of how many gay and lesbian couples we have in our church—so far, only two—the rules of any faith in God are still always pretty strict on one thing specifically... Adultery.

And based on what happened a few minutes ago, my internal guilt-o-meter is moving into the red.

Shelving those musings for now, I continue up the sidewalk in the direction of Kennan's house, past all the lively people, emblazoning all the important things Pride represents, like love, freedom, equality, Stonewall... how far we've come versus how far we still need to go.

Ken didn't go to Arizona State with the rest of us, but our mutual friend, Lou, did, and I think Lou is technically the one who invited me today. He invites me every year, I'm assuming because he just invites everyone on his friends list, or at least everyone from our old circle. I haven't seen most of these guys since college. Some of them stayed in Arizona after school, some moved to other places. And then some of us moved to New Mexico. Like me, Lou... and Tate, apparently. But to be fair, Tate is from here.

And me? Well, I moved here because I met and fell in love with a girl from ABQ my senior year of college. Desiree.

We moved to South Valley and got married a year after graduation, and since then, we've built a life together. A life that very much *appears* perfect...

My spiraling comes to a quick halt when I spot Tate, coming out of a bar across the street. My stomach twists, and I pick up my pace, rushing to try to catch up with him. But then two guys exit the bar behind him, sticking close, like they're all together. Tate is talking to them over his shoulder while walking, as if he's leading them somewhere...

In the direction of Kennan's party, it would appear.

Slowing down, I continue to walk in the same direction while watching them. The guys look kind of familiar, but I can't quite place where I might have seen them. They're not people from our old circle of friends.

One of them looks to be about our age—mid-thirties—with light hair like mine. Tall, and built. And the other guy appears slightly younger, with dark hair. He's holding the hand of the other guy, leaning into his side and smiling, while the older blonde scowls at Tate. Even from afar, I can tell he's not thrilled to be in Tate's presence. But still, he's following him. *I wonder why.*

I walk behind them for another block, around a corner, and sure enough, they head right inside the address that I have for Kennan's house. Pulling in a deep breath, I follow them, keeping enough of a distance, because I'm not sure how this will shake out, and I'm highly nervous.

I don't know how Tate will react to me following him to the party, especially now that he's apparently brought friends. I can only hope they're not his... *dates* or something.

The thing about being alive in the twenty-first century is that whether or not someone remains in your life doesn't prevent you from keeping tabs on them. Social media allows us to stay up to date on what people are doing, even if you haven't spoken to them in years. Which is exactly why I know the basics of what Tate's been up to since college.

I wouldn't say I *cyber-stalk* him or anything. We're actually not even friends on Facebook, so as far as that goes, I can only see so much. But over the years, I have to admit I've peeped his Instagram account a few times, and that's how I found out he's a very successful investment banker... And much to my internal chagrin, an unapologetic canoodler of many, *many* different men.

I know it's none of my business. I lost the right to care what Tate does with his free time when I abruptly ended our friendship junior year of college. Still, I've found that whether I want to or not, I can't seem to stop myself from occasionally playing the Insta-creep game, checking up on him, and *hating* the way witnessing his open sexual escapades feels in my chest.

I'm not sure what it means that I'm so invested in what Tate's been doing—and who he's been doing it *with*—over the years since we stopped talking, but honestly, my concern worries me. It feels awfully similar to the way I started fussing over him in college; an uncontrollable urge that ultimately led to me rushing out of his dorm room in the middle of the night with swollen lips and hickeys on my chest.

Gulping, I knock on Kennan's front door, though Tate had just walked right in. Naturally, no one answers, so after several seconds of shifting and feeling foolish, I do the same. There are a few people inside the house, but it sounds like most of the party is happening out back. I follow the noise, my hands shaking at the idea that I might turn a corner and bump right into a glaring Tate again.

"Holy crap! You made it!" a familiar voice calls out, and I peer in its direction. It's Lou, and he's trotting over to me with his arms open.

Forcing a smile still weighted by angst, I return the hug Lou's giving me while subtly peeking over his head for any sign of other former college friends.

The advantages of being taller than most people. Good views.

Lou pats me hard on back, then pulls away. "I can't believe you actually showed! It's been way too long."

"I know..." I sigh. "How have you been, Lou?"

"Great," he answers, his usual eager smile now framed by a few more age-lines, though he still has that same auburn hair buzzed short like in college. "Beckie starts kindergarten this fall, and Josh made the soccer team. Good thing he got Kara's athletic skills."

Trouble

I puff a chuckle as he pulls out his phone and starts showing me pictures of his kids. To which I give him the obligatory *aww*s and *they're growing so fast*s.

"How are you doing? And hey, how's Des?" he asks, sounding genuinely interested.

Lou's a great guy. Kind and perpetually upbeat.

"She's good." I nod, muscles tightening. I hate that it happens, but I can't stop it. "Still running her folks' flower shop."

"That's great." Lou glances around. "You've met Kennan before, right?"

"Maybe once or twice."

"Well, he's around here somewhere. Pretty much everyone is out back. And just a heads up, it's like half-naked dude soup." Lou throws his head back in laughter, which has me gulping down unease, struggling to smile awkwardly. "We're probably the only straight guys here!" He jabs me with his elbow, and I wince.

"I... I don't mind," I mumble while Lou drags me through the apartment, toward the door to the back patio.

"Shit, you know who just showed up, actually?" Lou gasps, and my stomach bunches. "Tate Eckhart! I haven't seen him since graduation."

Saying a quiet prayer for strength, I meander out onto the deck with Lou, overlooking the rest of the party happening beyond the veranda. It's quite the setup. This place is huge and super nice. Having this kind of outdoor space in the city is rare. *Kennan must be doing well for himself.*

There are lights and rainbow decorations strung up everywhere, grills going, tables of food and a bar area with bottles of liquor and coolers. Music is blaring out Lady Gaga, guys are dancing and laughing. And *yes*, there are very few females. While I'm looking for girls like it's a *Where's Waldo* book, my eyes land on the dark hair and immaculate jawline of my bathroom buddy from earlier...

My former best friend.

Tate's talking to Kennan, who's showing the guys Tate brought over to the food. And I'm just shivering in place like it isn't almost ninety degrees out.

This was a bad idea. I don't know if I can face him again after what happened through that hole...

The two guys split off, leaving Tate and Kennan alone. More guys are coming up to them, talking to Tate. He's Mr. Popularity at this party, and it doesn't surprise me. He's always had a lot of friends.

19

But seeing him in this atmosphere, talking to these muscular dudes giving him obviously flirtatious looks, I can't help uncomfortably wondering if they're really just his *friends*, or if he knows them more intimately.

Chewing on my lower lip, I'm still sort of lingering, all of my insecurities bubbling to the surface as Lou tugs my arm, bringing us down the steps.

"Tate!" he calls out, yanking me in Tate's direction. My palms are instantly clammy, and I feel a noticeable flush crawling up my neck. "Look who I found!"

Tate's face turns, and his casual smirk falls right off his mouth.

Lou doesn't release his grip until we're standing right in front of Tate, and the tension is so instantly thick, it's like an extra fifty degrees of humidity was just dumped into the air around us.

But Lou is oblivious to it. "How long has it been?" he chirps. "Thirteen years??"

"*Fifteen*," Tate grumbles, dark irises set on mine.

We used to joke about how we have the exact same color eyes. Tate would say mine were *copying* his, and we'd both laugh about it.

I miss that. I would take the friendly teasing and laughter in a heartbeat over the hostility he's now shooting me through those similar dark brown eyes.

Tate peeks at Lou, then back up to me, cocking his head. "I'm surprised you're here."

"Why's that?" I ask him, quietly, hoping my tone isn't giving away all the hidden stuff between us.

"I didn't know pastors came to gay parties." His gaze narrows, lips curved into one of his smirks that I'm sure everyone else would see as friendly or playful.

But I know him better than that. This one in particular has a bite.

My mind scoots around his accusatory tone, though, and focuses on his words. If he knows I'm working at the church, that must mean he's been keeping tabs on me as well...

Interesting.

"*I* do." I shrug. "And... maybe more should."

Tate blinks at me, giving me that look again; the one that makes me feel like I'm withholding information.

"They totally should!" Lou cheers, sipping his beer. "So Tate, I hear you're almost as rich as Kennan now," he teases, grinning.

20

Trouble

Tate's smirk grows a little less strained. "Please. I'm *way* richer than that queen."

Lou laughs, and my lips twist into a tiny grin. But when Tate's eyes land on my face once more, it slips away.

"How's your wife?" he asks me, the question alone popping my pulse, not to mention the knowing way he's glaring at me.

"She's, um... good." I clear my throat.

He purses his lips. "Mhm..."

Someone shouts Lou's name, and he taps me on the shoulder. "Be right back."

He staggers away, leaving Tate and me just standing here, staring at each other, radiating all kinds of awkwardness.

This is already not going well.

"Look, Tate, I wanted to apolog—"

"I need a drink," he cuts me off, turning and darting away.

Naturally, I follow him. Something I tend to do without even noticing. Tate grabs a cup off the table and pours brown liquor into it. Tilting his chin upward, he raises a brow at me, like he already knew I followed him without having to check first.

"Are pastors allowed to drink?" he asks in an almost scoffing tone.

"Yea, but I don't really... drink much," I tell him.

He turns to face me fully, sipping from his cup. "You've changed a lot."

My head slants. "Not a *lot*..."

"Yea. A lot." He keeps the cup up by his lips, eyes locked on my face over the rim.

I can't help but shift on my feet. It feels like he's assessing me. *Studying* me, and all the little differences between the man standing before him and the kid he used to watch movies and play games with.

"You've changed too," I murmur.

"No, I haven't," he retorts. "I'm still exactly the same wild mother-fucker I've always been. Except *now*, I'm not ditching classes with you to smoke weed and play frisbee. I wear suits and drive a Maserati, and I fuck *a lot*. I'm an adult who lives exactly the way he wants to live." He pauses to lean in. "You should try it sometime."

My heart feels like it's being squeezed behind my ribcage. "What makes you think I don't live the way I want to?"

He laughs dryly. "Do I need to remind you of the glory hole?"

Heat creeps up to my cheeks. "No, but—"

"Lance, listen. You and I both know the reason we stopped talking," he

21

goes on again, talking over me. "Now, if that's something you want to keep ignoring forever, that's your prerogative. But I can't waste my time fawning over people who don't know who they are, or what they want. It's a habit I thought I'd broken..." His eyes flick left for a second. "But I guess I need to work at it a little harder."

My forehead lines. "What does that even mean?"

"Nothing. Never mind." Tate shakes his head. "It's been great catching up, but I'm gonna go mingle. And you should too." He arches a brow at me. "It's what you came here for, right?"

"I came here to see old friends," I tell him honestly, projecting over the tremor that wants to shake my voice. "I'm being serious, Tate. I was hoping you'd be here so I could tell you..."

"Oh God..." he sighs petulantly, but I ignore him.

"So I could *tell you* how sorry I am. About how we left things..."

"It was a long time ago, Hardy," he huffs. "It's fine to leave things in the past."

I know I shouldn't say this... There are so many reasons why I should just keep my mouth shut right now. But I *can't.*

The words come up like projectile vomit; like a symptom of standing so close to him again and looking at his face.

"But I never stopped thinking about it," I whisper.

Tate's eyes round. He blinks, and I witness his jaw clenching.

My lashes flutter, and I shake my head. "I mean, our friendship... And how I treated you. How I... disappeared."

A flicker of something hurt-adjacent flashes in his eyes, something I've seen once before, and it stabs me in the chest. But he covers it up quickly and rolls his eyes, turning away from me.

"Don't worry," he grunts. "I'm over it."

Before I can say anything else, Tate storms away—*again*—leaving me standing alone with my heart thumping...

More confused than ever.

Chapter Three

Tate

15 years ago...

"**H**ell freaking yea!"

Chuckling, my eyes shift. "I take it from your celebratory tone that you passed?"

He's not even paying attention to me. Just shimmying around in the hallway in front of the board containing our midterm grades.

I won't say I don't get it. The urge to dance myself is pretty strong.

Econ305 is one of the hardest classes I've taken in my three years here at Arizona State, though at this juncture in my college career, none of my classes are *easy*. Still, I feel like I've done nothing but study for the Econ midterm, and then stress over grades being posted, for the last six weeks.

Seeing that 93 next to my name is immensely satisfying.

My friend, Justin, is doing the cabbage patch, and I'm laughing at him, when my phone buzzes in my pocket. Amusement falls away, because I think I know who it is, and I've been avoiding her calls for a few weeks. But when I pull out my phone, mild relief washes over at the sight of my best friend's name instead.

"Are you watching me??" I answer the phone with a grin.

"That shirt looks great on you," Jake teases, and I snort. "No, but seriously... how'd you do??"

"Ninety-three, kid!" I tell him excitedly, and he cheers in my ear. "Top ten percent of the class."

"Not that your head needs to get any bigger, but I'm proud of you, Trouble."

I can hear Jake's smile in his tone, and it makes me all warm everywhere. It feels good to be recognized for my hard work... Impressing people, and such. I guess I enjoy making them *proud*, which is something I really only get from my friends. And maybe my mom...

When I actually return her calls.

"How about you?" I ask Jake while waving to Justin, mouthing that I'll catch him later. "You ace that test about circuits or whatever the hell stuff I barely understood when you were telling me about it?"

Jake laughs. "I passed, that's all that matters. I mean, it's a trade school. As long as I show up and don't electrocute myself, I'll get a degree."

I shake my head while walking the halls. Jacob Lockwood is my best friend in the world, and he has been since we were kids, which is why it sucks that we're currently going to school in different states. He stayed behind in New Mexico, where he's learning to become an electrician, while I decided to pop on over to Arizona and go to business school.

I've never been one for working with my hands. My mind is my best asset, and at this point, I only have another year and a half before I graduate and put my love of numbers to good use.

"Hey, you're learning a trade that'll land you a sweet job," I tell him, striding out of the building in the direction of the quad. "Electricians make bank."

"Mhm. And if not, my best friend can always support me," he jokes. "Since he's gonna be super rich and all."

I roll my eyes, grinning. *That's the goal, anyway.*

"I'm just glad midterms are over and I can finally breathe again," I sigh. "These past few weeks have been hectic. I need to blow off some steam..."

"Is that... a euphemism?" Jake grunts, and I cackle.

Okay, so... here's the thing.

I'm gay. One might even say, I'm gay... *as fuck.*

But I've really only just started coming into my own, properly exploring my sexuality and all that.

Growing up in our small town in New Mexico, I was one of probably three gay kids. I say *probably* because only one of them was actually *out*, and the other—this kid, Bobby Turner—was a football player I used to make out with on occasion. He was actually my first kiss; my first real *anything*, as far as messing around with boys was concerned. But it was highly impor-tant to him that everything we did remained on the *downlow*.

Trouble

Yea. It was that *kinda thing.*

I've known I was gay since puberty, but all of my best friends back home are straight. So while I never necessarily felt like I needed to *hide* my sexuality, I also wasn't exactly itching to come out. Until senior year of high school, when I finally told my friends, and my mom, that I like dudes.

They were all fine with it. My friends have always been super supportive, even if they don't really understand the *gay thing* much. Still, I have to appreciate them for loving me no matter what. It could definitely be a lot worse.

The problem was that being the only gay kid in a sea of straights felt a bit isolating. I acted out a lot as a youth, for many reasons, the main one being that I always knew I was different from all my friends. I felt like if I made a name for myself, as a rambunctious troublemaker, then maybe they wouldn't feel inclined to see me as a stereotypical queer boy when I eventually came out.

It was a whole thing. And quite possibly the reason I decided to attend college out of state. I wanted to meet new people, experience new things...

Like dick.

That's not to say I've been slutting my way around the ASU campus, because that's not entirely factual. I've only just *finally* become comfortable enough with my sexuality to date guys openly. Not many... Just a few, here and there. School is still really important to me, so I tend to focus on that more than anything. But I did lose my virginity last year... So, that was cool.

Alright, it was more than cool. It fucking *rocked*. But the guy I lost it to is a notorious manwhore, so it didn't go any further than that one instance, despite my shameful attempts at getting him back inside me, following the v-card punch.

I'm still learning how to play it cool with guys, okay?? This shit doesn't happen overnight.

"I mean, yea. I'd love to celebrate the end of midterms by getting some great dick," I sigh to Jake over the phone. "But so many of the dudes here... aren't my type."

"You're just being picky—"

"They're all bottoms," I cut him off pointedly.

He pauses for a moment, before murmuring, "There's no way that's true..."

"It is, I swear! ASU is lousy with bottoms." I pout. "I feel so unoriginal."

Now it's Jake's turn to laugh. "Are you sure you're not just hung up on someone you can't have...?"

The pout turns to a scowl as my pace slows. "I don't like what you're insinuating."

He chuckles, then sighs. "Look, I'm not gonna come down on you for doing that thing we all know you do, where you chase unavailable straight guys..."

"Oh, good. I appreciate that," I mutter, sarcastically.

"Maybe you should try venturing off campus," he goes on making his point. *I swear to God, the dude just loves giving advice, whether you ask for it or not.* "You said you've been meaning to go to that club..."

Pursing my lips, I consider his words. Yes, there is a pretty hot gay club in town that people are always talking about. And *yes*, I have managed to secure a fool-proof fake ID.

Maybe Jake is right... Maybe I'm only getting so far here because I'm always surrounded by the same people. Branching out a bit could be just what I need to clear my head.

Get some *perspective*... in the form of a big, thick, *juicy*—

"Lance," I mumble, eyes widening as they lock on the guy jaunting from across the quad, right in my direction.

"Okay, I think that's the *opposite* of what I was just saying..." Jake mutters.

"No, he's here. He's walking over." Can't miss the sudden breathiness in my voice. Or the fact that my hands are miraculously sweating out of nowhere. "I gotta go. I'll talk to you later."

"Tate..." Jake says my name in an admonishing tone I'm quite familiar with.

"*Jacob*," I mimic his voice, smiling and waving back when Lance starts waving at me. "I'm good, don't worry. I'll text you."

"Go out and meet *new* people! Stop pining—"

"God, will you just shut up??" I hiss into the phone. "*Love you*, Beavis!"

Jake sighs in my ear. "Love you too, Butthead. Call your mom!"

Grumbling, I hang up on my mother hen of a best friend, tucking my phone away as the tall, gorgeous drink of water strides up to me, grinning.

"Hey," Lance huffs, like he's out of breath.

Man, he really just ran right over here...

Because he's excited to see me!

Okay, stop.

"Sup?" I croak, then cringe at how stupid I sound.

Trouble

"Not much. Just coming back from bio lab," Lance says casually. The sparkle in his brown eyes, and the way the sun reflects off his halo of messy blonde hair, prompt a tightness inside my chest; a reaction I worry is specific to him. "How'd you do on the Econ midterm?"

"Crushed it." I grin, and he laughs like he's happy for me.

So, so happy... for me.

"T! That's awesome!" Lance cheers, stepping forward.

I'm just fluttering, breathlessly waiting for him to wrap those huge arms around me and pull my body in close to his. I'm fucking *shivering* for it.

Of course, he doesn't do that. He shoots his hand out and grabs mine, in one of those straight guy high-five, half-hug things.

Ugh. He's painfully hetero. It's not fair.

Lance backs up, but our fingers stay entwined for a few extra Mississippis, the connection of our mingling flesh causing me to bite my lip.

I know what you're thinking. The same thing my best friend was accusing me of not two minutes ago. And *fine... you're both totally right.*

I am very much hung up on my good pal, Lance Hardy.

But it's not my fault. It'd be impossible *not* to swoon over him night and day. *I mean, look at him!*

He's so tall, with the body of some kind of professional athlete, though the only sports he plays are things like volleyball and frisbee... Purely recreational. Silky golden hair all strewn about and hanging in his eyes—*which are almost the exact same bronzy shade of brown as mine, I might add.* His sharp jawline and pillowy lips, stunning Colgate smile... Broad shoulders, long, sculpted arms, big hands... lifting and raking the honey-colored strands away from his face.

I'm telling you. This man is *beyond* beautiful. He looks like he was made in a lab.

For the specific purpose of driving his needy gay friend completely insane.

Lance and I met freshman year. Your standard college meeting story... We were at a party. Some of his friends knew some of my friends, so we all merged into one group. Of course, I noticed Lance right away, because how could you not? And honestly, at first, I assumed he was your typical frat bro, since he definitely looks like one.

But once we started talking more, I learned that he's actually super smart. Interested in history and environmental studies—two things I've never excelled in. But Lance grew up in a religious household—his dad is a pastor. Pretty much the opposite of me and my mom, and all of my friends.

Still, despite our many differences, with his shy quietness being initially startled by my sarcastic sense of humor and mischievous brand of tomfoolery, we somehow clicked. And over the years, we've actually become quite close. Close enough that I consider him one of my best friends here at school.

Someone I can confide in, about most things, so long as they don't involve how unbearably fucking *gorgeous* I find him to be, and how I'd love nothing more than for him to ruin me with his giant body. *Call me crazy, but admitting something like that might muddy our friendship just a tad.*

Naturally, because the universe hates me, Lance is straight. He doesn't date or hook up that often, since he's an introvert who doesn't seem to register how fuckhot he is, which saves me from having to swallow down gallons of jealousy on the regular.

Still, it does happen on occasion. And I guess it's fine, since I've been casually hooking up myself, here and there. The problem is that I haven't connected with anyone the way I have with Lance; on a level that isn't strictly physical.

Not that I'm looking for a boyfriend or anything. I just think it might be cool to have both... the toe-curling orgasms *and* the stomach butterflies. I can't help wishing my friend was open to some bisexual experimentation, because I just *know* it would be pure fire. And then, instead of returning from my dirty, sweaty hook-ups to hang out with Lance, we'd already be together. *It would be the perfect setup.*

Nevertheless, I know better than to fixate on it. Lance is my friend, and that's all he'll ever be. I have to be fine with it.

The fact that he thoroughly enjoys fussing over me like a protective mama bear is just an added bonus.

"So... where are you off to now?" I ask him, clearing my throat to expel any notes in my voice that could betray my forced nonchalance.

"I was gonna grab something to eat, then chill for a bit," Lance replies blithely. "You going to Justin's party tonight?"

"Actually, uh..." I blink up at him, trying to remember everything I was just thinking before he walked over here and scrambled my brain. "I was thinking of going out."

His forehead lines. "Out?" I nod hesitantly. "Where?"

"There's this club I've been wanting to check out," I tell him. "Christian goes there all the time. He loves it."

The sight of his Adam's apple bobbing in his throat distracts me enough that I almost miss his next question.

"Christian... So it's a gay club, then?" His eyebrow arches. I nod again.

Christian is an acquaintance. I wouldn't call him a *friend*, since the only time we hang out is when we're both drunk and in the mood to suck each other off. He's a bit wild, and like most of the snooty queens at this school, he feels that college parties are *beneath him*.

Christian is also the one who got me my fake ID, and he's assured me many times that getting into Element—the club he goes to every Friday night, like clockwork—will be a sure thing.

I tilt my head at Lance. "Well, that's how being gay works... If you don't show up to a certain number of functions annually, they revoke your membership."

He chuckles, and I grin, chomping on my bottom lip to keep it under control.

"Like Scientology?" He smirks.

I laugh. "Exactly."

"Okay, that's cool." His eyes jump around for a moment. "We'll miss you at Justin's..."

God, what kind of hellish fork in the road is this??

I *really* want to go to the club; to be around other gays, drinking and dancing, and rubbing our dicks together. But then I also want to stay here on campus with my friends... because that's where Lance is.

And he clearly *really* wants me to go to Justin's...

Is it just me, or is he pouting right now??

"You'll survive one night without me," I tease. "Hey, maybe Bree will stop by. You two can feel each other up some more." He huffs, shaking his head while I nod. "Walk this way with me?"

I don't have to wait for a response. I simply start walking away, and Lance follows. It's been this way since I've known him. Lance is like a sweet, loyal puppy dog. I wish it meant something more, but I really think he just prefers to befriend more outgoing people who will order him around so he doesn't have to think.

Striding toward my dorm side by side, there's some tension in the air. I'm almost positive it's all coming from me; a symptom of trying to act like I don't despise every lucky bitch who gets to fool around with my good buddy Lance Hardy. And because I'm not a fan of uncomfortable silences, I start babbling nonsense.

"I think I figured out where I fucked up on my statistical analysis test," I mumble. "There was this whole section about analyzing market trends... And I remembered that the day we learned about that stuff,

Tucker Hilson was watching porn on his phone in class. I swear to God... *Porn.* Obviously, the sound wasn't on or anything... But he sits right next to me, and I could *see* people fucking on his phone screen. And it was crazy, because literally that morning, I'd heard a rumor about Tucker's sister doing OnlyFans. I'm not sure if she actually does, but then I couldn't stop wondering if he was watching his own sister getting fucked. I mean, like... there's no way that's a coincidence, right?! Anyway, then Professor Imani said *aggressive growth*, and I almost fell out of my—"

"Tate, I just had a thought," Lance interrupts my story that I don't think he was even listening to, turning wide eyes on me. "Maybe I could come with you. To the club tonight."

I nearly trip over my own feet.

Okay, I must have misheard that.

"I'm sorry... what?" I peek at him.

"I've never been to a gay club before..." He shrugs.

"No... I'm sure you haven't." The bewilderment in my gaze is palpable.

"Do you need to be gay... to get in?" His brows furrow.

It takes me a few generous seconds of reeling before I answer. "I mean... I guess not. It's not like they make you kiss a man at the door just to be sure..."

"Right," Lance chuckles. "I think it might be fun... to go with you. For like... support." The look on my face must be giving away how confused I am by this turn of events, because his eager little smile falls off and he seems suddenly crestfallen. "Unless you don't want me tagging along."

"No, no, it's not that," I murmur. "It's just... well..." He's really staring at me, giving me the puppy dog eyes that have me squirming. "Are you sure it won't be weird for you? Since, ya know... you're not gay...?"

Jesus, why am I sweating??

"Tate, you're one of my closest friends," he says sincerely. "I always have fun with you, no matter what we're doing."

I nod, still puzzled by the fact that he *actually* wants to come to a gay club with me. "Alright... but you realize there'll be shirtless dudes grinding all over each other, making out... et cetera?"

Lance purses his lips. "I'm a little offended that you apparently think I'm some pearl-clutching homophobe who can't handle being around guys kissing."

"Of course I don't think that..."

I just didn't know you actively wanted *to be around it.*

Trouble

"Come on, T," he sighs. "If I go to Justin's, it'll be the same old thing. Flat beer, Post Malone, and flip-cup."

"As opposed to vodka sodas, Gaga, and twerking," I snort, and he grins.

"*And* without you there, it's a guaranteed snooze fest."

I'm ninety percent sure he's cajoling me right now, but whatever. It's true.

"I *am* the life of most parties..." I hum, considering it.

Could I really bring my straight friend to a gay club with me? The guy I crush on in secret...

I won't be able to go full-skank if he's around. That's a fact.

But this is *Lance* we're talking about. I love spending time with him. He's awesome, and pretty much one of my favorite humans. I'm sure it won't be weird...

It's not like he'd judge me or anything. Plus, we've both seen each other flirting with people before, and it's never been a big deal. Which just goes to show how hopeless it is for me to be lusting after him in the first place.

The unfortunate truth of the matter is that we're just friends, and we'll never be anything more. But at least I have a straight friend who's taking an interest in my lifestyle and being supportive of it. *What more could you ask for?*

"Look, if you think having me there will cramp your style, I get it," he says. "You can tell me to fuck off, T. We all know you're not afraid to do it."

I huff, and he shows me an eager smile. "Alright, Hardy. It's your funeral..."

My first trip to a gay club, and I'm bringing a breeder.

Starting out strong, Eckhart.

Lance's face lights up in obvious thrill. But then his forehead creases again. "Wait, not my *actual* funeral...?" I smirk at him. "Tate??"

Chuckling, I roll my eyes, slapping him on the arm. "You'll be fine." My gaze slides down his frame, and I purse my lips. "As long as you don't wear those." I point to his shorts.

"Pants??" he gasps.

"Those are some fabric shy of *pants*, friend." I give him a look. "And yet somehow too long to be classified as *shorts*."

He laughs, shaking his head. "Okay, fine. I'll wear the gayest clothes I own. Happy?"

My lips form a patronizing pout. *That's sweet. He dresses like a Mormon, but he's hot enough that it doesn't matter.*

Sauntering away, I wink over my shoulder. "Just remember... if you're not in mesh and glitter, you're doing it wrong."

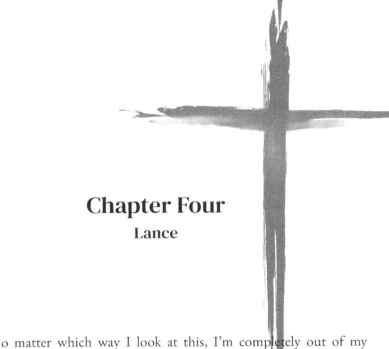

Chapter Four
Lance

No matter which way I look at this, I'm completely out of my element.
Stepping out of the Uber, my eyes slide up to the awning above the club.

Element. That's funny.

Thankfully, human emotions can be easily hidden behind a fake smile, because I'd prefer not to let the line of people waiting to get in, or my friend, Tate, who's smiling animatedly and waltzing over with confidence, see how much anxiety and doubt I'm currently experiencing.

I still don't really know why I thought this would be a good idea. I've been going over the decision for several hours, since I left him and went back to my own dorm, where I paced for way too long, showered, and took an even longer amount of time getting dressed. All the while, I was contemplating what kind of maniac I must be, to be willing to put myself into a situation that will undoubtedly make me uncomfortable on many visceral levels.

But all the neurotic obsessing just led me back to the same place. The place my thoughts always go, where they've been going for the last however many years...

Tate Eckhart.

He's the kind of friend I never had before I came to Arizona State. The kind who always intimidated me. Outgoing, witty, charming as hell, with the uncanny ability to make people do things without so much as lifting a finger.

I swear, the guy could talk Colonel Sanders into going vegan. And effortlessly, too.

Tate is so inherently different from me in so many facets of life, and I think that's why I've never been able to stop myself from gravitating toward him. He's this charismatic presence that lures you in, and before you know it... you're *chasing* him.

"Come now, Hardy," Tate calls to me, and I pull myself up out of the depths of my inner turmoil, stepping over to him with trepidation in every footfall.

We get into the line, which is moving pretty quickly, much to my chagrin.

I'd like a little more time, please.

I have no idea what I'm doing, thanks.

Tate pulls out his wallet, removing a driver's license. Peeking at it, my brow lifts.

"Lorenzo Mateo Gianluca?" I can't help laughing while I read the name.

"That's me." He grins wickedly.

"That's the most Italian name I've ever heard in my life," I murmur.

"I've got a little Italy in my veins." He shrugs. "More Irish, though. But we won't mention that right now."

I force myself to smile, fingers wiggling at my sides while I subtly watch him, observing all his details.

Stop it. I shake myself out of it quick.

Tate holds up the license. "Can't you see the resemblance?"

Awkwardly, my eyes shift between his face and the picture. The only real similarities I'm seeing are in the dark hair and dark eyes. Lorenzo definitely doesn't have the pretty lines my friend has. But that's not something I'm going to voice... because it sounds weird.

So I just nod while my heart thumps. And mutter, "I guess."

Tate looks at the picture again, pulling a purposeful pout. "We'll just say I got fillers after this was taken."

"And lost, like, thirty pounds," I chuckle quietly.

He beams. "Lorenzo got a glow-up."

"Stay on planet Earth with me now, Trouble." I shoot him a teasing smirk, and he bites his lip.

It looks like some subtle flush is coloring his face, and I have to assume it's from the excitement of where we are. I know Tate hasn't been to many strictly *gay* places. Coming here tonight was important to him.

That must be why I wanted to come along... Because he's my best friend, and I'd like to be a part of this experience with him. To let him know I support him, no matter what.

That explanation would make sense, right?

Shifting on my feet, I glance around, watching all the people, talking, laughing, flirting. Overall, it's good that I'm finally going out, off campus. I just turned twenty-one last month, and I've yet to come to any clubs. I went to a bar with some friends on my actual twenty-first, but it wasn't as fun, since the rest of my friends who aren't legal yet couldn't come. Instead, I end up just going to the liquor store and sneaking booze back into the dorm for our usual parties.

Tonight is something I need; stepping out of my comfort zone. I've always been a quiet guy. I fall into friendships with people wild enough to force me out of my shell, and thank God it happens; otherwise, I might turn into a total hermit.

That's why I'm so fascinated by Tate. He could be plopped into the middle of a room full of strangers, and he'd come away with five new best friends.

It's a little overwhelming to think about now. I don't want him to feel like he needs to dampen his rainbow energy just because I'm here. At the same time, if he winds up meeting someone and ditching me, I have no idea what I'll do.

God, this is stressful.

What the fuck was I thinking coming here??

We reach the bouncer by the door, who barely gives our IDs a passing glance before he stamps our hands and motions us inside. Taking a deep breath, I follow behind an obviously excited Tate, wiping my sweaty palms on my jeans. My insecurities are immediately turned up to full blast, and we just freaking got here.

The club is dark inside, colorful lights beaming from the back, where the dance floor is. Remixed pop music booms, the bass rattling my veins. There are people *everywhere*.

I'm sure it's nowhere near as packed as it could be, but still, it's a pretty full house. Bodies all over the place, ninety-nine percent of them men. I see a few girls sprinkled in, but they're few and far between. The rest are dudes, of varying shapes and sizes, and amounts of clothing.

Keeping up with Tate is difficult. He's maneuvering through the crowd effortlessly, and I'm stumbling to stay close, muttering, *"excuse me,"* and *"sorry,"* every two seconds. It's clear Tate is headed straight for the bar, and the second we get close, I hear a loud wail.

"Baby T!"

My eyes land on Christian—Tate's random hook-up friend, who apparently invited him to this place—standing by the bar, squished in between two slender, shirtless guys. Tate strides up to Christian and they fake kiss each other's cheeks. Then Tate turns to check for me, waving me closer.

"I'm so glad you came!" Christian cheers to Tate, before glancing up at me, his forehead lining in obvious confusion. "Lance Hardy... Never expected to see you here."

"Hey, Chris." I grin, knowing full well he hates being called that.

He pins me with a withering glare, before returning to Tate. "I thought you were single."

Tate peeks at me nervously. "Oh, no. No, no, he's just along for the ride." I swallow a thick gulp of awkwardness. "My bodyguard. Right, Hardy?"

I nod slowly. *This is already weird.*

They all know I'm not gay... and they're understandably just as perplexed by me being here as I am.

Christian introduces us—mostly Tate—to his little friends, and we order some drinks. I keep trying to hand Tate my credit card, but he won't take it. He never lets people pay for him, even though he has no money. But that's just another thing about Tate; his strong sense of personal pride.

I guess growing up without a dad will do that to you...

Either way, he's determined as hell to be rich and successful someday, and because he's *him*, I have zero doubt he'll get there. *If anyone could do it...*

Just as I expected, it doesn't take long for me to start feeling invisible. Okay, not necessarily *invisible*, since a lot of people are looking at me. I'm getting flirty smiles and whispers from pretty much every direction except that of the people I actually know. But it doesn't help me, because I'm not here to pick someone up.

I'm here for Tate. And he's already becoming preoccupied, chatting and laughing with Christian and his friends.

I'm thinking up ways to get Tate's attention that don't make me feel like a clingy loser tugging on his shirt, when he spins around to face me. His eyes shift, and he mouths, *"Let's go."*

He doesn't need to elaborate. I can read the look in his eyes. *He wants to ditch Christian.*

Tate grabs my arm and pulls me along, dragging me toward the other side of the club. Nestled just outside the dance floor, he says something to me, but I can't hear him over the music.

Leaning in, he speaks by my ear. "So, what do you think?"

I move in closer myself. "It's... cool." My voice is gruff, though I'm trying to project over the noise.

Tate pulls back and gives me a look, eyebrow cocked like he's not surprised by my answer, but he still thinks it's ridiculous.

"You wanna dance—"

"Don't feel like you need to stay with me."

We both speak at the same time, then stop and stare at one another.

He leans in again. "Hardy, it's a club. You have to at least *try* dancing and having fun."

"I am having fun," I assure him, but I know he doesn't believe me.

I don't think I believe me either.

This is just so... not my scene. I want to support Tate, and be a part of what he's interested in, but I'm not sure I have it in me. And I can tell this is more his *thing* than the same old campus parties. But he does the chill stuff for me, so I should probably make more of an effort to enjoy this. For him.

If I want to keep him, I have to try.

Keep him as a *friend*, I mean.

Lord, I'm already exhausted.

"I'm a terrible dancer," I admit sheepishly, just barely loud enough for him to hear me.

But, of course, he catches it and smirks. Then he eases his body into mine. And suddenly, his hands are on my hips.

In an instant, my lungs are collapsing.

Calm down, psycho. It's just dancing...

Tate is almost flush against me, our faces close, breaths mingling warm and fruity from the booze. He's watching me intently while I'm freaking out because my heart is beating too fast, and I don't want him to get the wrong idea.

But we've never really been this close. We've hugged before, because we're *friends*. But this feels different...

I can smell him. His cologne, or whatever that scent is... it's invading my senses. His eyes are observing my face with that curious confidence he always possesses, and I'm only just now seeing something I've never noticed in them before... A flicker in those deep brown eyes that looks like... desire.

Does Tate want...?

His fingers dig into my hips.

He smells so good. He's so close...

This isn't what I had in mind when I asked to come here with him... Is it??

I don't think so...

I'm so confused.

Deep down, in a place I never allow myself to dwell, I know I like spending time with Tate more than my other friends. That distinction is overwhelming. Because there's a reason...

But I can't think about it.

I can't feel these tingles beneath my skin. I *can't* give in to the inexplicable urge to hold him back.

I'm always chasing him...

His lips brush my ear, and I shudder. "Move with me, Sunshine."

My hands hover over his lower back, fingers trembling. And my mouth opens to ask why he's calling me that...

But someone slams into his side, knocking him away from me. A drink flies through the air.

"What the fuck?!" Tate growls.

Darting forward, I reach for him. "Tate! Are you okay??"

"Oh my God, I'm so sorry!" A guy pushes in front of me, taking Tate by the elbow while he wipes away spilled booze. "Are you alright?? My idiot friend just—"

"I'm good, I'm good," Tate grumbles, shooting the guy and his friend an annoyed look. "You're lucky I decided against Prada tonight..."

The guy chuckles, eyes gliding over Tate slowly. It makes my stomach feel yucky.

But it only gets worse when he says, "Let me make it up to you."

And Tate's eyes sparkle at him, the corner of his mouth quirking.

Um... what's happening?

I guess my presence suddenly comes back into focus, because the guy's eyes dart to me, and he says, "I'm sorry. Are you two...?"

Tate glances at me briefly. "No. He's just a friend."

Just a friend...

Why does that sound bad when he says it? It's the truth...

The guy smiles at Tate, wide and charming, chock full of obvious interest. He says his name, but I can't hear it. Because now they're talking *only* to each other. Having this hushed conversation, huddling close together in the darkness and neon lights, enveloped by smooth beats.

This is why Tate came here. To meet someone. To drink, and flirt, and dance... Probably hook up.

And I'm just his quiet, straight friend, looming like a shadow.

I'm gnawing on my lower lip, when the stranger turns to me, then his friend. "Bar! Drinks on me."

I can't even think about the fact that I still have a full drink, because my eyes are stuck on the stranger's hand on Tate's lower back as he guides him away from me.

The sudden stiffness in my muscles feels unhealthy. I don't understand why my stomach is all bunched up, but I don't like it. And the avoider of all things heavy or potentially confrontational in me wants to tell Tate I'm going home, or even quietly slink away without saying anything.

But I can't do that. Not to Tate. Especially not when *I* asked him for this. And I definitely can't leave him alone with a stranger who seems to really like touching him.

So I follow after them, toward the other bar. Like his silent bodyguard.

The next hour goes by slowly. I feel every second of it, standing around, watching Tate and his new pal—whose name I still haven't gotten—talk, and laugh, and flirt, blatantly, right in front of me, as if I'm not even here.

Not that it should matter... But for some unknown reason, it's winding me up into a giant rubber band ball of stress and anxiety.

The guy's friend eventually scampers off to go grind with some other guy, making me an official third-wheel. In Tate's defense, he was trying to include me in the conversation at first. But *conversation* quickly faded into whispers, salacious chuckling, and roaming hands. None of which involve me, because why would they?

By the time he and Tate move out onto the dance floor, I'm a full-on shadow. Lingering on the sidelines, sipping drink after drink, rebuffing advance after advance from miscellaneous men.

I don't know what I'm doing. It makes *zero* sense for me to still be here. But then the thought of even going up to Tate right now, interrupting his fun to tell him I'm taking off, makes me even more miserable inside.

And then, of course, there's the part of me that refuses to leave him alone, because *who even is this guy?? Where did he come from??*

What if he's some kind of murderer or rapist or something?

I couldn't possibly leave my best friend alone with this chump, to be taken advantage of and potentially harmed. Nor can I take my eyes off of them for one second.

Without even realizing it, I've killed three drinks, just watching them like a hawk, jaw working to a steady grind at how the dude is greedily feeling Tate up like it doesn't mean a damn thing.

Is this really what Tate wants?? To be manhandled and grabbed at like a possession?

I know he likes to hook up casually. He's never actually had a boyfriend since I've known him, and I never noticed it until now, but I think part of me has relished that fact. Because I don't like what I'm seeing right now.

There's no conceivable reason for me to be feeling the way I am. But the confounding frustration in me is stretching. Growing thinner, and *thinner...*

And when the guy's hands glide down to cup Tate's ass roughly, it snaps.

Slugging back the last of my drink, I slam the glass down on the bar and push off, stomping over to my friend. Weaving through bodies, I'm fuming.

I don't think Tate is drunk or anything. He's certainly consumed more alcohol at campus parties than he has tonight. But he must have a buzz going, at least. I can see it in his movements, and the way his eyelids are visibly heavy. It's pissing me off more than it should.

This guy has been plying him with alcohol to get him loosened up, and I don't appreciate it.

I just need to talk to him for a minute. Find out if this is really what he wants...

If it is, I'll leave him alone to hook up with the dude. It's not my concern, as long as he actually *wants* it.

But if he's even the tiniest bit unsure, then I can't allow this. I just can't.

As soon as I get close, Tate spots me, vibrant smile widening. "*Heyyy!* There's my friend!" He grabs my face, pinching my cheeks and poking me on the nose.

"Hey, T... Are you a li'l drunk?" My concern is apparent, but I'm trying my hardest not to sound like a huge buzzkill.

Tate makes the *just a little bit* gesture with his fingers, and I frown. My eyes slink to his handsy pal, who's dancing beside us, still pawing at Tate's waist.

My teeth are grinding to dust.

Leaning in by Tate's ear, I ask, "Do you actually like this guy?"

Tate shrugs, sipping his drink. "He's okay."

"Well, maybe we should go... dance over there." I nod in any direction that's away from this fool who's pissing me off with his sneaky fingers.

"You wanna dance with me?" Tate bites his lip, blinking a hazy gaze up at me.

I swallow hard to mask how obviously uncomfortable I am. "I will... I'll dance with you. If you just come over here..."

I try to take him by the arm, but he jerks, lifting his hands in the air and shimmying around. He's singing along to *Teenage Dream* by Katy Perry, his drink sloshing everywhere as he twirls.

Sighing, I rub my eyes. "Tate... I need to talk to you..."

But the guy wraps his arms around Tate's waist, pulling him close. Pulling him *away* from me. They start dancing together, though it seems like Tate is more interested in rocking out to this stupid song.

Something rubs on my ass, and I whip around, shooting a bemused look at a short guy who's trying to grind on me.

"Wow... you're *tall*," the guy says as I scoot away from him.

"Yea, thanks, but I'm not..." My voice trails when I turn back to Tate.

And it gets lodged in my throat at the sight of him and the guy... kissing.

Oof... This doesn't feel good.

I think I might throw up.

My inexplicably mortified gaze is locked on Tate and the guy, mouths moving together in deep, heated kisses, and I just can't take it anymore. I feel fucking *sick*, and it's so confusing, so painful, I need to get away. *Fast.*

Staggering through the waves of people dancing, my pulse is pounding in my ears, my vision blurring. I'm unsteady on my feet, but I manage to make it off the dance floor, leaning up on the wall for a second to catch my breath.

This sucks. I don't want to be here.

I feel like the biggest moron on the planet. And it's all my fault.

This was my idea. I mean, what did I think was going to happen??

What was I expecting from tonight??

Digging my fingers into my eyes, I struggle to breathe. I just don't fucking know...

I don't know why I wanted this.

Chin swiveling back toward the floor, I search for Tate one last time. But I can't see him over the crowd of bodies, jumping and singing along to

Trouble

Dancing on My Own. I shake my head and swallow my stupidity, leaving the club and this dumb-ass night behind.

Outside, people are stumbling around, laughing, smoking cigarettes and making out. And I'm all alone, feeling foolish and hurt and thrown by why I even feel these things in the first place.

Taking out my phone, I pull up Uber, ignoring the ache in my chest that's just making me hate myself more. Sniffing, my shaky fingers work on the screen.

"Lance!"

I nearly drop my phone.

Peering over my shoulder, I blink as Tate shuffles over to me. Alone.

"What happened to you?" he asks, pushing back messy strands of dark hair with his fingers.

His cheeks are flushed, lips all puffy and pink.

Burning nerves rise from my gut up to my chest.

"I'm going home," I mutter, returning to my phone.

"Why? It's still... early," he hiccups.

"Because. This was a stupid idea," I scoff. "I don't know why I wanted to come here..."

"You didn't have fun?"

I peek at him. He's pouting.

My forehead creases. "No, Tate. Believe it or not, I wasn't having fun watching you hook up with that guy."

"Oh..." His head tilts. "Well, you could've just danced with us or something..."

I laugh incredulously. "Yea, that sounds like even less fun."

"Hardy, I told you what it was gonna be like coming to a gay club with me," he huffs. "You fucking *begged* me to tag along, and I knew, I fucking *knew* you were gonna be bored—"

"I wasn't bored!" I bark at him, and his eyes widen. "I was having fun when it was just us..." His throat dips as I take a breath, rubbing my face. "Never mind. Just go back inside and hook up. It's fine. It's what you came for, and I'm just ruining it."

He's quiet for a few heavy seconds, during which I feel like *everything* is crumbling around me.

"Why are you mad...?" His voice comes out soft, curious.

My lips part, but I've got nothing. No single explanation would make sense.

"I really don't fucking know," I sigh, fiddling with my phone some more, finally ordering the Uber.

"Hardy..." he breathes, stepping closer.

"My Uber will be here in five minutes," I grunt.

He nods, chewing on his lower lip. But he doesn't move. He's just standing next to me, rubbing his arms.

"Go back inside, Tate," I mumble.

He shakes his head. "I don't want to."

"Yes, you do," I argue. "It's why you're here..."

"No, it's not," he whispers. "Not... necessarily."

"That makes no sense."

"Yea, no shit." He scrapes his palms over his face. "Nothing about this night makes any fucking sense."

"I'm sorry, T." My gut is rolling with regret. "I didn't mean to ruin your night. It's all my fault. I just thought..."

"You thought what?" he asks impatiently when my words dissolve. "Tell me."

"I don't know... I guess I just wanted to hang out with you," I murmur. "And this definitely wasn't the place to do it."

"But we were hanging out... and you didn't seem into it, so..." He blinks round, glassy eyes at me, and I'm just stiff.

The things I want to say are idiotic.

How can I tell him that I wanted it to be just the two of us? That I expected him to, what? Stay with me all night??

He was obviously looking to hook up, which isn't something I can give him...

I feel like I'm shaking inside, and I don't know why.

Maybe I do...

"I really wish you'd just... go back in," my voice grates.

"I don't want to," he says again, gazing up at me with intensity in his gaze.

The same shade as mine...

We don't speak again, just waiting in tense silence for the Uber to arrive. Surrounded by voices that aren't ours, drowning our unspoken words.

Tate and I get into the Uber, and I slump over, staring out the window, wishing I knew what the hell was going on inside me. And that I wasn't so afraid of it.

Trouble

It feels like Tate is staring at me, so I turn my face, just in time to catch him looking away.

"I am sorry, T," I mutter. "I just... You're my friend. It's selfish as fuck for me to want you all to myself..."

His face springs in my direction. "Is that what you want?"

I recoil, from my words and the way he's gawking at me. "I think that came out wrong..."

My gaze goes back out the window, my heart pounding in my ears.

I startle when I feel fingers gliding over mine.

Obviously, I know they're his. And I'm too damn terrified to look. But it feels too good for me to pull away.

Our fingers are locked the entire rest of the drive back to campus, and I'm so confused, and scared, with heated shame rising up my neck.

I like this.

But I can't *fucking like it...*

Chapter Five
Tate

When the car stops, our hands finally let go.

I feel high right now, honestly. I feel like my drinks have been laced with some sort of hallucinogen that floods you with the dopamine of crawling closer to something you've wanted for years, that's been just out of reach.

I never expected this. When Lance asked if he could come to the gay club with me tonight, never in my wildest dreams would I have predicted it going down the way it did.

Sure, he follows me around, and he clings to me more than any straight friend I've ever had. But I always just assumed it was because I'm the shit, and everyone loves hanging out with me. I've told myself that for years, like a mantra, because thinking anything else would be setting myself up for disappointment.

But tonight, in the club, Lance Hardy was acting almost like... we were on a date. He was nervous and jittery. Every time I'd look up, he was watching me.

At first, I thought he was just uncomfortable being around so many gay dudes. Or that he was anxious about being around so many strangers in general, with added loud music and lots of dancing. Lance doesn't go out. He's not a club kid, not even a little. It's understandable that Element would set off his introvert alarm bells.

But then the way he was hovering around me and Sean—the guy who spilled his drink on me—staring at us flirting and touching... It was the behavior of someone who was just a wee bit jealous.

But that couldn't be, could it??

I mean, why would Lance Hardy be jealous of a guy I was making out with...?

Unless... he wants to make out with me himself.

Truthfully, I was feeling pretty nice in that club. Sean was good-looking, and he liked touching me, which was flattering enough that I definitely would have let him plow me like a cornfield.

Still, when we were kissing, my eyes couldn't help creeping open to check for Lance.

'Cause, ya know... he's hot.

And maybe I was a *teeny bit* curious to see how he'd react to such things. I won't say I was blatantly *trying* to make Lance jealous, because that's an immature game. But if you're bored, and all the pieces are there... might as well play.

And sure enough, Lance bolted. He seemed really upset...

The way my heart leapt and my stomach flipped, you'd think they were circus acrobats.

So I told Sean I'd be right back—with no real intention of coming back —and chased Lance outside to try to read the situation a little better.

And now, here we are. Back on campus, walking to my dorm after just holding hands in the backseat of an Uber for fifteen minutes.

I still have no clue as to what's going on. I don't know if my *straight* friend is actually not as straight as I thought. I don't know if maybe he's confused or questioning things... Or if it's the unlikely possibility—*the one I'm secretly hoping for*—that he's just so into *me*, he might be willing to overlook the fact that I'm not a girl.

I sure as shit don't know why that thought is so appealing to me. Maybe I'm a huge narcissist or something. But if I could be the only *guy* Lance Hardy is attracted to, I'd give up booze and cigarettes for the rest of my life.

My thoughts are swirling while we walk up the path toward my building. I can somehow feel the tension in Lance's strides as he walks behind me. I'm desperate to turn and look at him, but I'm trying to play it cool. Be as *aloof* as possible. Still, when we reach the front of my residence hall, and I spin to face him, I just know I'm giving off a severe amount of burning intensity in my own eyes.

Lance is shifting on his feet, and I'm chewing my lower lip, wondering if I should just go for broke. I want to test out my theory. I *need* to get him upstairs with me... more than I've ever needed anything.

Lance starts to mumble, "Well... Goodnight, T. I'm sor—"

"I think you should come up," I cut him off.

Fuck being aloof. Throw all those goddamn cards on the table.

He looks like he might collapse. "W-what??"

I step up to him. He steps back.

God, you sexy straight boy... Stop being such a tease.

"Hardy, I want you to come inside with me," I murmur firmly. "And I think you might... want that too."

"No, I'm..." he croaks, then clears his throat. "I can't."

"Yes, you can," I hum, reaching for his hand again.

It felt so motherloving *good* to hold it in the car... *Who knew holding someone's hand could make my chest flutter and my dick hard at the same time?*

"We're friends, Tate," Lance mutters. "That's it. I know I acted crazy tonight, but I'm not—"

"It's okay if you're scared." My head slants, fingers brushing over his. "Because we *are* friends, and maybe that makes you feel like you shouldn't want more. Or maybe you feel like *God* wouldn't approve..."

He swallows visibly. "God has nothing to do with it..."

"Bullshit," I rasp, toying with his fingers. "Then tell me why..." He blinks a startled gaze at me. "Tell me why you wanted to come to the club with me. Tell me why you hated seeing me with that guy..."

I know I'm coming on strong, but I can't help it. I've been crushing mercilessly on this dude for nearly three years in secret. The slightest whiff of interest from him has officially set me on the trail like a bloodhound.

Whipping his hand away from mine, Lance backs up, noticeable fear glistening in his eyes. "I didn't hate it..."

"Right," I scoff. "That's why you ran out of there like you were fleeing a burning building."

"I was just... giving you some space." He purses his lips, stubborn, gorgeous idiot he is.

"I think you cockblocked me for a reason." I arch a brow, slinking closer to him. "The night isn't over, Hardy. Come upstairs and we'll hang out... Just the two of us."

He backs up again. "You're drunk, Tate..."

"I'm not drunk." My eyes stay on his.

Trouble

"You went to that club looking for dick," he grumbles. "And you found it with that guy. You should've stayed with him."

"But I don't want him..." I move into his space once more, crowding him. And this time, he doesn't move away. He's frozen, shivering in place, eyes gaping while my fingertips slide up his chest. "You knew why I wanted to go out tonight, and you just *had* to come with me. You pitched a fit when you saw me kissing someone else... I think it's pretty clear what that means."

My face inches, our mouths so close that chills are scattering all over my body.

"We're just *friends*, Tate," he manages to grunt. "I'm not—"

"You don't have to be," I interrupt him with a purr. "Just be you, and I'll be me... And we can be us, *together*."

He really seems like he's considering my words, and I'm fucking *flying*. I don't need him to figure out his sexuality. None of that matters right now. What matters is that I get him upstairs to my dorm room, alone. So we can explore whatever it is that made him so jealous in the club.

"We shouldn't..." His trembling hands hover over my waist, like he's desperate to grab me and hold on tight, but he's fighting it tooth and nail.

"Who gives a fuck about *should*..." My fingers glide up to his jaw. "Come to my room with me, Sunshine. You can have anything you want."

"You're trouble," he whispers shakily.

A soft sound rumbles from my chest, our lips barely a breath apart. He's going to give in to this. I *need* him to...

I can't just be his friend anymore. Not when he's this giant, nervous, six-foot-four hunk of quivering need, *begging* to unleash his forbidden desires for the first time.

Sin with me, Sunshine...

We both know I'm damned either way.

A sudden sound snaps us out of our trance. Voices, and footsteps.

Lance's face rears back, and he shakes away the lust fog. There's a group of people walking up the path from the quad.

And because he's *straight*, and afraid, he steps out of my grip.

"I'm sorry... I can't." His eyes are shining remorse as he stumbles away from me, storming off in the direction of his dorm.

"FML..." I mutter to myself, pouting and kicking rocks the whole way inside my building.

This fucking blows. An hour ago, I had two guys who wanted to kiss me. Now, I have none.

Maybe Lance didn't even want to kiss me in the first place. Maybe he really did just want to hang out as friends, and being in the club, watching me hook up, was too awkward for him. And I just obliterated our friendship by coming onto him like a raging horndog.

Fuck, what did I do??

Inside my dorm, I wander into the dark, empty bedroom. My roommate, Nick, visits his girlfriend on weekends, which means I have the place to myself a lot. It's the whole reason I invited Lance up, knowing we'd have privacy. But right now, the thought is bumming me out even more.

I'm spending the night alone, instead of with the one person I've been consistently dreaming about having in bed with me every night for a long time.

Mulling around in a state of gloom, I get undressed and pull on some sweatpants. Jake was right. This crush is no good. And not that I want to admit it, even to myself, but I know it's the reason I've only ever hooked up casually. The one thing that's been standing in the way of me developing an actual relationship is this incessant pining.

I tell myself I'm not interested in having a boyfriend. That college is for fooling around and exploring my sexuality the way I couldn't back home. But in this quiet, dimly lit dorm room, with my beckoning thoughts on full volume, I recognize the lies.

I do want a relationship... with the person I can't have.

The guy I drop everything to spend time with. The one I search for at parties, and in every crowded room. My *friend*, who knows more about me than pretty much anyone—except maybe Jake—who stays up with me until sunrise, just talking and laughing...

He calls me on my bullshit, but also encourages me. Believes in *me*, the kid who came from pretty much nothing; the lonely boy, brought up by a lonely mother, with big dreams of becoming rich and successful, and proving every person who ever doubted him wrong, desperate to show the world he's better than the father who didn't want him.

Lance Hardy sees past the smirks, and the sarcasm, because that's who he is. A ray of sunshine...

He's *good*, and I'm just... Trouble.

Lying in bed, I'm staring up at the ceiling for a while, replaying every second of tonight over and over in my head until my eyelids start to droop. But a knock at my door wakes me up.

I slink out of bed and over to the door, opening it hesitantly, just a crack.

Trouble

And when I peek through, my heart launches into a steady gallop; off to the races.

He's here...

He came back.

My Sunshine might just want some trouble after all.

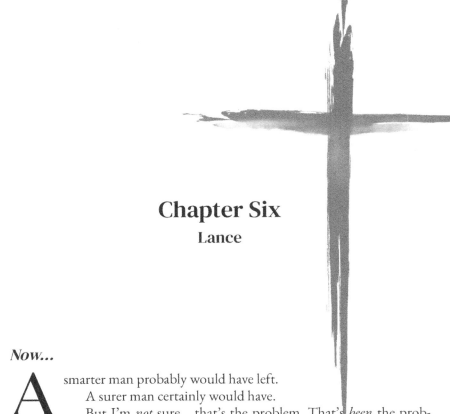

Chapter Six
Lance

Now...

A smarter man probably would have left.

A surer man certainly would have.

But I'm *not* sure... that's the problem. That's *been* the problem, for longer than I care to think about right now.

Maybe I can fool myself into thinking I came here just to see old friends... But deep down, I know that isn't exactly true. Which is why, instead of coming straight to Kennan's house, I went to the club first.

When I arrived in ABQ a few hours ago, I summoned all of the courage I could muster, picked a gay club, and forced myself to go in. But the moment I set foot inside the place, my chest felt like it was on fire.

There were eyes on me instantly, from all directions. Flirty smiles, winks... It was just too much, too fast. So I rushed into the restroom and threw myself into an available stall, just to get some privacy. To be alone for a second and think.

Was I making a huge mistake??

Had I just been fooling myself thinking I was ready for this... Confronting my inner hang-ups in such an ostentatious manner?

Was I ready for it? Would I *ever* be ready??

So much doubt was swirling inside me, I was about to leave and never look back. And that's when God sent me a sign... through a glory hole.

Trouble

I guess that's what they're called... I didn't know that until Tate said it earlier.

What kind of coincidence is it that it ended up being *Tate* on the other side of that wall? The guy responsible for the cancerous mass of confusion that's been living inside me for nearly two decades...

For all my equality and acceptance sermons, maybe a part of me still doesn't think God actually works that way. Have I been lying to everyone around me this whole time?

It's a test. It has to be a test.

Because this isn't just about my sexuality... There are so many more layers to it than that. It's also about the fact that I'm *married*. Isn't God supposed to lead me out of temptation and back to my wife?

I feel like such a hypocrite. Preaching acceptance for all forms of love, but only for people other than myself.

All of this nonsense waging war inside me has driven me to drink. I wasn't lying to Tate earlier when I told him I don't drink much. I haven't since college. *I guess there are a few bad things I haven't done since then...*

Taking a large swig from my bottle of beer, I glance around the party. The sun is setting, bringing on a nice breeze, a reprieve from the earlier stifling heat. The ambiance of the twinkly lights above our heads is nice, but I can't enjoy it. I'm too busy watching Tate from afar... Like a total stalker.

He's been blatantly flirting with guys for the past hour, since he brushed off my apology yet again. And I've just been standing around, pretending it's not driving me crazy, when in reality, I couldn't tell you a single thing anyone else has said to me since I've been here. Every conversation I've had has gone in one ear and out the other because I'm too busy eyeing my former friend, and the hands of various guys he's allowed to wander all over him shamelessly.

Maybe I *have* changed a lot since college... I'm sure we all have. But Tate isn't immune to it himself. He seems more hostile than he used to be... More closed-off.

Tate's always been clever, witty, and unapologetically wicked at times. But he never used to stuff down his emotions. At least, not with me. I hate to think I made him this way... That he's forever shelved his vulnerable side just because I got scared and turned my back on him.

I know he doesn't want to hear what I have to say... That much is clear. But I refuse to believe he was just looking for a meaningless hook-up in that bathroom stall. Sure, it would fit his M.O., but it felt like more than that.

I can't leave without confronting what happened... if for no other reason than preserving my own sanity.

My stomach twists up into a painful knot when I see Tate following a few of his *friends* inside the house. They're all touchy feely, whispering things to each other that I know would kill me if I heard. It's obvious they're going inside to hook up.

And I just can't have that.

Stalking back inside the house, my hand squeezes into a fist when I see one of the guys, a large shirtless man with very tanned skin and elaborate muscles, shoving Tate up against the wall. He plants a kiss on Tate's mouth while the other guy, a slimmer dude with a shaved head, runs his hands all over the two of them.

"Tate," I growl, stomping over, radiating emotions that feel familiar, but I still barely know how to process them.

Tate's eyes open, and he peeks at me, pulling away from the hungry kisses of his aggressive pal. He scowls at me and sighs, sifting his fingers through his hair.

"Excuse me for a moment, boys," he says to the guys, who are casting me curious, judgmental looks. "I just need to deal with something real quick." He glances at the guys and pouts. "Don't start without me."

"No promises," the shaved-head man says, taking the hand of the bigger guy and dragging him into a nearby room.

The door slams shut behind them, and I hear laughing from inside.

"Wow." Tate purses his lips at me. "Still cockblocking, all these years later."

I know exactly what he's referring to, and it has me chewing on the inside of my cheek so hard I taste blood.

"A threesome at Pride seems pretty cliché, don't you think?" I step up to him until we're only a foot apart.

"Actually, there are two more guys in that room already." He tilts his head, giving me a cocky smirk in response to my obvious look of concern. "This is how we party, Hardy." His smirk widens, and I force myself not to react to his little rhyming joke. "Jeez, lighten up. It's *Pride*... It's a celebration."

"So you only do stuff like that during Pride?" I cock a brow.

He rolls his eyes. "Why are you here?? Why are you policing what I do? And why do you even care??" His sudden burst of emotion twists me up. "You *left*, remember? *You* did. We haven't spoken in fifteen years, Lance. You can't just show up out of nowhere and start throwing all these questions and accusations at me..."

"I'm not accusing you of anything, Tate," I say firmly. "I just want to explain. Running into you in that bathroom was—"

Voices cut into my words, and my face springs in their direction. There are too many people around. I need some privacy to get my head on straight... To talk to him and fix this.

Grabbing him by the arm, I drag him up the hall and around a corner. Then I push him against the wall. His eyes widen up at me, and I witness his Adam's apple bob in his throat sheeted in stubble. It makes me feel things... but I shove it all down.

"I was just as shocked to see *you* coming out of that stall, trust me," I continue in a tone that's hushed, but assertive. "I didn't come here to confront you or anything, but honestly, I'm glad I ran into you." He huffs and rolls his eyes again. "More than glad. For fifteen years, I've been *hating* how we left things."

"Then why haven't you reached out??" he hisses. "You live in New Mexico now, Lance. You know I live here too. In fact, you probably even know that I only live, like, a few hours away from you."

I can't help how my lips curve. "Someone's been cyber-stalking..."

"Please," he scoffs. "Don't flatter yourself. I just so happened to scroll across a few measly details." He pauses and licks his lip. "You mean to tell me you haven't checked up on me... at all?"

There's something about the subtle dip in his voice, the rumble of it with us standing so close... The heat burning in the air around us.

"Maybe a little..." I hum. He smirks triumphantly. "But you never friended me on Facebook..."

"You didn't either," he says pointedly. "And we all know why..." I give him a blank look, to which he blinks slowly, like I'm testing his patience. "You're *married*, Hardy. You're married to a woman, and you work in a fucking church. Those are the facts. We aren't allowed to be in each other's lives, and obviously you want it that way..."

"Okay, first of all, my church is very accepting, so that doesn't matter." I pause, and his brows raise expectantly. "Second of all, why couldn't we be friends? Just because I'm... married..." I swallow hard. "We could be friends. Like we used to be."

"Then why didn't you reach out?" he repeats, speaking each word with conviction, like he knows the answer already.

I have nothing to say. I can't say it. I just... *can't*.

My eyes fall between us, and I lift the bottle of beer in my hand, killing the rest of it before setting it down on the floor.

Tate watches me carefully. "I thought you didn't drink anymore..."

"Yea, well..." I sigh. "Being around you stresses me out."

He laughs, and it brings a confusing tickle to my gut. "I guess some things don't change, hm?"

"Do you forgive me?" I whisper, blinking at him. "For leaving...?"

"Like an asshole?" he adds, and I chuckle.

"Yea... like an asshole."

He inches in closer to me, and my heart begins to race. I back up, but he grabs me by the wrist.

"What do you want me to say, Hardy?" His hand feels like a branding iron searing into my flesh.

"I want you to tell me the truth."

His grip on my wrist loosens, fingers sliding over mine.

"Truthfully?" He eases in close until our chests bump. Then he taps the band on my ring finger. "I wish this wasn't here."

The tremble in my limbs has jacked up to a full shake. I bite my lip to make sure it's not visibly quivering.

"You were right..." I croak. "A lot has changed since back then, Trouble."

His head cocks. "Maybe not that much..." He leans in closer, lips brushing my ear until I'm crumbling. "You're still following me around because you can't help yourself."

Fuck...

Fuck, this is so bad.

This is so painfully awful, because it feels *amazing*, and it's just reminding me of how amazing it felt back then, too.

But it's not supposed to. It *can't*, especially now.

God... did I ruin everything when I left??

"Tate..." I murmur, shivering so hard I might collapse while the heat of his body sinks into my pores. "We can't. That's what's different... This time, we *can't*."

"Then why were you in that bathroom?" His warm breath on my ear sends chills rushing all over my body.

The feel of his muscles brushing mine through our clothes, the way his fingers are slowly sweeping up and down my arm... The way the fingers on his other hand seem to have appeared on my lower back...

It's just like last time. It feels *exactly* the same, only now it's about more than just the things I've kept hidden. Us being friends, me being drunk and horny and confused...

This time, it's *also* wrong because I'm married. It's so very *forbidden*...

And my dick hasn't been this hard in fifteen fucking years.

I gulp. "That was a mistake..." I lie.

Of course, he's not buying it. "Try again." His tongue swipes my earlobe, and my lashes flutter.

"I was just using the—"

"No..." he cuts me off in a softly salacious voice that's now living in my brain. "Why did you *really* come here today... *Sunshine*?"

Fuck, I missed him calling me that. Why have I missed it so much??

"I..." My voice grates out as my hand inches up, twitchy and nervous, to rest on his waist. "I wanted to see... how it... felt."

"Mm," he rumbles, pushing his hips into mine. I feel the outline of his erection on my own, and I groan quietly, forehead dropping to his. "Was it the first time? Since we..."

I nod fast. "Mhm. Yes."

"Fuck..." he growls quietly, shaking his head like he's angry at himself. "Why is this always what I want? You fucked me up, Hardy... Like, *bad*."

Remorse clenches between my ribs. "I'm sorry, Trouble... I promise, I am."

Tate pulls back just enough for our eyes to lock. We're so close, the tips of our noses are almost touching. "This confusion of yours can only go on so long."

My lips part, but I can't speak. I'm at a loss...

Before coming here today, I'd spent years convincing myself it wasn't that bad. When I'm at home, living my comfortable, quiet little life, everything seems fine.

But just being near Tate Eckhart again throws a wrench in between the gears of my denial.

"I don't... I don't know what to think." I fumble for words, shaking head to toe. "I'm married, T. I'm married and I—"

"Please," he breathes, chin wobbling. "I can't listen to you talk about your wife. I just can't."

My chest hurts, like someone's stabbing me. I remember the fight, pacing in front of the door to his dorm room that night. I remember giving it up, and knocking...

I remember the *feeling* of it all, like it happened five minutes ago.

The nervous, trembling ecstasy of him opening the door, and me walking inside. And every single second of what happened after that, like the scariest, most incredible bliss I could never have imagined.

I didn't run away because I was scared of wanting him. I ran because I was scared of how good it felt that *he* wanted *me*.

A sudden noise interrupts our moment, and both of our faces slope in its direction. It sounds like hushed voices. Then a groan.

Tate's brows furrow, and he takes me by the wrist again, this time pulling me along with him. We turn a corner, and there's a sunroom; an open space, like a living room of sorts, without a door. We both peer inside at the same time, and I actually gasp out loud, then slap my hand over my mouth.

It's Tate's friends, the blonde guy and the dark-haired guy he brought over here. They're in the room...

And they're clearly about to have sex.

"Oh my God." Tate releases a hushed chuckle, shaking his head. But his eyes are wide, obviously intrigued by what we're seeing.

He bites his lip.

I bite mine too, watching Tate watch them for a few heavy seconds before my eyes slide back into the room.

They're both naked. The younger dark-haired guy is hovering over the blonde guy, who's lying on some piece of furniture with his legs wrapped around the other guy's waist. They're kissing, deep, heavily passionate, hungry... downright ravenous, while the younger guy rubs lubrication onto his dick.

My cock is straining against the front of my pants. I've never seen anything like this before... in real life. *I may or may not have watched a few videos...*

But this is totally different. This is happening right in front of my eyes.

My dick was already hard before, from the tension between me and Tate. But now, it's practically about to snap off.

"Those are my friends," Tate whispers. "Ben, the blonde... I grew up with him. That's Jake's brother. And his husband, Ryan... we sorta hooked up." My face snaps in Tate's direction. "Like, a bunch of times."

Blinking at him, I pry my eyes away to look inside the room once more. That's why they looked familiar... I've seen them while making my rounds on social media.

Of course, creeping our mutuals never showed me a scene like *this*. The dark-haired guy—*Ryan*—is pushing his fingers inside his husband's ass. It looks insane, but I can't even be concerned with that right now, because I'm too busy buzzing with jealousy.

That guy...?? Tate hooked up with him??

He's... fucking gorgeous.

"When did you hook up with him?" I whisper accusingly.

Tate peers up at me, biting a smirk off his lips. "Last year. Before they got together."

"Were you into him?" I grunt, and he shoots me a look that says *Quiet.*

Tate scoffs, "I'm never into anyone, Hardy. I don't do feelings."

My blinking becomes rapid.

Tate flashes me some very brief vulnerability, before inching his mouth up to my ear again. "Do you like watching them?"

Gulping a mouthful of saliva, I glance at the couple, who are now actively fucking. Ryan is pushing his severely impressive erection inside Ben as their hands rush all over one another, so deeply lost in their obvious connection that they don't even care there's no door to the room they're in, and anybody could walk by and see them.

The sight kicks a swift pang into my gut. That kind of passion... lust... *love*. The desperate desire to have someone right then and there... I've never felt that before.

My eyes creep back to Tate.

Okay... maybe once.

Tate slips his hand gingerly over my erection, and I tremor. "I guess it's a rhetorical question."

"Tate... we shouldn't—"

"Blah blah blah," he rumbles, working on the button and zipper of my shorts. "*Shouldn't* can suck my dick. And I'll suck yours." He shows me a cocky grin while I just stare at him, dumfounded. "Aren't you aching just a little, big beautiful ray of sunshine?" His lips dance along my jaw while his fingers slip inside my now open pants.

I'm *shivering*... burning, sweating, and throbbing deep inside, in a place where only he can seem to reach. And his lips are creeping awfully close to mine...

I think Tate's about to kiss me, and it snaps my fear back like a boomerang reflex. I grab his throat, and he groans softly. But I'm only trying to keep him from kissing me...

I think.

"Tate." I shake my head.

"We didn't get to finish what we started in the bathroom." He pouts.

His hand cups my erection over my boxers, a greedy hiss leaving my lips. "I thought you wanted me to forgive you..."

"I do," I huff, glancing over his shoulder at his friends who are really going at it, grunting, skin slapping, moaning into each other's mouths. My cock jerks hard in Tate's hand, and he purrs. "Are you saying this is how...?"

He nods slowly, rubbing my cock so good it's leaking all over me inside my boxers.

This is so bad... but it feels *so* good.

God forgive me...

I can't stop.

Not this time.

"I'm gonna drop to my knees now, Lance," he whispers. "I need to get reacquainted with the best dick I've ever had in my life."

My head is spinning, whirling and twirling around his words, and the sexy tone of his voice, the heat between us, and the live porn happening only a few feet away. I release Tate's throat, my fingers sliding up his neck and into his hair as he gracefully falls to his knees.

My eyes are on him and his on mine as he peels my boxers down just enough to get my dick out. The second it's in his hand, my eyes flutter shut and I bite my lip.

This is so much better than earlier. Because this isn't just a faceless hole. It's *Tate...*

My Trouble.

Deep brown eyes sparkling, pink lips parted and waiting... That wicked tongue of his.

"Say you want it just as bad as you did back then." He rushes out the words on a clearly eager breath, his chest heaving with anticipation.

I nod timidly, a palpable flush in my cheeks while my entire body trembles. "I... I do. I want *more*, Trouble."

He smirks, then extends his tongue, swiping at the underside of my swollen tip.

Groaning, my head falls back, and I chomp on my lower lip to keep myself quiet. Tate wastes no time sliding my cock deeper into his mouth, teasing me with that tongue, and I'm going out of my damn mind.

I should've known... I should've fucking *known* it was him earlier from the way it felt. I haven't stopped remembering the feel of this mouth on me in fifteen years. And believe me, I've tried. Every time my dick was in the mouth of someone else—a few other girls before I met Desiree, and then

Trouble

hers on the rare occasion—I would force my mind not to dwell on how it never felt as good as *this*. This mouth...

This mouth is trouble.

"Ffuck..." I thread my fingers in Tate's dark hair while he sucks me, slowly, deep into the back of his throat, but not like he's trying to choke himself on it. It just happens, as if he wants to swallow me whole; to fit as much as possible because he wants every inch of me inside him.

"T-tate... *Tate*..." I ramble, quivering as the tides of pleasure build higher and higher in my loins. "Tate, you suck like n-no one else."

He rumbles on my dick, vibrations of the words he won't pull off long enough to speak. But I know it's probably something cocky, because that's the way he is. He's always been this way...

The outgoing and confident to my quiet and unsure. The wild to my timid. The no fucks given to my polite over-thinker. It's what made us such great friends back then, I think. Because he always had the stuff I didn't, and I liked having it when I was with him.

I think maybe I missed it *really bad* all this time.

The burn from stopping earlier has been immediately replaced by a rushing high. I'm not even paying attention to his friends anymore. I'm just gripping his hair and flicking my hips against his face, riding his warm, slippery wet mouth, ready to explode down his tight throat. *Just like he let me in his dorm bed back then.*

"*Fuck*, Tate, what are we doing...?" I whisper, the same words I breathed that night while I touched him with shaky fingers. "I never want my cock to not be in your mouth, baby..."

Tate groans, and I peel my eyes open to catch him rubbing himself over his pants. Spit is running from his mouth while he slurps up and down, his free hand reaching into my boxers to play with my balls.

Tate is sucking my dick... Tate had sex with that guy in there... Tate doesn't do feelings...

Tate feels *like he should do feelings, though... with* me.

I'm seconds from bursting when voices and footsteps snap my eyes open.

Tate's friends have apparently finished fucking, and are now fully clothed, staring at us with wide, shocked expressions.

Whipping back, I pull out of Tate's mouth, stuffing my cock away as fast as possible. It fucking *kills* already. I was literally just about to come.

Fuck me... This is what I get. Welcome to blue ball hell.

"Hey, guys," Tate says casually to his friends, wiping the back of his mouth.

I'm fucking *mortified*. I'm sure my face has never been redder... And then there's Tate. Completely unaffected. Like this happens to him all the time.

Does this happen to him all the time?!?!

The guys are gaping at us, Tate's former fuck-buddy, *Ryan*, sharing a sliver of my awkward sentiment, while his husband, Ben, is just glaring at Tate like this is somehow all his fault.

"This is... really embarrassing," I grunt, rubbing my eyes while I attempt to get my bearings.

I'm a married man, for fuck's sake.

"Is it, though?" Tate cocks a brow up at my face, slowly rising from the floor.

My jaw clenches, our eyes locked as he counters my severity with his own stubbornness.

Uh, yes, Tate. It's embarrassing for me, because I don't do shit like this on the regular!

"I'm Ryan." The kid steps forward with a smile, extending his hand to me.

My gaze slips off of Tate onto the hand. I stare at it for a second before he snatches it away, his cheeks flushing pink.

Right... he was just fingering his husband's ass with that hand.

This is lovely.

But I can't forgo my manners, because it's who I am. So despite the immense awkwardness, and my inner rampant jealously, I murmur, "Um... I'm Lance." And I wave at him.

Waving?? You look like an idiot. They just saw your dick!

Ryan gestures to Ben. "This is my husband—"

"Were you watching us?" Ben barks at Tate.

Tate simply smirks at Ben, still that nonchalant guy he's always been. The one I was just swooning over moments ago...

But maybe that was just the impending orgasm talking.

It had to have been. Because this whole *no big deal, someone just caught us fooling around* thing is so not me. *Not even close.*

Tate leans into my side, and my heart thumps. But I ignore it.

I can't have this.

"If you didn't want anyone to watch, why'd you do it in the room with no door?" Tate asks Ben snidely.

Trouble

He has a point. But still...

I don't know what kind of drama these three have going on, but it's a bit much for me to process. Between this angry guy being a childhood friend of Tate's, and his husband being Tate's former fling, I just can't deal. I feel like I might pass out.

"So, how do you two know each other?" Ryan asks kindly.

He seems really nice, which has my mind desperate for details on the nature of his history with Tate. But there's no way I can get into it all right now. Not when they just caught us... And I'm married. And *straight*... I think.

I'm a man of God, who's not supposed to be adultering. Like, at all.

"I, uh... I should actually be going," I blurt out, running my hands through my hair. I turn to Tate and huff, "I'm sorry. I can't..."

But that's all I get out. My voice dries up, and I spin away from him, stomping up the hall as fast as I can.

I don't know what I was thinking... Or wasn't.

Yea, that's the problem. I wasn't thinking.

I lost my head being near him again, after so long. Temporary insanity. It happens.

But my stomach is churning, the entire walk back to my car.

When I get to it, I hop in and sit there, staring at the steering wheel for almost twenty minutes before I finally work up the courage to turn on the engine... and drive home.

Chapter Seven
Tate

I feel like an idiot.

And I'm telling you... I *hate* feeling like an idiot.

If there's one thing I can't stand, it's doubting myself. I have no room for it. I pushed away those types of insecurities years ago. Now, I like to focus primarily on how awesome I am, and living my best life.

This whole self-doubt and reflecting on the past thing is making me want to puke, then slap myself in the face.

Fifteen years ago, I fooled around with one of my best friends. And then he took off. Quite literally *ran* away from me, never to be seen or heard from again. And ever since, I've spent every waking moment making sure I *never* find myself in a situation where I feel so helpless and hurt and *stupid* ever again.

So I'm sure you can understand why Lance Hardy running away from me now, *over a decade later*, would make me want to gouge my own eyeballs out of their sockets. Bumping into him in that bathroom was like a massive *fuck you* from the universe. Or *God,* as Lance might say. Though I'm sure he would tell me that God *loves me,* and would never tell me to fuck off, and blahdy blahdy blah.

But if that's the case, then why would I be presented with the one person I've been actively trying to forget about for years? Of all the people on this big, blue spinning rock, why would I find myself on the other side of a rickety bathroom stall wall from *Lance Hardy*?

Ditching him at the club felt really good, I must admit. Giving him a taste of his own medicine. I've certainly fantasized about it enough... Maybe not so much recently, but definitely during my remaining years at Arizona State. I dreamt about seeing him, telling him off and sauntering away with my middle finger aimed at his stupid, beautiful face. And I got that opportunity, earlier today.

Unfortunately, I'm *an idiot.* And I squandered it, letting him nudge his way back into my world... *And my mouth.* With his deep brown eyes, and his shiny, tousled blonde hair. His huge behemoth body, all sculpted everywhere... Something he so blatantly takes for granted by being a fucking *pastor.*

He could be a model or a football player, or a hot fireman who slides down a pole with his shirt off.

Lance is just *too* goddamn hot. That's the only reason I entertained his bogus apology. His dick is too perfect to never let anywhere near my body again. And of course, because God *does* hate me, I dropped my guard, instantly regretting it when he ran off yet again, leaving me standing around like the moron I am—like *I* was supposed to do to *him*—with confusion in my chest and a dull throb between my legs.

Well, you know what? Fuck him.

It's Pride. The last thing I want to be doing is wallowing with blue balls. *I'm too awesome for that.*

Let's just chalk it up to a wrong place, wrong time scenario, and find me someone else to sate my need to be ridden raw. Because it's *never* going to be him.

End of story.

After Lance took off, I brought Ben and Ryan back to Xquisite with me. *I know, I know.* Returning to the scene of the crime makes it seem like I'm not as over it as I swear I am. But really, I just like this place, and I know everyone here. Nick is bartending all night, so worst case, I can just get drunk and wait for him to get off, so he can... *Well, yea. You get the picture.*

The only tiny sliver of positivity to the whole Lance debacle is that it's pulling focus from how potentially awkward it could be hanging out with the Lockwood's. I haven't seen either of them since two Christmases ago, when I spent nearly twenty-four hours getting railed by Ryan, and then Ben punched me in the face.

I *personally* wouldn't say there's bad blood between us, especially since everything worked out swimmingly for the two of them, and their wife. But still, Ben and I have never really gotten along. We've merely tolerated each other because his brother has been my best friend in the whole world since childhood. *A very straight best friend, whom I've never hooked up with, I might add.* And Ryan... Well, Ryan is a good kid. Our interactions were always casual, because casual is what I do.

Did I like spending time with him? *Fuck yea, I did.* But the entire time we played our occasional hook-up game, he was madly in love with someone else, *and* that someone's wife. So it doesn't matter that I could have maybe slipped, unintentionally, into something else with him...

He's just a friend. A friend who's put his dick in me a few times. That's it.

We can keep our distance again starting tomorrow. But tonight is still Pride, and Pride is meant to be celebrated in gay clubs with queer friends.

The bass is thumping my veins while I flirt with Nick over the bar. He's pretty much a sure thing, but do I really want to wait until he gets off work to get laid? *No, not exactly.* I'm wound up, frustrated, and feeling too many things that are too real for me... And it's all Lance Hardy's fucking fault.

I need a distraction. Like, *now.*

Turning over my shoulder, my eyes land on my *friends*, Ben and Ryan, who are kissing and touching, giving each other smoldering sexual looks. The sight of it twists a knot in my gut that I just can't overcome, no matter how much liquor I dump on it. I've never seen the two of them together like this... Not in person, anyway.

I've seen pictures on their Facebook and Instagram pages, of them swooning over each other. Photos of them with Jessica, and baby Ethan. They're in love, and it's interesting to witness, considering the last time I saw either of them, there was mainly only hostility and a very unsubtle fiery longing coming from both sides.

What a difference eighteen months can make, I guess.

Normally, I couldn't give a good goddamn about seeing people behave so painfully in love right in front of me. But for some reason, right now, it's spreading this singe up to my chest like heartburn.

I need to get away from it... *All of it.* From the hand-holding and googly eyes, the tender, heated kisses and eager touches. All these people and their fucking *feelings*...

Bleh. Gross.

Get me some dick, please. Stat.

Tugging my phone out of my pocket, I open Grindr to find dozens of new matches and messages. This is good. This is what I should have done from the start. Simple sex, no complications.

No potential of accidental run-ins with closeted former friends.

Trouble

Tapping on a message from someone with the username **SinfulSeth**, my thumbs work quickly to type out a response to his, *Hey, sexy.*

I've barely sent my reply before a dick pic pops up on the screen. Followed by the standard, *Top or bottom?*

Biting down on the inside of my cheek, I answer him, then ask if he's at the club. To which he responds that he is. My chin lifts, and I look around, wondering how close he actually is to me. My eyes dart left, and I spot a guy, pretty much right next to me, on his phone.

His eyes jump up to mine, then fall to his phone once more.

SINFULSETH

Are you standing next to me?

TLOVESTHED

That depends. On a scale of 1-10, how hot is the dude you're looking at?

The guy next to me laughs, his eyes slinking over again before he begins typing.

SINFULSETH

100

Turning to him, I stuff my phone into my pocket and murmur, "Good answer."

He tucks his phone away too, giving me a gradual once-over, while I do the same to him. He's definitely hot. Tall... Not as tall as a certain someone we're not thinking about, but still, maybe an inch taller than me. He has brown hair and nice lips, a perfectly trimmed beard. Definitely looks like he could pin me to something, which is really all I'm looking for.

So I tilt my head and ask, "You wanna get outta here?"

His lips curl wickedly. "I thought you'd never ask."

Killing my drink, I set the empty glass down on the bar, casting one last lingering look at Ben and Ryan. They're off in their own little world. *Good for them...*

No goodbyes needed. I take the hand of my new *unmarried* friend—at least, I'm assuming he's not married, but then how would I really know—and drag him with me, out of the club and into a cab.

My hotel is only five minutes away, but it's still more than enough time for **SinfulSeth** to slide his hand between my legs and whisper purely filthy things into my ear. When we get up to my room, he's slamming me up against the door before I can even attempt to reach for my room key.

"I bet you look damn good on your knees," he growls into my mouth, and for some unknown reason, all I can see in my mind is me on my knees...

Earlier, in the hallway at Kennan's house. With Lance humping my face and whining those delicious, nervous noises.

Shaking it away, I get us inside the room, and we immediately start stripping. Shirts and pants come off while we attack each other like ravenous animals. It's perfect, and *exactly* what I need...

Until my phone starts ringing, in my pocket on the floor.

My movements slow, but Seth, the gentleman, grabs my jaw to hold my mouth where he wants it. "Bend over, beautiful. Let me see what you're giving me."

Normally, words like that would have me shivering in anticipation. But right now, the hunger I usually feel when I'm about to get dicked isn't as strong as I'd like it to be. Still, I turn around, closing my eyes at the feel of lips on the nape of my neck.

He shoves me forward, and I gasp, bending at the waist and bracing my hands on the nearest piece of furniture; a chair. His hands are all over my ass, gripping and squeezing as he slowly lowers my fitted black boxer briefs. I take in a deep breath, focusing on staying in the moment; on the thrill of my overactive need to be turned out.

My phone starts ringing again.

I gulp. "I'm just gonna..." My hand inches to the floor, reaching for my pants.

"Don't you dare," he growls, pushing me onto my knees and immediately kneeling behind me. "You're mine right now."

"'Kay..." I sigh, panting just a little.

Seth licks a line up my spine. "Condom?"

"In my... pocket."

He reaches into the pocket of my pants to grab a condom. And my phone slides out with it.

Then it's ringing some more.

"Someone's looking for you..." he chuckles breathlessly, tearing the condom open with his teeth.

"Yea..." I mumble, my eyes shifting to my phone on the floor.

It's a New Mexico number I don't recognize. And my gut tightens at the idea that it might be...

No. No, absolutely not. It can't *be him...*

Trouble

Why would he scurry off again like a frightened animal, only to call me repeatedly?? That would be sincerely fucked up.

But now that the thought is in my mind, it won't go. I can't focus on anything Seth is doing because I'm too busy wondering who the hell is calling me over and over and over...

"Hang on," I mutter to Seth, grabbing my phone and sliding to accept the call. "Yes...?"

"Tate..."

Jesus Christ.

My eyes close, and I rub them hard, a sigh of bewildered frustration leaving my lips. "How did I know it would be you...?"

"I'm *sorry*, T," Lance whispers in my ear, and my teeth grind so hard I can hear them snapping.

"Why are you doing this to me?" I grunt. "I'm getting motion sickness..."

"I know," he grumbles, sounding exhausted. "I know, it's fucked up. I shouldn't be—"

"Hang up the phone, baby," Seth whispers while kissing my neck, grinding his cock between my cheeks.

"Who's that?" Lance asks in a suddenly sharp tone. "Are you with someone right now??"

I bite my lip. "What's it to you?"

"I'm losing wood here, man," Seth sighs, backing up.

"Tell him to leave," Lance growls, and my dick throbs.

"Seriously??" I huff, straightening and watching over my shoulder as Seth stands up and gets dressed. "Now you're cockblocking me over the phone?!"

"Thanks for nothing," **SinfulSeth** hisses as he stomps out of my hotel room, slamming the door behind him.

But I can't even be mad about it. Because no matter how hot he was, the tiny spark of excitement he took with him when he left was *nothing* compared to the intense buzz happening inside me right now...

From this Johnny come lately motherfucker on the phone.

"You are such an insufferable dickhead," I chuckle indignantly, rolling onto my back on the floor.

"Is he gone?" Lance mumbles in my ear, and the sound of his deep, rumbly voice, laced with his usual uncertainty, *and* some possessiveness that makes no goddamn sense, sends the most ridiculous wave of desire crashing in the pit of my stomach.

It's so familiar... All of this. *How can it still feel this way so many years later??*

I thought I was over it. I was *sure* that I was...

But apparently, all it took was him waltzing back into my life to undo all the stitches.

"Yea. Thanks to you, I'll never get laid again," I scoff.

"Doubt it," he speaks quietly.

"What do you *want*, Hardy?" I ask, my patience for his shenanigans wearing extremely thin. "You've officially ruined my entire day. Is this how you say *I'm sorry*?? Because if so, I think you're seriously missing the point of an apology."

"I... I shouldn't have left, okay?" he rumbles. "I got scared again, and I fucked up, T. I'm sorry, but this is... really difficult for me..."

"*What* is?" I pry, wishing I could reach through the phone and strangle the words out of him.

He goes quiet for a moment, just breathing in my ear, and it reminds me that I'm naked. My eyes fall to my dick, resting half-hard on my abs.

"There's more I wanted to tell you before, but I got... distracted," he hums.

My dick jerks, and I slowly slink my hand down around it. "Distracted, hm? How'd that happen?"

"Come on, Tate..." he huffs. "You know damn well how distracting you are."

"I've always distracted you, haven't I?" My fist curls and pulls gently on my cock as it fills and thickens in my palm.

"You have... and I just don't get it."

The depths of his voice reverberate in my brain, sending chills all over my body. My nipples are pebbled, chest moving with rapidly increasing breaths.

I'm the one who just doesn't get it... *How is this turning me on more than the hot as fuck dude who wanted to rearrange my organs??*

Talking on the phone with a married straight guy who used to be my friend... An indecisive, anxious, fluttering beast of a man who doesn't know what the hell he wants.

"Well, you have me right now," I breathe, tugging slowly on my cock. "You've chased away yet *another* attempt at an orgasm for me, so why don't you just spill it?"

I hear rustling, and I grin because I can tell even from over the phone that he's fidgeting around, all nervous.

Trouble

"Seeing you today... brought all that stuff from the past rushing back," he tells me. "I thought I'd shoved it down, but it turns out, maybe, it wasn't... buried deep enough."

Fuck... don't say buried deep *to me right now...*

"What the fuck are you so afraid of, Sunshine?" My voice comes out breathy from the feel of my hand sliding up and down on my rigid erection.

Some more rustling happens before he whispers, "You."

"Me?" I huff a laugh, and I can picture him cracking a smile in my head.

"You've always scared me, Trouble."

"Great... So I scare you, and because of that, you're going to keep chasing guys away from me forever..."

He hums into the phone, and my balls are *aching*. "You shouldn't be with any of those guys..."

I chomp onto my lip, squirming while I jerk my dick harder. "It's just sex, Hardy."

"You shouldn't have *sex* with them, Tate..."

"Why not?"

"Because..."

"Because *why*?"

He makes a little whining noise that has precum pulsing onto my abs. "Because I... Because *we*..."

"Fuck me, just say it, you delicious tease," I grunt, feverishly humping up into my hand.

"Tate... are you..." Lance's voice cuts out into a salacious whisper. "Are you touching yourself??"

A breathy chuckle leaves my lips, and I lick them. "Why... does that *scare* you?"

"Um..." he stammers.

I squeeze my cock tight in my fist. "Thanks to you, I'm not getting laid. I gotta get my rocks off, Hardy..."

"Tate..." he whimpers, like I'm physically hurting him. I love it a little too much. "Come on."

"*Come on* what?" I let a moan slip through my words. "Come on my abs? Come on your... cock?" He whines again, and my back arches. "Come on the bed while you stuff me full like we all know you want to..."

"Mmmff," he grunts, voice becoming a bit uneven.

"Are *you* touching yourself now, Sunshine?" The second the words leave my lips, I know they're true.

Lance groans quietly in my ear, a sound meant only for me as he takes a few generous seconds to work up to the sweet treat of a gasped, "Yes."

My eyes roll back in my skull. I have no idea why this is the hottest thing ever, but it just is. It's crazy how much simply *talking* to him makes me feel like a kid again; a wide-eyed nineteen-year-old, coming into his sexuality, with a friend whose every subtle movement turned into an aching fantasy.

The thing is, I never would have acted on my intense sexual attraction to Lance back then. Before that night, I totally could've kept him as a friend... One I happened to find *beyond* fuckhot, and may have dreamed about letting ravage me many, *many* times.

But *he* came to *me*, confused and sexually charged, needing something he could only get from me. Or maybe something he only *wanted* from me.

It was like a dream come true. But it fizzled out way too fast.

Now I've been reacquainted with all the things I felt that night, and I'm desperate to chase the high; grab onto it and suck the life out of it until we're both sweaty, and sated full.

"Tell me..." I purr, quickly putting him on speaker so I can use both hands. "Tell me what you're doing for me."

"Ffuck... *Tate*..." The way he says my name is downright pleading, and it's driving me wild. "This is..."

"What's wrong?" I groan, cupping my balls while my other hand works fiercely on my cock. "Is your wife asleep next to you?"

"No," he scoffs defensively, and I chuckle.

"Then tell me what you're doing..."

He hums, but eventually gives up the fight and mumbles, "I'm... stroking my cock."

"Mmm... good. Me too."

"Yea?"

"Yea. I'm doing it slow... The way you did it for me that night, in my bed."

He purrs, "Ohhfuck... *Trouble*."

"Remember?"

"Of course I fucking remember," he growls. "It felt *so* good... touching you while you touched me."

My chest flutters. "What else felt good that night?"

"K-kissing you," he whimpers. My dick is so hard I can feel the veins pulsing in my hand. "Biting your sweet lips and swallowing your little moans..."

Trouble

My head is getting all hazy as I breathe, "You always wanted to kiss me, didn't you, Sunshine?"

"Maybe..." he murmurs, and I roll my eyes, grinning when he corrects, "*Okay*, yes." Slipping my fingers up into my mouth, I suck on them, getting them nice and wet while he speaks hushed, timid lust into my ear. "I still remember pinning you to your bed with my hips... rubbing our dicks together."

"Fuck yea," I hum, sliding my hand between my thighs, parting them wider. "Remember what you did next?"

"*Uhh...* Tate..."

"I'll take that as a *yes*," I rumble. "Tell me, babe... and maybe I'll do it to myself right now."

Lance makes a purely greedy sound as my body trembles in wait. "I... put my fingers inside you."

Chewing on my lip to keep the groans in, I writhe by myself on the floor of my hotel room, slipping my fingers between my ass to tease my rim. "You fucked me with them, didn't you, baby..."

"*Yea*... I did. I fucked your tight, warm hole with my fingers." His panting is picking up.

"Why didn't you just use your cock?" I whine, stuffing a finger inside myself with a grunt. It burns from lack of proper lubrication, but I don't even care. My toes are curling. "I was *dying* to feel you fucking me deep and hard..."

"I know..." he whispers, practically choking as the sounds of him stroking himself echo in my ears. I stuff another finger into my ass, jamming them as deep and hard as I can, relishing in the delicious hurt. "Because you're *my* Trouble, aren't you, baby?"

I'm nodding, without even realizing it. "Uh-huh."

"*Fuck*, I should've just fucked you back then," he breathes unsteadily. "I wish I did..."

"Fuck me... now..." I gasp as my thoughts cloud into a fog of impending climax.

"Are your fingers touching that sweet spot for me, Trouble?"

"Mhmm..." I'm gnawing on my lip, shaking at the burn and frustration of my own fingers only being able to give me so much.

I want more... so, *so much more.*

"You want it deeper, don't you?" He growls my exact thought, and I mewl. "You want it bigger? Thicker, longer... Hotter and harder. You want it driving all the way up inside your beautiful body until you just can't help but—"

"Fuck fuck *fuck*... Lance, I'm *coming*," I rush the words out on garbled moans as my dick erupts, spilling hot pulses all over me.

Oh God, yes. Finally...

Shivers overtake me while I spin and spin through my sweet release, winding down from being wound up tight all damn day, as Lance croons by my side.

"That's good, baby. Listen to you... coming for me. You're gonna make me bust, my sweet, wicked Trouble..."

"Push it in my mouth," I sigh, fingers trailing through my cum, bringing it up to my lips. "Feed your orgasm between my lips like you did that night..."

"*Ffuck...*" he groans, voice snapping.

I suck my own flavor from my fingers while my ass clenches on the others, still buried as deep as they can get. "You taste like my Sunshine..."

He gasps, then whines, "Fuck me, *Tate*, I'm coming. Swallow it..."

"Every *drop*... baby, throb it on my tongue." I scoop more of my cum up, sucking dizzily, hungrily, lapping it up like it's his.

Lance is making all kinds of noises, bursting and coming over the phone, until he finally fizzles down and lets out a quiet purr. My big beast of a man...

Fuck... What the...

As the high begins to wear off, my eyes creep open slowly. Pulling my fingers out of myself, I blink at the ceiling, letting out a tired breath.

He's *not* mine.

He isn't now and he wasn't back then.

What am I doing...? Why am I letting him back into my life?

This could never go anywhere, so really... what am I thinking??

"Tate..." he whispers, and I recognize that tone. It's exactly how he sounded the last time we fooled around, right before he split like a log.

I can't do this. I cannot keep doing this to myself...

"Hardy..." I grumble, sitting up and shaking my head.

"Yea?"

"Don't call me ever again."

I end the call and power off my phone.

Because trouble is as trouble does.

Chapter Eight
Tate

Work is the ultimate distraction. But the good thing for me is that I also happen to love my job.

Sure, it's stressful. Any booming career usually is. Really, I wouldn't want it any other way.

I can do most of my work remotely, and being that I'm sort of the *relationship guy* for our firm, I tend to travel a lot.

I know, right? Me... the relationship guy. The irony is not lost.

I have a place in Corona, mainly because it's near where I grew up, and I like to have a home base near my mom just in case she needs me for anything. We're not super close, but other than my *found family*, she's all I've got. My in-state work travels are mostly to Santa Fe, where I have a penthouse rental. I also have a place in New York City. But a majority of my life is spent in hotels, traveling all over the country, sometimes the world, to land important accounts for my firm.

It's fun and it makes me bank, so you won't find me complaining. This is very much my lifestyle. Unattached bachelor, jet-setting all over the place to schmooze people much richer than me, in order to help myself and my coworkers get richer ourselves.

This is *Tate Eckhart*, as real as it gets.

Tate Eckhart wears expensive suits and has a drawer full of Rolexes.

Tate Eckhart sips scotches older than he is.

Tate Eckhart hasn't flown coach since he was twenty-two.

Tate Eckhart doesn't have time for relationships or feelings or reminiscing about past secret liaisons with straight former friends, because Tate Eckhart is all about work, and looking good, and curling guys' toes with his incredibly honed blowjob skills.

The love of my life is me... vices and all.

Fuck it. Tate Eckhart is *a vice, goddamnit.*

Call me shallow as a puddle. It's fine, I'm good with it. In fact, I should be *thanking* Lance fucking Hardy for ditching me in college. He showed me that falling in love is for the simple, the weak... The people without any bigger dreams or goals. Codependent fools with no aspirations.

I mean... I'm not saying I loved *him or anything. I only used the word to make a point.*

Whatever.

The *point is* that he did me a favor, and now I'm returning it. By ignoring his calls and pretending he doesn't exist.

And he's definitely been calling. For days since the lapse in judgement that led to phone sex, Lance has been calling and texting me nonstop. I still have no idea how he got my number... *Probably from Kennan, that loose-lipped lush.* Either way, it's irrelevant. I'm not answering any of his obsessive attempts at contacting me, because it's a dead end.

Whatever forces led us back into each other's lives were horribly misguided. Even if I thought I wanted a relationship, which I *don't*, I'm too busy. And Lance is too straight. And too married.

And too... He's just too everything I'm not.

I'm sure he's stuck on the idea of me back then. That's the only reason he's doing this... Chasing after me like he thinks he wants something he wouldn't want if he saw its ugly, unpolished realness. The Tate from back then doesn't exist anymore.

This is me. And why would someone like him... want someone like this?

My phone ringing distracts me, and I shake myself out of my thoughts, peering at the long granny-ash of the cigarette I've just been holding for minutes while I stare off into space. Stubbing it out in an ashtray, I pick up my phone and slide open the door from the balcony of my hotel room, stalking back into the air conditioning and out of the stifling humidity of Houston in July.

Noting the name on the screen, which does not say *Don't be an idiot*—the contact name I saved Lance's number under in my phone—my lips curve as I swipe to answer.

Trouble

"Sup, bestie?" I pad over to the mini fridge for a bottle of the cold-pressed juice I love.

I'm on detox for the next few days so I can go hard again this weekend.

"Oh, so you still remember me?" Jake deadpans, and I chuckle.

"How could I forget you, precious?"

"I assumed you had... since you've been radio silent for days," my best friend scolds. He does it in a nice way, but still. I recognize the tone well.

Although Jacob Lockwood is the same age as me, he's always acted more like my protective older brother. *And he's much less grouchy than his older brother.* Truthfully, Jake and I couldn't be more different, but it seems like that's how I choose my friends. Shakes things up, I suppose. Plus, I like being the wild one of the group. It makes me feel special.

I've known Jake and Ben, along with the rest of our close-knit group of friends, since middle school. And I'm the token gay guy. Well, I *was*... until Ben decided to upstage me and come out as queer. *That dude's always been a show-off.*

"What are you talking about??" I huff to Jake on the phone in between sipping my juice. "I tagged you in that hilarious Instagram reel of the guy pretending to fuck his gas tank with the pump nozzle."

"Yea, and as much as I appreciate you tagging me in videos of thirst traps on Insta, it doesn't count as conversation," he mutters, and I laugh. "I expected a call after Pride. How was Kennan's party?"

My mind instantly and unwittingly flits to Lance's big, beautiful cock thrusting between my lips. And then, of course, I recall the image of Jake's older brother getting railed by his husband, aka my former fling.

"Uneventful," I mumble.

"With you?? It never is," he chuckles. "Spill it, Trouble."

My stomach flutters, and I cringe. *God-fucking-damnit... Now that nickname has been completely sullied for me.*

All of our friends have always called me *Trouble*, since we were teenagers and I filled Mr. Janson's desk drawer with frogs. Lance didn't even know about the nickname when he called me it in college... Naturally, it just made me like him even more.

What a prick.

"Are you bored or something?" I grumble.

"I don't have to be bored to want to know what's up with my best friend," Jake croons. I roll my eyes. "Unrelated, I have a twenty-minute drive to pick up the girls from a sleepover."

A chuckle puffs from between my lips, then I bite the bottom one. I don't know why I'm hesitant to tell Jake I ran into Lance at Pride. It makes it seem like I'm harping on it, which I so am *not*... I just know what mentioning it is going to do.

Still, I tell him everything, so...

"Okay, I guess one sort of interesting thing happened." I gulp.

"I knew it. Go."

"I, uh... I ran into Lance." Jake starts coughing hysterically in my ear. "You alright there, buddy??"

"Sorry, I choked on a sip of my coffee." He clears his throat. "You ran into *Lance*...? At Pride??"

"Yea. It was weird." I purse my lips, ignoring all the crazy happening inside me.

"Did you guys... talk?" Jake asks, and I know he really means, *Did you guys hook up?* Because he knows me all too well, and he also knows *all* about my history with Lance Hardy.

Meaning, he knows exactly how into Lance I was in college, and how devastated I was when he ghosted me.

Okay, devastated *is a bit much. It makes me sound way too sad-boy for my liking.*

"We talked a little..." I explain, pacing around the living room of my hotel suite. "He sorta wanted to... apologize, I guess." I pause and shake my head. "But who cares, right?? I mean, fuck him." Jake is quiet for a few heavy seconds that have me gripping the phone tighter and tighter in my fist. "Please agree with me."

"It's definitely a long time coming," Jake finally speaks, though his words don't placate me one bit. "He should've apologized years ago." I'm chewing my bottom lip raw. "Is he still... married?"

"Of course he is." I roll my eyes again, feeling saltier than a New York City pretzel.

"What was he doing at Pride?" Jake huffs.

"What do you *think* he was doing at Pride..."

It's beyond obvious. Lance has been questioning his sexuality since college, and I'm willing to bet he would have let *anyone* suck him off through that glory hole. The fact that it was me was just some twisted joke put on by the big dude in the sky he loves so damn much.

"Do you think he came to see you?"

My jaw tightens. "Jacob, I love you, but please don't say things that make it hard to do so."

"Dude, come on. It's not crazy," he states firmly. "Maybe he was telling himself he went just to see how he felt about it, but it's not out of the realm of possibility that he was secretly hoping he'd run into you. He obviously knew you'd be there..."

"Whatever. None of this fucking helps me." I rake my fingers through my hair. "He's a pastor and he's married to a woman. I don't have time for any of these closet games."

Jake pauses for a second. "Hang on... Did he tell you he's been thinking about you?" I go silent for a second, and Jake gasps. "There's more to this story you're not telling me, isn't there?!"

"Why do all of my straight friends love gossip more than I do?" I scoff.

"Okay... I have a confession," he says, bunching my stomach. "He friended me on Facebook. Like, a year ago."

My lashes flutter. "Is that right...?"

"Yea. And I accepted him, *mainly* because I figured it was only a matter of time before he asked about you."

"That is just so..." My voice trails before I quietly ask, "Did he?"

"Well, *no*," Jake murmurs.

My chest tightens, a physical reaction I really don't care for. "See? Told ya."

"Yea, but he always likes every picture I post of you," he goes on. "Actually, he *only* likes my pictures of you."

Now my heart is doing a weird thump. Because it's clearly a fucking moron.

"That doesn't mean anything..."

"Maybe not... Or maybe it means he's been itching to get in touch, and has been working himself up to it."

"Look, this is all very third grade," I huff. "I gotta go get ready for a meeting."

Jake sighs, like I'm being too stubborn and it's irritating him. "Fine. I expect to hear the rest of this Pride story, though. The unabridged version. Are you coming home this weekend? For the party?"

My brow furrows. "What party?"

"Oh... Ben said he was going to invite you. I assumed he already had..."

"Please. Your brother rarely invites me to things unless Jess talks him into it."

"No, she wouldn't. It's a surprise anniversary party for Jess and Ryan. On Saturday."

"Well, I guess my invitation got lost in the mail," I mutter.

"Trust me, he'll call you. He said he was going to."

Nyla K.

"If he does, I'll be there."

"Even if he doesn't, you should come by Sunday. The girls miss their Uncle Trouble."

The sound of Jake's audible grin tugs my lips into one of my more genuine ones. I don't need to settle down myself, because I already have a family. *And they're pretty cool.*

"Alright, I'll talk to you soon, Beavis."

"Later, Butthead."

My conversation with Jake has me nostalgic for hours. All throughout my meeting with our new clients at the Houston office, I can't stop thinking about my life, and my friends... How different we are. All the ways I've *changed*.

I wasn't lying to Lance when I told him I really haven't changed much since college. I haven't in the ways that matter, like my personality and who I am. My pride in myself, my confidence, and the strength I find in Tate Eckhart, the successful gay man.

I guess in a lot of ways, I'm lucky I've never had to struggle with my sexuality the way some people do. Sure, I don't have any real family outside of my mother, and she's not without her issues. But still, she's always loved and accepted me.

The same goes for my friends. Of course, I have a ton of gay friends, but I also love my group of corny, straight, married pals, with all their kids and their parent-problems. The idea of getting married and having kids has never appealed to me, but I still love hanging out with them, the same way they love hanging out with me, despite how they might never truly understand the life of a wealthy, single gay man. We all love and accept one another *because* of our differences, not in spite of them.

Maybe I don't do *feelings*... but I *do* feel things. *Sometimes.* Right now, I hate to admit it, but I'm feeling a lot. And I guess... not all of it is awful.

Back in my hotel room at the end of the night, I'm tossing my stuff into my bag. My flight back to New Mexico leaves at seven in the morning, which means I'll need to leave the hotel by five. Doesn't matter to me, though. Us bankers are early risers by trade. Like farmers, only our crops are those sweet, green, dead presidents.

Maybe I'll even squeeze in a workout before I leave.

Sauntering around the hotel room with a glass of scotch, I have Grindr up on my phone, as usual. There are a bunch of guys in my area, and I'm wondering if maybe I should go meet up with one, or more. I could use the release... I'm a bit more anxious than usual, and I refuse to think about *why*.

Trouble

Opening a message from a guy who looks like exactly the kind of present I need to get my mind off the past, my eyes barely get to take in the perverse things he's written, when an incoming call flashes over it.

Don't be an idiot.

I roll my eyes. *Thanks for the reminder, past Tate. I* will not *be an idiot.* Swipe to ignore.

A few seconds later, a text pops up, and I growl. *I will not read you.*

My mood is souring fast, and I really fucking hate Lance Hardy for killing it the way only *he* can. He's been cockblocking me since that night... The first time I ever went to a gay club, and I made the mistake of bringing my *straight* friend.

I'll just have to settle for fucking myself tonight. *No matter. I'm an excellent fuck.*

Traipsing into the bedroom, I plop onto the bed and pull up PornHub on my phone. I'm absentmindedly scrolling through videos for a few minutes when something catches my eye. Squinting at the screen, I click on the video, watching the bodies move. They both look *very* familiar, one more than the other. Their faces are blurred, but rather shoddily, because a few errant movements and I'm able to catch their profiles.

"Holy fuck..." I gasp, eyes widening.

It's Ben and Ryan. *Jesus, these two...*

They clearly have some very strong exhibitionism kinks going on in their marriage. First, fucking in wide open rooms for the whole world to see, and now posting videos of them fucking on the Hub... for the *actual* world to see.

Chewing on my lower lip, I'm watching Ben smash his cock into Ryan and shivering at the revelation that apparently sweet Harper is quite versatile, when a new text pops up at the top of my screen. My eyes jump, expecting it to be from fucking Hardy. But it's not.

It's from my friend, the amateur pornstar.

BEN

> Hey... I'm throwing a surprise anniversary party for Ryan and Jess on Saturday. If you're around, you should come.

I can't help snickering to myself. Because he said *come*, and I'm a child.

Nyla K.

Thanks for the invite, Lockwood. Wouldn't miss it for the world ;)

Ugh.

I laugh to myself at his response. *God, he hates me. It's so much fun.*
When I close out his text, my eyes linger on my unread messages...
Don't be an idiot.
Don't...
I click on them... Because clearly, I *am* an idiot, and I just can't fucking help it.

DON'T BE AN IDIOT

T... please. I really need to talk to you.

DON'T BE AN IDIOT

It's important. I need you to listen to me...

DON'T BE AN IDIOT

Trouble, don't be like this.

DON'T BE AN IDIOT

It was never supposed to be like this with us...
Remember? Me and you... we're so much more.

A frustrated breath leaves my lips as I smack my phone face down on the bed next to me.
It doesn't matter what he says. None of it.
Maybe we were more back then... Or we *could* have been.
But it doesn't matter now. Because one very big thing *has* changed since college...
The door to my heart closed permanently when he slammed it shut.

Chapter Nine
Lance

15 years ago...

I*'m in a dream...*
That's how it feels when he opens the door.
The look on his face, the sparkle in his eyes, washes away my guilt, uncertainty, and shame. Like a baptism, I'm cleansed of all reasoning that I *shouldn't* be doing this by that one look, the relief and elation I can feel through his dark gaze.

I paced in front of Tate's door for minutes, contemplating what a fool I am. Scolded myself for hundreds of seconds, telling myself to turn back, just *leave* before I made things worse.

It doesn't matter how badly you want it...

It's wrong. No good can come from knocking on that door.

Tate is too important. This will only hurt him in the long run.

But the thing is, it's been building for a long time, this *want*. I carry it around in my chest every day. I don't know what it means for my sexuality that I've been stuffing down feelings of desire for my closest friend since pretty much the moment we met.

But that's still only the *second* most complicated part of this whole thing...

The first is something that evaporated the moment he opened the door.

Naturally, I'm still nervous, fighting to steady my racing pulse as I wander inside the dorm room, and Tate closes the door behind me, locking it. I turn to face him, eyes falling over his exposed torso; all the curves and slopes of muscle that prove him to be a *man*. A strong one, with size and definition I've never looked for in partners before.

Masculinity isn't something I thought I found alluring... until right now.

Tate still hasn't said a word. But when my gaze snaps out of the blatant ogling and rises back to his face, he's biting his lip, looking at me with the same hunger I can feel in my bones.

Has he always looked at me like this?

Is he just horny and wanting to hook up, because he didn't get it from that guy at the club? Or does he want me the way I secretly want him?

Is this a new attraction... or are we finally being honest with ourselves, and each other...?

Tate looks like he wants to lunge, the way his eyes are blazing and he's tugging his lower lip between his teeth, fingers twitching at his sides. But he's not moving, and I think I know why.

He put himself out there earlier, and I took off. I know Tate well... He's not going to do it again. *Leaving* is a big deal to Tate Eckhart.

So I force my feet to move, stepping into his space until I can feel the heat radiating from his solid frame. I'm dizzy in an instant, the lust fog swallowing me up as I lift my shaky fingers. Their tips ghost over his smooth flesh, running through the lines of his abs and up to his chest.

He gasps, and I hum, our eyes locked the whole time.

Cupping his jaw, I angle him upward, hovering my mouth over his. I'm used to bending to the people I kiss, since they're usually girls I'll have a good foot on. But Tate is on my level. He's *tall*. Still a few inches shorter than me, so that I can tip his chin like this... But taller than anyone I've been this close to.

It's mesmerizing.

I can't believe I'm doing this... I can't believe I'm letting myself do it.

"Tate..." I whisper his name on a shivering breath, watching his dark lashes flutter as his eyes close.

"Mmm..."

Mine follow, our noses brushing while I graze his cheekbones with my thumbs. "Why did you call me Sunshine?" I don't notice that he's gripping my shirt in his fists until he tugs the material, untucking it from my pants. "What does it mean...?"

"It means you make my boner grow like a flower." He smirks, sliding his flingers up under my shirt.

Trouble

I hum a reprimanding chuckle. "Stop messing around, troublemaker." I nip at his full bottom lip with my teeth, and he gasps. "Tell me the truth."

"That *is* very true..." He pushes his hips into mine. I can feel the shape of him, long and hard beneath those fitted sweats. "But... being around you is like being in the sun." I think he's nervous, saying these words to me. *Tate's never nervous...* It squeezes my chest. "You're bright, and warm. You... make me happy."

My lips are quivering. "I *want* to make you happy... I want to make you feel good, Tate."

He whimpers, "Please make me feel *so good*, Sunshine... I need you."

Our mouths are so close, we're sharing the same breaths. My pulse is popping off inside me, and I'm *shaking* for him...

Taste... I need a taste.

"What if I kiss you...?" My words dance on his lips. "Will that make you feel good?"

He nods fast. "Uh-huh."

"You want me more..." our mouths brush, "than that guy in the club?"

"Please," he rasps, fingers slinking from my abs up to my chest. "I'd throw him off a bridge for one little flick of your tongue on mine."

A chuckle rumbles out of me. "That's not very nice, Trouble."

Parting my lips, I feather them over his again, and he whines, "*Fuck*, stop teasing me, Lance. I'm so fucking hard, it hurts." He grips the nape of my neck, trying to pull my mouth to his.

"I'm afraid if I kiss you... I won't be able to stop," I tell him, hoarse and shaky. "*Ever.*"

"Good," he breathes. "I expect devotion..."

Groaning, holding, eyes closed, I'm so ready to lose myself in this.

"God, forgive me," I plead on a whisper, tugging his face as my lips fall...

And I *sink* into him.

Our mouths melt together, a fast chill zipping up my spine. We're kissing... I'm *kissing* Tate Eckhart.

He's already the sweetest thing I've ever tasted.

In an instant, I'm burning alive, chasing the luscious little pants and mewls he's giving me, like delicious breaths of sugar. Keeping it slow, because it feels *euphoric* this way, I suck his soft lips sensually between mine, grazing them with my teeth. When my tongue feathers his, a moan follows, and my cock leaks inside my pants.

Seriously, this feels *too good*. It's not supposed to feel this good kissing someone... Especially someone you're not supposed to kiss.

But it does. It feels like bliss, ignited. A scorching blaze of passion flowing between our ravenous mouths.

Before I know it, we're moving. Tate is dragging me with him toward his bedroom, our kisses growing deeper, *hungrier*, despite the uncoordinated steps that have us almost tripping over one another.

Tate falls backward into his bed, yanking me on top of him. I quickly kick off my shoes while he frantically unbuttons my shirt, tearing it open and shoving it down my shoulders. I don't want to stop touching him for one second, but I manage it long enough to rip my shirt off and throw it somewhere. Then they're right back where they need to be, on his neck and his jaw, in his hair.

Wow... Kissing him feels incredible. The burn of his stubble, my aggression he's matching in spades. It's like we're fighting fire with fire, and dissolving into one another. I don't think my dick has ever been harder... From *kissing*.

I could come from this, I swear.

Tate is writhing beneath me, spreading his legs wide so I can kneel and thrust in between his thighs. My cock is stiff as it seeks out the rock-solid shape in his pants. I groan at the feeling of grinding two long, hard erections together. Both throbbing and desperate to be freed from the prisons of our pants.

His hands grip and squeeze my pecs, dragging down to unbutton and unzip me. We sound like feral beasts, grunting and panting, lips viciously sucking, clothes rustling. It's erotic music to my ears.

Making out with Tate... In his bed...

I'm kissing a guy. This is crazy...

Tate and I are kissing. His tongue is in my mouth...

And he's pulling my pants down...

"Jesus, Lance, you're such a good kisser," he rasps in between my sensual tugging of his pouty lip between my teeth, my tongue sinking in lick him deep. "Why have we not been doing this, like... every day?"

"I don't know, but you taste amazing," I whisper, fisting his hair. "Sweet, delicious Trouble..."

"It's Colgate." He smirks. "Minty fresh."

"You're so *fresh*, aren't you?" I stop kissing long enough to peek down at him while his fingers tease my happy trail. "Being all sexy and tempting... Making it impossible for me to resist kissing your *perfect* fucking mouth."

Trouble

He whines, lashes fluttering. My eyes travel down his creamy complexion, taking in the smooth, taut lines of muscle, glancing between our bodies at the outlines of our full dicks. His is much more visible than mine, since I'm wearing jeans. Still, we're both obviously turned the fuck on, and as nervous as I still am about doing this, my curiosity has broken free of its chains.

I want him to touch my dick. I want to touch his...

"Take off my pants," I demand, soft and gravelly.

Tate pushes my jeans down over my butt, getting them around my thighs before I have to wriggle out the rest of the way. Now, I'm in only my boxer briefs. And I'm so hard, the head of my cock is poking out.

"*God*, I just knew you were fucking huge," he purrs, reaching for my erection.

The moment his fingers graze it, I let out a shivering groan, and a pulse of precum comes with it, seeping onto his abs.

"Look at you... making a sticky mess on me." He cups my balls, and I shudder again. "I'm leaking for you too, baby."

Oh, fuck yea. Baby...

I fucking love that.

Grasping his jaw, I kiss him rough. "I love how you touch me... baby."

Tate chuckles, a raspy-sexy thing, nipping my lip. "Oh, *baby*, you make my cock so fucking hard."

"Yea?" My fingertips trail the waistband of his pants, tugging them away from his skin. I peek down, then back up at his flushed face, cocking a brow. "Are you naked under here?"

"Of course," he hums. "Gotta show off that dick-print."

Something hot and tight rises from my stomach up to my chest, and I growl, "I don't want people seeing your dick, Tate."

"Why not?" he teases, playing coy, like the wicked troublemaker he is.

"Because..."

"*Because...?*" He tilts his head on the pillow, biting away his cocky Tate-smirk.

"Don't fuck with me," I mutter, breathlessly, attempting to choke back my irrational jealousy. "You know why..."

"Mmm... no, I don't," he keeps going, pressing my buttons on purpose. "You haven't even officially met my dick yet."

I sit back on my knees, and grunt, "Then let's remedy that, smartass."

Yanking his pants down, I swoop them off his legs, leaving him completely naked and squirming before me.

I might actually burst into flames.

Look at his body... I mean, damn. *He's an Adonis. I never knew a naked man lying beneath me could look so... beautiful.*

I'm sure it's just Tate. I can't imagine feeling this way about anyone else. I can't imagine *doing* this with anyone else. I trust him, and I care about him, and...

Fuck me, he's just so fucking sexy.

Does this mean I'm attracted to men? Or am I just forever enamored by my good friend, the troublemaker?

Either way, it doesn't matter. I want exactly what I told him I did... To make him feel good.

I want to watch him feeling so unbelievably good for me.

Pushing my boxers down, I crawl out of them, pinning Tate to the bed with my hips. Our dicks are resting together, both stretched, long and thick, tips all shiny with arousal.

"Your cock is so nice, baby," I whisper, kissing him softly while we touch each other everywhere.

"Thank you..." he mewls, dazed.

"It's mine, okay?" I flick his swollen lips with my tongue, rubbing his thighs, my fingers teasing closer to his dick. "Tell me this big, sweet cock is only mine, Trouble."

I curl my fist around it, and he groans, "*Fuck*, baby, it's yours. My dick is all yours, Lance."

"Can I play with it?" I watch his head tipping back as my fist moves up and down, building to a gradual stroke. "It feels so hot and heavy in my hand..."

"God, fffuck yes," he pants. "Work this cock, baby."

My lips drop to his throat, where I kiss and nip his creamy skin, licking the mound while it dips. "Mmm... you like it slow?" He nods. "And *tight*?"

"*Yes...*"

"Fuck my fist, Trouble."

His hips move, rocking into my hand while I suck and bite him. I barely even notice that I'm humping his leg until he reaches for my erection, tugging it to match the tempo I'm giving him.

This is *wild*. I never imagined jerking off a dick that wasn't mine. But Tate's velvety smooth skin pushing in my palm is unbearably hot. As illicit and captivating as his fist working up and down on my own aching cock.

We fall back into kissing, thrusting into one another, our fists bumping while we stroke hard, but slow, rubbing our wet tips together and whimpering in unison at the sensation.

We're both sweating, *writhing*, naked in this bed that's barely big enough for the two of us. It's the most erotic experience of my entire life, and I'm just trying to focus, because I feel like I could come any minute, but I don't want this to end yet.

"Baby..." Tate grunts, kissing down my neck and chest, biting me and sucking my flesh with force. "You feel so *fucking* good..."

"*Mmm*... T-tate," I stutter when his lips cover my nipple, and he suckles gently, swirling his tongue around and around. "God, what are we doing...?"

"What we should've been doing for years," he purrs, lapping at my sensitive peaked flesh. "Fuck me, Lance. *Please*... I want this big cock inside me."

The nerves at what he's saying make me lightheaded. I'm dizzy and drunk on this, desperate for more of him, but also knowing that I *really* shouldn't do it.

"I want you in between my legs..." he goes on, feathering his tongue all over my chest, pulling my cock, squeezing my balls. "Pump me *full*, baby... Fuck my ass with every swollen inch."

"*Mmmff*..."

I wanna fuck him...

God, I wanna fuck him so bad.

"My hole is *so* needy for you, Sunshine," he mewls. My free hand grabs a fistful of his ass, so hard I'm sure I'm bruising him. "It's warm and tight... *aching* for your big, dripping *wet*—"

"F-fuck, shit, *Tate*." I smack his hand away from my dick. "Stop... you're gonna make me come."

He grins lazily, kissing my lips slow. "*Mmm*... no coming unless it's inside me."

I grasp his jaw, holding his face still. "Your mouth is filthy." I swipe my fingers along his puffy lips. "I should come in here..."

Tate groans, parting his lips to lick my fingers. I tug my lower lip between my teeth, watching in fascination as he does it again, this time curling his tongue around them.

"*Suck*," I growl, pushing them forcefully into his mouth.

He grunts, but immediately starts sucking up and down on my index and middle fingers, nice and sloppy. Our eyes stay locked the entire time, sharing the same thought, verified when he spreads his legs open wide.

Nyla K.

Okay... so maybe I can't put my dick in him...
But I don't see the harm in using my fingers. That's not as bad, right?

While Tate throats my fingers, I use my free hand to tease his nuts, his eyes drooping when I spread apart his plump cheeks. Impatiently, I yank my fingers from his mouth, moving them in between. His chest is fluttering, beautiful body flushed everywhere.

Clearly, he needs this. I was never positive what position Tate liked to play in the bedroom... But any time my mind has ever mischievously wandered there, I always secretly hoped he liked to *receive*.

And I guess he does. Because when my slippery fingers dance over his rim, he melts before me, releasing a shivering breath of thrill. The feeling of his hole relaxing under my touch has my dick pulsing onto his pelvis.

"Tell me... if I'm d-doing it wrong, okay?" I mumble, racked with eager nerves as my fingertip nudges into him.

"Please, just put *any* part of your body inside me before I die," he whimpers, rocking against my hand.

"Tate..." I stuff my finger into his ass. We groan together. "Ohh, *baby*, take it..."

"Lance *fffucking* Hardy..." His chest heaves while my finger rests inside the hottest, tightest little spot I've ever felt. "Give me more. Finger my ass... *m-more.*"

I'm burning the hell up, balls drawn tight and achy as I slide a second digit into him, pushing them both as deep as they'll go.

"*Uhhh...*" Tate's back arches, ass clenching on my fingers. "That feels *so* fucking good, baby."

"Yea?" I draw them back, gliding in deep again.

His dick twinges out precum onto his abs, and I'm drooling.

Holy fuck, that's so sexy.

"Your f-fingers..." he gasps, hips chasing the feeling of my hand working in and out. I can't stop marveling at how scorching hot and *inconceivably* tight he is. "*God*, they're fucking incredible..."

"This hole is too small, baby," I groan, pumping my fingers into his ass, rough and deep, while I rub my cock all over him. "I can't believe you wanted my dick in here..."

"Trust me, I still want that more than—*fuuuck*—anything." He holds my hips, spreading his legs as wide as possible. Giving me his ass to finger-fuck almost brutally hard. "Mmm... your big cock stroking in me like this... I'd probably come in seconds."

"Because you love being fucked, huh, sweet Trouble?" I hover over him, jamming fingers into his hole over and over while he cries and trembles.

"Uhhfuck... *yes*. Lance, that's my... Your fingers are... on m-my... *ohh, God*, right there!"

"Baby, your ass is so *warm*. I love feeling you inside..."

"Keep going..."

Tate's dick is bigger, harder, and more engorged than I ever thought possible, pulsing out arousal every time I move my fingers in a certain spot.

It must be his prostate...

"You are so fucking sexy, Trouble... all messy for me." I kiss the words onto his quivering lips. "Taking my fingers like a good boy. You feel it on that sweet spot, beautiful?"

"Uh-huh." He nods, biting his lip. "Right there, baby... holy fuck, I'm so close."

"Yea?" I grind my body into his, stretching him open and swirling my fingers until he's sobbing. "You gonna come on my fingers?"

"Yes... *yes yes yes....*" His toes are curling, hands clutching me for dear life while I work between his legs. "Fuck me, baby... *Fuck me, fuck me harder*, Lance, I'm gonna come..."

"Fucking *come*, Trouble," I growl the words into his mouth, muscles straining like I'm fucking him with my whole body. "Show me how that big dick comes for me..."

Tate's ass clenches tight. His eyes roll back. "Mm... I'm... Fuck, I'm *coming*!"

Eyes falling between us, I watch as his dick erupts, keeping our bodies close because I want it all over me. Warm spurts shoot from his huge, masterpiece of a cock, hitting me in the chest and dripping onto his abs.

It's the hottest thing I've *ever* witnessed. Nothing compares to this.

Kissing Tate, I swallow his moans and hoarse whimpers while his hole contracts on my fingers. His entire body is quaking, shivering in my arms.

And then he liquifies beneath me.

Damn, that was... Wow. Beautiful. Perfect. Hot as fuck.

I want to make Tate come all day, every day. Forever.

Pulling my fingers out slowly, I massage his legs, and his hips, holding him close and breathing him in. The high of getting him off has me weightless.

"You're even more gorgeous when you come, you know that?" I croon, and he exhales, running his fingers down my back.

"Hardy..." he whispers with wonder in his tone. I gaze down at him, biting my lip. *He's, like... really fucking perfect.* "Let me suck on your cock, baby."

"Um... what?" I blink.

"Mmm... you thought we were done just because I came?" He lifts a dark brow, smirking. "How very selfless of you, Mother Theresa." I cackle, and his grin widens. "I want... that big, *delicious* dick... thrusting between my lips." He rolls on top of me, pinning me on my back. Then he drops below my waist, licking up traces of his cum as he goes. "I've been fantasizing about sucking you off for *years.*"

My cock jumps, and Tate chuckles, kissing my inner thighs.

"Really...?" My fingers sift through his messy dark hair.

"Oh, yea," he hums. "Big time, you sexy giant."

A rumbling laugh leaves my lips, but it dissolves into an uneven groan when his warm, wet mouth slips over the head of my cock. It's already the best thing I've ever felt in my twenty-one years of life.

Tate's lips move farther down my shaft, and I'm seeing stars.

"Fffuck... *Tate...*" I croak, holding his face in my hands. "Baby, that feels —*uhh suck me...*"

I'm not even making any sense. But I also can't hear what I'm saying, my pulse pounding so loud in my ears. Tate is just slurping up and down on my dick, taking me as deep as he can until I'm sure he's about to choke.

His fingers toy with my balls, eyes watering, saliva flowing while he bobs, sucking and *sucking.* Legs parting wider, I fist his hair to guide his perfect mouth. I barely even notice that I'm fucking his face until my tip glides down his throat and he does this little gag that turns into a jagged moan.

"Shit... I'm sorry, baby," I breathe, releasing his hair.

He sucks off with a wet pop. "Shut up and keep riding my throat, Sunshine." Pouty lips tease the underside of my head. "Feed me your orgasm."

"H-huh...?" I shiver.

His mouth slopes back onto my cock, and I'm winding, panting, and *purring* for him, eyes trying to close. But I can't miss one second of this view; Tate Eckhart sucking my cock like a *master.*

It briefly has me wondering how many guys he's done this to...

Jealousy burns my lungs. Until I remember his words...

He's been wanting to suck my dick for years...

He's always wanted me. My friend, *Tate... This guy who is so blindingly beautiful, and smart, and funny... Sexy. Sinful. Perfect.*

Trouble

He wanted me all along...

And when I glance down to watch him sucking the life out of me, and find him stroking his cock—already hard again—it's more than I can handle.

The orgasm rushes up, and my balls burst, flooding his mouth with pulse after pulse that he swallows without hesitation. I barely realize that my legs are wrapped around him.

"Baby, I'm coming for you... *Tate*, I'm *coming* so... *hard*."

The sky is falling all around us, bathing us in cosmos of shimmering pleasure. I'm shaking, gasping for air, until the world eventually evens out and Tate pulls his mouth up my dick, releasing a tired exhale.

Peering down at him, I watch his head fall to rest on my pelvis, his fingers trailing up and down his softened cock.

My forehead lines. "Did you come again?"

"Yea..." he sighs dreamily.

"That's *so* hot," I hum.

Lifting his head, he gazes up at me. In the low light, his eyes look so much darker than that smooth brown I know they are.

Same as mine.

Tate crawls over me, curling his warm body of firm muscles up on mine, letting out a breath of pure contentment. "You're really fucking awesome, Hardy."

I rumble, but he's not smirking, or teasing. I can see in those eyes that he's being real with me.

"So are you," I whisper, stiffening from the sudden heaviness in the air.

What we just did... How can something bad also be the most amazing thing I've ever felt?

"You know how your eyes are copying mine?" His lips twitch.

I huff. "I was born first, but sure."

He chuckles. My words echo.

"Well, maybe that means we're supposed to be... something." His lashes flutter as he lies down on my chest, cheek resting over my heart. "Maybe it's so you can see me the way no one else does... And I can see you." He lifts my hand, playing with my fingers. And now my pulse is steadily speeding up. "Because I definitely see you. I see every perfect thing about you, Lance Hardy. You're... my ray of sunshine."

Oh, God...

I'm... *suffocating.*

Burning in my eye sockets has me blinking over and over. My throat is closing up, and I can't breathe.

Fuck...

No. This is so bad...

Tate...

"Baby..." He sounds soft and so sweet, I just want to cling to him and never let go. *Why... Why the fuck does it have to be like this??* "I'm not saying I... expect anything," he goes on, opening his heart up for me like a treasure chest. But I *can't* fucking have it. "I understand how scary it is, you know that. But I really like you... a *lot*. I like you so much, baby, and I want more of this. *Us*. You make me so *happy*, Lance."

Fuck... Fuck fuck fuck!

Tate... Baby, I want that too...

Shit. Fuck my life.

I have to go...

I'm breaking the fuck down here.

I'm starting to squirm as Tate lifts his chin. He takes one look at me and his brows furrow. "Are you okay?"

"No," I grunt, wriggling out from under him. "I'm so sorry, T... But I just... I have to go."

Jumping up, clearing my throat to hide the emotion bubbling over, I rush to get dressed, doing everything in my power not to look at him. But I *feel* him staring at me like a laser searing into my flesh.

"Wait... Right *now??*" He sits up. "Why??"

"I can't do this." I gasp for air, hustling into my clothes as quickly as possible.

"I don't understand..." Tate's quiet voice shudders with pained confusion.

I'm not right for you, Tate... The words lodge inside my throat. *I can't be what you need.*

The only thing I manage to expel is a weakened, "You mean so much to me, baby..." before my voice gives out.

I'm about to fucking lose it.

God, why the fuck did I do this??

I'm such a fucking idiot...

Ignoring reality for one blissful night in secret is fine. But what happens tomorrow, when I can't keep away from him? And the next day, and the next.... When I *need* him more and more, because I can already feel it happening.

Trouble

I will fall so easily for him, I know it. And he'll fall with me...

And I *can't* have that.

When it all comes crashing down—which it will—it'll destroy him, and he doesn't deserve that.

There's no hiding this kind of sin.

"You're really doing this...?" Tate croaks, pushing the emotion out of his tone to bark, "Are you *really* fucking doing this right now??"

"I'm just not... I can't..." Giving up, I rub my eyes. "I'm *sorry*, Tate."

He's silent for a moment, hurt lining his face, before he mutters, "At least have the decency to look me in the eye while you—" His shaky voice gives out.

And as much as it *kills* me, I shoot him one last glance.

When our eyes meet, an entire lifetime of possibilities passes between us, flitting up into the air and evaporating like smoke. I see his sadness shifting quickly to anger, though the pain lingers visibly just beneath his surface. He's masking it, because it's what he does.

His pride is all he'll show to the outside world, covering the truth of his insecurities...

I'm abandoning him, too.

Tate scoffs and shakes his head, biting down on his lower lip. He grabs a pillow, hugging onto it to cover himself. "Whatever... You're welcome for the orgasm," he sniffs. "Hopefully, it didn't turn you gay, you fucking coward."

Ouch...

I've just been stabbed in the chest.

I'm *bleeding*...

I want to scream. Run to him and fall on my knees, cry and beg and tell him it's not what he thinks. That he doesn't understand...

But I can't. I can't tell him the truth if I don't even understand it myself.

So instead, I leave. Rushing out the door as fast as I can, each step slaughtering me more than the last.

Running from the first person I've ever loved...

My troubled heart left behind.

Chapter Ten
Tate

6 months later...

"Uhh... fuck yea. Fuck me *harder*."
Bang. Bang. Thud. Thud.
Slap slap slap slap slap.
These are the magical sounds of me getting turned the fuck out.

"You take cock like a champ, baby." A swift palm cracks down on my ass cheek, and I purr.

My bed is slamming against the wall, my head being stuffed into a pillow while some dude named Jose pounds into me from behind, jostling my organs around with his big ol' dick.

It feels *stupefyingly* good. In fact, I'm high on it.

Soaring through the clouds, tears seeping from my eyes at the sensation of being so motherfucking *far* away from emotional connection, the costs of shipping it back to me would be *astronomical*.

Six months ago, I fell prey to the same Hallmark bullshit so many humans insist is one of life's *greatest gifts*—*I beg to differ*—and it cost me one of my best friends.

After our secret *liaison*—which is just a fancy way of saying he crept into my dorm in the middle of the night and did lots of gay stuff with me —I confessed my feelings to Lance Hardy, who, prior to me cracking open my chest and offering him my heart, had been someone I thought I could actually *trust* in this world. But instead of reciprocating, or showing even the slightest modicum of respect for me, or our friendship, he darted out of my room, and subsequently out of my life, like he was escaping sudden death.

The *first time* I put myself out there in raw vulnerability turned out to be the most painfully devastating rejection of my existence, shy of my birth father skipping out on my mother when he found out she was pregnant.

And what's worse, I've had to go on living and breathing at the same university as the person who showed me how horribly misguided I'd been in thinking I wanted to be with him.

Yea... Lance Hardy still goes here. He's still *present* at Arizona State, still friends with all of my friends. But I don't see him. I suppose if there's one thing to be grateful for in all of this, it's that I haven't so much as peeped his gorgeous, evil face once since he dressed hastily in the dark and scurried away.

Shortly after what happened between us, I found out that Lance had transferred to one of the other ASU campuses, and because we're in two completely different programs, we share no classes. The only reason I know he's still alive is because despite how stabby it makes me, my so-called *friends* occasionally drop his name into conversation. And every time it happens, I get flashbacks that tear apart my insides like PTSD.

His hands treasuring me, our lips ravenously moving together, breaths ringing through the dense desire in the air...

Me, telling him I wanted us to be something more.

And him... telling me he had to go.

So from that moment on, I've done everything I can to convince myself I don't give a shit about *feelings*, and just do me.

Over the summer, I took an internship at Morgan Stanley. It's a coveted position, granted to only four students a year... And I was one of them. I spent three months learning the ins and outs of the banking world, developing my portfolio while practicing my hot-shot swagger and getting coffee for the richest dudes in the Southwest.

The internship was tough, but I loved every second of it. And most importantly, I learned that burying yourself in an all-consuming line of work is the *best* possible way to avoid dealing with emotional turmoil. Though, equally important is the other big life lesson of the last six months. Something my former friend is personally responsible for teaching me...

Fuck love. Fuck relationships. And fuck as much as possible.

Never again will I concern myself with emotional investments... Only financial ones. The only *opening up* you'll get from Tate Eckhart will be that of the *face down, ass up* variety, like with Jose here.

Just think of my heart like Circuit City. Closed for good.

And who needs love anyway, when you can just get fucked?

I like getting fucked. Getting fucked is fun. It feels *good.*

You know what doesn't *feel good?* Having your heart ripped out of your chest while it's still beating. That's what *love* gets you.

No, thanks. I'm set.

I'd rather have my prostate milked like a California dairy cow by a bunch of hot studs. Safely and responsibly, of course.

Ten minutes and two fabulous orgasms later, I'm stretching out in bed, catching my breath. Sweaty, sore, and sated. And expecting a knock on my door any minute from campus security, to deliver a second verbal warning for fucking too loud.

I sit up as the guy I met two hours ago saunters over, grasps my chin, and presses a soft kiss on my lips. *Uncharacteristically sweet for someone who slapped my ass red and spit in my mouth.*

"It was nice meeting you," I breathe, backing away from his touch.

He chuckles, eyes lingering on me before he gets up and gets dressed.

"See ya around, hot stuff." He winks, then leaves.

And I flop backward onto the bed. My fingers brush along the sullied sheets I need to change, fighting mercilessly against memories that want to creep in.

I can't let them. I won't.

The thing about hot sex with strangers is that it works in the moment. But like all distractions, it fades fast. As soon as the orgasm wears off, you're alone again. And that's when reality starts poking you in the chest.

You're not fine...

It still hurts...

Acting like a slut won't stop you from thinking about him.

Blinking heavily, I force myself to focus on something other than the fact that my heart clearly has a hex on it, which started the moment I was conceived. Picking up my phone, I tap on Instagram and start the mindless scroll.

Because social media is just wonderful for improving your mental state.

My friends know that Lance and I don't talk anymore, but that's the extent of it. While I'm sure it'd feel great to release my inner petty bitch and put him on blast—tell everyone we fooled around, then he freaked out and ghosted because he's a closet-case and a bad friend—I won't stoop to that level. Mainly because I'm very committed to proving how little I care.

As far as I'm concerned, Lance Hardy doesn't exist anymore. My dorm room door may as well have been the door to another dimension. When he stepped out of it six months ago, he vanished for good. And now, he's dead to me.

My scrolling slows when I notice a picture posted by my friend Lou. I can tell right away it's from this big group camping trip he went on last weekend with a few of our other friends. He tried inviting me, but barely got the words out before I declined.

My exact response was, "The only tents I pitch are in my pants, Kemosabe."

I guess they must have had fun, based on this picture of them all huddled together in nature.

It actually takes me a few seconds to notice it... There are a bunch of people in the photo. But when my eyes land on a very familiar blonde giant, with his arm slipped around the waist of a pretty girl, my blood runs cold.

Pulse immediately racing, a sweat breaks out across my forehead.

"Fuck..." I whine, rubbing my eyes.

Pain, aching and ferocious, radiates in my chest. It feels like the jagged lump that used to be my heart is splintering and cracking.

Why the fuck does it still hurt so bad?? It doesn't make any sense...

I'm over it. I've moved on.

I'm awesome, and I don't need this shit.

I'm fine.

Peeking at the screen, I can't look away from my former *friend*, wearing that smile I remember swooning over endlessly. Sweet, charming, yet humble, framed by vast dimples. His hair has grown out a bit, silky golden strands hanging by his ears. And there's at least a few days of stubble lining his immaculate jawline that twists my gut into an agonizing knot because of how sexy it is.

How can he look so good when he's the epitome of a flaky, awful shithead who walks out on the people he's supposed to be there for??

"Ugh!" I hiss, ready to chuck my phone at the wall.

But then I glance at the photo again, eyes hardening to a severe glare at the girl he's hugging into his side.

Who the hell is that...?

I've never seen her before, but she very well could go to ASU. I'm not exactly known for paying special attention to females. Still, the way she and

Lance are standing so close together is gnawing at me like a flesh-eating bacteria.

Checking the accounts Lou tagged in the picture, I find hers...

Desiree Dixon.

Chewing my lower lip, I tap on her profile, falling swiftly into the well of behaviors you're never supposed to entertain when you're trying to get over someone... Cyber-stalking their new acquaintances.

Desiree *is* a student at ASU. She's an ecology major... *Like Lance.*

She's a botany enthusiast...

Like Lance.

And she's from New Mexico...

Like me.

This bitch.

I know I should stop looking. This is the opposite of a good idea, but I just can't look away. I'm unleashed, and going full obsessive-ex right now.

Scanning her posts, one catches my eye, and my chest caves. Amidst the dumb pictures of flowers, food, and dogs, is one of her... and Lance. Together.

She's sitting on his lap, kissing his cheek. He's playing with her dark, curly hair... smiling.

The caption reads:

He makes everything better. *red heart emoji* *couple emoji*

I feel sick.

Dropping my phone on the floor, I jump up and run to the bathroom, barely making it to the toilet before heaving my guts out. Gagging and gagging, I'm expelling the drinks I had earlier, eyes watering. Heart *crumbling.*

He's seeing someone...?

He has a... girlfriend.

Sputtering for air, I wipe my mouth, trying to breathe, *struggling* against these bullshit fucking emotions that are flowing up out of me worse than the vomit. It's no use... I'm exhausted. I'm so tired of pretending I don't care when obviously I do.

This crutch I've made out of partying and casual sex isn't strong enough to hold me up... I've barely gotten myself upright since he left.

Tears stream down my cheeks while I whimper, breaking the fuck down like such a fucking loser. I can't believe I'm crying over him on the bathroom floor. I just don't get it...

He didn't want me. He threw away three years of friendship because he's a coward, and he's not worth my time. I shouldn't be heartbroken. I should be glad I dodged a bullet.

But I'm not. Six months later, and I'm still just as sad and angry and confused as I was that night. Because I never got any closure...

He just ran away. That's the problem. We crossed a line, and for me, it was *life-affirming*. No matter how much I hate to admit it, I haven't felt anything even close to what I felt with Lance in my bed... Kissing, stroking, squeezing, panting, sucking, groaning, sweating, and *coming*. *God*, coming so *fucking* hard, it was like an explosion of the best pleasure I've ever felt, and I *know* he felt it too. Giving in to what we both clearly wanted was a revelation.

But he left me forever wondering, which makes the whole thing so much worse.

I'm shivering all over, gasping, cradling my skull and rubbing my temples. *It doesn't make any sense...*

Was he struggling with his sexuality...? Was he really that scared to like fooling around with a guy as much as he did??

I know his family is super religious, and his dad is a pastor. But Lance always told me they weren't *those* kinds of church people. The ones who condemn gays and throw scriptures at us, as if some poorly worded jargon from thousands of years ago will somehow change our biology. Lance said he believes that God loves everyone, no matter what.

He could've just been trying to make me feel better... Because I was always a little hostile toward his faith. Particularly since I've never had faith in any power higher than myself and my own inner strength.

God is just a father... And fathers leave their sons to fend for themselves. *Or be crucified.*

Maybe Lance is okay with being bisexual... Since he clearly still likes girls. Girls like Desiree...

My thoughts are swirling, pounding inside my head like a migraine as I get up on shaky legs and wash my face.

Of course she's beautiful, because why wouldn't she be? And Lance is happy with her, because the more likely possibility is that he left because he didn't want *me*.

He could handle fooling around, he could probably even handle liking it...

But he couldn't see past knowing *I* have feelings for him.

Had. Put that fucking shit in past tense, bitch.

Fury swiftly crawls up my throat to mingle with the sadness. Frustration still lives inside me every day, thanks to Lance Hardy, because I'll never truly know what went wrong. Why he always seemed so into me until he wasn't. Why he had to dip out in the middle of the night and cut me off completely.

And if all he wanted was a secret, illicit gay romp to hide away in the dark, well... I guess I gave him that. And now, he can settle down with his *girlfriend*, and pretend it all never happened.

Swallowing down the anger, the depression, the loss, and the debilitating abandonment, I get into the shower and clean up. Then I get dressed, and head downstairs, out into the chill of winter.

I wander around aimlessly, smoking cigarettes and searching for someone to help me drown this terrible ache. And I don't even know how it happens, but at some point, I wind up on my knees with my accounting professor's dick in my mouth.

Build up this wall around yourself, Tate.

Bury the pain beneath layers of protective coating, so you never *have to feel again.*

Forget closure. Lance has moved on, and so will I.

Except that my life is going to rock so much harder than his ever could.

Because I don't need love when I have lust. I don't need a father when I can land a Daddy.

And I don't need Sunshine... when I do much better in the dark.

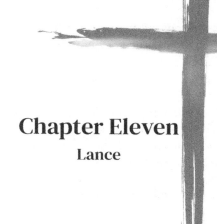

Chapter Eleven
Lance

2 years later...

"Are you alright, son?"

My eyes lift from my phone screen at the sound of my father's voice. He's walking over to where I'm seated on the back patio of Des's parents' house in South Valley, New Mexico. We've been living here together since graduation while we save up for our own place.

And the wedding.

Both of my parents are from New Mexico. We moved to Arizona when I was too small to remember it, but they moved back a couple of years ago. And now we're all just hanging out in South Valley... Me and Des, my mom and dad, my sister, my future in-laws. One big happy family.

Yes... Happy.

Happy...

Happy?

You ever notice how saying a word over and over makes it start to sound wrong...?

Pulling one of my polite, casual smiles, which are feeling increasingly forced lately, I watch my dad take a seat beside me. "I'm good."

Sipping from his glass of lemonade, he gazes over the backyard. And I continue to stare at him, my fingers digging into my thigh so hard they begin to ache.

"You really found a good one with that Desiree," he says calmly. It's his standard tone.

My father has this tranquility to the way he speaks. Like a confidence in his words, an easy charm that makes you want to listen to him. I can count on one hand the number of times he's raised his voice. He doesn't need to. He can get his point across effortlessly with just his words and his commanding tone.

I guess that's what makes him such a great pastor, preaching to a congregation that hangs on his every word of God.

Humming an indifferent sound, I myself am barely listening to his words right now. I'm lost in my thoughts. And there are many of them... all cluttered up, clogging my conscious mind.

"She'll make a great wife, son." He tilts his face in my direction, giving me a half-glance.

But his brown eyes wrench my gut.

It hurts... I still can't bear looking at my reflection in the mirror. Seeing that color irises is a dagger to the heart.

"You'll have no trouble building a beautiful life together."

Heart lurching, my betraying eyes fall to the phone in my hands once more.

Trouble...

"I'm sure we won't..." my grungy voice trails, "have any trouble."

I force an exhale while staring out at the flower garden Des planted here. It's the only thing giving me comfort lately. The summer rays draping over the vibrant purples and blues...

The sunflowers.

They're my favorite. Reaching up high, like they're trying to get as close to the sunshine as possible. It reminds me of that story I heard years ago... about why they follow the sun.

Adoration and loyalty, above all else.

I suppose I can understand the patience in staying just out of reach... Now that I know how hard it can be to keep your distance.

God feeds and nourishes us with His warmth and light. Like a father should.

My eyes shift.

My lips part. But I can't release the questions on the tip of my tongue.

The point of me leaving, and starting this life, was to *prevent* disaster, not invite it. It's been the most difficult thing I've ever done. And it's not getting any easier.

Trouble

I fear it never will.

"So Des was telling Mom you're working on the guest list," my father interrupts my vexing thoughts with more words. "What kind of numbers are you thinking?"

"We're keeping it small," I mumble.

I can't deal with a big wedding. Honestly, I just want to get it over with.

The word *introvert* has taken on a new meaning for me. Over the last few years, I've recoiled into myself. I've grown quieter, less social. I relish my alone time, but I know I can't have it constantly, being engaged and all. So I spend time with Desiree, and our families more than friends, play-acting the gregarious fiancé, son, brother.

But I don't feel it.

I feel as though I've lost my shine... Or that I left it behind, with someone who's most certainly thrown it away and forgotten about it by now.

"Are you planning to invite any of your old friends?" Dad asks, and my gaze flings his way. "Anyone from back home, or from... Arizona State?"

I can't even fight off how paranoid that question makes me. It's very possible he's just asking because he's my father, and he's curious. But I can't stop remembering the time I came home during sophomore year, regaling my parents and my sister with tales of all the new friends I'd been making at ASU...

Gio Hardy has always been difficult to read. My mom likes to say he has a *permanent poker face*. That's not to say my father is *emotionless*. He smiles and laughs, he frowns when something upsets him, and his forehead creases when he's confused, or thinking deeply. But he only does those things when *he* wants to.

I'd hate to think that it's calculating, because he *is* my father. We're not as close as he is with my sister, but we don't have a bad relationship either. He just holds it all close to his chest, and over the last few years, I've taken to scrutinizing his behaviors.

Like the time his poker face slipped.

"I only keep in touch with a few of my friends from college," I answer, as calmly as I can manage, though the trajectory of this conversation is working up a lot of unresolved things...

Things I've been holding on to for quite some time.

I was so wrecked for so long; broken and miserable, a cloud of gloom following me everywhere. I hated myself *so* deeply for what I did to Tate. I still do, and on some level, I think I always will.

103

But I hated the *circumstance* more than anything, and that resentment still burns like acid inside me, triggering anger and sadness every time I think about him...

Every time I torture myself by looking him up on social media.

Shaking it off as best I can, I add, "We're not that close."

"What about your friend Tate?" my father asks.

The reaction to hearing his name out loud is still so strong, it's visceral. Especially from the lips of my father.

"I haven't spoken to Tate in years," I mutter, clearing my throat before the emotion slips out.

I can't believe it's still there, and it's still so *strong*.

I was really hoping meeting Desiree, dating her, and marrying her, would start to taper off the agony just a little bit.

I guess no such luck.

"Really?" His voice has a lilt at the end, like he's surprised by this information. "I thought you two had been close."

Peeking at my father, I watch him carefully, wishing like hell he would just be honest.

"We were." I shift to face him. "But we had... I don't know, a *falling out*, I guess."

There it is... the reaction I've been waiting for.

It's subtle, but I caught it.

He's relieved that I don't talk to Tate anymore.

Sighing, my dad leans forward. "Lance... the unfortunate truth is that people come in and out of our lives. It can't be helped. You'll always lose friendships, make new ones. Because we're forever changing and growing, which leads us down different paths. Sometimes, God brings people together so they can help one another. Sometimes, he brings us people who will hurt us, as a test of our strength. To make us stronger."

I'm not breathing.

Lifting his glass, he takes another sip of lemonade. "It's all part of God's plan, son."

He shows me a warm smile, and I mirror it, though I feel like something inside me is festering. I've been unsettled for so long, I barely remember how it feels to be content.

I'm in an emotional war zone, with landmines everywhere. A single step in any direction could decimate myself and everyone around me.

Eventually, my father goes back inside, but I stay out. I walk to the garden, and stand beneath the sun, hoping to absorb the light I've lost.

Trouble

My fingers brush over the yellow petals, and I whisper, "Forgive the sins of my father..." I allow myself just a few more minutes of missing Tate Eckhart before adding, "Forgive *me*."

Chapter Twelve
Tate

Now...

Nothing like a lazy Sunday afternoon in your hometown.

The party at the Lockwood-Harper's last night was pretty fun. *Say what you want about those fools, but they sure know how to throw a proper shindig.*

I would never admit it to anyone, but I'm happy to be back in their lives. I like how easily I was able to slink back into the fold with Ben, Ryan, and Jessica, as if the past eighteen months of me steering clear never happened. I do believe the time apart did us some good; spared us the drama and all. They spent it forming their little family, which yea, I guess is sorta cute. And I spent it... being me.

As usual.

Naturally, Jake and his wife, Laura, wouldn't allow me to drive all the way back home last night, after having a few too many cocktails at the party, so I crashed in their guest room. Their twin daughters jokingly refer to it as "Uncle Tate's room" because I probably stay in it consistently more than any of their other guests.

And now I'm just... thinking. Sitting out on Jake's back deck, staring at the cacti and various stone sculptures they have bordering their yard.

I love the Southwest. I do. There's a reason I always keep coming back to this place.

But I also love traveling. I love my independence. It's something I'd never be able to keep up if I were... attached.

My throat feels a little thick, but I swallow it down with a mouthful of Laura's famous lemonade.

My phone pings with a message, but before I can open it, it starts ringing. It's my assistant, Troy.

"Go for awesome," I croon into the phone, smirking at how witty I am.

"Hey, so I didn't want to bother you earlier because I know you probably had a late night..." he starts. "But something was delivered to your place this morning."

"Okay..." I mutter. "So? I'll get it later when I go home."

"The person who delivered it was asking all kinds of questions," Troy continues, his tone a bit more sheepish than usual.

"Just tell me what's going on," I huff. "I'm not in the mood to decode your conversational riddles."

"Right, um," he breathes into the phone. "A guy brought you flowers."

"*Flowers??*" My brow arches up to my hairline.

"Sunflowers," he adds. "They're actually really pretty." Troy is swooning, but I'm just confused. "He was asking Luis if you were home, and if he could bring them up, so Luis called me. He sent me a picture of the flower delivery. I just texted it to you—"

"Troy, I don't give a fuck about the flowers," I bark. "Who is this intrusive delivery person?"

"His name is Lance."

My stomach flops harder than Gaga's ARTPOP album. "Wait... he showed up at my house??"

"Yea. Do you know him?" Troy has this hopeful lilt to his voice that makes me want to gag.

I sigh. "Unfortunately..."

"Alright, well, he was really insistent on needing to see you..." he trails.

"And...? What did you tell him?"

I can practically picture him fussing with that bow tie he always wears. "I told him you went to see your family for the weekend."

"Troy..." I hum his name patronizingly. "Did you tell him *where*?" His silence answers the question for me. "Goddamnit..."

"I'm sorry! But he seemed really distraught," he whines. "He said you guys are old friends and that he's desperate to speak with you, but you're not returning his calls..."

"What if he was a murderer?!" I hiss. "He could be some stalker trying to hunt me down and cut off my face so he can wear it around town pretending to be me, and you just fucking *told him* where I am?! Jesus, Troy, I thought we talked about this..."

"He didn't seem like a murderer..."

"Yea, neither did Ted Bundy." I rub my eyes. "Fuck my life."

"Tularosa is a big town. It's not like I gave him an address."

"You don't know this guy... He's like a dog with a damn bone." I flop back in my chair. "Shows up out of nowhere after fifteen goddamn years and now he wants to follow me everywhere... Jesus, do I need to have *Not Interested* tattooed on my forehead??"

"Wait a minute..." Troy murmurs. "Is that the guy...? Your old friend from college??"

At that moment, Jake saunters outside, casually grinning and sipping his lemonade.

I glare up at him, barking into the phone, "Stop talking to Jake about my life." Then point at my best friend. "And you. Stop telling my assistant things!"

Jake takes a seat, shrugging. "He asked me why you're such a lonely hermit. I felt inclined to answer honestly."

"I hate both of you," I grunt, hanging up on Troy.

"What happened?" Jake asks, smirking like the meddling old lady his thirty-four-year-old father of two clearly embodies.

"Lance showed up at my house," I mumble, opening the text from Troy. "With flowers."

My eyes scan over the picture he sent me... Sunflowers, in a cute clay pot. With a card.

I wonder what the card says...

No. I don't care *what the stupid fucking card says.*

I'm not some desperate girl on Valentine's Day. I don't want flowers from a guy who won't leave me alone... No matter how theoretically thoughtful it might be.

Tall, gorgeous, broad-shouldered annoyance... With his sharp jaw and his deep, sexy voice...

Who apparently knows me well enough to know that *no one* else has *ever* given me flowers before...

Damn him.

"Aww! Let me see!" Jake snatches the phone from me, checking the picture. He pouts. "Oh my God, he *loves* you!"

"He does not *love me*," I scoff. "He's peeking out of the closet while remembering the only other guy who's ever touched his dick. It's just a physical reaction, or attachment or something..."

"Right." Jake shakes his head, tossing my phone at me. "Keep telling yourself that."

"Ugh, I need to leave..."

"Why? So you can go home and smell your flowers...?" He snickers, and I narrow my gaze at him.

My phone starts ringing again. *I swear to God, I'm about to throw myself onto a cactus.*

"It's your brother," I huff to Jake, swiping to answer. "Yellow?"

"Tate? Hey, man. How's it going?" Ben rumbles in my ear. *It's amusing how straight he still sounds.*

"I'm just peachy, thanks for asking. How can I help you?"

"Look, uh... are you at my brother's?" he asks, more interested in me and what I'm doing than he's ever been before, which is odd.

My eyes flit to Jake, who's leaning in on the table like he's desperate for a tea spill. I shoo him away with my hand and whisper, "Go play with your kids, for Christ's sake. Yes, Ben. I am at your brother's. Why? What do you need?"

"Oh, nice," Ben says. His shifty tone has me narrowing my gaze. "So just wondering... that guy Lance... what's up with you two?"

There's a distinct scowl forming on my lips as Jake snatches my phone again, putting it on speaker, and placing it on the table.

I glare at him while my lips curve wickedly. "Lockwood, is this your way of asking if I'm single? Because trust me, what with my history with your husband, I really don't think it's a good idea..."

I grin snidely at Jake, who fakes a laugh.

Suddenly, there's a new voice barking at me through the phone—Ryan Harper. "Um hello, Tate. My husband is not hitting on you."

My head tilts. "Oh hi, Ryan!"

"Hey. So this guy Lance—"

"Oh my God, whatever you do, *don't* tell him where I am." I breathe my exasperation out loud. "I'm trying to freeze him out so he gets the hint. I'm a fucking idiot and I can't chase straight, closeted guys anymore. It's, like, *beyond* fucking toxic."

I shoot Jake a look, to which he nods like he gets where I'm coming from.

But then a familiar brogue rumbles over the receiver, "Tate..."

My eyes widen. Jake's eyes widen.

I mouth, *"He's there?!"* And Jake shrugs, appearing baffled by this turn of events.

How the hell did he find Ben's house??

This guy is, like... nuts.

"Oh... fuck." I rub my eyes and groan, "Dude, boundaries! I can't believe you came all the way down here!"

"I'm sorry, I just..." Lance's voice trails for a moment, before he whispers, "I needed to see you."

This is all so overwhelming. It's been easy to brush him off with the distractions of work and living my life. But now that I'm here, and *he's* apparently here... and my best friend is staring at me with fucking swoon all over his face... I just don't know what to think.

I swallow hard and ask, "Why?"

"To say I'm sorry," Lance speaks firmly. "And to tell you that I've been... thinking about you. About *us*."

I shake my head. "Yea, I told you, that's not—"

"I mean before," he cuts off my rebuff. "I was thinking about you before I saw you at Pride. For, like... a while."

Jake is motioning all around with his hands while I'm just blinking at my phone, flustered as hell and *hating* it.

I don't get flustered... I *fluster*. I'm not the one who should be feeling this way. But at the same time, I can't help how my chest is melting inside like the ice cubes in my drink.

I hear people chattering in the background of the call. A female voice shouts about *forgiving him* and *accepting the love.*

I'm not even sure who it is, but my head still wobbles swiftly. "You guys don't get it, okay?" I say to all the random individuals who are apparently listening to this embarrassing conversation go down. "It's not that simple..."

"Can we at least talk?" Lance asks, his tone deeply pleading.

I can't believe he can sound so rugged and masculine while he's basically begging.

Begging for *me*...

"No," I grunt.

"Tate, I'm already out here," he breathes softly. "I drove for hours on the off-chance I might be able to track you down. I won't stop until you agree to see me."

Jake pouts at me, and I hear Ben grumble, "Okay, that's really fuckin sweet..."

Trouble

My face falls into my hands, and I hiss, "Jesus Christ, fine! Anything to get rid of the audience commentary! I'll text you the address."

"Thank you, T," Lance murmurs, and I hate that I can hear the beautiful, beaming smile in his voice. "I can't wait to see you."

"Yea, yea..." I mutter and hang up the phone, peering at Jake.

He's quiet, staring at me for all of two seconds before he chirps, "You're gonna fall in love."

I roll my eyes. "God..."

"You're gonna get married." He keeps teasing while I grab my phone and shoot up from my chair, stalking away from him. But of course, he follows me, shouting, "Tate Eckhart has a *boyfriend*!"

"Grow up!" I snarl, stomping into the house. I go straight to the guest room and lock myself inside, staring at my phone.

Am I really going to do this??

It's *so* much pressure...

I mean, damn. I was anxious about things with Lance before, but now that all of these people are involved, I'm really freaking out.

I don't do this. I don't do... boyfriends.

I do other people's boyfriends.

And speaking of, what the hell happened to Lance's wife?? Why is he all gung-ho about this when he's still married??

I guess for that reason, more than anything else, I text him Jake's address. Because I need answers. I need closure on this. I can't have him following me around like a lost puppy anymore. We need to figure this out once and for all. And I'm going to stay strong...

I'm not going to let him weasel his way in with his pretty eyes and soft, pouty mouth, and giant muscles. That hair the color of vibrant sunshine...

I shake my head. *Stand firm, here, Eckhart. You got this.*

I wind up pacing the room for ten minutes until I hear Laura's voice call out, "Tate! You have a visitor!"

"Yea, Uncle Tate! You have a visitor!" The twins mirror their mother's words, and I'm cringing down to my soul.

This is so fucking awkward.

Taking a deep breath, I leave the room, marching toward the front door. I can already see him out there, through the narrow windows on either side of the door; all squirmy with his hands stuffed into his pockets. As if he isn't built like a professional wrestler.

Whipping open the door, I grit my teeth. "Oh, hey... It's my stalker."

Lance presses his lips together, like he's trying to suppress a sheepish smile. I can feel eyes on my back, so I step outside and nod. "Let's talk out here. Away from these nosey parkers."

Trudging around the side of the house, my heart is leaping against my ribs, but I'm pretending it's not. I can hear Lance following me, keeping up easily with my long strides. I don't stop until I get us into the backyard, between the house and the pool house, where I'm sure no one can see or hear us.

I stop and spin to face Lance, folding my arms over my chest. Classic aggressive stance. *I mean business.*

"Okay... You got me." I lift a brow, and he blinks. "I'm here... *You're* here, for some reason. Talk."

But Lance doesn't say anything. He shakes his head subtly, stepping forward.

I back up.

"Spill it, man..." I grunt, backing up more while he keeps inching his way into my space. "What was... *so* important..."

My nerves are rattling, and I gulp as he pushes up close to me. I startle when my back hits the side of the house.

"W-what, Hardy?" I stammer, peeking up at his face. He places his hands flat on either side of my shoulders, caging me in as my lips tremble uncontrollably. "What do you... have to say for yourself?"

His warmth is coating my entire body as he traps me against the wall, mouth hovering over mine. "I've said enough. No more words, Trouble..."

My head shakes, arms lying limp at my sides.

What is happening...?

"No more *words*," he breathes, brushing my lips with a minty purr, "until I get what I came for."

My mouth opens, but no more words...

Because he kisses me first.

His sweet, soft, hungry mouth melts over mine, and my head instantly fogs. I can't remember *anything* I wanted to say to him; none of my witty remarks or snarky attitude. They're all gone. I'm too busy vibrating, parting my lips with his like an instinct as they tease and suck and capture. A soft whimper escapes me, and he eats it up, nibbling on me, growling in between sweeping his tongue into my mouth.

He groans, and my cock jumps against where he's writhing into me.

"*Fuck*, baby," he sighs, like this is it; *this* is all he's wanted for fifteen fucking years. His hand slides up my neck and cups my jaw while he devours my mouth like he's been *starved*. "I never forgot how good you taste... my sweet, sexy Trouble."

"Mmmff..." is all I can make happen, arching up to him. I hadn't even noticed, but my hands are gripping his sides for dear life.

"You're my blessing, T... Did you know that?" he rasps while licking my lips, sucking them, *bruising* them with possessive need. "I'm meant to have you... You're supposed to be *mine*."

Drunk on sensation, I glide my hands up his chest, cupping the hard stones of his pectorals beneath his shirt, feeling his heart jumping into my palm. I can't stop feverishly kissing him back, because *fuck*, it just feels so good. It feels like nothing I've ever gotten from anyone other than him, and it's spinning my head off my body.

"Finally speechless, smart mouth?" He grins on my swollen lips, brushing them over and over, nipping, sucking, toying with me until my cock is aching painfully between us. I feel his, solid and pushing against the front of his pants. All I want is to free the beast and let it rock my fucking world... But that's the problem.

Because wanting him is simple... The trouble is with the rest of it.

"But you're married..." I gulp, my voice trailing as his hooded gaze hungrily eyes my mouth. "Right?"

His forehead lines, and he nods woefully. "But it doesn't stop me from wanting you. It never has. I want *you* more..."

I give my head a little shake, our eyes locked in the seriousness of what's going down right now. "This is fucked..." My fingers give in and reach, touching his sharp jaw, combing through the silken strands of golden hair as I admit, "I missed you."

His eyelids droop, and he drops his forehead to mine. "I missed you so bad, baby..."

Shoving my lips back onto his, I kiss him like I'm already fully addicted. I guess maybe I have been... This whole time. And it's been lying dormant.

Waiting for him to show back up.

This is too serious. Too much...

I'm not equipped for any of it.

"I just want what I never got back then, Sunshine..." I grunt breathlessly.

"I want it too," he groans as his large hand slinks between our grinding bodies to cup my cock. A strangled gasp leaves him, and he tugs my bottom lip rough with his teeth. "I want to make this come... for only me."

Fucking motherfucker...

There's absolutely no way I can say no to this guy. I never could. And maybe he's just going to run again... In fact, I'm sure he will.

But we've both changed. He knows what he wants, even if it still scares him. And I know enough now not to expect anything.

It can be just sex... Just an experience, I'm sure it can.

He needs his first time... And I need him to fill me up with all those rays of Vitamin D.

I smirk at my thoughts, and he grins. "What's funny?"

"Nothing, just thinking..." My eyes shift. "We could go in there." I nod toward the pool house.

Lance pulls back to give me a quick look of uncertainty. "Can we really do that...?"

I shrug, tracing his muscles through his shirt. "We've always been good at keeping secrets."

Yanking him by the arm, I drag him over to the pool house, shoving him inside and closing the door behind us. There isn't much in the way of furniture in here, but it's private and that's all I'm looking for in this burning hot moment.

"Tate... are you sure about this?" he mumbles as I pull him over to a chaise lounge. "I think I owe you some... answers." He gasps while I start ripping at his clothes.

"No talking." I lift my shirt over my head, shoving my pants down. "I just need to see..."

"See what?" he asks while I get him out of his shirt and open his pants.

But rather than responding, I kiss him.

I know what I'm looking for here, but I don't want to admit it out loud. Not to him... Not *yet*.

"You said you wished you fucked me back then," I purr into his mouth. "Do it now."

He kisses me slowly. "Only if I have you, baby..." He pulls back to gaze down at me. "Do I have you?"

It's such a heavy question. One I refuse to answer in any fashion. I just want him to fuck me... I'm shaky for it.

Avoiding a response, I spin in his arms. He tries to turn me back around, but I lower myself down onto my stomach on the chaise.

His chest covers my back as he kisses my neck. "I want to see your face, gorgeous..."

Biting my lip hard, I shake my head. *Too intimate...*

I'm... No. I can't do it that way.

Trouble

Pushing my hips back, I rub my ass on his cock where it's sticking out of his pants. "Please, Sunshine... Will you fuck me? I *need* it."

I can feel him hesitating, but not out of his usual fear. This time, he's trapped between wanting to unleash on me, and wanting to make love to me. I need it to be the former.

Lance shoves his pants down around his thighs, taking his long, perfect cock in his hand and running the head in between my cheeks until I'm shivering.

"What if someone finds us?" he whispers, biting on my shoulder, hard, until I whine.

"Mmm... right. You're a married man," I taunt him with a sharp, salacious tone. "Afraid of getting caught having gay sex, *Pastor*? What would *God* think...?"

My taunting works, because he growls, pushing me down roughly into the chaise. "You're so much fucking trouble, aren't you?"

"Trouble you can't get enough of, apparently," I hiss at the sound of him spitting into his palm. "Decade and a half and you're still chasing me... *Wanting* me."

"You really do want me to fuck the attitude out of you, huh?" He runs his thick shaft up and down over my hole while I whimper. "I never stopped wanting you, Tate. And I'm gonna need more than just saliva to get this dick in you."

"*Fuck*..." I hum, lifting my head enough to peer around the room. My eyes land on something. "That looks like lotion."

Lance pauses. "It's sunscreen..."

"Whatever, just use it."

"Is that... healthy?"

"Who *cares*... Coat your dick and push it inside me, breeder."

He snarls, "Fucking wise ass," then smacks me hard on the butt, causing me to yelp.

A deliciously growly chuckle rumbles from his chest into my back as he inches lower, dropping kisses and bites all over the skin of my shoulder blades. I'm going out of my goddamn mind with each sting of pain from his teeth, and the burn from where his palm just connected with the flesh of my ass cheek.

Squirming away, he grabs the tube and squirts some SPF 30 into his hand. It smells like the beach, and I can't help laughing quietly as he strokes it onto his big dick.

"You think this is funny, troublemaker?" he growls, swirling fingers over my hole before stuffing one inside me quick.

I gasp. "It's important to protect yourself against the sun..."

He goes quiet. I peek at him over my shoulder. The dumfounded look on his face has a giggle slipping out before I can stop it. I bite my lip to cover the sound, but it's already out there. And now he's grinning, *beaming* at me.

"You're so fucking cute." He grasps my jaw and kisses me slowly, rocking his hips into me from behind, rubbing his silky cock on my tender cheek while his finger plunges in and out.

I scowl. "Don't get sweet on me, Hardy. I'm not your boyfriend..."

"Mmm... Right," he whispers, biting my lip gently as his finger slips out. "But you're adorable. I want you to be *mine*."

"Don't care," I grumble. "This is just *sex*."

He sighs, gliding his dick between my cheeks. "But I find you oh-so *sweet*, Trouble. Remember that I knew you before you were a hotshot."

"That was a... *uhh* long time... ago..." My voice goes uneven, interrupted by breathless groans as the fat head of his cock slips around over my hole.

"Doesn't matter," he hums, rippling into me. "You're still the same Tate to me. Beautiful, sexy, warm... *Tight*..." He gives his dick a shove, and the crown slips in. I gasp out loud. "This is what I should've done back then... Made you mine, baby. All *mine*..."

"*Ffuck*," I whine as he thrusts in deeper, collapsing on top of me. "Holy fuck, so good..."

"This is perfect." He shudders with his lips on my neck. "Your body fits me *perfect*, just like I knew it would."

"God... Lance." Tears are seeping from my eyes already, it feels so incredible. His dick is so big, so *so* thick, and hot, and *hard*, tearing its way inside me... Bare. "You... fuck fuck fuck, *yes*... You should've put on—*mmm don't stop*—a condom." I arch up to him while he sinks in more, deeper, tunneling his way inside my body. "I never... *fuuuck*... without condoms."

"I trust you." His voice shakes. "Mmm, feels like *heaven*, baby. I can feel everything... Every warm, soft ridge of you sucking me in."

"Fuck *yes*... Give me every inch." My head is spinning.

I don't give a single fuck about the condom. It just feels so blissfully perfect... It's like this was how we were always meant to fuck. Him pumping his massive bare cock into my ass. Me clenching on him, holding and squeezing him. Him riding me, slow and deep, kissing my neck and my lips and my jaw, whispering things like, "I love this feeling, T. You're the best... sweetest, tightest little hole I've ever fucked. You wanna be mine, don't you, baby? You want me to fuck your breath out forever?"

"Yesss... *God, yes*. Fuck me harder, baby," I groan, lifting up to him as much as I can while he pins me down with his weight. "You fuck my ass better than anyone..."

He growls, picking up the pace just a bit until his skin is slapping against mine. My cheeks feel raw and red, but I love it, the soreness. The way he's stretching me open and jamming at my prostate over and over until I'm leaking sticky pulses everywhere.

"Baby... I might..." He stops to tremor, reaching a hand around to grab my cock in his fist. "I might come. I can't help it... you feel *too good*."

"Good... *please* fill my ass with your cum. It's all I want..."

"I wanna be the only one who comes in you..."

"You are... you will be. I promise..."

He whines, biting down hard on my flesh while he strokes my cock furiously to match the tempo of his hips. My eyes are rolling back in my head, fucking forward into his hand and back against his dick, riding it with my ass until everything starts to blur.

"Tate... *Tate*..." he grunts.

And then I feel him... throbbing into me *deep* while he sobs into my back.

It's the most amazing thing I've ever felt in my entire life. I can't help how my balls draw up, and I cry with my face smashed into the fabric. "Fuck, I love this... I love it, I *love*... baby, you're making me come so hard!"

We're both quaking, growing and gasping and panting. His hips buck into me as he milks out every drop, draining his balls in my ass while I shoot my own hot pulses all over myself and this poor chaise lounge. Lance's hands rush, caressing my body; rubbing my cum into my muscles, all the way up my chest, teasing my nipples and sinking his teeth into the nape of my neck.

I'm gasping for air, struggling to breathe for more than just the way this intense orgasm knocked the wind out of me.

It wasn't a fluke.

Everything I've been pushing down for fifteen years... The memory of how badly I always wanted him. It wasn't bullshit. *I didn't build any of it up in my head.*

He's exactly *everything* I always imagined he'd be before he took off.

I'm no longer left wondering what could have been, because this is it... He's my ray of sunshine.

God, I am so fucking fucked.

I'm shivering with nerves. I've never felt so attached to someone after sex, but my body physically doesn't want to let him go as he pulls out.

"Shit... This is a big mess," Lance croaks, cupping my ass and massaging it in his large hands. "Now I understand the appeal of the condom."

"Yea... that and the whole safety thing," I huff.

"Baby," he croons, nestling up in front of me, pulling my naked body into his. His pants are still down around his calves, but he doesn't seem to care. "You're *perfect.*"

I swallow hard, unable to pull my eyes away from his, despite how fucking intense this is.

No one's ever looked at me like this before...

His fingers push my hair away from my forehead while I just blink at him, dazed and confused.

"I'm not letting you get away this time," he whispers, dropping a slow kiss on my lips.

"Hardy... *you* were the one who ran. Not me," I mumble pointedly, feeling all twitchy from the emotions building up in my chest with nowhere to go.

"I know." He nods. "And I'll never stop being sorry for it. But you've always been mine, T. It just took me way too long to figure it out."

I want to ask him about his wife. What he plans to do about her... And if this is really *real.*

They never leave their wives... *And would I even want him to??*

The truth is that the tables might have turned. Now *I'm* the one who's afraid.

Afraid that he might still be the only one I can't shake.

In this moment, I don't think I have the slightest clue what I want. *Well, maybe one thing...*

"I need a cigarette," I rasp, and he grins.

"Mmm... my Trouble," he hums, kissing me softly.

Oh yea... Big fucking trouble.

Chapter Thirteen
Lance

I t's odd... This difference.

Because it doesn't feel *new*.

This change is like something that's always been there; a seedling buried deep within my soil that's only just now been given the opportunity to sprout.

I feel awake. I feel alive.

I feel... horribly, terribly *guilty*.

Watching Tate stand up, naked, the contours of his sculpted body like a statue of Greco-Roman perfection, my eyes follow him as he wanders toward the window of the pool house and cracks it, lighting his cigarette where it rests between his puffy lips. Right now, he looks just like he did when we were younger... Hair all tousled around, a youthful glow to his face.

I guess the only difference is that he's frowning. That *Tate smirk* is gone, and I can see the contemplation in his eyes. I swallow hard.

It reminds me of the night I left him.

As great as I feel inside, this is still very bad, just like it always has been.

The second we walk out of here, his friends are going to know what happened between us. Which wouldn't be a big deal in any other situation, but I'm *sure* they also happen to know I'm married. There's no way Tate didn't tell his best friend. He's not known for keeping his mouth shut.

My thoughts begin to swirl over everything that's happened in the last week... Seeing Tate again for the first time in so long, when he was never far away in my thoughts. It sparked a need in me, something that's probably always been there, but for some reason only *he's* ever truly been able to drag up to the surface.

I wish things were different... I wish I could demolish the wall that's been built between us over the last fifteen years. But I just don't know how to do that. *I built most of it myself.*

Standing, I step into my boxers and stride slowly over to Tate, watching him stare out the window at the swirling smoke from his cigarette. Dropping to my knees beside him, my fingers are instantly twitching with the desire to just touch him and never stop. The sensation is overwhelming... It scares the shit out of me because I've never felt it for anyone but him, and I just don't understand how that's possible.

God wouldn't allow such things... Would he??

"Tate..." I whisper his name, unsure of what I'm supposed to say.

I'm confused, and you're the reason.

I've finally come alive, thanks to you.

Even though it's wrong, all I want in the world is to seal myself to you forever.

Would you even want *that?*

His face slopes in my direction, our brown eyes locking while we both breathe visibly. Mine flick briefly to the bite marks on his neck.

"This isn't going to work..." he mumbles, dark brows knitting together. "Is it?"

My lips part, but I can't speak.

Because I don't want to lie to him with truths.

He can always tell, anyway.

Before I can even try to answer, he sighs, "It's okay," chin dipping as he swallows, gazing at the cigarette between his fingers. "I don't need it to."

"What does that mean?" I ask softly, his words and the tone he's using gripping my gut like a vise.

His lashes flutter as he peeks up at me once more. "I'm used to casual sex..."

My head shakes like an instinct. "I don't want you to be used to casual sex, Tate."

You deserve so much more...

"What about if it's with you?" He blinks.

Wait...

He's... not going to run out of my life? To get me back for what I did to him??

120

Trouble

The notion of it makes me so light, I could float up into the air.

I wasn't lying when I told him I didn't want to let him get away again. All I've been able to think about since I bumped into him in that club is how amazingly *not random* it was. There was absolutely no way this is a coincidence, running into him again after all these years, when not a single day passed that I didn't think about him in some capacity. Choosing *that* club, of all the clubs in ABQ... And *that* bathroom stall, at *that* moment...

Things don't happen by accident. There's a plan in motion, and I can't stop remembering my father's words from all those years ago...

God brings people together.

After everything I did to try to escape him, Tate still wound up back in my life. If that's not a sign, then I don't know what is.

It's still wrong... That part hasn't changed. But pushing him away nearly killed me, and I won't do it again.

I don't think I could if I tried.

"Are you saying that's enough?" I reach forward and take his hand in mine. It's so much bigger than a woman's... I remember thinking the same thing that night, in the backseat, before everything changed forever. Holding it feels like picking up the forbidden fruit. "Is that... what you want?"

Tate sucks in a breath, tossing his cigarette out the window. And he whispers, "Thank you for the flowers... Sunshine."

He's not running.

That's all that matters right now.

A smile of the fullest, most untamed joy I've ever felt hijacks my lips, and I lean in quick, kissing him greedily. Possessing him with my mouth. Lifting our joined hands, I hold his up to my chest, right over my heart, cupping his jaw with the other. He feels unsure, but only for a moment before he whines the most deliciously needy sound between my lips.

Suddenly, I'm twenty-one again, back in his dorm room, kissing him for the first time. Giving up my reservations, abandoning the fight, for *him*.

Because, damn me if you need to... But this feels way too good to stop.

I'm feral for this feeling, nostalgia mixed with brand new blinding thrill. I love it so much I can barely contain myself, sucking him and feeding him my tongue. He tastes like fruit and cigarettes. *Sweet poison.*

"You're going to get me in so much trouble." I grin on his lips.

He rumbles, deep and sexy from within his chest. "I think that's what you want."

"You have a point," I pant, touching his chest, feeling how hard and defined he is there. How much bigger he's gotten since we were young, stupid kids. "I'd love to get *into* you again, *Trouble*."

He laughs in my mouth, and I grin, flushing at how incredible it feels to make it happen.

"Wanna go for round two, Sunshine?" He straddles my lap, clinging to me like a vine.

"Baby, fucking you a thousand more times wouldn't even scratch the surface," I purr, holding his waist, fingers easing down to squeeze his perfect ass. "Not when I should've had you every day for the last fifteen years."

Tate falters. I feel it happening, his kisses slowing and the rocking of his hips coming to a gradual halt.

Fuck... I shouldn't have brought that up.

He's always going to hold my leaving against me. And I don't blame him. I tore apart our friendship.

I should've tried harder to stay friends, despite not being able to be with him. But I wasn't strong enough, just like I'm not strong enough to stay away from him now that we've somehow crashed back into one another's lives. I knew back then there was no way I'd be able to see him all the time and not shove him up against a wall to kiss these soft, pouty lips, or sneak into his dorm room at night when no one was around and spread him open.

The floodgates had burst. There was no *just friends* after that.

And so, I feel like I owe him *some* explanation for all this... Especially now that we're technically older and wiser.

And he's naked, in my arms, with my cum in his ass.

"Tate..." I breathe slowly to keep from dumping it all out at once. "I must have dialed your number a hundred times, baby... When we were still in ASU." He starts chewing on his lower lip, forehead resting on mine. "I can't even tell you how many times I walked to your building and just stood outside..."

He shakes his head a little, pulling back. But I hold his face to keep him close. Our eyes open and lock, the tips of our noses almost touching while we stare at each other for many moments of silence.

Finally, he whispers, "What the hell were you so afraid of, Hardy?"

I swallow, caressing the rough stubble on his jaw. "I told you already... *You*."

It's not the entire truth, but it's not a lie, either.

Trouble

Tate looks like he wants to say something, but he's keeping himself in check. It's new, a tactic he uses to stay guarded.

Shifting, he releases an exhale. "We can't stay in here like this. Jake will murder me if he finds out we fucked near the twins' pool toys."

I chuckle, nodding and playing with his hair. "When can I see you again?"

"How about the first *Neversday* of *No Thanks*-uary?" he quips, then shakes his head. "Sorry. Force of habit."

Another laugh bursts out of me, and he purses his lips. "Baby... be serious. I need more, Trouble."

"Oh, you'll get it." He cocks a dark brow. "What about your *wife*?"

My stomach bunches, and I frown. "I don't wanna think about that. Just tell me when I can see you..." His silence has me pouting. "*Please,* baby? How about tomorrow?"

He stares at me for a second. "I'm in Santa Fe tomorrow..."

"I can come there." I brush my lips on his ear. "I'll *come* wherever you want, sweet stuff."

"Wow... first time fucking a guy and you're already fiending. Never would've predicted that," he mutters sarcastically.

I grip his ass hard, and he whines. "*Okay*, Tate. You were right, I was wrong. You're smart, I'm stupid. You're perfect, and I'm a fuck-up... Should I keep going?"

"I'm really enjoying it." He grins. "But I'm not kidding. We probably have five minutes before Jake comes out here, and there's no lock on that door."

"Then tell me when I can see you," I growl, sucking his neck rough, leaving a purple bruise.

"I'll have my people call your people," he croons, pressing a kiss on my lips before hopping off me and standing up.

I don't really like how flippant he's being. It's just reminding me of how often he does this exact thing with guys who aren't me. But there's also not much I can do about it right now. I do need to get dressed and get the hell out of here, being that I've been gone all day and I still have a long drive back home.

At least that's a few hours for me to come up with something to tell Des about where I've been...

Tate and I put our clothes on, all the while subtly peeking at each other. The air in the room is a bit too tense for a post-orgasm atmosphere, though I definitely get why. Everything between us is completely unstable. Tracking him down didn't actually resolve anything, aside from us *finally* having sex, a desire many years in the making. Not that I followed him out here to get laid. I came to talk, which we admittedly didn't do much of.

But I can't be too upset about it. I had sex with *Tate Eckhart*.

I'm fucking *weightless*.

Unfortunately, everything aside from the mind-altering sex is highly uncertain. I can't lose him again, but I also can't keep him. I don't think I'm capable of being *casual* with him... But we can't be more than that either.

It's like we're in a relationship purgatory.

"Tate..." I call to him as he's wandering to the door, but he ignores me, brushing his messy hair back with his fingers.

He yanks open the door with a sigh and steps outside while I stalk after him, back in the direction of the driveway, where my car is parked. When we get there, he spins to face me. I step closer to him, but he inches away, stuffing his hands into his pockets.

"Alright, well... that was fun," he mutters, refusing to look at me. "Get home safe..."

Get home safe??

Fuck... He's trying to get rid of me.

If this is casual *Tate, I don't like it one bit.*

"So, I don't get to... say hi to Jake?" I ask hesitantly, trying to keep at least some of the hopefulness out of my voice.

Tate clears his throat, gazing down at his shoes. "I don't see the point."

"You don't...?" My stomach is crawling up into my throat.

"I mean, he's just going to grill you about your wife and make everything awkward as shit," he grumbles. "It's what he does. He's like a nosy, overprotective brother. I'm saving you from extreme discomfort, trust me."

"You shouldn't let me off the hook, Tate," I murmur, easing closer to him again.

Finally, his eyes lift to mine. "It was just *sex*, Hardy... I don't—"

His voice cuts out when I thread my fingers through his.

"Oh good, you're still here."

A voice pulls my gaze away from Tate, and I glance up as Jacob Lockwood is striding over to us, smiling. We've only met once before, in college. He came out to visit Tate for a weekend, sophomore year. He's a nice guy. We got along well.

A few years ago, I friended him on Facebook, just to see what would happen. And to my surprise, he accepted. Because of that, I know what he looks like now—pretty much the same as he did back then, only with a touch of silver in his dirty blonde hair, and a few more smile lines around his blue eyes. I know he's married, with twin girls, and that he still lives in his hometown of Tularosa, as does his brother, Ben—the one whose house I showed up at earlier when I was driving around this unfamiliar town in search of Tate.

I still can't really think about him, or his husband, without remembering them fucking at Kennan's party. But regardless, they're nice guys. They were super helpful and supportive before, despite how stalkerish I was being.

Jake struts over to us, eyes flinging between me and Tate as he tosses out his hand. "Great to see you again."

We shake, like mature adults.

"Likewise." I smile politely.

"So..." Jake folds his arms over his chest. "Did you kids get a chance to—"

"In high school, Jake peed his pants in gym class, during a flag football game!" Tate barks.

"Dude!" Jake chokes out a scoldingly baffled laugh, gaping at his friend.

Tate shrugs. "Sorry... This is really awkward for me. Now we're even."

I can't help grinning at the two of them. Their friendship is adorable, and highly entertaining. *But only because I know with full certainty they've never even come close to hooking up.*

"Okay, first of all, I told you I *had* to pee, and you jumped on top of me anyway. So that was totally your fault," Jake defends himself. "And second of all, *why* is this awkward for you?"

They squint at each other for a second, and Jake's lips twitch, like he already knows why.

Eventually, Tate gives up and rolls his eyes. "Ugh, whatever. We fucked, okay?! *Jesus...*"

My eyes widen, and I gasp, "Tate!" Jake smirks triumphantly, peeking at me with a raised brow. I cover my face with my hands. "God, help me..."

"Don't ask Him for help," Tate mutters. "He's mad at you."

Huffing, I shake my head at him. "You didn't have to tell him that."

"Oh, yea. Like he's gonna believe you came all the way out here so we could *talk*," Tate scoffs. "Use your head, Hardy."

"I think that ship has sailed," Jake mutters in amusement. But it falls, his brows furrowing. "Wait, *where* exactly did you... do it?"

"We didn't—"

"Pool house," Tate speaks over me.

"Tate!" I bark again.

"You had *sex* in my pool house?!" Jake whisper-shouts at us.

"Don't act so scandalized." Tate tilts his head at his friend. "You and Laura do it in there all the time. It's the only place you can get any privacy. You might as well just turn it into a fuck-shack."

"This is mortifying," I grumble.

"I'll say." Jake aims a stern glare at me, then Tate, folding his arms over his chest. "You're both adultering. Not cool."

"*Adultering* isn't a word," Tate interjects. "It's called *committing adultery...*"

"You would know," Jake quips.

"*And* it's really none of your business." Tate ignores him, pursing his lips.

"Like hell it's not!" Jake gasps. "You did it on my property."

"What are you gonna do? Call a priest?? We've already got one right here." Tate gestures to me.

"I'm a *pastor*, not a priest," I grumble.

"Tomato, *tomahto*." He shrugs.

"Look, you're both grown-ups," Jake starts, and I can see what Tate was saying about the overprotective brother thing. *I feel a scolding coming on.* "You can do whatever the hell you want, but I'm just going on record... I think this is very reckless."

"Duly noted." Tate grunts, shoving his friend away, toward the house. "Say goodbye! Lance is taking off."

Jake peeks at me over his shoulder while Tate pushes him. "See ya around, Lance. Oh, and if you hurt my friend again, I'll smite you myself."

"Shut *up*... God, you're so embarrassing," Tate mutters, their bickering trailing as Tate walks Jake to the front door.

The two of them are whispering so I can't hear, but I'm too distracted and uneasy to care. Running my fingers through my hair, I exhale slowly, trying to shake off that ordeal. But Jake is totally right...

What the hell am I even doing??

This is wrong on so many levels. Regardless of my feelings for Tate, the secrets and inner tumultuous thoughts I've been dealing with since college, my wife doesn't deserve to be cheated on. And Tate doesn't deserve to be strung along or played with like a toy, no matter how much he insists it doesn't bother him.

He may not do "feelings" with the random guys he hooks up with, but he and I are different. We have a history. Whether he wants to admit it or not, there's something here.

When he comes stomping back over to me, he looks flustered. I expect him to have some smartass remark on deck. But instead, he just breathes, "Sorry about that..."

I blink at him, a bit perplexed. "That's okay."

I try to get closer to him again, but he slinks away, leaning up on his car. "I gotta go. I have an early meeting tomorrow."

My brow arches. "It's six-thirty..."

"You don't know my routine." He squints at me. "I like to pamper myself on Sunday nights."

I bite my lip. *He's so cute...*

Just as stubborn and self-involved as he was back in the day. Negative qualities in other people that happen to be charming and sexy on Tate.

"Tate, don't make me keep begging." I push into his space, trapping him against the door of his fancy foreign car. "I want to see you again, baby. I *need* to..."

My hands cup his face, holding his jaw still so he can't look away. Our eyes melt together, and I see all the doubt and worry in his, like it's reflecting my own back at me. I have very little confidence in most of what's happening here.

The only thing I *know* is that the second I drive away... I'm going to miss him like crazy. After all, I missed him for years when he wasn't mine. And when I saw him at Pride, it turned me possessive and needy all over again, like the last fifteen years never happened. Now that he's given me even the smallest sliver of him, I'm dying for more.

Tate's lashes flutter when I drape my mouth over his, kissing him slowly.

But he pulls away before it gets started. "Go home to your wife, Lance."

Those words... they're like a dagger to my heart. The harsh reality they carry churns acidic discomfort in my gut.

But I force myself to let him go, not without first resting my palm over his heart and whispering, "I'm not going to stop trying, Trouble. Because we both know you're *mine*."

I feel him shiver, but he wiggles away from me, trying to disguise it as he opens the door to his car and slinks inside. Backing up, I move over to my truck while Tate's vehicle roars to life, and he quickly backs out of the driveway, peeling off without another word.

God, what am I supposed to do with this ache?

Nyla K.

My head is cluttered as I hop into my Ford F-150, pretty much the opposite of Tate's sleek black Maserati. He probably bought that because he's rich now, and he likes to have nice things... Whereas, I bought mine because it was affordable, and convenient for running things to and from the shop when Des needs help, weekend trips to Home Depot for miscellaneous DIY projects, things of that nature. It fits the image I've built of myself.

The married man who works at the church, who knows everyone in his town and waves hello to them at the grocery store, who spends his free time working around the house to keep busy...

What would it even look like, bringing Tate into that?

How could it ever work?

The truth I feel, weighted in the pit of my stomach like a large stone, tells me it couldn't. Tate wouldn't fit into my life, and I wouldn't fit into his. There are too many things keeping us apart, and I hate it. Even if I could get him to stop fighting me, it wouldn't make a lick of difference.

We're not *supposed* to be together.

I'm quiet and despondent the entire drive back to South Valley. Just cruising, with music from one of my playlists on at low volume, lost in my thoughts. Still, the nerves don't return until I pull onto my street.

I really wish I'd been able to clean up a bit before coming home. I can smell Tate on me, and I'm not sure if it's something Desiree would notice...

Fortunately for me, when I pull into the driveway, my wife's car isn't there. She must be at the shop. She spends a lot of time there, because she loves it. To be honest, I like it a lot myself, but not because it's her parents' shop, or because she works there. I've just always loved flowers and plants. Growing beautiful things, watching them flourish, then making something out of them that people can enjoy. I guess you could say it's a passion of mine.

Inside the house, I head straight for the shower, thoroughly washing off the smell of sex. Then I get dressed in fresh clothes and head back out... to the flower shop.

South Valley Florists is less than five miles from our house. The store has been in Des's family for two generations. Her parents left it in our care when they retired, under the guise that we'd pass it onto our children someday.

That's a topic I'm already too stressed to think about right now.

Parking, I hop out of the truck, hands sweating, muscles bound up in tension. I try to focus on breathing as I make my way inside the store through the backdoor. There are no lights on in the storefront, since it's closed. Only a dim glow coming from the back room. I wander slowly, taking in a breath as I peer inside. I spot her right away, sitting on the floor in front of a bunch of planters, dirt lining the already dark skin of her hands and arms.

She's a beautiful woman, my wife. Just as stunning as the day I met her, the summer before senior year of college. I remember it like it was yesterday...

I was *miserable*. Six months had gone by without one of my closest friends, and I'd done nothing but replay the last time I saw him in my head, probably thousands of times. I missed Tate so much, I spent most of my time wallowing, trying to focus on school and fight off the devastation of self-inflicted heartache I barely even fully understood.

It sucked. Big time.

I was here all summer; at the new house in South Valley with my family, moping and brushing off their every attempt at getting me to *talk about it*, or join in on family activities. All I wanted to do was sulk around outside, fussing with the garden and existing in a never-ending state of gloom.

Until one Sunday, the last one before I was due back in Arizona for the new semester, my father badgered me into coming to church for his sermon.

Of course, I was less than enthusiastic. My faith had fallen away over the years, and I just didn't want to sit around people, listening to my father preach about *love* and *selflessness* and *honesty*. I was too angry, and sad, and truth be told, a little afraid that all the good partitioners would be able to read my sins the second I stepped through the door.

But despite all that, I agreed. Because I was lost... and in desperate need of being found.

I was uncomfortable for most of the sermon, fidgeting in place, guilt and shame burning me under the eyes of the Lord. More than that, I was in agony... because I was in love with someone I couldn't have, and it hurt so motherfucking bad.

When my father led us in prayer, I bowed my head, squeezing my eyes shut as hard as I could, struggling to hold back the tears.

Please take away this pain... I begged in my mind. In my heart, reaching out for faith, for *strength*. Deep in my weakened soul, I was *pleading* for salvation.

Show me the way... Guide me, Father, because I don't know what I'm doing anymore.

Nyla K.

I miss him. The tears crept from behind my eyelids. *I love him. I can't help it, God, please help me...*

Show me the way...

My heart was *begging* God for a sign, foolishly hopeful that He would bring Tate back to me. That He would tell me it was okay; I could love trouble, and He wouldn't hate me for it.

Amen.

The sermon ended, and I composed myself as much as I could before wandering up to see my father. He was speaking to a couple, who he introduced me to as Mr. and Mrs. Dixon. And a moment later, a young woman walked up to join us...

Their daughter, Desiree.

"Hey," Des says now, pulling me out of my vivid memory.

And our dog, Sunny, barks, prancing around where he's tied by his leash to the leg of a table, I'm guessing so he doesn't get into the dirt and make a mess.

Desiree is glancing up at me from the floor, and I feel like I'm acting weird, just standing around in the doorway.

Is this how I normally act?? Why do I feel like a totally different person...?

"Hey." Stepping over to her, I give Sunny some quick love on his fluffy head before I drop to my knees to check out what she's doing. "You been here long?"

"If I said no, would you believe me?" She side-smirks, and I chuckle. Lifting an orchid, she places its roots into a pot, scooping up dirt in her fingers and packing it around the base. "How was the cookout?"

"The what?" I grunt, bemused, before remembering the lie I told her about where I was going. "Oh, um, it was fine. Fun."

Wow, you sound so fucking guilty.

Swallowing down a mouthful of it, I grasp some dirt and help her, using my hands to distract myself from the nerves shaking me inside out.

"How are your friends?" my wife asks casually.

I sure as shit don't feel casual as I mumble, "They're... good."

I told her Kennan was having another party, hoping it was a good enough cover, since she doesn't know him. Still, my stomach is churning while my mind rushes through the likelihood that she'll mention this to any of our friends from ASU.

"That's good," Des sighs, sitting back and brushing the dirt from her hands, observing the orchid in its new pot. She peeks at me, amber eyes sparkling. "I missed you."

The way I gulp feels like a painfully slow, deliberate pause before I'm able to respond. "I missed you too."

She smiles, full lips framing white teeth. Just like that first day, when I met her in the church. When she appeared, as if from out of nowhere, like the answer to my prayers.

"'Kay. Let's go home." She stands up, holding out a hand to me.

Gazing at her from the floor, part of me feels like this is still the way I'm supposed to go; the path God is illuminating, to keep me out of trouble.

Over a decade ago, Desiree was sent to me, like a blessing and a curse. The way she floated into my life, this beautiful, sweet, fun girl, felt like a testimony to the faith I knew I couldn't lose. I saw her as an angel, sent by God to ease my pain. It wasn't a coincidence that she showed up at that very moment. She even went to Arizona State.

It was His plan, for us to start dating at school, for her to help me move on from the torture I'd been feeling for six long months since I closed the door on Tate.

Desiree opened a new one, full of possibilities that were *good* for me. I could see it all, laid out before my eyes. A future I could have, with someone I was *supposed* to have it with.

But God doesn't give with both hands. He holds them out, in opposite directions... and you can only choose one.

Being with Desiree, falling in love with her, getting married and starting this life we've been building for years... it's the right direction on paper. But the wrong one beneath the surface.

My heart wanted to go the other way.

It's very possible that while I've been able to ignore the pleading inside me, God still heard it. It's also possible that He's testing me... And based on what happened at Pride, and what I've been chasing ever since, I'm failing miserably.

But I can't help it... I don't feel like I ever stood a chance on this path.

And even though I know my heart doesn't want it, I take my wife's hand. I let her help me up, dust myself off, and go home with her. Because I've gone too far in the opposite direction.

It might be too late to turn around.

Chapter Fourteen

Tate

I f I told you I never mix business with pleasure, I'd be lying.

Not that I make a habit of it or anything. But doing what I do, it's bound to happen. I'm basically a professional schmoozer, using my natural charisma to charm rich people into handing their money over to my firm.

Honestly, it's the job I was made to do, so it's only natural that it would occasionally overlap with another *skill set* of mine.

"If JDX doesn't lift soon, they're fucked," Pierce says with confidence, sipping from his second glass of the meal.

It's barely noon, but this is pretty average when any of the partners get together for lunch. We just sit around drinking and talking shit about other firms.

We're basically Mad Men.

And I get to be Don Draper. Only with way *less interest in vagina.*

"Oh, they'll take a bath, for sure," Z adds, leaning back in his chair while ogling our waitress. "Just wait until we get onto the green this weekend. Henderson's gonna be all bitter, overcompensating by putting his dick on the table... Betting his kids' tuition so no one at W thinks he's a bitch. If he only knew they have no intention of signing with him."

I'm only half-listening, my eyes lingering on my iPhone until someone says my name.

"Can we expect to see you Saturday, Eckhart?"

I glance up at Truman, tilting my head.

Trouble

"I'm sorry, all I heard was *dick on the table*," I mutter, smirking as they chuckle.

My amusement is a bit forced, since I'm currently using large amounts of willpower not to focus on the messages that have been popping in all morning, joining the nice little collection of texts I refuse to respond to. Usually, I'm chiming into the conversation much more, but I can't help it. I'm distracted, and I have been all week.

My fingers twitch with the desire to reach for my phone where it's resting beside my plate. Instead, I stuff them into my pocket like I'm putting them on timeout.

"Come on, man." Z uses his most persuasive tone. "We could use your expertise at swooping in and sealing the deal when no one's looking." He sneers, and I purse my lips.

"We've been over this." I lift my glass to sip. "You goddamn geriatrics are not getting me onto a golf course. It's literally the most boring place on earth."

"But you're weirdly good," he whines.

"I know, it makes no sense." Truman shakes his head. "He never plays, then shows up once a year and cleans everyone out."

A laugh rumbles from my chest. *Yea*, I guess I'm good at golf, and it annoys them because I don't know shit about it. I just hit the ball, and it flies, then shrug like Elle Woods. *"What, like it's hard?"*

"I told you, I don't play sports." I murmur, and they collectively become a symphony of scoffing and eye-rolling. "Now, if you need me to show up at the bar and help you close, all you have to do is ask nicely." Lifting a shoulder, I give them my coyest of smirks.

Pierce leans in on the table, shooting me with a teasing glare. "Tate, will you *please* come to the club on Saturday and use your magical powers to secure PD Holdings?"

Lolling my head back, I groan. It's partially for show, since I would love nothing more than to add this account to my ever-growing list of conquests.

But then... *Golf? Really??*

It's so unbearably dull.

Unfortunately, a lot of business is conducted on the green. It's just a thing. Typically, I let the guys here do all the boring stuff while I hang out at the bar. Then when they bring the client inside for a drink, I *sweep the leg*, so to speak, and *put 'em in a body bag.*

Karate Kid references make my job seem more exciting.

Nyla K.

Because really, it's just a lot of talking. Spouting numbers and percentages, taking subtle jabs at other firms while making sure not to outright *slander* them. That and entertaining; plying the client with booze and gourmet food, laughing at their stupid jokes, and pretending to be interested in whatever inane shit they like to brag about.

Actually, it's a lot like flirting. *The client* is like a super hot dude with an insane body, who's dumb as a stump and has the personality of a block of cheese. The same amount of acting is required to seal any deal. Fortunately for my firm, I'm *very* good at feigning enthusiasm for the purposes of getting into hot dudes' pants.

Or in the case of our clients, securing thirty percent of their capital growth.

"*Fine*, I suppose I could stop by and help your follow-through," I sigh.

Z scoffs, rubbing his eyes. "I bet he doesn't even know he just used a golf term."

Truman snorts while Pierce flops back in his chair, and I wink at him.

The thing is, to *me*, my job is very exciting. Ever since high school, I knew I wanted to be in finance. I grew up on the poorer side of the middle class, and like with most things we covet, the lack of available money just made me want it even more.

Being that my *dad*—otherwise known as the dipshit who stuck around just long enough to impregnate my mother, then vanished forever—wasn't around, my mom had to work two jobs in order to keep a roof over our heads and provide just enough for us to get by. We never went hungry or anything like that. But we didn't have nice stuff. Really, we didn't have much *stuff* at all, and as a kid with friends who had loads of it, I was always on the outside looking in.

Add to that the fact that I knew with full certainty I was gay the second Lindsay Tran kissed me at a pool party when I was thirteen, it became abundantly clear from a young age that being *different* was something I'd never escape.

So I had a choice. Either fall back into mediocrity and let bullshit insecurities consume me—*which, let's be real, has never been my style*—or embrace my uniqueness, build confidence in it and use it to drive toward the life of luxury I've always wanted.

I'm sure you can guess which way my cookie crumbled.

My friends didn't start calling me *Trouble* because I raised a lot of hell as a kid, though I was certainly no angel. I earned the nickname by being a purveyor of wise-ass remarks, an epic sweet-talker, and a notorious champion in the field of emotional coercion. And I'm sure listing off these traits now makes it sound like I was a tiny sociopath in the making, but I swear, it wasn't that bad. I just learned how to get what I wanted on my own, since life gave me zero handouts, and I was brought up to only truly ever rely on *myself*.

As soon as I realized I was also pretty damn good with numbers, my plan took shape. Because what profession springs to mind when you think of shallow, overly narcissistic men who love money only second to the power that comes from manipulating people for it? *If you're imagining someone like Leonardo DiCaprio as Jordan Belfort, minus the excessive drug use and blatant thievery, you'd be spot on.*

I wanted to wear suits that cost more than a year's rent. I wanted to drive a fancy, foreign car, and travel the world making deals. I wanted to talk *dollars and cents* to prove how much of it I was worth, and I wanted to be envied the way I'd been envying other people my whole life. Call it a symptom of my very obvious Daddy issues, or a desperate need for control. *Whatever. Fuck it.*

That seat at the head table was *mine*, and I decided I would do everything in my power to take it. *Within vaguely ethical reason, of course.*

I was on my way toward this lifestyle when Lance rejected me, which made diving in headfirst even easier. After that, I chose business over personal, vanity over vexation, and settled into the role of a lifetime that wasn't *supposed* to be mine.

Being that I'm the youngest partner in my firm's history, I'd say I nailed it. The ultimate victory for a fatherless gay kid who used to get his clothes from Goodwill.

What can I say? I'm a determined motherfucker.

Still, I won't tell you it's all champagne and caviar, because getting to where I am now was far from easy. I had to work extra hard for the respect of my colleagues, being gay and all. A lot of the senior partners are old dudes who, before they met me, assumed all gay men were only interested in fashion, Broadway, and sucking each other off in truck stop bathrooms. And I'm only interested in *two* of those things. *I've never been one for musical theater.*

During my early years, I begrudgingly spent a lot of time in strip clubs, discussing market trends while paying girls to dance away from me. I took my licks like a champ, paid my dues, and dealt with my fair share of homophobic comments. But never once did I think of calling it quits. It's just not in my nature.

Eventually, the partners realized that I actually knew what the fuck I was talking about, and that me loving dick didn't prevent me from *also* loving money just as much as they do.

At this point, it's been years since they've dragged me to a strip club, because they trust me emphatically, and my work speaks for itself. In fact, *I* call the shots when it comes to most client meetings now. I'm often tempted to bring them to a drag show or a leather bar or something, just to fuck with them. But instead, we gravitate toward any place that has scotch older than me.

And the ironic part of it all is that I'm not the only man in this firm who likes dick... I'm just the only one who admits it out loud.

Pierce's cheeks are a bit pink as he tosses back the rest of his drink, and Z pays the bill. Truman is already up and storming out of the restaurant, barking at someone on the phone. And I'm just chewing my lower lip, watching my phone screen light up again, another message buzzing.

God-fucking-damnit...

I'm going to end up reading them. I know I will.

I don't stand a fucking chance, especially when every vibration of the damn device feels like it's happening in the pit of my stomach.

Don't be an idiot...

Don't be an idiot...

Don't be an idiot.

Buzz buzz buzz.

Don't be a buzzing idiot, you idiot.

My phone is telling me exactly what to do, and yet I can *feel* myself deliberately wanting to disobey. I just really want to know what he's saying that's so motherloving important.

Probably just more pleading to see me... Same stuff he's been saying for the past few days.

I can't stop thinking about you.

I still feel your body on me, baby.

You know you're mine, so just stop fighting it.

Meet me somewhere, Trouble.

Honestly, Lance Hardy has to be the neediest married man I've ever slept with. I guess I understand why... being that we have a history and all. But if anything, that makes it worse, because I still don't *understand* any of it.

I don't get why he ran away from me all those years ago, or why us bumping into each other at Pride set him off the course of the straight, virtuous life he'd been living since. *I mean, if he's really been thinking about me over the years, how hard would it have been to pick up the phone?*

Maybe he *does* actually love his wife, despite the way he was acting before we parted ways at Jake's... after he fucked me to tears like I used to dream he would back in college.

Or maybe it's just not as easy for Lance to live his truth as it is for me.

I'll admit to a certain degree of ignorance when it comes to marriage, monogamy, and fearing life outside of the closet. I'm not familiar with any of those concepts, so I can't really empathize with what he's going through.

Sure, before I came out, I was definitely nervous about how people would treat me. But it turns out, I've surrounded myself with exactly the right support system. I pay no mind to the bigots of the world, because the way they think doesn't affect me. It's never going to change who I am, so why give them the satisfaction?

My time is far too valuable to be squandered on close-minded morons.

But Lance isn't me. In fact, in a lot of ways, he's the opposite. He's gentle, contemplative. He *worries* about other people, to the point that he actually wants to save their eternal souls.

I can't even fathom that level of human compassion.

It's possible that even the thought of admitting he's gay, or bi, and uprooting his simple, comfortable life is far too scary for him to consider. Or, there's the more likely possibility that he just wants to have his cake and eat it too...

His wife being the cake, and me being the one he eats.

Either way, I don't know why I'm even thinking about this. I need to forget about it and move on with my life. I need to remember who I am *now*, who I became as a result of Lance fucking Hardy and his goddamn uncertainty.

This is who I dreamt of being when I was younger; a ruthless wolf of fucking Wall Street. In all those images of a future Tate I used to concoct, not once was there ever a significant other attached. It was always just me, living it up with my black Amex and a closet full of suits. Traveling and being bougie.

No commitments to anything other than my kick-ass career, and *myself*.

Lance can claim that I'm *his* all he wants, but we both know it's not the truth.

No matter how much it felt that way when he was—

Nyla K.

"I'm gonna need a smoke, please," Pierce murmurs by my side, and I flinch.

Shaking myself out of my thoughts, I pull a pack of cigarettes from my pocket while we all stagger out of the restaurant, plucking two between my teeth. Lighting them both at once, I suck in some smoke before handing one to Pierce.

I only smoke when I'm drinking, or when I'm severely stressed, both of which happen pretty often. Sometimes I'll sub in a weed pen, but definitely not while I'm at work. This job requires me to be fully lucid.

Booze doesn't count. Tying one on is inherently part of the gig.

Though, I prefer not to get blasted in the middle of the day, like ol' Piercey boy, here.

The four of us walk the three blocks back to the office, Pierce and I smoking side by side while Z scampers behind us and Truman power-walks ahead. We tend to stick together because we're closest in age. I'm still the youngest, but Pierce is only a year older than me. Truman is forty, and Z— short for Zurkowski—is forty-three.

Pierce and I are the only partners of the four of us. The other two are on their way, but it's not something that comes easily. It takes a lot of hard work, lots of long hours; years of putting your job above all else. Some of the guys can't hack it, and it usually always boils down to whether you're willing to sacrifice having a family for your career.

This isn't exactly groundbreaking stuff. Single guys will always get ahead faster than those with wives and children, because when you're single, you have no obligations.

My time belongs to *me*, and I choose to give most of it to my career. I'm a workaholic, and I like it that way.

Less time for thinking and emotions, and all that riffraff.

Back upstairs, on the thirty-fourth floor of the building, we part ways, heading back to our respective offices. Pierce pats me on the back, stumbling into his, which is across the hall from mine, immediately closing all the blinds. I'd be willing to bet good money he's going to fall asleep in there, which just has me shaking my head as I amble into my corner office and shut the door.

Making my way over to my mini fridge, I pull out a coconut water, drinking it quickly in hopes that it'll combat a potential headache from the day drinking. Gliding over to my couch, I plop down and stare while my phone burns a hole in my pocket.

Trouble

Theoretically, I could go home. I have no more meetings until next week. Any work left to do can be done from my condo at this point.

A flicker of something causes me to shift.

I wonder what Lance is doing...

I wonder if I should...

Closing my eyes, I exhale swiftly, expelling that thought.

Stop. You don't need to see him. You don't need to be thinking about him.

Yes, the sex was absolutely fucking mind-blowing, but that doesn't matter. There are a million other guys to have hot sex with, none of whom will saddle you with all sorts of complicated emotional baggage and painful memories. Guys who aren't married, or afraid God's wrath will strike them down for putting their dick in me.

Ugh. I knew this was going to happen. This is exactly why I fought tooth and nail to ignore him after Pride. Because part of me *knew* that if we did finally cross that line and have sex, it would turn into something so stupidly fucking cumbersome. And that's exactly what happened.

I've slept with *a lot* of guys. I won't share the actual number, but to put it into perspective, if I had a dollar for every dick that's been inside me, I could buy plane tickets, or a decent-sized flatscreen. *A few hundred McDonald's cheeseburgers.*

And out of all those penises, not a *single one* has managed to weasel this kind of antsy emotional reaction out of me. Maybe there was one who almost got under my skin the tiniest bit...

But that's irrelevant. All bullets were dodged, and it was for the best.

The point is that Lance Hardy already wreaked havoc on me years ago. I refuse to let him do it again.

So despite how *epic* the orgasm was, no matter how badly my nuts are now *aching* with the desire to feel him pinning me down and biting my neck and stuffing me with that sweet, *perfect* cock again, I will not call him. Nor will I read his many, many text messages.

Don't be an idiot.

That's why I haven't changed his name in my phone... And I'm not gonna. Because now that we fucked, and it felt like *that*, I'd be an even bigger idiot if I kept going back.

Deciding that going home is a bad idea, I settle in for a long night here at the office. I have more than enough work to keep my mind occupied. That's the way it should be.

My work distracts me from feeling things, not the other way around.

I make a few calls, get on some Zoom meetings with Tokyo and Berlin.

I work on projections for the W account, and when hours have passed and it's dinnertime, I DoorDash sushi and eat it while I work.

A standard day. Truthfully, I like working here at the office. I also don't mind working out of hotels while I'm traveling. And it's not that I *don't* like working at home, but something about being in my condo feels suffocating at times.

But I don't want to think about that, so I don't.

I just keep working, well into the evening, until the next thing I know, it's dark outside and my back is stiff from pacing around the room. Stretching out, I check my watch.

Damn... it's after nine.

Well done, hustler.

I can see through the glass that pretty much everyone's gone home for the night. The lights are dim out in the hallway, and I haven't seen or heard anyone for a while. It's not unusual for people, specifically partners, to linger here well into the night. But today was an early day, and I guess not everyone enjoys working for thirteen hours straight.

Amateurs.

Tossing my work cell down onto my desk, my eyes slink over to my personal, and I bite my lip. I kind of want to check Grindr, to see if anyone good is around, but I'm afraid the second I unlock the thing, my dumb fingers will go directly into my unread texts.

They're thirsty like that.

I'm contemplating this when I hear footsteps. Then a quick knock on my office door.

Before I can even say *come in*, it pushes open and Pierce peers in at me. "Shit, you're still here?"

"Burning the midnight oil," I sigh.

His lips twist as he leans against the doorway. "You know you can't get a promotion, right?"

Huffing, I shake my head. "Please tell me you haven't been asleep this whole time..."

I guess he takes this chitchat as an invitation, striding into my office and going straight for the cabinet where I keep the good scotch. "I was on two hours of sleep this morning. Drinks at lunch didn't help..." He takes out two glasses, pouring liquor into both. "But hey, it's Friday."

My brow lifts, and I smirk. "It's Wednesday."

His face freezes, shifting into a puzzled look of realization. "Oh, shit..."

A laugh puffs out on a breath as I purse my lips. But he just shrugs indifferently, stalking over to hand me a drink. We clink and sip, my eyes gliding over him briefly.

A memory of us drunkenly pawing at each other at the Christmas party last year springs to mind.

Josiah Pierce is *straight* as far as the rest of the firm, and probably the rest of the world, is concerned. I don't know his situation, other than that he was engaged—*to a woman*—when he started here, but it ended and now he's single. He goes out to bars with the guys, and talks about hooking up with the ladies... And who am I to question any of it? I don't exactly *care*. What he does is his own business.

All I know is that he sucks dick rather enthusiastically *for a straight guy.*

I try not to hook up with coworkers often, because talk about complicated. But it does happen on occasion. Josiah is *very* fucking cute, and he has a great dick. Not to mention, fooling around with him falls under that highly inconvenient weakness I have for curious straight dudes...

I don't *want* to find it so unbearably hot, but I can't help myself. *It's my toxic trait...*

Well, it's on the list.

Our eyes lock for a moment and his shift away first. "So... what are you working on?"

His cheeks are slightly flushed as he wanders over to my desk, rifling through my papers.

The first rule of hooking up with coworkers is the same as the first rule of *Fight Club*. You don't talk about it. Talking about it just makes it more real, when you're supposed to act like it *never happened*. So the fact that Pierce and I have done some very satisfying secret gay stuff together has never been openly discussed.

Ignoring tension is easy to accomplish when other people are around, and we're focusing on work. But when we're alone like this, it can become difficult not remembering him eating my ass while I gave him sloppy head. It certainly brings a different sort of vibe to the room, which is annoying me because of how much I've been dealing with this shit lately from *other* parties.

"I was just finishing up some shit for W," I tell him casually, killing the rest of my drink. "It's pretty much good to go."

He peeks at me. "You don't need help?"

I blink a few times, then mutter, "I'm good. I'll probably just call it a night."

Pierce is quiet for a moment, visibly chewing on the inside of his cheek.

And it's becoming obvious that he, too, is feeling the burn, though he doesn't seem all that bothered by it.

"You're driving all the way back to Corona tonight?" he asks curiously.

I shrug. "I guess I could stay in town if I need to."

He nods, eyes falling to his glass, swirling the liquor around a few times before slugging it back. Then he whispers, "Maybe you should..."

Oh, boy...

Sweet Josiah wants some dick.

I can't say I'm not flattered. And even though I know I shouldn't mess around with a partner at my firm—physically *in* my office explicitly—I won't deny that the idea of letting him fuck me up against the glass window is *very* appealing.

But something is missing. Some of the sizzling excitement, or the hunger... *Something* about it doesn't feel right, and I can't put my finger on why.

Clearing my throat, I try shaking off my sudden malaise. "Yea... I'm pretty wiped." He's giving me a wide-eyed look that's unnerving me even more for some reason. "What are your plans for tonight?" I ask, trying to keep it friendly.

"Nothing much," he hums, then holds out his glass. "Refill?"

Sighing, I take his glass, ignoring the way he's watching me while I pour us another round. I'm all up in my head right now, and I can't figure it out. I was just thinking about finding a random hook-up for the night... And here it is.

I should be flirting with him. Hell, even skipping the segue and dropping to my knees, since he seems like he's good to go. But something is stopping me.

A normal person with morals would assume it's because we work together, but I know that's not it. After all, it didn't stop me from hopping on his dick the last time.

So what changed?

Why am I so apprehensive right now?

Bringing the drink to Pierce, I keep some distance between us. His eyes are running over one of my projections, finger trailing the paper in a seductive motion I've never seen anyone use while assessing financial documents.

"Did you factor in Q2 on this?" he asks softly.

"Uh, of course," I grunt, because *duh. I'm not a hack.*

His eyes lift to mine, brow cocking. "You sure?"

Frowning, I push him out of the way, rifling through the papers to locate something that will shut him up. "See?" I point to my numbers. "Right there. Don't question me."

Grinning, he sips slowly from his glass. He's already close, but now I can feel him inching closer. Easing himself behind me, he leans over my shoulder, practically resting his chin on it.

"Hmm... those are some big numbers." His mischievous tone slinks into my ear as his hand does the same to my waist. "If you land this, you might finally be able to buy that island off the Maldives shaped like a penis."

I can't help chuckling, though I'm way too warm and my throat is all scratchy. Attempting to squirm out of his hold proves ineffective when he grips me tighter, and pulls me in *closer.*

Turning my face slightly, I peer at him. "Whatcha doin, JP...?"

His breath brushes my cheek as he purrs, "Let's fuck."

No, thanks.

My spine stiffens. But not at his request. At my goddamn knee-jerk reaction to it.

No, thanks?? When have I ever said no thanks *to a hot guy who wants to ride it raw??*

I swear to God, it feels like my stomach is in knots, and I'm actually *shaking.* The way I'm behaving, you'd think I'm...

Oh, fuck.

My heart thumps while my mind reels.

Guilty. I feel guilty...

I don't want to fuck this dude because he's not...

Don't be an idiot!?!

Whipping back my drink, I swallow down the burn, releasing a jagged breath of bewilderment. *This is so fucked.* Now, *I'm* cockblocking *myself.*

My body is repelling random hot guys who aren't Lance... *The fucker got into my head.*

He incepted his cockblocking ways into my brain!

Pierce pushes me into my desk, grinding his erection against my ass. "You're so fucking hot..." He reaches around my waist, going for my belt.

But I grab his hands, stopping him. "Look, I don't know if this is a good idea..."

Jesus, what the fuck am I doing??

I can't believe I'm actually trying to stop him.

"But you feel so good," he rumbles, and the sensation of him, rock-hard and smashing against my ass has me trembling.

143

Fuck, I wanna get fucked. I want it so bad, but...
But I don't want it with him. Because he's not... Lance.
Ew. I hate myself right now!

My mind is choking on the thoughts, gagging on them, because I can't *believe* I'm even *thinking* such ridiculousness.

He ruined me. Lance Hardy fucking ruined me, that damn gorgeous married asshole!

"Pierce, I can't," I grumble, wiggling out of his hold.

He gives me a look of wounded confusion. "You don't want to...?"

God, this is awkward. How can I shoot him down in a way that won't make shit super weird between us at work??

"No, it's not that," I attempt sincerity. "I just remembered I have to go..."

"Go where?" He blinks.

My mind is blank. I can't think of *anything* other than Lance fucking Hardy, and it's turning my brain to mush.

Lips parted, I'm about to throw out the first thing that comes to mind, when a noise from outside my office stops me. Footsteps and voices.

Oh, thank God.

Pierce's eyes widen in momentary horror as he fixes himself up fast, darting away from me. A couple of the senior partners walk by, barely sparing us a glance. Clearly, they're more invested in their conversation, oblivious to the fact that they just narrowly avoided catching their employees having sex.

But I can't even think about that right now. *I gotta get the hell out of here.*

Grabbing my stuff, I mutter, "Goodnight, Pierce," flashing a very brief, uneasy smile of reassurance to pacify the dude, before rushing out into the hall.

The entire elevator ride down to the garage, I'm dazed and perplexed. Once I'm tucked securely inside my Maserati, I'm finally able to breathe again, but it's not comforting. Not even a little.

I'm twisted the hell up right now.

I don't belong to Lance Hardy, and he sure as shit doesn't belong to me. We're just old friends who fucked. That's it.

Why am I so fixated on it... On him??

"Fuck it," I mutter, giving up my resistance as I pull out my phone and open my texts.

Trouble

I need to see what he's been saying... What he has to say for himself and this *disease* of sudden neediness he's infected me with.

Ten unread messages from last night to about an hour ago. Eyes scanning over them, a tight heat of delusion spreads up my chest.

DON'T BE AN IDIOT

Miss you, baby

DON'T BE AN IDIOT

Sweet dreams, troublemaker

DON'T BE AN IDIOT

Good morning T...

DON'T BE AN IDIOT

I dreamt about you last night

DON'T BE AN IDIOT

Beautiful day, isn't it?

DON'T BE AN IDIOT

I hope you have a good day at work... even though you're ignoring me

DON'T BE AN IDIOT

Tateeee....?

DON'T BE AN IDIOT

The least you could do is respond... Or even just read my messages

DON'T BE AN IDIOT

Can I see you tonight?

DON'T BE AN IDIOT

I know you want to gorgeous...

Dropping my phone into the cupholder, I rub my eyes.

What the fuck, man??

As anxious as I'm feeling, as uncharacteristically fluttery as my heart is right now, I'm simultaneously swept up into a twister of frustration and fury.

Where the hell does he get off?? Coming at me like an obsessive, clingy lunatic??

He's the one who ran out on *me*. He fucking destroyed my heart when he left. I fucking loathe even admitting it, because I could've sworn I was over it, but it's fucking true. *That shit hurt like hell.*

And now he just shows up, casually sidling back into my life and turning everything upside down. Acting like he wants—no, *needs* me. Like he's been poisoned and I'm the antidote.

But it's all bullshit.

He doesn't want me. If he did—

No. I shake my head. *Fuck that. I'm not even going to think about it, because it's pointless.*

Snatching the phone back up, I tap his contact, ready to call him and chew his ass out. But I pause.

Man, it would be so much more satisfying to yell at him in person...

After all, we never had that big blowout.

In college, he just left. Then at Pride, I was too busy reveling in how good it felt to see him again, ensnared by his beauty and his annoyingly sexy apprehension.

Every interaction since the glory hole, I've rationalized it away as *Tate doesn't do feelings, so who cares?*

But I *do* have feelings. *Like, right now, for example.*

I feel fucking pissed.

I deserve at least *one* opportunity to tell him off, and I'm too wound up to wait.

Pulling out of the parking garage, I call my assistant over the Bluetooth.

"Hey, boss," Troy's voice chirps through the speakers in my car.

"I need you to find Lance Hardy's home address for me."

Two can play this game, Sunshine.

Let's see how you like being tracked down... And how you'll explain this one to your wife.

Chapter Fifteen
Tate

The drive to South Valley is about an hour. But the time spent cruising the highway does nothing to subdue my rage.

Troy came through, as he always does. And by the time I'm pulling onto Lance's street, I'm vibrating.

This is *actually* crazy.

I kind of can't believe I'm just showing up at his house like this...

I've never done anything like this before. I don't show up at dude's houses to confront them, because I've never cared enough about anyone to do it.

But let's be clear. This isn't some Say Anything, love declaration type shit. I'm not Lance.

I'm here to give him a piece of my mind, that's all.

Cruising up the dark street, everything is silent; motionless, like a world on pause. It's not even eleven at night, but it seems fitting that a place like this would *shut down*, in a sense, after dark. It's obviously a quiet little neighborhood.

I can just imagine the families who live here... Children and dogs running around, playing in their yards. Not unlike where I grew up; where Jake and all our friends still live.

I have nothing against it, I just wouldn't be able to live here myself. I need to be in a city, where I can let the loudness surround me and enjoy the chaos. I need to travel, see places, experience things. *Break free.*

I need to be able to spread my wings.

Nyla K.

This... Living in a place where everyone knows your name, same faces every day...

It's not me. It's *Lance.*

He's the small-town guy. Working in the yard, waving to people when they say hello.

After all, he's the local pastor... A respected member of the community.

I wonder what they'd think if they knew...

Counting the numbers on the houses, I slow down when I spot his. It's normal, pretty much identical to all the others. But I can tell right away it's his because of all the flowers in front. The yard is decorated with color, various gardens and accents visible even in the low light.

Lance always loved his flowers. Trees, plants, pretty much all fauna. It's his thing.

I suppose it's his wife's thing, too. They have that in common. *Shared interests...*

I bet they have a few.

My stomach feels gross as I cruise up to his house, eyes lingering on the sunflowers in his yard. The sight has me gulping down emotions I don't want to deal with.

I choose not to pull into the driveway, instead parking farther up, by the edge of his property line. Not that I'm *hiding...* I'm still mad as hell, and I don't care who sees me.

But actually being here, in front of his house, knowing his wife is inside... it's bringing on a wave of nerves that has me trembling with sudden apprehension for this plan.

What do I do?? Should I go knock on the door? Just start yelling his name on the front lawn?

It's late... I don't really want to make a scene.

Fuck that. Make a scene! Be the drama. You deserve it!

Head all cluttered with nonsense, I decide to pick up my phone and send him a text; two words that will hopefully have him shitting his pants.

ME

I'm outside.

I can barely sit still. My knee is bouncing rapidly while I chew on my lip, fussing with my hair in the rearview mirror. Within a minute of sending it, my text is read.

Oh, shit... Here we go.

Trouble

The typing bubbles pop up, but then they disappear. This happens a few times while I'm choking on the adrenaline crawling up my throat.

I need to walk... I need to move.

I can't breathe.

Stepping out of the car into the cool air allows me to calm down a little. Until movement draws my attention to the house. Lance's face appears in a front window, and as soon as he sees that I am, in fact, here, his door is opening and he's flinging himself outside, padding his way down the walkway.

Okay, now, be strong.

Don't let him hypnotize you with his pretty face and perfect hair and huge, god-like muscular body.

Remember why you came here... To give him the business!

"Tate... What...?" Lance whispers as he strides over to me, barefoot, wearing only some blue pajama pants and a white t-shirt. *Fuck, how does he make boring straight-guy jammies look so good??* "What are you doing here? How did you find my house...?"

Face bathed in surprise, and some noticeable delight, he gets up close to me, like he wants to touch. But he stops himself, face springing left and right.

I fold my arms over my chest. "I have my ways. Probably similar to how you found the Lockwoods' address... Or *my* address. Or my *phone number*." I narrow my gaze. "Easy to be a stalker these days, huh?"

His lashes flutter, and it looks like he wants to smile, but is holding back.

"Why are you here?" he asks, dark eyes boring into mine. "You didn't respond to any of my messages..."

"This is a face-to-face conversation," I grunt.

Immediately, something washes over his features, like he's bracing himself for pain. "What conversation...?"

I gulp.

Don't cave. You're mad, remember?!

Who cares if he seems happy to see you??

Yell at him! Tell him off!

Heart racing, I force out words in a mumble, "You fucked me up."

I wanted them to come out much more aggressive, but my tone isn't cooperating. I can't find enough voice to yell at him, my boiling anger from before having retreated into confusion. And hurt.

The things I've kept tucked away securely since the night he left.

Lance doesn't look confused at all, though. In fact, he almost nods, *agreeing* with my accusatory statement.

"You fucked me up big time when you took off," I croak, even though I *despise* admitting this to him. "You were one of my closest friends, Lance. And you fucking *vanished* without a word... That shit fucking hurt." I pause to let it sink in, but not so long that he thinks it's his turn to speak, because it certainly is not. "But I got over it, you know? I moved on, built a life... A life I fucking *love*, by the way. And then you reappear out of fucking nowhere, and *ruin* me all over again..."

Scraping a hand over my face, I shake my head, emotions bubbling to the surface. "You just couldn't leave me alone, could you?? Instead of showing up back then, or never showing up at all, you waited fifteen *fucking* years... Until I was settled and over it. *That's* the moment you decide to stroll back into my life like nothing happened?? Seriously, what the *fuck*, Hardy?!"

Rage is gaining more traction inside me, my volume increasing with the resentment spewing from my lips. Lance glances around again, as if he's worried his neighbors might hear us. It fucking *sends* me.

"I can't even fuck anymore without thinking about you," I hiss. "You're in my head, like some kind of child filter that blocks all the good stuff. I should be getting railed against a desk right now! But instead, I'm *here,* in your boring little neighborhood, yelling at you! It's *fucked!*" My chest is heaving, muscles too tense. I start pacing in front of him because I can't stand still anymore. "This is all so fucked. *Fuck you* for turning my mind against me..."

"Tate..." He steps forward, reaching.

But I smack his hand away. "Don't fucking touch me! We're not fucking it away this time!"

"Lower your voice," he growls, glaring just a bit.

It makes my dick twitch, and I hate that it does.

"What's wrong? Afraid your neighbors will find out you've been fooling around with a guy??" I seethe. "What about your wife... Is she inside?" My face swings in the direction of the house. "I should go have a chat with her, shouldn't I?"

Marching toward his driveway, my fists are balled, and I'm shaking. Lance grabs me by the waist before I make it a foot, hauling me backward.

"Alright, that's enough," he grunts, opening my car door. "You're acting crazy."

"I'm not leaving!" I gasp, fighting against him. "This is a long time coming, Hardy. I reserve the right to freak the fuck out on you! I never got to back then..."

"I know!" he whisper-shouts at me. "You have every right to lose it on me, Tate, but can we not do the whole screaming in the street thing?? Back then, it would've worked, but we're too old for this shit now."

"Fuck you," I breathe, ripping myself out of his grip. "College Tate wants me to be dramatic as fuck. If I had a drink, I'd be throwing it in your face!"

"Next time, I promise," he huffs, grabbing me again as he tries to push me into my car, but I fight against him some more.

"I'm not leaving," I teem.

"No. You're not," he growls. "Just get in the car, please, so we can talk."

My movements slow, and I allow him to guide me into the driver's seat. He closes the door, jaunting around to the other side while I sit, quaking in place.

Ugh, fighting with him is infuriating.

He's so *calm*... It's like arguing with a mannequin. *Completely unsatisfying.*

Still, I somehow feel his composure pacifying me. I'm still angry, but rather than raging out on him like I would have as a kid, I'm more collected. Because *he* doesn't want to fight. He wants to listen to me talk.

Damn him and his mature, adult communication.

Lance settles into the passenger seat, turning to face me. We stare at each other for a moment, draped in shadows as the dome light fades overhead then goes out. I swallow, refusing to acknowledge how good he smells now that we're in a confined space. But it's mingling with the smell of my leather seats, and it's goddamn intoxicating.

Focus. "What do you have to say for yourself?"

His forehead lines, eyes shimmering remorse. "I'm—"

"*Not* an apology," I cut him off with a snarl. "I want fucking *answers*, Hardy. What am I supposed to do with you now??"

He's quiet for a few seconds, gaping at me. "It's very complicated..."

"Yea, no shit," I scoff.

"But that doesn't change anything," he says softly. "It doesn't stop me from wanting you... It never did."

My anger is retreating further, back into the hopeless abyss of fear I can't let him see.

Petulantly, I flop back against my seat. "You just *had* to fucking show up, didn't you? I was doing so well..."

Lance reaches over and takes my hand, playing with my fingers. "I'm sorry for stressing you out, Trouble."

My eyes slink to his and my jaw tightens because *fuck me*, he's just *so* goddamn gorgeous. "Your cockblocking powers are telepathic now. I can't even fuck without thinking about you..."

Visibly stiffening, he squeezes my hand tighter, until it hurts. "Who were you with??"

The jealous rage burning in his eyes has me squirming. "No one. I mean, I *would* have fucked my coworker, because he wanted it. But I couldn't..."

"Did you hook up with him??" He looks like he's on the verge of losing it, tormented fury etching his face. "Please, Tate, tell me you didn't..."

"I didn't!" I bark. "I just told you, I *couldn't*, because I can't stop thinking about *you*, you insufferable idiot!"

Lance releases a long *whoosh* of relief, his lips curving slightly. "I'm sorry..."

I roll my eyes aggressively. "Yea, you really seem broken up over it."

"I can't help it." He tries to scoot closer, held back by the center console between us. "I'm not sorry that you didn't get to fuck someone else, Tate. I want you all to myself."

"That's just it, though," I hiss. "I'm not yours. I can't be yours, Lance, don't you get that?? You have a wife. *She's* yours. And you have some stupid fucking bearded asshole in the sky telling you that you can't want me. So I'll never be yours, and you'll never be mine." I blink hard, pursing my lips. "Not that I want that anyway... I'm just making a point."

I'm finding it difficult to look at him right now. He has this puppy dog pout thing happening that's driving me insane. *Someone so large shouldn't be allowed to make that face.*

"Tate... it's not..." He stops to chew on his full bottom lip. "It's not what you think..."

"I don't know what the hell that means," I sigh, exhausted from all of this.

He tugs me closer by my hand, his other lifting to cup my jaw. "It means that I want you regardless of whether or not I'm *supposed* to..."

My heart is thumping faster by the second. I feel like such a moron because I can't stop myself from leaning into his touch. I know I didn't come here for this... I should be smacking him and storming off. But I just can't fight it... The *attraction*. The chemistry that moves between us like a current.

Trouble

I'm overflowing with memories, new and old; sensations, good and bad.

The high of being with him that first time, and the hurt of him leaving. The illicit, lustful burn of him *now*, how it felt when his body pushed inside me, bare, unrestricted... But also, the aching confusion of knowing that forbidden sex aside, this will never be on *my* terms, and not understanding why that upsets me so much...

"Do you want me, Trouble?" he whispers, pulling me even closer until our lips are hovering.

My brain is *pleading* with my mouth not to release the words, but it's too late.

It does whatever it wants, always has.

"I wouldn't be here if I didn't," I tell him, soft and raspy, trembling in a fervent heat that somehow gives me chills.

"I'm so glad you're here, baby," he hums.

And before I can even think about pretending to protest, his lips part and cover my lower, sucking it in a gentle, sensual kiss that melts me into a goddamn puddle,

It's just so *passionate*, the way he's kissing me, slowly, grazing my mouth with his, rumbling these luscious little sounds and swallowing my much more submissive whimpers. Erotic and deep, his tongue pushes into my mouth like he's savoring me.

I'm coming undone.

No... No no no, this is too... romantic. Too cherishing.

This is how you kiss someone you...

No. Bad.

Reaching for his jaw, I grasp his face and kiss him harder, fisting his hair. I need to rough this up a bit. Make it purely carnal and nothing more.

"*Mmf...* baby," he groans between my lips, fisting my shirt. "You're hungry, aren't you?"

"Starved." I climb over the center console, trying to get as close to him as possible in the cramped space of my coupe.

Fuck it. I want sex.

He's already fucking up my head... Might as well fuck my body, too.

I can't even try to act like the sex we had the other day wasn't the best sex of my life.

I just need to get him inside me again... That'll make it less confusing.

He just needs to fuck me because it's the only part of this that makes sense.

"Baby, we can't do this here," he gasps in between my voracious kisses while I'm attempting to crawl onto his lap.

"I don't fucking care," I rasp, reaching for the control to move his seat as far back as it'll go.

This really won't be easy. He barely fits in this car. He's so tall, his head almost touches the ceiling.

"Tate, I'm serious," Lance rumbles, then grunts when the seat reclines, and I finally manage to straddle him. "We're right in front of my house... Anyone could see us. My wife is inside..."

"No one will know what we're doing..." I purr, sucking on his lips while my hands run down his chest to lift his t-shirt. "The windows are tinted."

He whines a noise of protest, though he's still kissing me, holding my waist where I'm seated on top of him. "Let's go to a hotel, baby. We'll have more space... I can take my time with you."

Fuck, that sounds good... My cock jerks at the thought.

But I'm too impatient, too needy, too wound the hell up. And the second we stop, this becomes real. What we're doing... The *reality* of the situation. If that switch flips, we go back to hurt and frustration.

This, fucking in a car in front of his house... It's just hot, forbidden sex, plain and simple.

It needs to be just sex.

Pausing, I rest my forehead on his, panting over his lips. "Fuck your neighbors, fuck your wife, fuck anyone who might see us. *Fuck* the consequences, Sunshine... And just fuck me, right now."

Lance lets out a shivery sound that thumps my balls hard, sliding his hands down to cup my ass and squeeze until I grunt. "Trouble... Always *so* much fucking *trouble.*"

I feel amusement dancing on his lips before he attacks mine once more. Our kisses are instantly ravenous, feverish licking and sucking, panting breaths bouncing off the interior of my Maserati from how rough we're eating each other alive.

Ripping his shirt over his head, I whip it off while he works on my pants. He unbuttons my shirt, and I wiggle myself free with his hands roaming all over my front, tracing the lines of my abs and my chest, brushing his thumbs over my nipples until I'm shivering.

"You have the most beautiful body," he hums while I kick off my shoes and try to get my pants down with barely any room to move. "I wanna see all of you... Every delicious inch."

"Yea, well... That's not really an option in here," I huff, basically planking over him. "Push my pants down. Just shove 'em off..."

He chuckles seductively, peeling my pants down, with my boxers, over my ass and down my thighs. "You and your sexy tailored suits... Your ass looks mouthwatering in these pants, baby. My dick was *aching* the second I saw you."

"Mhm... I pay top dollar to make sure my ass looks perfect in everything I wear," I tease, kicking my way out of them the rest of the way until I'm naked and perched over him in the passenger seat of my Maserati.

Believe it or not, I've never been naked in this car before. I've actually never had sex in here... I've had sex in other people's cars, and in my old cars. I've gotten, and given, some good head in this car. But this will be the first official fuck of my GranTurismo.

I reach for the waist of Lance's pants, but he snatches my hand, and I peek up at him.

"I don't want you showing your perfect ass to anyone else, Trouble," he growls, grabbing me by the cheeks and pulling me into him, his finger grazing the crack of my ass. "This sweet treat is all mine."

The possessiveness has me throbbing. But I can't help the teasing smirk on my lips as I hold his neck, toying with the short hair at his nape.

"My ass is God's gift to humanity, Sunshine," I croon, flicking his bottom lip with my tongue. "It wouldn't be fair to hoard it all for yourself."

Lance squeezes me harder, *tighter*, so rough I can feel bruises forming already. A quiet yelp escapes me as he pulls me in so that my erection is on his abs. "Don't be a brat. You know this ass is mine." He grips tighter. "*My* fingerprints on it."

Releasing one cheek, he moves his right hand around front to fist my cock, giving it a slow tug.

"This big dick is mine too..." he whispers hoarsely. "Nobody else touches what's mine, troublemaker. Understand?"

Eyes closed, my head tips back at the sweet sensation of him stroking me, like he's putting me in a trance. But then he grips tighter, yanking my dick hard enough that I grunt, eyes snapping open.

"Tell me you understand, Tate," he rumbles, sounding so dominant and scary, my balls are buzzing. I love how his timidity floats away when we're alone like this, and he's just feral for me.

I nod quick. "Yea, fine. I understand."

He squints up at me, leaning forward to press a kiss on my chest. His soft lips trail to my nipple, tongue fluttering over it until I groan. Lapping and licking and sucking, he's making me *wild*, stroking his fist up and down my cock while my eyes flutter shut again.

Until a sharp sting springs them back open, and I gasp. "Ah!"

He just bit my nipple. And I mean *hard*. Not one of those playful nips. This one hurt.

But he immediately picks back up licking, soothing the pain away. It feels so damn good, my cock leaks a pulse of precum.

"Mmm..." he hums. "This time, say you're mine... and *mean it*." Our eyes connect, and he bites me again. *Harder*.

"*Fuuck*!" My whine turns to a moan as he tends to my nipple, throbbing from the pain and dripping wet with his saliva.

"I'm waiting, Trouble..." He bites the underside of my pectoral muscle until I flinch.

"It's yours," I gulp. "All of it. My ass and my dick, and whatever else you want." My voice ripples with the way he's kissing closer and closer to where my dick is standing up straight, engorged and bobbing. "I'm... *yours*."

Lance hums out of satisfaction, releasing my erection. "I'm yours too, baby." I tilt my head down at him. "I know you don't feel it, but I am. Me and you *only*, Tate."

I bite my lip. "Fuck me, Hardy, *please*..."

He leans back, reclining like we have all the time in the world. Not like we're sitting in a car parked suspiciously in front of his house, with me naked on his lap for any passersby to see.

I mean, the windows are tinted, but they're still windows, *not two-way mirrors.*

"We'll get to that. Right now, I'm playing with you," he sighs. "The way you play with me by not answering my texts."

I scowl at him. "You know why—"

"Yes, I do, but that doesn't make it hurt any less," he says pointedly, and I freeze. "I'm not one of your random fuckboys, Tate. I don't just text you when I'm bored. If I say something to you, it's because I mean it." *Okay... Wow.* His fingers trail up and down my sides. "Are you punishing me...?"

"No, I—"

"Tate," he cuts me off, kissing a little bite mark he made on my chest. "It's okay... I get it. You're punishing me for disappearing. And I deserve it."

I gulp. "Maybe a little..."

"I hate it," he whispers. "I hate that I hurt you, and I hate when you shut me out. Forgive me?"

I blink down at him as he taps his finger to his bottom lip. And I obey his wordless command, pressing my mouth to his, like I'm enslaved to him. We groan in unison, kissing slow, but hungry. *Deep*, our tongues touching and tasting.

"I don't know what to do... with this," I whimper, head spinning.

I'm barely even aware of what I'm saying, or why I'm offering him truths when I'm terrified of doing it. But I can't stop myself.

He's always been able to crack me open.

"I know... Me neither," he pants. "Just use me, baby. Make yourself feel good." Holding my ass once more, he squeezes, guiding my hips. "Rub your cock on me, nice and slow."

Whining a raspy moan, I rock my hips, rubbing my aching erection on his abs. Even just the friction of his warm, smooth skin on my dick feels incredible, and I'm leaking.

"You're making me all sticky, Trouble..." He leans back, letting me writhe into him while I kneel over his thighs.

My dick is reaching up to his chest, dragging through his muscles until I'm panting, draped over him with our mouths brushing sensually.

"This feels so good," I purr, kissing him softly. "Do you like it...?"

"I think I could lie here for hours with your pretty cock rubbing all over me," he hums, lips trailing from my jaw down my throat. "Lean back, beautiful."

I'm not sure what he's going to do, but my head is all hazy, and I just want to chase the high of this bad thing we're doing that's fogging up my windows.

Reclining a bit, I hold his shoulders while Lance tugs his pants down to his thighs, his giant, perfect dick springing out; so big, and *thick*. I'm instantly clenching in hot, aching need to get that thing inside me again.

"Tell me you have lube," he rasps, sounding every bit as lust drunk as I'm feeling.

I nod fast. "In the glove box." His brow arches, but before he can even say it, I add, "I've never fucked in this car before... Just so you know."

One of his blindingly beautiful smiles shines up at me, his hands traveling up my ribcage. He makes a hungry noise, lowering to kiss my nipples again, licking the swells of my muscles, biting me over and over.

"*Mmf*, you're a biter, huh?" I shiver, my cock pulsing. "Are you teething?"

He chuckles. "I don't know what it is about your sweet skin, but I just want to bite you..." He does it again, and I hum. "I like the way it makes you tremble."

"*Fuck*, Hardy, I need you inside me. I've never felt a cock as perfect as yours moving in my ass..."

He whines softly, sucking and kissing down my abs, shifting me backward on my knees, I think so he can get to the glove box.

But then he pauses. His eyes slide up to mine, and they're sparkling, something like mischief; a frisson of delighted, nervous thrill as they fall back down... Below my waist.

Hungrily eyeing my erection, his mouth inches lower. I'm not even breathing as his breath warms my flesh, brushing the slick tip of my cock.

Holy fuck... He's getting so close to it. Is he actually going to...?

Lance's gaze slides up to mine again, and his lips ghost over the head.

I whimper. He groans.

He does it again, barely even a touch. Just a swipe of his mouth on my dick, and I'm falling the fuck apart.

"Baby..." My fingertips stroke the nape of his neck. "Holy *fuck*..."

He kisses my crown softly, and my dick lurches up to his mouth.

Grinning, he hums. "So, so pretty..." Tongue extended, he swipes it over the fat curve, his lashes fluttering. "So *sweet*, Trouble, my *God*..."

"*Uhh yes*... Kiss me more." I dig my fingers into his hair. "*Baby*, kiss my cock..."

He does. He *kisses* the head of my dick, so slow I'm in agony. But it feels *fantastic*.

The teasing, the warmth, how apparent it is that he's never done anything like this before... it's all winding me up so tight, my dick has literally never been harder. I can feel every vein thumping.

"Fuck, *Tate*..." He feathers his tongue, swirling it around and around like he's licking a lollipop. "I never... knew this would feel so good..."

Gripping my hips for dear life, he gasps as his parted lips slip over the tip, sucking it into his mouth. I cry a garbled noise, balls contracting, throbbing precum on his tongue. He moans, sucking out my arousal and sliding me in deeper.

He likes it... Good God, he really loves sucking my cock...

Resting his forehead on my abs, he sucks vigorously, slow but hard, on just the first inch of me. And I notice that one of his hands is missing...

Peeking down, I spot it between his legs, rubbing on his balls, fisting his cock.

He's touching himself while he sucks my dick... Because he fucking loves it.

Holy motherfuck... This is the dream. The holy grail of forbidden fantasies...

Straight guy giving his first blowjob in the car with his wife right inside, and loving *it.*

Is it possible to die from overstimulation??

"*God*, Sunshine, your *mouth*..." I whimper, holding his jaw, watching him with stars in my eyes.

Lance sucks and *sucks*, his tongue massaging my length while breaths puff from his nose and groans of curious hunger rumble around my shaft. He's not throating or chasing or swallowing me whole. This is so different, a million times better than the best head of my life.

He's *exploring*... sucking on me because it actually feels *good* for him, and he wants it.

This is not a job... This is all pleasure right now.

Saliva runs down my inches while Lance Hardy *makes fucking love* to my dick with his mouth, and the sensation is unrivaled. When he cups and squeezes my nuts, I'm about to come. I don't think I could hold back if I wanted to. Thankfully, he slurps off before I have to tap him on the shoulder.

"Baby, I need to stop," he says, breathlessly. "If I keep going, I'll come." Kissing my abs, he peeks up at me while I pull my bottom lip between my teeth. "I need to bust inside you, beautiful."

"*Fffuck*..." I shiver, touching his lips. "Shh... You might make me come if you say another word."

He chuckles and bites my fingertip, looking like the sexiest most mystifyingly gorgeous married guy I'm not supposed to have.

Lance lifts me, going for the glove box to get the lube. As he opens it and squirts some onto his fingers, I shift on his lap, stumbling to turn around and face the windshield.

"What are you doing?" he asks.

I peek at him over my shoulder. "I wanna ride you reverse cowgirl." I smirk, popping my butt out.

Eyes falling to it, he growls like an animal, swiping wet fingers between my cheeks. "But I... wanted to see your... face." His sentence is broken up by how much he's lusting over my ass, watching his own hand as it works lube into my hole.

A raspy hum leaves me. "I can still look at you. But this way, you get to watch my ass bouncing on your dick."

Another ravenous noise. "Baby, your ass is *so* fucking sweet." He leans back again, tugging his fingers out of me. "Come sit down on my cock, princess."

Scowling at him over my shoulder, I'm trying to pretend I'm not quaking from how sexy his taunting is while he chuckles wickedly, using both hands to hold me open.

This is going to be so fucking hot...

And much less intimate than fucking face to face.

I just don't think I can handle it that way... Looking into his eyes while he's inside me is way too real.

Reclining a bit, I let him position his dick up to my hole, and I'm far too impatient to do this gradually. Still, I'm savoring every second of the curve nudging up to my ass before shoving myself backward on it, until my hole sucks him right in.

"*Fuck...*" Lance shudders.

Hungrily, I sit down slow, welcoming him inside, inch by inch.

"Unghh!" My eyes roll back in my skull, dick flinching and dripping all over the place. "*Ohhhfuckyeaa...*"

I can feel him twitching in me, and I'm *trembling*, sweating already, with my cheeks resting on his pelvis and every swollen inch of this giant monster cock buried in my ass.

"T-Tate..." he croaks, gripping my waist. "This is... *holy fuck*, I'm so deep..."

"Oh yea, it's way up there," I gasp, shifting and purring. "Wow, baby... *Damn*, what a long fucking dick..."

Lance groans then growls, sitting up and holding me from behind. "Ride me, Trouble. Fuck me good with this warm, tight cunt."

Fuck fuck fuck...

The mewls pouring from my lips might be embarrassing, if I cared right now. But my mind is all fuzz. As soon as I lift up, then push back down, I'm on a mission.

I mean, I've fucking *owned* this position before. It's my bread and butter. But something about Lance's dick inside me this way is lighting the holy *fuck* out of my prostate. I'm all sensation, moving up and down on his every rigid inch, gripping the dashboard with white knuckles while I hump the life out of him.

Up and down... *Up*... and *down*.

Swiveling my hips...

Trouble

Dropping it like it's hot, and *smack smack smacking* us together like I'm in a goddamn rodeo.

The sounds inside this car are wild. Grunts and whimpers and cries, the skin slapping, the wet milking of his thick cock in my hole... The rawest animal fuck noises ever, so salacious, they're overpowering the confined space. This sordid music is turning me out just as much as him stretching me and jamming forcefully at my prostate again and *again*.

The car is rocking, every window fogged to the max from the sticky heat in the air. It's highly obvious that we're fucking like maniacs in this vehicle, but I couldn't give a single shred of *fuck*.

I'm too busy writhing on my knees, grinding Lance Hardy into the leather while he holds my ass open, watching me work him in and out, my thick cock bobbing up and down as I go, slapping against my abs.

"Baby, fuck *yes*." He sits up suddenly, wrapping his arms around me with his chest on my back, our muscles slipping and sliding with sweat. He bites down on my shoulder, hard enough that I sob and my dick weeps. "My Trouble's got such a *tight* ass... Pump my cock in this perfect hole. Just like that, baby... *Fuck*, Tate, you're fucking the life outta me."

"God, Lance, I'm so close," I whine, hoarse as fuck, damn near losing my voice. "Your big dick feels so good, and I'm so... fucking... *close*."

"Yea?" he gasps, turning my face to kiss my lips while we smash our bodies together. I nod fast, eyelids drooping, muscles stiffening, balls humming. "You gonna come all over the place, sexy thing?"

"*Fuuck... yes*. Fuck my ass..." I'm bouncing on him so hard, my brain is shaking up like a soda can. If he pops that top, I'm gonna explode.

"This fucking ass?" he growls, smacking his palm down on my ass cheek.

I cry and clench. "Ohh God, yea... Hit me again."

Rumbling, he slaps my ass once more, and I grunt a garbled sob.

"*Fuck*, the way you squeeze my dick..." His voice tremors. "I'm gonna pour so deep in you, baby."

"*Mmff*... come... come in me." Gravity swallows me up and I fall. "Fuck, I'm *coming*..."

The words have barely rushed from my lips as my dick shoots, heavy pulses spraying everywhere. No one makes me come as hard, or as *fast*, as he does, and it's deliciously mesmerizing. I'm crying and shaking, clamping and *coming*, so fucking hard I can barely breathe.

"Mmmyeaa, that's it, love. Ride it out," he croons, fisting my hair, dropping kisses all over my neck and shoulders. "You're so pretty when you come. Look at that big, beautiful dick pulsing for me..."

"God... fuck... can't... stop..."

My hips are still moving, desperately rocking on him in fluid motions because it feels *so damn good*. His dick brushing on every electric nerve inside me, controlling my orgasm enough that pleasure is washing me from head to toe in waves.

Lance's fingers trail through the cum on my skin, caressing my aching cock with its slickness as he groans out loud. "I love feeling you come, Tate... *Uhh*, I'm gonna bust, baby..."

"Come for me," I plead hoarsely, slumping back against him while he fucks up into my hole with rough, shallow thrusts. "Come in my ass, Sunshine."

"Ohh, *fuck*!" he snaps, holding me close and bucking into me. I can feel him swelling, filling me with hot pulses. "*Fuck fuck fuck*, I'm coming so hard for you. I fucking *love* coming in you, Trouble *baby*."

"Nothing feels like you do..." I whimper, exhausted and sated and buzzing all over.

Lance goes from groaning to purring, petting me and kissing me everywhere as he comes down from the high. His tight hold stays coiled around me for minutes. And we just breathe, recovering from that marvelous insanity.

Finally, he sighs, loosening his grip just enough. "What kind of unicorn are you...?"

Chuckling, I snort by accident, then laugh harder, my hole clenching on him as I do because I can't help it.

"Shit, love, that feels so good," he breathes a tired laugh, massaging my ass with strong, coveting fingers. "Tighten on it while I pull out."

I do so as he slides his cock out of me, spreading me and running his fingers up and down my hole while his cum tries to seep out. Biting my lip, I peer at him over my shoulder, watching him stare like he's transfixed. He pushes a finger into me, and I gasp as he stuffs his cum back inside.

"What are you doing back there?" I yawn and shiver.

"Never you mind what I'm doing," he teases. A cackle bursts out of me. "You're so fucking hot, T. I can't even deal with how sexy you are..."

"Flattery will get you everyw—wait! Don't get cum on my seats!" Serenity is shoved aside as I scramble to close my legs, toppling over the center console.

Trouble

Lance laughs out loud. "Baby, you're gonna need to clean the car. It's just a fact."

"Son of a bitch... This is Italian leather," I grumble. "Will you please grab some wet wipes out of the glove box?"

"Do you have an entire pharmacy in here or something?" He snickers while rifling through all of my items.

"It's good to keep supplies on hand."

"I see you have condoms..." He pulls them out, cocking a brow.

"Some good it did me," I sigh. "I can't stop letting you in bare."

His deep eyes glisten as he bites his lip to cover a purely adorable grin. "Only me... Right?"

I roll my eyes, refusing to respond. But I think the flush in my cheeks is answering for me. I strictly *never* have unprotected sex. It's a point of pride. I may be a wild little slut sometimes, but I like to be responsible with the things that are most important to me... My body, and my money.

But then Lance Hardy comes along and literally *comes*... inside me. As if I really *do* belong to him... And I'm fucking feral for it. All of it.

The feeling, the notion of him claiming me... Hell, even the mess. I can't understand why, but with him, it feels right.

Even though it's not.

Using the wet wipes, we get cleaned up, then redressed, which is somehow more difficult than getting out of our clothes. And of course, once we're dressed and sitting side by side again, reality smacks us both in the face, hard and fast.

It's the curse of the orgasm... The one drawback to blinding pleasure. Inhibitions lowered, you do and say all kinds of crazy shit. But as soon as your balls are drained, a big ice-cold bucket of *holy fuck, what did I just do?* is dumped over your head.

Lance and I peek at each other. I gulp a dry mouthful of awkwardness while he chews on his lower lip.

I have to break the tension... It's stifling.

"Your pajamas are cute," I whisper.

It makes him smile, beyond bright and so gorgeous. "Yea?"

I nod. "You look like a hot stepdad."

The smile shifts to a bemused frown. "I don't know how I feel about that..."

Chuckling, I bite my lip to keep my own grin in check.

Alarm bells are ringing in my head.

Danger! Danger!

Too much swoon!
Heart eyes! I repeat, your eyes are officially heart-shaped!
Get out before you ask him to dinner and a movie!

Lance reaches over, taking my hand. He lifts it to his lips, kissing the top before he sighs, "I guess I should go..."

Swallowing feels like my throat is full of broken glass. "Oh... right. Okay."

I snatch my hand away. *Idiot.*
You're an idiot. *Just like your phone told you not to be.*

"It's not like I want to," he says solemnly.

"But you have to. I get it," I grumble, struggling to locate my unaffected tone. The one I use before slinking away after casual sex.

Where is it?? I usually keep it right here...

"Tate..."

"Just a heads up, you might want to shower before crawling into bed with your wife," I mutter, hating how fucking bitter I sound.

"Baby, please," he hums. "Look at me."

"I'm good."

He grasps my chin, forcing me to make eye contact. And as much as my head is screaming for me to pull away, I fucking *can't.* "Do you want me to stay...?"

My brows furrow. "In the car?"

His lips quirk. "Just... with you. Wherever. Do you *want* me to stay with you?"

Staring at him, my pulse is flying, the sound of it echoing inside my skull. I feel all hot and itchy inside my skin...

It shouldn't be such a difficult question, but it is. It's impossible to answer.

"I... I don't..." Shaking my head, I mumble, "It doesn't matter. You *can't.* You have a wife, a job, and a faith that have nothing to do with me..."

"Deflecting," he rumbles, holding my face still when I try to jerk away. "It's a yes or no question, Tate. Nothing else matters. Do you... want me to *stay?*"

Blinking at him, I'm frozen with his eyes holding mine captive.

I don't understand how he can even be asking me this... How he can say none of that stuff matters?

Of course it matters. This isn't a fairy tale, it's real fucking life. And even if he thinks *he wants to give up everything to be with me... Well...*

That makes even less sense.

Apparently, his sex-fog doesn't wear off as quickly as mine does, because he's talking crazy.

I hate how he gets under my skin like this... Burrowing beneath my layers and weaseling his way back into places that have been shut down for a long fucking time; since *he* fucking shut them.

Jake said us doing this is reckless, and he was right. But not because Lance is married, or even because *God* is probably judging the fuck out of us right now.

It's because something about simply being *near* him makes me want to forget all the things I learned the hard way and crash back into his warmth... his sunshine. Like we're still those same foolish kids in that dorm room bed.

But we're *not*. Our lives have changed, too drastically to just ignore.

I can't be reckless like that anymore... Not this time.

We all remember how that turned out for College Tate.

So I subtly shake my head, even though the way his brows are immediately crushing together and his bottom lip is jutting out has me cringing inside.

God, I hate his fucking sad look...

"No..." I grumble, then clear my throat, because the word comes out rather betraying of my stern indifference. "I don't. You were right... You should go. We *both* should."

Lance's fingers slip off my face, his throat bobbing in a visible swallow that has me looking down, at anything other than him. *I just can't...*

"Alright... Can I just ask you one more thing, then?" he whispers, and my jaw tightens.

Come on, Sunshine, just get out of the car...

Don't do this to me right now.

"I'd rather you didn't..." I hum tiredly, rubbing my eyes.

Naturally, he ignores me and asks anyway. "What *do* you want?"

Taken aback, my gaze flings back up to his... Because of all the questions he could ask, this is one I didn't expect.

"We've been over this," I sigh, "I want *sex*, Hardy. Because I like feeling good with no strings attached. I know that's probably a foreign concept, being that you apparently don't do *anything* casually. But some people don't need a *relationship* to validate themselves. My self-worth is based on being boss as fuck, twenty-four-seven, three-sixty-motherfucking-five, and I don't need to carry anyone else's baggage, or expectations. I love money, and dick, and being awesome, and that's all. Sure, it's fun and hot in theory while we're fucking, but I don't actually *belong* to you, Sunshine. I never did, and I never will."

At the end of my little tirade, I feel like I just ran an emotional 10k. I'm somehow exhausted and jacked with so much adrenaline, my hands are shaking.

The way his eyes are all sparkly and rounded has some remorse creeping in, but I swallow it down fast and rough like a big pill.

Whatever... Maybe that was harsh, but he needed to hear it.

Lance blinks at me, pursing his lips. His head tilts, and he actually looks a little more frustrated than hurt this time around. "That's a cute speech, Tate. Do you rehearse it in the mirror in case one of your Grindr hook-ups gets clingy?"

Um... what?

My mouth drops open, lashes fluttering in perplexity.

But before I can even think of what to say, he leans over the center console, lining his face up with mine. "I already told you, I'm *not* your fuckboy booty-call, or a dick attached to some random meathead you met at the gym. I know you... The amount of time we spent apart is irrelevant. I *still* fucking *know* you, Tate, and I know for a fact you wouldn't drive all the way out here in the middle of the night to make a scene if there wasn't something about this you can't shake."

I'm dumbfounded right now.

I feel like a total buffoon, just sitting here, chest thumping, gaping at him without the slightest clue what to say.

I can't believe he's calling me out like this... And he couldn't be more wrong!

I'm not here because I'm into him. I'm here because...

Because I...

Goddamnit!

"Don't flatter yourself," I mumble quietly. "It was on my way home..."

He huffs a breathy chuckle, shaking his head. "I'm not saying I have the answers, baby. I definitely don't. But don't pull that heartless robot shit with me. Because we both know it doesn't apply where we're concerned." Brushing his fingers through my hair, he presses a soft kiss on my bottom lip. "I'd like to know where you stand, Trouble. It might make this a little easier... on us both."

"If you're waiting for some declaration of love, don't hold your breath." I scowl as he pulls away, not without first brushing his thumb over my lip.

Trouble

"You can keep fighting me if you want..." He opens the door on his side. "As long as you also keep showing up."

Lance hops out of the car with a soft smile on his swollen lips, offering me a little wave that's so adorable, it makes my stomach turn. He closes the door, and I watch him walk away, back to his wife, inside their quiet house...

Surrounded by lies and sunflowers.

Chapter Sixteen
Lance

"'For I know the plans I have for you... Plans to prosper you, and not harm you. Plans to give you hope and a future...'"

My chest tightens, but I push past it. "'Then you will call upon me, and come to pray to me. And I will listen...'"

Fingers twitching, hands sweatier than they should be, I blink hard at the words I'm reading, although I most certainly have them memorized by now.

"'You will find me when you seek with all your heart...'" My voice gives out, and I clear my throat. *Get it together,* Pastor... "'I will be found by you, and will bring you back from captivity. I will gather you from all the nations places where I have banished you... And bring you back to the place from which I carried you into exile.'"

Slapping the book shut, I mosey from behind my lectern, forcing myself to focus. "What do you think God means by this?" I pause for a moment. "It seems pretty self-explanatory, no?"

A few people chuckle.

"God was passing a message to His people in Jerusalem through the prophet, Jeremiah... That we know. Basically, He was giving them comfort. *Assurance.*"

A few hushed *amens.*

"God has been telling us, since, well, before Jesus came along, that all we—as His people—need to do is have faith in His *plan*... That it'll all come together in the end, right?"

My eyes flick, and I see people nodding.

"Okay, now, let me hit you with a *but...*" My lips quirk. "Isn't that a lot easier said than done? I mean, in this particular instance, in the book of Jeremiah, the Jews had been *exiled*. Driven from their homes, families torn apart, lives destroyed... And God is just saying, 'Hey, chill out. As long as you have faith in me, everything will be fine.'"

The smirks on the faces of the younger crowd are visible. But it's usually at this point in my sermons—the part when I call God out a little, just to make my point—that the older members of the congregation appear a tad uneasy.

As if I haven't been doing this for years, and I'm about to launch into some shocking blasphemy.

It's only one of the *constructive criticisms* they've given me since I took over, though probably the one with the least grounds, considering that I always come full circle in my sermons. The way I see it, I'm not here to reinforce the ideals of God-fearing people set in their ways. I'm here to give encouragement to those who need it most...

The *unsure*. The lost, and the doubtful... Those who are struggling with their faith, facing obstacles in their lives. *They* need this more than people whose minds have been made up for decades.

We're not going to think about the fact that I'm definitely preaching to myself right now.

"Whether we'd like to admit it or not, I'm sure many of us have felt this way before," I go on. "When something bad happens, it's human nature to react negatively. Get upset, experience anger, or fear... To desire answers and a resolution. Human beings are built with a logical side, and that side is the one seeking the comfort of a *physical* plan. You know what I mean... Something tangible we can look at and say, 'Okay... *This* is how my problems will be solved.' But God doesn't always give us that, does He?"

Very few people shake their heads, and it makes me want to laugh... How much they actually believe they're sinning for questioning their creator. It's still baffling to me...

I've never known God to condemn questions. *Ask, and ye shall receive, right?*

He's not saying, 'I'll give you whatever you want.' He's saying, 'I'll answer any questions you have for me.'

But that's a whole other sermon I think went over most of their heads.

"In fact, He rarely does," I continue. "Admittedly, God expects us to serve Him in faith, whether His plan brings us joy or pain. Just look at the

Jews... They suffered in many ways, for many reasons, and God's only answer to them was, 'Have more faith.'"

Pacing slowly back and forth, I wring out my hands, desperate to keep my own inner turmoil out of my words and give off a confidence I'm not quite feeling.

"I'm sure what you *don't* want to hear is me saying if the Jews could do it, then we have no right to complain." I force down my smirk, shaking my head subtly. "But herein lies the point... It's not about following God *blindly*. Faith *is* comfort. In faith, we find inner peace, self-awareness, and acceptance. The purpose is not to expect Him to wave his hand and solve all of our problems, it's to teach us that when they're *not* solved—because, let's be honest, rarely will they be—we'll still persevere."

I pause to gulp as a few more people say *amen*, even more eyes widening to the realization of what I'm telling them.

"The lesson is for us to remain steadfast in God's plan, and know that regardless of where it takes us, we serve an ultimate purpose. The pain we experience helps us grow, the mistakes we make teach us lessons for the future... So that when He says, 'My plans will prosper you, and not harm you,' we understand that even if we come to *physical* harm at times, it happens for the greater good of the will of God."

The *amens* grow a bit louder, movement in my peripheral encouraging me on.

"We will always find Him when we seek with our hearts, because He's *always* there, in our hearts. And it's our responsibility as His children to have faith in that, with absolute certainty, even when times are tough. *Especially* then. That *faith* is our reassurance brings us from lost to found... No longer blind, we *see*."

Murmurs and chants of agreement clamor up to me, gasps of enthusiasm and praise ring through the room. But I'm busy staring at the flowers that line the platform edge...

The sunflowers.

Clearing my throat once more, I stalk over to the lectern and mumble, "And on that note... let us pray."

Leading everyone in prayer, I can't help asking God for strength myself. I've been feeling like the ultimate hypocrite for days while putting together this week's sermon, and now that I've actually spoken it out loud, I'm afraid a giant neon sign is flashing *FRAUD* on my forehead, or my nose will start growing like Pinocchio.

Preaching *faith in God's plan* feels like a wash... Because I don't understand His plan in the slightest. I'm more confused, right here and now, than ever before, and all I want is exactly what I was just telling everyone not to ask for... A clear sign of what the hell I'm supposed to do.

When the prayer is over, the band launches into their rendition of *"What a Beautiful Name,"* followed by one of our congregation, Penny, who comes up to read a poem she wrote. After that, we pray some more, for our friends and family, anyone who needs it, which is when things tend to get heavy.

To be honest, despite how long I've been at this, I still fumble through a lot of it. I try to bring so much openness to the way I preach, but it's not always up to me. There are old traditions I can't escape, and during these times, I feel like I'm just standing back, phoning it in.

Maybe I just feel like that *now*, because of how much uncertainty is radiating around my life. But now that I'm questioning things, it's difficult to remember a time when I didn't fidget uncomfortably at people speaking in tongues.

By the end of the final song—sorry, *hymn*—I'm exhausted, and so ready to just go home and take a nap. Unfortunately, thinking I'll be able to just slink away after the service is a foolish notion on my part. I'm expected to stand around and *talk* to people, then join my father while *he* stands around and talks to people, because everyone wants to talk to him. After all, he's the OG.

I'm just the hippy who took his place.

It's also nice out today, which means lunch with the family after church; our weekly trip to my dad's favorite restaurant with Desiree's parents, the seven of us sitting around, talking some more.

Talking, talking, talking...

By the time this is over, I don't want to speak again for days.

"Great work, sweetie," Desiree says, grinning as she walks up to me, pushing onto her tippy toes to kiss my cheek.

I show her one of my standard smiles in response, though it's taking much more effort to move the muscles in my face than usual. Curling an arm around her waist, I hold on to her loosely, fighting, *struggling* to push down all my doubts, my confusion, my rampant, raging *guilt*.

It's amazing they can't smell it coming off of me like sulfur...

I could swear I was burning alive from being the biggest sinner around.

"Wonderful sermon," Des's mother, Patricia, says with a smile as she and her husband stride over to join us. "Very moving."

"It was powerful," my father-in-law, Clark, adds. "For a moment there, I wasn't sure where you were going with that."

His lips are curved to display his exterior manners, but I can tell beneath the surface, he feels my interpretations were a bit too loose for his rigid, black-and-white-with-nothing-in-between Christian views on the Bible.

"Expanding into modernist thought is smart," my father says to me, turning from where he'd been giving his regards to the Lucas's. "Reaching into new territory will certainly ensnare the youth."

He shows me a tight smile that doesn't quite reach his eyes. I don't need him to voice what he's thinking. I can hear it clearly without words...

Not something I'd ever do personally, but I respect where you're coming from.

My muscles are tense, as is my gut. I've had this big ball of stress living inside me for the last few days, since I watched Tate drive away through my living room window. And it's only gotten worse, with every moment leading me to right now. Each step I've taken in my regular, boring life since he showed up feels like it's weighted by so many things I'm not supposed to be thinking or feeling. And now that I'm standing in the church where I work, with my wife, and my father, and this *family* who knows nothing of my secrets... I can't help how anxious even just breathing right now is making me.

"Such beautiful words, honey." My mom smiles at me and rubs my back.

Her support isn't forced for pleasantry's sake, which I have to appreciate. Sometimes I feel like she's the only one who actually gets me... Though I'm sure if she knew the truth, that would change.

Ignoring the *adults*, since they're stressing me out, I peer down at my sister, offering her a thankful grin. "I'm glad you could make it today."

Ellie tilts her head. "Well, I didn't have much of a choice. Mom dragged me out of bed." I chuckle while our mother shoots her a scolding look, to which she hums, "Kidding, of course. If I'm in town, there's no way I'm missing you speaking. Since, you know... You barely do it outside of here."

"Little sis has got jokes." I purse my lips, yanking her ponytail playfully, to which she smacks my hand away while I grin.

"Alright, children. That's enough," my father sighs in amusement. "Let's go eat. I'm starving."

With that, the alpha patriarch has spoken, and we all leave the church, piling into our respective vehicles to drive to lunch. Ellie chooses to ride with Des and I, which I fully understand. Although we're certainly not kids anymore, being around our parents just has a way of making us all feel like we're teenagers again. At least on our own, we can speak freely, without worrying about sugarcoating everything for their often-stifling sake.

Desiree's parents are a lot like mine. Kind, loving, and just supportive enough, if not slightly emotionally detached. The Dixons are every bit as religious as the Hardy's, in a way that doesn't come off as necessarily *strict* to an outsider, though you pick up cues here and there; factors that make you feel like you must be on your best behavior around them.

They're not blatantly judgmental, and you won't catch them outwardly condemning things. But certain topics of conversation will get raised brows and subtle looks, the kind that almost guarantee they'll be talking about you as soon as you're gone.

And the thing is, when I was a kid, I never used to see my parents that way. I always thought they were so understanding and open. But that's the kind of youthful naivety you grow out of when you become your own person, and realize that your parents only wanted you to be *who you are* if it falls within the bracket of their beliefs.

It could be worse... I know it could. I should be grateful that I still have both of my parents, and that they were never abusive or negligent.

At the same time, it's difficult to see past the secrets I've been obsessing over, and the lies I know could destroy my family with a few confessed words.

"So, Ell..." I glance at my sister in the rearview mirror. "You excited for the semester to start?"

"Please," she huffs, rolling her eyes. "As much as I love my job, I'm never ready for summer break to end."

I chuckle. "I bet. It sounds like you had a great one this year."

"It was incredible," she sighs dreamily.

My sister is a professor at UNM, teaching social sciences at the under-grad level. She's super smart and works really hard, so we don't get to see her often during the school year. Summer break is really the only time she makes her way out to South Valley, and even then, it's not as much as when we were younger.

Now, she spends her free time traveling and tending to her thriving social life. Which is what leads me to my next big brother inquiry.

"And how's Marcus?"

Her eyes flit to mine, and I have to smirk. Ellie hasn't had many serious boyfriends over the years. She's always been sort of allergic to commitment

—kinda like a certain someone I can't think about right now. But a few months ago, she started dating a guy named Marcus, a writer and a podcaster, who's so very *different* from my lone-wolf sister, it's almost crazy that they managed to fall into *anything*, let alone an actual relationship.

Personally, I think Marcus is good for Ellie. There's something to be said for finding someone who keeps you on your toes, shakes things up. Your *opposite*... More like your other half, who will give you the things you lack, and let you be what they're missing.

Gulping, my fingers dig harder into the steering wheel while I shift my thoughts.

"He's... good," Ellie answers my question hesitantly.

I can tell right away something is off, because she's fidgeting and her face is flushing, the way it used to when I'd catch her in my room trying to cover up something of mine she'd broken.

"Oh, Elisa, you're a terrible liar," I croon. "What's going on?"

My sister breathes out steadily, rubbing her eyes. "Alright... I don't want you to freak out, okay?"

Suddenly, my stomach is twisting into an even bigger knot of stress. "Okay..."

"I didn't want to tell anyone yet, because it's still really early," she mutters, chewing on her lower lip.

I swallow a painfully dry gulp, peeking at Des, who shoots me a look in return.

"I'm... pregnant," Ellie says, and I almost swerve off the road by accident.

The entire vehicle is silent for a full three Mississippis.

"Oh... Wow," Desiree lets out a quiet, tense version of what I think is supposed to be a *cheer*, though it comes out more like a question. "Congratulations, Ellie..."

I've never been stiffer in my life, my fists locked in clenched white knuckles around the steering wheel.

God, no...

This is going to be just treacherous.

Shoving down how selfish I'm being, I glance at my sister in the mirror, who's staring at me with wide eyes, as if she's holding her breath for my reaction.

"Ell, that's..." I pause to gulp. "That's great news. Congratulations."

She exhales, nodding slowly. "Yea... I mean, it was a shock, to say the least. Obviously, we haven't known each other that long, Marcus and I..."

Trouble

"Well, all that matters is that you're happy about it," Desiree says.

My stomach is churning so hard, I think I'm going to be sick.

"Are you?" I ask Ellie, forcing myself not to sound like I'm interrogating her.

It's just that she's my baby sister. And *okay*, she's not *actually* a baby at all... She's twenty-five. But still, I was ten when she was born, so no matter how grown-up she gets, I'm always going to remember holding her tiny body, pinching her chubby cheeks, changing her diapers and feeding her little spoonfuls of mush.

My sister grew up into a strong, independent woman, and I love that for her. Plus, she's never been hung up on the idea of having kids just because it's what society expects of her. Honestly, she's never even mentioned wanting to be a mother.

"I am," Ellie replies softly. "I'm scared to death, but I'm also... excited? I guess..."

"How's Marcus dealing with it?" Des asks my next question, because I'm still a little shell-shocked.

"He's onboard. Neither of us expected this, but we're just gonna go with the flow and see it for what it is..." My eyes lock with hers in the mirror once more before she murmurs, "A blessing."

I don't think I could say another word if I wanted to. I'm just *stunned*, my mind frantically running through this information.

I'm happy for my sister, of course I am. And Marcus is a great guy. I'm sure he'll make an excellent father.

But this is the kind of thing that will undoubtedly bring about a lot of change...

And again, not that I'm *trying* to be self-centered here, but it's almost *guaranteed* to rain a shitstorm of questions and expectations right onto me. Whether I want it to or not.

When we get to the restaurant, I'm so anxious I'm practically vibrating.

Ellie stops me on the way in and whispers, "I won't tell Mom and Dad. Not yet, anyway." I blink at her, jaw tight. "I hadn't planned on telling them until after my first ultrasound... And I really don't think telling them now would be... helpful." She tilts her head. "Right?"

My eyes soften as I'm overcome with appreciation for my awesome sister, and how much she loves me. Wrapping her up in a tight hug, I whisper, "You can do whatever feels right, Ell. This isn't about me, it's about you. And I'm so happy for you, I just want you to know that."

She nods against my chest. "I know. I love you, Sir Lancelot."

I chuckle, kissing her hair.

"Look at my beautiful babies," my mother sighs, walking over to us. "I love seeing you together."

Releasing my sister, she shoots me one last look—a slightly nervous one, though I can tell she's pushing herself to portray confidence. *I know the look well.*

We all walk into the restaurant together, joining my father, my wife, and her parents. We're seated at our usual booth by the window, which gives me some minute solace for the moment. Being able to look outside and see the sun is distracting me from how uneasy I am.

We order our food, chatting casually for a bit. As it does, the conversation eventually goes from small talk to today's sermon. My father has strong opinions on the way I'm running the church, that much is always clear. He's been retired for years, and you'd think that would force him to loosen the reins a little. But even with his own projects taking up a lot of his time, he still manages to focus a lot of attention on his son, who was supposed to follow in his footsteps, but instead wound up taking a metaphorical sledgehammer to the foundation he'd built over the course of his time at South Valley Pentecostal.

"It's good to see some new faces on Sundays," Patricia says cheerfully. "A lot of them started out coming Tuesday evenings, right?"

I nod, chewing and swallowing a bite of my sandwich before I respond. "Turner and Kelsey really came through with the marketing. They've been reaching a whole new crowd on social media."

"Social media," Clark scoffs. "Back in the day, we used to walk around town handing out flyers. Now all you have to do is click a button."

"Convenience is the way of the future," my father mumbles, in a way that makes it impossible to tell if that statement was meant as a compliment or a complaint.

"People are looking for something different," Desiree cuts in, showing me a soft smile as her hand slides supportively onto my thigh. I swallow hard, because it feels much heavier than it should. "Something that stands out, and makes coming in worthwhile."

My father lifts a brow. "The word of God isn't enough?"

"That's only one part of the message," I grumble, locking our eyes. "The point isn't simply to drill things into their heads and make them feel like they're being brainwashed. It's to give people a reason to love attending church. To make them feel accepted, wanted, and show them that showing up is more than simply *showing up.*"

Trouble

His head tilts. But I don't back down.

This is the same argument we've been having since I took over. My constant fight to convince him that there's more to being a pastor than just *preaching*. I know he knows I'm right, but like Des's father, he's stuck in that old-school mindset.

Doing this was never my dream. Sure, I've always been spiritual, but I never saw myself *working* in a church. The main reason being that as a kid, and even into my twenties, coming to church felt like a chore. And who wants to be in charge of something that bores people?

I always saw my father's job as similar to a high school teacher. Some teachers stick to the material, because they feel that it speaks for itself. But if you want to engage your students, so they actually *retain* what you're teaching, you need to think outside of the box.

When he came to me about filling his shoes when he retired, I told him point-blank that I was never going to be him; if I was going to teach people about God, and faith, I would do it my way. He reluctantly accepted at the time, but I can tell he's never really understood what I'm trying to accomplish.

It makes the whole thing that much harder. Because while I do enjoy shaking things up within the church, sometimes I just wish my career didn't feel like such a fight.

And now that I'm facing an existential crisis in other aspects of my life, I'm finding myself reminiscing about all the things I used to love... before I set out on this path of the *righteous*.

"I have to say, the arrangements in the church today were just lovely," my mother redirects the conversation, casting a kind smile at my wife. "You've truly outdone yourself, Des."

The tension between me and my father dissolves a bit, and we go back to our food, while Desiree accepts kind words regarding her job.

"Thank you." She nods appreciatively. "The sunflowers this year have been absolutely stunning. They're our top seller."

Biting the inside of my cheek, I ignore the nervous flutters in my stomach.

The sunflowers are gorgeous...

"We're very proud of the beautiful work you've been doing, sweetheart," Clark says to Desiree.

My eyes flick to my father. *You see, Dad? That's how you support your kids when they take over your business.*

In a way, Des and I are in the same spot. Her parents retired and put her in charge of their flower shop. The only difference is that Des loves running the store, whereas I've never been completely sold on my feelings toward being a pastor.

I guess that's why I spend my free time gardening, growing things for her to sell. It's always been my passion, and I'm grateful to have that outlet... Thanks to my wife and her parents.

You're just being dramatic...

The forbidden stuff you've been dabbling in is causing you to question all the decisions you've made over the last fifteen years. Because you're confused and unsure of where this unexpected path is bringing you...

Don't write off the comforts of the life you've built.

Don't question God's plan.

Don't think about what could have been...

"And just think of how fulfilling it will be to pass this onto your children," Patricia adds, ripping me out of my inner pep talk.

I feel Desiree still at my side, but I force myself to act natural and keep eating.

Unfortunately, these prying parents of hers aren't done.

"Yes, when *can* we expect some grandbabies?" Clark asks while chewing. "My knee is getting impatient. I can't wait much longer to bounce a sweet little cherub-faced angel, grandpa-style."

He chuckles, and Patricia squeals.

But I'm frozen in uncomfortable tension.

Peeking at Des, I find her glancing at me.

"We already have a baby, Dad," she teases. "Or did you forget about a certain adorable fox terrier with a pizza addiction?"

She rubs my leg in calming motions, and I force a huff that's supposed to sound like a laugh.

"Oh, yea. How is Sunny boy?" Ellie asks. I can tell by the look on her face she's trying to help me out with another subject change.

"Sweet as ever," Des answers fondly. "Definitely a handful, but we love him, messes and all."

"Sunny is a very nice pet, dear, but a dog isn't a child," Patricia says pointedly. As if we didn't fucking know that. "You can't imagine the joys of bringing a child into this world."

I can physically *feel* my blood pressure rising.

"You two have been married for over ten years," Clark keeps going, keeps *pushing*, and I'm about to snap. "None of us are getting any younger..."

Gulping back the words that are trying to rise from my throat, I flinch as Desiree's fingernails dig into my thigh.

"It really would be nice to have a baby around to spoil," my mother mumbles. But when our eyes meet, she adds, "When you're ready, of course."

"Why wouldn't you be ready?" Clark stares, primarily at me. "What's the hold-up, anyway?"

"It's not that..." My voice creeps out, but I clamp my shivering lips shut.

Glancing at my father, who's suspiciously quiet during this conversation, I find him swirling the iced tea around and around in his glass.

"Dad, can you just leave it, please?" Desiree mutters tiredly. "It's not the right time..."

"Son, if you're waiting for the perfect time, it'll never come," Clark says, again, addressing only me. "Sure, babies can be a handful, but it's all worth it when you get to watch them grow up into amazing little humans."

"Dad," Des barks, softly, but still.

Fuck, she's gonna break the skin.

"I thought you said you were trying," Patricia joins in, the two of them double-teaming us. "Have you been to a doctor?"

Desiree rubs her eyes with her hand. The one that's not squeezing circulation out of my leg. "I really don't think this is the time or place for this conversation..."

"Listen, we're all family here," Clark argues. "We're just wondering..."

"You two would make wonderful parents," my mother says.

"Children are the future..." my father mumbles.

I'm going to fucking pass out...

"Alright, enough!" Ellie snaps. "The reason they don't want to talk about it is because—"

"Ell, no." I shake my head at her. "You don't have to..."

"It's fine," she whispers to me, then sucks in a breath. "It's because I'm pregnant. I just found out, so I was waiting to tell you guys... But I told Lance and Des in the car."

My mother's face is immediately swept up in jubilation. "Oh my... Elisa. Really??"

Ellie nods, glancing at our father. He shows her one of his stoic smiles, taking her hand in his.

"Darling, I am so happy for you," he says. "And Marcus...?"

"Marcus is excited." Ellie grins.

We share one last look as the table erupts in congratulations and prying questions, all now directed at my baby sister.

She just took a baby bullet for me. And I'm so beyond appreciative.

But the moment the squeals of delight and talk of marriage and weddings dies down, I can feel the unspoken words hovering in the air above our table.

Your little sister is having kids before you.

It's so suffocating, I'm asking for the check while they're still finishing their food.

I have to get out of here. I just can't deal with this right now...

On top of all the other bullshit running through my head, here's yet another piece of the complicated puzzle. Because sure, Ellie saved me from having to answer for myself *today*. But what about the next lunch?

How much longer can I hold off these questions?

Desiree and I have been married for over ten years. The assumption is that we'll be starting a family. This isn't a new topic. Our respective parents have been grilling us about it for years now, and it's getting harder and harder to slither our ways out of it.

Outside of the restaurant, I say goodbye to everyone, quietly thanking my sister with a kiss on the cheek, and a demand that she keeps in touch every step of the way, if not with our parents, because they're too much, then at least with me. And then I tell Des I need to head back to the church for a bit, to finish up a few things. It's not unusual, being that I have an office there and all.

But right now, the look on her face is very clear... She's worried.

Concerned that I'm going back just to get away from her, from everyone, really. That I'm internalizing and shutting down, as I do.

But my wife, unlike her parents, knows when to let things go. And she agrees to have her parents drive her home while I slink into her car and drive back toward South Valley Pentecostal.

The entire fifteen-minute ride is spent obsessing. Fixating on all the noise building up inside me, so loud I can barely hear the songs playing on the radio. What it all boils down to is that I have absolutely no idea what I'm doing.

Here's the truth... I've always wanted to be a father. Objectively, I love the idea of raising a child. Caring for someone other than yourself, teaching them, molding them, and watching them grow into their own individual person... Regardless of how much Clark was pissing me off before, it sounds amazing. *Totally my thing.*

Trouble

But the harsh reality is that I don't want to make a child with someone I don't love.

Wow... That is so heavy.

But it's true. That's not to say I don't love Desiree. I *do*, in a surface way that feels completely superficial.

She's my friend, my savior. The person who showed up right as I was asking God for a sign, to guide me in the right direction.

But she's never made me feel the way I do with him. *No one has.*

As wrong as it might be, this quaint, pleasant little life is completely devoid of sunshine... without my Trouble.

Chapter Seventeen
Lance

The sun is setting as I drag myself out of my office.

I've been here in the church for hours... working.

And by *working*, I mean stalking Tate on social media.

I can't help it anymore. I spend more time lurking around his socials than is considered normal behavior, and even though it hurts my heart more often than not, I can't seem to make myself stop.

I love feeling connected to him, even when we're not. I love knowing what he's doing even when he won't answer my calls or texts—*which he still won't, by the way.* I've probably sent him fifty messages, since the night we fucked in his car—*I texted him to make sure he'd made it home safe*—to this morning—*I asked him if he was ever going to stop running like I did.*

All have been read. All have gone unanswered.

It's starting to weigh on me more and more each day. Because I still feel like seeing him at Pride was a sign from God... But him pushing me away is too, and it hurts like hell to accept that maybe the *sign* was for me to move on. Finally. For *good*.

I never stopped thinking about Tate over the years. Not once. Having this affair fizzle out in such an agonizing fashion could be God's way of showing me that it never would have worked between us, even if I'd stayed.

But I don't want to accept that. I just can't rationalize that we would *finally* get our blinding, brilliant, beautiful moment, only for it to burn out in a matter of weeks.

Trouble

The stress of the whole *wife and baby* thing, mixing with Tate being so frustratingly out of reach, has me wishing I had some booze to take the edge off. Of course I don't... Unless we're talking about the blood of Christ...

I think I've sinned enough.

I just finally put my phone away, after scrolling Tate's Instagram for *way* too long. He hasn't posted much recently, but there was a new picture of him from yesterday. He was golfing.

Apparently, it was for work, and based on the caption, he doesn't particularly enjoy it. But he's good at it, somehow, which doesn't surprise me. Tate's good at most things other people struggle with. Effortlessly talented, and aloof enough to always be shrugging it off with a confident smirk. I'm sure some people find it infuriating. But not me. I'm swept away by his borderline narcissistic ways.

In the picture, he was wearing the *Tate* version of a golf outfit—fitted gray slacks, a polo shirt with some kind of design on it I couldn't make out because I was too busy ogling how *long* and *defined* his arms looked, pristine white sneakers, and a black cap that was literally just that, but because it says Balenciaga on it, probably cost him more than my monthly mortgage.

Needless to say, I'm *still* swooning over how adorable and sexy he looked, smirking next to a few other partners from his firm and their new client, with a cigar in his mouth.

He's just so monumentally *different* from me, and it's definitely part of what lures me in so desperately, like a moth to his lavish flame. None of what he does, or buys or wears, are things I would ever want for myself, and yet I find him so fascinating because of it. That and I hold an unrivaled sense of pride inside myself for him, and the fact that he *actually* did what he set out to do. He became that rich, successful man he always said he was going to be someday; doing what he loves while supporting himself and relying on no one.

I still remember when we used to stay up talking, walking around just outside of campus, smoking joints and drinking from a shared pint of whiskey, discussing the future. He'd say, *"I'm gonna have it all one day, Hardy. Just you wait and see."*

And he did. He *does*, have it all.

All but the one thing I wish he wanted... The one thing I wish I could give him.

Wandering around the quiet space of the church, I admire the flowers and the way they brighten up the room, even as the light begins to fade. My fingers brush over the yellow petals of a sunflower.

A buzz in my pocket distracts me from the softness. It's a Facebook notification.

Tate Eckhart accepted your friend request.

Blinking in disbelief, my lips slope into a purely dopey grin as I click on his profile.

I can't believe he accepted me as a friend... I really didn't expect him to.

I never tried to add him over the years, because I knew it would just bring on more torture I was already wading through every day, missing him and pretending I wasn't. Not to mention, I didn't want him to know I was still thinking about him...

Man, all of that really went out the window, huh?

I finally sent him a request when I was looking for him, stalking every available avenue to bring him flowers, which *yes*, I can now admit was extremely creepy. But regardless, he never accepted me—*no surprise there.*

I guess he's had a change of heart.

Maybe he does want to be friends again...

I bite my lip. *Yea, right. That totally wouldn't work at this point.*

Tate uses his Facebook less than he uses his Instagram, that much is clear from looking at his profile. However, he is tagged in quite a bit, especially by Jacob, who's been a Facebook friend of mine for years, which was helpful when I was being a weirdo stalker. He actually just tagged Tate in a picture earlier today, of his twin daughters on inflatable pool floats. One is a unicorn, and the other is a slice of pizza, and the caption reads:

Thanks for the gifts, Uncle Tate!

Tapping to like the photo, I scroll up and notice that Tate posted a new status update. Just now.

Tate Eckhart: *Love getting weird looks from the guys who detail my car. No, that's not really dried smoothie, sir, and I'll thank you to stay out of my personal affairs ;)*

A snort flies out of me while I shake my head at my phone. There's so much to unpack from that one stupid post... Like that fact that he *did* have to have the interior of his Maserati detailed after we fucked and got cum all over the passenger seat.

Also, he used the word *affair*.

I can't help wondering if him finally accepting my friend request right before posting this means something.

Did he want me to see it? Is he talking to me without talking to me?

Why is he so damn frustrating?? Can't he just answer my texts, or call me back for once, instead of posting something on Facebook that clearly alludes to what we did? Is he still punishing me with these passive aggressive games? Trying to see how much I'm willing to grovel for him...?

Or is he purposely trying to keep me at a distance, even though I know he doesn't want to?

Clicking the blue thumbs up, I like the photo while striding over to light a few of the candles lining the edges of the room. I could just turn the lights on... Or I could go *home*, since there's really no reason for me to still be here.

But I think I need to stay.

I need to talk to God... Just me and Him. Let Him know that I'm sorry for how much I'm pining when I'm not supposed to, but that I just can't make myself stop.

Because you don't want to... I hear Him telling me.

"Oh, you're good," I huff, slipping my phone away.

But the second it touches the inside of my pocket, it starts ringing.

And when I tug it back out, I fumble at the name on the screen.

"Hello?" I answer so fast, I almost drop the thing.

"Really? The *first* person to like my post?" Tate croons into my ear. I'm immediately covered in chills. "I literally just accepted your friend request. Were you watching my profile?"

I swallow. "No..."

"You're the worst liar in the history of liars," he teases. "And that's *including* former presidents."

I chuckle softly, leaning up against the wall. "Yea, well... You obviously posted that for me, Trouble. They manage to get the stains out?"

He laughs, and my heart thumps aggressively. "Yes, they did, thanks for asking. Between them and my dry cleaner, I'm running out of local businesses who don't know how slutty I am."

I know he's messing around, but the way my gut tightens at the thought of him with anyone else continues to overwhelm me.

"So... you've obviously been thinking about me," I rumble, and he

185

chuckles. "Why don't we call time of death on this back-and-forth game and just meet somewhere?"

"Hmm... and why would we do that?" His voice is smooth, deep and sultry, like decadent dessert for your ears.

"Because I want to see you," I tell him honestly, absentmindedly grazing sunflower petals some more. "And I know you want to see me."

He releases a breath. "Boy, you really think you've got me pegged, huh?" I nod, even though he can't see me. "Tell me, Miss Cleo, what am I thinking right now?"

It's wild how even just *talking* to him, flirting and listening to his delicious, rumbly voice has me practically writhing.

I'm in the *church* right now... I'm not supposed to feel this way, in *here*, of all places, but I'm buzzing.

"You're thinking about how good it feels when I'm inside you," I murmur, peeking at Jesus on the wall. *So sorry about this one...* Tate stifles a sound, and I lick my lip. "And about how good it felt when you... were inside me."

Tate breathes heavily, clearly trying to cover it up while my own face is burning from the memory of slipping his cock into my mouth, now at the forefront of my mind. It's making me dizzy, and my balls are already aching.

The first time I've ever done that... And it felt *so* damn *good*, I think I could have come, just from sucking on him.

"You're pretty naughty... for a man of God," he whispers.

I gulp again, swallowing down a thick helping of guilt. I'm getting used to the taste. *Honestly... I don't hate it.*

"And you're too much trouble to keep teasing me like this," I hum. "What's wrong, baby? I thought you weren't afraid to be *bad*..."

Tate is quiet for a moment, before he says, "I just needed to be sure you could handle it."

An easy grin rests on my lips while my head tips back. This *is* bad... It's so unbelievably wrong, but I'm not strong enough to fight it.

My attraction to him is like a Godzilla-sized monster, wiping out all traces of remorse and responsibility. I don't want to lose this feeling again... Even if it destroys all other aspects of my life.

It's worth it. Keeping him is worth giving up *everything* else.

"Tell me you missed me," I rasp into the phone, breathy and keyed up.

"You know I did," he mumbles, petulantly, like a stubborn, sexy thing I need more than oxygen.

"Now tell me where you are," I demand. "Unless you want me to come find you again..."

"I do like it when you chase me..." I hear some noises, like a car door opening and closing. Then his connection changes, as if he just switched from Bluetooth to his phone. "I guess I also like coming to you. Is this door locked?"

My brow furrows, lips parted to ask him where he is and what he's doing.

But then the door to the church opens.

And he's standing right there.

Blinking at me, with his phone held up to his ear.

"Guess not," he murmurs, silky voice in my ear and reaching from the opposite end of the room.

My hand slips away, releasing my phone with a *thunk* onto the floor as my feet bring me to him. Uncontrollably, I'm being pulled in his direction, *magnetized* to him, just like I always have been.

Tate...

Tate's here.

He showed up again. He came... to my church?!

This is crazy. It's bad, and so reckless.

He shouldn't be here with me when I can't control myself around him.

Tate tucks his phone away, biting his smirk off as he closes the door behind him. And I'm striding down the aisle, with my heart slamming in my chest.

He's *here*.

"Thank God," the words slip from my lips right as I'm grasping his face, hauling his to mine.

The kiss is fast, frantic. So instantly frenzied, his back ends up crashed against the door while I suck on his sweet mouth and he feeds me his eager sounds. His hands land on my chest, desperately fisting my shirt as our tongues tangle and our breaths echo.

"I can't believe you're here," I pant, nipping his bottom lip then kissing it a whole bunch of times, my fingers on his jaw and in his hair. "I can't believe you actually... showed up, *here*... for me."

"Neither can I," he whispers hoarsely. "I was sure I'd burst into flames the moment I stepped through the door."

Chuckling, my lips brush his, kissing slowing. My hands running take in the feel of every inch that makes him up. So masculine and defined. He's all sharp angles and curves of muscle. Rough stubble on his jawline, broad shoulders, slim, tapered waist, firm, taut ass. Big hands, bigger dick.

He's a *man*, even more than he was when we were in college, and it's enough to have me reeling and simultaneously falling to pieces.

"You wanna burn, baby?" I kiss the words over to his ear, sucking the lobe between my lips. "Because that can be arranged."

Tate whimpers, eyes closed, head resting back against the wooden door while I toy with his ear and glide my hand between us to cup his thick cock. "Are we alone in here?"

I nod, dazed and crazed and needy as hell, sucking on his neck and throat. "Not that it would matter, right?" Pulling back, I watch his eyes flutter open. "You want the danger, don't you? That's why you keep showing up places where you know we could get caught..." He bites his lip, rumbling a greedy sound while I fondle him over his pants. "I think you want to get me in trouble, Tate... Because it turns you on."

"Maybe you do know me, Sunshine." A lazy grin slopes his lips, and I hum before kissing it hungrily.

I've never felt so unleashed. Having him here, in the church where only a few hours ago, I was preaching the word of God to my congregation, my family, my wife... the place where my father preached for so many years... it feels like a fever dream. The lust of impending sin is palpable, like a thick cloud of smoke surrounding us.

And I must be the worst pastor in the world, because I'm inhaling deep and holding it in.

Slipping my fingers through Tate's, I pull him off of the door and drag him up the aisle. My pulse is pumping like a heavy bass line, skin burning beneath my clothes while my mind filters through hectic thoughts.

All the truths, and the lies... I don't care about any of them. When I'm with him, it's as if all that matters is *us*. I'm sure that's very unhealthy, but like an addict with his drug of choice, the craving outweighs the consequence.

All I want in the world right now is his salacious brand of distraction.

"This place is actually... really beautiful." His voice stops me, and I turn to face him, standing before the pulpit with his hand in mine. "It's not what I expected."

"What did you expect?" I ask him softly, reaching out to brush his clavicle, exposed by the open collar of his dress shirt.

He steps back, and I release his hand, watching as he glances around the room, twirling and observing the space.

His brows knit. "I'm not... sure. I think I went to a church once when I was little, but I don't remember it much. I think it was bigger... Colder. Less light, more judgement." Dark eyes look past me. "There were no flowers..."

I let my gaze linger on him as he takes a seat in the first row of pews, remembering all the times he's told me he doesn't believe in God...

God doesn't want people like me, Hardy..." His voice flutters through my memories.

Plucking a few sunflowers out of one of the hanging vases, I saunter over to where he's sitting. His chin lifts, gazing up at me while I hold them out to him, echoing the words I spoke many years ago. "God sees only the soul, Tate." He takes the flowers as I tower over him, grazing his neck with my fingertips. "And yours is beautiful."

He blinks. "You're also not what I expected..."

"No?" I plop down by his side, unable to stop touching him.

He shakes his head. "You're not wearing the black shirt with that white collar thing."

I laugh softly. "Those are for priests."

"I still don't understand the difference," he rumbles.

"It's complicated," I sigh. "Different sects, different rules, different..."

"Rituals?" He cocks a brow at my face.

"*Traditions.*" I take a sunflower from him, tapping it against his chin. "We don't wear collars, we don't take confession..."

Turning to face me, his knees press into mine while he smirks. "I don't call you Father?"

Chuckling, I shake my head, making a cringey face. "No. Definitely not."

Tate leans in closer, humming over my lips as his hand travels up my thigh. "What about *Daddy*?"

My cock jerks hard between my legs, the rapid rush of blood making me lightheaded. Snatching his hand, I shove it possessively onto my dick and he groans.

"Are you here to *tempt* me, Trouble?" I growl, pressing him against me so that he can feel my erection through my pants, already big and stiff, just for him. "Test my willpower with your wicked ways..."

"That depends..." he purrs, massaging my cock. "Is it *forbidden* for you to suck me and fuck me until I'm sobbing your name like a prayer?"

A hungry sound escapes me as his dark eyes glisten with mischief. "Oh, yea." I nod. "Big time."

"Mmm... then call me the serpent," he croons, and I laugh a rumbly one.

God... How am I not supposed to love him??

I mean, I know You say to be evenly yoked in relationships and whatnot, but he's just perfect, and You know he is.

I feel like You made him for me.

If that's not the case, then feel free to smite me down right now, but I just... can't stop. And I'm sorry...

But I can't.

Urging forward, I capture his lips once more. Kissing Tate's mouth feels like heaven. This is *actually* what heaven feels like, I'm sure of it; the sensation of his soft lips on mine, his warm tongue teasing in between, and the way he clings to me, desperately, like he's afraid he might slip and fall away from this pleasure. It's all so *fervent*, every movement of us sucking and panting and pawing at one another like animals.

I force myself to back away from his kiss, enough that he releases a frustrated whine, eyes hooded with need. It has me grinning wickedly.

"You're no more of a sinner than I am, baby." I drag a sunflower down his throat.

His hungry gaze is on my mouth as he trills, "How are you gonna repent, Sunshine?"

I rumble a sultry laugh. "Maybe you could help me... *atone* for my sins."

"Well, we are in God's house..." He squirms from his visible erection.

Sinking onto my knees on the floor, I begin untying his shoes. "The door is unlocked..." I arch my brow up at him. "Anyone could walk in here at any moment."

"That's hot," he whispers, watching me closely.

Once I get his shoes off, I go for his shirt. Kneeling between his legs, I pop each button while he leans in to let me kiss his lips softly. I push the expensive material off of his shoulders and down his arms, dragging my lips over his throat and humming at the feel of his soft skin and rough stubble, the cords of muscle beneath it.

"Take mine off, baby," I whisper, lost in his smell and the warmth of his flesh.

Tate opens my shirt, wantonly touching me, tracing the curves of my chest while his legs wrap around my waist. Shrugging out of my shirt, I grab one of the sunflowers, trailing it over his nipple until he purrs.

Trouble

"Lie down on your back," I command, and he does, without hesitation, melting horizontally on the wood.

Climbing onto the bench before him, I drop the sunflower onto his chest, captivated by the sight of it heaving for breath beneath the elegant yellow petals. Slowly, I remove his socks before moving to his pants. Unbuttoned, and unzipped, I peel them off his long legs, adding them to the pile of his clothes on the floor. I'm sure I've never been harder, and a lot of it has to do with how bad this is...

I wasn't exaggerating when I told him anyone could walk in. It's true. The church doors are known to stay open because it's a place of worship. It's more than a little dangerous to be fooling around with Tate here, out in the open like this. Especially since everyone—mainly my wife—knows I'm here.

There might be something seriously wrong with me, though, because the thrill of knowing this is *wrong* and *dangerous* has me leaking in my pants almost as much as the sight of Tate, splayed out on the wooden bench in nothing but his black boxer briefs and my favorite flowers.

"You look so good, baby," I praise, using the flower to brush his skin some more. Tracing the lines of his chest, and his abs, then over the prominent outline of his massive cock. "Truly a gift from the heavens."

Tate whimpers when the flower ghosts over his erection, lashes fluttering, fingers twitching, likely with the need to touch something.

"You're so beautiful, I'm *aching* for you, Tate," I go on, pushing his legs apart to wedge myself in between.

"You're such a fucking tease," he whines as I stroke his body with the sunflower, as if it's my paintbrush and he's my canvas.

"You like it?" I lean over him, sweeping his lips with the petals, my mouth only inches away.

"*Fffuck...*" He arches up to me, breathing heavily, pushing his dick into mine through our clothes. "Yea... I do."

"You love how I cherish your body... don't you, Trouble?" I bite his neck, and he flinches.

"Uh-huh." His throat dips. "Feels... mmm*good.*"

Scraping my teeth down his chest, I kiss his nipples, sucking and licking and biting them while he writhes beneath my punishing mouth. His legs are trapped under me, so he can barely move his lower half. All he can do is fist my hair and grip my shoulders, and tremble for me.

Because he's *mine.*

"You love how it aches and *burns...* when I play with you like my sweet toy," I croon, nipping the pink little point that's now dripping in my saliva, brushing it over with the sunflower to soothe my sting. Then I move lower, biting each stone of his abs, hard enough that there are reddish indents in his skin from my teeth. "Tell me..."

"Tell... you...?" He gasps when I peel his boxers down just enough for his dick to poke out.

"Tell me you love what I give you that no one else does, gorgeous thing." I caress the head of his cock with the flower. And then with my lips. He groans a shivering sound. "Tell me how *good* it feels when I save you."

"Fuck me... *Sunshine*..."

His voice is a hymn.

Suckling at the tip of his cock, my eyes roll back in my skull and his hips buck. I yank his boxers lower, ripping them down his thighs so I can get more, suck him *deeper*, this perfectly thick shaft, solid as stone wrapped in velvety skin, sliding on my tongue.

"Oh God, *Lance*... Suck my dick, baby," he rambles with his fingers combing through my hair. "I *love* what you do to me... So, *so* good..."

Groaning on his dick, I suck him harder, rougher and sloppier, saliva spilling as his inches lurch down my throat. This is deeper than last time, and I love it. I feel like I need him all the way back there, gliding past my fucking tonsils.

The swollen, dripping crown of Tate's delicious dick grazes my gag reflex and I try to swallow, my throat clenching on him. He hisses, holding my jaw, thumbs caressing my cheeks.

"*Mmmff*... if this is church, I should've gotten baptized years ago." His dark eyes meet my watery ones, and he bites his lip, whispering, in a barely audible voice, "You doing okay?" I nod, bobbing on him, using my tongue to cradle his length. "You want me to forgive you, Pastor?"

I nod again, eyelids growing heavy, my balls throbbing almost painfully with how fucking aroused I am. I still can't believe I'm actually sucking a dick... Tate's dick.

I'm giving Tate Eckhart head in the church...

I'm so hard, I might burst through my pants.

Tate's dark lashes fan atop his cheekbones. "*Fuck*, baby... Maybe I get your whole *possessive* thing now..." He cups my face while my lips stroke him up and down, working and chasing and *sucking* until my jaw is sore and my head is spinning. "I want this mouth for only me... No one else."

My chest is on fire. I can *feel* the raw emotion I'm shooting at him through my hazy gaze, and I think he can feel it too. Because he's not smirking, or teasing, and the way he's petting my hair and my face, and staring at me... It's like he's experiencing something he never has before, and he both loves it and is terrified of it at the same time.

His head falls back with a groan. "God, *Sunshine*, you can fucking have me as long as you never take this mouth away again."

Slurping up and off his cock with a pop, I pull in a much-needed breath.

Tate scowls down at me with flushed cheeks. "You've gotta be kidding me right now..."

Grinning, I rip his boxers down his legs the rest of the way. "Mmm... I just love playing with you, beautiful." Shoving his legs open wider, I plant slow kisses up his inner thighs. "But I told you... I'm not letting you get away this time."

Picking up the sunflower once more, I use it to tease his cock, which is stretched up to his navel, veins pulsing so hard I can practically see them. I inch my mouth closer, pressing a delicate kiss on his balls.

"Jesus fucking Christ," he shudders, head dropping back onto the wood again. But then he lifts it and blinks remorsefully at me. "Sorry..."

"We'll let it slide," I hum, licking and sucking his nuts until he's quaking. My tongue feathers down them while I hold his ass in my hands, lifting and pushing him up. Then my lips sneak curiously between his cheeks. "Take this repentant tongue in your sweet little ass, baby."

Spreading him open, my tongue extends to flutter over his hot, clenching hole. He groans, and I mewl, both of our bodies racked with shivers as I go in for another strong lick.

"Uhh *fuck*, L-Lance." His body is already liquifying in my hands, hips chasing my mouth, desperate for more. "I used to fantasize about you eating my ass... But—*ummff*—this is so much better."

"Mmm *mmm*..." is all I can say with my face buried between his cheeks, my heart swelling at his words.

Lips sucking, tongue lashing, in an instant, I'm fucking *feasting* on him, and it's *divine*. I can't believe I'm actually eating his ass, and although I've never done it before—to anyone—I have some moves locked and loaded. Because honestly...

I've wanted to do this to him for a *long* time too.

"Unnghh, baby... Ohh, *baby*, eat it," he moans, hoarse, with his fingers tugging roughly at my hair. "Fucking lick my hole... Just like that... *Fuck*, your tongue is *heaven*."

Reaching down with shaky fingers, I hastily undo my pants, opening them just enough to get my dick out. It's fucking *throbbing*, pulsing and *dripping* from the head while I ravish Tate's tight hole, stuffing my tongue in as my hand glides up to fist his cock.

And now I'm jerking him and eating him, the most obscene noises of wet suction, flesh beating and ravenous grunting ringing out through the church.

"No one's ever tongue-fucked me like this, Sunshine," he pants, writhing against my mouth, holding me deep in his ass by my hair.

"You're so fucking sweet, T," I huff, out of breath.

Then I bite him. Right on the rim.

'Cause why not?

"*Ah!* Fuck," he whines, and I can see the chills sheeting his entire body. "The *biting*, Lance..."

"Sorry, my delicious feast." I grin wickedly.

"Yea right," he gasps. "You're not—" I bite him again, on the swell of the ass, and he hisses, "Godfuckindamnit!"

"Shh... There there." Licking and licking, I soothe the pain, leaving his asshole soaked as I nuzzle his balls, biting them until his shudders, covering them with tender kisses. "I love this." I nip my way up his nuts, then his cock, tongue slipping out to toy with his wet tip. "You're so tasty... I can't help wanting to eat you alive."

"Fuck you and your little love bites," he growls, squirming to give away how surprisingly good it feels when I hurt him just a bit.

He looks like a dream come true right now. I have to stop for a second and just admire the sight of him... Blushed skin glistening, covered in bite marks and yellow sunflower petals. Dark hair all mussed up, moist, shivering pink lips.

"Tate..." I croon, shoving my pants down farther, running my hands up his thighs, then his hips. "No one has ever been as hopelessly fucking *gorgeous* as you."

The mound of his throat bobs. I assume he's about to flip over, as he does. Give me his backside, to hide from the obvious emotion that flows between us when we're lost in this beautiful sin together.

But this time, he doesn't.

Instead, he reaches for me, and pleads, "Come here..." Lowering, I let him take my face in his strong hands. "Save me, Pastor."

Crawling over him, I trap his body beneath me on the wooden surface. It's narrow, and we're a bit too big to lie on it fully, but it doesn't even matter. I have one foot on the floor, the other knee beside his hip and I'm holding him to me, cradling his warmth and his size and the yearning trembles I feel in his limbs as we grind our slick, swollen cocks together.

In a slow sweep, my lips overtake his to kiss him deep. And he kisses me back, apparently not giving a single fuck that I was just slurping on his ass. Tate eases his tongue into my mouth, and I stroke it with mine, simultaneously trying to reach for something in my pants.

"Fuck..." he grumbles. "My lube... it's in the car." His fingers dig into my shoulder blades while I bite his lip. "*Mmf*, whatever. Just fuck me raw, I don't even care."

"I love your dedication," I chuckle. "But I have... something. Something we can use..."

My fingers slide over the small glass bottle in my pants pocket, pulling it out.

"*You* have lube?" He grins on my mouth. "Please tell me you've been carrying it around with you just in case."

Rumbling another soft laugh, I hold up the bottle of oil. "It's not quite lube, but it'll definitely work." Tate takes it from me, looking it over while I kiss his throat. "Smells a lot better too..."

He unscrews the top, the scents of cinnamon, myrrh and cassia immediately flowing out. "What is this for?"

"It's for sanctification," I explain to him, pouring some out onto my fingers. "Anointing oils signify humility, and dependence on God. We don't use them much, but we still have them... Mostly, I just like the smell."

Slipping my hand between us, I swipe my glossy fingers over his hole, and he gasps.

"So using them for sodomy is probably considered... *mmm—*" his voice cuts in a shaky hum when my finger slides into his ass, "—sacrilege..."

I kiss his lips softly. "Yea... Probably."

Tate's eyes flutter as I work the aromatic oil into his body with one finger, then two.

"You're determined to drag us both to Hell, aren't you?" he whimpers, rocking against my hand.

"Sweet Trouble..." I hum, pushing my cock against his. "If you only knew. Pour some of that onto your fingers... Use it to make my dick wet for you, baby."

The way he whines and rumbles is so erotic, he's driving me insane. Just like the feel of his slippery hand as it fists my shaft, stroking sacred anointing oils onto my erection. The smell is intoxicating, working up the haze of forbidden lust in my brain, and the tension of carnal hunger in my muscles.

The sun has fully set, leaving us bathed in darkness. Only the glow of the candles surrounds us, giving an erotic ambience; heady joined breaths of illicit thrill, the slip and slide of wet skin, and the vast desire shining up at me in his gaze.

For someone completely sober, I'm drunk on this sacred moment. On *him*.

Wrong and right be damned with me... Because I've *fallen*.

Throne broken, asunder from righteousness in the house of the Lord.

Retrieving my fingers from within Tate's body, I ease myself between his thighs while my forehead rests on his.

"I... I should..." he stammers, twitching fingers on my chest. "I need to... turn over."

"Shhh," I hush, kissing him softly while I guide my cock up to where his body is waiting for me. "I'm gonna fuck you so good like this, baby."

"Lance, I c-can't," his voice has taken on a vulnerable lilt. "It's too... much."

The very tip of my dick is resting right at his threshold, eager to rush inside. But I pause to hold his face and caress his hair.

"Stop running from me, Tate." My hoarse plea melts into slow, lush kisses while his tense muscles begin to mollify.

"Just flip me over and nail me to this bench, Hardy," he whines petulantly. "Face to face is—"

"What you need," I cut him off. "Passion..."

"Fuck *passion*..."

"And hunger..."

"Fuck *hunger*..."

Grabbing his hands, I pin them over his head. He mewls, eyes glistening as I flick my hips just enough that the silky head of my cock nudges into his hole.

His eyes roll back, and he groans. It's the most mesmerizing sight and sound of my existence.

"This is how *I* get to fuck you, baby," I growl, sinking deeper into his body. "Only me... watching your face while you fall apart."

"*Fffuck*," he gasps, his dick moving and leaking on his abs from the feeling of me entering him.

"Open your eyes," I demand breathlessly, blazing inch after inch into the grip of his body. "Look at how fucking sexy this is... Your man between your legs, filling you with his big cock."

Tate whimpers, but his eyes creep open and his chin dips. He glances down as my pelvis is hitting his cheeks, his nuts resting flush against my skin. I continue holding his wrists with one hand, while the other brushes down his arm and his side. He flinches like it tickles, and I bite my lip, touching him sensually all over.

"I love being able to watch my fingers teasing your beautiful body, baby," I tell him, toying with his nipples.

"*Fuck*, that feels..." His voice trails when I draw back a few inches, pushing back in him nice and deep. "Ohhh *so good...*"

"And I get to watch your pretty cock weeping for me." My hips move again, back then forth, rocking into him while his dick jerks and twinges. "So hard and *long* when I'm all the way inside you... Showing me how much you love me fucking *deep* into your ass."

"*Mmm*, I love it so much," he purrs, chewing his lip. Forcing his eyes open so he can watch.

Honestly, he looks mesmerized by the sight. Overwhelmed, maybe a little... I'm guessing because he never lets anyone fuck him this way. Face to face... It *is* much more intimate. And I'm elated that he's giving up just a little bit of fight for me. Shutting out all the noise of this thoughts—like I am.

Letting me inside more than just his body.

"I know you do." My thrusts pick up gradually in pace as I work into him slow, but as deep as physically possible, stretching his ass open around my girth. I'm *claiming* him; fucking him like he's mine, because he *is*. "Tate... my hot, tight hole to fuck... You feel *incredible*, baby. And you look even better."

"Sunshine..." he rasps, legs wrapped snugly around my waist while I stroke in him. "*Uhh* this is so fucking hot..." Our eyes lock, and his throat dips. "Keep watching me..."

As if I could look anywhere else.

Grunting, I fuck between his legs, jostling his body forward and back with my demanding thrusts. My fingers play with his cock and his balls, teasing his sweet, sticky flesh. And all the while, his gaze is gripping me as tightly as his ass squeezes my dick.

He looks like a *masterpiece*, splayed out, draped in candlelight and surrounded by sunflowers.

"I knew you wanted my eyes on you, gorgeous." I lean down to kiss his lips, giving him a rough buck that feeds me a guttural groan. "You belong to me, Trouble. You belong with me between your thighs, kissing your lips and punishing your sweet spot."

"*Fuck fuck fuck.*" He squirms, back arching. "You're so right... I'm all... fucking... *yours.*"

Snarling, I bite his mouth, bruising him with kisses as the fucking gets harder, *rougher.* The skin slapping grows louder, as do our grunts and groans and the crude wet sounds of my dick pumping his ass, tolling like depraved church bells.

"Mmm... you fucking *look* like mine." I nip down his neck and chest, sucking his nipples, jerking his cock and really just praising him with rough pleasure and sweet pain.

Finally releasing his hands so that I can touch him all over, I grip the underside of his thigh, angling him for the deepest penetration possible. Tate grabs my face and hauls me back up to his mouth for more slippery kisses.

"Fuck me," he pleads, hoarse and insatiable. The sound of his voice draws my balls up tight. "Fuck my ass, you filthy fucking preacher."

"Yea? Is this my luscious little cunt to fuck?"

He sobs. "*Guhhyess...* Yours. All yours..."

"Who owns it?"

"You own it..."

"Yea...?"

"*Fuck yea.*"

Sitting back a bit, I grab his calves, straightening his legs and holding them up so that his feet are by my head. My eyes are stuck on the sight of my cock diving deep, aiming for his prostate and watching with hooded delight when his dick pulses more precum. There's a nice little puddle accumulating on his abs, and it's the hottest thing I've ever seen in my life.

"Lance *fucking* Hardy... goddamn, no one's ever—*fuuuck*—no one's ever hit it like you do," he cries and groans and growls, toes curling on either side of my face. "You fuck my ass like a god."

"You're blaspheming, sexy troublemaker." A bead of sweat runs down my temple, every muscle in my body straining from how *thoroughly* I'm working on him right now. I bite his ankle, and he whines. "Beg for forgiveness."

"Unnghh I'm sorry." He cups his balls. "Forgive me, Daddy, for I'm... sinning. *Fuck*, I'm gonna sin *so hard* on your cock..."

"I can't with you." A hoarse chuckle gusts from my lips while I lick and bite him some more, everywhere I can reach.

I think I'm biting his foot, but I can't even tell. I'm fucking out of it, hypnotized by this hot, sweaty, debauchery we're engaging in that has me so close to ecstasy. Pounding into him over and over, I'm rushing to get him off before I explode.

"Sun... *Sunshine,*" he sobs, hot hole clenching on me. "I'm *sofuckingclose!*"

"You're practically screaming," I hiss, taking his hands and pressing them up to my chest. "Someone's gonna think you're being murdered..."

"I am," he gasps. "Fuck, you're killing me with that big cock, baby."

I push my fingers up to his lips. "If they come to help... all they'll find is a needy slut with his ankles in the air." I stuff my fingers into his mouth, and he grunts around them, sucking greedily. "Having his pretty ass wrecked by the fucking pastor..."

Tate moans my name, muffled by my fingers in his mouth. I'm about to come and collapse, my head clouded and my balls *aching*.

Leaning down, I hover over him while my hips move, slamming him with furious thrusts. "That's what you want, isn't it, Trouble? You want everyone to see me owning you... So they know that you're *mine*, and I'm yours." He nods frantically, eyes rolling back in his head. "You want me all to yourself, huh, beautiful?"

I pull my fingers out of his mouth, and he whimpers, "*Lance*... fuck, I'm gonna come..."

"Not until you answer me."

"Mmmffuuck *yes*... Yes, that's what I fucking want." His hands grip my neck. "I want—*uhh*—I want you back. I want you... *mine.*"

My heart jumps, chest throbbing as hard as my loins.

"I'm gonna come so deep in you, baby," I breathe on his lips, swallowing his cries. "Spill this seed in your cunt and make you mine forever..."

"Fuck fuck *fuck*, Lance, I'm coming!" he wails, clamping around me like a vise. "I'm *coming* on your cock..."

"Come on my cock, baby... Give your man what he needs."

Tate releases a garbled stream of curses, immediately followed by hot flowing orgasm. Shooting everywhere, my chest, his chest, drenching us both in cum. With his hole gripping my cock, I can feel the contractions. My hazy gaze slinks down to watch his abs clench while he grinds his hips against mine, rubbing his balls all over me, writhing his wet cock between our bodies. It's the single *sexiest thing* I've ever seen. And it sends me toppling over the edge.

"Holy *fuck*, Tate, I'm coming..." I manage to croak while the heavens fall, and I fist his hair and bite his lips.

Everything slows down like we're underwater as my dick shoots off inside him, pulsing wave after wave of an orgasm so strong, I feel like I'm having a seizure. My hips ripple into him in shallow pumps, stroking it out to feed him every drop.

"*Mmmmyeaa...*" his breathless purrs echo in my brain. "I *love* feeling you come in me..."

"Baby, I'm so yours..." I ramble, barely even cognizant of what I'm saying. "I belong to you, Tate... You're my salvation, baby. *Fuck*, it feels so *good* pouring into you... breeding this hot body."

I think I've blacked out. I don't even know where I am anymore. All I know is that my knees are raw, and my voice is hoarse, and I'm sated, fuzzy and calm. Filled with the most sweeping sense of comfort I've ever experienced.

It's like all of my problems have melted away, and I'm finally at peace. Awake, alive.

In love.

Don't ask me how, but after years of worship in this building, this is the first time I've felt true *faith*...

Fucking Tate Eckhart in the most desecrating way possible.

"Ayy-*men...*" Tate sighs, sounding like he's losing his voice. His body goes slack while I'm still catching my breath, absentmindedly nuzzling my lips along the sweaty flesh of his throat. "You know you can't actually get me pregnant, right?"

I snort, and his chest moves with a rumbly chuckle. Lifting my face, I gaze down at him, attempting to contain my psychotic grin.

I love you.

Okay, don't say that.

Instead, I kiss him, to keep the words in. But they're definitely still *there*. Right on the tip of my wicked tongue.

"Hardy... I'd love to keep basking in this unholiest of post-coital afterglows, but you're kinda crushing me."

"Sorry, baby," I croon, kissing him one, two, three more times before finally getting up.

I pull out of him slowly, watching the space between his legs while I help him sit upright.

Trouble

Tate groans and winces, frowning at the bench. "These things are not made for fucking on."

"No, they're certainly not," I rumble in dazed amusement.

Tate stretches out his arms and cracks his neck while I just keep staring at him, completely confounded.

I brush my fingers along his shoulder. "You have flower petals all over you..."

He grins and huffs, shaking his head.

Deciding I need a minute with my thoughts, I kiss his cheek, then stand up. "Hang tight, love. I'll go get you something to clean up."

He blinks at me, but doesn't speak. Simply nods and watches me as I jump into my pants and stagger off toward the bathroom. I feel light as air, a direct contrast to how I was feeling before he showed up. All the stress is gone, which is troubling, since theoretically every time we're together I dig myself deeper and deeper into a hole of treacherous sin.

Why is it so easy for me to come alive with him and no one else?

Why has nothing ever felt more right than doing the wrong things in the wrong ways with the wrongest person?

What is it about Tate Eckhart that makes him feel like my true salvation?

Shaking my head, I splash some water on my face, then gather some damp paper towels for him.

"This'll have to do for now," I tell him as I wander over, pausing when I find that he's gathered up all the sunflowers we were fucking with into a little pile.

"Have you ever really looked at a sunflower?" he murmurs. "They're actually pretty disgusting."

I chuckle, taking a seat next to them. "I guess they're not the prettiest flower..."

"No, not really." He cleans himself up, then steps into his boxers. "That thing in the middle is—" he mimics a gag, "—thoroughly appalling to look at."

I peer at him while he pulls up his pants. "Because of the holes?"

"Ew." He shivers. "I'm gonna puke."

I laugh. "If you hate them so much, why'd you let me drag them all over you?"

He grins and bites his lip. "I don't *hate* them... I think despite that one creepy factor they're actually... really fucking nice."

I can't help beaming. "So you liked the ones I sent you?"

He rolls his eyes. But then he mutters, "Yea... I did. They're still going strong, by the way. And they smell *amazing*."

"They symbolize loyalty... and adoration." I blink up at him, and it's hard to tell because it's so dark in here, but I think he's blushing.

I shift in my seat. "The story goes that Clytie, a nymph, fell in love with Apollo, the God of Sun. At first, he loved her too. But when Apollo began looking at another nymph, Clytie was overcome with jealous rage. She told the other nymph's father about it, and he buried his daughter alive as punishment."

Tate blinks wide eyes at me. "I'd call that an overreaction."

I chuckle. "Lil bit. After that, Apollo was so angry he turned Clytie into a sunflower. But she was still in love with him. Her love for Apollo was so strong that, even as a banished flower, she couldn't help watching him move across the sky every day. And that's why sunflowers follow the sun."

Tate stares at me for a few heavy seconds, during which I have absolutely no idea what's running through his head. But I know what's in mine...

It's the same thing that's been in there since the moment I left him behind.

I'm in love with you, Tate... Still just watching you move across the sky.

Finally, he clears his throat. "Uh... bathroom?"

"It's right back there." I nod.

Tate picks up the rest of his clothes and shuffles off, while I sit next to his pile of wilting flowers, wondering how long he'll disappear for this time.

I want to believe the things he said while we were fucking, but I can never be sure if it's just sex talk, or if he really means those words...

I want you back...

I want you... mine.

Struggling with my undying want for Tate Eckhart is fading off. Each time we're together, I grow less and less concerned with the consequences of loving him. I know it's awful to say, but clearly there's no limit to the types of fucked up shit I'll do just to be with him. Even if it's just physical... to *him*.

It's more than physical to me, but that only makes things more complicated. The fact that we're fucking alone is liable to destroy lives and hurt people, but I just *can't stop*. It's to the point where I just committed a terrible, awful act of sacrilege... And I'm barely even batting an eye.

I'm sure I'm going to Hell.

"I'm sorry..." I whisper, "I'm sorry I'm not the man You thought I was. I'm sorry I'm not... *good*."

Tate comes sauntering back, and I can immediately tell he wants to bolt. Fidgeting around in place, eyes flicking to the door.

Standing up with a sigh, I grab my shirt and slip it back on, buttoning it up slowly. There's nothing I can do to keep him from running off... Shy of tying him up in the basement, I have no way of keeping Tate Eckhart, a fact that feels every bit like a knife between the ribs.

"I'm glad you found me," I tell him quietly, scooping up the flowers. "I really... needed you today."

"I'm... um..." His eyes fling around the room like he can't say what he wants to while looking at me. "I'm glad I got to see you, too."

My lashes flutter. *Fuck*, I want to hold him so bad right now. Just cling to him and never let go. But I'm afraid he'll push me away, and it'll hurt too bad.

Still, I can't stop from inching closer. I've already proven myself unable to play it cool.

I push into his space, and he doesn't back away. So I brush my fingers through his hair, to which he releases a shivery breath.

"It's getting late..." I mumble. "I'm sorry if I kept you from your Sunday night pampering again."

His lips quirk, but he visibly crushes it. "Actually, I'm working from home tomorrow, so..."

"Oh..."

"I'm back in Santa Fe on Tuesday for a big meeting," he says, as if he might just be making conversation. But then his eyes lift to mine. "I'll be at my condo tomorrow, though..."

My forehead lines. "In Corona?"

He nods. "Uh-huh..." He swallows visibly. "So... maybe if you wanted to... come by..." His voice is so low I can barely hear him.

"What was that?" I snap teasingly, and he scowls.

"You can come to my place," he mutters, then adds, "If you *want*, I mean. Like, if you're not... busy." He sighs, rubbing his eyes like he's exhausted. "Jesus, this is annoying. Never mind. I give up."

Laughing, I meld our bodies together, cupping his jaw with one hand, brushing him with sunflowers in the other. "Let's try that again, Trouble."

He glares at me, but when I raise my brow, his eyes soften and he takes a breath, vibrating some palpable insecurity. "Lance... would you like to stay over at my place tomorrow?"

My heart is practically exploding out of me. I'm instantly swept away, like we're on a magic carpet or something.

"See? Was that so hard?" I smirk, and his jaw tenses.

"I'm seconds from withdrawing the invitation," he grumbles. But I feel his fingers ghosting over my lower back.

"I would *love* to stay over at your place tomorrow, baby," I tell him in a confident rasp that has his eyes falling shut and a tiny hum creeping from his lips.

My mouth brushes his, a tender kiss overflowing with so many things I never knew a kiss could hold. Tate kisses me back, leaning into me much more than he usually allows himself to. His arms circle my waist, and he clutches me to him, panting while our tongues touch and we just float in this mystifying well of illustrious sensation.

And this time, when I go to break the kiss, he's fluttering like he's not ready for it to stop.

"Do you—" his voice starts as a bated breath before he gulps, "—wanna come over now?" A chuckle rumbles out of me, my smile damn near breaking my face the way my heart is about to break my ribs. Our faces inch back, eyes reopening as my thumb slides over his puffy bottom lip. "Last time, you asked if I wanted you to stay…"

"Did you?" I stifle my crazy-person smile.

"No…" he huffs, so clearly lying, and I find it beyond adorable.

"But this time you do…?"

He gapes at me for a moment, like he's totally out of his element. "Do *you?*"

"Baby," I hum, chest buzzing with delight while I caress his jaw, combing fingers through his dark hair. "There is nothing I want more in the world than to stay with you. But we should probably play it safe, right?"

He blinks at me, nodding without much conviction.

"My wife knows I'm here," I go on. "She's probably already wondering why I'm not back yet."

"She sounds annoying," he mutters, and I chuckle.

"I'll come over tomorrow," I tell him with another soft peck to his full lips. "We'll spend the whole night together. No pool houses, or cars, or churches… Just me and you, in your bed." A hushed growl of anticipation moves up his throat. "How's that sound?"

At last, he graces me with one of his Tate smirks, though this one seems brighter than usual; framed by a nervous excitement I haven't witnessed in fifteen years.

Trouble

"So... a good old-fashioned, friendly sleepover?" His brow lifts. "Like when we used to crash at Justin's because we were too drunk to make it back to our dorms."

I laugh, then bite my lip. "Exactly. Only this time, I won't be afraid to make a move."

He grins. "You mean, you're bringing your A-game?"

I shake my head. "Mm-mm, baby... I'm bring my D-game."

Chapter Eighteen
Tate

ere's something about me...

H I don't typically have *guests* in my condo.

I don't host dinner parties, or really any kinds of parties, for that matter. Even the sex parties I've been to take place *off campus*, so to speak. On the rare occasion that I bring random hook-ups here, it's more of a *wham, bam, thank you, man* type situation.

In theory, it's because I'm really not here all that often. Traveling for work keeps me in hotels, or at my place in New York. Mostly the penthouse in Santa Fe. Altogether, I probably spend a week or two here each month, give or take. So the last thing I'm trying to do with my limited time in this condo is entertain company.

The *real* reason, though, as I'm sure you can guess from my blatant commitment allergy, is that there's no one I like enough to have cozying up in my place. It's very much the epitome of a bachelor pad. In fact, all of my places are. They're designed for me and me alone, with the exception of guys I bring over just long enough for them to give me the business before I kick 'em to the curb.

Sometimes I let them take a shower... But only if I'm in there too.

Actually, the last time someone stayed over was when Ryan showed up here on Christmas Eve. *And we all remember how that turned out...*

Suffice it to say, me inviting Lance to spend the night is exactly as uncharacteristic and bizarre as it seems. And because of how infrequently it happens, I'm feeling a tad edgier than usual.

Trouble

Why did I invite him over again??
I'm still a bit fuzzy on the details...

I remember us boning in the church... And how spectacularly filthy, unholy and fuck-tastic it was. I mean, we got it on in God's house... While He was watching.

Doesn't get much freakier than that.

Then I remember Lance telling me that story about the sunflowers, looking all rumpled and sexy, talking about Greek mythology, like the hottest, nerdiest golden-haired giant to ever exist.

And the next thing I knew, he was touching my face and kissing me, and I was practically begging him to come over.

When the hell does that happen?? Seriously... I'm really asking!

I've done nothing but think about Lance Hardy since the moment he popped back up out of nowhere, and now he's got me doing things I *never* do... Chasing him all over the place, showing up at his house and his job, inviting him to stay over at my condo like some needy fool who's desperate for a *boyfriend*. It makes no sense...

Why is it so easy for me to be casual with literally everyone else in the world?

What is it about this guy that makes me feel like I'm nineteen again??

Is it just because we used to be friends? And good ones, at that. I'd considered him a person I could trust back then; someone who knew my dreams, my fears, my deepest, darkest secrets. And he definitely still knows all those things... Let's be real, he's not exactly the type to forget stuff.

Or is it because, once upon a time, I thought, for a very brief lust-driven moment, he could be something more?

I've been trying hard to keep things easygoing between us, but I feel like the more I fight wanting to be around him, the stronger the urge becomes. It doesn't even feel like I'm in control of my own actions anymore.

I'm being guided by a need I don't understand...

Lifting my pen to my lips, I suck in a long drag, holding it, then expelling pungent smoke into the air. I'm sitting in a chair on my outdoor terrace, smoking and staring. The weather is beautiful, summer heat fading as the sun goes down between the other buildings in the complex.

My phone rests on the table in front of me, still open to the text from an hour ago, telling me he was on his way. We never really discussed what time he would come over, and honestly, I have no idea what'll happen once he's here.

Of course, we'll have sex. That's a given. But my concern lies *in between* the fucking and sucking. Even if I keep him inside me for a majority of his time here, we'll probably still need to stop and, like, eat, or use the bathroom.

What will it be like when we're not preoccupied by getting each other off?

My mind drifts to a memory from a year-or-so ago...

I was sitting right here, at this very table, smoking, like I am right now. Only I wasn't alone. There was a hot, heartbroken twenty-one-year-old sitting opposite me, staring off into space, like the state of his existence was so bleak, he could barely even fathom how he'd wound up here.

I *hate* admitting this to myself, let alone anyone else, which is why it's something I've held so close to my chest it's basically woven itself into my fibers. But the reason I invited Ryan Harper over here that time he called me, all torn-up and so clearly devastated from the loss of something I didn't even understand at the time, was that I actually... kind of... liked him.

Just a little, okay?? Let's not make a federal case out of it.

Here I'd thought I was being sneaky and hilarious, sleeping with my best friend's niece's boyfriend. What I *didn't* anticipate, though, was him being so cool, and sweet, and fun... With that insatiable curiosity I love in former straight guys, and a dick that just wouldn't quit.

Seriously, it did not want to quit fucking me. That dick was working overtime...

Needless to say, I unwittingly inserted myself into something that ultimately got me punched in the face by a dude I've known since I was twelve.

That's what I get for playing with fire. It was my own damn fault, which is why I *should* fucking know better. Sleeping with Ryan while he was hung up on Ben isn't *exactly* the same thing as getting involved with Lance, but they're different branches on the same general tree.

Lance is married, and not that I even want to think about it, but he doesn't seem like he actively *hates* it.

They never leave their wives, it's just a fact. And now that I've thrown myself at him on more than one occasion, why would he? He knows he can just keep fucking me on the side, lying to his wife—which is clearly part of the thrill—while keeping his boring, religious lifestyle intact for the rest of the world to see.

Sure, he talks a big game, about wanting me more than he wants her, and us *belonging* together, but those are just words. Actions will always speak louder. Regardless of whether Lance Hardy seems enamored with me when we're together, he still has a whole ass reason for leaving me back in the day that I barely understand, and it's enough to keep him rooted in his denial, forever locked into his *image* of the small-town preacher with the beautiful wife and the cozy house in the suburbs surrounded by sunflowers.

Gaze drifting across the terrace, I admire mine; the pot of sunflowers he sent me, all faces aimed in the direction of the sun. *Just like Lance said...*

Clytie following Apollo... The one who got away.

Chasing after something that will never belong to you... I know the feeling.

I hear the buzzer for my intercom from inside, and my heart leaps up into my throat. Naturally, I swallow it back down where it belongs, annoyed that it's being a spazzy fool, forcing myself to meander as slowly as possible to the door.

"Who is it?" I stifle a smirk with my finger on the intercom button.

"Special delivery." Lance's voice comes over the speaker, and I hate how much my stomach is already flipping and flopping.

"Hmm... I didn't order anything." I continue being a brat, because I can't not.

"You got me," he rumbles a sigh. "But while I have you, are you aware that Jesus Christ died for your sins?"

A laugh bursts out of me. "Oh God... I told you people I didn't want any more of those pamphlets!"

He giggles, a sound that's somehow growly and cheerful at once. "Really?? Not even if they're being brought up in my pants...?"

"Idiot," I murmur through my own chuckles, buzzing him up.

Pacing for the two minutes it takes the elevator to reach my floor, I'm radiating nervous energy. I have no idea what to expect from this little rendezvous.

Sex is one thing. A thing that makes sense for my current lifestyle. But my fuck-friend staying the night??

I didn't smoke anywhere near enough weed for this...

A knock on my door brings my pulse to a rabid thump. And when I open it, I feel an instant flush in my face that makes me want to hit myself.

"Hey, Trouble." Lance shoots me with a smile that's somehow shy and oozing swagger at the same time.

"Hi, Sunshine," I grumble. Trying not to sound too breathy has me overcompensating with aloofness.

I motion for him to come in, but he doesn't really make it. He takes one step, and then he's pinning me to the doorway, dropping his lips onto mine before I even have time to process what's happening.

"*Fuck*, baby, I missed you," he hums, fisting my shirt and my hair while his mouth overpowers mine.

"Mmmff..." The very uncool sound flees me, my arms lying limp at my sides.

I'm hypnotized. Transfixed. The way he kisses me is like... *Wow.*

I know for a *fact* I've never been kissed like this before, by anyone but him. Like he's sucking out all of my hesitations and internal hang-ups, replacing them with nothing but *yearning*. Physical, yes, but also... a longing for something deeper.

Some crap that only *he's* ever made me want. And I feel stupid all over again.

But *good* stupid... if that makes any sense.

Surely, it doesn't.

My hands finally spring to action, but only enough to grip the waist of his jeans. He purrs into my mouth, biting and sucking, feeding me his tongue, *slowly*, like it's my reward for being a good boy.

Goddamn... I'm so fucking hard right now.

"See? I don't need words." He grins on my lips. "The way you're kissing me and trembling is your way of saying... *I missed you too.*"

"Don't be a buzzkill, Hardy," I huff, body melted to the wall as he chuckles, brushing his lips on mine.

When we finally pull apart, I have to get my bearings for a second, which is long enough for him to duck out into the hallway and pick up a paper bag.

My brows furrow. "What's that?" His head slants, and my chest tightens. "You didn't bring me... anything. Did you?"

"Why?" He smirks. "Would that be bad?"

I shrug. And he chuckles, sauntering past me inside the condo like he owns the place. I'm frowning as I close the door, not without first peering out into the hall to make sure none of my nosy neighbors were watching that little interaction.

Piss off, Mrs. Federman. My gentleman callers are none of your concern.

Lance is already in my kitchen, setting the bag down on the marble island. He peeks at me before pulling out some flowers.

I roll my eyes, pursing my lips, because there's no way I'm setting this moronic smile free.

"For you, my beautiful, stubborn man," he croons, shoving them at me.

I take them with a huff, no choice but to admire them, since they're in my arms and all. There are a few more sunflowers, sort of floppier than the ones he gave me last time. Plus, some pink and purple ones that smell amazing. I have no clue what they are, but I'm sure Lance does.

I'm sure he knows all about how to grow them, what their meanings are, and any funny little anecdotes that make them seem like more than just *flowers*.

He's... a hot botany nerd? Is that a thing??

"Thank you..." I mumble, feeling like a red-faced buffoon, clutching a bouquet of wildflowers to my chest.

Okay, but why am I getting all squirmy when he brings me flowers?? I'm not a fifteen-year-old girl going on a first date.

"You're welcome." Lance shows me a polite grin, before proceeding to remove more things from his bag.

I can't even help how I'm gaping at him like he's lost his mind.

"Steaks..." I mutter.

"Uh-huh." He nods. "And potatoes. Asparagus. Plus, all the ingredients for my famous béarnaise sauce." He winks at me. "Hope you're hungry."

Fluttering. I think that's what *every* part of my body is doing right now. Especially my eyelashes. Blinking and blinking, I haven't the slightest clue how to process this.

"Wait..." I'm pretty sure my eyebrows are in my hairline. "You're going to... cook? Here??"

"As perceptive as ever," he teases. But I'm still just standing here, gawking like he just pulled human meat out of that bag. He chuckles, head tilting in puzzled amusement. "It's alarming to me that the idea of someone cooking a meal for you gets this kind of reaction."

Swallowing, I shake myself out of it. "Yea, well... *usually,* when guys come over, the menu consists of but one word... I'll give you a hint. It starts with *s* and ends with *ex.*"

"Oh, I'm familiar with the concept," he counters, shuffling around in my kitchen, opening drawers and cabinets, locating things I didn't even know I had. "Worry not, my darling Trouble. I assure you we'll get good use out of that word for dessert." He gives me a sultry look. "And most likely breakfast, too."

Chills sheet my skin, but I ignore it, watching him take out knives and pans.

Is that a freaking garlic press??

"Okay, have you been in here before??" I gasp, and he laughs.

Stepping over to him, my eyes widen at the sight of him deflowering my pristine kitchen, which has only ever been used when I make smoothies. Or sometimes toast.

"Have *you*?" he retorts.

"I didn't know you were going to... do this." I gulp, hovering anxiously.

He peeks at me. "You thought I was only coming over for sex?"

Well... yea. I shrug.

Lance sighs, rolling up his sleeves. "This is a date, Trouble, whether you like it or not. So I'm going to make you dinner, you're going to eat, and then I'm going to spend the rest of the night between your legs, feeding you in *other* ways." He faces me, propping his hip against the counter. "You think you can handle that?"

The way I've been completely flipped upside down is making me lightheaded.

I nod subtly, and he grins, poking me on the nose with his fingertip.

"Good. Because I'm starving, for dinner *and* dessert. I'm gonna get started on this first, unless you wanna give me a tour or something?"

I shake my head. "Seems like you're already more than comfortable here..."

His smile widens. "I can make myself at home anywhere you are, love."

Did I hit my head?? I feel concussed.

I guess expecting him to show up and make a beeline for the bedroom was foolish on my part. Lance Hardy doesn't behave the way normal guys do. He's an aberration.

Still, I didn't predict *this*... Him wanting to cook for me. I'm so thrown off, all I can do is stare at him while he opens up packages of ingredients and starts chopping things.

"Do you, uh... need any help?" I ask hesitantly, not that I'd know how to help him if he did.

Of course, he calls me out on my insincere offer. "In college, you could barely heat up Top Ramen." He sneers. "Has that changed?"

I shoot him a salty look. "*Actually*, it has." He lifts his brows, intrigued. "I can make grilled cheese. *And* I'll have you know, I've become quite the master at heating up Eggo Waffles."

He laughs, and my insides quiver.

Damn him.

"Tell you what..." He pauses what he's doing to slide a possessive hand onto my ass, pulling me closer. "Why don't you pour yourself a drink and stand there looking pretty." He pats me hard on the butt, and I hum. "I've got this."

Trouble

Attempting to scowl isn't really working. I'm pretty sure I just look horny and obsessed. He leans in to press a soft kiss on my jaw.

And I'm melting, like a slice of garlic butter on a thick, juicy filet mignon he's making... for *me*.

❋

As much as I wanted to resist it, I'm feeling beyond nice right now.

I killed two and a half scotches while Lance was cooking, and two glasses of red with dinner—I opened this crazy expensive bottle of Bordeaux I got as a gift from a client, mainly for myself, since Lance continues to insist he doesn't drink anymore. I poured him a glass, but I've only seen him take two sips.

Anyway, the booze mixed with the weed from earlier, and the general high of being on an honest to God *date* with Lance Hardy, have managed to dial what few inhibitions I do have way down.

The food was fantastic. *Who knew the dude could cook better than most of the gourmet chefs I've paid to feed me?*

Really, I shouldn't be surprised by any of Lance's hidden talents. He's always been an enigma, and it seems like in the time we were apart, he's only gotten more interesting, which is unfortunate for my attempts at down-playing his attractiveness.

We've already been talking for hours, and I'm still desperate for more. I don't remember the last time I felt this needy for *conversation*...

Actually, I do. *It was fifteen years ago.*

None of this bodes well for *keeping things casual*, but I'm drunk, and fuzzy, and on a date with a purely *fascinating* married pastor who's still the exact same person I used to call my friend, only somehow... different.

The sun has set, and we're sitting outside on the terrace. I'm smoking, and Lance is lounging on the chaise, watching me.

"Seriously, though," he starts with a relaxed grin. "No one's *ever* made you dinner before?"

"Obviously, people have made me dinner." I roll my eyes. "In restaurants. When I pay them." He chuckles, shaking his head. "No, I mean Jacob and Laura do. Jess usually cooks every time we all go over for dinner parties or holidays..."

His deep gaze seems permanently fixed on me. "They're your family."

It sounds like maybe it was supposed to be a question, but there's no need. He knows the answer.

213

He knows I have no *actual* family, aside from my mother, who I don't see that often. My friends have always been my family.

"The Lockwoods pretty much took me in," I murmur after swallowing another gulp of oaky red. "We had to lean on each other a lot. Especially when they were kids and their parents died." I glance down at my glass, swirling the liquid around while I take a drag from my cigarette. "It was a tough time." My eyes lift. "But you already know all of this..."

"You're right," he hums. "I do."

I let out a steady exhale. "Other than that, *no*. No man has ever prepared a meal for me before."

His lips twitch. "Whose fault is that?"

I suppress a grin. "I feel like you're insinuating that it's mine, but I don't see how that's possible. I'm a delight."

He laughs softly. "I'm just saying, I highly doubt no man has not *wanted* to wine and dine you. You just never gave them the chance."

"You complaining about that, Hardy?" I cock a brow. "Because the way I see it, you get to own this *first*. You must be pretty pleased."

"It's only fair..." He smirks. "Seeing as how you've stolen so many of mine."

The way we're talking feels light, but the topic of conversation is venturing into heavier territory. It's catching me, but I'm still buzzed, so I'm not overthinking as much as I probably should be.

As soon as my cigarette is out, he nods me over. "Come here."

Why do I love the way he orders me around so much? That commanding tone and that dominant sparkle in his eyes that sneaks out from behind his quiet layers. It makes me weak in the knees when I thought they were much sturdier.

Standing up from my seat, I take the couple of steps to the chaise and plop down next to Lance. He immediately folds me into his big arms, tugging me by the waist until I'm lying, curled up against his side. And because it's the easiest thing to do, I nestle in even closer, resting my head on his shoulder.

It just feels so *good*, lying with him out here. I don't want to be loving this as much as I am.

"Tell me about the kid," Lance's voice rumbles into me. "Ryan."

My toes wiggle at how obviously jealous he is. "What about him?"

"Cut it out, Trouble," he scolds, though I can hear his grin. "You know what I mean... How did you manage sleeping with a guy your best friend's brother and sister-in-law ended up marrying?"

I sigh, "You know Ben and Jessica's daughter, Hailey?" He nods. "Well, Ryan was dating her first. Like, before any of us knew him. She brought him home for Thanksgiving, and *apparently*... he and Ben started having an affair."

Lance is quiet for a moment before he breathes, "Wow... juicy."

I chuckle. "Yea. But none of us knew about it. That part is important. They were hiding it, I guess... Trying to act like it never happened, when I ran into Ryan at this sleazy bar outside Santa Fe. And ya know... one thing led to another..."

He shifts. "Okay... So, you hooked up with him, and then he got together with Ben?"

"Not *exactly*."

"Tate..."

"I don't know the specific timeline of how things happened between them. All I know is that Ryan showed up here a few weeks later like a lovesick puppy, and... Whatever, I was bored. So we had lots of sex, I brought him to the Lockwood's Christmas Eve party, which turned out to be a bad idea. I got punched in the face and we left."

His fingers stop running up and down my back. "Someone *punched* you??" He sounds outraged, and I snicker. "Who??"

"Ben," I huff at the memory. "Maybe I was pushing his buttons a little..."

He's silent again for a second before he snorts, "That sounds like you."

"Yea, well, it was just *so* clear that Ryan was infatuated with him, and Ben was acting like a stubborn idiot. If I hadn't intervened, he might not have admitted his feelings. I deserve, like, a medal or something."

"Oh, yea. I'm sure you're the hero in that story," he scoffs.

"Anyway... Ryan stayed here that night, and shit was definitely tense. The next morning, he left, and I didn't see him again until Pride. Right after I ran into you."

Lance grasps my chin, tilting my face so I'm forced to look at him. "Did you like him?"

I'm purposely keeping my gaze as snarky as possible. "Not to be a broken record here, but it was just *sex*, Hardy. We fucked a lot, that's it."

"That's not what I asked you..."

My chest tightens, and I purse my lips to hide the fidgets from talking about this. "*Ugh.* No... I mean, he's cool and everything, but it... it wasn't like that."

"I thought you never invite guys to stay over," he mumbles, intense vulnerability in his eyes. "It just... seems way less casual than your usual M.O."

"Except that I have a weakness for guys I can't have." I glare at him. "Clearly."

"So you *did* have feelings for him..."

"Why am I the one being scrutinized here??" I grunt defensively. "I think it's your turn to answer some questions, *Pastor*. Let's start with, where does your wife think you are tonight?"

"With you," he answers, fully serious.

I stare at him for a moment before I scoff. "Yea, right."

"I'm not lying," he insists. "I told her I was going out with some of the ASU guys for a birthday party, and that I'd probably end up crashing with you instead of driving home."

My body is reacting in a bunch of strange ways to this information. I'm nervous, and confused, excited and upset, pleased *and* displeased... I'm all the fuck over the place.

"Okay, well, that's still not the truth," I mutter.

"I know," he sighs.

This whole situation is throwing me off my game. Having him here, *talking*—not fucking—the obvious jealousy coming from both sides, the nostalgia of being reunited with someone who meant so much to me before, and the extreme satisfaction of falling into whatever this is with him being as easy as breathing.

I can't tell if my mind is playing tricks on me, or if this is really happening. And because of that, I find myself wanting to ask...

"Do you..." My voice fades, and I grunt, "Never mind." Lance pulls my face to his, kissing my lips softly. Dragging out the rest of my stupid question. "Do you love her...?"

Ew... I hate how much I sound like I care right now. Like my happiness is riding on how he answers this fucking question. It's so stupid...

"I... can't tell," Lance replies timidly. "Which probably means I don't. I think I love her as a friend... She's a great person. But it's just so complicated."

"How?" My forehead lines. "How is it complicated?"

"I have no other frame of reference for that emotion..." He gapes at me, running his thumbs along my jaw. "Just one. And nothing else compares to that."

My skin is suddenly all hot and itchy.

"Are you sleeping with her...?" I have no idea why I'm asking him this. I don't really want to know if he's been plowing his wife in between plowing me.

"We haven't since before Pride," he says, and somehow, I know he isn't lying. But it only makes me feel better in terms of jealousy, not clarity.

"Hardy, I just..." I squirm out of his hold. "This is all a bit much. I thought you were going to come over and we'd just fuck until we passed out. But now we're talking about this heavy shit, and I'm just... not equipped for this kinda thing. You know that."

"I *don't*, though, Tate. I don't *know* that." He grabs my hand to keep me close. "I told you, I know *you*. The you who was my best friend in college. The you who told me I made you happy... before I ran out and ruined everything. That's still *us*, T, regardless of how long ago it was. So I'm sorry if this makes you nervous, but you have to know I've never felt about another person the way I've felt about you, from back then to right fucking now."

Honestly, I might be having a panic attack.

The words he's speaking are so sincere, as is the twinkle in his dark brown eyes. It's confusing as shit, because I just don't understand why it took fifteen years for him to say this to me.

Blinking at him, I focus all my energy on ensuring my voice doesn't shake. "Then why did you get married?"

He takes in a breath, letting it out slowly. "Desiree showed up in my life when I was fucking *miserable*, Tate. She was the first piece to the puzzle of my new life. And it's a good life, I won't lie. It's nice, and safe and comfortable... No trouble."

I'm chewing on my lower lip, fizzling angst swarming my gut like rabid butterflies of uncertainty.

"If I never ran into you at Pride, I could've lived that life forever," he goes on. "I'm *sure* I could have. But then I never would've felt this." He presses my hand up to his chest. "The way my heart races when I'm with you... The way you thrill me to my bones, and make me feel alive. I've never gotten that from anyone or anything but you. So the thing is, whether it's wrong or not, turns out I don't *want* to live a life without trouble..."

Fuck me...

This is *so* overwhelming, I don't know what to think, or say. I'm just sitting here, frozen.

And sure, maybe there's a part of me that wants to just give in, because fighting it is *really* difficult. But he's also not the only one who's built himself up a nice, comfortable life. They're different, sure, but the purpose is the same.

"I... I don't know if I can be... what you want," I tremble out the words. "You don't know that it ever would've worked with us. The night you left split us in two different directions... We're too far apart now."

His eyes hold me with a knowing sparkle. "Tate, look... I know you're pushing me away on purpose, because you're scared, and I get that. I'm scared too. But I just want you to know that I didn't choose her over you. I settled for her because I couldn't have you."

A growl of frustration leaves my lips from the flood of emotions crashing through my chest that I'm not used to dealing with, and I drop my forehead to his. "I hate that I still don't understand why you left..."

"I know, baby." He cups my jaw, lips parted while he shivers, like he wants to tell me more. To explain himself.

And this time *I* kiss *him*, stopping it before whatever it is can derail this even more. Sucking on his lips, I'm desperately fleeing to him like he's my safe haven from all the bullshit he's also responsible for.

The truth is, I'm not sure if any explanation of what happened back then would make me feel better right now. The past is the past, and we can't change it. He dug himself into this hole and he'll have to find his way out.

For now, all I can do is take the parts of him that are available to me, believing his words that they're the important parts; the parts he's been saving for me.

"This wasn't supposed to be an emotional bullshit night," I mumble on his lips.

"I know, baby, I'm sorry," he rasps in between kisses that are getting hotter and deeper by the second, his hands sliding down to cup my ass. "Why don't we migrate into the bedroom, and I'll make it up to you."

"Mmm... what about dessert?" I writhe into him, purring at the feel of how hard he is already.

Lance nips my bottom lip. "You *are* dessert, Trouble... My favorite sweet treat."

"I'll never say no to being eaten," I murmur, and he chuckles.

Before I can even process what's happening, he's standing up and hoisting me—rather effortlessly, I might add—over his shoulder, as if I'm not six feet, one hundred and eighty-five pounds, carrying me inside while I force my startled glee into annoyance.

"This is fully ridiculous." My voice is choppy from the way he's manhandling me. And you won't catch me admitting it, but I just know my face is flushed because I kinda like it... Lance Hardy hauling me around like his *property*.

"No backtalk," he scolds, smacking me on the ass.

I yelp, then huff, "You're going the wrong way. That's the guest room."

"Oops. Sorry... I didn't go this way when I broke in."

A laugh bursts out of me, and he chuckles, patting my butt some more. Inside my bedroom, he tosses me down onto the bed, immediately dropping his hands down on either side of my hips to cage me in.

"What a dork," I hum breathlessly, biting my lip while I gaze up at him with desire I can't hide anymore.

"Mmm... You like it, don't you, sexypants?" He grins, eyes falling to my mouth.

"More or less." I lift my foot to run it up his leg.

He eyes me hungrily for a moment before whispering, "Strip."

He straightens, staring down at me with his brow raised. I'm fully gaga for the growly demands, and the cocky dominance that comes out of him when we're alone and being naughty. In my mind, I'm choosing to believe this side of him only shows up for me.

I make quick work of removing my clothes, expecting him to do the same. But he doesn't. Instead, he wanders around the room, poking at things.

"There's something I'm dying to do for you," he says, glancing at me over his shoulder. "We should probably put a towel down."

My lips slope into a wicked grin. "Oh *my*... Are we gonna get *messy*?" He smirks and nods. A chill runs through me. "There are extra linens in the hall closet..."

Lance wanders off, and I'm just lying on my bed, naked, with my dick throbbing from the anxious thrill in my bloodstream. He comes back with a sheet, spreading it out over my bed.

Then he points. "Lie there. On your stomach."

"'Kay..." I breathe, crawling to the middle of the bed.

"Now, I need..." His voice fades as he goes to my nightstand, opening the top drawer.

His eyebrow cocks, and my face flushes. "That's not mine. I don't know how any of that stuff got there!"

He chuckles, rather erotically, rifling through my personal... *belongings*, if you know what I mean.

"Wow, you have no sense of boundaries, do you?" I mutter, fidgeting in place.

He pouts at me. "But I wanna know what's in your sex drawer..."

"Are you looking for something specific?" I grin.

"There's no shortage of goodies in here..." he murmurs, wide eyes returning to the contents of the drawer. "Please tell me you use this stuff alone."

"I'd rather not lie to you, Hardy."

Shooting me a glare, he picks up a bottle, stepping over to the bed. "My plan was to pamper you... But now I'm thinking you need to be punished."

"I'm okay with either." I blink up at him.

Lance tugs his shirt over his head, tossing it onto the floor. He kneels on the bed behind me, stuffing my face down into the sheet. I grunt, and my dick pulses. "We'll come back to your extensive collection of sex toys. For now, I want you to relax, baby." I hear him opening the bottle, positioning himself over my thighs. "You have a big, important meeting tomorrow. Let me get you nice and loose."

"How dare you," I gasp.

"Shhh..." he rumbles, dropping warm, slick hands onto my shoulder blades. "No more talking, troublemaker." His fingers brush up my skin, and I purr as he leans over me to whisper in my ear, "Your man's gonna rub you down."

Sweet Caroline... This is already so damn hot.

Kneading my shoulders with his strong hands, I'm unable to keep my eyes from drooping shut. I can't believe he's actually giving me a massage... Another thing I've never gotten from a man. Except the ones I pay, of course. At spas and whatnot...

The occasional bathhouse in Amsterdam and Ibiza.

But this is already so much better than that. Because this is *Lance Hardy*. A guy who's most certainly never massaged another man before, rubbing me with baby oil, digging his fingers into pressure points that have me groaning uncontrollably.

"Fuuuck..." The words flees my lips into the bed.

"That feel good, beautiful?" he breathes, pressing into my muscles just hard enough that it aches, relieving my stress in the best way.

"Mmm*yeaa*," I moan, liquifying beneath him. "Magic fingers..."

He chuckles seductively, working down my back slowly. I'm being lulled into a trance by his hands. When he gets to my ass, I'm so blissed out, I barely recognize his sneaky fingers grazing the crack.

But he doesn't go inside. He massages down the backs of my thighs, then my calves, bending my knees so he can rub my feet.

"You have nice feet," he mumbles, kneading my arch.

"Mhmm..."

"They're so big," he sighs, pushing his crotch into my leg.

I can feel his erection, big and solid, through his pants, like it's begging to be freed. And the idea that he can become so turned on just by rubbing me has my hips subtly humping into the bed.

"The things I could do to every inch of your body, Tate..." He sighs, dropping my foot.

The unmistakable sound of a zipper sends a zap through my loins. His shifting around tells me he's getting naked, and now my tranquility is joined by unbridled excitement and fervent lust.

Lance squirts a generous helping of oil onto my back. And suddenly, he's draping himself over me, dragging his chest along my slippery flesh.

"*Uhhh...*" I groan at the feeling of his firm pectorals writhing into my back, like he's massaging my body with his. "Fuck, *Lance...*"

"You feel so good, T," he hums in my ear, sucking my lobe between his lips. His erection settles in between my cheeks, and I purr. "Slippery wet and *so damn hot.*"

Arching my back, I push my ass against his crotch, whimpering when his big dick wedges deeper between my ass, his velvety shaft sliding over my hole. "Let me massage your cock with my ass, baby..."

"Mmm *fuck*, you know just what I want, baby," he croons while I rock my hips, forward and back, stroking his every rigid inch between my cheeks. "That's it, love. Use that sweet ass to stroke my dick."

"Wetter..." I plead on a hoarse breath.

He lifts a bit, and I feel a gush of warm oil being drizzled below my waist, dribbling and flowing into the crack of my ass. Squeezing it rough in two handfuls, his dick is slipping and sliding in between, making obscenely wet sounds.

My balls are thrumming, cock leaking where it's trapped between my abs and the bed. *Those hands...* They're just so *strong*, and *large. Manly as fuck...* Kneading down my ass, my thighs and my calves once more.

He grabs my ankles in both hands and pushes them forward to bend my knees, holding my legs apart as he drags his cock, ever so *slowly*, up and down between my ass cheeks. As he draws back, the swollen head glides over my hole, and I whimper.

"I might just... slip in you, baby," he whispers raggedly, his voice made of burning arousal. "By accident."

"Uhhm *please*," I gasp, not giving a fuck how needy I sound.

"But *baby*, I'm not *supposed* to," he taunts in a salacious tone. "This is just an—*mmm*—innocent massage."

He's really teasing my hole with the tip of his dick now, and I'm going out of my mind. I need that thing inside my ass right this instant or I might die, rocking my hips back against him to try to get it in. But clearly, he's toying with me on purpose.

At this point, I'm not above begging. *No shame in my game.*

"Please... *Please please*, Lance," I whimper. "Just... fucking *fuck me*, baby. I need it... Fuck my ass like only you do."

Lance growls, yanking me closer by my legs until his dick is *really* crammed in there. When his hips rear back, that sweet, fat curve nudges my rim, and I shudder, relaxing my muscles as much as possible. And because of the abundance of baby oil coating his dick and running like a river down to my balls, it actually slips inside me. Just the tip. Sucked right in.

"*God yesss...*" my voice snaps.

"Oh, no... Would you look at that," he hums. "We're so *wet*, my dick accidentally slid inside your tight little hole..." I can hear a wicked grin in his breathy brogue as his fingers caress my calf muscle. "How very unprofessional..."

"It's all good, dawg," I croak, shivering and trying to play along with his little game, though my hips are moving in an obvious, shameless attempt to get him deeper. "*Fffuck*, maybe just... push it in more..."

But he's holding me in place by my legs, and he's not moving. Just kneeling the exact distance away from me to keep only the tip of his dick wedged inside my ass. *So I'd say about nine inches, give or take.*

God, baby, you give, I'll take. I'm burning alive right now.

"I should really... focus on this massage," Lance's resolve for this teasing game is audibly cracking, and it's so sexy, I'm leaking everywhere. I love hearing him fall apart for me. "I'm supposed to be... *uhh*, rubbing you down. Not fucking you in the ass."

"Mmf, you're making me crazy," I groan, but he ignores me, picking back up where he left off with the massage.

His fingers work on my muscles, sensually rubbing my feet and my legs, all the while with just the head of his cock resting inside me, buried snugly and beyond frustrating, because all I want is for him to shove it hard and deep. Fill me up with a ravaging drive. But he won't. His hips remain stock still, ensuring his dick stays right where it is.

Fucking torturous man.

"Please, Sunshine..." I resort to begging again, mewling with my fingers digging into the bed. "I'm *throbbing*, baby..."

"I'm sorry, my love." Lance drops my legs and leans over my back. As he does, his dick finally slides in *deep*, every hot, slick inch burrowing into my ass. I cry out of dizzying pleasure with him pouting on the nape of my neck. "I'm doing a bad job of unwinding you. Looks like I'll have to stop..."

Swiftly, he tugs his cock out all the way.

"*Come on*, man..." I whine, shivering and hoarse from the derailed pleasure.

He chuckles, like the sadistic sex monster he is. Then he slaps my ass. "Flip over. I need to do your front."

"Do what to my front...?" I bite my lip, rolling onto my back.

"Massage it, silly." He grins, arching a brow as he settles between my parted thighs. Running his hands up my thighs and hips, he releases a ragged breath. "Look at you..." His fingers graze my erection, and it flinches. "So *big*. All stretched and swollen and dripping sweet like candy for me, baby."

"You should totally suck it," I purr, and he hums.

"I'll get to that, sexy Trouble." His fingers dig into my waist. "But first, lemme praise what's mine."

"Ohh..."

Hands rushing leisurely all over me, he massages his way up my hips, my abs, and my chest, taking his time on my pecs then playing with my nipples. My body has never buzzed so hard in my *entire life*. Seducing me with his touch, he's driving me purely *wild*. Caressing my arms, my hands, then back down my torso, avoiding my dick to knead my balls tenderly.

God, I think I'm gonna come... This feels so frustratingly good.

Suddenly, he's moving back a bit. He grabs my feet and pushes them together. Then he thrusts his cock into the space between my arches...

Fucking my feet.

He's... fucking... my feet.

I'm *falling the fuck apart.*

"Ohh yea, that's fucking good," he groans, eyes fluttering shut, head tipping back.

I bite my lip, watching with hooded lids while he thrusts his giant dick between my feet, *in* and *out*, the head dripping as he goes.

"Lance... I'm gonna *die* if you don't fuck me," I heave. "*Please*, Sunshine, I need you..."

His eyes creep open. "You need me to take care of you, baby?"

I nod frantically. "Yea... Yes, *please*, my God... My ass is fucking *aching* for your big cock."

"Mmm..." he hums, eyes glistening down at me with deviance. "I suppose I could break the rules just this once." He bites his lip, and I breathe through a moan.

Whatever this erotic little game is driving at, I'm here for it. I'm fully positive I've never been so turned on in my life. And the hottest part is that it's only partially role-playing. Most of this is just straight up *Lance Hardy, the secret sex wizard*.

My hands are reaching for him, desperate to pull him closer. Greedy with desire, I curl my fist around my erection. But he smacks it away.

"Uh-uh. No touching," he scolds, finally stopping with the foot fucking to yank me closer. "Lift your hips, baby. Rest this sweet ass on my legs."

Sitting my behind on his thighs while my shoulders are still resting on the bed, he fists his erection. And before I even know what's happening, he's guiding it all the way inside me. Inch by aching inch, barreling into my ass until I'm filled to the brim and seeing stars.

"*Fuck yesss*, Daddy." My back arches and my cock throbs. "Fuck fuck *fuck*, that's good dick."

He growls, "You like it, baby?" I nod fast while he pumps into me. "You like this dick deep in your greedy hole?"

"Fuck me, I love it." My eyes roll back in my head as he fucks into my prostate.

All that teasing and toying and torturous foreplay has brought me right up to the edge. And now he's fucking me, slow, but achingly *deep*, rippling those hips to work his perfect cock in and out. He's *possessing* my body, gripping my waist, shuffling me back and forth like his fucktoy while I'm just gazing up at him with hooded lids, barely containing my lust-drunk fixation.

I can't *believe* I protested fucking face to face before... Because lying on my back while he moves between my legs is seriously an otherworldly pleasure.

"Take this dick baby." *Slap slap slap.* "Take it deep, my perfect little slut."

Fuck, where has his filthy mouth been all my life??

Cries are pouring from my lips on every breath, my hands covering his on my hips. "*Unngh*, L-Lance... You... fuck... so... *good*."

Smacking harder and *harder*. Hole clenching, muscles coiling.

Leaning down abruptly, he slurps my cock between his lips, and my toes curl.

"Oh, fuck me." Shocked at what he's doing, my chin dips, and I watch him in awe as he sucks my dick while pumping me full.

His thrusts are *hypnotic*. He's riding me like a sexy fucking cowboy in a rodeo or something, all the while hunched over, suckling the first couple inches of my cock, jamming into my prostate so thoroughly, it's like he's *literally* fucking the cum out.

I'm... so fucking close...

"Come in my mouth, Tate," he groans over my crown. "I wanna swallow you... Feed it to me, baby, *please*."

My balls draw up, because he's actually *begging* for me to come in his mouth.

This man... This fucking man, I can't...

"Fuck me harder..." I sob. "*Harder harder*, I'm gonna... *come*."

My entire body breaks into chills, the most intense orgasm washing over me like a tidal wave. My ass clamps on his cock as my dick throbs between his soft lips, shooting heavy streams onto his tongue.

He groans while his throat adjusts, swallowing every pulse like he's *dying* for it... For *me*. He's fucking *swallowing* for me, and my head is spinning. I'm sweating and aching and *coming* so fucking hard, I can't breathe.

As soon as I'm done, he sucks up my tired cock, lifting me onto his lap so that I'm upright and straddling him. Gripping my ass, he holds me close, lashing my lips with his tongue. "Ride me, baby. Suck the cum out of my cock with that sweet hole..."

Cupping his jaw, I kiss him fast, pushing my tongue into his mouth to taste myself while I bounce on his lap. Grinding with him all the way inside me, I swivel and stroke, up and down on every rigid inch until he's crying into my mouth.

"Uhh, Tate... holy*fuuuck!*"

I feel his cock bursting inside me, spilling deep while I ride it out. The feeling of him soaking my insides has me clutching him for dear like while even more cum leaks from my dick, dripping all over us.

Fuck... shit... motherfucker...

Multiple... orgasms... can't... breathe...

Where am I??

225

"Sunshine... what are you doing to me?" I whimper breathlessly, brushing my fingers through his soft hair while we both struggle for air, foreheads resting together.

"Just showing you how good we work, my Trouble love," he sighs, voice raspy and as perfectly spent as I feel.

Mission accomplished, pal.

Eventually, he pulls me off his dick, lying me down carefully like I'm his filthy prince. Then he rubs my back, my ass and my legs while I bask in it... This bizarre, *euphoric* feeling.

It's not the first time I've fucked in this bed—not by any means—but it's sure as shit the first time I've been fucked *and* cherished this thoroughly, left feeling this mollified by someone's presence.

It's the first time I've wanted someone to stay.

He belongs here... touching me like this.

"How was the massage?" He lies down next to me, wearing a sleepy grin that's purely gorgeous. "Relaxed?"

Yawning, I nod, touching his chest. "You should always be here..."

I don't even know what I'm saying. But I'm just so *serene* right now.

And I know it's because of him. Not even just the sex, but the way he smells, and feels, and looks at me.

Those brown eyes, reflecting back my own wonder, hold me as tight as his big arms around my waist. And he hums, "I couldn't stay away if I wanted to."

Chapter Nineteen
Tate

"Hold still."

"S-sorry..."

My fingers slide up his wet flesh, cupping the firm, plump cheeks of his peachy butt.

I'm telling you, this guy's ass... Yowza.

He flinches again, and I rumble, "Stop moving, Hardy. You're squirming away from my mouth..."

"Sorry, baby, it's just—*ummff*—intense," he whimpers, then groans. "It tickles—ahh, *Tate!*"

I can't stop the grin from taking over my lips. Lips that are currently buried between the taut cheeks of my sleepover buddy.

Yes, I'm eating Lance's ass. He's never been eaten out before, so naturally, I had to volunteer my services.

After the unbelievably sensual, ball-exploding massage sex last night, we cuddled up in my bed and dozed for a bit. Unsurprisingly, we both woke up in the middle of the night with raging hard-ons, rutting them together like we were sword-fighting. In the dark, he opened my legs and fucked me slow, and I don't want to admit it, but I came so hard I was crying actual tears into my pillow.

We fell asleep again to more tangled cuddling. He actually held me all throughout the night, and not once did I kick him away or wriggle free. I'm going to pretend it was because I was assed out and exhausted from all the delicious fucking, but in the back of my mind, I know that's not the reason.

It felt... good. Really, *really* fucking good. Sleeping in his arms, enveloped by his warmth, the cadence of his heart rocking me deeper and deeper into a lulled slumber so peaceful, I woke up feeling fifteen years younger.

But despite the serenity, waking up with Lance Hardy humming random songs and peppering my neck with kisses was a bit alarming. Mainly because of how easy it feels... Doing this with him. These things I don't do... *Ever.*

Why does this romantic, coupley shit just happen so naturally with him? Honestly, it's as if my body acts this way with him on impulse, and it's so strange I feel like I've been in a fog since last night.

Rather than attempting to figure it all out, though—because that seems like a lot of work—I yanked him into the bathroom for tooth-brushing. He used mine, another super intimate thing that's grossing me out with how easily I offered it to him. Followed, of course, by sexy shower time. Which is where I decided I just couldn't not taste his sweet little virgin *never been licked* ass.

"Sunshine, you're clenching," I giggle, then clear my throat because I sound *way* too smitten right now. "Relax and let me slide it in..."

Propped up against the shower wall, palms flat, ass popped out for me, he peers over his shoulder. "You just mean your tongue... right?"

Grinning, I squeeze his cheeks in my hands, spreading him open and fluttering my tongue over his rim. His eyes fall shut, and he groans.

"Mhm. I'm a bonafide bottom, baby," I rasp into his ass, licking up and down, methodically stroking his hole with my tongue. "But that's not to say I wouldn't enjoy—" my index finger creeps, grazing him until he puckers again, "—popping a digit in here. At some point."

"You can... if you want to," he rumbles, wiggling his hips like he's getting used to the sensation of me loving up on his sweet ass with my mouth. "I trust you to always make me feel *oh so good*, Trouble love."

It's interesting how that statement makes my chest feel like it's full of cotton candy.

"Mmm... Lance Hardy isn't opposed to a finger in the butt," I croon. "Duly noted."

Kissing and kissing, licking and sucking, I get lost in eating him, pushing my tongue into his hole as deep as I can, until his knees start to buckle. And when I'm sure he's nice and wet, saliva running down his balls like a stream, I nudge the tip of my finger into his ass.

Just a little... to see what he does.

"Uhhfuck!" he gasps, rough voice echoing inside my shower stall.

"That okay?" I peek up at him.

He nods fast. "Y-yea... I think... Mmm... I think it feels... nice."

I chuckle, licking around where my finger is probing him. "If you refer to having your ass penetrated as *nice*, you might be a top."

"Keep licking, smart mouth," he purrs. My tongue swirls and swirls, finger moving in and out gently. "*Ohh*... I can only imagine what it would feel like if your dick pushed inside me. Fuck, I might die."

And for the first time in my entire life, the thought of putting my dick in someone lingers for more than a split second.

I just love getting fucked way too much to ever top... But Lance Hardy is a giant, beast of a man. With the tightest, most gorgeous ass I've ever played with.

It might be totally hot to fuck his hole... Ride it deep and come in him... Fuck me, I think I just came a little.

Literally, my balls just throbbed so hard, precum is flowing from my head like it's weeping.

Pushing the images out of my brain to be fantasized about later, I grasp his cock in my left hand, aiming it down between his legs. Painting down his perineum, tonguing his nuts, sucking them, angling my face to slurp them up. He's trembling and I'm high on this, knelt behind him in the shower, feasting on him like he's mine.

Whoa... possessive much?

Focusing on my *job*, I lick down the length of his shaft, so engorged, it's like work holding it downward this way. My lips suckle at the head before I advance, throating his many inches like he's literally feeding it between my lips.

"Fffuck, Tate... your mouth is fucking lethal," he whines, huge body shivering as the water pours down his immaculate frame.

I can feel him relaxing, muscles finally easing up. So I make my move, shoving my finger in deeper and pressing on that spot I'm all too familiar with offering up myself.

As soon as it hits, Lance's entire body convulses. A stream of unintelligible words leaves his lips, his hole clenching so hard on my finger, I can't even move it.

"Tate, *Tate*, fuuuck me, I'm fucking—"

His voice cuts into a garbled cry, his dick spraying cum down my throat like a fucking hose.

In my mind, I'm laughing. Because *yea... seems about right.*

That's God's gift to gay men, Pastor. Proof of why these butts are made for fuckin'.

Gulping him down, I'm reeling. Remembering how sweet he tastes, and how good it feels to swallow for him while he falls apart.

I missed this... Fuck, I missed making him come in my mouth.

All the blowies I've given, and not once do I recall my heart thumping as fast and as desperately as it does with Lance Hardy's perfect dick shooting off between my lips.

It takes me a moment to notice that he's stroking my wet hair, and I'm fingering his hole in tender, almost cherishing motions, the other hand massaging his balls. It's so erotic when he gets off with me.

Hungry, animalistic, with even more passion.

It also takes me a moment to notice that this closeness I feel to him isn't fully terrifying me like it should.

Letting him go, his dick springs out of my mouth with a heavy, tired bob, and I gaze up at him, pulling my finger out of his ass. He blinks down at me, throat dipping in a slow swallow as his fingers grasp my chin.

"How was your breakfast?" he asks, in a deeply commanding tone that has me quivering.

"So good," I breathe. He takes my hand, standing me up, then crowding me until my back is against the wall. "How was yours?"

His lips brush mine. "Life-changing."

I whimper, melting into the stone tiles as he kisses me deep, holding my jaw to keep me still, like he's making sure I don't miss one second of whatever he's trying to profess with his lips on mine.

We stay in the shower, just kissing and panting for minutes on end. Until he finally pries off of me, reacquainting us both with reality.

"I'm sorry, baby," he murmurs quietly, petting my face. "I don't wanna make you late."

My brain is so lust-fogged, I barely even understand what he's saying for a moment. "Oh... right." I blink, clearing my throat. "Big meeting today."

Lance grins, pressing a soft kiss on my bottom lip. Then he hops out of the shower.

What the hell...

This guy is distracting on a molecular level.

Following him out, I can't miss the opportunity to ogle him dripping wet with a towel wrapped around his waist. But it's not until I'm drying off myself that I notice how rock-hard my own cock still is.

Trouble

Padding from the master bath into my bedroom, I find him staring at me, smirking when his eyes fall to the way my dick is tenting my towel.

"You gonna be able to work like that?" He arches a brow.

It makes my nipples hard.

"Wouldn't be the first time I've handled business with full wood," I tease.

He narrows his gaze at my face, and I bite my lip.

God, I love that look. Why is it so much fun to push his buttons??

That crazed, jealous twinkle in his eyes rocks my nuts like an earthquake.

"What time do you have to leave?" His head slants.

"Ten," I answer, glancing at the clock.

It's nine-thirty now, which will leave me just enough time to get dressed, have a juice, and stop for my Starbies on the way to Santa Fe. In all honesty, I should have left last night, but for whatever reason, I decided having a sleepover with Lance in my condo was more important than getting to work early and unfettered.

Nothing is *ever* more important to me than work...

So this is... *peculiar.*

Yea, let's go with peculiar.

"So no time for me to help deflate that...?" His puffy lips twitch at one corner.

Stepping up to him, I touch his chest, tracing the perfect curves of meaty pecs. "I might have a few extra minutes... in the interest of you properly draining my dick. You know, making sure my head is clear and all."

"Right..." he hums, eyeing me with amusement. "Actually, I think I have a better idea."

My fingers brush his nipples. "Listening..."

Lance turns away from me suddenly, going for my nightstand drawer. I watch him in confusion, interest piqued. I'm not sure what his obsession with that drawer is, but I have to assume it's something to do with his jealousy, paired with the fact that he probably doesn't possess a drawer full of sex toys and copious varieties of condoms and lubes in his own home.

When he turns back to me, he's holding up a butt plug. One of the fancy ones, with different stimulation settings that can be controlled by an app on your phone.

I gulp.

"Instead of me getting you off now, I want you to wear this." His eyes sparkle with thrill. "All day."

Blink.

"I'm sorry... I think I blacked out for a second..." My lashes flutter. "Did you just say you want me to wear a plug in my ass *all day*? As in, the entire drive to Santa Fe, at work, during a super important investor meeting...?"

He nods enthusiastically. "Uh-huh. That's what I want."

As insane as it sounds, I can't help how my balls are vibrating like that toy right now.

I've never done this before... Used this specific type of toy at work. And the thought of it is *enticing*, to say the least.

At the same time, this has the potential to completely humiliate me at the office. I mean, that plug can be intense. *What if I can't control myself and I shoot in my pants during the meeting??*

"Hardy, I don't..." My voice trails, and I shake my head. "I don't think I want to be rock-solid with my asshole vibrating during this meeting."

"Hmm... I'm sorry, baby"—he cups my jaw, leaning in to whisper over my lips—"if I made you feel like this was negotiable."

Christ on a carousel, who is this man??

I'm quaking from head to freaking toe right now. The way he's venturing into casual Dom territory has my ass clenching and my dick pointing at him through the towel, as if I asked it who's calling the shots. Who's in control...

Who I *belong* to.

Him, right there. The married guy holding a vibrating butt plug, oozing confident authority over my *anatomy.*

Lance tugs at the towel around my waist until it falls to the floor, pooling at my feet. Then he nods toward the bed. "Chop chop, Trouble. On all fours. Or you'll be late for work." He smirks.

Chewing my lower lip, I find myself following his command without even thinking. I crawl onto my bed on my hands and knees, presenting my ass before him like he owns it.

Okay, who are you kidding?? He so obviously does.

I hear him rifling through my drawer some more, most likely locating the perfect lube. And when he comes up behind me, I'm shaking, fighting to collect my jumbled thoughts and control my shivering breaths.

"Baby..." he croons, swiping a slick finger between my cheeks. "You are *so* beautiful, I can't stand it."

My heart thuds, chest tight and bursting open from his words.

He pushes lube inside me with one finger, then two, working in and out to wet me up and stretch me out, before pressing the smooth object up to my hole. Then he leans over my back, reaching around my body to fist my cock with his left hand.

"Open for me," he growls softly, shoving the plug inside with mirrored grunts, then groans from us both. He bites my shoulder and kisses my neck, sighing, "Good boy."

"Fuck me..." I choke and shudder, the ache of fullness and my body stretching around the toy drawing up my balls something fierce.

Lance teases my cock with his fingers, squeezing out beads of precum. "I love how much harder that just made you." He releases my dick and straightens, patting me on the ass. "You might wanna bring a change of panties just in case."

Glaring at him over my shoulder, I can feel the flush in my cheeks. Over my entire body, in fact. I'm instantly burning alive, which doesn't bode well for this experiment.

He winks at me, and I growl, though it turns into a purr because *goddamn...* this thing feels *intense* already.

Taking my hand, he helps me off the bed to stand up. I wobble for a second, and he chuckles. "Don't worry, baby. You won't be the only one suffering. I'll be going out of my mind all day knowing your ass is full without me."

"Good," I grunt, trying to sass him, though my voice is way too hoarse.

He runs his hands up my chest, touching me sensually. "Under no circumstances are you to come, or remove that until I see you. Your next orgasm comes from *me*, and I want to take it out myself. Got it?"

I squirm in front of him, whining, "But I'm gonna be aching like fucking *crazy*, Hardy..."

Pouting, he pulls me closer to him by my neck. "I *know*, baby... It's gonna be *so* fucking hot. I can't wait to feel how badly you're squirming..."

"But so... when will I see you?" I breathe anxiously.

"I'll come to your place in Santa Fe tonight." Lance kisses down my jaw. "Meet you after work and... give you some relief."

That sounds like the best thing ever...

Can we just fast-forward to that moment please??

"Okay." I nod fast. "So tonight, then? My place..."

I've completely abandoned ship pretending I don't want him around. It's like the second he shoved that plug inside me, I forgot every qualm and hesitation I'd been clutching for dear life. The concerns about where this is going, and how any of it could ever work... They've all but fizzled away, and now, I just want *more*. I'm counting the seconds until I see him again and he hasn't even left yet.

"It's another date, baby." He grins. But it fades, and he peeks down at me. "And this should probably go without saying, but you will absolutely *not* be giving this body—my body—to anyone else. Is that clear?"

"Even if they're super rich?" I tease, like the snarky idiot I am.

A growl leaves his lips, and he grabs a handful of my ass, *hard*. Hard enough that it jostles the plug, and I yelp.

"Trouble..."

"I'm just... kidding," I gasp, falling into him. "I won't be with anyone else. I promise."

The way he stares at me, our eyes locked for a few heavy seconds that feel like hours, has me shivering for a whole new reason.

So, I'm not... hooking up with anyone else now??

He's... it?

"Gorgeous, sexy, perfect," he pants, kissing me in between each word. I'm just... *melting*. Like a slutty little ice cube beneath his rays of sunshine.

"Baby, please..." I whimper, pawing at him. I'm not even sure what I'm begging for.

Not a great sign that it's been two minutes and I can barely control myself. And if he's doing this as a way to turn me into an even bigger junkie for him, it's clearly working fast. Seriously, he's got me wrapped around his finger right now.

I think he's bested me at my own game, and the craziest part is I can't even tell if I'm mad about it. I'm just so *eager* to get this day over with so I can be with him again.

Touché, Sunshine.

"Get dressed, baby." Lance finally releases me so that I can get ready. With literally ten minutes to get my damn act together.

I rush around the room, doing only the essentials of my skincare regimen, slipping into my easiest ensemble that still makes me look like the powerful, successful boss bitch I am, though all the while I'm flinching and humming when the plug moves a certain way, sending shocks through my loins.

And he hasn't even turned it on yet!

This is going to be the greatest test of my willpower I've ever experienced.

But the wildest part of this whole thing is that I'm actually... excited. To see if I can do it. To play this sexy game with him.

But mostly... I think I like that it means I'm guaranteed to get him back later.

Straightening my tie in the mirror, my eyes are on him, freshly dressed back in his clothes from yesterday, but still looking positively delicious. He comes up behind me, reaching around to take over fixing my tie. Obviously, just an excuse to grind his crotch into my ass, pushing the plug to ghost over my prostate.

"*Fuck...*" I gasp, and he hums.

"I'll see you tonight." He kisses my neck. "And Tate..." My eyes meet his in the mirror, and he holds up his phone, displaying the app that controls the plug. *So he must have familiarized himself with it... Lovely.* He smirks wickedly. "Good luck with your meeting."

I'm in fucking *Hell.*

All seven circles. *Eight,* even.

They need to add another one specifically for people wearing elaborate sex toys in secret while surrounded by twenty of the richest, stuffiest old straight men ever invented.

The drive to Santa Fe wasn't bad. I was squirming in my seat, but at least it's comfortable. I actually got used to the feeling of this foreign object in my body and almost forgot about it for a bit.

But as soon as I got to the office and started walking again, the burn returned with a vengeance like gonorrhea. And when I reached my office, I was hit with a wave of tingles that had me toppling over onto my desk.

The vibrations had started.

I have no clue how Hardy knew I'd just reached my office... For all I know, this thing could have a GPS tracker in it too. Honestly, I wouldn't be surprised. It's *that* kind of toy.

Twenty different levels of vibration settings, pulsing and an extension that can literally thrust the head part deeper inside you. All to be controlled by the master of your domain.

For a servant of God, Lance Hardy sure is resembling a sexy golden-haired spawn of Satan right now.

The vibrations started out mild, calm enough that I could still communicate. But he was gradually increasing them the more time went on, so that by the time the meeting was about to start, my teeth were chattering, and my face was all flushed. I had to scurry off to the bathroom to splash some water on my face and make sure my dick was tucked securely into the waistband of my pants, held in place by my belt, so there was no chance of it popping up to say hello in front of the investors from Singapore.

At this point, the meeting has been going on for a solid hour—though it feels like four—and I'm not sure I've heard a single word anyone's said.

Something about hedge funds... market... shares... I think?

Lots of numbers, that's for sure.

God, my dick is hard.

"If you feel the projections are solid, we'll move forward," one of the investors says. I can't even tell who it is, all of their faces are blending together.

My partners all nod in agreement, looking to me.

"Yes... solid," I croak, and shift in my seat.

Solid as a fucking rock.

Lifting my glass of water to my lips with trembling fingers, I sip slowly, distracting myself from the increase in voracity of the buzz below my waist; the way the pulse of it is fizzling up my spine.

"I've seen nothing but growth, and we're quite satisfied," my boss adds.

I cough into my glass, choking while I fidget.

Thankfully, no one really bats an eye.

"Tate will be handling the overseas merger," he adds, droning on about my proposal while I tug the collar of my shirt away from my neck.

I'm on *fire*. My balls are throbbing, and my ass is clenching, and *holy fuck*, I swear to God, they can probably *hear* how loudly this thing is vibrating. It's all I can hear, as if it's happening inside my head.

"We look forward to working alongside you." The investors all look at me.

My fingers dig into my thighs, and I manage to grunt, "Likewise."

The performance of a lifetime, I'm telling you.

I deserve an Oscar. Or an Adult Film Award.

They start discussing my upcoming trip to New York right as the asshole controlling my asshole decides to explore the *thrust* function.

The rounded tip of the plug starts fucking deeper into me, grazing my prostate. A sound I can't control flees my lips as my dick pulses precum into my navel. They glance up at me.

I somehow manage to control my squirming and mutter, "Wall Street," because it's the first thing that comes to mind, and the only two words I can produce right now without moaning.

Trouble

My boss nods. "Right, the Wall Street partners will see to it that every-thing moves smoothly."

Fuck me, that was close.

Thankfully, the fucking stops after only a few minutes, and I can breathe a little easier, though my bones feel like they're vibrating, and I'm all sticky inside my clothes.

The meeting is *way* too long. It should've ended an hour ago, but the investors love hearing themselves talk, so it just goes on and on *and on*, so that the moment my boss *finally* stands, I'm leaping up out of my seat.

I manage to shake everyone's hands, though I'm sure my palms are much sweatier than I'd like them to be, rushing out of the room first and making a beeline for my office. Once inside with the door locked and the blinds closed, I collapse onto my couch on my stomach, the only position that's mildly comfortable. My balls are so tight, they feel like they might rupture, and before I know it, I'm grinding my hips into the cushion for some relief. But I have to stop, or I'll come.

God, I wanna come...

I wanna come so fucking bad.

This is agony! What time is it?!

I check my watch. It's almost five. That means I can get away with slinking out of here soon. Wiggling my phone out of my pocket, I send a text to Lance.

ME

You're the devil.

DON'T BE AN IDIOT

Why...? What's wrong? *winky face*

I growl out loud. *This fucking guy...*

ME

I have never been so uncomfortable in my life... When are you coming over???????????

DON'T BE AN IDIOT

Lol. Text me the address, I'll leave right now

I send him the address to my penthouse. He only lives about an hour away. If he leaves now and doesn't hit any traffic, I could be coming all over him in ninety minutes tops.

Nyla K.

ME

Please hurry sunshine

DON'T BE AN IDIOT

I'll be there soon, Trouble *eggplant peach and three water squirts*

Fuck, even the emojis are turning me on.

I gotta get outta here.

Wincing as I stagger to my feet, I rush to my desk, gathering my things. I press a button on my desk phone. "Troy, get in here."

Less than thirty seconds later, the door handle to my office is jiggling.

"Boss? It's locked," Troy calls through the door, and I roll my eyes, hobbling over to unlock it.

My assistant creeps inside, closing the door behind him.

"I have some business to attend to, so I'm leaving," I grunt.

Troy nods. "The meeting went well?"

I ignore his question. "Leland is probably expecting me to go to dinner with them, but I can't. So if he comes by, just tell him I... had to run out. And maybe I'll join them later. But I won't. Obviously, don't *tell* him that, but just..." I pause, flustered. "Be convincing."

Troy raises a brow. But, of course, he doesn't comment on my behavior. He simply nods. "You got it. You need anything for tonight? For whatever you're... doing?"

His lips twitch, and I glare at him. "If I need something, I'll ask for it."

"Right." He grins, annoying me with his knowing smirk and his stupid bowtie. "It's just that there's nothing on your calendar, so I wasn't sure what business you could be—"

"It's the business of noneya. Ever heard of it??" I snap. "Also, I might be late tomorrow..."

"That's cool, boss." He shrugs, eyes sliding me up and down. "You want some water, or something? You look flushed..."

"I'm fine," I bark, shuffling papers into a binder. "Just do your—" My voice cuts out abruptly when the plug starts thrusting again.

The papers fly out of my hands, fluttering everywhere while I grip the edge of my desk, breathing like I'm going into labor.

"Jesus," Troy gasps, rushing over to pick up the papers. "Are you sure you're alright??"

"I'm... f-fine." It comes out like a whimper, my cock leaking all over me. My knees are buckling. I'm about to fall down.

238

But then it stops, and I let out a long exhale.

Troy is giving me the most bewildered look ever.

"Give me those." I snatch the papers from him, tucking everything into my bag.

Straightening, I walk as normally as possible out of the room, though I'm sure I look like Kermit the frog.

I don't even care. I just need to get home. Once I'm *home*, I can sit down with a bag of ice on my biscuits and wait for the beautiful demon who's causing me all this discomfort.

On my way out of the office, I run into Josiah, who stops like he wants to talk to me. But I just keep walking.

Nope. No time for that.

The drive to my penthouse is agonizing. I get stuck in traffic, so a ten-minute drive turns to thirty, and by the time I get inside my place, I'm ready to collapse and cry and ejaculate all at the same time.

Dragging myself over to the nearest piece of furniture, I strip down to my boxers and curl up on my side. My hand grazes my cock, and the feeling is so intense, I have to force myself away, otherwise I *know* I'll come.

I turn on the TV and smoke some weed to distract myself. Checking my phone, I see no new texts from Hardy, but it's not even six yet, so he's probably still driving.

My eyelids begin to droop, the pulse in my dick and balls lulling me into a fevered daze that slowly puts me to sleep.

Baby, come home... I think someone on TV is saying.

I miss you, I need you. You're all I think about...

I'm Clytie, reaching up for the sun, just out of reach. My feet are buried in the dirt... I can get high enough.

Dig them up... Pull out the roots, and go get him.

You make me so happy...

"God sees only the soul, Trouble... And yours is beautiful."

We should be... more.

Eyes creep open, lids heavy.

It takes a moment for my groggy haze to wear off. But when I lift my head, everything is dark. No lights, and the sun has set.

The clock reads...

Eight forty-five??

I sit up fast, drawing attention to the object inside me. My forehead lines when I realize it's no longer buzzing.

Nyla K.

Grabbing my phone, I blink at the screen. No missed calls or texts from Lance.

What the hell...?

He should have been here hours ago...

My fingers work quickly.

> ME
>
> Hey... sorry, I fell asleep.
>
> ME
>
> Where are you?

I chew on my lower lip, hoping he didn't show up while I was sleeping and leave. But that wouldn't make any sense... He would've at least called or texted me. Plus, Lance isn't exactly the type to come all the way out here, ring my doorbell once and then take off. The dude would probably scale the building to get inside.

He's nutty like that.

So why isn't he responding??

Getting up, I grab some water, then a scotch, all the while jittering with nerves on top of nerves. They're stacking up inside me with every passing second I don't hear from him. Minutes go by before he even reads my texts. But still... he doesn't write back. Which means he's *alive*... He's *okay*. He's just not responding to me.

> ME
>
> What the hell, Hardy??

This time the text is read right away. But I don't get a reply. Not even typing bubbles. Nada. I'm staring at my phone, waiting for an answer, and getting *nothing* back.

He's fuckin' ghosting.

On my second drink, I decide to call him. It rings twice, then goes to voicemail.

"Hi, you've reached Lance Hardy. Please leave a message, and I'll get back to you. God bless."

Mouth agape, I'm fully stunned. Dumbfounded. Bam-fuckin-boozled.

He just sent me to voicemail.

Lance Hardy is ignoring my calls...

I can't fathom this right now.

Trouble

Even if something came up, the least he could do is text me and let me know he's not coming. I mean, it's common courtesy. Instead, he's deliberately ditching me. Blowing me the fuck off, and not in the way he was *supposed* to tonight.

I'm wound so fucking tight from wearing this goddamn plug in my ass for twelve motherfucking hours, being vibrated into an early blue-ball grave. And now, on top of that, I feel like a fucking moron.

Like the biggest *idiot* on the planet.

Because I actually believed he was going to show up, and I was *excited*. Not only to get some relief in the form of his giant, muscular body and his massive dick, taking care of me the way he promised he would, but also to see his face. Watch him smiling at me and listen to him talk while he touches me all over like it's his favorite thing.

I wanted to fucking see him tonight, goddamnit. And now he's a no-show, and I'm just the idiot who got his hopes up. *Again.*

Rubbing my eyes with my fingers, I'm as emotionally exhausted as my body is coiled and ready to blow. I should just take this fucking thing out of me and come already... End the charade.

But I don't want to.

I want him to do it...

I'm fucking pouting. *Ugh, what a loser you are.*

ME

> I don't understand why you can't just tell me you're not coming. It's not that hard.

It's ten-thirty, and now I'm four scotches deep, and I'm spiraling.

ME

> Lance... you promised.

The booze is working faster than usual because I've barely eaten all day. I'm swimmy, and my nuts are aching so bad, they have their own heartbeat.

"Get this thing out of me..." I whisper to myself, rushing to the bathroom.

I can't have this plug inside me anymore. It's just making me feel even stupider.

One more twitch with it burrowed in my ass and I'll really *fucking hate myself.*

In the bathroom, I pull the plug out, maybe a little too fast, whining and tossing it into the sink. Chills sheet my flesh from the sudden emptiness. My body feels weird now that it's gone.

Rolling my eyes at myself, I wash the thing off and stuff it away in my nightstand with the rest of the toys I keep here. It's a bigger collection, because I have a lot more sex around these parts than I do back home. Which reminds me...

My dick is fucking *engorged*. Like, *huge* and tumescent, veins popping, head swollen. I need a fucking orgasm, and since Lance fucking Hardy clearly won't be showing up, I suppose I should just go out and... get laid. *Right?*

The sound of my phone ringing snaps me out of my thoughts and I run —I freaking *sprint*—to go answer it, skidding around the corner on two-wheels like Scooby Doo. But when I reach my phone, disappointment washes over me at fucking Pierce's name on the screen.

Motherfucker.

"What?" I answer, then cringe because I should've just ignored it.

Goddamnit.

"You didn't show for dinner!" Josiah yells over loud background noise that sounds like a bar.

He's obviously out drinking.

"So what?" I grumble, cupping my cock and pouting like a real baby.

Why didn't he show up...?

He said he was going to...

"Come get drunk with me," he slurs into the phone.

"No," I huff, pouring myself yet another scotch and taking a giant gulp.

I can get drunk right here, by myself... In Morontown.

"Come on, T..." he whines in my ear. "Please?"

My head is circling all of this bullshit. My aching balls, Lance blowing me off, Josiah drunkenly purring in my ear.

I should just meet him and get it over with. Get fucked and prove that Lance Hardy doesn't matter, because he *doesn't.*

All of that bullshit from last night, and this morning, was just smoke in mirrors. It was all an act. He hypnotized me for the fun of it, and because he's clearly an immaculate liar, I fell for it.

I actually believed that he could be... That *we...*

Fuck this.

"I'm... tired," I mumble, and it's the truth. I am...

So very tired.

"Then I'll come to your place," Josiah says quietly.

"What about your straightness?" A tipsy grin tugs at my lips, before I bite it off.

"If anyone could make me forget about it, it'd be you..." he hums.

My dick jumps. I want to have sex... *That's what I want.*

No feelings or attachments or broken promises. No waiting by the phone for a married, closeted Jesus-freak who's *never* going to be what I need.

Inside my chest is caving as I swallow another gulp from my glass.

"J... let me call you back," I mutter, hanging up before he can say anything else.

I need to make one last call before I close the door on this man for good. Because I'm drunk, and drunk Tate is too obsessive to remember all the reasons he stopped being this way.

One more fucking chance, Lance...

And then you're done.

Placing a call to his phone, I pace while it rings, and rings. And *rings*.

This time, he's not sending me straight to voicemail. But it doesn't seem like he's going to answer either. Sipping my drink and circling the room, I wait for the inevitable voicemail, his sexy brogue instructing me to *leave a message.*

But instead, the call connects... To silence.

I check the screen. "Hello...?"

A breath sounds in my ear, like a sharp inhale. And then a melodious female voice responds, "Hello..."

My stomach crawls up into my throat. "Um... hi..."

"This is Desiree Hardy. Lance's wife," she says. "How can I help you, Tate?"

Chapter Twenty
Lance

S *hit is going south.*

In all honesty, I should've been prepared for it. It's my own damn fault for being so cocky and careless. Assuming I could just keep disappearing under the measly excuse of *hanging out with friends*, and not have to answer for any of my odd behaviors that have popped up seemingly out of nowhere.

After all, I've been married for a while. Des and I have been in a relationship for fifteen years. The entire amount of time Tate has been out of my life, she's been in it, and over the course of that long span, I can count on one hand the instances in which I've *hung out* with friends from college. Based on my personality, it's totally suspicious that, out of the blue, I'd reunite with people I haven't seen in over a decade and start spending loads of time with them.

Although, if we're being *technical...* That is, more or less, exactly what I'm doing.

Still, it's been my alibi since Pride. And on paper, it doesn't seem that odd. But when looking at it through the eyes of my wife, paired with a palpable shift in my emotional state and a lack of interest in all things *physical* with her, I can understand her skepticism.

Realistically, this affair smacked me upside the head. I went to Pride expecting to test the limits of desires I've kept locked up tight for years. And yes, that *is* what happened... But God chose to throw me a curveball, and now I'm in this so deep, it'll be downright impossible to dig myself out.

Trouble

Spending the night at Tate's was the best time of my entire existence. Every moment we're together is better than the last, and the complex reality is that the love I had for him when we were kids has only gotten stronger. After lying dormant for so long, it's sprouted up and bloomed into the most beautiful, yet thorniest of flowers.

I never stopped loving Tate Eckhart. I can admit that now. The difference is that now I'm *in love* with him, despite the clawing reasons why I shouldn't be, which have only multiplied over the years.

The Desiree factor is but one of them. Unfortunately, it's the one currently giving me the strongest stress-induced migraine.

Leaving Tate's yesterday, I was on a cloud. Buzzing on him, and *us*, while naively assuming I could just pop home for a few hours before heading back out to see him again, without providing any real explanations to my wife.

Go ahead, you can call me a dumbass. It's fully justified.

The bliss-bubble popped, however, when I attempted to broach the subject of leaving again with Des.

She was asking me what I wanted for dinner, while I was grinning at my phone screen like a deranged lunatic. Tate had texted me, clearly feeling the burn from the way I'd been going at him with that plug. All day, I was like a puppet master, controlling his torturous and inconvenient pleasure. Increase vibrations here, throw in some pumping there. That toy is next-level intuitive, and *I* got to be in charge. Commanding over his body from a hundred miles away.

I freaking *loved* it, and I absolutely couldn't wait to see him, to reap the benefits of how needy I was clearly making him. I messaged him that I'd be on my way to him soon, all the while working up the nerve to put on a solid performance for my wife.

I don't like lying to Desiree. Truthfully, I don't like lying to *anyone*, but the abysmal fact is that I've gotten pretty good at it over the years. If I could choose, I would say *fuck it*, and just tell the truth. Lay it all out on the table, because I'm sure it would feel *so* good to get this stuff off my chest.

But there are consequences to being honest. Ones I'm not prepared to face.

Responsibility I'm not yet ready to take.

So I asked Desiree if we could eat early, because the guys wanted to get together again, hoping she would just shrug it off and concede, like she has every other time I've told her that's where I'm going. And she kind of did, although this time she was a bit more questioning.

245

"Really? You're hanging out with them two nights in a row?"

"Don't the guys have families? Their wives are okay with them going out every night?"

"It just seems strange... You've been spending so much time with them lately..."

I was able to brush it off by explaining that since I don't drink, I'm their designated driver. That I wanted them to be able to let loose and have fun, safely and responsibly, without having to worry about taking Ubers all over the place. A weak ass excuse, no doubt about that. But it was enough for her to give me the indifferent shrug I was looking for, and continue the rest of our rushed meal in silence.

We've just finished eating, and I'm anxious to get a move on, knowing it'll take me over an hour to get to Tate, and I already told him I was leaving. I'll probably be a little late. Hopefully, he won't be too upset.

As soon as my dishes are in the sink, I rush upstairs to get ready. But when I come back down, Desiree stops me in the foyer.

"Are you really going out with the guys...?" Her eyes are intense, though her tone is calmly inquisitive.

Gulping over immediate nerves, I mutter, "What do you mean...?"

She shifts in front of me, visibly uncomfortable, and it's making me tense all over. "I don't know, but something has been off lately, babe. You've been going out so much, and it's just... making me nervous. You never go out, it's weird."

My pulse is racing faster and faster.

"Sweetie, I..." I pause to find my voice again. "Sometimes it's good to get out, you know? Be with old friends..."

Lord, I hate myself. So much.

Desiree doesn't look at all satisfied with my answer, and now I'm getting dizzy.

"Okay, don't be upset..." she murmurs. I didn't think it was possible for my eyes to get wider, but when she lifts my phone from behind her back... *Welp, I was wrong. They're much wider.* "I only looked at a few texts..."

"Des, what the..." I gasp, reaching for my phone. She tugs it back. "Why would you snoop through my phone?? That's such an invasion of... privacy." My voice is shaking. "How'd you even get into it anyway??"

"I know your code." She shrugs.

Well, I guess I'm just an idiot then.

I'm beyond speechless. Frozen, standing there with impending doom dumping over me like a waterfall.

Trouble

"Why is Tate asking you to come over?" She blinks at me.

"We're... meeting at his house," I lie, fast.

"Why is he so desperate for you to get there?" Her brow arches.

Stomach bunching up painfully, the adrenaline of being caught has my limbs trembling. "He's just being stupid," I force myself to scoff casually, as if to say *'That's just Tate being Tate. He's such a goofball.'*

But beneath my blithe exterior, I'm really freaking the hell out.

She read my texts...

I know I don't have the right to be pissed, but still... I really didn't see that coming.

Thank God I deleted my past messages to Tate. The much more incriminating ones that show how blatantly obsessed I am with him. But the ones from today are still there, and my paranoia is running rampant through all the ways our conversation could allude to us fucking.

In my mind, it seems *really* damn obvious.

Desiree stares at me for a moment, blankly, like she doesn't believe a word I'm saying. It's throwing me off big time, mainly because she's never been the jealous or suspicious type before. I'm not used to this.

Then again, I've never given her a reason to be up until now.

"Lance..." she whispers my name quietly, as my heart crawls up into my throat. "What were those emojis for?"

The fucking eggplant and the peach, holy fuck, I'm so screwed.

"Des, I have no idea what you're talking about," I grumble, forcing my fear into anger as I go for my phone again, but she keeps snatching it away like I'm a fucking child. "Give me my phone. This is enough now."

She glares at me. "Just tell me why Tate is acting like he's going to *die* if you don't show up there immediately..."

Mind you, my wife doesn't know Tate *at all*. They've never met, despite the fact that Desiree also went to ASU. I'd never met her either before I did, which isn't unusual. It's a big school. But regardless, she doesn't know his personality, or what's considered normal behavior for him.

Still, for her to even be *mentioning* Tate is aggressively churning my gut. The lies I've been spewing to her revolved around a group of us hanging out. Only seeing texts from Tate puts the spotlight on him, which isn't good.

"He's just... He's going through something right now." More sour lies pour from my lips. "He was my best friend in college, Des. I'm... worried about him."

God, forgive me...

I'm such a fucking piece of shit.

Her eyes soften, and for a moment, I think she might let it go.

But then my phone chimes in her hand. Twice. Two new incoming texts.

Both of our eyes fall to my phone. She lifts it to read the messages, and I lunge.

"Desiree, come on!"

"You're being so shady!" she gasps, whipping away from me with my phone clutched to her chest. "Why can't I see what he's saying?? What are you hiding??"

"Fine," I huff, raking trembling fingers through my hair. "Whatever. Read whatever the fuck you want. You'll see how crazy you're being."

The words I'm speaking directly contradict how I'm losing my shit inside. My knees are actually wobbling, and I think I might fall down.

She reads the texts while I scowl at her.

"Well??" I hiss. "Anything juicy?"

Please please please, Tate... Don't say anything.

I'm *sweating* beneath my clothes, guilt and angst rushing in my veins like poison.

"He just said that he fell asleep, and he's asking where you are," she murmurs.

A breath of relief washes through me as I take on a new tactic. "Babe, what's wrong?" I try redirecting the conversation, stepping closer to her. "Why are you acting this way?"

"You're the one who's been acting different lately, Lance," she says quietly. "It's like ever since you started seeing your old friends again, something has... changed."

"Nothing has changed," I whisper. "I'm still me, I just... I like spending time with people from my past."

That's sort of true...

Desiree looks like she wants to say something else, but refrains.

My heart rate is jacked up, my body vibrating with the need to just leave and get to Tate like I told him I would. But it's probably not an option anymore.

But I at least need to get my phone back and explain to him what's going on.

"I would never snoop through your phone or ask you to show me your texts..." I grunt, rubbing my eyes.

"I wouldn't care, because I have nothing to hide!" she snaps, and I bark back.

"I'm not hiding anything!"

The phone chimes again, and I cringe.

Desiree checks it. I'm starting to lose my composure, which I really hate, since I am at fault here. But she's being nuts, and I don't know what to do.

"Des, give me my phone back," I repeat in a growl.

It starts ringing, and I don't even need to see the screen to know who's calling.

"Answer it." She holds out the phone. "Put it on speaker."

"Fuck no. I'm not doing that," I hiss, reaching out and swiping to decline.

"You're unbelievable..." She shakes her head.

"Why?? *Why* am I unbelievable?? He's my *friend*, Des, I don't see what the issue is. You're being—"

"What?? What am I being?" she seethes.

Smart... Intuitive. Totally correct to call me out on the lies I'm so obviously peddling.

"You're being crazy," I murmur, *loathing* myself down to my marrow for gaslighting my own wife.

The woman who's done nothing but stick by me for years while I've struggled internally and shut down. Desiree is practically a saint for putting up with my aloof, emotionally closed-off ass, and how do I repay her? By cheating on her with the man I probably should have been with this whole time, lying to her face about it, and accusing *her* of being crazy.

Burn in Hell, Pastor... You're truly the worst.

"I don't think I'm being crazy, Lance," she says calmly, and it scares the shit out of me.

At least if she's spazzing, I can use it to fuel my own frustrations... But this calmness makes it seem like she already knows all the answers to her questions, but refuses to let me off the hook until *I* cop to it.

"You've been acting strangely. Something is up. You can't tell me it's not." She pins me with a pleading gaze. "Just *tell me*, Lance... The lying will only make it worse."

Gulping over the sandpaper of my throat, I stare at her, my entire existence flashing before my eyes.

And the thing is, I *want* to tell her. I so badly want to tell the truth, *finally*, after so many years of stuffing it down. I'm sick of it... Physically *ill* over the lies I've been choking on. My soul is exhausted...

I've been tired for fifteen years.

But I just can't make myself say the words... I *can't* get them to come out.

Even just the first part... The easiest part.

It won't work, and I hate myself for being such a fucking *coward*.

But I'm scared. I am. I'm terrified of the ripple effect turning me and him into rubble.

Instead, I sigh, rubbing my eyes hard. "Fine... You don't want me to go out tonight? I won't." I shoot her a look, every bit as frayed and worn as I feel. "Happy??"

"No, Lance... I'm not happy." She shakes her head. "I just want you to just tell me what's going on..."

The fear and loathing I have for myself is gnawing at my insides. "Nothing is going on, Des..."

"Are you having an affair?" She blurts the words out, and my knees nearly buckle.

"Why... would you think that?" My head is spinning. I'm so dizzy, I might collapse.

"Please," she huffs. "You don't even *like* going out, Lance. Why would you suddenly start going out with someone single, like Tate?"

I blink over and over, mouth hanging open, words dried up.

"Is he, like, your wingman? You guys go out and meet women together??" Her wide gaze sparkles accusatory hurt at me. "Is that what's happening? I deserve to know the truth..."

Scraping up the words, I mumble, "Tate's gay."

And so... am...

I stare at her with my heart screaming in my chest.

"Oh..." She looks momentarily surprised, as if she wasn't expecting that for some reason. "Well, he could still help you meet girls."

"I assure you, that's not what's happening," I mutter, rubbing my face.

"But the emojis..." she whispers.

"Fucking emojis..." I scoff, shaking my head. "At least just let me text him back and tell him I'm not coming." I reach out for my phone.

She blinks her amber eyes at me. "I'll tell him."

This is completely fucked, an even thicker guilt now clogging my chest. Not only am I lying to and hurting my wife, but I've dragged Tate into my mess of a marriage. He doesn't deserve to be in the middle of this shit. And now, he probably thinks I'm ditching him on purpose, ignoring his calls and texts, and my wife is going to start interrogating him??

Fuck this... I'm ruining his fucking life all over again.

Before I can even figure out how to respond, Desiree pushes past me with a huff, stalking toward the stairs.

"Des, come on!" I chase after her, but she's running.

She darts into our bedroom while I'm still stumbling up the steps, slamming the door right in front of my face. I hear the lock click as I'm grabbing the handle, jiggling it over and over.

"Desiree..." I knock on the door. "This is insane. Can we please just talk about this??"

I keep knocking, but she's obviously ignoring me, and I'm spiraling. So many treacherous emotions are ripping me apart from the inside, as I lean up against the door with my face in my hands.

Our laptop is in there too. I can't even log into my phone somehow and intercept anything.

I'm just... fucking done.

None of it matters...

My wife is going to find out. She's going to tell her family, and they'll tell my family...

And it'll all be over.

You knew this would happen... You knew someone would find out eventually, and you'd have to explain yourself.

What did you think? You could just cheat on her forever while stringing Tate along in hopes it would just work itself out?

What the fuck is wrong with you??

Puffing out of defeat, I march down the stairs, heading outside for some fresh air.

Everyone's going to find out. The truth will be revealed, and when it is... it might mean the end of me and Tate Eckhart forever.

Honestly, that's the only part I care about. The relief of coming clean to Des will feel good, of course it will. But as soon as she tells my family, well... There's no guarantee I'll be able to hold on to Tate after that.

I just needed a little more time... to be with him and show him how *good* we are. So that hopefully when it eventually blows up, he might not be as inclined to run.

But I was sloppy. Chock it up to me not knowing how to have an affair, I guess.

Nyla K.

I never wanted to hurt anyone... All this time, I've only been trying to protect him.

Desiree and I don't speak for the rest of the night.

Nor do I get the chance to speak to Tate.

Not once does my wife open the door to our bedroom, or come downstairs, which leaves me to sleep on the couch. Fortunately, I'm so exhausted from the drama, the guilt, and the worry weaving around my every fiber, I end up passing out cold pretty quick, though my sleep is anything but easy.

All night, I'm tossing and turning, my unconscious mind fighting in a war that's lasted nearly two decades.

When my eyes reopen, sun is beaming into my face through the bay windows. Groggily, I sit up, rubbing my face and fisting my hair, wondering if last night was a dream. Or a nightmare...

But, of course, it was real. Because if none of that had happened, I'd be waking up in Tate's bed this morning. Spooning him, rubbing my morning wood on his perfect ass, listening to the way he breathes when he's both calm and needy at the same time. I'd be feeling his strong body, staring deep into his eyes, that iridescent shade of chocolate brown like mine, wishing I could convince him to admit his feelings for me, even though it probably wouldn't make a lick of difference.

I'd still be stuck, regardless.

Summoning the energy to lift myself off the couch, I shuffle into the kitchen for much-needed coffee. And I find my wife already standing there, sipping her tea. Staring at me again, with my phone resting on the marble island between us.

"Morning..." I grumble, moving around her to make some coffee, all the while squirming with the need to lunge at my phone and call Tate immediately. Explain myself and hope to God he's not too pissed at me for blowing him off without a peep.

Fuck me... The plug.

He was wearing that plug all *day* because of me. I was supposed to ease his suffering.

What if he had someone else do it... because I never showed up??

Now my stomach is coiling up with nausea for a whole new reason.

Hopelessly full of dread and sorrow, I go about placing a K-cup into the machine, grabbing my mug. Then I peer at Desiree, because she hasn't said a word yet.

"I guess we should ta—"

Trouble

"I spoke to Tate," she interrupts me, and I drop the sugar bowl, dumping a pile onto the counter.

My eyes widen, muscles stiff as I gape at her. "You what..."

She blinks. "He called last night, when you were asleep."

Lashes fluttering, anxiety rising. "Okay..." She continues to watch me closely. "What did he have to say?"

"Lance, I think I owe you an apology," she sighs, still far too calm for my pinging nerves to handle. "You've just been gone so much lately... Staying out at night, coming home the next day all rumpled. And you've been distant... I mean, I know you're not one to open up much, but it seems like ever sense you went to that party in Albuquerque, you've been much more closed off. Not to mention, we haven't slept together since then..."

I swallow the bile wanting to rise in my throat, forcing myself to turn away and clean up the spilled sugar with shaky hands.

"I guess I assumed you were having an affair," she goes on. "Being that all the signs kinda pointed to that, ya know?" Facing her again, I cock my head, lips parted, ready to lie. But she keeps going before I can. "But there wasn't any evidence of that in your phone... or on your socials."

A quiet breath leaves my lungs, some relief unbunching my shoulders.

"Really, the only person you've been talking to is Tate," Desiree chirps, sipping her tea, eyeing me over the rim of the mug. "I watched your phone all night, and he was the only one who called."

And there it goes... All traces of comfort evaporated.

"Okay..." I croak again. "So you... answered?"

She nods. "Yea, I did."

"And?" I hold my breath.

"He confirmed what you said," she replies. "That he's been going through some stuff lately, and he just needed a friend."

My chin bobs. *Wow... Tate came through, corroborating the story without any direction.*

Not sure why I'm surprised. He's infinitely smoother than me.

I hope he's not too upset... About calling my phone and getting my wife.

Knowing Tate, he's probably livid, and ready to write me off, which has my lungs shriveling up like old balloons.

"That's good then," I mutter, trying not to make the words sound too much like a question from someone who's dying inside.

"It is," Des says softly. "And I am sorry... for accusing you. For snooping."

253

"It's... alright," I breathe, letting myself relax once more. "I should probably call Tate, though. Apologize for blowing him off." I wince internally at my choice of words.

"No need." She grins. "He's coming over for dinner tonight."

Fucking motherfucker... I think I'm having a heart attack.

The machine beeps that my coffee is finished while I stand stock still, gawking at my wife with my mouth open.

She invited Tate to dinner here... And he said yes??

What the fuck?!

Desiree sips from her mug again, patting me on the arm. "I'll cook. I want to make your famous béarnaise sauce."

Okay, this is entirely fucked up right now.

The way she's been eyeing me, the tone of her voice... it's still accusatory. Maybe I'm being paranoid, but it seems like she knows something is up, and that *apology* was just to get me to drop my guard.

She knows. She fucking knows. And now she invited Tate to dinner to what... confront us both?? Watch us together and see how we act??

This is going to be the worst dinner of my life, I can already tell.

Des saunters away, peeking at me one last time over her shoulder. "I can't wait to finally meet the infamous Tate Eckhart."

Oh, yea. That's it. It's official.

I'm lodged, miserable, in purgatory.

Chapter Twenty-One
Tate

R*emind me...*
Why am I doing this again?
Taking one last drag of my cigarette, I stub it out on the ground, striding up the walkway. I'm sure I *look* calm. Blaise. Unaffected...

It's just the way I am.

Not to toot my own horn—*which sounds totally dirty, by the way, and exactly like the kind of thing I'd enjoy doing*—but I'm pretty damn good at embodying the façade of someone who doesn't give two shits. It's part of what makes me so great at my job. I play the part of the ruthless, superficial bachelor playboy extremely well.

And that's not to say it's all an act; it's certainly been my identity for long enough that it *feels* hella real. But the notion that I'm *emotionless* is still just a front I put up to keep everything copacetic. It's also something I believe in, since being overly emotional has never helped me in any way, shape, or form.

I'm like a method actor, living and breathing this image, even when it becomes harder and harder to keep reality from pushing through the surface. And now, more than ever, I need to remain vigilant about it; keep my guard up as high as it goes. Because lately, I've been letting that shit slip, and based on where I am right now, I can't afford to reveal my carefully protected vulnerabilities from behind this mask. No matter how badly they want to get out.

Glancing around at all of the flower gardens, I can't help remembering the last time I was here. Parked right over there on the street in front of this house, with Lance inside my car, quite literally fucking me senseless.

I don't know what it is about his dick that just fucks all the logic out of my brain, but it's most of the reason I'm here right now. Aside from knowing that declining Mrs. Hardy's invitation would probably make me seem even guiltier than I so clearly am.

Is she aware of what happened that night in my Maserati...? Has she known since then??

She didn't allude to anything like that last night, when she answered his phone. But I mean, why would she? Why come at with me accusations over the phone when you can invite me over for dinner and do it in person?

I'm not sure if that's what tonight is about... Desiree made it seem like she just wanted to meet me because I'm her husband's friend, with whom he's been spending an almost suspicious amount of time recently. But over the course of the five-minute phone call that sobered me right the fuck up, I could *feel* the unspoken words traveling over the line.

You're sleeping with my husband...

You turned him gay.

Maybe I'm just being paranoid. Honestly, I hope I am, because having dinner at the home of a guy I've been sleeping with just so that his wife can confront me about being an adultering whore sounds like the least fun thing ever.

Maybe she really does just want to meet me. It's understandable. I'm cool as shit.

And if that's the case, then my being here only solidifies the *real* reason I've shown up tonight...

I'm a troublesome pot-stirrer extraordinaire who can't stop myself from playing with fire like a slutty li'l pyro.

Pausing in front of the door, I take a deep breath. I'm wound up beyond belief right now, both in stress and nearly two days of pent-up, unreleased *tension*. At this point, a light breeze runs the risk of launching me into an orgasm or a panic attack. Or both.

Hardy texted me this afternoon—*finally*—to apologize and I guess try to gauge my mental state, what with being blown off by him and then sneak-attacked by his wife. But he was much more ambiguous than he usually is with his messages, which leads me to believe his wife might actively be checking his phone. Another red flag being waved over this whole stupid dinner, which should have me running in the opposite direction.

Trouble

But you know me... I'm like a bull. Something about the color red just has me charging right towards them thangs.

My response was as follows:

> I'm fine. I'll see you tonight.

Because, fuck it, right? The way I see it, even if blowing me off wasn't his choice, it's still his *fault*. He's the one who's married, not me. *He's* sneaking around, and doing it very poorly, I might add, being that it's only been a few weeks and his wife already probably knows everything. At this point, I don't owe him anything, but he owes me *a lot*, so I'm here to collect.

Sure, maybe the sneaking around turns me on like the roar of a five-hundred horsepower engine, but that's not *all* I'm doing this for. Clearly... because I'm sure sleeping with any other married man in the world would be less complicated than doing it with Lance Hardy. But I'm here.

I will endure whatever awkwardness is about to happen tonight, if it means letting him know I'm serious as balls about this affair.

Your move, Sunshine.

Ringing the doorbell, I shift on my feet, wishing I'd brought my weed pen with me. I smoked a little in the car, to calm my nerves, but I'm pretty sure a horse tranquilizer wouldn't stop this anxiety from bunching me up in knots.

I hear footsteps inside the house, and then the door swings open, revealing the tall, large frame and beautifully helpless features I see every time I close my eyes, whether I want to or not. Taking one look at him, I have to smirk.

Man, he looks stressed.

"Tate," he breathes, and I don't want to admit it, but my stomach flips quite foolishly at the relief in his tone.

"Here I am," I sigh, cocking my head.

He looks like he wants to say so many things, eyes etched in unease, but also alit with need, aimed right at me. He clears his throat and puts on a polite smile, visibly forced, as he steps aside, motioning for me to come in.

"It's so good to see you." His fingers brush my lower back. When I cast a glare up at his face, he clears his throat and mutters, "I mean, thanks for coming."

"Mhm." My chin bobs around, taking in the inside of his home.

Lance is already fidgety as hell, his huge body fluttering about like he doesn't know what to do with himself. We're barely out of the foyer before he steps in front of me, leaning in to whisper frantically, "How are you? Are you feeling okay?? Baby, I'm *so* sorry about... I mean, I never meant for it to go down like this, and I know it's all my—"

Holding up a hand to cut him off, I glance behind him, where I'm guessing the hallway leads to the kitchen, based on the smells and sounds of food being prepared.

"Hardy, you are by far the *worst* adulterer I've ever met." I keep my voice as low as possible. "But it doesn't matter. Let's just get this over with, okay?"

He blinks down at me, gaze glistening with remorse. I can see it very clearly... He feels bad. I get it. He doesn't need me making him feel worse... *Chances are this experience will be punishment enough.*

But by the end of this night, he'll need to seriously evaluate the state of his affairs—*literally*—and decide what the hell he wants to do next.

And then I'll need to decide if I can ever see him again.

"Are you terribly upset with me, baby?" He pouts, and I want to fucking die.

Goddamnit, why does he have to be so fucking sexy?? He's like an adorable, giant puppy dog who keeps peeing all over everything. You wanna hate him, but you just... can't.

Oh my God, he's fucking Marmaduke.

"Yea. I am," I grunt, mostly for show, because I have to at least *pretend* I'm not obsessed with him. Especially right now, considering where we are... and who's in the next room. *He deserves to grovel some more.* "Are you gonna keep talking to me like that with your wife around? I just need to know if I should expect to find crushed glass in my food..."

He bites his lip, fingers twitching at his sides. "I wanna kiss you so bad."

"Ugh." I roll my eyes, pushing past him so he can't see how much he's getting to me.

Keep it cool, Tate.

Play hard to get... Remember? You used to be good at it.

Lance shuffles ahead, showing me into the kitchen. The moment I step through the doorway, it's like I'm hit with a wave of tension. I've never felt anything like it before, but I'm so insanely *uncomfortable* all of a sudden...

Because Mrs. Lance Hardy is *right fucking there*, just as beautiful and radiant as the pictures of her online I've come across during my occasional cyberstalking ventures.

Darker complexion of visibly smooth skin, waves of brunette hair flowing down her shoulders. A figure that I'm sure straight guys go all *Pepé La Pew* over. But to me, it's just spurning the nausea in my gut.

Cool, so she's gorgeous, and she has an amazing body...

A body Lance has touched... and kissed... and fucked... probably thousands of times...

I think I'm gonna be sick.

Pausing her gliding between the stove and the island, she glances up, pinning me with vibrant eyes. Her full lips curve, just a bit.

"Oh, hi!" Brushing her hands on an apron covering a stunning sundress, she rushes over, extending one to me. "This must be Tate! It's so great to finally meet you."

The nerves taking me over feel primal. Despite my brain telling me to be confident and cocky and carefree, my body is having an entirely different reaction. As if it knows I'm doing something wrong, and it's too much for even my well-rehearsed haughty arrogance to overcome.

My stomach rolls as I take her dainty hand, shaking it robotically. "Hey... Desiree." Her smile shifts. "Nice to... meet you."

This is who Lance really belongs to... Like, legally.

This is who swept in and scooped him up when he should've been mine.

Clearing my throat, I focus on using every weapon in my wealthy investment banker arsenal, pulling a fake grin out of my ass while I hold up the bottle I brought. "I wasn't sure what you were cooking, so I brought scotch. Highland Park... It's fifty years old."

"Ooh, fancy," she chirps, peeking up at Lance.

He, too, looks like he might throw up.

"I know the preacher over here doesn't drink." I nod toward Lance. "So you guys can just use it as a decoration or a conversation piece if you want."

Desiree giggles. The sound is so melodious and feminine, it reminds me of a Disney Princess. "Don't be silly. Let's open it up! Make a toast."

She brings me to the counter, pulling out some glasses.

"I'll sit this one out," Lance grumbles, and she shoots him a look.

"Nonsense." She smiles. "One never hurt."

While Desiree is pouring, I peer at Lance, who's hitting me with some kind of burning intensity in his gaze, like he wants me to read his mind and understand what he's trying to get across wordlessly. I'm not telepathic, and as history would show, my skills in reading Lance Hardy specifically are notoriously shoddy as best. But if I had to guess what this particular look meant, I'm still just getting one word... A word he's gotten pretty used to saying to me at this point.

Sorry.

So to that, I give him back something I'm *sure* he can read, because it seems very obvious.

You should be.

Desiree hands me a glass, then hands one to Lance, holding hers up with a perfectly polite grin. "To old friends."

She clinks her glass on mine, then on Lance's, and I try to ignore the way it feels like she's scrutinizing Lance and me as we tap our glasses together.

"Cheers," Lance grunts, taking a pretty big gulp for someone who claims not to drink.

I say nothing, just toss it back, praying for my high scotch tolerance to take the night off. I'll need a significant buzz to get through this, that's for sure.

Distraction... I need a distraction.

"It smells amazing in here," I feign interest in the food. "Can I help with anything?"

"Thank you. And no, don't be silly." Desiree sets down her glass, barely having taken a full sip. "Babe—" She glances at Lance, who straightens like a private. "Would you be a lamb and just watch the sauce for a moment while I give Tate a tour of the house?"

Lance's eyes are rippling with uncertainty that he's obviously trying to hide. They spring to me for a split second, before he nods, inching over to the stove and picking up a wooden spoon.

I want to be offended that he's really going to leave me alone with her, but I can't blame him. *I guess him wanting to follow me around everywhere would be pretty sus.*

Desiree tilts her face upward to cast me a sweet smile, taking me by the arm. "Off we go."

She drags me along, and I subtly peek over my shoulder one last time at Lance.

If she kills me, donate my penis to science.

We wander together through the house, Desiree showing me around like we're in a museum, not a regular two-story home in South Valley. She brings me upstairs, and I start freaking out even more at the idea that she's literally going to show me their bedroom...

That's a move, right?

This is our *bedroom, where* we *have sex because he's* my *husband... That kinda thing?*

But instead, she pauses in front of the closed door, facing me. "Are you a dog person?"

I'm thrown off for a second, before I mutter, "Uh... they're cool, I guess."

She chuckles. "But you're not allergic or anything...?"

"No, no." I shake my head. "My best friend has a dog... Slater." I pause with her staring up at me. "As in A.C... From *Saved by the Bell*." I clear my throat. "He's a German Shepherd Rottweiler mix. Super sweet... well-mannered..." My voice trails, and I gulp.

Okay, you can stop rambling about Jake's dog now.

"That's cute," she says, slowly opening the door to reveal a bedroom. Her and Lance's bedroom. She gestures to an adorable dog who, the moment he sees us, jumps off the bed and scurries over. "This is Sunny. He's a smooth fox terrier. We keep him in here when we have company, because he likes to hog everyone's attention. Isn't that right, Sunny boy??"

His name is... Sunny?

Why am I not surprised...

Desiree bends to scratch behind his ears while the dog licks her all over, little tail wagging like crazy. The dog is cute, I'll give him that. Probably half the size of Slater, with white fur all over, save for some dark brown and tan on his face and ears. He seems wary of me, casually sniffing my hand when I hold it out.

The dog barks, and I flinch.

He knows.

"Sunny, shhh," Desiree scolds him, petting his face.

"Did you, um... Adopt?" I ask, out of my league when talking about pets *and* children, because it's so far beyond my realm of knowledge.

I'm cool with my friends' kids, because they've known me since they were babies as *cool Uncle Tate*, who gives them cash for their birthdays. But dogs can't be bought, and I don't think this one likes me very much.

Yes, I'm sleeping with your daddy, okay?? Get over it.

"We had an ASPCA rescue event at the church, and Sunny was just the sweetest thing." Desiree smiles fondly. "We couldn't possibly not take him."

Interesting...

I've been not-so-casually wondering for a while now why Lance has no kids yet. Based on my own experiences being friends with married couples, it seems like that's what they do. He and Desiree have been married for a long time... And back in school, he used to always mention that he wanted a family someday.

He likes kids, and I'm sure he wants to have his own—yet another reason we're so vastly different. But the way Desiree is fawning over the dog makes it seem like he's their *kid*... Like maybe they're going the fur-baby route instead of trying for actual children.

I wonder why...

Did Hardy change his mind about wanting a family?

Or is Desiree the one pumping on the brakes?

Saying goodbye to the pooch, Desiree closes the bedroom door, and we head back downstairs.

"I'm sure this is all pretty boring compared to your place," she says. And as much as I want to feel like she's sizing me up or something, I'm getting nothing but kindness. "Lance says you're a hugely successful banker. Like one of those Wall Street guys, only out here." She chuckles, and I huff, rubbing my neck.

"I do alright for myself," I murmur, keeping it humble, for probably the first time ever. *Call me crazy, but I just don't think bragging about how rich and awesome I am will help in this situation.* "It's a stressful job, but I love it. Traveling and whatnot..." She's watching me closely as I follow her back up the hallway toward the kitchen. "I'm actually heading out to New York on Friday, for a week. This big account we're trying to lock..."

Her face lights up as if she's excited for me, but I can't tell why.

"Babe, did you hear that?" she gasps as we rejoin Lance in the kitchen. "Tate's going to New York for a week!"

Lance's eyes lock on mine, and I see the surprise and mild hurt in them, most likely because I hadn't mentioned the New York trip to him yet. I planned on telling him about it last night when he came over, but then that never happened...

And for reasons unknown, I'd been considering asking if he wanted to come with me... At least for a couple of days.

But now that his wife is involved, I doubt that's a possibility. *I imagine he won't be able to get away much after this...*

My stomach is sour as Lance rumbles, "Really? That'll be fun..."

"It's not really about *fun*," I grunt, going for some more scotch. "It's about work."

He blinks at me, and my head tilts subtly.

"Wow, New York City..." Desiree sighs. "I've never been, but it seems very exciting. Are you there a lot?"

"I have a place there," I tell her. "I split my time between New York and

Santa Fe, with lots of other scattered trips in between. Houston, Chicago, Atlanta... I never really know where they're going to ship me off to next."

"That sounds like quite the life," she says.

I take a long sip from my glass, the burn distracting from the way Lance is casually peeking at me. "Keeps me busy."

"I imagine it's pretty difficult to make a relationship work," she adds.

Lance scrapes the pan on the stove burner, loudly, then mutters, "Sorry."

Desiree pushes him out of the way, taking over with the food once more. "But I'm sure settling down isn't even on your radar, hm?" she continues to pry, politely enough, but still.

It's making me highly uneasy.

"Not... really. No," I grumble, eyes flicking to Lance. "I don't have time for relationships."

I witness him gulp, and my jaw sets.

I told you that.

"A chronic bachelor traveling the world, living out his dreams," Desiree chuckles gleefully. "What are you doing hanging out with this guy?" she teases, nodding toward Lance.

I feel like my stomach is going to crawl right up out of my mouth. Lance is gaping at me, shooting me with many emotions, and I'm stuck drowning in them all.

I know his wife is going for playful jeering, but there's something about that question that seems sincere.

What am *I doing hanging out with Lance?? It still doesn't make a lick of sense.*

Was that the purpose of tonight? To show me once and for all how much we'll never work?? The clash of lifestyles??

"Des," Lance rumbles with a hint of admonishing in his tone.

"I'm just saying," she goes on. "You two are so different. It's pretty amazing that you managed to reconnect after all these years." Her gaze jumps to mine. "Most friendships just fizzle out after college... As people's lives move in different directions."

A rush of confidence sweeps up my spine. Because I don't like what she's insinuating.

Sure, I know in most cases she's right. And maybe this is all fodder for marking her territory and proving how little I belong in her husband's life. But I resent the fact that just because people chose different paths, they can't remain friends.

"Actually, most of my best friends are married with kids," I hum directly.

She arches a brow. "So it's just you and a bunch of married guys?"

Now we're cooking, sister.

"I have single friends, don't get me wrong. But the people I'm closest to all have families. And maybe I like it that way. I mean, dare to be different... right?"

I lift my glass, winking at her before I toss it back.

Mrs. Hardy is staring like she's not sure what to make of me, and I'll be honest, it's a teeny bit satisfying. I like that maybe she thought she had me figured out, and I'm proving her wrong. And I know it's probably petty and inconsiderate of me to want to show her up, in her own home, when I've been sleeping with her husband... But I can't help it.

She invited me here. She had to have known what she was doing on some level. Whether she's simply jealous of me because Lance has been spending time with me as a friend—this elusive single guy with too much money who gets to travel the world as a career—or she has some inkling suspicions of the kind of *hanging out* we've actually been doing, is irrelevant.

She's trying to control the situation; control *him*. And she's doing a shit job, which is pissing her off. That's the vibe I'm getting from Desiree Hardy.

Showing me a smile that doesn't reach her eyes, she clears her throat and switches off the stove. "Well, dinner's ready. Babe, will you please set the table?"

Determined to keep shoving babe *in my face, it seems.*

I'm not going to admit it's making me feel a little stabby.

Lance just grunts a response, shuffling toward the dining room. I follow after him.

"Let me help."

"Nonsense," he sighs, like he's exhausted. "You're our guest."

"I insist," I reply. *Insistently.*

In the dining room, Lance busies himself setting the table while I mosey around, fiddling with things he's already set up. Freshening both of our drinks, I slide his glass closer to him with my index finger.

"You need this," I whisper.

"No, I don't..." he mumbles, peeking toward the kitchen. "I need to stay sharp."

I tilt my face in his direction. "Worried?"

Trouble

"Tate, stop messing around," he huffs, keeping his voice down. "This is fucked..." He pauses to rub his eyes. "I'm just—"

"I hope everyone's hungry!" Desiree bursts into the room, interrupting whatever he was going to say.

It wouldn't take a psychic to figure it out this time. He's struggling with this...

Because underneath the lying and the sleeping around, he's a good man, and stuff like this doesn't come easily for him.

Shutting down my defensiveness for the first time since we ran into each other, I'm allowing myself to see things clearly...

He's in *way* over his head.

"What do we have here?" I ask, taking my seat as his wife delivers a plate in front of me.

"Halibut with roasted potatoes and asparagus," she says, sitting down across from me, which puts Lance by my side. Not sure if she did that so she can watch us, but it's interesting. "And Lance's famous béarnaise sauce."

I choke on my sip of scotch.

So she made almost the same meal he made for me at my house? That's... weird.

Glancing at him while he takes a slow seat, I watch Lance for any sign that she might know he made me dinner at my house. But he just looks miserable, and it's really dragging down the mood in the room.

"Looks great." I force a smile.

Desiree appears pleased with herself, but still not exactly cunning. The fact that I can't tell what's going on here is giving me a subtle migraine.

Picking up my fork, I'm all set to dig into my food, when Lance scoops up my left hand. I'm startled enough that I drop my fork, glaring at him, then his wife as she takes my right. They're already holding hands, bowing their heads...

Oh, right... Saying grace.

"Thank you, Lord, for this beautiful meal among family and friends," Lance says, swallowing visibly. "We ask that You bless it, let it be nourishing to our bodies. Praise and glory for Your sacrifice, Lord. Amen."

"Amen," Desiree says, reopening her eyes.

"Uh... amen," I grunt, shivering when Lance's hand slides out of mine.

I can't miss his little smirk and the quiet rumble of a chuckle, because he knows I don't do religious stuff. He didn't ask me to say grace when we ate at my place. Although now that I'm thinking about it, he did bow his head for a few seconds himself.

"Tate, you've never been in the church?" Desiree asks, picking up her fork to dig in.

"No, not me." I take a small, tentative bite. It's delicious... *Doesn't taste poisony.* "I just wasn't raised that way, I guess. My mother's never been religious. Or spiritual, for that matter."

My mind spins around a memory that's been coming back to me more and more recently... Of being in a church with my mother.

I don't think we were there for any type of service. In fact, I remember feeling unwanted. Like we weren't supposed to be there...

"I don't mean to pry..." Desiree says. "You can tell me it's none of my business." I wave her off. "But what about your father?"

Lance coughs, shooting a look at his wife. "Des, come on..."

"It's fine, really," I tell him before answering her question. "I never knew my father. He left my mom before I was born."

"Oh, I'm sorry," she says, and I think she really means it.

I shrug. "It's been nearly thirty-five years. I'm over it." She nods, the three of us going back to eating in silence that feels way too thick. "Anyway, it was always just the two of us. No aunts or uncles or cousins... Not even any grandparents. I think there were at one point, but none I ever spent any time with." I release an exhale. "Just me and Mom..."

The woman I haven't even spoken to in months.

Guilt rises up my throat, but I swallow it down forcefully.

"That's why your friendships are so important to you," Lance murmurs, and when I glance up at him, he's side-eyeing me with some assurance. Like he wants me to know that my friends can be my family, and that's totally okay. But then he balks, eyes flinging to his wife before he adds, "Right?"

"Yea," I breathe, shifting in my seat. "It is."

"Well, on that note, I've gotta ask," Desiree speaks again, and I feel myself bunching up once more. "What do you guys do when you go out on the town?"

Her tone is curious, but overall, still pretty easygoing. Regardless, I don't know how to answer because I don't know what Lance has said to her already.

Peering at him, I watch him focusing on his food while shooting me subtle glances. I look to his wife again, and she's just staring at me.

Trouble

I guess she needs me to answer this question... To see if it's similar to what he's told her?

"It's pretty much exactly what you'd expect," I whip out a fake chuckle and smirk. "I'm the wild one, and the rest of the guys are boring... Especially this marshmallow." I nod in Lance's direction.

He finally gives me a full look, lips curving in amusement.

I continue to eat in between improvising. "If Kennan comes out too, that's a different story. Because, ya know..." My voice trails, but Desiree is watching me, brows raised in wait. "He's also gay and crazy."

She giggles, though she seems intimidated by the *gay thing*. Who knows why... Maybe she doesn't know a lot of gay people. Or maybe she suspects she might know one better than she thinks.

"Kennan's wild." Lance finally joins the conversation, crunching off a bite of perfectly cooked asparagus. He peeks at me. "Maybe wilder than you."

"He's just loud and extra. There's a difference," I murmur. "I like to let loose like an adult, whereas he still acts like he's twenty-one." Forking a potato, I point it at him. "They call that *Peter Pan Syndrome*."

Lance huffs, a small grin becoming a bit less stiff. Seeing it eases a bit of my own tension.

"Which one is Kennan again?" Desiree asks, and I look up.

Shit, I forgot she was there for a second.

"He's the one who had the Pride party," Lance answers. "In ABQ."

"And he didn't go to school with us?"

Right... I also forgot she went to ASU.

It's still weird to me that she went to the same college as us, but I can't for the life of me ever remember seeing her until she started dating Lance, at which point I went to great lengths to avoid ever seeing them.

"No, he's friends with Lou," Lance says, then turns to me. "Still fuzzy on exactly how those two met."

A laugh bubbles out of me. "Why? They're so similar," I tease, and Lance chuckles. "Kennan decorated the offices for Lou's firm. I guess they just hit it off. Lou's always been cool like that... Seeing people's personalities, rather than superficial traits." I pause, swallowing a bite before adding, "Like you."

Lance blinks at me. "No room for prejudice," he mumbles. "Love is love, right?"

Except when it comes to dating one of your best friends, though... right?

I think he's reading my mind right now, because he's giving me another one of his apologetic looks, like he wants to explain himself, but can't get his voice to work. And in this moment, it's stirring me up more than usual.

Because I always assumed Lance took off on me because he was afraid of admitting he liked guys, scared of what his family would think... The usual stuff. But the more time we've been spending together recently, the more that explanation is feeling like only a fraction of the truth.

"I'm sorry..." I pull my eyes away from Lance to peer across the table. "We've been talking about me for too long. Tell me about you. What's Desiree all about?"

Lance's wife seems all too pleased that I'm involving her in the conversation, launching into talk about her parents' flower shop, where she works and Lance helps out, none of that surprising me in the slightest. And she does talk a lot about her and Lance *together*, but mostly as it pertains to their families.

I'm probably projecting, but they seem more like two separate people whose lives are connected by others, rather than a happily married couple. And I would know, because I know a lot of happily married couples. Everything about Lance and Desiree feels like an *image* for the sake of their families and their community.

As if they're actors in a play, putting on this performance for the rest of the world.

And I'm the theater critic who ain't buyin' it.

As we finish our food, the conversation slows, and I ask Lance, "Hey, how's your sister doing?"

I've never actually met Lance's sister, but he's always spoken very highly of her. The other day, when he was over, he told me that she's unexpectedly pregnant. He seemed to feel a certain type of way about it, but wouldn't allow himself to say anything unsupportive.

"She's good," he replies, leaning back in his chair. "I spoke to her yesterday. She has her first ultrasound next week."

"At least she'll probably be able to work through this semester," I comment, purposely trying to impress him by proving I was listening and retaining the details he shared with me. "Before it gets too uncomfortable, or whatever..."

Lance shoots me another content little smile that reminds me to slow down with the scotch. I'm already warm and fuzzy enough as it is.

"Look at you, trying to sympathize with a pregnant lady," he croons, and I grin.

But then I glance at his wife. *Was that a little too flirtatious?? I can barely tell...*

Flirting for me is like breathing.

"Oh yea, Ellie's pregnancy was quite the surprise," Desiree says. "It brought up more than a few questions."

I blink at her. "What kinds of questions...?"

"For Lance and I." She chuckles, gazing fondly at him. But when I glance his way, he appears wildly uncomfortable again. "Since Ellie is younger, I guess everyone was expecting me to go first."

I swallow thickly, my stomach twisting. "Well... everyone does things on their own time."

"Or God's time," she adds, smiling at Lance. Then she stands up with her plate. "Who knows? It could happen sooner than *we'd* planned, too."

I feel my face go ashen, and I'm trying hard to control the look of horror that wants to break out. I wish I could speak, provide some kind of normal, casual response, but my mouth is just hanging open. And Lance seems to be having the same problem. Except that he's also gaping at his wife like she's lost her mind, and I really wish I knew what that look meant.

Desiree comes over to get our plates, and I manage to produce words in a robotic tone. "Let me... help with those."

"No, please. You sit." She brushes me off. "I'll bring some coffee and dessert."

She squeezes Lance's shoulder on her way out of the room, leaving us both sitting here like a bomb of awkwardness was just dropped on the table.

My eyes follow her back and forth as she moves about the kitchen, until I shake myself out of it and peer at Lance. He's chewing on his lower lip, eyes round, forehead lined.

Reaching over, I slide my hand onto his thigh. I don't know why, it just happens.

His face flings in my direction, and I whisper, "Are you okay?"

"No..." he breathes, blinking hard. "No, I'm very fucking *not* okay. I don't know what's going on... This whole dinner is just..." His voice cuts out, and he covers my hand with his, linking our fingers. "I can't do this anymore, T."

My spine stiffens, chest clenching so hard I almost cough. "Can't do... what?"

"This," he whines in a hushed tone. "Lying and hiding and... whatever the hell she's playing at."

"Do you think she knows?" I ask, so quiet, it's barely audible.

But, of course, he hears me. "I'm not sure, but I'm telling you right now, this isn't how she usually acts. Something is up..."

"She's probably jealous, or threatened," I tell him. I can feel him shaking, even just from holding his hand.

It fills me with the inexplicable need to comfort him; to make him feel alright again, because despite everything, he's always done it for me. Squeezing his hand tighter, I hear him exhale slowly, as if it's working, and just being able to hold my hand gives him some solace. It fills my chest with warmth, until my mind circles back to what his wife just said.

"Is she... trying to get pregnant?" I ask him nervously, awaiting his response like the test results for a terminal illness.

"No," he answers sincerely. "In fact, she—"

His voice evaporates fast when Desiree comes back into the room with pie and coffee. Our hands fly apart even faster.

"Honey, will you get us some cups?" she asks, setting everything down.

"Sure." He shoots up and staggers off.

And the whole time his wife is asking me about coffee or tea, milk or cream, talking about peach crumble something or other, I can't stop thinking about what he was about to say.

In fact, she what??

This whole babies thing is freaking me the fuck out, man.

I mean, sleeping with a married guy is all well and good, but if his wife is *pregnant*, I feel like that changes things just a tad.

I'm tense as hell. I don't think I've ever been this tense before, and never over any type of *relationship*. Bound in nerves like rope tying me up, left to focus on the *ridiculous* way my hand is missing his with every second he's out of the room.

When he comes back, we have coffee and some kind of peach cobbler thing that's really fucking delicious, but I can't even enjoy it because I'm too busy spewing angst from every pore in my body.

Lance's wife is talking, but I can barely hear her. I'm up in my head, muscles bunched, heart heavily pumping through it all. Watching Lance out the corner of my eye, I see him tapping his fingers on his thigh under the table, most likely counting the seconds until this excruciating evening is over.

I know the feeling.

Extending my foot like some knee-jerk reaction, I gently nudge it on his. He looks like the contact surprised him, but he doesn't react much. So

Trouble

I push my foot into his a little more, and his eyes flit to mine. Only for a second, but that one look is enough to have me buzzing.

I just want to be done with this too.

I want it to go back to being just *us*... Hidden away if we have to be, but I can't deny that no one gives me *comfort* like he does, deep in the faraway corners of my soul. And no one else ever has.

It's only him.

Inching closer, as subtly as possible, I run my foot up his ankle, then his calf, caressing him with it, because I can't use my hands to touch him. It would be too obvious. I continue grazing his leg with my shoe because I can't not, studying the wide plane of his chest as it moves with unsteady breaths. It's the way he always breathes when we're together. Excitement flowing from his lungs, but still, he's at ease.

With *me*.

Because he's... mine.

He should be mine, not hers.

The sudden possessiveness is crawling through me, and I don't know why. Maybe it's because his wife is right there, talking about the life they've made together since he left me, and knowing that he still found his way *back*.

Regardless, I just can't take it anymore.

I need him to—

Lance's hand slides onto my thigh. And it startles me so much, I jump and knock over the cup of coffee I'm holding. Dumping it all over myself.

"Shit!" I gasp, jumping out of my seat like that's going to do anything. "I'm so sorry..."

"Oh, that's no problem," Desiree hops up, rushing over while Lance is just smirking at me.

I scowl down at his beautiful face. *Jerk... he totally did that on purpose.*

Desiree hands me some napkins, but my shirt and pants are soaked with hot coffee. "That'll probably stain..." she says. "I can try to soak them for you."

"That's okay," I breathe. *Just one of many Armani suits.* "I should probably be going, anyway. It's getting late, and I have a bit of a drive home."

"Nonsense. You can't drive all the way home like this." Lance stands up from his seat. *And he's a giant once more.* "I'll get you something to change into."

"Not necessary," I grumble, my words coming out defensive because I'm still all wound up and jealous and the longer I stay here, the more I run the risk of doing something even stupider than dumping coffee on myself. "If I can just use your bathroom to get cleaned up..."

"Of course. Top of the stairs," Desiree says while clearing the tablecloth. "Honey, will you bring the dishes to the sink? I'm going to get this into the laundry."

Lance peeks at me like he doesn't want to leave me, aching my chest and confusing me more.

Darting away from him, I climb the stairs quickly, stalking into the bathroom. At the sink, I grip the counter, closing my eyes and taking a deep breath.

What the hell am I doing...?

Coming here was a huge mistake. All it got me was irrational jealousy, even achier blue balls, obsessive thoughts about Lance's wife getting pregnant, and a ruined suit.

"You're doing great, you know that?" I scoff at myself in the mirror.

A soft knock on the door pulls my attention. "T?" *It's Lance.* "You okay in there?"

Scowling at the adorable concern in his voice, I unbutton my shirt. "Leave me alone, Hardy." Unbuckling my belt, I open my pants, using a towel to dry off some of the coffee.

"Just let me get you some clean clothes to wear," he murmurs. "Please?"

Huffing out of frustration, I stomp to the door and whip it open. "You'd like that, wouldn't you??"

His gaze seems to be stuck between my exposed torso and my open pants as he bites his lip. "Huh...?"

"My eyes are up here," I grumble, rolling them when his finally lift.

Flushed, he stares at me for a couple of seconds during which I *feel* every agonizing twitch of hunger and need that have been coursing through me for days, since he was supposed to come back to me, but instead we wound up *here*, in this fucked up situation.

Eventually, he turns and strides into his bedroom. And I take slow steps to follow him, walking farther away from rational thought, and closer to what I really, *really* want.

Inside his bedroom, the dog is scurrying around him while he digs through a dresser.

"You want, like, jeans? Or are sweats okay...?"

I'm quiet until he turns around, and my default sassy humor used to disguise my vulnerability comes out. "I'll take anything as long as it's Prada. Or Gucci."

Lance's lips curl into a grin that he purses away, thrusting some sweatpants in my direction.

Stepping closer, my brow furrows. "I can't wear those... You're huge. They're gonna fall off."

This time he chuckles, eyes falling down to my crotch once more. "I don't think you'll have a problem filling them out, big boy..."

Fuck. Me. Hard.

The spark in the air has turned into a full-blown blaze.

"You shouldn't be looking at me like that, Sunshine..." I breathe, shrugging out of my shirt. "The door is open... and your wife is downstairs."

"I know... but I can't help it," he croaks, stifling a hoarse whimper when I step out of my pants, and he sees what I'm wearing. My favorite Andrew Christian jock. "Sweet Mother Nature..."

Humming a growly sound of aroused amusement, I ease myself up to him, biting my lip and *burning* from head to toe. I feel the heat coming off of him too, only a few inches of space separating us. He flutters closer until we're all but sealed, ravenously ogling the sight of my erection and my ass in the jock.

"Give me the clothes, Lance," I whisper, tauntingly.

"Hm...?" he replies, engrossed, as his covetous gaze lifts to my mouth.

"Unless... you want me to stay like this," I hum, going for broke and sliding my hands up his chest.

He groans softly, leaning in to brush his lips over mine. "Fuck, baby... We *can't*..."

"Then stop." I'm seconds from bursting into literal flames, from the torturous heat between us, and the fact that I'm *definitely* going to Hell for what I'm about to do.

And so is he. Because he drops the clothes onto the floor and grasps my jaw in his big hands. "You know stopping isn't an option with you."

Fuck it.

Lifting my mouth to his, I kiss him, quickly enough that he gasps. But he immediately returns it even faster, and *harder*, thrusting his tongue between my lips to thrash mine.

"Damnit, Tate, you taste so fucking good," he growls, ripping at my hair while I tug him by his pants, walking us backward until my legs hit the bed. "This is so, *so* bad..."

"I know." I crash onto my back, pulling him on top of me, where he immediately settles between my legs, rubbing his clothed erection against mine. "It's fucking *deplorable*. Take your dick out and fuck me..."

Lance is biting and sucking my lips viciously as I open his pants, pushing them down just enough to get his dick in my fist.

He purrs, nibbling his way down my neck while his hand cups my cock. "Baby, you're so hard... Tell me you haven't come since the last orgasm I gave you."

Lifting my hips to push my dick harder into his hand, I rasp, "You said to wait for you... So I did."

Groaning, low and jagged, he abruptly flips me onto my stomach, squeezing my ass in two fistfuls. I whine and he scolds, "Shhh... *Quiet*, sexy love. My wife will hear us."

"Fuck, I'm gonna come so fast..." I writhe beneath his body weight, face smashed into the bedding.

"You look incredible, T," he praises, spreading my ass open and running his fingers over my hole. They're wet, I'm guessing with his saliva. "You wore this for me?"

"Call it wishful thinking," I whimper as he opens me up wider, lifting enough to spit between my cheeks, massaging it into me.

"You're such a naughty little slut," he hisses, spitting some more, pushing it inside my ass to really get me as wet as possible with no other available lubrication. "You know there's no way for me to resist you... Even with her right downstairs. She could come up here any second, but I *can't* fucking *help* myself. I'm all fucking yours, Tate, and you know that."

"I'm yours too, baby... And you promised you'd take care of me." My heart is slamming in my chest, mind all foggy and devoid of the sky-high stack of consequences. I'm just squirming under him, pushing my hips back while he strokes saliva onto his cock and grinds it between my cheeks. "I wore that fucking plug *all day*, but you never showed up... God, I was *aching* for you, Sunshine, and I still am... Down to my fucking core."

"I know, baby." He pouts on the nape of my neck, kissing gently as he pushes his crown up to my hole. "Let me make it up to you... Soothe that sore spot with this big dick that belongs to you."

"*Ohhfuuck please.*" I grip the comforter in my fists. "Please fuck me, Sunshine... Fuck me in the ass right where your wife sleeps."

He groans, as quietly as possible, nudging his giant erection into me. "Mmm, Tate baby, you're so much trouble... Open that ass for me. We gotta make this quick."

His head surges inside my hole, my eyes rolling back in my skull. "*Uhhh*... n-not a p-problem, baby. Just touch it once and I—*fuck*—I swear to God, I'm gonna sh-shoot everywhere."

Trouble

"Good boy." He thrusts into me hard, and deep, filling me with every solid inch until I'm seeing constellations.

His pelvis taps on my cheeks as he bottoms out, my ass burning from the lack of proper lubrication. But I don't even care. It feels *miraculous*. Having him inside me again... It's like my missing piece has been snapped back in. Everything is right with the world... *Well, not* right, *but you know...*

I'm high, not only because I'm in serious need of this release, but also because I *have* him. He's *mine*, fucking *me*, with his wife right downstairs.

It probably makes me evil, and awful, and disgusting... But I can't help it.

Trouble is as trouble *fucking* does.

Lance draws back and drives back in, again and *again*, building his rhythm fast, fucking me deep and raw, while trying to keep the sounds of his skin slapping mine to a minimum. As soon as his swollen cock starts lancing my prostate, I have tears rolling down my cheeks.

Apparently, I'm being too loud, because he covers my mouth with his hand. Knelt behind me on the bed, gripping my hip with the other, he pumps into me rough, biting my shoulder to keep *himself* quiet.

The dog barks, and he snarls, "Shh! Sunny... shut up. Mother... *fuck*, baby, you're so tight. I love this ass so damn much." I groan behind his hand, winding and coiling. "My warm, perfect little cunt... You want me to bust in you, gorgeous?"

I nod fast. "Mm mmm."

"You want me to send you home with an ass full of cum?"

I nod again, arching up to him, hole clenching, balls heavy and throbbing.

Fuck... fuck fuck fuck...

His hips are smacking into me, our pants and hushed grunts creating sinful music. And maybe it's too loud... In fact, I'm *sure* it is. But the thrill of getting caught just makes it that much *better*, *hotter* and *dirtier*, rushing my orgasm even *faster* to the surface.

"Mmm, *Tate*, I'm almost there," his voice cracks. "Come with me, baby." His left hand leaves my waist, reaching around to caress my stiff cock. "Come *hard* for your man."

My body seizes as a wave of blinding euphoria pulls me under. I'm sobbing, *wailing* behind his hand, buzzing in heavy contractions as I come almost violently, shooting so hard it hurts. My dick sprays pulse after pulse of cum for him while he catches them in his hand.

"That's it, baby... You come *so good* for me, Tate. My love, you're...

275

sucking... it... *out*." He gasps, and I feel his dick swell and throb, filling me up as he bucks his orgasm deep into my body. "Oh God... *Oh yes*, baby, you have no idea how good it feels to come in you..."

Licking and sucking and biting my neck, his entire body feels like it's convulsing on top of me. We're both spinning, whirling and twirling, crumbling to bits together in his bed, his big cock spilling in my ass like it belongs to me, and I belong to him...

Because I do.

God... I definitely *fucking do.*

"Gorgeous, you're *everything*," he whispers, ragged, finally removing his hand from my mouth and dragging the cum-soaked one up in its place. "Lick it up," he commands.

And of course I do. Because it's filthy and fucking *perfect*, just like him, and us, together.

As soon as my cum is in my mouth, he grabs me by the jaw and kisses me fierce, lapping and sucking my flavor from my tongue, whimpering as he goes.

"It should've been you," he breathes almost frantically. The desperation in his kiss, and his words, has even more tears seeping from my eyes, emotions I can no longer hold back forcing their way out. "*Fuck*, Tate, it's always been you, baby."

"Mmf... Lance," I mewl, falling the hell apart here. "Lance, I... I..."

"Tell me you love me," he whispers a plea.

I'm *terrified*, crying nervously into his mouth.

It's... always been... him.

"Lance! Can you bring Sunny out?!"

Fear jolts my limbs at the sound of his wife calling him from just down the stairs.

"Fuck, shit..." I grunt, yanking away from his kiss.

But he's not sharing my sense of urgency. In fact, he's still just lying on top of me, softening dick still resting in my ass while his fingers comb loving through my mussed-up hair.

"Lance, get up!" I wriggle beneath him. "She's gonna come up here."

"I don't even fucking care anymore," he sighs, part dazed and part exhausted. He sounds sated, but his tone is dripping with melancholy. Like he's not ready to give up our moment. He doesn't want it to end this time... Maybe ever. "Don't take this away from me, T," he begs hoarsely. "I don't care about *anything* but you... And I wanna hear you say it."

I shake my head and whisper, "Not like this..."

Trouble

He pulls back enough for our eyes to lock. My face is melting from the way he's looking at me, seeing the emotions streaming down my cheeks. He swipes them off with his thumbs.

"Tate..." His gaze bores adoration into me...

Looking at me the way Clytie looks at Apollo, no doubt. I gulp.

He's gonna say it...

Oh God... I think he's going to...

"Lance?!" Desiree shouts again.

Lance sighs, lifting himself up on shaky arms, pausing for a moment to play with my hair before he pulls out of me and stands up. Breaking the spell, but not fully. There's still an invisible string tethered between us. I can feel it, and it's choking me up.

I'm not ready for this... Am I??

"Your dog was literally watching us have sex," I grunt by way of shifting the heaviness, eyeing his dog while I scramble up quickly. I'm jittering all over at the notion that his wife might walk upstairs any second since he's not answering her. "He saw the whole thing. What if he's a nark?"

Lance chuckles, grasping my chin and pressing a soft kiss on my lips while I squirm.

"I have cum running down my leg, baby," I whine hoarsely, and he chuckles again.

"Mmm... hot." He grins, still looking at me with a world of emotional ferocity behind his eyes.

"You really want her to find us like this?" I jerk away from him, picking up my dirty dress shirt and using it to wipe myself up a little.

"It doesn't matter," he replies softly. "*Nothing* else matters, Tate. Only you..."

"You keep saying that..." I grumble anxiously, dressing in his clothes. They're so *not* my style at all, but they smell like him and I'm basking in it. "But it's fucking bullshit. It all *matters*, Hardy. Otherwise, you wouldn't still be hiding it. You wouldn't have ditched me last night, and you wouldn't have... left me back then."

He gives me a wounded look, and I swallow.

This is all just... crazy. All of it.

What the hell are we doing??

Lance brushes his fingers through my hair. "I'm not afraid anymore, baby... Back then, I was scared shitless. But *now*... I just want you. I want to *stay* this time, Tate, and give you everything I should've given you back then. I want all this—" he gestures around the room, "—only with *you*."

I'm still as stone, just gaping at him with my mouth hanging open.

I don't... know what to say.

Is that... Could we really...?

Footsteps are coming up the stairs. My heart slams.

Lance kisses my forehead, and whispers, "Don't go yet. I'll walk you to your car."

Then he darts out of the room, and I release a quivering breath.

I can't stay to say goodbye... This is too intense. I need to get the hell out of here. Especially knowing damn well I won't be able to look his wife in the eye after having just fucked her husband in their bed while she was feet away.

I hear their voices, and then more footsteps, only they're now descending the stairs.

The dog is sniffing me. I glance down at him, and he barks.

I narrow my gaze. "You didn't see a thing, got it?"

He barks again, and I huff.

If Lance doesn't tell his wife tonight, this damn dog probably will.

"Sunny! Come on, boy! Outside!" Lance calls from downstairs and the dog goes running.

Rubbing my eyes, I leave the bedroom with a handful of my sullied clothes, tiptoeing down the stairs and making an immediate beeline for the front door.

Just as I'm reaching for the handle, though, a female voice stops me.

"Are you in love with him?"

My shoulders slump, eyelids dropping in a slow blink.

So close...

Wordlessly, I shake my head. But she asks again, "Are you...?"

I clear my throat. "What is *love*, anyway? I mean, really—"

"*Tate...*"

Finally, I peer over my shoulder, giving her my most contrite look of admission. "Maybe a little..."

Her face is framed visibly by many serious emotions. Some angry, some devastated, some... guilty, it seems, which is throwing me off.

"Have you always loved him?"

Exhaling my surrender, I nod. "Probably... yea."

Desiree bites her lip. "Does he love you...?"

"You'll wanna talk to him about that," I grunt, turning away, going for the door again. As I pull it open, I mutter, "I'm sorry..."

And as I'm walking out, she replies, "Me too."

Chapter Twenty-Two
Lance

Confessing the truth, *honesty*... it's freedom.

Even just *deciding* to finally come clean is like a wave of serenity washing over you, assuring a great gift of gravity when, at long last, you speak the words. It's a fast lift of weight from your shoulders, to blissfully assuage the agony of all your festering lies.

Outside in my backyard, I'm watching Sunny scamper to and fro, peeing on things, my lips curved into a pleasant smile. Because this is it...

This is the last night that I will spend saddled with the sickness of these secrets.

I'm going to tell my wife the truth.

I'm going to tell her I want a divorce.

I'm going to tell Tate that I love him.

No. I'm going to tell him that I'm *madly in love* with him, and that I always have been.

I will tell him, with the fullest sincerity in my heart, that I never *wanted* to leave him fifteen years ago... And then, I'm going to tell him why I did.

The joy of confession is no doubt a much-needed comfort, because under no circumstances does telling the truth dissolve your problems. If anything, it begins the long, hard road to rebuilding everything you mangled and destroyed with your lies. This delightful feeling is a conduit... Which is good.

Because my groveling will be damn-near insurmountable.

There's no way to know how Tate will react to what I have to tell him.

He's already so closed-off because of what I've done, what I made him into. I can only hope the truth also gives *him* some peace... Peace we can both revel in while we hopefully move on from this, together.

The sound of a car engine roaring to life stiffens my spine, snapping me out of my reverie. My brow furrows.

That sounds like Tate's car...

Whistling, I call for Sunny. "Come on, boy! Let's go."

He scampers after me, following me back inside the house. And when I get there, Desiree is standing in the foyer, staring at the front door. My gut is immediately churning with unease.

"Where's Tate...?" I mutter, stalking up the hall, glancing in all the rooms as I go. My heart falls. "He left, didn't he?"

Desiree turns slowly to face me. Then she nods.

I rake my fingers through my hair. *Fuck... This sucks.*

He wasn't supposed to leave. I wanted to tell him...

The urge to go after him is strong, but I hold myself back. I can't go to him until I start releasing all of this shit into the open. He deserves to have me unsaddled; all secrets revealed, all truths laid out for the world to see and make its judgements.

I don't fucking care anymore... What I told him upstairs was the truth.

I don't care about *anything* but him...

He is *all that matters.*

"Des, look, we need to talk..." I mumble, stepping up to her.

Her eyes are shining at me like she already knows. It's helpful, yet it isn't. Because I'm glad telling her about me and Tate will be a bit easier. But still, the wreck is inevitable.

My wife nods again, slipping out her small hand to collect mine. She links our fingers, yanking me along into the living room. And I go with her, since this is clearly going to be awful, and we might as well settle in, get comfortable, and prepare for the emotional demolition.

She brings me to the couch, releasing me as she motions for me to sit. I do. But rather than sitting down beside me, she suddenly lifts her dress up over her head, tossing it onto the floor.

Uh... what?

My eyes are wide, mouth agape to display my sheer bewilderment as she stands before me in only some skimpy panties. Breasts out, nipples pert from the chill of the central air, or maybe even the adrenaline of whatever the hell is going on. She drops onto her knees on the couch, straddling my hips and grabbing my face.

Trouble

"Des, wait—"

That's all I get out before her lips assault mine and she kisses me fast. *What in the holy fuck?!*

Hands flying to her waist, my fingers dig in as if I might try to pry her off of me, but she's gripping my jaw and kissing me so hard it's like her mouth is a vacuum sucking me in. I don't think she's ever kissed me so *aggressively* in twelve years of marriage...

But then I remember something, from when we first started dating...

Back when I was still actively hung up on Tate, spending every waking minute trying to stuff down the misery of not being with him, she used to climb on top of me the way she is now, and just take over...

Basically, she would do all the work while I'd just lie there, taking it; the pleasure that, sure, felt good for my body in some ways, but never reached anything deeper.

It's always been this way with my wife. I can admit that now. I've been able to get off purely because my body reacts to the superficial stimulation. But on the inside, I'm empty.

No amount of sex or fooling around with women has *ever* lit me up the way a single touch from Tate Eckhart does. Whether that means I'm gay, or just hopelessly in love with him, remains to be seen.

Either way, this isn't doing anything for me, and I'm done pretending it does.

Lifting my hands up to my wife's, I rip them off of my face, dipping out of her hungry kisses and sucking air into my lungs. "Desiree, stop! I don't want this... We need to *talk*."

"Shh... No talking." She grips my shoulders, shoving her tits into my face. "I can do this... It's fine. I can still be what you need, Lance."

"What?? No. *Stop*," I grunt, struggling away from her. But she literally grabs my jaw and stuffs her nipple into my fucking mouth.

Rage, helplessness, and a tickle of fear claw at the inside of my chest, because this doesn't feel right *at all*. It feels *so bad*, and she's not *stopping*, despite how obviously uninterested, and downright appalled I am, ripping at my clothes, opening my pants and trying to pull out my cock.

She's gone fucking crazy!

"Enough!" I roar when the anger overpowers my normally level-headed instincts. I shove her off of me forcefully and she crashes onto the couch, scrambling to get up. "I *don't* want this!"

"Yes, you do!" she sobs. "Just come in me. We can make a baby, I promise we can! I know that's what you really want." Her hands slither along my chest and my neck while I smack them away, stumbling back and pushing her off every time she tries to climb back on top of me. "I'm sorry I made you wait so long..." she whimpers. "It's my fault... I wasn't sure. But now I am! *Please* get me pregnant, Lance, I want you to!"

"What in the fuck is wrong with you?? No! That's *not* what I want," I growl, grabbing her wrists and holding them still. "*Yes*, I did want a baby... I probably still do." I pause with my pulse racing, gulping over the words I'm about to say. "But not with you."

Desiree's face falls, something powerfully impotent shimmering in her eyes. She looks hurt; of course, she does, but there's more to it than that. I also see rejection, or worry? As if she thinks this is what she's supposed to do and she's failing...

Shaking it off, she rips out of my hold and slithers onto the floor, kneeling between my legs. "Fine, then you can have my mouth. Come on, baby... I'll show you it's just as good..."

She gets her hand inside my pants and around my cock, which is limper than a wet noodle, pulling it out fast and dropping like she's actually about to put her mouth on me. But I grab her face quick.

"No. No no *no*, I'm gonna insist that you *don't* do that," I rasp, heaving from all this craziness.

"Why not?" she whines, extending her tongue.

I push her back again, growling, "Because I just fucked Tate!"

My wife's face goes still, wide eyes gazing up at me, long lashes fanning as she blinks.

Heat rushes to my face, and I swallow hard. "I fucked him, so please don't try to... put my dick in your mouth." Uncomfortably, I clear my throat while she finally starts to back up. "I mean, that's not the only..." I shake my head. "Whatever, the point is that I don't want what you're trying to do, Des. I'm *sorry*, but I just don't." Her eyes fall shut as she sits back on her knees, covering her face with her hands. "This is what I wanted to talk about, by the way," I hiss, fisting my hair. "If you'd just *listened* instead of attacking me like a wild animal, we could have avoided this awkwardness right fucking here..."

"How long..." she mutters. I inhale deep, releasing it slowly. Her hands fall away from her face, and she peers up at me. "How long have you been sleeping with him?"

"Only a few weeks." My voice is low, weighted with guilt. But I'm trying to project; push past the severe discomfort of this situation and just tell her the fucking *truth*. "It started... after I ran into him at Pride." Something like relief washes over her features, and she nods. Until I add, "But I've been in love with him since before I even met you."

Her chin drops. And she nods again. "Yea... I know."

My head slants, forehead lining in confusion as she grabs her dress, slipping it back on. But she doesn't come up to sit on the couch. She stays parked on the floor, kneeling before me.

"You used to say his name in your sleep, you know..." She huffs, shaking her head a little, eyes set on the floor to purposely avoid my gaze. I'm surprised, and not, by what she's telling me. *Tate Eckhart has been invading my dreams for a long time.* "A *lot* when we first started dating, actually. Over the years, it faded... And I thought it was because maybe... you were moving on." Finally, her eyes lift. "Maybe you were learning to love me in his place."

I swallow a heavy gulp of remorse that slides roughly down my throat. Speechless. Just staring.

"I should've known." She looks back down at her hands. "I should never have agreed to something so damningly futile."

My head swivels. "No, Des, it's *not* your fault... This is all on me. I shouldn't have tried to stuff you into a hole in my heart that you didn't fit in." She releases an exhausted sigh, covering her face again. And for a moment, I think she's crying. It slices me open, and I lean forward. "Please don't blame yourself... This is *my* fuck-up, Desiree..."

"Did you know that I transferred to ASU?" she mumbles behind her hands.

My lashes flutter in bemused blinking, at the subject change and her words. *She never told me that...*

"Senior year," she scoffs derisively. "I mean, who the hell transfers schools during their senior fucking year??"

"Wait, I thought—"

"I was all set to graduate from New Mexico State," she keeps talking. Something about her tone is twisting me up in knots. "Honestly, I would've stayed. You and I could have done long distance. Your family was in New Mexico... I'm sure it could've worked. But they didn't want to take any chances. So they paid for my tuition, housing, expenses... All of it. Just to keep us together. To ensure we *stayed* together... as in physically."

Baffled by her words, my head is spinning. I'm finding it hard to breathe, and my heart is beating a lot faster than it should.

"Who..." I croak. "Who's *they*?"

Her face slants slowly, wide eyes meeting mine. "Your parents."

The floor disappears out from under me. Like a trapdoor opened.

And I'm *falling*...

"Hold on..." I mutter, rubbing my eyes, because I must be hallucinating. "I don't understand..."

Desiree straightens, breathing in and out slowly, like she's preparing herself for something painful. "Remember the day we met? In church, after your dad's sermon..."

I nod. I can do nothing more than that.

"A few weeks earlier, my parents had invited yours over for lunch after church," she murmurs. "It seemed normal at first. Just having the pastor and his wife over, polite hosts, enchanting guests. Light conversation. Your mom and dad said they had a son my age, casually mentioning that you were single... And that they really wanted you to find the... right girl." She gulps over the words. I'm not breathing. "Like I said, it was pretty normal. But after they left, my parents told me that your parents wanted to set us up. That they wanted me to meet you."

She pauses for a moment. "It was a little weird... But then, stranger things have happened. So I agreed. But right before church that day, they told me not to say anything... About any of it. They made me swear never to tell you they were setting us up."

A stupefied gasp leaves my lips as I sit back, gaping at her, undoubtedly an expression of utter perplexity on my face.

What the hell is she... talking about?

Our parents were... what? Trying to arrange our marriage?? Without me knowing about it??

"The first meeting went well," Desiree goes on, brows knitted. "I liked you right away. I thought you were caring and sweet. And gorgeous, obviously. I could definitely see myself dating you. But it was also clear that something was up. Underneath your polite smile, you seemed a bit sad... Like you were wrestling with feelings you were trying like hell to overcome. I recognized it right away as heartbreak... And I told my parents I didn't want to pursue a guy who was clearly in love with someone else."

She peers up at me while my skin breaks out in chills. "I promise I didn't know about Tate until we'd already been together for a while. I never would have agreed if I knew you were... Or that it was..." She's scrambling for words, tripping over her own tongue. "They just told me you were hung up on someone who was bad for you, that was it. They said you *needed* me to help you forget, and move on. And I guess I... liked the idea of fixing you. Of holding your brokenness together. I thought I was *helping* you, Lance, I swear!"

Her face is contorted in guilt and sorrow. But I can barely see... My vision is blurred by ardent rage, confusion and hurt, rising in me like a tide.

My voice scrapes, "So you mean... you never would've gone along with fabricating a relationship if you knew I was in love with a man?"

She swallows visibly, tears springing to her eyes. But I'm finding it very difficult to process sympathy right now.

My hands are shaking, my chest is on fire, and there's so much loud noise inside my skull, I want to cover my ears and curl into a ball.

Is this really happening...? She's saying...

It was all a lie. This whole time. Every moment of us... That sign from God...

It was a fake. Forged by people trying to control the outcome.

My parents pushed Desiree into my life at exactly the right moment... to get me away from Tate.

Or... my father *did.*

Let's face it, I know for a fact this is all his doing.

"Why would you go along with that...?" I croak. "To save me??" My head shakes in disbelief. "Talk about a messiah complex..."

She sniffles. "I'm so sorry, Lance. I can't even express how s—"

"Did my father tell you about Tate?" I cut off her forced apology that I'm now seeing, just like everything else, as shiny, hollow plastic, with nothing underneath. Desiree pales, blinking back tears. "Did he *specifically* want you to keep me away from *Tate*...?"

"He never said it was *Tate*." Her head shakes while she chews on her lower lip.

And I'm fuming so hard, it feels like I'm breathing fire. Honestly, I don't know if I even believe a word she's saying now...

I can't tell what's a lie and what's real anymore.

"Desiree!" I snap, and she flinches. "I need you to tell me *exactly* what my father said!"

"He just said that he... or the *person* you had feelings for... was bad for you," she squeaks. "That they were hurting you, but you couldn't see it. And that I needed to do my best to keep you... Keep you with me, and away from them. I only found out later it was... a guy. Someone you'd been close with in college." She whimpers, crawling over to me. "I promise, Lance, he *never* said it was about keeping you from..."

"From what? Being gay? Being with a man??" I bark, and she sobs, covering her face again.

Jumping up from my seat, I begin pacing around the room, red splashing behind my eyes. I'm furious, enraged, confounded and so fucking *sad*... So *angry* at my own damn family, and the woman I'd thought was my *partner*...

But mostly, I'm mad at myself. For being played.

I'm hurt and helpless and so pissed the fuck off at myself, I could retch... For allowing them to so easily manipulate me.

My father is... There's no other way to say it.

He's a *monster*.

My mind flashes back to that awful time, when I was dying inside over losing Tate because I thought I *had* to.

Meeting Desiree in that moment was like the perfect antidote to my sadness.

Come to find that it was all orchestrated by my father. Because he's fucking selfish. A hypocrite of epic proportions... Pointing out the speck in my eye when there's a log in his.

Ripping my hair in my fists, I growl out loud while Desiree cowers on the floor. "This isn't happening... This is... it's fucking *crazy*. I can't... I just..."

My voice gives out as my lungs fight for air. If I don't calm down, I might pass out.

"Lance, please... Just relax," Desiree whimpers, reaching for my leg. "Let's talk about this. We can talk—"

"*Talk?!* Why talk now??" I roar. "You've been *lying* to me since day one! Did you ever even love me??"

She blinks up at me, tears tumbling down her cheeks. "Did *you*...?"

Staring down at her, my seething glare turns hopeless. Because she's right.

Maybe she's partially at fault for going along with my father's despicable scheme, but I never truly loved her either.

I thought I did. For a while, I convinced myself that I loved her... But it wasn't real.

Not the way it is with him.

My mind is sifting through so many thoughts, years of memories all cluttering up inside my skull. I can still barely fathom why someone like Desiree, someone beautiful and smart, would marry someone she didn't love, and who she knew didn't love her.

Trouble

Just to feel like she was rescuing me from the evil gay love of my life?? It's fucking ludicrous.

But more than anything, I'm *shocked* at how far my father was willing to go to preserve his image... His version of the truth.

I've gotta hand it to him... He's calculating as hell. Downright diabolical.

Wanting Tate out of my life because he couldn't stand the thought of me being gay is fucking *abhorrent*. And still, he'd rather be *that* than what he is...

I'm sure he could rationalize that he did it to protect me.

The same way that I've convinced myself I was protecting Tate...

Scoffing out of desolate rage, I shake my head. "This is so fucked up..."

My heart feels like it's bleeding.

"Lance, I know I messed up..." Desiree's voice slithers up at me from the floor. "I lied to you, and our relationship was built on those lies, yes. But I did love you... Maybe not all the way, but it wasn't all fake." My eyes fall to her. "I shouldn't have kept all of this from you, but what did you expect me to do?? Regardless of how it started, you're my *husband*. All I wanted was for you to love me even a fraction as much as the person you couldn't have..."

"That's just it, though," I rumble, exhausted and heavy, like a million pounds of weight is crushing my soul. "I *could've* had him! If it weren't for the interference and the enabling, I probably would have realized sooner that nothing else mattered... You not loving me and me not loving you, it's all irrelevant. Because I *love* him, and I always have. Whether it's wrong or not means fucking *nothing* when it comes to him."

Crashing onto my knees before her, I shake my head. "I'm sorry, Des. I am. I'm sorry I cheated. It was wrong, and you didn't deserve that. And I'm sorry you felt like you needed to save someone who didn't need saving. But we both chose to ignore the truth and keep burying ourselves in lies. Maybe my father started it, by manipulating us into thinking this was the right way... But it's *not*. And we should've had the courage to admit that."

She nods, wiping tears from her eyes. "You're right... What he convinced me to do was very wrong, and I knew that going in. I ignored every single sign over the years that I wasn't the one you wanted. I fought it hard, stupidly thinking if we were together long enough... maybe it would become real."

"I did too..." I rub my eyes. "It wasn't only you. I stuffed down so much because I thought I *had* to. I should've been stronger. I just..." My voice fades into a broken gasp. "*Fuck*, I just wish I hadn't walked away from him..."

And now we're both crying, softly, sniffling and hurting. For two different reasons that are oddly similar.

"And to think I wanted a baby..." I scoff sullenly, shaking my head. "Don't get me wrong, of course I would have loved our baby, but... we would've been doing it for the wrong reasons."

Desiree cringes, squeezing her eyes shut. "I've never been sure about raising a child to begin with... But I considered it. I mean, your father thought I should..." My gut rolls with these words. "A baby was supposed to... lock you down even more, I guess. But the thought of bringing your child into this world, and you abandoning us to be with another man..." She shakes her head. "I mean, it's not about that, but I just knew you didn't really want a baby with *me*. And, God, Lance, trying to keep you in love with me, even on the fucking surface, was exhausting enough without adding a child to the picture..."

My heart has fallen down into my stomach. It's being burned and digested.

Looking at her now... I'm not convinced this woman ever even *liked* me. Every single moment of this relationship has been forced. From denial, to settling, and everything in between.

Staring at the floor, I ask, "Did you ever cheat?" My eyes lift. "It's okay, you can be honest. I did..."

"No," she mumbles. I can't tell if she's lying, but it hardly matters. "Our sex life was fine for me. And I didn't mind that you were... imagining someone else." She fiddles with her fingers. "In a weird way, it was a turn-on... Because I got to have you."

I blink. "That's kinda messed up, Des."

"Yea..." she sighs. Blankly.

This girl might be a sociopath.

"What would you have done if you'd gotten pregnant?" I ask quietly, discomfort tightening my chest again. She refuses to look at me, fingers twirling in her lap. "Desiree...?"

Her eyes flick to mine briefly, shifting back down as she whispers, "I was taking birth control all along..."

Glaring at her, I scoff, "So you lied about that too, then? Why am I not surprised..."

There's some very clear, very miserable guilt on her face all of a sudden, and it's making me sick to my stomach.

Trouble

My brows furrow. "That was it, though... Right? Just the birth control...?" She still won't look at me. "Desiree... tell me that was it." She bites her lip to cover an aggrieved whimper. "Please tell me you didn't..." My voice dies as her eyes finally lift to mine.

She doesn't need to say the words. I can see it all over her face.

She... did.

She fucking...

"No... *fuck*..." I rub my eyes so hard I'm seeing spots. My stomach turns violently, and I scramble to my feet. "I think I'm gonna be sick..."

Rushing to the kitchen, I dry-heave into the sink with tears flowing from my eyes and a persistent ache in my chest. It feels like I've been shot.

"Lance! Please!" Desiree wails, chasing after me. "Just look at it from my point of view!"

I'm dizzy. I can't see through the haze in my vision as I wobble. She dashes up to me, grabbing me by the arms while I try to push her off.

"Your *point of view*..." I groan, smacking her hands away from me. "You had an *abortion* without telling me..." Emotion steals my breath. "You made that fucking decision with *my* child! Dammit, Desiree, I'm your *husband*, not some random guy! How could you do that without even a discussion??"

"Lance, I'm *sorry*," she sobs quietly, pulling on my arms.

Yanking away from her, I stagger out of the room.

Gotta get out of here...

Too much. This is... too... fucking... much.

Stumbling up the stairs, I march into our bedroom, going for the closet. Like magnets, my eyes land on our bed, in the spot where Tate and I—

My fucking heart.

I just wish he was here so bad. He's the only person I can trust in this world...

And I've done nothing but hurt him.

In the closet, I'm shaking as I grab a travel bag and start throwing things into it.

"W-wait..." Desiree swings into the room. "Where are you going??"

"I'm leaving," I rumble. "I'm going to be with the man I love. The person I should have been with this whole time."

She's just crying and crying, while I'm packing and packing. I can't fucking do this... I can't stay here for one more second. Not now... Not with all of this bullshit in my head.

Not with her, knowing she's just a pawn in my father's game, one with her own hurtful, reckless agenda.

None of us are innocent here, but I feel like I've been on the receiving end of a fifteen-year inception. The only person who's blameless in all this is Tate. He hasn't deserved a single bit of the emotional turmoil I've put him through, and it's high time I give him what he *actually* deserves. The truth.

And a promise that I'll never run or put fucking *should* before my feelings for him ever again.

Desiree watches me pack, sniffling and nodding. No pleading words, no beckoning consolations. No argument. I think she knows this marriage is dead.

Apparently, it's been slowly rotting for quite some time.

"I'll send for the rest of my things," I grunt, taking my bag, pausing one last time to look at the bed.

And in it, I don't see years and years of sleeping with her. I don't see the shell of myself, the robot my father had programmed, who laid with her, and fucked her, and kissed her while feeling nothing.

I see none of those memories based on falsified *divine* intervention.

All I see there now... is *him*.

I see his beautiful face, and his stunning, perfect body. I hear his shivering breaths, fighting for the courage to tell me that he loves me too.

I know he does. I've known it all along, and I only wish I hadn't been such a fucking idiot all these years... A simple-minded, weak, spineless fool, who was too afraid to push past what other people saw of him.

I've run from the truth for far too long. I've hidden behind the veil of righteousness. Purity...

It doesn't exist. Bad things, *wrong* things can be beautiful too. In fact, they can be every bit as beautiful as the good.

My affliction, my *trouble*, can bring me more peace than any forced virtue I thought I needed. He *does*.

And if anyone, even God, has a problem with me loving him... Well, they can just fuck right off.

Chapter Twenty-Three
Tate

"Hurry hurry hurry! I'm about to burst!"

"Remind me again why you couldn't just use the restroom at the bar," I grumble with my key in the lock while Troy does his pee-pee dance next to me.

"I would have," he squirms, "if I'd been fortunate enough to get there before the guy whose bowels apparently exploded." I make a face, pushing open the door to my penthouse. "I would've needed a gas mask to go in there."

"Okay... gross." I shoot him a horrified look while he darts inside, practically shoving me out of the way. "Just make it quick. I don't want you lingering like you *always* do when you're here."

"I think this is only the second time I've been inside in five years!" he exclaims while running up the hall to the bathroom.

"And yet you have the floor plan memorized," I scoff.

Shuffling over to the fridge, I pull out a bottle of water, sipping long.

I might be a little drunk. Not *wasted* or anything. Just casually tipsy, in an effort to hide my feelings and remind myself of how little I care. About everything.

I *definitely* don't care that a few hours ago, I was confronted by the wife of the man I've been sleeping with. Nor do I care that I had sex with said man in their marital bed while she was downstairs, and it was the hottest, most toe-curling experience of my life, which is saying a lot coming from someone who's had a five-way.

And I'll tell you what... I sure as shit *do not care* that I'm so afraid of my feelings for Lance Hardy that the mere notion of him coming clean about our affair to his wife and opening a door for us to become something real had me fleeing his home without saying goodbye and peeling out so fast I left a strip in front of his house.

Honestly, Lance Hardy who? I barely even know who that is.

Worst of all, I had an entire hour-plus drive home to sit in my Maserati and stew about the events of tonight. Meaning, that by the time I got back to Santa Fe, there was no hope of me just falling asleep. And because I didn't trust myself not to do something immature like hook up with a random dude just to prove how single I still am, I called my assistant to see if he wanted to meet me for a drink at the bar around the corner from my place.

Naturally, Troy was free and overly enthusiastic about the prospect of drinking with me. Who knows, he might not have even been free, but he's just that dedicated to impressing me.

What a nerd.

No, I kid because I care. Troy is actually the perfect assistant. He's twenty-five, with the energy of a puppy and the loyalty to match, single, and he rarely dates, which means he's basically married to his career— always a plus in any PA. Degree in finance, he's also enamored by the stock market and has a real passion for PR.

Not to mention, he acts like working for me is like working for Taylor Swift, which does wonders for my ego.

As soon as I got back into the city from Lance's, I went straight to the bar, where Troy and I drank several drinks and blathered about the upcoming New York trip. I must say, it was a great distraction from the looming fodder in my brain, despite Troy's not-so-subtle attempts at tricking me into spilling details about what's been going on with me lately.

Ever since Lance showed up at my place that day with flowers asking all kinds of questions, Troy's been more meddlesome than usual. Acting like he needs to know every aspect of my personal life to do his job properly, when really, he's just nosy.

Not that I can necessarily blame him. It doesn't take a homicide detective to spot the sudden changes in my behaviors over the last few weeks. I've been inattentive, and moody, and conveniently absent from the places I used to frequent before Lance Hardy ruined my ability to canoodle with strangers. I also haven't texted him in the middle of the night for a condom run in weeks, or pinned him my location in case I go missing.

Trouble

You know, the standard duties of a personal assistant to someone like me... i.e., a slut.

I haven't done any of it since Lance resurfaced, and the most disturbing part is that I don't miss it. I actually turned off my Grindr notifications. *Me... Tate Eckhart.* The dude who used Grindr more than Google.

It's fucking weird. So I don't blame Troy for wondering what's been up with me. If anything, I blame *myself...* For being an emotionally stunted weenie.

The whole thing makes me feel like I'm barely holding on to who I was. Like a child with a balloon, the string is slipping through my fingers. But I can't tell if it scares the shit out of me because it's a bad thing... Or if I'm worried it might be the best thing that's ever happened to me.

A sudden beep startles me out of my thoughts. It's the security system, alerting me that someone just used my code to get into the building. Brow furrowed in confusion, I check the clock. It's almost two in the morning.

Who the hell would be using my code at this time of night?

Not many people have it, though I've been known to hand it out to miscellaneous hot guys whose dicks are nice enough to earn them a standing penetration invitation.

Dangerous? *Perhaps.* Irresponsible? *Most definitely.* But just add that to the list of foolish things I've done in the name of getting laid.

Wandering over to the door, I drink some more water and wait for whoever it is to show up. And sure enough, only a minute later, my building's state-of-the-art security system is pinging and telling me someone's outside my door.

I press the button to turn on the camera. And my water bottle slips from my fingers when I see Lance Hardy... standing out in the hallway, holding a bag.

He's so tall, the camera only shows him from the mouth down... All I can see are his pouty pink lips on the screen.

Ugh... What are those things doing here?!

"Shit..." I grunt at the puddle of water on the floor.

"Tate?" he calls through the door, and I jump.

Shit! Fluttering around, I try to remind myself to breathe.

I'm not prepared for this...

I ran away from him earlier for that exact reason!

Steeling my nerves, I unlock the door, pulling it open and painting on the most aloof expression I can muster.

His forehead lines in concern. "Are you okay? You look like you're about to throw up..."

"Nice to see you too, Hardy," I grumble sarcastically.

He grins, a soft, beautiful thing full of so much relief and delight, it makes me all hot and itchy under my clothes.

"What, uh... are you doing here?" I ask stupidly, biting the inside of my cheek.

His head tilts, and he stares at me for a second before he murmurs, "You left without saying goodbye."

"How rude of me. Goodbye," I chirp, closing the door on him.

He breathes a laugh, grabbing it and pushing it open while I purse my lips to dampen my smirk. "You gonna invite me in or what, Trouble? I came all the way here..."

"Showing up unannounced at two in the morning." I shake my head, opening the door wider for him. "Booty call much?"

He steps inside and nervously, I back up. "Your booty is way too perfect for a measly *call*." His brow cocks. "This is more of a booty *visit*."

Chuckling, my eyes fall to the floor. "Watch out."

He looks down, frowning at the puddle of water on the floor. "What happened here?"

"I saw you... Got a little too excited, had an accident," I quip, and he cackles.

Okay, it can't possibly be normal to love making someone laugh this much.

Lance strides inside, dropping his bag with a thud. *That sounds heavy...*

He wanders over to the kitchen, grabbing some paper towels, using them to clean up the spilled water while I just shift on my toes, busting at the damn seams.

Why is he here in the middle of the night?

Why does he have a bag?

Why is he once again just making himself right at home in my place??

And why do I love it so much...?

"You don't have to do that..." I mumble, watching him carefully.

He's in the same clothes he was wearing earlier, and he looks just as gorgeous, if not a bit more tired.

"I don't mind," he hums, peeking up at me. "Something tells me I'm responsible for it anyway."

"What are you *doing here*, Lance?" I ask again, impatience bubbling over. "And what's with the bag?"

Standing up slowly, he stares at me with layered emotions framing his face. His lips part, but before he can speak, footsteps come from behind me, carrying a chirping voice.

"Sorry! I got distracted using your Peter Thomas Roth serum. You can add that to my Christmas list if you—" Troy's words cut off abruptly when he notices we're not alone. "Oh... hello. Who's this now?"

My eyes fling between my assistant and Lance, widening when I catch Lance's features quickly morphing from shock to despair. I can actually feel him stiffen from where I'm standing, see the vein in his neck start to throb as his face takes on a much angrier glow. His sudden raging jealousy is palpable, and it makes my balls ache, my stomach flutter, and my nipples hard all at once.

God, why is that look so fucking hot??

He shoots me a wounded glare, snapping me out of my ogling. "Lance... It's not what you think."

"Ohhh my God! *This* is Lance?!" Troy squeals, and I roll my eyes.

"This is my assistant, Troy," I explain to Lance, easing over to him carefully. His frown melts, and he blinks. "Remember? You spoke to him that day when you were stalking me..."

Lance's rage subsides, and he takes a breath. "Right... How could I forget?"

I don't know why, but his possessiveness is so endearing, I find my hand sliding onto his shoulder without even realizing I'm doing it. He peeks at me, biting a sheepish smile off his lips. Remembering myself, I snatch my hand back fast.

"*Wow...* It's *so* great to finally meet you!" Troy gushes, scampering over to shake Lance's hand. "Tate talks about you all the time."

"*What?!*" I cough.

Lance's face lights up. "Really??"

"Well, not with his mouth," Troy smirks at me. "But with his *eyes.*"

"You're an idiot," I grumble.

"Anyway, I'm so sorry to intrude!" Troy gasps. "Tate didn't tell me he was having company..." He peers at me, tilting his head in that damn knowing way, like he's catching me eating carbs when I'm supposed to be doing keto.

"No, no. It's my fault," Lance says politely. "I kind of just popped in... unannounced." He clears his throat. "I hope I'm not interrupting... work stuff?"

"It's fine." I glare at my assistant. "Troy was just leaving."

"Right," Troy gathers himself, though I can tell it's *killing* him not to ask what's going on here. *I mean, come on. I don't even know what's going on here, and it's my situation!* "I just needed to use the bathroom, which I did, and now I will... exit. The premises."

He shoots me a look, swooning over Lance's obvious debilitatingly good looks and Viking body, while also annoyingly demanding answers. *Awful ballsy for someone who works for* me.

"It was nice meeting you." Lance smiles, a bit strained.

I feel his pain. *We desperately need to talk, and Troy just ain't gettin the hint.*

"You too! Hopefully, we'll be seeing much more of each other." Troy grins, scuttling toward the door. "Tate, I'll text you the itinerary. Let me know if you need anything else for the trip!"

"Yea, uh-huh, whatever. Just *go*," I hiss.

His eyes fall to Lance's bag briefly. "Luggage. Neat. Are you coming to New York??"

"Um..." Lance shifts awkwardly in place. His fingers are wiggling, and he looks like he's going out of his mind.

"Troy!" I snap. "Get fuckin' lost before I strangle you with your goddamn bowtie!"

He smiles wistfully. "Isn't he just the best? Greatest boss on earth, that's what I always say."

"I'm sorry, I just can't..." Lance grunts.

For a split second, I think he's going to take off. Like the awkwardness is getting the best of him, and it's not what he signed up for. It has me powering up a death look at my assistant, ready to *Roadhouse* kick him right out of the apartment.

But then Lance turns, quickly grasping my face in his hands, startling the hell out of me as he lays a kiss down on my lips that's somehow both ravenous and romantic at the same time.

It's *so* unexpected, a shocked gasp flees my mouth, slipping right into his. Unfortunately for me, it sounds embarrassingly moany. But I can't even dwell on it because my heart is melting and my soul is whimpering, and *God fucking damn, since when does* one kiss *render me so fucking useless??*

I can't even move my hands. They're just lying limp at my sides while Lance Hardy owns the fuck out of my entire body using just his sweet, pillowy lips.

Tugging my lower in a deliciously slow fit of possessive suction, his fingers glide down my neck, shoulders, arms. Then he takes my hands in his, lifting them and draping them on his chest. He sucks off my mouth to break the kiss, bringing with it a breathy purr I can't keep in.

Lashes fluttering, I watch him lusting after my lips like he didn't even want to stop, our foreheads resting together while we breathe and he caresses my jawline.

"We've never done that in front of anyone before..." he hums in fascination. "*I've* never... done it."

It takes a moment for my brain to defog, and process what he's saying.

Right... My assistant is still hovering over by the door. I know that because I can feel him staring at us.

And Lance has never kissed me in front of anyone... Nor has he kissed a guy in front of anyone. Because I'm the only guy he's ever kissed, and I love that.

So... does this mean he's...

"Sweet tea in Savannah..." I hear Troy gasp. "That was the most romantic kiss I've ever seen in real life!"

"Shut up, Troy," I whisper breathlessly, gazing at Lance as he inches back enough for our eyes to meet.

His heart is flying beneath my palm.

"*That's* why I'm here, baby," he breathes, brushing my lips with his thumb, tender and light, like a butterfly kiss. "Because I'm done keeping us a secret. I'm done sneaking around, I'm done staying away... *Never* again, Trouble. Not a chance in hell. You've been mine since that night in your dorm, my first taste of you... I swear, I touched heaven when I kissed you, baby, and it's still there, every time, like an awakening that keeps waking me up. You're my *truth*, Tate... And I can't stand the thought of hiding you for one more second."

I could collapse right now if he wasn't holding me up. I could pass out if he wasn't feeding me confidence in his words through that shimmering gaze that's *possessing* mine. If I had a breath to breathe, it would belong to him too.

Every single part of him has every single fiber of me wrapped around him like tendrils, and the only thing that tells me I'm not dreaming is the thumping of his heart in my hand.

A heart he's apparently just offering right up to me, on a silver platter.

My hand, his heart... His question, and my answer.

And I'm fucking scared. I've never felt fear this strong, just from *standing* here and taking the confession of this man... my lost preacher.

But I think... the fact that I'm afraid means it's *worth* something.

And despite everything, even knowing how much it fucked me up last time, I think I might want to open up for him again...

Let his light back in.

My chin does a quick, nervous bob. Breathing shallowed, trembling just enough for him to feel it, I whisper, "You should kiss me again."

His lips sweep into a breathtaking smile. Fitting, because he's taken mine.

"I might never stop," he says, tickling my mind with familiar words.

"Good." My fist curls around the fabric of his shirt. "I expect *devotion*, Sunshine..."

"It's all yours, Trouble," he hums, pulling my mouth to his.

And now he's kissing me wild, feral, but slow enough that I forget my own name, along with the fact that my assistant is still in the room.

Until he releases a jubilant squeal. "Oh my *God*, it's like a movie! I'm crying actual tears!"

Lance starts laughing into my mouth while I growl to disguise how squirmy and mortified I am.

"I promise, all you have to do is give him a light shove and he'll fly across the city," I grumble.

Lance presses two more soft kisses on my bottom lip before turning to Troy and raising a brow. "Goodnight, Troy," he croons while sliding a possessive hand down my back. "Get home safe! I'm gonna throw your boss over my shoulder now."

Troy instantly flushes, and I have to bite back my giant swooning smile.

"Okay, okay. I'm going." Troy lunges for the door, taunting on his way out, "Just a heads up, his ring size is a nine."

Over the last fifteen years, I've lived exactly the way I wanted to; the way I told myself was the pinnacle of *awesome*.

I climbed the highest mountain, man. Rose to success.

I made my first million at twenty-six and I've been steadily rising since. *Acquiring a taste for the lap of luxury, and grinding my ass on it, if you know what I mean.*

I travel to dope places, I wear dope clothes, I do dope things. I have sex with *dopes*, I guess, but they have big dicks, so it never mattered. Because *pleasure* was the catch, and *I* had it on *my* hook, not the other way around.

Trouble

I've been calling the shots in my own life. And it's been fun, I can't deny that.

But the last thirty-six hours have been a *revelation*, and now I'm sincerely looking over how I've spent my time, like... *Did I really think that was it??*

Just money, fast cars, Rollie on my wrist and a slew of faceless bodies... It's great, yea, but the enjoyment is always limited. I reached its peak already, and there was nothing more after that. I couldn't get higher.

This, though... This is a high that has no zenith.

Sure, I know it's only been a day, but this *feeling* is already better than anything I've experienced in my thirty-five years of life. Because it comes from somewhere deeper than material possessions and superficial bodily encounters can reach. Not to mention, its responses are triggered by the most bizarre, unexpected things...

That might be the craziest part. The fact that I can get the same blissful feeling kissing Lance Hardy that I got from driving a McLaren F1 around a track at one-hundred and eighty miles per hour—*which, yes, I actually did*—is almost mind-boggling. That something as simple as making him laugh, or making him come, registers the same magnitude of dopamine earthquake as the most exciting things I've done—swimming with sharks in Costa Rica, skiing the black diamond in Telluride, sitting next to George Clooney on an airplane and having him tell me he liked my shoes—I'm telling you, it has my head spinning.

With this newfound realization, though, are occasional splashes of regret. Because if I'd *known* I could feel this way from something so theoretically mundane as watching him *sleep*, I would have chased Lance Hardy down years ago and dragged him back into my life.

Regardless, it doesn't much matter. Because feeling this way *now* is more than enough to put the years without it into perspective.

I know what it is... This *sensation* when I'm with him, the flood-like high that's better than a million sunset yacht parties in the Hamptons. I'm not stupid... It has a name.

But I'm not gonna say it.

Not yet.

And it's not because I'm *scared*...

Okay, fine. It is.

I am fucking scared. In fact, I'm petrified. Of saying it myself, of him saying it... I'm just scared all around. I'm more afraid of *that word* than any of the other crazy, reckless shit I've done in my life.

Nyla K.

I'm afraid that saying it will jinx this.

I know it sounds dumb, but I can't help the way I feel. I'm worried that as soon as *those words* are out in the air, everything will fall apart.

Irrational? *Maybe.* But still technically *possible.*

I'm almost positive that saying it while feeling it would be cathartic as fuck. It's like when you're coming and you scream out, *"I'm coming!"*

Saying the words in that moment isn't *necessary*, but it really enhances the experience. *Communicating your feelings, and such.*

But then imagine, if you will, that you're about to start coming, so you yell out, *"I'm coming!"* And then someone runs in with a machete and chops your head off.

Perhaps an extreme example, but you get where I'm coming from.

Saying the words is like inviting disaster.

It's fear of the unknown. And maybe I'm also afraid of the *word* itself in this context; its meaning and its consequences. Because I've never said it to anyone before—I've said it to my friends, and my mom, but that's very different... That's not *this* soul-igniting sensation of nervous joy and euphoric dread—nor have I felt it in this capacity. The only time I've ever even come close was with Lance... Lance from the past.

College Tate might've been feeling this for college Lance before he ran away. It wasn't spoken out loud, but sorta close. Feelings were confessed... And then my heart got shattered. *So yea... Maybe my fear isn't totally ridiculous, after all.*

Basically, I've spent the last thirty-six hours actively preventing myself from saying those words to *present Lance*, out of fear that I'm not ready, and it's too soon, and as soon as I say it, one of Elon Musk's satellites is going to fall out of the sky and crush him right in front of me or something.

And believe it or not, it's been difficult. There were a few instances when it felt like the words might spill from my lips like a sieve, whether I was ready or not.

Like when Lance told me everything that happened with his wife; the devastating conversation that led him to my doorstep.

We were lying on my living room floor, because apparently in the heat of the moment, making it all the way to the bedroom felt like way too far a journey. My head was on his chest and his heart was jumping up to touch my cheek, our legs tangled the way his fingers were swirling around in my hair.

Sated. *Happy.*

Trouble

Sure, my mind was plagued with many questions, but the moment felt *way* too good to spoil with serious talk.

But I guess Lance couldn't wait, because he whispered, "I left her."

That part didn't surprise me. What *did* surprise me, though, was the almost unhinged way my stomach flipped upside down and my heart started skipping rope in my chest at the notion that Lance Hardy might not be taken anymore.

Playing with his fingers to give the impression of playing it cool, I said, "Talk to me, baby."

And then he spilled his guts. Told me the whole story of what happened after I left his house, about Desiree coming onto him, him coming clean about the affair, Desiree confessing that she'd been goaded by Lance's parents to pursue him, manipulate him, and ultimately serve as their puppet in some horribly misguided attempt at keeping him *straight*. Or as a means to keep him away from *me*.

Like *I* was responsible for turning him gay.

And we still wound up together, anyway. How's that for serendipity?

Right then, those scary words were marching up the back of my throat, like soldiers treading up a battlefield. But they came to a halt when, in a hushed and saddened tone, he brought up the abortion.

I could tell he was trying to downplay it, to make himself feel better by acting like it was no big deal. But I've known him for a long time. He was severely hurt... *I'm sure he still is.* The way his voice shook ever so slightly in sorrow, the squeeze in his grip as he held me to him. The knowledge that his opportunity to become a father was taken from him without even a discussion cut him deep.

"You know I always saw myself raising kids," he'd said softly while I kissed his neck and played with his hair, giving my full attention to his words. "I'm relieved, I suppose, because I don't want a child with her, but..." He exhaled roughly. "I just wish it didn't have to happen like that."

In that moment, I was going to tell him. I really felt like my attempts to control the words were futile. They were going to roll off my tongue, whether my brain thought I was ready or not.

Lance was mumbling to me while my shivering lips grazed his throat. "I can't believe I'm with you right now, T... I can't believe, despite everything, I get a second chance to show you how happy I can make you... No matter what."

"Mmm..."

"Whatever tries to stand between us, we can overcome it, baby. You're the piece of me I've always needed, and when I left you, I felt like half my heart had gone missing. And the reason why is because, well... Tate, baby, are you listening?"

Lifting my face to glance down at him, words spilled from my lips. "Come to New York with me."

I know, right? I totally bitched out.

But like I said, I was scared. And I still am.

Lance and I spent that entire night and most of the following day wrapped up in each other. And there were a few more times when I felt like I wanted to tell him the *truth* about how I was feeling.

When he agreed to come to New York with me, and his cocoa irises twinkled with excitement because he'd never been there before.

When he drew me up to slow orgasm with the most sensual, worshipping head of my entire life.

When he giggled at the *Ace Ventura* hairstyle he gave me in the shower while washing my hair, or when we were lounging around in our underwear, eating takeout and teasing each other like we were still college friends, only *better* because now we kiss and play with each other's dicks.

Or last night, outside on the terrace, when he pushed my legs open and slid inside me so deep I came *crying*.

But I didn't. I haven't worked up to it yet, and part of me feels like I'm waiting for him to say it first. *Probably a little immature, but that's the least of my worries right now.*

I'm *falling,* for the first time, and it's scary... Because it's so much more consuming than I thought it would be.

And now we're in New York City, a trip that's supposed to be about business, but has somehow turned into an escape for me and my very newly separated... friend? Fuckbuddy? Lover? *Ew.*

Wait, I've got a good one... Disciple of my Dick.

Nailed it.

"Baby... this place is..." Lance's voice is dripping with wonder as he twirls around my stunning three-bedroom luxury apartment in Hell's Kitchen. "*Wow*... Nice work, Trouble."

Pursing my lips, I croon, "You like it?"

He inches up to me, being coy with his sex eyes. "It's a total dick magnet."

My head tips back in a haughty laugh that has him beaming. "Mmm... Is this dick magnetized?" I slide my hand between his legs while he hums and kisses my jaw. "Because I might just have a magnet of my own it can stick to."

"Sounds gay... I'm in," he chuckles in my ear while I spill more raspy giggles.

"You can't say that until you're divorced, Straighty," I tease, and he pouts.

"But that could take months. I can't wait that long."

Holding him by the waist, I pull back so I can look at his beautiful, perfectly chiseled face and just revel for a minute because this feels *so different*, and I can still barely even comprehend where it came from.

It's like a dream... In fact, it's more or less the *exact* dream I used to envision back in college. Different setting, different circumstances, but still... It's me and him. Flirting and touching and gazing at each other like if we look away for even one-second we'll go blind.

I might have gone completely loco en la cabeza. But I'm finding it extremely difficult to care how ridiculous I'm being when he's looking at me like that. Like I'm quite literally the *only thing* on the planet that matters.

"I know some great lawyers," I mutter while he brushes my hair back with his fingers. "Not that I'm trying to... rush you or anything. Obviously, it's totally your call, I just... I can help. If you need it. Which you might not. So whatever. Forget I said anything..." I let out a flustered breath.

Alright, chill, love virgin. Jesus.

Lance chuckles, dropping a soft kiss on my lower lip. "You're so fucking cute."

I roll my eyes, trying to remember my edge. "Come on, Hardy. Don't make me bring you to Times Square, spin you around, and leave you there."

He laughs harder. "I'm obsessed with you, Tate Eckhart. I can't help it." I force a scowl, to which he sighs, "Sorry. *Yes, please*, Trouble. I would love any assistance you can provide in making my divorce quick and painless." He pokes my nose with his fingertip.

Gulping, I try to remain professional. "Are all of your assets joint?"

He nods. "Yea, but it's pretty much just the house, and she can have that. We don't have, like, properties, investments and such." My head slants, and he huffs. "I'm way, *way* below your level, T. I've got a few grand to my name, that's it. And Desiree makes more money than I do."

I don't know why, but this surprises me for a moment. I remember always seeing these priests and ministers rolling around in Mercedes and

BMWs, scoffing to myself, because maybe I'm wrong, but doesn't that money come from the churchgoers? And aren't they giving it... to *God*?

At the same time, Lance behaving the opposite way makes perfect sense. He's not that kind of person at all, and he doesn't care about money or material gains. He grew up comfortable, and he's never strived for anything bigger than just that. Comfort, and happiness.

He's just an overall humble, kindhearted guy. Pretty much the opposite of me.

"I don't care about anything," he goes on. "As long as I can pay the legal fees, I'm good. I can probably stay with Ellie until I find a place of my own."

Or you could move in with me...

My lashes flutter. *Whoa... That's a bit fast... isn't it?*

Then again, I do have two places in New Mexico... Maybe he could stay in one, and I'll stay in the other. So it's not like we're rushing into anything...

My face must be giving away my hectic thoughts, because he smirks and taps my temple, "Whatcha thinkin' about, Trouble?"

"Nothing," I grunt defensively and clear my throat. "Listen, if you need money for anything, I've got you covered."

He scoffs. "Nice try, but I'm not taking your money."

My head tilts and I show him a cocky smirk. "Well, who do you think is paying for this lavish trip to the Big Apple, Sunshine?"

He squints at me. "I can pay for my own stuff..."

"What about the plane ticket?"

His jaw ticks. I find it *unbearably* sexy. "I'll pay you back for that."

"Stop," I groan, rolling my eyes and cupping his jaw with my hands. "I'm just playing with you, Hardy. You're not paying for shit. I invited you here because I wanted you to see New York. I want you exploring the city with me and fucking my brains out in this gorgeous, almost *unfathomably* expensive apartment." He snickers, gripping my ass hard until I grunt. "I wanna wine and dine and sixty-nine you, dirty preacher."

"You're incorrigible, Mr. Eckhart," his deep voice rumbles into me. I'm hard as stone.

"I'm sure you knew that when you started chasing me all over New Mexico." I grin, to which he gives me a snarky look. "But just so you know, this is still a business trip. Meaning, I will have to do some work while I'm here..." He pouts. "But it's a small price to pay for my clients who are paying a much, *much* bigger price."

"Mmm... deliciously ruthless." His lips hover over mine while he rubs his cock on me through our pants. "My sexy big bad wolf of Wall Street." I growl and nip his lip, to which he laughs. "When do you have to work?"

"Quick brunch meeting tomorrow, and then I'm all yours until Monday." I speak the words easier than breathing, though I stiffen once I've said them.

Am I really... All his?

Are we really doing this?

I'm still so nervous, radiating anxious energy like electricity coursing through my veins. But I think I like it.

Because that's the thing about scary shit... *It makes you feel alive.*

"What do you want to do tonight?" I ask him. "Anything at all. You name it."

I've never seen him look so thrilled. *Definitely not in this decade.* He has this youthful zeal to his face right now that reminds me of when we were kids. It's intoxicating.

"Well, first off, I think I need a proper tour of your bedroom, hotshot." He smirks, running his lips over my ear. "And your shower."

"That's a given," I hum, and he chuckles.

"We have some time to kill before we're meeting Troy for dinner, right?" His tongue flicks the lobe and my cock jumps.

"You're forgetting we're in a different time zone, Sunshine." I grin. "It's seven-thirty."

"Oh... crap." He pulls back, frowning. I have to laugh. "Dinner's in an hour! We gotta get a move on!" He starts dragging me along toward the bedroom. "We have to shower, and I need to make you come at least three times. Then we have to get ready... and I haven't unpacked any of my clothes yet..."

"Lance." I can't stop giggling. It would be embarrassing if I wasn't already embarrassing the shit out of myself by being so goddamn smitten. "We don't *have* to go to dinner with Troy. He's my assistant; he'll do whatever the hell I tell him to do. You want him to get us dinner and deliver it here on a horse?"

He stops panicking and peeks at me, snorting a rumbly laugh. "That's not necessary. But I would like to have dinner with you... Just you."

Biting my lip, I nod slowly. "Done. What else?"

"I want to take my time with you in the shower." His eyes are burning flames of desire at me, sheeting me in chills. "Make sure you're fucked thoroughly and your balls are drained by the time we leave this apartment."

"Mmm... sounds like a plan," I purr.

"So that means we'll need a couple hours." His forehead lines. "Can you find us a place to have dinner at, like... ten?"

Smirking, a breathy chuckle leaves my lips. "In the city that never sleeps? There might be a place or two."

He purses his lips, smacking me on the ass. I gasp as his gaze softens from dominant desire to something much more poignant.

He slithers his fingers through mine. "And then I want you to take me out. Show me New York, baby... I wanna see this fast, loud, hectic city with you."

"Nothing would make me happier." I squeeze his hand.

"Tate... In all honesty, I just need to thank you for a second," he whispers.

"We just got here, Hardy," I chuckle. "At least wait and see if you even like it."

"I know I will..." He drops his forehead to mine. "Because it reminds me of you now. No matter what, we'll always have this memory, baby." His tone is suddenly serious, and it's tightening up my stomach. "Whatever happens, this right here is a dream *you* made for us. You turned an awful moment in my life into something beautiful, T. I'll always be grateful for that."

The way he's speaking... There's something beneath his words that I just can't place. So many emotions I'm hearing and feeling from him, mixing up with my own into something heavy between us. Good *and* bad, right and wrong.

Sunshine... and *Trouble*.

Pushing away the seriousness, I smirk. "If you're looking for ways to make it up to me... my cock is soaking wet right now."

Lance hums, holding my face, giving me one last lingering look before his eyes glisten wickedly.

Then he drops to his knees. "Dinner is served."

Chapter Twenty-Four
Lance

T his city is *alive.*

I know I've heard people say that before, but actually being here, *feeling* it myself, really has me appreciating New York for all that it is.

Sure, it's loud, dirty, crowded, and sometimes highly overwhelming. But in spite of all that, people still *want* to be here. I mean, they actively choose to be in this expensive as hell place with all its issues, on *purpose.* There has to be a reason, right?

Yea, that's what I'm discovering right now... There is a reason.

It's magic.

Experiencing New York City for the first time with Tate is like having my very own *Trouble Tour Guide.* In fact, I already called him that, twice, and he's not finding it as funny as I am. Still, he's the perfect person to show me around this city. He's been here hundreds of times, so he knows the best places, or the places he knows I'll like. Plus, he has the energy of someone half his age, which is refreshing. It reminds me that despite my introverted qualities and the dull life I'd settled into, I'm *not* just a boring, married pastor.

I'm still young, and now that I've broken free from the chains of denial that held me down for years—*or at least, I've started to*—I can finally *feel* young again, too. I can run around having experiences in this chaotic, sparkling city, with a man who's like this wild place personified. I can finally *live*, and live the life I should have been living this whole time...

With Tate.

"That was... *fucking* incredible," I sigh, hanging back on my way out of the restaurant to follow Tate's lead.

I know Manhattan is a grid, but it's still only my first day here, and I have no idea where the hell I am or where I'm going.

I get the sense people on the sidewalk don't like that.

"Told you." He peers both ways before choosing a direction, striding confidently up the block. "Best ramen in the city."

We just came to this little hole in the wall near Tate's building for dinner. A Japanese place with a sushi bar and various ramen noodle bowls. I wanted to try something we don't get the best of back home, and fresh sushi is definitely that.

The sheer number of restaurants near Tate's place alone has my head spinning. *How does anyone ever decide what to eat here??* It's a smorgasbord of different cultures and ethnicities and specialties all laid out like an indecisive person's worst nightmare.

Still, not a bad problem to have. I've already selected four more places I'd like to try before we go home.

Scampering after Tate, I pluck his hand into mine, and he shoots me a nervous look. *I love making him look like that.*

He's been loosening up exponentially with the affections and coupley stuff since I showed up at his place. Honestly, I feel like he loves it deep down, and he *wants* to give in very badly. But he's still unsure, which is fine. He can go at his own pace, as long as he knows I'm not going to stop holding his hand. It's all I've wanted to do for over fifteen years, and I *finally* have it.

It'll take more than a scowl from a sexy, dark-haired dude with perfect lips to make me let go.

"I'm not from here." I blink at him, controlling my teasing grin. "I might get lost."

Tate's pretty lips swoop into a smile, and he lets out a laugh. "Great. First day back in New York and I'm stuck lugging around a six-foot-four Swedish tourist."

"Can we go to Ikea?" I tease.

Tate snorts. "If you wanted meatballs, baby, why didn't you say so?"

Chuckling, I shake my head at him while he smirks, tugging me along up the street. The weather is positively *gorgeous* right now. The summer air is beginning to cool off, not just for the night, but in general as the season winds down.

Trouble

I can imagine that New York City in prime summer can be like an over-crowded version of Hell, though I think I would still love to experience it. New York Pride in particular. *I assume it's like a much bigger ABQ Pride, plus a hundred more tons of rainbow glitter.*

Actually, I really want to experience *all* the seasons here... Fall's crisp air, strolling through Central Park with the leaves changing. Winter's luster, watching snow fall from inside of your cuddly warm apartment, ice skating and the Rockefeller Tree. Springtime, when everyone comes out of hibernation.

It seems like the city would have a whole new personality for each season.

I wonder if Tate will bring me back...

Casually peeking at him while we walk, I think about everything that's happened over the last two days. All the changes... Big, core-shaking ones. Honestly, I think if I didn't have Tate right now, I'd be freaking the hell out. Which I suppose is the *exact* reason I didn't even think twice about showing up at his house.

Because despite everything that's happened between us, the emotional pain I caused him in the past, the frustration and confusion I've caused him in the present... he still opens the door for me. He's still my friend, even if we were never really *just friends* in the first place, but two guys with crushes we were too afraid to act on.

We're supposed to be *more*. That's the plan, fucked up or not.

And while I'm positive it's entirely unhealthy to jump from a decade-long marriage straight into a committed relationship with someone as love-repellant as Tate, I don't exactly have much of a choice.

It's always been *him*. That's the part I wish I'd been able to see the whole time. My father could push a million pretty girls my way... But I'm fully certain I would end up back with Tate Eckhart every time.

He's my Apollo... And I'm just Clytie, following him from one side of the sky to the other.

"Don't think I don't feel you staring at me," he mutters, shooting one of his little smirks and eyebrow-cocks my way.

"Sorry," I rasp. "You're fun to look at."

"Well, that's a given."

"You're also too cocky for your own good," I say in a faux-scolding tone.

He chuckles. "Also true."

"Where are we going now?" I ask, because he seems like he's bringing me somewhere specific, though he hasn't mentioned what we're doing tonight.

I told him I wanted him to show me New York *his* way. I'm sure I'll get a chance to see a few of the *sights*, as they say, since we'll be here for a few days, and I'll need to keep myself entertained while he's working. But right now, I'm just excited to be here, and be here *with Tate*.

"I'm bringing you somewhere I know you'll enjoy," he answers, stifling an obviously excited grin.

"Okay..."

That could be literally anywhere at this point.

Wandering up the street, fingers linked, Tate weaves us effortlessly in between bodies. And I'm buzzing from how good it feels to hold his hand in public. We pass a few guys holding hands, laughing and shoving each other playfully. One of them looks me and Tate up and down, giving me a rather sultry smile accompanied by a wink. I can feel my face flushing, because he's really good-looking. In fact, a decent percentage of the guys around here are *really* good-looking, and they're also not shy about blatantly checking you out, or publicly displaying their affections for one another.

Tate said his neighborhood is a bit of a *gay hot-spot—and not just because he lives there. That was his joke.* But it's like Pride happens all year round here, which is exactly how it *should* be. Rainbow flags hanging outside various restaurants and bars. And the... *What did Tate call them? Beefcakes.*

Actually, I think he said *"Certified Angus,"* and then made a crude gesture with his hands that had me laughing and shaking my head at him, because he's just too much.

Either way, the point is that going from being a *straight*, married man who literally works for God, to gallivanting around a place called *Hell's Kitchen* with the guy I'm currently fucking, is both overwhelming as shit, and invigorating beyond belief. It feels like this is an experience I *need* to have right now. An experience I was trying to have at Pride in ABQ, but not really knowing how to go about it.

As it turns out, sticking my dick in that glory hole was the best decision I ever made. *Go figure.* And now, here I am, with the guy from the other side of the wall, holding his hand out in the open and not feeling guilty about it.

Well, maybe just a teeny bit... But that's only because we still haven't had that talk.

Trouble

I've been putting it off, simply because I don't want to put a damper on our trip, or stress Tate out when he's supposed to be working.

But I'm gonna do it. I swear.

"Eye candy?" Tate's voice cuts into my thoughts, and I peek at him while he pulls me off to the side, positioning us in a short line that appears to be for the bar we're standing in front of.

He's watching the group of guys I'd just been looking at while they walk by, discussing our physical attributes loud enough for us to hear. I can't help but feel flattered. Especially because the *jawline for days*, as they've so aptly named Tate, is with *me*.

Grinning at him, I take his chin between my fingers. "All the sugar I need is right here."

His face flushes a little, though he turns away purposely in an attempt to hide it, fussing with his wallet. We're already moving up to the door, showing our IDs to the bouncer as Tate croons over his shoulder, "Hold that thought..."

Focusing on the loud music coming from inside, which sounds like *The Devil Went Down To Georgia—an odd choice of music for Manhattan, no?* —I glance up at the sign right before I'm yanked inside.

Flaming Saddles?

As soon as we step inside the cramped bar, the name makes perfect sense. There's cowboy decor hanging up everywhere. Red light bathes the bodies all huddled together in a space that's probably smaller than Tate's living room, every set of eyes aimed up at the guys in cut-off jean shorts and cowboy boots dancing on the bar.

Think Coyote Ugly, but make it gay. That's exactly what Flaming Saddles is.

"You were saying?" Tate shouts to me over the music, distracting me from the denim-clad butt shaking right above my face.

Seriously, I'm not sure my eyes have ever been wider. *This definitely isn't what I expected when I asked him to show me around New York.*

Tate slinks up to the bar to order us drinks, which apparently *can* be done while men are dancing on it, and I'm so hypnotized by the stomping of the cowboy boots and the twirling of the hips that I barely even remember to be nervous about letting go of his hand.

To say this place is crowded wouldn't be doing any justice to the sheer number of men packed into the confined space. I find it both exciting and overstimulating, and the introvert in me wants to cling to Tate for fear of losing him and having to maneuver my way through this experience alone.

A moment later, the song ends, and everyone cheers just as Tate is turning around with two plastic cups. He hands one to me, leaning in close. "You don't have to drink it if you don't want to."

His lips brush my ear when he speaks, sending chills all over my body. Lifting the drink without a thought, I sip, needing the distraction and, let's be real, the alcohol. *I'm far too new to the gay New York cowboy scene to be in here sober.*

Liquor burns its way down my throat, providing me instant comfort as Tate takes my hand again, shouldering his way through the bodies while I'm muttering, *"excuse me,"* and *"sorry,"* every two seconds, like the well-mannered, church-going boy I am. When we reach the back wall, Tate is chuckling through my uncanny feeling of déjà vu.

"You're too polite for New York," he says to me over the random pop music that's now playing.

He goes to pull his hand away, but I squeeze it tighter, lifting it a bit so I can admire the way our hands look together.

"This is not at all the type of place I'd expect to see you in." I grin, inching my body closer to his.

It's exhilarating, being in a place like this, ninety percent dudes, all touching and flirting and dancing. And this time, *I'm* one of them.

I'm no longer on the outside looking in... I'm *inside*, with Tate. It's mesmerizing.

"Flaming Saddles is a rite of passage," he says. "Plus, I kinda wanted to bring you to the gayest place around and see how nervous I could make you."

Glancing about the room, my brow lifts. "This is pretty gay."

Humming a rumbly chuckle, he brings our joined hands down, finally managing to untangle our fingers, but only so that he can place mine on his hip.

Then he walks his fingers up my torso, leaning in to brush his lips on my ear again. "Are you *nervous*?"

"Always," I rumble back, shaky hand sliding down to his butt.

Out of habit, my eyes shift. But then I remember that no one here cares what we're doing. In here, I'm not married, or the pastor, or Gio Hardy's son. I don't have to worry about someone I know seeing me and lying to excuse my behavior, or hiding what I'm doing out of fear of what people will say.

Being with Tate and being *me*—the *real* me—is met only with acceptance, and it won't be long until the confidence I have right here and now extends past this tiny room.

I'll get there. Soon enough, the *world* will be my Flaming Saddles, and I won't give a tiny rat's ass about the approval of strangers.

One step at a time.

Tate seems like he might want to dance, and regardless of whether I still can't dance for shit, I'm desperate for a do-over of the last time we were in a club together. But just as I'm about to attempt it, the music changes and everyone cheers.

Tate pulls back, winking at me before his gaze moves to the bar. The guys are back up there, only now they've multiplied. A line of hot dudes with bulging biceps, and *other* bulges, are performing a choreographed number to *Pour Some Sugar on Me*.

It's pretty amazing, but I can't stop staring at how *narrow* that bar is. *Seriously! How do they not fall off??*

We watch the show in amusement, clapping and cheering for every hip swivel, boot stomp and ass drop. Tate gives me the eyebrow wiggle, and I stick my tongue out at him while we sing along, commenting on which guys are the hottest versus who have the best moves. Overall, it's a very entertaining performance, and without even realizing it, I've managed to kill my drink.

I feel great. Wonderful, even. *I could definitely get used to this.*

"Let's go," Tate says, draining the last of his cup and dropping it off on a nearby table.

"Wha—why??" I whine, though I don't think he can hear me. Or he's not listening.

He's just dragging me toward the exit while I watch two of the guys launching into their next dance.

Outside on the sidewalk, I can breathe a bit easier. It was more than a little stuffy and sweaty in there. But still, I was having a great time.

"Why'd we leave?" I ask Tate while he yanks me along like a distracted puppy.

"That's a one-drink kinda place," he says, as if it's common knowledge. "Two max."

"I thought you said it was a rite of passage..."

"It is, but you can't dance there."

My stomach flutters. *So he does want to dance with me...*

"I guess it was pretty small..." I mumble, quaking a bit at the idea of going somewhere with a wide-open dance floor, where everyone will be able to see how clunky and uncoordinated I am.

Tate's face shifts to show me a side-smirk. "I hate to burst your bubble, Hardy, but we're in Manhattan. Everything is small here. But what we lack in space, we make up for in twenty-dollar drinks."

I laugh. "Hey, you know what they say... It's not the size that counts, it's the way you use it."

"Says the dude with the Louisville Slugger in his pants," he chuckles.

A couple of guys overhear that comment as we're passing them, whistling and hollering, "Get it, girl!"

Tate cackles while my face turns beet red.

So much fucking trouble, I'm telling you.

A few blocks and one avenue down, Tate brings me inside a club very different from Flaming Saddles. Equally small and crowded, this one is much darker, and there's no one dancing on the bar, though the bartenders are shirtless, with chiseled muscular torsos on display. Just beyond a narrow hallway is a dance floor, visibly packed with men grinding on each other to the thumping beats of techno-remixed pop music.

"Based on your wide eyes, I'll assume you'd like another drink," Tate sneers, and I give him my most anxious scowl. Followed by a nod.

Chuckling to himself, he weasels his way up to the bar, slithering in between two guys who look like they've been waiting for drinks. But Tate completely disregards their snarky looks, leaning over the bar to tap his cheek against that of an incredibly attractive bartender.

My forehead lines, and my stomach twists, watching them chat and laugh. Clearly, they know each other, and judging by the way the bartender is looking at Tate, I'm willing to bet they're more than just *old pals*.

I can't take my eyes off of Tate and the dude who really has no business being that attractive. *It's unfair, honestly.* And my mind rushes back to college, to the night in the club, when Tate was flirting with various guys. Then it jumps ahead, to Pride in ABQ. The party at Kennan's house; more flirting, touching and teasing, and the wordless invitations he's so good at.

Really, it's just Tate being Tate. His personality hasn't changed in all the time I've known him. He's still the same confident, charming man who captivated me way back when at a party in a mutual friend's dorm room. And more than anything, I'm just grateful to have another chance at being around him, fluttering nervously in his orbit.

I never won't be jealous where Tate is concerned, but I guess if we're going to enter into any kind of relationship, I'll have to get used to it.

Trouble

Because he's a very... *popular* guy. I assume being out with him will mean occasionally running into men he... knows.

"I guess you have to be sleeping with the bartender to get a drink in here," a voice croons from my right, and I peer down.

There's a man standing next to me with severely wandering eyes and no sense of personal space. I stare at him for a second until he nods toward Tate.

My blinking becomes rapid. "Oh, no... Actually he's—"

"Wow, you are *huge*," the guy talks over me, grinning. "And stunning. Let me buy you a drink. Assuming I can work some magic myself..."

"No, thank you, I'm good," I mutter, as politely as I can manage. "I'm actually with someone..."

My eyes fling to Tate, and I bite the inside of my cheek. *Did he forget about me? Is he ditching me?? Is he really going to flirt with that dude right in front of me and—*

Tate turns, waving me over, rather urgently.

"I guess that makes sense," the dude at my side is mumbling as I slink my way up to the bar.

Sidling up behind Tate, I drop my hand onto his waist. He peeks up at me, smiling, and hands me a drink.

"Lance, this is Jeremy. We go way back," Tate introduces me to the bartender, who's twirling from the register with his change. "Jeremy, this is Lance. We go way, *way* back." Jeremy casts me a brief, appraising look, followed by a fake grin before handing Tate the bills. But Tate waves him off. "That's for you, love."

Calm down... Remember, he's with you.

Jeremy gives Tate a swooning look, his eyes bouncing between us. A small frown tugs at my lips. *What is this dude's problem??*

"Jeremy here didn't believe that I was with someone," Tate says to me, shooting Jeremy a petty smirk.

Oh, would you look at that? It's my old friend Possessive McJealousy. Haven't seen you in all of five minutes!

Melting my chest against Tate's back, I lean in to kiss his neck. "What's so unbelievable?" My eyes lift to Jeremy's, and I cock a brow.

Pretty confident display for a guy who still has a wedding band on his sweaty, trembling hand.

"Oh, *gee*, how much time you got?" Jeremy teases.

"Ha ha." Tate rolls his eyes.

Nyla K.

And now I feel like a straight-up caveman. I think I'm seconds away from peeing all over Tate. *Metaphorically, of course.*

"Baby, let's go dance," I purr the words right by his ear, trying to be casual with the way my overprotective gaze is flitting to this hot shirtless guy who goes *way back* with *my* Trouble.

Tate spins a bit in my arms. "Lance Hardy wants to dance??" he gasps, and I purse my lips.

"You owe me one from fifteen years ago..." I hum. "*Lorenzo.*"

Tate bursts out laughing, and all the yucky green jealousy fizzles away.

Because maybe he's hooked up with a lot of Jeremys over the years, but I know for a fact I'm his only *Sunshine.*

"Okay, *Footloose*, lead the way," Tate chuckles, turning to wave at Jeremy, who's already off flirting with a new customer.

"Pretty sure it was Swayze last time," I tease, taking his hand. And this time I'm pulling *him* along, toward the dance floor.

"I have no shortage of references, Hardy, you know that."

I try to stop along the edge of the vastly crowded area, but Tate won't let me. He shoves me forward until we're wedged right in the middle of the floor, literally surrounded by muscle and testosterone. And sweat. *Lots of sweat.*

The music is good; it's loud enough that I can feel the bass inside my chest, songs I vaguely recognize, though I don't listen to this poppy stuff much. I'm more of a mellow music guy, regardless of the time period. I like The Doors and Bob Dylan, to Hozier and Cigarettes After Sex. Really, anything you can zone out to.

Tate, on the other hand, has always liked music you can dance to. Case in point, whatever song is playing right now, he knows the words to it, and he's singing along while swaying around in front of me. Not loud or anything, but his lips are moving, and I'm finding it very sexy.

Releasing my inner hang-ups about not having the first clue how to dance, I slip my free hand onto his lower back, wishing I wasn't holding this stupid drink and could use both. But either way, Tate seems overjoyed. This has always been his thing; dancing, letting loose surrounded by guys. And I'm sure in the past it's been about meeting someone and hooking up, but obviously it's not *just* about that.

This whole thing, where we are, this piece of culture we're living in right now... It's not about sex. Maybe parts of it are inherently sexual in nature, but more than anything, it's about *freedom.* From judgment and oppression... Freedom from bigotry and societal expectations.

Trouble

For the first time, I actually *get it*. They're not just *words* anymore. I can see it before my eyes, feel it in my chest.

And I'm a part of it, here and now. *Finally*, I've arrived.

I'm... gay.

Yea. I'm definitely gay.

Slugging back my entire drink in three gulps, I toss the cup onto the floor while Tate cackles.

"I'm not holding your hair back tonight!" he yells at me over the music.

"Sorry..." I murmur with my head spinning, grasping his face. "I needed both hands for this one."

Dropping my mouth onto his feels so different in this moment. It feels heavier, with the weight of so many confessing emotions behind it, but still somehow light as air. Kissing him here, within the thumping music and colorful lights, is enchanting.

But it's also *real*. It's honest.

It's freeing of shackles I've worn my whole life without even realizing it, and it's stepping from darkness into a light I never knew was waiting for me.

I'm kissing Tate Eckhart deeper and needier through a slideshow of choppy images in my head, and it feels like an actual revelation come to fruition. Seriously, I can't believe the things I'm remembering right now...

Boys in school calling me gay for liking flowers...

Butterflies when my best friend in middle school tackled me in the backyard.

Ryan Reynolds. Yea, that's it. Just... Ryan Reynolds.

Losing my virginity to Kara Dellacourt while her brother, Alex, was asleep across the room... He always had the prettiest smile.

"Whoever lives in love lives in God, and God in them."

My heart is on *fire*. But in a good way. I can feel the reality of all these things I've buried for way too long. I only wish I hadn't wasted so much time on fear, and doubt, and misunderstanding the will of God, when really, it's so simple.

Love.

Love is just... love.

Breaking my lips away from Tate's, I'm pulling in air like it's the first time I've truly breathed. He hums a sweet sound that I can feel more than hear, his hand clutching my chest as if he might fall down.

Blinking at me, his eyes glow in the dimmed light while he sucks on his lower lip. And I can tell I'm probably blushing at how *intense* that just was.

But I feel... *fucking great*.

"Thank you..." I whisper.

I'm not sure he heard me, but I think he read my lips because his mouth slopes into a bemused, yet fully delighted smile that makes him look twenty years old again. He chuckles, shaking his head. Then I laugh back, pulling him in for more kisses.

And we're just dancing, and kissing, surrounded by guys who are doing the same.

It's *beautiful*. Not wrong.

It could never be wrong... *Not this kind of love.*

A familiar song starts playing. My stomach flops, and I'm reeling.

Tate finishes his drink so he can touch me while he hums along and writhes into me. But I just can't stop kissing him, because this is bordering on miraculous.

I can't believe this song is playing right now...

"I should've done this back then," I murmur into his mouth.

"Yea, you should have," he teases, grazing his fingers up and down my back in between singing the lyrics.

"No, I'm serious, Tate." I rest my forehead on his. "How different would our lives be if I'd just—"

"Everything happens for a reason," he cuts me off, and I blink at him. "You're the one who's been saying that to me, Hardy. It's *true*. God... had a plan."

I chuckle. "Are you preaching to me now, Trouble?"

"We're in a gay club. This is my house of worship." He winks.

"Okay, baby." I beam, holding his waist. "Show me what you got."

"You asked for it!" he cheers.

And then everyone breaks out into a collectively bellowed chorus of *Teenage Dream* by Katy freaking Perry.

I'm blasted.

Lit, as the kids would say.

Do they even say that anymore? Probably not.

Leave me alone, I'm almost forty.

Regardless of the terminology, I'm a bit wasted. But not from booze or narcotics, or any sort of ingestible substance.

Right now, I'm high on *life*, and *love*, and most of all, Tate Eckhart. *My very own designer drug.*

Trouble

Okay, maybe I've got a slight buzz on, because I don't drink and I had two scotch and sodas. But still, it's not about that. I'm all fuzzy and warm, with zeal in my bloodstream from this incredible night in New York *mothafuckin'* City.

Honestly, I don't like to get bogged down by age, because in a lot of ways, it's a state of mind. It's good to be mature and responsible when you get a little older, but it's also good to keep a sense of whimsy. And that's something I've definitely lost over the years.

I mean, shit, I'm only thirty-five, but I've been living like a retired old fart.

Turning into my father.

Coming on this trip has helped me reclaim my youth. I feel like a kid again, stumbling down the sidewalk with Tate, hands linked and swinging while we laugh it all off. It's just fun for right now, and I need this. Especially knowing the bevy of serious shit that's waiting for me back home.

Adult stuff... Like divorce, moving...

Switching careers?

I haven't actually decided on that last part, but I'll need to figure it out by the time we get back. Because I'm sort of blowing off my job to be here, and I'm assuming me not showing up for church on Sunday will present a lot of questions.

I have every intention of answering them, but not right now. Call it selfish and immature, but I just wasn't in the mood to explain myself to anyone before I left. So I didn't.

I texted my sister from the airport, but all I said was that Des and I split up, and that I was on my way to New York with a friend. I just wanted her to know that I was alive in case people started freaking out. Basically, I said, *don't worry, I'll explain everything when I get back*, and then I turned my phone off.

I know, it's a little dramatic. But I think I deserve a few days of blissful, unfettered silence before I strut back into my formerly quiet life as a whole new person.

I'm sure it'll be confusing for some people; people who believed that the rather convincing *Lance disguise* was the real me. For others, it'll probably be much less of a shock.

Mainly my family... My father. *I can only assume they've been waiting for the other shoe to drop.*

Regardless, I'll have to think carefully about what my next steps are, as far as my career goes. Because I'm not saying I've stopped loving God, or the church. I'm not even saying I haven't enjoyed what I do. It's just that preaching what I *believe* in has always felt monumentally more difficult than preaching what everyone expects me to preach. And I think I'd like to see what my life can look like when I'm no longer fighting.

There's so much more out there... Where I am right now is evidence of that.

"I cannot believe," Tate hiccups, stopping outside his building to fish a cigarette and lighter out of his pocket, "you drank, *and* danced tonight."

"Hey, I used to drink in college, remember?" I sway in front of him, watching him flick the lighter over and over.

"Oh, I remember." He grins with a cigarette between his teeth, eyes meeting mine. "You used to do more than that. Remember the time we made a bong out of an eggplant?"

Chuckling, I shake my head. "Yea... vaguely. I remember being so high, I ate an entire birthday cake."

Tate is laughing so hard he's almost falling down. "Whose birthday was it??"

"I don't know, but they definitely didn't get any cake," I snort, and he cackles.

"Man... You really sucked the life outta that eggplant." He goes on flicking his lighter.

I squint at him. "What's that supposed to mean?"

"It means the signs where all there, Hardy," he sneers.

"You're still just as much of a smartass as you were back then," I grumble through a grin.

"Yea... and you're just as much fun as you were back then." He peeks at me. "You just needed your Fairy Tate-Mother to remind you of how awesome you are... The real you, I mean."

"Okay, fairy," I snicker, and he winks. "I think I've already more than adequately voiced to you how much better my life is with you in it. At this point, I'm just waiting to hear it from you in return."

His face grows a bit serious, some sudden nerves visibly framing his features, though his eyes are sparkling. "What do you wanna know...?"

Stepping in closer to him, I grab the lighter from his hands and light it, holding up the flame to his cigarette.

"Did you miss me?" I ask on a breath, our gazes locked, igniting themselves. He blows his smoke away from my face. "You know I did..."

"How much?"

Trouble

"A lot."

"How much is *a lot*?"

He pauses for a moment. "As much as someone can miss something while still technically being able to survive without it."

Humming, I stuff his lighter into his front pocket while he bites his lip. "Did you ever check up on me?"

"I feel like you're asking me questions you already know the answers to." He grins, and I shrug. "*Yes, Lance*, I cyber-stalked you. Just like you cyber-stalked me."

I'm chuckling, until a sudden cloud of gloom creeps over me. I don't want it to, but it does. Because I know how I used to feel when I'd look him up on Instagram, or see Jacob's posts about him on Facebook. More often than not, it wasn't great.

If he felt even a fraction of that sadness because of me, I deserve to be gut-punched.

"Did you... really hate me?" I whisper, then swallow. "A lot?"

Tate stares at me for a beat, taking a drag. When he releases the smoke, his eyes fall to his shoes. "I really wanted to..." My heart splinters as he glances at me once more. "But I couldn't."

"Why not?" I mumble. "You should have..."

I sure as hell did.

"Because, Hardy," he huffs. "Maybe I didn't *fully* understand why you left, but I still got it." My stomach falls, weighted by the truth like I swallowed a bowling ball. "What kind of person would I be... What kind of *gay man* would I be if I couldn't empathize with that struggle?"

My lips part, but my brain is still fighting.

Is now the time...?

Am I really going to do this right now?

What if he takes it badly??

What if this ruins everything??

"Baby," I shiver, pulling him to me by his neck, fingers in his hair and on his beautiful face, because he's just so *perfect* and I don't deserve him. "I... I need to... tell you..."

"Sunshine..." He tosses his cigarette and cups my jaw. "Stop. It's okay, trust me. You don't have to say it right now if you don't want to." He kisses me softly, and I'm crumbling. "You took a huge step today, babe. You were out in public with me, kissing and being happy. Really, that's all that matters."

321

My entire body is trembling as I nod, leaning into him because he's *so good*. So much better than me. He's not the trouble, *I* am.

I can't even tell him the truth when he's standing right here, waiting for it.

"Whenever you want to say the words, I'm here." He brushes his lips on mine. I can taste him already, like cigarettes and sugary fruit. I don't know how Tate's always been able to make tobacco taste good, but he does. It somehow enhances his flavor and his delicious scent. "I really do forgive you, Lance. I'm not holding a grudge, I promise."

Say it.

Just tell him. He deserves it.

No matter what.

"Tate, I love you," I rasp, the wrong words, onto his sweet mouth. I feel him stiffen, and then quiver. "I'm in love with you, baby. I mean... there was never any question, was there? It's always been you, no matter what."

"*Fuck...*" he breathes, hands sliding down to my chest.

At first, I think he's afraid to look at me. But when I take his chin and lift his face, his eyes meet mine. And they're illuminated. Pupils blown out like he's high.

"You don't have to say anything." My voice is barely audible.

He bites his lip, staring at me in blazing silence before he whispers, "We should... go inside."

Nodding, I give him one last lingering look before letting go of his face. He turns and stalks inside the building, and I just shuffle after him, hoping I didn't really fuck up and scare him away.

That's not even the scariest thing I could have said.

I refuse to regret saying it, though. He knows I love him; he's known this whole time... *Hasn't he? How would he not??*

I feel like it's super obvious.

Passing the security desk, I'm rushing to keep up with Tate, who's practically running to the elevators. He uses his code to call the elevator, awkwardly fidgeting in place, eyes glued to the screen. It's actually kind of cute... He looks frazzled, which isn't a way he looks often. The fact that I made it happen by telling him I love him makes me feel a little better.

Like maybe...

He might feel the same.

Or at the very least, he sincerely enjoys having me love him.

"Tate," I murmur, stifling a grin. Stepping up to his back, I trail my finger along the nape of his neck.

Trouble

He visibly shivers and clears his throat. "This elevator is so slow... It's like, just because it's late, they only have the slow one working..."

I bite my lip. "Baby... are *you* nervous now?"

His chin lifts to show me a scowl. "I don't know what you're talking about. I'm just annoyed about the elevator."

"Really...?" I hum, lowering my lips to his neck. "You sure it has nothing to do with the fact that I *love* you...?"

Tate whimpers, clearing his throat again to mask it. When the elevator finally arrives, he dives inside it like he's narrowly escaping an explosion, and I follow him in slowly, instantly crowding him in the corner. Peeking up at me, his throat dips.

"You look like you want to say something," I rumble as he presses the button for his floor.

He blinks at me. And then he presses a different button, for the fifth floor. His apartment is on thirty-five.

"How do you know?" he asks softly.

I raise my brow. "Know what?"

He presses another button. *Six.* "That you... love me...?" Tap tap. *Seven, eight.*

My lips swoop into a grin. "It's pretty hard to miss, Tate."

He tilts his head.

Tap tap tap.

Nine. Ten. Eleven.

The elevator is only just stopping at the fifth floor, doors slowly opening, pausing for many generous seconds.

"You are..." I ease my body into him until his back is sealed to the wall, "The most... beautiful..." *Twelve.* "Sexy..." *Thirteen.* "Mesmerizing thing I've ever encountered." Reaching out, I swipe my finger up a row of buttons, illuminating them all. Tate grins, tugging his lower lip with his teeth. My right palm falls by his shoulder, caging him in while the left presses even more buttons. "Loving you is the easiest thing I've ever done, baby."

"I'm so fucking hard right now," he whispers.

The way we're gazing at each other feels primal, chests heaving, breaths echoing inside the elevator while the doors slowly close. As soon as they touch, I attack him, grabbing his face and kissing him so hard I think I might have bit him by accident. But if I did, he likes it.

Tate writhes, *grinds* his cock into mine, fingers digging into my sides.

323

"Hang on," he breathes, stopping our kisses just long enough to press the remaining buttons. I laugh out loud, and he beams. "Okay. Proceed."

"My troublemaker," I croon, nipping down his jaw, sucking on his earlobe. "You want me to fuck the cum out of you real quick?"

"Fuck yea," he groans, head tipped back while my mouth bruises the smooth flesh of his neck.

"Too impatient to wait until we're inside your place, hm?" I bite him. "You need this dick right fucking now, don't you?"

"God yes, *Lance*... Give it to me."

"Beg," I growl, cupping his erection, pulling on the shape of him through his pants.

"Please..." he purrs. "*Please please,* fuck me."

"Hmm... Not quite convinced," I sing, wrapping my fingers around his thick shaft.

His lashes flutter as he begs, "Please, Lance... I *need* you to fill my ass. *Please*, baby, I'm desperate for you."

"That's what I love to hear." Spinning him fast, I shove him into the wall, trapping his body against it with mine. "Such a needy little cockslut. Pleading to get fucked in the elevator, where anyone could see..."

"Mmhmm..." He pops his ass out, dragging it along the length of my cock.

"Say it," I demand softly. "We're running out of time, Trouble... Any minute now, someone could show up."

"*Fuck*, I'm a needy little cockslut," he gasps, when I rip his pants and boxers down below his ass.

"Keep going." I reach into his pocket for the lube I know he has.

"I'm *so* desperate for you, Sunshine..." he whimpers. "I want your big cock in my ass right here. I don't care who sees."

"Well, that's good." I rip open the lube with my teeth, pouring it onto my hand. Peeking up into the corner, I stuff my wet fingers between his cheeks and rasp, "Say hi to security."

Tate is dazed, panting and quaking as he waves at the camera. "Hi, security. *Ohh*... ooh, baby, touch it..."

Chuckling wickedly, I pull my fingers back, and he whines. "No time. Sorry, love." Stroking lube onto my cock, I quickly nudge it between his cheeks. "Open up wide."

Surging forward, I drill into him, *deep*, filling him with every inch in one long thrust. Tate groans, and I slap my hand over his mouth.

"Too loud, cockslut," I hiss. "The doors are open."

"Sorry..." he murmurs behind my hand.

Gripping his hips, I pull back, then slam in, repeating the motion to develop a fast, punishing rhythm. His ass is so tight, it's squeezing the life out of my cock. It feels so good already, my eyes are rolling back in my head. *Could also have something to do with being in a public elevator, with cameras on us.*

"Baby, this is so fucking hot," I grunt, slamming my dick into him over and over, pounding him against the wall with the elevator doors wide open, revealing hallways of his building.

I've yet to see anyone, but we're already in the twenties, and if we end up going back down, we'll most definitely be met with some very livid security personnel. But for some reason, that thought makes it even hotter.

Knowing we could get caught, and not giving a single fuck. The urgent need for one another that demands to be satisfied, right here, right now... It's intoxicating.

Sliding my hand away from his mouth, I grip his throat, sweating through my clothes as I mash our bodies together, bucking up into him roughly.

"*Mmf* the way you take this dick..." I rasp. "You're *perfection*, sweet Trouble."

"Ffuck me... *Lance*," he gasps, gripping the wall for dear life, baring his hips against my ravaging thrusts. "T-tell me... you love me again." I groan, hoarse, and he trembles. "Say it while you fuck my ass."

"I love you, Tate." I bite the words onto his neck, sucking and kissing his sweet skin while my hips smack into his cheeks, turning them all pink. "I love you so hard, so *deep*... Deeper than my cock could ever reach."

"You should... t-try," he groans, shuddering when I hit his prostate. "Fuck me deeper, baby. Spread me open and stretch me wide..."

My balls quaver. "Such a filthy mouth." I kick his legs apart farther, squeezing his ass, holding him while I stroke every swollen inch in and out. Watching my body disappear inside his is purely captivating. "My Trouble's slutty little ass loves cock, doesn't it?"

"*Ohhyeaaafuck...*" His back arches, cheek resting on the wall. "Yours, baby."

Reaching over, I slam my fist into a bunch of buttons. "We're gonna get caught, naughty thing," I breathe raggedly, with a wicked curl to my lips. "They're gonna find you in here, full of dick, panting like a dog in heat."

"*Mmmm...*" He presses his lips together to control his whines.

325

"I need you to come for me, baby," I grunt, fisting his hair. "Let me see that pretty dick shoot all over this elevator..."

"Uhh, Sun... *Sunshine*..." His voice is shattered, broken words falling from his quivering lips as he reaches between his legs. "I'm... almost... *fuck*..."

Smacking his hand away, I fist it for him, big dick all slippery with precum, throbbing in my palm. "Baby, you're so hard, and thick... nice and wet for me. I'm gonna fill you with *so much* cum, my love..."

My heart is leaping into his back, chills sweeping over me, my loins coiled up and ready to burst. Glancing left, I catch someone coming out of their apartment, turning toward us just as the doors are closing. I'm not sure if they saw... but they might have.

And it has me riding Tate's hole so hard, I think I might break him.

"Fuck, Lance," he gasps, tightening all over. "*Fuck fuck fuck*..."

"You gonna bust, baby?"

He nods fast. "Yea..."

My hips work harder, and *harder*, muscles straining. "You want me to come with you?"

"*Yea*..." He's thrusting into my hand, fucking my fist while I bite his jaw and neck.

"Wanna feel my big cock filling your warm... *tight*... *perfect* little cunt?"

Tate sobs a stream of hoarse curses as his dick pulses, thick arousal drenching my hand and the elevator wall. I can feel his orgasm like it's my own as his body blooms for me. *So* beautiful and so sweet, he's sucking me right over with him.

"God, I fucking love you, Tate..." My forehead falls to his shoulder while I push and push and *push*. "I love how you come for me... I love how it feels to... *fall* with you, baby..."

"Come in me," he cries softly, singing the words like a mantra. "*Come in me come in me come in me*..."

"I'm coming in you, baby," I whisper, snapping in half.

My balls contract, aching almost painfully as I swell and throb, filling his tight ass with wave after wave. Capturing his lips, I swallow his jagged sounds, holding him so hard I fear I'll crush his ribs.

"Feel how much I love you, Trouble... Feel it deep."

"I... I..."

"You're *mine*, Tate. All fucking mine."

"I'm... all... yours."

Breathing heavily, I force myself to get it together enough to shift him just as the elevator doors are opening in the lobby. I crowd him into the corner, rapidly tapping the close button and the button for Tate's floor over and over. By some minor miracle, there's no one standing there. But just as the slow ass doors are closing, I spot someone over by the security desk.

"Fuck..." I gasp, and it turns into a chuckle when the doors finally shut. I drop my head onto his back. "That was close."

"Hmm...?" Tate is so dazed he has no idea what's happening. I don't even think he knows what planet he's on right now.

My heart is soaring, chest cracked open with everything I am just spilling all over him.

I love this man... I fucking love him, more than I ever thought possible.

"You're so beautiful," I whisper, kissing the corner of his mouth. Straightening a bit, I tap him on the ass. "I need you to clench for me, love."

"Mm-mm," he yawns, propped against the wall. "I'm going sleepy-bye."

"Tate." I smack his ass harder, and he whines, aiming a tired scowl at me. "Focus. Squeeze that perfect hole. You gotta hold the cum in until we get inside your place."

"*Fuck me*, you're making me hard again..." he whimpers, wiggling his ass.

"Mhm, and there'll be plenty of time for me to tend to your big, beautiful dick when we get inside. But right now, you have to clench for me..."

"Aye aye, captain," he giggles, squeezing his ass while I pull out of him.

"Good boy," I breathe, patting his ass before tugging his pants up for him.

The way he's flushed and disheveled right now is hypnotizing. He's like a dream come true.

"Okay, that was... crazy," he sighs. "I can't believe we—ohh God..." His face tilts toward the camera. "This is gonna cost a pretty penny to smooth over, I'm sure."

Zipping up, I bite my lip, folding him into my arms. "So... you're going to use your wealth and connections to sweep this little indiscretion under the rug?" He purses his lips to contain a wicked smirk. "That's hot."

He laughs, cocking a brow. "You like that?"

"Mmm..." My lips decorate his throat. "Will you tell me all about *stocks* and *bonds*, sexy man?" He chuckles while I grin on his flesh. "How *big* your investments grow..."

"Oh, baby... my growth is *substantial*," he purrs while I rumble into him. But then he glances down and frowns. "I came on the floor..."

"Uh-huh," I croon.

"Should I... do something about it?"

I pull back to give him a look as his mouth quirks. Then we both burst out laughing, shaking our heads because this is wild.

We just fucked in an elevator... Best night of my life.

Finally arriving at his floor, *for good*, we stumble over to his place. I have to press my lips together to keep from laughing at the way he's walking.

Tate scowls, shoving his keys at me so I can open the door.

"I'm sorry... It's just so cute," I swoon. "You got a good hold on it, or is it... trying to escape?"

"Go ahead. Keep making jokes," he grumbles while I snicker. "One of these days, I'll switch things up just so I can fill you with cum and see how you like it."

The words, and hearing *him* say them, have my dick moving in my pants, a significant flush creeping up my neck. I distract myself by opening the door and stalking inside. Tate comes in after me, locking it behind him.

"I saw that reaction, Hardy." He smirks. "A little *curious*, are we?"

Grasping his face, I kiss his lips softly, humming as I go. "I love you so much, Tate..." He releases a mewl of a raspy sigh, lashes fluttering up at me as I pull away. "But you're *my* cumdump."

He gasps, feigning outrage while I chuckle wickedly. "If I wasn't desperately holding on to your load right now, I'd storm off."

My head falls back in a laugh. "Here, baby," I murmur, undressing him. "Let me get you cleaned up."

Tate bites his lip while I remove his clothes, leaving a trail of them on our way to the en suite. I get the shower running, undressing myself while he stares at me.

"Overall, pretty amazing first night in New York," I breathe through the most contented sigh ever.

"Drinks, dancing and elevator sex... The full Hell's Kitchen experience," he rumbles in amusement while I beam. "You're one of us now."

Taking his hand, I bring him into the shower. Beneath the warm flowing water, I gaze over his beauty, and the noticeable blush still on his cheeks.

"Hardy... um..." he starts, fidgeting in place. I can't tell if he's squirmy from the cum, or something else.

Trouble

Slinking my fingers between his ass, I touch him, sensually, teasing his slippery, puckered hole. "You can let go now, Trouble."

I feel him relax as he leans into me, panting soft breaths. I'm lost in playing with him, admiring the way my cum slowly spills out onto my fingers.

"God, that's so hot..."

"Baby..." His tone is quietly inquisitive and nervous.

"Yea?"

"About what you... said..." he mumbles. "Before..."

My head tilts as I watch his gorgeous face. "That I love you...?"

"Yea." He clears his throat. "That. Um, I just... I want you to know that if I have a hard time... saying things like that, or whatever..." His voice trails off into a strained sigh.

He seems to be really struggling with this, and it's as adorable as it is worrying. Because I don't want him to stress about anything. I want him comfortable and happy at all times. And I want to be the one who makes him those things.

Whatever that means. As long as it's with *him*, I want it.

"I just mean I might be... bad at this," he whispers. "I've never done it before. I don't know how to..."

"Shh." I comb fingers through his wet hair. "I don't need anything else from you, Tate. You give me everything just by breathing." He pouts. "I love you exactly like this. What we are is *perfect*."

"But Sunshine..." He grabs my jaw, pulling my mouth to his. "You make me breathless..."

"Don't worry, baby," I hum onto his puffy lips. "I won't tell anyone."

We kiss slowly, beneath the running water, hearts beating in tandem. And although things are still chaotic and unsettled, between us, in my life and in our lives together, I'm at ease. The details don't matter... Nothing else does. *Just us.*

He set me free.

"Thank you for the best night of my life..." I hold him, with no intention of ever letting go.

And he whispers, "Thank you for... loving me."

Chapter Twenty-Five
Tate

This past week has been a whirlwind of glorious fuckery.

It's still strange... having Lance around like this. Spending all this time with him, out in the open. Behaving in ways I've never behaved with anyone before, and actually... loving it.

But I think the weirdest part is how *normal* it feels. How effortless it is. Holding his hand in restaurants or while we're walking down 9th, stopping so he can kiss me frequently, usually under the guise of wanting to taste something I've eaten, or as he likes to say, *get his fix.*

"I'm jonesing real bad, Trouble. Don't let me starve..."

That sorta thing.

The constant swoon-filled glances and lip biting and fuck-me eyes, the rabid smiles and teasing touches, and the laughter. *Oh, the laughter...*

Don't tell Jake, but I don't think anyone's *ever* made me laugh the way Lance does. He has this sense of humor that's unexpected, as if you're not prepared for him to be as funny as he is, so it throws you off, and you're laughing, but also gawking at him, because how can someone who looks like he does also be low-key hilarious?

Not only that, but making him laugh is probably one of my favorite things ever. Because he doesn't give them out sparingly. You have to earn them, like a rare and valuable currency. And it turns out I'm just as skilled at raking in Lance Hardy's deep, sexy chuckles as I am regular money.

Doing all of this and more with him just comes naturally. It's as if the time we spent apart never happened, and we just slid right back into our groove together. We're exactly where we would have been if he'd never run out of my dorm that night, more or less, and it's crazy. Intense as hell, but somehow it just works.

The more I've thought about it, the more it makes sense that Lance would be the only person to draw me into a real relationship, because he's the only person I ever wanted one with. And sure, it was a long time ago, back when I was still young, dumb and full of... *well, you know.*

Admittedly, I never actually got over those feelings. They were always there; I just got really freaking good at stuffing them down. And because Lance wasn't in my life, it didn't matter. I could avoid it and just focus on being me, *sans feels.*

But now that he's back, and shedding his own disguise—his marriage—I guess my shields have come down. I can stop pretending I don't want him, and *have* him. For real.

It's a second chance; an opportunity to finally see what would've happened if he'd never left. And not only that, we sorta get to be kids again. *Kids with adult money, which is way better.* Merging our college selves with our present selves; having the goofy fun times we used to have together as friends, only with a *lot* more touching.

As it turns out, the excitement had nothing to do with the sneaking around. We're still every bit as insatiable for one another, except now, we're like that in the open too. Free of worry about getting caught, yes, but more importantly, free of *internal* worry. Because now we both know where the other stands.

All of this to say, nothing is perfect. There are still a lot of things up in the air. Starting with the fact that Lance sort of just split on his life and his responsibilities to run away with me to New York. *Is it weird that that makes me all fluttery in the balls?*

I'm sure people have been looking for him. He just doesn't want to be found, which is fine for right now. *That's tomorrow's problem.*

I'm having too much fun on this *business trip slash mini gay-cation slash new relationship training camp* to be bothered with the stresses of what things will look like when we leave New York.

I mean, shit, maybe we should just stay here.

Honestly, it's not the worst idea. I love the city, and clearly, so does Lance. He could find something to do for work... Something to occupy his time. And until he does, he could be like my sugar baby. My giant, still married, *hasn't-even-technically-said-he's-gay-yet* sugar baby who's the same age as me. *We might need to come up with a better term for that.*

Nyla K.

Yea, how about boyfriend, *you fuckin neophyte.*

Regardless, it's a moot point for the moment, because I don't even know if that's something Lance would want. We haven't talked much about where he sees this going after we get back, even though it's our last night. We've been too busy screwing and holding hands to discuss the *serious*.

Although yesterday, he did express a desire to leave the church...

"In a perfect world, I could get divorced, come out, and still be a pastor there," he said last night while we were lying in bed with our legs tangled, touching like it was going out of style. "But I know it'd never work out that way. Not with Desiree's parents being such well-respected members of the congregation, and the community. And certainly not with my father still around, reigning over the place like it's still *his*."

I listened to his voice and his words, absorbing everything while my chest ached just a bit for my ray of sunshine.

I never noticed it before... how much of a grudge Lance holds against his father. Even before we found out about the secret marriage arrangement, I always knew their relationship was a bit strained, but he never told me why. He used to say they were just *very different people*, and that his father does things that he *would never do*.

I suppose now it makes more sense... His father is a closet-homophobe, which is almost worse than an out-and-proud homophobe. At least you can just avoid the ones who are all *in your face* about it. But the ones who keep their hate buried beneath surface smiles and fake support—the *no rainbows after 11:59 on June 30th* type shitheads—are much more vindictive.

Then again, I've never had any patience or tolerance for fake people.

"It sucks, because I know a lot of them need me," Lance went on about his congregation. "That's the *only* reason I took the job. Because I wanted to make a difference in the community. Let the people who have felt marginalized know that God loves all of us, not just the stand-sit-kneel Christians."

"Then keep going," I told him softly. "Fuck the haters." His lips curled into an elated smile. "Stay and fight for what you believe in, Hardy. Let your people know that it's okay to be a gay, divorced, disappointment in the church. After all, if you're pissing people off, that just means it's working. Pretty sure Jesus said that."

He laughed, and I swooned—*naturally*—unable to resist batting my lashes at him. Then he grabbed my jaw and whispered, "And you'd be okay

332

with that? Dating a pastor...?" His thumbs brushed along my cheekbones. "You're not exactly a believer, Tate."

My stomach fluttered at the notion of being in a *real* relationship with him, which somehow seemed even more illicit than the affair. And that he was actually considering *my* feelings as a factor in his major life decision... It was downright fascinating to me.

If it's possible, I might know even less about being a *boyfriend* than I know about religious faith. *I'm the freaking Virgin Mary when it comes to having a monogamous relationship.* But just because I'm not used to things, doesn't mean I'm *opposed* to them...

"If God is okay with me, then I'm okay with Him," I said quietly. "And if those people wanna chase us out of South Valley with pitchforks, well... I just hope they can keep up with my Maserati."

I winked at Lance while he laughed and rolled on top of me.

"What am I going to do with you..." he crooned, lowering his lips to my throat. "You're way too much trouble for this lowly pastor to handle..."

"If anyone could get me to behave, Sunshine..."

Real fingers trailing my lower back snap me out of my memories and scattered thoughts. Glancing up, I give Lance a smile while he delivers me a glass of scotch, lifting his glass of water to tap it against mine, a confident smirk on his lips.

God... He's just so *sexy*, it actually worries me. Because I can't guarantee that I won't succumb to even riskier levels of lewd and lascivious behavior than what happened in the elevator.

I mean, look at him... How can I be expected not *to hop on his dick in public?*

At this point, I'm gonna be handing out checks like bubblegum to get me out of the hot water he submerges me in just by being his delicious self.

We're out at a Wall Street bar for our last night in New York, which wouldn't be my first choice of activities, but it's sort of a requirement, being that I am here for work in the first place. The rest of the partners are here—*most of them, anyway*—along with Truman and Z, the lot of us celebrating yet another successful acquisition.

I'd considered not bringing Lance, but when I asked him, he seemed purely thrilled at the idea of me inviting him to any sort of work function, making it impossible for me to turn around and squash his joy.

Much to my surprise and relief, though, he's been holding his own. He doesn't know shit about finance, but that doesn't exactly matter. Neither do any of the other guys' dates. He's just here for moral support, which he's been giving me in his own stoic, convivial way, and to be *my* version of arm candy, as opposed to the *dates* brought by some of the other guys, between actual girlfriends, escorts and out-of-town sidepieces.

And then there's Lance... my married *boyfriend*, I guess, who talks about God for a living and was straight until about five minutes ago.

So even though Lance doesn't drink, for *me*, booze is entirely necessary. Especially since Josiah Pierce is also here, and the last time I spoke with him outside of work, he was begging to come over and lay the pipe.

"I'll finish this and then we can go," I tell Lance, taking large sips.

I don't want him to think I don't appreciate him being here for me, because I totally do. My bosses seem to like him. In fact, they're all sincerely impressed that I brought a date, a shocking turn of events none of us saw coming.

Even so, I've just about hit my limit on work-talk. I'm much more interested in seeing how many more positions me and Lance can pull off in my bathtub. *We're at four so far.*

"I'm fine," he says casually, though his eyes harden and his jaw ticks when he sees Pierce at the next table, laughing with Z and his *date*, whose boobs are so big they're practically in Brooklyn.

That's my bad. I made the mistake of telling Lance about Pierce and me occasionally doing the nasty, and now he's on high alert. I know I probably shouldn't have said anything, but in the interest of trying this thing called *honesty* out for size, when he asked, *"Which of these tools is the one you've fooled around with?"* I answered.

Of course, I explained to him that it was just a couple of drunken instances, reminding him, without shooting myself too badly in the foot, that unattached hook-ups had sort of been my thing before he popped back up and swept me off my feet. But because Lance Hardy has the memory of a damn elephant, he pointed out that I was pretty close to sleeping with Josiah again the night I showed up at his house.

So all evening, he's been watching the dude like a hawk. And while his jealousy and borderline toxic possessiveness has a tendency to make me drip like a leaky faucet, I'd rather just leave and spare us all the potential awkwardness.

"Yea, you seem fine," I mutter to Lance, sarcastically.

He shoots me a look. "I am."

"If you stare any harder, you'll give yourself an aneurism," I huff, taking another sip.

Squinting at me, his lips twitch. "I'm sorry..."

"Apology accepted. Let's go." I stand up fast.

"...*if* I gave you the impression that me loving you started when I said the words," he continues in a commanding, if hushed, tone, fingers slipping down to graze my ass. "It didn't. I've been in love with you for a long time, Tate, which means any motherfucker who's touched you over the years has been messing with what's mine. This asshole, the bartender the other night... all of them. Now, I can accept your past for what it is... Your *past*. But don't expect to put me in the same room with these pricks and have me *not* envisioning all the ways I'd like to chop their balls off. Because that—" he squeezes my ass cheek, and I flinch, "—won't happen. The most I can give you is a fake smile and dead eyes."

Blinking at him while trying to tone down the bewildered hearts in my eyes, an amused breath gusts from between my lips. "You're not like the others, are you, Preacher Man?"

He leans close. "Baby, you have no idea..." He winks, and my balls thump.

Seriously, though... Where on earth did this guy come from??

From the casual stalking and territorial nature to the filthy mouth, hidden kinks and dominant, primal fucking, I can safely say Lance Hardy is giving the *ultimate* camouflage.

Meanwhile, I'm high-key obsessed with the fact that I'm the only one who gets to savor the deliciously deranged filling beneath his discreet, shy-guy shell.

"That said, we can go whenever you're ready." He taps me on the butt, quiet, normal-guy mask back in place.

"I guess we could stay for another drink," I rasp, watching him smirk while sipping his water. "As long as we can stop for hot dogs on the way home."

Lance chuckles. "Not satisfied with the thirty-dollar crab cakes?" I shake my head. "You prefer your food to be served out of a metal cart on the side of the road?" I nod enthusiastically, and he laughs. "Good, because I can't go back to New Mexico without one last scrumptious street dog."

"Actually, there's a Papaya Dog three blocks from here." I grin, and his eyes light up.

"Okay, forget what I said." His eyes fall to my drink. "Kill that and let's go."

Chuckling, I sip more, faster, as Lance presses a quick kiss on my jaw.

"I'm gonna run to the restroom," he says, sauntering off, eyes lingering on me until they absolutely have to break away.

And mine do the same, gazing after him and just loving this... All of it. The affection and attention, the way it feels to be fawned over by him, to an almost stifling and psychotic degree. Honestly, it makes perfect sense for me, an only child who grew into a bit of a spoiled narcissist. Finally settling with someone who treats me like the human equivalent of a Fabergé egg seems pretty on-brand.

It feels good to finally have someone looking after me. I've been independent all my life, always supporting myself, and I do a damn good job of it. I don't *need* anyone for anything, but as it turns out, I guess there is something I *want* that I can't go out and buy, or find on Grindr.

After all, what's the point of all the riches if the king comes back to his castle and sleeps alone?

While I'm waiting for Lance, I pick up my personal cell, and either out of habit, or some kind of unconscious reflex, I tap the Grindr app. I haven't opened it in weeks, save for the night Lance stood me up, when I was annoyed and horny as fuck and just felt like being petty after his wife answered his phone. Of course, nothing came of it. I looked at a few messages from random dudes, dick pics and the same shallow comments and questions, reducing me to a *type* or a *position*. In that moment, it felt so forced.

And to be honest, that's probably a big reason why I decided to show up at Lance's the next day. Because I realized that the excitement I used to take from engaging with random men on Grindr wasn't all that exciting anymore. It had become average, predictable.

Lance Hardy isn't either of those things. Forbidden or not, he's always been able to shake me up.

That was when I reapplied it. I'm over splashing around in the shallow... I'm ready to dive into the deep end.

Give me a microphone, I'll Gaga this shit right now.

Mind made up, I'm about to delete this stupid app and never look back. But something catches my eye, and I click on it.

Son of a bitch...

Lifting my gaze, I narrow it at Pierce, who's still at the next table. He's on his phone, which now makes perfect sense, considering who just popped up in my immediate area.

TLOVESTHED

Really?

Trouble

I see the moment he reads the message in real-time, because his head pops up then flings in my direction. He looks around before returning to his phone.

JPDL8

Where'd your friend go?

I glare at him, and he peeks at me, grinning. Rolling my eyes, I'm about to exit the app again, but he sends another message.

JPDL8

If you're down lmk... I'll ditch the guy I'm talking to

"Ugh," I grunt, closing the app and deleting it.
There. It's done.
Exhaling swiftly, I chew on my lower lip. *Wow, this feels... kinda cool.*
Is this maturing? Am I mature *now??*
Looking around for Lance, I'm filled with a sudden urge to share this with him. To let him know that I'm officially off Grindr. And I didn't do it *for* him, but I did it for *him*, for myself to *have* him.
Because I lo—
"Why'd you log off?" Pierce's voice startles me, and I jump.
Jesus, he really just sidled up out of nowhere.
I back up, but he keeps inching in closer.
"Why are you on Grindr, you fuckin creep?" I rumble, just teasingly enough that I'm not insulting him outright.
He shrugs. "I'm bored. Gotta get it somewhere, right?" He smirks, and I roll my eyes. "I've been texting you..."
"And I've been ignoring you."
He pouts. But before he can continue bothering me, Truman and Z come staggering over to the table, red-faced and glassy-eyed.
"T-Money!" Z sloshes his drink around.
"Hey, Tate, where's your date?!" Truman snickers at his stupid rhyme.
"Yea, he seems like a cool guy," Z says, squinting and nodding his approval.
Pierce's hand appears on my knee, and I jerk away from it, glaring at him. "He'll be right back. Then we're taking off."
"Does anyone else find it sufficiently disturbing that Tate Eckhart has a

boyfriend?" Truman chuckles. "I mean, no offense, T, but it's like seeing a dog walk on its hind legs. It just seems unnatural."

"Hilarious," I mutter while they laugh at my expense.

"Well, I'm happy for you," Z slurs. "As long as you're happy."

"Happy... Already bored as hell," Pierce chimes in, shooting a fake grin at me. "Same thing, right, T?"

Okay, he's starting to irritate me just a skosh.

"Jealous," Z says to Pierce, winking at me.

I grin, nodding. "Yea, he sounds *super* jealous."

"Sure. That's why you're banging Manhattan Barbie while your wife is back home with the kids," Pierce says to Z. Then he turns to me. "And your boyfriend has a super visible tan line on his ring finger. Because relationships always *work* out, right?"

Leaning in, I seethe under my breath, "Studying my man a little hard for someone who's *straight*, no?"

His hand grazes my leg *again,* and I smack it away. "It's cute that you're trying, T. But you'll be back on Grindr as soon as he falls asleep."

My muscles are stiff, frustration pulsing through my veins. I shouldn't be letting this dickwad get to me, but I can't help it. I'm stubborn by nature, and this drunk fool doubting me is just making me want to prove him wrong.

"What about Grindr?" Lance asks, as he saunters up to me.

His tone is aloof enough, as is the slight slope of his lips. But his pretty brown eyes are sparkling with unease, and it makes me want to backhand Josiah Pierce across the face.

"Nothing. You ready to go?" I push into him, trying to leave, but he's not really moving as fast as I'd like him to.

"Lance! Stay for one more shot!" Z cheers.

"He doesn't drink," I grunt, peeking at Lance. "Let's *go*. Please?"

"Hey, Tate," Truman hiccups. "Satan called. He wants to know if he can borrow your ice skates... Since ya know, Hell froze over."

The three of them start giggling like idiots, and I'm scowling so hard my face might get stuck in permanent RBF.

"*Ah*, I get it." Lance tilts his face in my direction. "Because you're seeing someone." He cocks a brow.

My stomach is twisting and turning rather uncomfortably as I gnaw on my lower lip.

"See? He got it," Truman rumbles. "It was funny."

"*So* funny..." Lance mutters, looking only at me.

Trouble

He doesn't appear amused in the slightest, and I think I need to say something...

Or do something. To let him know how I feel.

Their stupid jokes are just that, *stupid jokes*. I deleted Grindr because I don't want meaning*less* anymore. I want meaning*ful*. And yea, maybe I've never had a relationship before, but doesn't that just make this first one, with *him*, all the more special?

Oh God. Is it romantic gesture time??

I'm so out of my league...

Sucking in a breath to steady my nerves, I tap my knuckles on the table. "Alright, assholes. It's been real. Oh, and one last thing..."

Grabbing a fistful of Lance's shirt, I haul him to me, kissing his sweet, startled mouth. I can't go too hard on him, or I'll forget the reason I'm doing this in the first place, but I make sure to flick his tongue and bite his lip, and give him one of those little moans he likes so much.

The peanut gallery is surprisingly giggle-free all of a sudden.

Sucking off his lips, I open my eyes as he opens his, our gazes melting together. His gorgeous face is all flushed, looking just like my friend from college who I always wanted to kiss like that.

And I hum, "I love you, Hardy. We're way past dating, don't you think?" His lashes are fluttering, like he's in shock, and it's the sweetest, sexiest thing I've ever seen. "Hmm... Look who's speechless now." I smirk, kissing him once more.

"Don't fuck with me, Trouble." His voice comes out hoarse, hands sliding up my chest.

Chuckling, I touch his jaw with shaky fingers. "Fully serious, Sunshine. I'm in... love. With you. I'm not seeing *someone*... I'm seeing *you*. Fifteen years, baby, and you're still all I see."

"God, Tate, I love you so fucking much," he breathes, rushing to kiss me again, fast and desperate, but cherishing all the same. Like he's grateful. He's thanking *me* for loving *him* with this kiss, and my knees are about to give out.

My dumbass coworkers are hooting and hollering and muttering things, but I've tuned it all out. Literally *nothing* else matters right now... Just him.

"You're gonna get laid so hard tonight, baby," Lance purrs, grinning into my mouth while I laugh.

"I guess Hell really has frozen over, huh?" I beam, playing with his fingers, high as a fucking kite on this spectacularly terrifying moment.

Nyla K.

He nods, kissing my bottom lip a dozen times.
Satan better get a fucking sweater...
'Cause Tate Eckhart is in love.

I'm pretty sure I floated all the way back uptown.

Lance and I both did. We basically rode a unicorn over a damn rainbow from Wall Street to Hell's Kitchen, touching and kissing and whispering *"I love you"* on repeat. A brief detour was made at Papaya Dog and, in a place that sells food made of ground-up animal parts, *we* still managed to gross everyone else out.

But who cares? Not me, and certainly not my man.

My... man...

Crazy.

We're swept up in it right now, and I've gotta say... the songs weren't lying.

Love feels really freaking great.

Somehow, we were able to keep our private parts to ourselves until we got back to the apartment—just barely. But once we were inside, it was a genitalia free-for-all. We spent the last three hours fucking our way across every surface of my apartment, and thankfully we ended up in the bathtub, because my muscles are sore as fuck, my skin is chafed like a motherfucker, and I can feel the bite marks on my ass cheeks so prominently, I essentially have his dental records on my butt.

Lance is slumped, with his back against the edge of my giant lavish bathtub. I'm curled around his front, dozing, with my face wedged into the crook of his neck, his fingers caressing up and down my back. The water is still pretty warm, only a few bubbles remaining, and the scent of gardenia from whatever fancy bath products we used lingering in the air.

This is bliss, right here. A tranquility I didn't know was possible from something as frightening as that four-letter word.

"T...?"

"Mmm..."

"Say it again."

Chuckling softly, I croon, "I love you," grinning lazily while my lips brush his skin.

Lance shudders, purring, "I love you, baby..."

Trouble

"This is by far the gayest moment of my life," I rumble, and his chest shakes. "And I've been to Boy Beach in June."

"Trouble," he whines in a softly scolding tone. "I don't wanna know about that..."

Summoning all of my remaining strength, I manage to prop myself up to look at him. "You know I haven't... been with anyone else. Right?" He blinks. "I mean, since we started sleeping together..."

"I do now." He gulps.

"I deleted Grindr," I tell him, tracing the muscles in his chest.

He breathes out slowly. "I didn't... You didn't have to do that, baby."

"I know I didn't *have* to. I wanted to. I wanted... to make this real." I keep my eyes on his to convey my sincerity, despite how much I'm shivering from it. "To give this a real shot. That's why I told you about Josiah, too. Because I want to be honest with you, Lance."

Something flashes over his face, and his throat dips. But he doesn't speak. Just stares back at me while I confess the things to him that have been holding me back from what I've wanted this whole time.

"I might not always be good at this, baby..." I whisper. "I need you to know that I might fuck up. I'm used to being by myself, being selfish. So I need you to promise you'll stay, even if I make it hard to." Pausing, I swallow, pulse rapping quickly as my insecurities resurface. "Just promise you won't... leave me, baby."

I hate how vulnerable I sound right now. I hate that I'm even saying these words, but my walls are down and I'm utterly defenseless.

I have no idea how to do this, and be *cool* about it. Instead, I'm just spilling my guts to him and just praying it won't frighten him off like last time. Because I only just lost my love-virginity, and I have no clue what I'm doing.

Lance takes my face in his hands, settling his eyes on mine; that same deep shade absorbing my own. "I will *never* leave you, Tate. Not this time... not unless you want me to."

"Why would I ever want that...?" I kiss him softly.

He breathes harshly over my lips, a sudden air of trepidation surrounding him. It's twisting my stomach right up.

I did, I ruined it. I freaked him out...

Goddamnit, Eckhart, pull yourself together!

"If you knew why I left..." Lance interrupts my internal struggle, purposely keeping his gaze averted while he speaks, "You might wish we'd stayed apart."

My heart is racing much faster now, nerves shifting from my own hang-ups to whatever has him so shredded all of a sudden.

"What are you talking about, Hardy?" I ask, voice laced with quiet concern.

"Fuck..." He rubs his eyes. "God, forgive me..."

Okay, what's going on...?

I'm stiff, itching all over with my pulse increasing steadily.

He shifts to straighten, finally making eye contact. "Tate, here's the thing... I know I should've told you sooner. I know that..."

"Told me what...?" I mumble, barely audible.

But he just goes on, "I fucked up leaving you the way I did, and I have to live with that. For the rest of my life, I'll have to exist knowing that I *left* you when all you wanted was for me to stay. I left knowing it was the worst possible thing I could do. But you have to understand where I was coming from, baby... I was *so* scared of my feelings for you. *Terrified*. Because I guess... they're wrong. In a sense."

Wrong...? Why??

Is this still because he's uncomfortable with his sexuality? Jesus, did his father really fuck him up that bad??

"When I got you back, I realized that it doesn't matter if loving you is wrong. It's *not* wrong, even if it is. This love, baby... there's no *way* it could be wrong. Not us." He places his hand over my heart. "No matter what, I *love you*, Tate Eckhart. And I will keep loving you until there's nothing else left. No. Matter. What." He looks like... there are tears in his eyes, about to fall. "That's why I should've told you... *Now*, in our present. Because I couldn't do it in our past, but now I fucking owe it to you to be honest, baby. I was just waiting for the right time..."

"L-Lance... You're freaking me out." I shiver as he takes my hands. I'm suddenly freezing, teeth chattering with fear. "You left me because you were... afraid of being gay. *Right??* I mean, wasn't that the reason...?"

His wide eyes are filled with so much regret as he drops his chin, shaking his head slowly. "No... that's not the reason, baby. I wish it was..."

The weight of something giant is hovering above us. Something huge and terrible, with the power to completely destroy everything we've built, today, over the past week, the past month... Hell, the past fifteen years.

In my gut, I can sense it. His words are going to change *everything*.

And I'm not ready. I'm not fucking ready to let this go yet...

Just give me a little more time... Please.

It felt so good to love him like this.

Trouble

My lips tremble as he wipes his eyes. Then croaks, "The reason I left, Tate, is because my father... is your father." He clears his throat. "We have the same... dad."

...What?

The rapid flutter of my eyelashes matches the dangerously fast pace of my pulse. I shake my head. But no words will come out. I'm just gaping in confused silence.

Lance doesn't say anything. He just sits quietly, fidgeting in place while I *stare*, dumbfounded. *No.* More than that...

My entire *life* is flashing before my eyes.

This makes no sense...

Why is he saying that? Is he fucking nuts??

"Lance..." I scrub a hand over my face. "What the hell are you talking about...? Is this supposed to be a joke?? Because it's really not fucking funny..."

"No, Tate, it's not a joke." His words gust from his mouth, as if he's exhausted from holding this in for so long. "I *wish* it was. But no, it's the truth."

"You're fucking lying," I scoff. "How would you even know something like that?? It makes no fucking sense. My dad left before I was born... I sure as shit don't know him, so how the hell would you??"

"I think he was... seeing your mom on the side," he rumbles like he's in physical pain. "I don't know the specifics, all I know is that I found some pretty damning evidence that my father, Gio Hardy, knows your mother. And he's... your biological father."

"What the fuck?!" An unamused cackle flies out of me as I leap up from of the water. "That's fucking *crazy*! Do you have any idea how crazy you sound right now??"

Stumbling out of the tub, I scramble to grab a towel, just narrowly avoiding slipping and breaking my skull open.

Maybe that wouldn't be such a bad thing right now...

My mind is spinning like a deranged carnival ride, whipping my thoughts all over the place. What he's saying makes no sense, and I'm teetering between anger, confusion... denial.

No. No no no. That's impossible.

There's literally no fucking way...

"Tate..." Lance hops out of the bath after me, dripping water everywhere.

"How do you know??" I snap at him. "What alleged *evidence* did you even find?"

Visibly shaking, he wraps a towel around his waist. "He keeps a storage unit off 303. I followed him there once... It's where he keeps all of his secrets."

Blinking, a bit of my initial hostility begins to trickle off. And now I'm just in shock.

Because I know he's not lying. *What would be the point??*

I can tell he isn't, but that doesn't make any of this better.

"What... was in it?" My voice creeps.

"Pictures... of you as a kid," he answers calmly, though it's obvious that even speaking these words is tearing him to shreds. "Pictures of him and your mother. Some financial papers that looked like receipts of payments... to your mom."

"Like... child support?" My stomach is turning so violently, I think I might be sick.

My mother never told me about any of this. She never told me that my father sent her money. *She never told me she sent him... pictures of me.*

In fact, she never told me a damn thing about him.

"Well, I don't think they were officially married," Lance mumbles. "But more or less, it seemed like he sent her money from the year you were born to the time you were eighteen." He pauses for a moment to glance at his feet. "He paid for some of your tuition, too..."

A memory springs into my mind... Of me applying for colleges and financial aid. I got approved for scholarships and grants, a few loans, to cover a majority. But there was still going to be a bill of at least a few thousand a year. And we were broke as fuck.

At least, I *thought* we were, until my mother surprised me with a laptop on my eighteenth birthday, and a card filled with cash.

"I have some money set aside," she'd said. *"It's not much... but it's enough to help pay your tuition."*

I remember being so excited, so grateful that she actually cared enough to do that for me. Maybe she'd cared all along...

Maybe she didn't regret me.

"I'm so proud of you, sweetheart..."

"Wow, holy fuck..." I cover my face with my hands. "I need to sit down."

The world around me seems to be toppling over, and I'm dizzy.

"Come here." Lance gasps, darting over and grabbing me by the waist. I find myself leaning into him for comfort, his strength and his warmth and his smell, as he walks me into the bedroom like I'm some kind of invalid.

Snapping out of it, I rip away from him, pinning him with a seething glare.

"So... that's it then?" I hiss. "Your dad just also happens to be my dad? No big deal??" Lance stares at me like he hasn't the slightest clue what to say or do, and it's making the situation feel even more hopeless. Crashing my butt down onto the bed, I breathe out roughly, gazing uneasily at my hands in my lap. "Gio fucking Hardy, huh...?" My eyes lift to his. "Was there ever a DNA test or anything? How do you know for sure?"

"Tate..." He shakes his head, tone almost patronizing as he steps over carefully, taking a seat next to me on the bed. "I know this is a lot..."

"*A lot?!*" I scoff. "No, it's not a fucking *lot*, Hardy, it's a shitstorm of epic proportions!"

"I know, I know." He shakes his head. "I *know*, Tate, but—"

"*Was there* a fucking paternity test?!" I cut him off with the same question I'd really like a fucking answer to.

He stares at me. And I don't want to see it...

I *don't* want to see his eyes right now, because they're way too similar to my own.

Fuck my life. This is fucked.

"Yea, there was," he mutters.

A choked sob of rage and despair leaves me as I rip my hair in my fists. "Well, that's just fucking perfect... The first time I fall in love, and it's... tainted." I sniffle, feeling Lance stiffen at my side. "What did the deadbeat have to say for himself?"

Lance shifts. He's silent for a moment before whispering, "I never brought it up..."

My face whips in his direction. "Hold on... So you *found* the skeletons in his goddamn closet, and you didn't even expose them? You said *nothing??*"

"I wanted to... I *tried* to, so many times." He shivers. "But it would've destroyed everything. My family..."

"So *what?!*" I shout.

"My mother and my sister, I mean." He shakes his head. "They don't deserve that, T..."

"Oh, and *I* do??" I hiss.

"No. No, that's not what I'm saying..." I can see him shaking from where I'm sitting, but not in rage like me.

He's being swarmed with guilt, like a million tiny earthquakes happening all over his body. I don't want him to feel that way, because realistically, this isn't his fault.

But I just don't understand how he could have kept this to himself.

How the fuck could he let that asshole get away with this??

If it was me, I would've been flipping tables and shit.

But we're so different, me and him. He's never had the confidence that I do. And clearly, he lets his father—*our father? Ugh, kill me*—manipulate him a lot.

"So is that why... he..." My voice cuts out. I can't even speak, I feel so nauseated, swallowing down the bile trying to rise in my throat. "That's why he really wanted to keep us apart, isn't it? Because he knew..."

This is too much. Too much core-shaking information is being dumped on me, and I can't breathe.

Lance nods. "It would appear so..."

Anger sweeps through me again, and I snap, "You're being entirely too cavalier about this right now, *bro.*" He flinches like I just shot him, and I growl, flopping onto my back. Covering my face with my palms again, I murmur into them. "I need you on my fucking level right now, Lance, because this shit is *seriously* fucked up. The guy you have feelings for is actually your half-brother! Because *our* father is a scumbag who's been hiding an illegitimate child from your family for years! Get fucking pissed right now, Hardy! I mean, God, don't you *care??*"

"Of course I fucking care!" he barks.

I peek up at him, watching him use every ounce of his strength to hold it together. For me...

He's doing this for me...

He's been holding this in... all these years... because he loves me.

I'm in love with my... brother?

God, I'm gonna throw up.

"I've been fucked up over this for *years*, Tate." His voice tremors. "Since the day I found that storage unit, I've been living in constant torment. I *know* I should have told you, because above all else, you deserved to know who your father was, but..." His words dissolve into a choked sound that splits my heart right down the middle. "But I was falling in love with you. And I was selfish, okay?? I didn't want to give it up. I didn't want to give *you* up."

Falling onto his back beside me, he stares up at the ceiling, while I stare at him, searching for any and all differences I can find between us physically.

Trouble

There's no shortage of them... Really, our eyes are the only similarity we share, and it gives me the tiniest sliver of solace in this moment.

I've never seen his father before...

I wonder if I look like him.

"As soon as we hooked up, I knew it was over." He sighs, broken. "I knew I'd made a huge mistake, and I was afraid, Tate. So I did the only thing I could think to do... I left. I couldn't believe I'd let myself do something so... immoral." He lets out a breath. "And I couldn't deal with how much I *loved* it."

Rolling onto my side, I lift my hand like an instinct. Like I want to ease his pain with my touch. But I stop myself, because I don't think it's right...

Knowing what I know now.

How can we possibly move forward together?? How could we ever love each other like this??

My heart is completely shattered as I whisper, "How long have you known, Lance?"

It's not accusatory, or carrying the anger I still feel inside. I'm curious, because I need to understand what he was thinking.

He turns his face to meet my gaze. "I found out halfway through sophomore year."

"Lance..." I whimper, closing my eyes.

I don't even know what to say anymore.

"I'm so sorry, Tate," he rasps, with guilt seeping out of his tone. "But you have to understand... how much I already liked you at that point."

My stomach flutters. I know it's ridiculous. Clearly, my body can't comprehend the magnitude of this situation. My physical reactions are straight from the heart, and I guess love doesn't see right, or *wrong*.

He liked me when I liked him...

The whole time, during those college years, the parties and the late-night conversations, the walks around campus, the laughter, and youthful high jinks, I thought he was just my straight friend Lance. While I was pining for him... it turns out he was pining right back. Holding on to the secret of a lifetime, that would have obliterated everything.

I guess it still did, in so many ways. It tore him away from me when he left, in his misguided attempt to do the right thing. But somehow, we wound up back together, and now the truth is ruining us all over again.

It's so beyond fucked, I don't even know what to think.

"Tate, fifteen years ago, I was consumed by this information," he says, shifting his body to face me fully. "I let my feelings for you get the best of me that night in your dorm room, and it was the best and worst night of my whole life. I thought I was doing the right thing by leaving, holding the burden of the truth inside, *myself*, so it couldn't hurt anyone else. But then God brought me back to you... He put me in that bathroom stall for a reason, Tate. And that's when I realized that I didn't give a fuck if it's wrong. I *don't* fucking *care*."

He speaks the words with conviction, reaching for my hands. And this time, I let myself go to him. I let him place my palms flat on his bare chest, over the softness of his skin, and the hard planes of his muscle. His big, beautiful heart pumping the blood we share through his veins. It's so fucking fucked up, and maybe it *is* wrong...

But I still love him. I can't just turn that off.

Attraction, chemistry, *love*... they don't work that way. There's no off switch, or device to wipe my memory clean of everything that's happened between us.

I didn't choose for this to happen. It just did, and now more than ever, I can't cut him from my insides. He's a part of me, deeper than I thought.

"I told you, I'll never stop being sorry for my mistakes, baby..." he whispers, head resting on the bed while mine does the same, our brown eyes bonded together. "I have to live with them. Leaving, not telling you the truth, not confronting my father, and allowing him to force us apart because he's an evil, selfish piece of shit... That's my burden, and I'll own it. But loving you... Being with you, falling for you... That wasn't a *mistake*, Tate. It was a blessing. *You*... are my blessing."

His fingers slide up to my face, and my eyes close. "I... I don't..." My voice quavers, the doubt trying to fight its way back up because I'm afraid that letting go of it makes me a sick, twisted degenerate. "This is a mess, Hardy. I feel like you should've just stayed away..."

"But don't you get it, Tate?" He pulls me closer. "I'm like Clytie... Even though I betrayed you, and fucked up so royally, I'll still always love you... No matter what. You can run, I can run, it makes no difference. I never won't follow you across the sky, baby."

My lashes flutter, pulse jumping. "I'm not Apollo, Lance... *You're* the sunshine, not me."

"Trouble... if you think my world doesn't rise and set with you, then you haven't been paying attention."

Fuck me, I just...

I have to kiss him.

Rushing my mouth to his, he's already there, waiting. Just like he said.

348

Trouble

He's been suffering in the silence of his hollow life, feet buried in the dirt, face aimed up. Doing nothing more than existing when every breath is a lie and every truth is damnation.

I kiss the lips of my martyr, with his big, beautiful heart full of twisted love. The sin he just can't shake... I can't either.

And the whole time, as we breathe and move together in this delicious uncertainty, I can't stop thinking about how I was right. I called it from a mile away...

The moment I said the words, all hell broke loose.

Chapter Twenty-Six
Lance

Sixteen years ago...

"The house looks great, Mom."

"Thank you, sweetie." My mother smiles, setting down a tray of sandwiches on the outside table. "The patio came out beautiful, didn't it?"

"I must admit, I was skeptical of that contractor," my father grumbles without looking up from his newspaper. "Hiring such young guys..." He shakes his head, then sighs. "But they did excellent work."

"I told you." My mother shoots him a look, grinning smugly. His eyes lift only briefly to meet hers before slipping back down to the paper.

Taking a sip from my lemonade, I gaze out over the backyard of the new house, elbowing my sister. "You gonna help Mom with the garden?"

Ellie makes a face. "I don't know how to grow things."

"You can learn." I grin. "It's easy."

"For *you*," she retorts.

"He has a green thumb." My mom beams at me, handing Ellie a sandwich. "Always has."

"Ew! Your thumbs are *green?!*" my little sister squeals and starts giggling when I hold up my thumbs, pretending to check their color.

"When I come back for summer break, I expect to see this place swarming with colorful flowers." I poke her while she fights me off.

"Yea, right." She gives me some of her ten-year-old sass that has me

Trouble

chuckling, biting into her sandwich. "Do any of your new friends from school have green thumbs? Maybe they can come help!"

Like an instinct, my mind goes to Tate first. But if I'm being completely honest, it never strays too far from him.

"Nope, their thumbs are just regular. Like yours," I tease.

"My friend Rachel has pink thumbs," Ellie says while chewing.

"Elisa, don't speak with food in your mouth," Mom scolds.

"You mean she paints her *fingernails* pink?" My lips twist in amusement.

Ellie nods enthusiastically, making sure to swallow before she says, "I wanna paint my nails! Will you do it for me?"

"Sure thing, kid." I nod enthusiastically.

She's just the sweetest, and pretty much the main reason I come home as often as I do, which is really only during major holidays or longer breaks.

"And then I can paint yours after, right?" My sister's eyes light up.

"Boys don't paint their fingernails, Elisa," Dad grumbles, again, without even looking up.

Ellie frowns, and so do I, subtly glaring at him.

Really, Dad? She's a kid, for fuck's sake. Is it a big fucking deal?

But, of course, I don't say anything. I keep my inner thoughts to myself, and continue on with lunch.

It's spring break, and a few of the guys were going on trips to various party spots. But I don't exactly have money for that, so I decided to just venture to New Mexico, to our *new* home state, and spend time with the family. See how the renovations are coming along, hang out with Ellie.

There's always next year.

College has been great so far. I'm doing well in all of my classes. Still trying to figure out what I want to do with my life, but more than anything, being away from home has helped bring me out of my introverted shell a bit, which is all I could've hoped for.

I actually have a great group of friends now; a solid bunch of guys who have been texting me stupid pictures and nonsensical messages since we all parted ways for our individual travels.

The inside jokes in our group chat have me laughing to myself, shaking my head at how crazy they are. Lou sent a picture of Justin mooning someone out the car window, to which Tate replied something about *back bush* that has the chat flooding with vomiting GIFs and emojis.

"What's so funny??" Ellie chirps, nudging closer. "Can I see?!"

I move my phone away from her. "Sorry. Eighteen-plus content."

Nyla K.

She pouts.

"Lance." My mother gives me her admonishing tone. "Don't be looking at perverse things with your sister around."

"It's not my fault!" I laugh. "The guys are driving to TJ, and apparently it's getting rowdy."

My mother doesn't look amused.

"Do you have a best friend at school?" Ellie asks, swinging around the veranda now that she's done with her lunch.

Again... Tate.

My stomach feels a bit more fluttery than I think it's supposed to, but I ignore it. "I think we're all best friends. Gavin is awesome, he's my room-mate. He lets me use his Netflix password." Ellie's eyes widen in excitement. She only just learned about Netflix recently. "Lou is the smart, responsible one, but he still knows how to have fun."

"I thought *you* were the smart, responsible one..." Mom side-eyes me.

"There can be more than one responsible one." I stifle a sheepish grin for my mother before returning to my sister, "Justin is loud and crazy, but inside, he's just a teddy bear."

"Like Bam Margera?!" Ellie squeaks.

"Excuse me! How do you know Bam Margera?" My mom gasps at my sister in outrage while I cackle.

My phone pinging distracts me from Ellie's devious giggles.

> TATE
>
> Still regretting not going with those idiots?

I can feel myself smiling like a buffoon as my fingers work.

> ME
>
> Uh no. They're gonna get arrested. Or shot.

> TATE
>
> $20 says at least two of them come home with the clap.

Snorting, I purse my lips. "But I guess if I had to choose a *best friend*... it'd be Tate."

A fast, crinkling noise draws my attention to my father. When I look up, his newspaper is down and he's *staring* at me.

Trouble

"Tate Tate Tate Tate!" Ellie starts singing, prancing around us. "Lance has a best friend, and *Tate* was is name-oh!"

"Is Tate smart, or crazy?" Mom teases.

"He's both," I sigh, then clear my throat. "He's actually going to business school. He knows more about finance than most of the professors."

"That's interesting," my mother says, distractedly supportive as she cleans up.

"Yea, he's really cool..." I shift in my seat.

I feel like my face might be flushing, but I'm really hoping it's not. Especially because my father is still watching me like a hawk.

Over the entire course of our lunch, he's barely looked up from his paper once. But as soon as I mentioned Tate, it's like I somehow piqued his attention.

I can only hope it's not because I'm acting suspiciously.

In all honesty, I don't know what to think about the reaction my body seems to have to Tate. It's confusing, so I'm trying not to really focus on it. But it's hard not to when even just texting him gives me this unusual flutter in my stomach.

I'm straight. I've always been straight... *I think.*

But there are times when I feel like that label doesn't quite... fit. And being around Tate definitely unearths the most prominent of hidden desires.

"Where is Tate from?" my father asks, startling me with his brogue.

I blink at him. "Uh... he's from New Mexico, actually. Tularosa."

My father's features shift. It's subtle. Blink and you'd miss it. But there was a reaction, like an eye twitch or something, and it's throwing me off a bit.

"Hm," he grunts, a noise that I don't understand. "And how long have you known him?"

Okay, this is starting to feel like an interrogation...
Since when does he care about my friends??

Peeking at my mom, I watch her gathering up the remainders of lunch, carrying everything inside while my sister skips after her, singing Tate's name on repeat.

"I dunno... since last year," I mutter, playing it off like I don't remember the exact moment I first saw Tate Eckhart, because having my father's full attention on this matter is a tad overwhelming. "We had friends in common..."

He straightens, folding his newspaper on his lap like he's invested. But not necessarily in a good way. I can't pinpoint exactly why, but I don't feel like he's being *supportive* in his line of questioning. And his eyes have this nervous gleam in them I've never seen before.

"Why are we only just now hearing of him, then?" My father asks.

"I don't know, Dad. He's just a new friend." I shrug, unable to fight the defensiveness growing in my tone. "I didn't know I was supposed to alert you every time I start hanging out with someone new."

My father stares at me for a moment in silence. Then he exhales, shoulders unhunching. "Don't be silly, son. I'm just curious about your life. I'm glad to hear you're making friends and enjoying school."

He shows me a smile that doesn't reach his eyes; one that seems forced. Then he stands up, and wanders inside the house.

Brushing it off myself, I wander around the backyard for a while, checking out the garden potential until the sun goes down.

Still, that nervous look remains in the back of my mind for the rest of the day.

All throughout dinner, while Mom is talking about the house, and all the ways that South Valley is different from Tucson, in between Dad yammering about the transfer to SV Pentecostal and how much he's enjoying the congregation, I can't stop thinking about the way he was staring at me.

The way simply mentioning the name *Tate* sent this flash of dread over his features. It was as if he'd seen a ghost. It's just as odd as him trying to be subtle while prying me for information, which seems to be happening every ten minutes, give or take.

"Has Tate always lived in New Mexico?"

"What's his family like?"

"Does he come home for breaks often?"

"Where does he live?"

"Why did he choose to go to ASU?"

Honestly, it's more nerve-racking than it should be, for a few reasons. Mainly because my father has never been an overly chatty person. He likes to talk when *he* wants to talk, about what *he* wants to talk about, and that's it. I can probably count on one hand the times he's taken an actual interest in my life or getting to know my friends. He's a very closed-off person, especially where it pertains to me.

I think we spent more time together when I was Ellie's age, but even then, it was never emotional, or deep. The only things he ever talks to me about are the church, making sure I get a good job, find a nice girl, settle down and have kids. It's all of that *traditional* stuff, I suppose, because that's how he was raised.

God and family. That's all that matters to him, which is the other reason why his sudden interest in my life is alarming. Because my father's idea of *family* is very rigid, focused mostly on image and community. It's very *men should work and bring home the bacon, women should stay home and pop out babies*, and all the while you should be worshipping God and thanking Him for blessing you with the opportunity to these things. And not that this is something I dare voice to him... But I don't know if I necessarily share those views.

I don't think that's *me*.

The older I get, the more I feel myself being suffocated by this idea of the simple American churchgoing lifestyle. Hence the reason I decided to live on campus. Part of me would've loved to go somewhere farther away for school... Somewhere big and different, like New York. But I didn't have the money for that. So I settled for the best escape I could, and now I see why it was so important for me to do so.

I think I'm... different. I think I want to *be* different.

Still, I'm only just figuring myself out, and I don't want to have to worry about voicing this stuff to my family until I know what it is I even have to say.

But my father is good at reading people. He's the type of guy who can sniff out lies like a pig hunting for truffles. So part of me is nervous as hell, sitting here, squirming while answering questions about Tate, this shiny, fascinating new presence in my life. Because I'm afraid my father can totally tell there are details I'm choosing to exclude from my curt answers. Details I'm not sure he'd approve of.

By the time dinner's done, I'm racing up to my room—which is more or less the guest room in this house—so I can hide out and obsess in peace. Lying in my bed, it's not long before I'm on my phone again, because I'm a millennial. *Besides, what else is there to do around here?*

It seems as if the guys made it to Tijuana in one piece, and now the group chat has gone dark, I'm guessing because they're either out raising hell, or they've already passed out drunk.

Biting my lip, I pull up my messages from Tate, reading through them.

I miss him. I kind of wish I could just tell him that, but that would probably seem like something I'm still only working up to even thinking about considering. Pretty sure telling your friend you miss them after three days is considered odd behavior.

Nyla K.

But it doesn't stop it from being true, and it also doesn't stop me from wondering how he'd react to such things. *I wonder if he misses me too...*

I cringe at myself, and how hopelessly uncool I am.

We're friends. Just because Tate is gay—and not afraid to admit it—doesn't mean he's automatically interested in all of his male friends.

But in terms of me specifically...

Shaking it off, I type out a quick message.

ME

How's Nashville? Homesick yet?

TATE

Here are my thoughts so far: country music is terrible and I hate Jake for dragging me here, the food is excellent, there are so many bars that don't even card you... but unfortunately they all play country music so I still want to die.

I laugh out loud.

ME

Oh come on! Johnny Cash, man. It's not all bad.

TATE

Johnny Cash sounds like someone handed their grandpa a microphone

I'm giggling while frowning at my phone.

ME

That's really rude

ME

And a bit much coming from someone who listens to Kesha

TATE

You're all nuts. Kesha serves.

ME

eye-rolling emoji

TATE

The closest I'll get to liking country is Miley Cyrus.

Trouble

> **ME**
>
> I'm gonna pretend you didn't just say that...

> **TATE**
>
> OMG JAKE SAID THE SAME THING!!!!

> **ME**
>
> lol. Maybe I should be his friend instead ;)

> **TATE**
>
> You bitches are out. Next year we're going to MIAMIII

> **TATE**
>
> You down?

My toes wiggle at the thought of going to Miami with Tate... *The beaches and the clubs. The dancing...*

It's as thrilling as it is stressful to think about.

> **ME**
>
> I guess so

> **ME**
>
> Someone's gotta keep you out of trouble right?

> **TATE**
>
> Oh God.. what was I thinking inviting dad to spring break Miami??! *facepalm emoji* I take it back!!!

> **ME**
>
> HA HA ohhh Tate you're so FUNNY

> **TATE**
>
> ;-P

A knock at my door startles me, and I almost drop my phone. "Uh, come in!"

For some reason, I'm about to stuff it under my pillow. Until I remember that I wasn't doing anything wrong... I was just texting a friend.

My dad appears in the doorway, casting me another studious glance that has me holding my breath without knowing why.

"I just wanted to say goodnight," he says.

I nod, feeling like a child for some reason, rather than a twenty-year-old college student. "Goodnight."

Nyla K.

But he doesn't leave. He lingers, still staring at me like he has something to say, and is both actively trying to get the words out and hold them in at the same time.

"It's good to have you home, son," he murmurs with minimal emotion, which is how he always sounds. "Your mother and I are proud of you. Doing well in school, having experiences..."

"Thanks, Dad," I mumble.

"I hope you know that you and your sister are the most important things in the world to me," he says, uncharacteristically soft.

Blinking, bemused, I reply, "I do know that."

"Good."

My phone pings, and I flinch.

His brow arches. "Is that your friend Tate?" I feel like I want to lie, but I can't. So I just nod. "How's he... doing?"

My eyes are wide. "Good..."

My father releases a long sigh, gaze falling to the floor. "Funny how God brings people into our lives... isn't it?" His eyes lift, and I'm frozen.

I have no idea what he's talking about, but for some reason, I can't move, blink, or breathe. I'm just staring at him with anxiety rippling inside me.

Something feels... familiar. The glisten of his eyes, the etchings of his face...

"None of it is random..." he whispers. "Never a loose end left untied."

Why do I feel like I've seen that look before on someone else...?

Straightening, he exhales and taps the doorframe with his knuckles. "Goodnight, son. I love you."

Locating my voice, I manage to croak, "Love you too, Dad."

And on his way out, he whispers, "Remember that. No matter what."

I might be paranoid.

In fact, I'm *sure* I am.

There's no real evidence to support the way my thoughts have been running away with me over the last twenty-four hours, but I can't help it. I feel it in my bones...

Something is up. And I need to get to the bottom of it.

Ever since my father found out that I have a friend named Tate Eckhart who goes to ASU, he's been acting strange. It's all very subtle, things you'd never notice unless you were really paying attention, which apparently only I am.

There's been a shift in his demeanor. He's been cagey, more antsy than usual. That on its own is a sign of *something*, because my father is never anxious or jittery. He doesn't get *flustered*. He's an apathetic man of God, whose emotional reactions are reserved for the occasional designated moments. He doesn't cringe when he hears phones beeping, nor has he ever paid any attention to technology at all.

But ever since I mentioned Tate, I swear, it's like he's acutely aware of every moment I spend on my phone and every sound it makes, as if he's wondering who I'm talking to... Wondering if it's Tate. And I just can't figure out why.

What is it about Tate specifically that has him so invested??

Does he know Tate somehow?? It seems crazy, I mean... How the hell would my father, a married pastor in his forties, know Tate?

The way my mind is producing the most alarming of half-cocked theories is making me nauseous. But after watching my dad carefully, I can only deduce that he's hiding something. It seems super obvious to me now that I'm paying attention.

I don't know what it is, but his sudden weirdness just doesn't add up. And because it seems to have something to do with one of my best friends, I'm now desperate for answers.

When my father casually mentions that he's going out to run some errands, I ask if I can tag along.

To which he gapes at me for a solid two-seconds before declining my invitation by pawning me off onto my mother.

"I'm only running to the bank and the post office. Why don't you stay and help your mother pick out fixtures for the new cabinets?"

Honestly, him brushing off my attempt at spending time together isn't a sign of sketchy behavior, since he always chooses to run his errands alone. *Unless* it's actually a sign that he's been hiding something for so long, his elusive behaviors now seem normal...

Oh, yea. There's no possible way I can let this go.

I'm getting to the bottom of it. Right here, right now.

As soon as my dad walks outside, I holler at my mom that I need to run out for something. I'm not even sure what I said, but I'm out of the house and in my mom's car before she can question it.

Following my dad up the street.

Seriously, my adrenaline is already skyrocketing from the mere fact that

Nyla K.

I'm actually *tailing* my own father. Never mind the wild things my imagination is concocting right now.

I'm vibrating between rampant curiosity and impending doom while I drive, eyes locked on my dad's Altima to make sure I don't lose him, watching it cruise ahead of me. Past the bank. Past the post office. And onto the freeway.

I have no idea where he could be going, and the longer we drive, the more I'm beginning to panic.

Eventually, he leads me into the parking lot of a self-storage facility.

I park far enough away to ensure he doesn't see me when he gets out. Then I creep around the corner of the building, watching him wander up to a storage locker that looks to be about the size of a walk-in closer. He takes a key out of his pocket, using it to open the padlock on the door. But when he steps inside the unit, my view is cut off, and I have two choices.

I could run over there, bust him, and demand that he explain himself...

Or I could play this smart.

Go home, wait until later... and steal the key to his secrets. Then come back here to get the answers myself, before he has a chance to hide the evidence.

I choose the latter.

Because I want to see what's in there with my own two eyes, and I want to see it without giving him any leeway to lie or cover things up. No matter how scary it is, or how it could affect reality as I know it. I will find out the truth... No matter what.

The entire drive home, my head is spinning.

Why does my father have a storage unit?

What could he possibly be keeping in here that he couldn't store at the house?

The new house my parents just moved into has tons of storage space. I guarantee this is not practical. It's self-preservation.

But the most nagging question is why did me mentioning *Tate* seem to prompt his shady behavior?

My curiosity is officially piqued, and it's epically stronger than my fear, doubt, and rationality. There's no possible way I can go back to school and act like everything is normal.

I've already set off on this past... I need to find out what's going on and see it through.

Hours later, my father comes home. With groceries, I'm assuming to distract us from the fact that he was gone all day "running errands."

Trouble

Having this cloud of uncertainty over me all day is making me incredibly anxious. Even more so because every time I look at my father's face, all I can think is that he's hiding something so *serious* it needs to be kept under lock and key, miles away from here.

Impatience is bubbling over. But I manage to hold on, and keep my composure until everyone goes to bed.

And then I make my move.

I find the key to the storage locker in the glove box of dad's car, which is lucky considering it's only the second place I look. Part of me knows I should wait until tomorrow to go out there, since slinking off at ten at night could catch my parents' attention. But I don't care.

Can't wait. Need to know.

Leaving a note that I went out for a drive in case they wake up, I take my mom's car again, driving back to the same storage place. I walk the same direction my dad did, my heart thudding faster and faster with every step. My hands are shaking so badly, I can barely stick the key into the padlock.

Whatever is on the other side of this metal door... It might change my life forever.

I'm praying that it doesn't. Silently begging that it's something stupid like old collectibles, or materialistic bullshit, like expensive things he doesn't want my mom to know about.

Anything but the worst possible shit I'm seeing in my mind as the lock clicks open, and I slowly lift the metal door...

Seven hours on a bus.

I think I stared straight ahead at the seat in front of me the entire time.

Sleeping would've been nice. Being able to read, or watch movies on my iPad. Anything to distract my mind from the knowledge that's been living there for the last four days.

But *no*. As it has been since the night I left my father's secret storage unit, with my heart bruised and battered in my chest, my eyes dry and my temples throbbing, relaxation is frustratingly out of reach.

I can't eat, because the simple act of bringing food to my mouth feels exhausting. I can't sleep, because every time I close my eyes, I see the truth, hidden away in a metal box off of Route 303.

And the more I think about the gut-wrenching, heartbreaking, soul-crushing things my father has been hiding, the more my gut wrenches, my heart breaks, and my soul is crushed.

I was totally right... My life is *forever* changed. And I hate myself for it.

I should've just left it alone. What I wouldn't give for a time-machine right now...

If I could hop into the DeLorean with Marty and Doc, I totally would. God, if I could just go back...

I'd ignore my curiosity, stuff down my need for answers, and stay in the dark, cozied up with sweet, sweet denial.

I'd sell my fucking soul for blissful ignorance right now.

But instead, I'm stuck with the burden of information, and it sucks. *Sucks real bad.*

And what's worse, I didn't even confront my father about *any* of it. *What a fucking idiot I am!*

I think I was just so stunned, shocked down to my core at how directly the contents of that storage unit affected *me* and my personal life... I blacked out. And the next thing I knew, spring break was over, and I was on the bus back to school.

The lifeless husk who looks like me said goodbye to my family, concealing the festering disdain for my father and quietly slipping away.

Back to Arizona State. To face the truth...

In the form of my biological half-brother, Tate.

And because God apparently just *loves* playing games with me, when I open the door to my dorm room, I find my father's illegitimate son hanging out with my roommate and a few of our friends. A nice little get together...

And I'm in Hell.

"Hey," Tate says, following me into my room while I drop off my bag. "No love?"

My eyes slink in his direction, the open gash in my chest throbbing when I look at him. When I actually *see* him...

The scattered dusting of resemblance that now makes me want to collapse in pain.

Papers... Bank statements... A paternity test...

A photo of my friend *Tate with handwriting on the back...*

Your son Tate, age 2.

"What... do you mean?" I grumble, reminding myself not to take this out on him, because it's not his fault.

He owns not a single *breath* of blame for this fucked-up situation. In fact, this is *Tate's* devastation more than anyone else's.

"You haven't responded to my texts in days." He folds his arms over his chest. "I thought you went to Roswell and were abducted or something." He smirks, but I can't reciprocate.

"Sorry..." I huff, struggling to pull it together.

I need to figure out how I'm going to tell him...

What if he never wants to speak to me again?

What if he's so pissed off and angry at my father that, by association, he writes me off too??

I don't think I could handle losing him, as a friend, *let alone... someone I...*

God, this is so beyond fucked. Why are You doing this to me?!

Is it because I was noticing him as more than just a friend? Are You really that hateful, discriminatory higher power that closed-minded assholes like to say You are?? Because if not, then what's the reason??

Why would you take him away from me just as I was starting to feel something... more?

"Hardy... are you okay?" Tate asks, stepping closer to me, his snarky attitude fading away when he realizes that I'm clearly not doing well.

Taking in a quiet breath to calm myself down, I nod. "Yea... I just had a... weird break. My parents, just..." My words trail, and I shake my head. "It was a whole thing."

"Hm... So what you're saying is that you missed the shit out of me more than you thought you would?" He arches a dark eyebrow, and I can't help it.

I snort out a laugh that feels *so* beyond good, for a second, I'm weightless.

Nodding, my grin is uncontrollable. "Yea, I guess that's what I'm saying, T."

"Good," he chirps, reaching into his pocket. "Because I brought you a gift."

He holds something out to me. Blinking, I take it from him and look it over.

It's a magnet with a picture of Johnny Cash on it, giving the middle finger. And it says, *I live like Johnny Cash... Somewhere between Jesus and jail.*

Laughing out loud, I'm gaping at Tate in awe while he beams with pride.

"This is so fucking cool," I hum, flabbergasted that he got me something in the first place, let alone something so awesome.

"You like it?" he croons, and I nod. "Well, Jake dragged me to that godforsaken Johnny Cash museum... And when I saw it, I thought of you."

Snickering, I bite my lip. "We'll make a Cash lover of you, Trouble."

"Unlikely." He smirks.

"Thanks, Tate. This is really thoughtful." I stare at him with my mind warring against my gut.

"Don't mention it." He winks.

I feel my muscles stiffening, fighting the urge to step forward and wrap my arms around him. It's something I've definitely experienced before with Tate; the desire to be closer to him, to touch him, even just a little... Up until now, it was confusing.

Knowing what I know now? It's downright *agonizing*.

You need to tell him the truth... Tell him what you know.

That your father is also his father... That he's the brother *you never knew you had.*

But it's not that simple. I know it's not.

It never is.

"I'm sorry." I clear my throat. "I didn't bring you anything from New Mexico..."

"Yes, you did," he says quietly, tilting his head. My forehead lines, and he chuckles softly. "*You*, Hardy."

Biting my lower lip, I shift on my feet.

He's my friend... He cares about me, and I care about him. A lot.

And in this moment, I decide that it's more important than the truth. Because the truth is ugly, and complicated, and painful. But this friendship isn't any of those things. It's beautiful. Special.

It's a blessing, and my father's lies are a curse.

"Come on." Tate nudges me. "Let's go get a drink. I wanna tell you and your copycat eyes all about my annoying trip that I refuse to admit was actually kinda fun."

Huffing a timid laugh, I nod and follow him, thinking about our similar eyes, and the secret in their chocolate brown that he doesn't know.

I can protect him from the heartache I feel right now. After all, my father has caused him enough pain for one lifetime.

Tate has moved on. He's become a strong, amazing person, and he did it without a father. Look at me... I had a father, and I wouldn't say I'm any better off than Tate. He's everything I'm not; confident, outgoing, charismatic. All the things I wish I had, he has in spades.

Who needs Gio fucking Hardy, anyway? This quiet, emotionally distant, judgmental liar. Tate doesn't need that energy in his life, not after he's made it to where he is all on his own.

Why ruin it all by telling him this fucking truth?

Keeping this from him, from all of them, is the best thing I can do for *them*.

I'll hold on to this secret, swallow it down deep, to save the people I love from pain. And if it slowly erodes me from the inside, well then... So be it.

Better me than them.

Part of me knows it will, too. This truth will surely make me miserable. Because it means I can never have him the way I think I want to...

It's not right now. I *can't* want him.

But I have to be okay with it. *What other choice do I have, anyway??*

I can't change the facts, but at least I can keep Tate safe. Keep him *happy*.

If all we can be is friends, that's fine. I'll take it, and I'll be grateful.

Because at least I can still see him.

If this is all I can have of Tate Eckhart, feet buried in the ground, then I'll aim my face up at his light...

And just watch.

Chapter Twenty-Seven
Tate

S o I have this memory...
I didn't even actually remember it until I started seeing Lance. Mainly, the day I went to his church.

Unsurprisingly, I'm not a religious person. Neither was my mother, or really any of my friends growing up. Some of them were dragged to church with their families once in a great while on Easter Sunday. And there was the occasional *grace* said at big family dinners—mainly when Jess and Marie's parents were around. But outside of that, I grew up knowing nothing of church life, baptisms and communions, hail Mary's and penance, *et cetera*.

I read the Bible shortly after I met Lance in college, because I wanted to seem smart when he'd mention things about it. And yes, I realize, me reading the *Bible* to impress a guy I liked probably sounds like a *lipstick on a pig* situation, but I also kinda wanted to see what all the fuss was about. What was so important about this book that made it—and the characters in it—responsible for most of the world's division and war since the moment it was published?

Side note—Imagine God and Jesus going on a book tour...

"The Almighty Father will be signing at the Barnes and Noble in Glendale from two to four!"

Needless to say, the book wasn't for me. And despite some of the important messages you can take away from some of the stories, like be nice to people, don't be selfish, yada yada, I'm still no clearer on why a book written by a bunch of men *thousands* of years ago is supposed to dictate the way people perceive faith today.

But once more... I digress.

The point is that I've never been in a church before that day I surprised Lance at his. Or so I'd thought... But being in there brought up some flickers of a time when maybe I had.

It was long ago, but I don't remember the year. Still, I feel like I had to have been under five years old. It's that sort of grainy, disjointed slideshow in my mind that gives *first memory* type vibes. Who knows, I could've even been two or three.

All I know for sure is that I was actually *in* a church, and I was with my mother. She seemed stressed, or upset. I remember that vividly, because it's happened often since, and when I was a child in particular, it used to really twist me up in the gut. My chest would get all stuffy with anxiety, as if my mother's emotions directly affected my own.

It's something I've had to distance myself from over the years, because my mother is... Well, she's a complicated soul. Too emotional for her own good. And if I let her moods influence mine, I'd probably never leave the house either.

In these broken pictures, can see her dragging me along by the hand, which I guess means I was old enough to walk, but I must have been very small. Also, the inside of the church looked *huge*. To my adolescent mind, the ceilings were fifty feet high, all dark wood and cathedral stained glass; images of a man with a crown of thorns... *bleeding.*

It was terrifying. *I mean, do they actually expect children to be in there and not piss themselves?*

The rest of the memory is a blur, aside from the feelings. The confusion about where we were and why my mother was bringing me there, the fear of being somewhere strange, being yanked along by my arm with eyes on me. I remember feeling that everyone was staring at me like I didn't belong, and it had me tripping over my own feet.

I remember yelling, and crying...

And I remember a man.

I can't see his face, but the memory is of more of a *presence*. A tall, foreboding stranger with dark, scary eyes. And the sensation that he didn't want me there any more than I wanted to be there.

Unwanted. That's how I felt, and after that, I think I associated that feeling of being unwelcome with church, and *God.*

For a long time, I was sure that, like my own father, God didn't care about me. He didn't want me around, nor was he interested in whether I thought about him. We were just... indifferent. It wasn't until I met Lance that I felt the slightest bit less resistant toward a *higher power*. Because Lance Hardy was the first religious person I'd ever met who told me that God loved me, *no matter what*.

"God sees only the soul, Tate... And yours is beautiful."

It was sort of baffling at first. *Me,* of all people, befriending someone who loved *God*. And I'll admit, when we first started talking in college, I had a wee bit of attitude.

You know what I mean... When you're not a religious person and you meet a religious person, there's always that initial eyeroll.

Like, oh boy, here we go... They're gonna whip out the pamphlets and start telling me about how Jesus died for my sins so I shouldn't get drunk, or sleep around, or watch the Call Me by Your Name video. They'll probably scold me for using the Lord's name in vain, and Jesus H. Christ, I hate censoring myself. I'm an adult, goddamnit!

I suppose it's an offense stereotype that all religious people are judgy, obnoxious prudes, but when you're gay, it's just something you come across more than you'd like to. So imagine my surprise when Lance Hardy wasn't like that *at all*.

He's always been the kind of Christian who gets it. And I guess now I understand why...

Because he himself isn't perfect. He's so *imperfect*, in fact, that he's completely fine with the idea of pursuing a serious relationship with his own half-brother. And not only that, but he actually thinks God is okay with it. That God led us back together because it's part of His *plan*.

I'm not sure if I believe that. *At the same time, wasn't everyone in the Bible technically related? The first few books are basically all about distant cousins fucking and making babies.*

Either way, our relationship is hardly a poster for good behavior, what with all of the lying, and fornicating, and adultery. And now we're adding incest to the mix; a new layer to the epic casserole of *what the fuck* that is Tate and Lance.

We just got back from New York this morning. I left Lance at my place in Santa Fe, because it's where his truck is, pretty much immediately heading out. I have some important things to do right now, but even if I didn't, I think I would've left, just to get some distance and some perspective. To clear my head a little.

We've been attached like Siamese twins for the last week, and yes, it's been amazing. But that was before he dropped that truth bomb on me last night, and now I'm just sort of spinning. Like a satellite that's been knocked out of orbit. Twirling through the vacuous space without the slightest clue how to proceed.

I told Lance he could stay at my place if he wanted to, but he seemed to think going to his sister's was a better idea. Not that we're breaking up or anything... If we were even official to begin with.

It's just such a huge fucking *mess*... Him leaving his wife, me struggling with letting my guard down. Me finally *letting* my guard down and telling him I love him, only to then find out that we share DNA and a very fucking awful father, making learning how to be a boyfriend the least of my worries.

How do you move on from something like this?

No, I'm seriously asking. How??

Because I don't want to lose him. I don't want to give up the first love I've ever had just because it's weird and maybe a little icky.

Look, I'm a queer, sex-positive millennial, and with that comes a certain level of open-mindedness. I'm not saying you should date your family members, but... where's the line?

I didn't know Lance was my half-brother when I fell in love with him. It's not like we were raised in the same house or anything. I would never call his father *Dad*, and clearly, despite what he told me he saw in his father's storage locker, I still don't even really consider him my father.

A *father* is someone who's there for you, who raises you, loves you, cares for you unconditionally. A *parent*. As far as I'm concerned, Gio Hardy is nothing more than a sperm donor, and just because he also happens to be the splooge that made Lance, does that mean Lance and I can't be together??

It's not fair.

And yes, I realize that life isn't fair, but give me a break. I just found out the guy I love and have been sleeping with for weeks is my long-lost brother... I think I'm entitled to a few days of whining.

I'm not sure what's next for Lance and me. But if there's any hope of figuring this whole thing out, I need some answers. So I'm on my way to see the *other* person Gio Hardy left, and finally find out some of the details she refused to share with me when I was a kid.

I get to Corona in the afternoon, pulling into the parking lot of my mother's complex with a ball of nerves in the pit of my stomach. I haven't been here in a while, and on the surface, it's because I'm busy being a heartless workaholic bachelor with no time for tedious family visits. But that's not the real reason.

In truth, I'm not the cold-blooded narcissist I make myself out to be. It's just easier to play the bad guy than to admit that I'm vulnerable, and that beneath the designer labels and perfectly crafted façade is a man chock full of insecurities, many of which stem from this shit right here.

A father who didn't care about my existence enough to make a single appearance in my life, and a mother who never recovered from losing him... Who probably wasn't well enough to deal with such pain in the first place.

Peering at myself in the rearview mirror, I take a deep breath, holding it with my eyes locked on my own reflection.

"You did this on your own..." I whisper to myself. "You made it without them. Without *him*. It's almost like he... doesn't matter at all." I exhale slowly. "He doesn't matter."

Using my spare key, I head inside my mother's building. I bought this condo for her as soon as I started making steady money. At the time, it was a necessity. She was working two jobs and barely getting by. Not to mention she was drinking more and more to combat the mental health issues she's always refused to acknowledge.

Basically, Sloane Eckhart is a difficult person to have for a mother, especially without any other family around to serve as a buffer or take the pressure off. It's not that I don't love her, because of course I do. More than anything. But what are you supposed to do when someone you love prefers to struggle more than they want to be well?

My mother is emotional to a fault, and she always has been. It's probably why I lock mine up so tightly... Because I've seen what it looks like to overflow with so many feelings, the only way you can cope is by numbing yourself. Having *that* as my only parent... let's just say it wasn't long before *I* became the caregiver in the relationship.

So I got her a place where she can live comfortably, and where everything is taken care of. I pay for her food, her utilities, pretty much everything she needs, so that she doesn't have to worry about a thing. I visit her when I can, meaning when I can work myself up to it, and aside from that, she just does her own thing. Because she's not incapable of functioning, she's just... sort of broken.

When I knock on her door, it occurs to me that I probably should have called first. *Damn, Lance got me all used to the pop-in. I never used to do this before he came along.*

I hear my mother's footsteps shuffling up to the door, most likely checking the peephole. I wave at it, trying not to look as mentally vexed as I currently am.

She pulls the door open with a smile, and croons, "My darling son!" Delighted surprise covers her face. "This is so unexpected!"

"Hello, Mother," I rasp. "Long time, no see."

She smacks me playfully on the chest, and I chuckle. "Come in, wiseass."

Waltzing inside after her, I can't help swinging a scrutinizing gaze around, checking for any signs that she isn't doing well. The place looks pretty normal. Of course, there's a box of wine on the floor by the couch, and a full glass on the coffee table, but that's pretty standard. At least she waits to start drinking until after she's had her coffee. *Usually about noon.*

Overall, the place is clean, because I pay people for that, which she complains about endlessly. I know she can pick up after herself... The cleaning service is more for my own peace of mind. Having someone show up twice a week just to make sure she's good gives me comfort from a healthy, if slightly guilty, distance.

"If I knew all I had to do to get you to visit was stop asking, I would've lost your number years ago," my mom teases, clearing off the couch and tidying up the coffee table.

Faintly, I snicker. "You know me... unable to resist a little hard-to-get."

On the TV, she has Netflix paused. My mother is big into movies and TV shows. I pay for pretty much every streaming service available just so she can watch whatever she wants. It's really all she does. Binge-watch everything under the sun and play games on her phone. Well, that and coddle her cat, Linus.

"I was just watching this crazy documentary about a guy who killed his wife and kids," she says animatedly. "He hid their bodies for a week—*oh*, there's my boy!" She scoops the cat up off the floor. "Look who finally came to visit us. My *first* child. The one who doesn't need his mommy anymore." She makes the cat wave at me, and I shake my head.

"You been getting outside at all?" I ask, noting she's still in pajamas.

She sighs, like a petulant teenager, plopping Linus down on the couch. "Yes, dear. For your information, I've been walking with Mrs. Landerman every day. Today she couldn't make it, though. She had a doctor's appointment."

I purse my lips and nod, fidgeting in place.

"You look great, love." She smiles fondly, stepping up to fiddle with my collar and brush invisible lint off my shirt. "Always so dapper. How's work?"

"Great," I grumble, pushing past the way being around her always makes me feel like I'm still a kid. "I just got back from New York. Landed a huge account. Everyone's excited..."

"Good, sweetie. That's excellent." She brushes her fingers through my hair. "Seeing anyone?"

She asks it in an almost sarcastic way, because she's well aware that I don't do relationships. But honestly, if anyone in my life supports my desire to sleep around and avoid love, it's my mother. We may have our issues, but she's always fully accepted me for exactly who I am.

"I wouldn't trade you for anything," she used to say.

But now, when she asks me the question, I just see Lance. He's *every-where.* All up in my thoughts, stuffing me so full of him, he must be coming out of my pores.

"Actually, Mom, that's part of why I came to see you," I mutter, holding her hazel gaze. "Can we talk?"

"Oh... sounds serious." She spins to grab her glass of wine. "Let's go outside."

Nodding, I follow her to the terrace, watching her closely.

Sloane Eckhart is a beautiful woman. Long dark hair, petite, with fair features. Standing next to each other, you wouldn't assume she's my mother; maybe an older cousin, or even a sister. People are always surprised that she has a thirty-five-year-old son because she doesn't look old enough, though she did have me when she was only twenty-two.

It's just weird because I'm thinking about all of these different things now... Things I never would have given an ounce of thought to if Lance hadn't revealed the true identity of my mystery-dad.

How old is Gio Hardy? Is he much older than my mom?

Did they have some kind of salacious affair, and that's why he wanted nothing to do with us?

Was he... the man in the church from my memory?

My mother brings me out onto the terrace, plopping down at the table and grabbing her pack of cigarettes.

She holds it out to me, because usually this is what we do when I come visit. We sit out here, drinking and smoking, chatting about whatever to fill the silence. Except this time, I have some awkward stuff to bring up, and it's making me feel all squirmy and uncomfortable.

It probably goes without saying, but we don't typically have *deep* conversations. We don't dredge up the past, we don't talk about our feelings, and we *never* talk about my father.

Until now.

"I'm good," I decline the cigarette, digging my fingers into my thighs because I *really* want one. "I'm... trying to quit."

My mom lifts a brow while lighting hers. "Okay, I knew it." She exhales the smoke, and I'm *dying*. "You're in a relationship. That's why you want to talk, and that's why you're quitting smoking." Her lips slope into a cheeky smirk. *You see where I get it from?* "Spill the beans, Mr. *Never Gonna Settle*. Who is he??"

My knee is bouncing like crazy. This is about to get embarrassing as hell when I tell her who I've found myself falling in love with, and all I can think about is how *badly* I want to fill my lungs with goddamn nicotine right now.

"Fuck it," I growl, reaching for her pack. "I'll quit tomorrow."

Mom chuckles. "Oh, yea... You're my kid, alright."

Lighting the butt, I scowl at her. But it fades when I inhale the smoke, eyes rolling back like a fiend.

Mhm... That's the good stuff.

It's not like Hardy *asked* me to quit or anything. I've been thinking about it for a while, and dating someone who doesn't smoke—who barely even *drinks*—seemed like a good reason to, you know, like... be healthy.

It's barely been twenty-four hours since my last cigarette, which isn't a big deal, considering that I only smoke when I drink, or when I'm stressed... or sometimes after a particularly rough pounding. And right now, with everything going on... *Stressed* is an understatement.

It's just not a great time.

I'll quit when I quit, okay?! Lay off!

"Mom, listen," I breathe, slightly calmer now, though I'm still radiating nervous energy. "I didn't come here to tell you about my relationship..."

"But there *is* a relationship..." Her head tilts.

I roll my eyes. "Yes, *fine*. There is. His name is... Lance." Her forehead lines, like the name sounds familiar. I shift in my seat. "Remember... from college?"

My mother's eyes widen. "Ohh yea! Oh my God!" she squeals. "Wasn't he the guy you were moping about the summer before senior year?"

"Uh-huh..." I grunt.

"Awww." She pouts. "You were so sad when that ended. You never let anyone get close after him..."

"Yea, I remember," I snap. "It's my life, you don't have to recap it. I was there."

"Wow, you must really be smitten." She continues to poke me with her motherly teasing. "Getting all defensive."

"Ugh..."

"So, you're back with Lance..." She leans in like I'm about to give her the scoop. "Is it serious?"

I purse my lips, scowling at the table. "I guess we're... in love..."

"What was that?" She sneers. "I can't hear you."

"We're in love, *okay?!*" I growl. My face has never been hotter. Seriously, you could fry eggs on my cheeks. "I love him, and he loves me, and you'd *think* that would mean we could sail off into the sunset, right??"

Her brows zip. "Well, maybe... What's wrong, Tate? Why are you getting upset?"

"Because..." I huff, rubbing my eyes. "I found something out that really just... rained bullshit all over my goddamn parade."

My mother is quiet, just watching me, waiting for me to elaborate.

Sucking in a deep breath, I steel my nerves. "When you got pregnant with me, did my... father..." It's not a good sign that I'm choking on the words already. "Did he have another family? Like a wife, and a... kid?"

Her face is still, eyes wide and shining unease. It takes her a moment before she eventually mumbles, "Why?"

"Just answer the question, Mom." My tone is stern, because I need to know what she knows, regardless of how uncomfortable it is.

My mother takes a large sip of her wine, then a drag of her cigarette, and I'm growing more impatient with each ticking second.

"He did," she finally says calmly. "I didn't find out until after I was pregnant with you, but yes. Apparently, he was married, and he had a baby. A son."

Nausea wafts over me as I drop my head into my hands. It feels a million times more real with my own mother confirming it.

"Fuck me..." I grunt behind my palms.

"Tate, why are you asking me this?" she rasps. "You know I hate talking about—"

"Lance's last name is Hardy," I mumble, slowly lifting my face. "Lance Hardy... Does that name mean anything to you?"

An audible gasp flees my mother's lips, shock and appall filling her gaze. "What... I don't..." Shaking her head, she glances down at her fingers.

But I just can't let her shut down on me. Not this time.

Slapping my hand down on the table causes her to jump. "Mom! I'm gonna need an answer right now... Tell me my father's fucking name!"

"It's Gio..." she whimpers. "Giovanni Hardy. So what?? It's a common last name, I'm sure it doesn't mean—"

"Lance's father's name is Gio fucking Hardy," I breathe, closing my eyes. My temples are throbbing already.

The silence seems to last an eternity, until she clears her throat. "Where is this coming from, Tate? Did you... did you meet him?" Her voice is small, shaky, and riddled with fear.

"No," I rumble, smoking the shit out of my cigarette. "Lance found out... He found a bunch of Gio's things he'd been hiding. Bank transactions, pictures of me... a fucking paternity test." My mother gasps, trembling as she lifts her glass to her lips, chugging the rest. "Can you please tell me the truth, Mom...? Tell me what you know, because I'm..." My voice cracks and I exhale. "I'm freaking the fuck out here."

I can see the tears welling in her eyes, and now I'm crumbling for another reason.

Leaping up, she darts back into the house, returning with the box of wine and another glass. She pours me some, and I can't even be bothered by the fact that I'd never usually drink this cheap shit.

I'll take anything at this point.

Once she's sipped from her fresh glass and I've downed about half of mine, she says, "I met Giovanni when I was twenty years old, working at the diner. You know the White Sands on 54? Anyway, he came in a few times, and we used to flirt..." She's staring into her glass, visibly jittering. "He was a very noticeable man. Charming, good-looking... The whole tall, dark, and handsome thing."

Okay, Mom. I get it. He was hot.

"He was older than me, but not by much," she goes on. "At the time, I think he was thirty-two. But I fell for him... hard and fast. There was no avoiding it, really. He made me feel so special, and it was like he... understood me. When no one else did." She pauses to exhale slowly. "So we began seeing each other, and it went on for about two years. I thought we were going to get married. I was even living with him at the time..."

She pauses to take a sip and light another cigarette. I barely notice that mine has a long-ass granny ash thing going on. Stubbing it out, I reach for another while she peeks at me.

"Gio was always pretty religious," she says on a breath. "Something he mostly got from his family, though they were all Catholic and he considered himself less devout, I guess. But six months before I found out I was pregnant, he started working in the church. I thought it was odd because he'd never seemed like he wanted that, and when we were together, he was always talking about breaking free from organized religion. But all of a sudden, he was spending all of his time in the church, and he began growing distant. It drove me crazy that he had this whole other life... one I wasn't a part of, and one he clearly didn't want me to be a part of."

My mother's eyes gleam with sadness as she sniffs. "When I found out I was pregnant with you, I was so happy. I was sure Gio would be thrilled... He said he wanted children. But when I told him, he was so... cold." Her shoulders slouch, as if she's still weighed down by these memories. My heart is *aching*. "He blamed me for being irresponsible. Said it wasn't a good time, and he stormed off. When he came home the next day, he told me it was over. He said he would take care of us financially, but that he wanted..." Her voice trails into a pained gasp. "He wanted no part of raising you."

"Jesus fucking Christ..." I breathe, stunned and pained and *angrier* than I've been in probably my whole life.

My mother glances up at me. "This is why I never wanted to tell you about him, Tate. When you were little, you used to ask questions about your father... And there was no way I could tell you who he was, knowing he wanted nothing to do with you. It would've broken your heart. Still, I was so angry at him. I was fucking *furious*... I just couldn't understand how a man could be so despicable toward his own flesh and blood. I mean, not loving me was one thing, but to treat an unborn baby like that, I just..."

She wipes her tears away. "One day, I followed him. I was pregnant and hormonal, and I was convinced there was someone else. He wouldn't tell me outright, but I knew he was lying about something. That was when I found out that he had a wife, and a son. The baby was young... a newborn. I wasn't sure how long he'd been married... But the fact that he had a new baby with this woman, while he was with me for *two years*..."

Tossing back a large gulp of wine, she releases a ragged breath, shaking her head. "He's not a good man, Tate. He's selfish and irresponsible. And the fact that he worked in the church just rubbed me wrong..."

"Mom..." I croak, my voice crawling out of my throat for the first time in what feels like hours. "Did you bring me to his church? I have this memory that's been coming back... Of being in a church, and seeing a man there..."

She blinks tear-filled eyes at me. "Yes, I brought you once... You were only about two years old... I can't believe you remember." Huffing, her lips actually quirk a bit. "We'd been going back and forth for a while... Gio demanding that we do a paternity test before he gave me any more money. Being a real prick. One day, I just sort of... lost it. I brought you to the church when I knew he was there, and I made a bit of a scene."

I have no idea why, but this makes me chuckle. It's not funny at all, but I can just imagine the look on my asshole father's face.

"So clearly I got my love of the drama from you too," I murmur, and she smirks.

"Well, it had to be done," she says firmly. "But a few weeks later, Gio left that church. He took his little family and moved out of New Mexico completely. I honestly didn't think I'd ever hear from him again... But a few months later, I received a check from him in Arizona."

"Is that... when you started sending pictures of me?" I ask softly, hating the twinge of hopefulness in my voice.

It's stupid and purely pathetic that I still have this flicker inside me... This moronic desire to believe that even just the tiniest fraction of him was interested in knowing me.

"I'd been sending him pictures of you since you were born, sweetheart," she says, wearing a sad smile. "Because I was just so in love with you. I wanted him to see what he was missing. I wanted him to know how much of a scumbag he was for willingly turning his back on you. You were the most beautiful baby," she whimpers, shuddering as she speaks. Pressure is building behind my eyes. "The smartest little kid... A real hellion at times." She grins, and I snort a wet laugh. "But you were perfect. Just the right amount of trouble to balance out your magnificence."

My chin drops, because I don't want to cry over him. I hate myself for these feelings...

But I *love* my mother. She's fucking badass. *We both deserve better than him.*

"After a while, though, Gio started asking for pictures of you," Mom says, mouth set in a line, as if she doesn't want to give him credit for anything even slightly redeemable. "He would ask about your grades, and your interests. I barely even wanted to tell him, but I felt like I owed it to you, to show him how amazing you were. He even paid for some of your tuition... That laptop that I gave you for your birthday." My eyes lift. "I'm so sorry I didn't tell you it was from him, my love. You just have to understand where I was coming from..."

Reaching across the table, she takes my hands in hers. "Tate, you did this all by yourself. Everything you have, the smart, grounded, successful man you've become... that was all you. You never needed a father, especially not one who was too cowardly to be a part of your life."

"Mom..." my voice grates. "It wasn't all on my own. You raised me. *You* were there."

Smiling at me, her glistening gaze holds me tight. "Then out of all of my mistakes, Tate, you're the one thing I did right."

"Neither of us needed him." I squeeze her hands. "Fuck that asshole."

She chokes out a laugh that has me chuckling along. Sitting taller, she cocks her head. "Yea. Fuck him."

I can't help laughing. Although the amusement dies off when I remember why we're even talking about this in the first place. I think my mother notices, because her brows zip together.

"How is it possible that Gio's son is the man you fell for?" She blinks. "It just seems so... unlikely."

"Tell me about it," I grunt, raking fingers through my hair. "Especially after him leaving. I never thought I'd see him again... And when I did, it was like... Well, it was confusing as shit at first." My mom chuckles. "But then it just felt *right*... Even though it clearly isn't."

"Does he know? Your father..." she asks. "That you and Lance are...?"

"God no," I scoff. "I'm sure he'd have a heart attack and drop dead on the spot. Maybe I should tell him." I smirk, and she slaps my shoulder admonishingly.

"All I know is that Gio was fully aware that you went to Arizona State," she sips her wine. "He paid your tuition bills for three years..."

My eyes flick to hers. "Wait, he stopped after junior year?"

She nods. "Yea, but it didn't much matter at that point. I had enough saved, and you'd started your internship..."

My mother is still talking shit about Gio, but now my mind is racing.

It's odd that he'd stop paying for my tuition right after Lance and I had our little falling out... At the same time that he was enlisting Desiree as Lance's anti-Tate protection beard.

It seems like there's a piece of the puzzle missing. But unfortunately, I think we've hit the extent of my mother's knowledge on the subject. The only person who knows the rest is the asshole in question. *Great.*

"Mom... do you think I'm gross?" I ask on a breath. "For sleeping with my half-brother."

She laughs at my misfortune, and I scowl. "No, honey." She pouts, scooting in closer to squeeze my face like when I was a kid. I shake her off. "You didn't know. It's not your fault."

Trouble

But Lance did...

Gulping, I choose to omit that fact, since I don't want my mother to think he's a fucking weirdo.

Still, I can't help asking her the question I've always secretly been desperate to ask. "Do I look like him?"

An air of sorrow surrounds her as she shows me a glum grin. "A little, yea. You have his eyes. His nose... Maybe his cheekbones."

"Are you saying I got my hotness from him?" I scoff, then cringe, because *ew... That's my boyfriend's father.*

God, this is fucked up.

My mother narrows her gaze. "You got your hotness from *both* of us."

I have to laugh at that. Until it trails off once more into the misery of my current predicament. "Lance has his eyes too..."

"Well, Lance's mother also has brown eyes," Mom says.

And I don't know why, but that one comment gives my heart a jolt of much-needed comfort. Maybe it's not as bad as it seems... The similarities and all.

Maybe it doesn't matter, and we can just forget about it.

Based on what my mother told me about Gio Hardy, I think I'd rather just write him off as dead to me and pretend he doesn't exist.

But could Lance do that...?

I mean, Gio *actually* raised him. Regardless of whether he's a piece of shit or not, he's still Lance's actual father.

"Oh, honey, I can tell you're stressing over this," my mother smooths her thumb between my brows.

"Tell me about it," I grumble. "I'm gonna need Botox after all this bullshit..."

She rolls her eyes. "Look, the way I see it, you have two choices. You can end it with Lance because it's the *right* thing to do... Or you can say *fuck you* to the rules, and follow your heart." She sits back, lighting herself another cigarette. "I know which one I'd choose."

I squint at her. "Are you just saying that because you love the idea of Gio finding out his sons are banging?"

"Doesn't hurt." She winks at me, and I laugh. "Seriously, Tate... the fact that you're even talking to me about this tells me it's real, what you feel for him. You wouldn't be here if it wasn't." I gulp. "I think you know you don't want to give him up, and you're searching for reasons and excuses to ignore the truth. And, sweetie, if it's that important to you, then don't you dare let it go."

Overcome with warmth, and love, and confidence that I really needed, I lunge at my mother, hugging onto her tight. "Thanks, Mom. I love you so much... you know that right?"

"I do, baby," she says, stroking my back. "Whether I believe in it or not, I have to thank God for Giovanni, at least a little bit... Because he gave me the greatest blessing of my life."

Her words remind me of Lance's...

The ones he spoke to me, and the ones he wrote on the card that came with my sunflowers.

I'd love to stay and hang out more, but I have somewhere to be. Still, despite the emotional trauma being uncovered, today was exactly what Mom and I needed.

I don't think I need to avoid seeing her. In fact, I should probably make more of an effort. After all, she's the only parent I've got. And the only one I need.

Kissing my mother goodbye, I set out on my way. I know she's not perfect. She has her issues... *Who doesn't?* But she's a great mother, and she was there for me. Maybe she couldn't give me everything I needed all the time, but at least I *had* her, no matter what.

Everything else, I got from my found family.

Inside my car, I start it up, ready to head back to my hometown, to them. But before I do, I take out my wallet, removing the small, folded piece of paper...

Is it really a coincidence, running into someone you never stopped thinking about? Or is it just part of the plan? Either way, I'll thank God for the blessing.

I've missed you, Trouble.

I promise I won't run again.

Love,
Your Sunshine.

Chapter Twenty-Eight
Tate

"**D**on't take this the wrong way, brodie, but you need to drive that thing off a cliff."

Jacob rolls his eyes, though he's smirking as we saunter up the walkway.

"I'm just saying," I continue, "that vehicle is as unappealing to look at as it is to ride in."

"Tate... shut up," Jacob rumbles, ringing the doorbell.

The twins both reach up and start ringing it themselves, over and over.

Laura smacks their hands away. "Enough. Or I'll make you sit out in our terrible minivan while the rest of us have fun at Uncle Ben's."

The girls straighten immediately, which has me laughing. Even more so when I put two and two together...

"Oh my *God*, Uncle Ben's!" I gasp at Jake. "Like the rice guy! I just got that!"

"Really?" Jake huffs. "We've been saying it for like twelve years." Ignoring me, he shoots his wife a wounded look. "You think our minivan is terrible too?" He pouts, and she chuckles.

"It's pretty bad, Daddy," Stella says, and her sister giggles.

"Yea, Dad, it's *ugly!*" Stacey exclaims.

Laura laughs while I high-five them.

"Jury's out, Beavis." I wink at Jake.

"Yea, Jury's out, *Beavis!*" the girls shout as the door opens.

"Hey, it's my family!" Ben exclaims, eyes slinking to mine. "And Tate."

I have to snort. *We're besties.*

"Wassup, Uncle Ben?!" I holler, and he rolls his eyes.

Jake pushes his way into the house, hugging Ben. "Oh, thank God. They're ganging up on me out here!"

"No ganging up on my little brother." Ben gives the twins a fake look of scolding before scooping them both up and dragging them inside while they giggle hysterically.

We all pile into the house, saying our hellos to the visible attendees of this family get together. I know I was just here for the anniversary party a few weeks ago, but I'm happy to be easing back into dinner parties and game nights with everyone.

Despite past events that *could* have made things more awkward between us than they did, I still consider these people my family. The one I don't share blood with, but who know me and love me, regardless of how much trouble I am.

And that's *true* family, right? *Unconditional love.*

"Well, if it isn't the Lockwood's and their three kids," Bill smirks at me as he strolls into the room with our friend Greg following him like a shadow, as he does.

"Ha ha, you're so *funny*, William," I sneer, giving them all the standard half-hugs.

"My dearest friend in the world here won't stop ragging on my awesome minivan," Jacob gripes.

Ben cocks his eyebrow. "You know how much it pains me to say this, but I have to agree with Tate here. That old hunk's gotta go."

"Aha!" I clap while Jake scowls.

"*Old hunk??* Isn't that what I usually call you, babe?" Ryan's voice chirps as he swings into the room, casting a teasing smirk at his husband.

Ben glares at him, though his lips are sloped into a grin I might dare to say is a bit *sultry*. "Watch that mouth, kid." He slides his hand low on Ryan's waist. Then whispers something in his ear I'm glad I can't hear based on how it's making Ryan blush.

He bites his lip, composing himself as he comes to give me a hug. "Good to see you again, Tate." Ben only gives him one full second of contact before he's tugging him away from me by his belt loop. "We're so glad you're coming over again. Aren't we, baby?"

Ryan lifts a brow at Ben. So I fold my arms over my chest, giving Ben the same expectant look.

Ben rolls his eyes. "I guess you being here isn't a *tragedy...*"

Trouble

"Awww!" I throw my arms around him. "I knew you always loved me, Big Daddy Lockwood!"

Ben pushes me off of him. "Alright, that's enough. Don't make me punch you again."

"Ooh, *please* punch him again!" Bill cheers. "That was my favorite thing!"

"Yea, this past Christmas was so tame," Greg mutters. "No gay love triangles, no fist fights... We just *celebrated*, like... *happily*." He scoffs.

"Boring," Bill groans.

I laugh out loud, peeking at Ben. "You hear that, Lockwood? Your parties aren't the same without a dash of trouble."

I smirk while Bill and Greg cheer, Ryan laughs, and Ben frowns.

"You're the drama alright, Butthead," Jake shakes his head, shooting me a knowing look.

A look that says, *I'm still not over what you told me twenty minutes ago, about you being in love with your half-brother.*

I glare at him with my own look. *Shhh! They might hear your thoughts, idiot!!*

"Come on, drama queens. There's food and drinks in the dining room," Ben sighs, grabbing Ryan by the hand.

"Why do you guys call each other Beavis and Butthead?" Ryan asks over his shoulder while Ben tugs him along and we follow.

"Because he's blonde and I'm brunette," I chuckle, peering at Jake.

"And because they're two inseparable doofuses." Ben grins.

"Touché, *Daddy*," I sneer.

"Please. *Stop*," Ben growls, tension in his eyes as they flit to the other guys, mainly his brother, likely to see if they're reacting to me calling him that... As an indication that I may have blown up his spot about the video on Pornhub.

Of course, I didn't, because I think that would just make things weird between the Lockwood brothers, and there's already more than enough awkwardness to go around, what with Ben and his wife marrying their daughter's ex-boyfriend and me having slept with him a bunch of times.

Naturally, I had to let Ben and Ryan know I saw the video, when I was here for the party. But that, mixed with them catching me blowing Lance while watching them fuck at Kennan's party, is a little collection of secrets we can leave between us.

Or save for a rainy day, in case Ben decides to punch me again.

"He's *Poppa*, remember?" Ryan gives me a pointed look.

"Ah, yes. How could I forget," I murmur as we all file into the dining room. "Where is the Lockwood-Harper prince?"

"He's with his auntie and his cousin in the living room." Jess traipses around the corner, looking as radiant as ever, even in an apron, carrying a tray of food. "But I did hear him asking about you."

Chuckling, I stride over to where she's grinning teasingly, kissing her on both cheeks.

"Jessica. Stunning, as always."

"Thank you. Same to you. And thank you for the anniversary gift." She smiles at me, not even looking as she slaps Greg's hand away from the entrees, pointing at the appetizers.

"You're so welcome," I croon. "I knew you'd love it."

"He has no idea what it is," Jake calls me out. "His assistant does the gift shopping."

My gaze narrows at him, and he shrugs innocently.

"First year anniversary gift is paper," Jess hums sweetly. "It was a big, fat check." She winks up at me, and I laugh.

"Straight from the heart." I tap my finger on my chest.

"So Tate..." Ryan murmurs, lips sloped in a sly smirk. "We haven't seen you since the party..."

"Really? I could've sworn you were at my house last night..." I wiggle my brows at him, and Ben, whose eye is twitching.

Ryan rubs Ben's back while grumbling, "Funny. No, I mean, since your... *friend* came by." He looks like he's trying to contain his thrill, and it's making me itchy.

"Oh yea! We heard about your stalker," Greg mumbles in between chomping back appetizers like a garbage disposal.

"Word on the street is your old pal Lance from college showed up here looking for you," Bill sneers.

I swear to God, the guy is in more people's business than Andy Cohen.

"Word on the *street*?" I cock a brow. "You mean the cul-de-sac all you vanilla milkshakes live in?"

"Please tell me you've been seeing him." Jess pouts. "He seems so sweet, and *so* into you!"

"Son of a bitch, I just walked in the door," I grumble. "At least let me get a drink before you start hassling me."

"Come on, Trouble. Spill the tea," Bill whines. "We heard he's more smitten with you than Ryan was."

Ben glares at him, jaw visibly clenched in displeasure. "Never gets old."

"Well, that's not really a fair comparison." I smirk. "Ryan was my soulmate."

I wink at Ryan, and he rolls his eyes. Ben is clearly about to erupt, which makes all of this incessant prodding the slightest bit worth it.

"Jake already told us Lance went over there so you guys could *talk*," Greg adds.

"That's an interesting way to describe sex in a pool house," Ben says with a wicked grin.

"Excuse me! *What* happened in our pool house?!" Laura shoots her head in from the kitchen.

"Benji... there are children present." Jake glares at his brother.

"Yea, *Benji*. And I don't think you want to pull that thread," I hiss at Ben. "At least I didn't have an *audience*."

Ben's eyes widen.

"What audience??" Jake balks.

"Alright, that's enough..." Ben grumbles, pushing me like he's trying to shove me out of the room while I laugh.

"Isn't that guy married?" Greg points a spring roll at me.

"To God?" Bill adds.

"I don't have to sit here and take this third degree!" I spin, facing Ben. "If you want me to keep your discretions under wraps, I'm gonna need the good scotch..."

He glowers at me.

Ryan grabs me by the arm. "Let's go chat in the basement. Dinner will be ready soon."

Jess sighs, "Ten minutes in Mantown, then I expect you back up here and on your best behavior." She lowers her voice. "Which means no s-e-x talk."

"I should really go then." I smirk.

"Walk," Ryan grunts, bringing me downstairs to the basement Man Cave.

It's really quite the setup. Usually when we hang out here at Big Lockwood's, we end up down here, sipping scotch, playing pool, watching various sports games. I actually haven't been down here since last Thanksgiving... When I first met Ryan.

Peering at him, I watch as he moves around the bar with much more ease than that night, taking out glasses and pouring Ben's secret Macallan 35 that he hides down here so Bill and Greg won't drink it all. Ryan trots over, handing me a glass.

"Where's your husband?" My eyes slink to the stairs.

Ryan shrugs as we clink, taking a sip. "Dunno. I'm not his keeper." My brow lifts, and he laughs. "Just kidding. I think he's helping Jess."

I let out a breath, slugging back a generous mouthful of smoky liquor. Sure, I'm happy to be here. And yes, this is exactly the kind of distraction I need right now, although these friends of mine are meddlesome, bordering on intrusive, and aren't going to let me leave without badgering me for information to an almost unhealthy degree.

But at the same time, I think I might need that. Maybe it's time to talk some of this shit out, like I did with my mom.

Telling Jacob definitely felt good, even though we only had a minute to discuss before Laura came in griping that we had to leave or we'd be late.

"I wasn't being too demanding up there, was I?" Ryan asks, and I blink. "I mean, you don't have to tell me what's going on with you and Lance. It just seems like something's up, and I wanted to make sure you're okay."

And here I thought I was hiding my misery like a seasoned pro. Meanwhile, the twenty-two-year-old I've known the shortest time of all my friends saw through my act like cellophane.

I sip my drink again, killing it. "Man, they don't make booze strong enough, do they?"

"Tate..." he admonishes with a head tilt. "We can talk. At least, I hope we can. I hope it's not..."

His voice trails, and his cheeks flush, and it's just odd because I'm usually so good at being around people I've slept with and not giving a damn. Maybe Lance Hardy ruined that for me by making me feel things.

Goddamnit... stupid wizard, giving the tin man a heart like it's something he needs.

"We can," I sigh. "We can talk. It's not... weird. I promise." He blinks at me and nods like he's relieved. "And if it is, it's only because... I... I mean, we... you and I..." Pausing my fumbling, I take a breath, snatching his drink and downing it. "We had fun together." My eyes slink to his. "Right...?"

His lips curve. "Yea, we did."

Shaking off the embarrassment crawling around inside me, I grumble, "Anyway, it's just that things with me and Lance are complicated. We have a lot of history. He was one of my closest friends in college, but I always liked him. Turns out... he liked me too." I pause to marvel at that fact for moment. "But there's always been something standing in the way. I didn't know what it was until recently, and now I'm worried it's too big an obstacle."

Trouble

"Tate, take it from someone who's fallen for someone he isn't supposed to... Twice." He grins. "No obstacle is too big. The challenge is just rising above it... All the bullshit that's holding you back. Forget what people might think, forget about fear, and just focus on how that person makes you feel. If it's something stronger than all of those other negative emotions combined, then it's worth the risk."

Gaping at him, I can feel the blush on my face, the buzz of my nerves. Those reactions tell me that he's right. This gorgeous young kid with his mossy green eyes and perfect jawline... He was a pretty little steppingstone I didn't know I needed on my path toward the real thing. And I think I might've been that for him too, which makes me feel a lot better about everything.

Huffing, I rub the back of my neck. "I should've known I was going to fall for him all over again..." Ryan's eyes widen at my confession, but he's clearly trying to push past it. "Seeing him at Pride was like... I guess it woke me up. Don't get me wrong, I tried fighting it. He kept showing up, then I kept showing up... And even though it was wrong, it felt so unbelievably right, ya know?"

Ryan huffs, shaking his head in knowing amusement. "Oh, yea. I'm familiar with that sensation." He brings our glasses back to the bar, pouring two more. "Is he... still with his wife? No judgement, obviously. Been there, done that."

I chuckle as he hands me my drink. "Actually, he... left her." I sip, choosing not to divulge certain bits of the story that would turn this evening far more dramatic than I care to make it. "For me."

"Wow..." he whispers, gaping at me like he can't believe he's talking to *Tate Eckhart* about being in freaking *love*. "So what's the problem? You won, Tate."

"It's not a game, Harper." I shake my head.

"It *is*. Patience, falling, but not falling apart. Holding on... That's all of it. Game, set, match. Time to go collect your trophy." I chuckle, and he smirks. "Where is he now? Have you seen him since you got back from New York?"

"How did you—"

"I stalk you on Instagram," he says shamelessly, and I laugh.

"Um, he... came with me." I sip casually. "To New York..."

"You brought him on a trip?!" He looks befuddled, and it's pretty adorable.

"Yea..." I sigh. "It was the best week of my life, and now he's at my place in Santa Fe, just chillin' while I sort this out. Or maybe he went to his sister's, I'm not even sure..."

"You haven't talked to him?"

"We agreed to give each other some space... just to think."

"What's there to think about?? You love him...?" He lifts his brows at me, and I bite my lip, focusing on my glass. My head does the subtlest nod ever, but it still makes him cheer quietly. I glare at him, and he clears his throat. "Sorry. And he loves you, I'm assuming..."

"Please. I would never say I love you first." I scowl.

He rolls his eyes. "Okay, well... there you go."

"It's not that simple, Harper. Not everything is as easy as falling in love with your girlfriend's parents, okay??"

He cackles. "I can't even with you..."

Exhaling a long breath, I rub my eyes. "I've never done this before. I'm nervous... It's a big thing. Even just having him at my place is like... *crazy*. I usually kick people out right after sex..."

Ryan stares at me for a moment. "You let me stay over..."

My eyes widen and bounce to his. They're also unusually round.

"Yea, well... You were clearly desperate," I grunt, trying to be dismissive, but he's obviously not buying it.

"I've been wondering about that, actually..." he mutters, and I cringe.

Ugh... I was really hoping to avoid all this.

"All I've heard about over the last year is how much of a bachelor you are... How you don't do repeats, just sex, nothing more."

"What are you getting at, Harper?" I shift.

He stares at me until my eyes meet his. "It was just casual, right? Me and you..."

Unclenching my jaw, I roll my eyes and sigh to portray exasperation. But I decide to be honest... Because *fuck it*. Isn't that the point of all this? To stop hiding from the truth?

And my truth is that... I'm tired of fighting.

Embrace the trouble.

"It was casual, yes," I murmur. "But I might've enjoyed being casual with you... *more* than I enjoyed being casual with most others..."

Ryan's brows jump. He looks surprised, but also quite pleased. "So you're saying you... *liked* me?"

"Bleh. Don't be annoying." I scowl, and he laughs.

"Tate Eckhart liked me?!" He gasps, shimmying around. "Oh, damn. I thawed your icy little heart, did I, *Trouble??*" He starts poking me in the chest. "Tell Lance I said *you're welcome.*"

Groaning, I tip my head back while he pops and locks in front of me. "And this right here is why you never date twenty-year-olds."

Ryan laughs and stops dancing. "Look, Tate, in all seriousness, I've been meaning to apologize to you." My lashes flutter. "I used you, and it wasn't right. I'm sorry."

My lips form a little pout, because the kid is just too sweet for real life. "Ryan, it's fine. Like I said, we had fun—"

"No, I mean it. Christmas Eve..." He bites his lip, eyes falling in remorse. "That was fucked up. I still feel bad about it, and I just want you to know that you helped me. A lot." His gaze slides up to mine. "More than you know."

My chest tightens and warms at the idea that I was actually more than just a fuck to him. In every casual relationship I've had, it's always been just physical. Strictly sex and nothing more.

But I guess sometimes the sex *is* more. It doesn't have to mean love... It could just be comfort, or healing. It could be an awakening.

Just like my physical relationship with Lance woke up the love in my heart.

"You helped me reaffirm who I am as a bisexual man." Ryan grins. "You made me comfortable with my sexuality. And most importantly, you brought me back to the loves of my life. So for that, I'm eternally grateful."

I purse my lips to tone down my vibrant smile, tapping him on the jaw with my knuckles. "No sweat, Harper. It's what I'm here for." He chuckles, giving me a knowing look. I roll my eyes. "And you helped me too."

"Because I'm awesome, and my dick works miracles?!" he gasps, resuming his dance moves, while I laugh at him and shake my head.

Kids these days...

Sudden noise at the top of the stairs freezes us both. Footsteps.

Oh crap. It's Ben.

Grabbing a fistful of Ryan's shirt, I haul him close and whisper, "Listen up. Your husband already hates me, and I really don't wanna go for round two with his crazy jealous side. So why don't we just leave this little conversation between us, hm??"

Ryan nods fast, in obvious agreement with not telling Ben there might've been a flicker of something not-quite-casual-adjacent between us.

It hardly matters now, anyway. They're happily married, and I'm in love with Lance. Whatever happened between Ryan and me ended a while ago, and it was obviously for the best. We weren't what each other wanted.

Because I want...

Fuck, I want Lance Hardy.

Creepy or not, I don't give a fuck. I want him. I need him.

I fucking love him. No matter what.

Ben hops off the steps, wandering over to us with slightly suspicious eyes.

"Took you long enough," I grunt. *Going for gaslighting, of course.*

"Sorry," he rumbles. "I had to help Jess get everything set up. Then Jake started bothering about some random nonsense." Ryan hands him his glass of scotch and he takes a sip. "So... what's up?"

"Tate's in love," Ryan says.

And Ben spits his drink all over the place.

"You're what??" he croaks, gawking at me like we just told him I'm in love with *his* brother, not my own.

"To clarify, *not* with Ryan." I speak firmly, grinning at Ryan, who gives me a sarcastic thumbs up.

"Hang on... You're actually in love?" Ben blinks, ignoring my joke. "Like, you used the word *love*?"

"No. I did not," I reply, and he exhales. "But I *do*. I love Lance." Ben gasps again, and I roll my eyes. "Okay, God! Why is everyone acting like it's the craziest thing that's ever happened?? You spread your legs for your daughter's boyfriend while she and your wife were in the same house!"

Ben's face flushes, but he covers it with a seething glare. "We're not talking about me. This is about you, *Trouble*." I smirk. "Is it... for real?" I nod, and he peeks at Ryan, who's beaming. "So, when he showed up at our house, that was, like, the part of the movie where the guy races to the airport?"

Ryan chuckles while he grins.

I rake my fingers through my hair. "Not... exactly."

"He's still being a big baby about it," Ryan mutters.

"I told you, there's more to it than just happily ever after." I glare at them both. "You, of all people, should understand that."

"Is it because he's married?" Ben asks.

"Or a pastor?" Ryan adds.

"No. Believe it or not, those two things aren't the biggest hurdles we're facing." Sipping my drink, I pace around in front of them. "There are other... factors. Things I can't get into right now. But let me assure you, it's a doozy." I peer at them. "This might even make your taboo relationship look like third graders holding hands in the schoolyard."

Ben and Ryan share a look.

"It's killing you not knowing, isn't it?" I smirk.

"Yes!" Ryan whines while Ben chuckles.

"Tate... at the end of the day, you've never given a shit about what people think about you before. It'd be ridiculous to start now," he says knowingly.

My brow arches. "Are you actually... giving me advice right now?"

"You're ruining the moment," Ben mutters, and I laugh.

"He's right, though," Ryan says, slinking his arm around Ben's waist. "Fuck the way it looks on the outside. This love right here? It's beyond all reasoning, and worth every retribution."

Ben smiles down at his husband, the two of them sharing a wordless expression you don't need words to understand. He takes Ryan's chin in his fingers and kisses him softly. And it's a kiss I can feel myself now. It's odd... I never thought I'd be able to.

But now when I look at them, I don't feel annoyed by their love, or secretly jealous. I just feel Lance. His hands on me, and his lips possessing mine.

I feel him with me right now, because he's in my veins. And it can be wrong, or misunderstood by everyone in the world, but that doesn't matter to me.

I just want to be in love with him. I want what Ben and Ryan have, only *ours*.

"Guys! Dinner!" Jess calls from upstairs.

"Thanks for the drink, Lockwood-Harper's, Harper-Lockwood's... whatever you are." I huff. "If Lance and I can get to even a sliver of what you guys have, I'll be happy."

"Awww!" Ryan swoons, while Ben shakes his head. But he's grinning, like maybe he's a little bit... happy for me.

Heading upstairs, Ryan whispers to Ben, "Thank you for not punching him."

"I'll be honest, seeing him in love is really humanizing the enemy," Ben marvels, and I chuckle.

"You wanna hang out?" I peek at him.

Glancing at me, his lips twist. "Don't push it."

Dinner was great.

I definitely missed Jess's cooking.

All of us sat together, joking and laughing, and teasing one another mercilessly. It felt just like old times. I mean, *old* old times. Before Ryan came into our lives, before any of the recent drama. When we used to hang out as friends who have known each other for more than half our lives.

Unsurprisingly, Ryan fits right into it. Yes, he's much younger than the rest of us, but it doesn't seem to matter. He's a part of our little family now. And as we're all lounging around, stuffed full of coffee and dessert, I can't stop wishing Lance was here. So he could fit in too.

The thing is, I never cared about being the only single guy at all the parties and gatherings before. It's what I've been used to, basically forever.

But just because you've gotten used to something, doesn't mean it's what you want.

"You ready?" Jake asks quietly, since the twins are dozing next to him on the couch.

I nod, glancing around the big living room. Bill and Rachel left first, with their little one in tow, Greg and Marie took off with their daughter, Maxine, twenty minutes ago. Now it's just us; the Lockwood's, the updated Lockwood's... and me.

"I should go say bye to Jess." I stand slowly, stretching my arms.

"She's upstairs with Ethan," Ryan says from where he's draped over Ben's lap on the loveseat, both of their faces aimed at the TV.

I hover for a moment, until Ben's chin lifts. "You can go up there. She's just putting him to bed."

Nodding, I wander off to find the lady of the house. I'm trying to be as quiet as possible, since I don't want to wake the kid. I haven't been up here since before Ethan was born, so I'm just guessing his bedroom must be the old guest room. Sure enough, as I creep up the hallway, I hear singing. A soft, melodious female voice.

It's obviously Jess. She's singing a lullaby...

"You are my sunshine, my only sunshine..."

I peer through the crack in the door.

"You make me happy when skies are gray..."

Jess is sitting on a big chair, rocking a sleeping Ethan to her chest. It's a pretty heartwarming sight. But what has mine swelling and blossoming inside me are the words she's crooning.

"You'll never know, dear... How much I love you. Please don't take... my sunshine... away."

Trouble

My... Sunshine...

A flustered hum escapes me, and Jess looks up, obviously spotting me. So I walk into the room quietly, trying to play it off like I wasn't just out there listening to her singing to her son and freaking out about the lyrics to a damn lullaby.

"Hey," she whispers, smiling at me.

"Hey... I just wanted to say goodnight. We're taking off." Leaning down, I kiss her cheek. Then, for whatever reason, my fingers brush through Ethan's soft mop of wavy brown hair.

He looks so peaceful. *A cute freaking kid, if I ever saw one.*

"I'm glad you're back," Jess says quietly through her tranquil smile.

"I'm not sure if I ever left..."

Jess tilts her head up at me, and I feel like she's saying something. Something I understand, maybe for the first time in my life.

Winking at her, I say a silent goodnight to baby Ethan, my head swirling with various thoughts, like the mobile hanging above his crib. As soon as I'm out in the hallway, my phone buzzes in my pocket.

I don't even need to check. I already know...

> DON'T BE AN IDIOT
>
> Tell me this isn't it, baby...
>
> DON'T BE AN IDIOT
>
> Please just tell me I'm not gonna lose you again

Don't be an idiot.

My lips twitch, a soft chuckle rumbling from my chest.

So much for that idea.

I don't fucking care anymore. I just love him. I love Lance Hardy, whether he's related to me or not, and if that means I'm *an idiot*, or weird, or a fucking sinner, so be it. I can't stop loving him just because I'm not supposed to, and I don't care what that makes me... As long as I'm his.

On my way back downstairs, I finally change his name in my phone.

> ME
>
> You never lost me, Lance. You had me the whole time.

As I'm saying goodnight to Ben and Ryan, Ben whispers, "Say hi to Lance for us. And tell him I respect his game... Showing up here to win you back like that." He lifts a brow at me. "Takes balls."

Nyla K.

Huffing, I just shake my head, leaving with my best friends and their sleepy kids.

Balls, huh?

In the car, on the way back to their house, my phone buzzes again.

MY ONLY SUNSHINE

I miss you, baby. Come back and let me love you.

"Just out of curiosity, what time does church usually start?" I ask, an idea in my head and nervous anticipation in my chest.

"Why?" Jake peers over his shoulder.

My lips twitch. "I'm gonna show someone my balls."

He and Laura laugh, and she gasps, "In church??"

"Yea. Why, is that frowned upon?"

"I'd say so," Jake chuckles.

My smirk grows wicked.

Good.

Chapter Twenty-Nine

Lance

Y ou'd think after years of knowing the truth, obsessing about it
would get old.

But when it comes to fixating on Tate being my biological
half-brother, there's never a dull moment in my brain.

Honestly, I can't even remember a time when I wasn't beset by this
information. And now that Tate knows too, it's just... infinitely more
unsettling.

Over the years, my emotions on the matter have fluctuated. Sometimes
I'll be miserable, walking around under a gloom-cloud. A majority of the
time, prior to this past month or so, I've deep in denial, which I suppose
was part of the reason I fell so easily into the trap laid by my father to marry
Desiree. If I hadn't been so eager to pretend I wasn't in love with my
brother, I might have protested just the tiniest bit.

But all this time, the emotion I've tried hardest to stuff down is the
anger; the rage that pumps through my veins with nowhere to go. More
than anything, that's what I'm feeling right now. I'm fucking *pissed*.

I'm just so endlessly irritated that getting the guy of my dreams has
been convoluted like this. I mean, he told me he loved me. *Tate Eckhart* did.

*Seriously, anyone who predicted him ever saying those words deserves a
medal, because even I didn't see it coming.*

Being in New York with him was like a dream, so *naturally*, I had to go
and ruin it by dropping the *we have the same dad* bomb. But you know
what? I'm done blaming myself. *Not anymore.*

Nyla K.

My part in this has been absolved. I told the truth. All cards are now on the table, leaving only one person at fault.

Gio Fucking Hardy.

My father is such a life-ruiner, he's ruining our lives without even realizing it. That might be the worst part... Knowing that he's just sitting back, blissfully unaware of the cyclone of torment his children are experiencing because of him.

It's not fair. *He* deserves to be suffering, not us.

I had an honest to God *boyfriend* for almost a week. I *finally* broke free from the trance of a hollow marriage, and went to get my man. And to my own shock and awe, he was onboard. *I'll never forget the look on his face when he told me he loved me for the first time... I actually got to pop his cherry, for fuck's sake!*

We were *so* damn close, and that's why I'm currently enraged and stewing in self-pity. Because I should be with Tate right now, reveling in my long overdue gay awakening with the guy I've been in love with since college, holding his hand while he fumbles through learning how to be a boyfriend, like the adorable, sexy, perfectly *fuckhot* relationship virgin he is.

But no. Despite how well Tate took the news of us sharing blood, we parted ways when we got home from New York, because I guess he needed some *space* to *think*. I still don't really know what that means exactly... I didn't need space to think. I've had enough of that for fifteen years. I'm done with space, and I'm done thinking.

But I'm trying my hardest to hold it together, and respect his needs. I don't know when I'll see him again, or if he's really okay pursuing a relationship, regardless of this... *hiccup.*

On top of that, we're no longer the only ones freaking out.

I told my sister.

I know... way to put out a fire with gasoline, Lance.

But she had a right to know. Plus, I really needed someone to commiserate with me on all this.

When we got back from New York, I lingered at Tate's penthouse for one night, but being there without him was making me sad. So I called Ellie and asked her if I could stay here, at least while I got my bearings and figured out what the hell I was supposed to do next.

As usual, my sister's been great. She and her boyfriend, Marcus, even went to Desiree's to pick up my things. It wasn't much, just some clothes, books, and a few personal items. I'm leaving everything else behind with her, because none of it matters. My life is in shambles right now. Having my own TV or couch won't do me any good when I'm essentially unemployed and homeless.

I do kinda miss Sunny, though.

I feel bad for showing up and stressing out my pregnant sister. She should be thinking about exciting baby stuff, not worrying about her brother and the half-brother she just found out existed being in love with each other.

To her credit, Ellie is a trooper. Barely batted an eye at me coming out. *Not sure if that means she's just a loving and supportive sister, or if maybe she suspected all along...*

"You hardly touched your eggs," she sighs, plopping down next to me at the table.

"Sorry..." I grumble. "They're delicious, I'm just... too pissed off to eat."

I see her nodding in my peripheral. "Have you talked to him at all?"

The quiet, mystified curiosity in her voice tells me she's referring to Tate.

"We texted last night for a few minutes," I reply, still basking in the relief of Tate responding to my messages, assuring me that we're not over.

"Is he... doing okay?"

My gaze lifts to watch Ellie fiddling with her silverware. She's more concerned about Tate than anyone else in this scenario, which doesn't surprise me, because Ellie is amazing. She's always been sweet and thoughtful, with a great sense of humor and a no-nonsense attitude that I just *know* would mesh so well with Tate. I hope they get an opportunity to meet and spend some time together—*when either of them is ready, of course.*

I guess in theory, my sister thinking of my boyfriend as a *brother* isn't the weirdest thing ever. *The fact that he actually is makes it a little more peculiar...*

"I hope so," I hum, rubbing my eyes. "He said he was going to see his mother, but we haven't talked enough for him to tell me about it..." The silence stretches, and I move my hands away from my eyes to find her smirking at me. "What?"

"Nothing. I've just never seen you this way over anyone," she says pointedly. "It's cute."

I scoff. "That's because I was never really in love with my wife... Or *anyone*, for that matter." My knee is bouncing faster with every second I sit here thinking and talking about Tate. "I'm in love with him... Like, *hard*. I just wanna go find him right now and—" My voice cuts out, and I peek at her, blushing. "Sorry... Is this too weird?"

"Oh, it's super weird," Ellie laughs. "But also really sweet, and adorable, and messed up because I just want you guys to be able to be *happy* together." She lets out a breath. "I'm thrilled to see you finally in love, Lance. I'm proud of you for coming out, and I'm honored as fuck to be the first person you told." I chuckle, biting my lip. But her smile fades and she shakes her head. "I'm *also* fucking pissed at our piece of shit father for keeping this from us. But most of all, I'm so damn *angry* for Tate, it makes me want to retch."

I nod, eyes cast down. "Yea... it's fucking bullshit."

Ellie huffs a quiet laugh. "It's funny hearing you curse like the rest of us."

"I'm not a pastor anymore, Ell." My chin drops.

"Don't say that," she scolds, in a supportive way. "You should only leave if you want to, not because you feel like you *have* to."

"It doesn't matter..." I mumble. "They won't want me anymore after they find out I'm gay."

"You don't know that," she says firmly. "Give them a chance before you write them off."

Pursing my lips, I know she's right. "Either way, if he's there, I'm not staying."

My sister nods in agreement.

The sound of the front door opening and closing tells us Marcus has returned from the store.

"I'm back! And I got the good OJ," he announces, shuffling into the kitchen with a few bags. He sets a carton on the table in front of us, grinning at Ellie. "Sans pulp."

"Thanks, babe," she sighs, a bit despondently.

Marcus continues pulling things out of the bag. Bread, milk... Entenmann's donuts.

"Ooh, those are my favorites," I hum.

"I also got you this." He waves a small rainbow flag in front of my face.

Ellie chuckles while my eyes light up, a soft smile tugging my lips. "Where'd you find that?"

"At the store," he chirps with pride. *Literally*. "It's a bracelet. Or a... wristband?"

Stretching it out, I find that it is, in fact, a rainbow flag wristband. I can't stop myself from beaming as I tug it into my left wrist.

Trouble

My first rainbow accessory...

Turning my face up to Marcus, I gush, "Thank you. That was really sweet..."

"Don't mention it, pal." He winks, patting me on the shoulder. "I thought you could use a little pride today."

Ellie is swooning, giving her man heart eyes for being so thoughtful. But I'm just staring down at my new wristband. It reminds me of Tate. Not just because he's *gay*, but because he's *proud*. He's always been proud of who he is.

No fucks given. That's Tate. Unapologetically himself, and not even having a deadbeat father will change that.

It also reminds me of our time in New York; how happy we were. Dancing and kissing in the club. *What I wouldn't give to go back...*

But that's just it... Wishing I could turn back time isn't solving anything. We're *here*, on this path, set forth by God. We have to adapt and conquer as necessary.

What are my next steps, Father?

Where do I go from here...?

Ellie's phone chimes, and she checks it. "Oh, boy. It's Mom." My eyes spring. "She's asking if I've heard from you yet."

I huff out of annoyance, chewing on my lower lip. "I wonder if Desiree told them anything about Tate..."

What would Tate do right now if he were me?

"If she did, Mom never said anything," Ellie replies. "All she's saying now is that they're worried about you, and that Dad is doing the sermon again today..."

A sudden chill rushes over my skin, like a burst of air through an open window.

That's it...

That's what Tate would do.

I jump out of my seat. "I'm going."

"Going where??" Ellie looks confused.

"To the church. I'm going to see Dad. I'm gonna confront him, like I should have years ago."

Rushing toward the guest room, I'm shivering, with nerves; fear, anger, and the tiniest sliver of excitement.

I've always wished I was more like Tate in certain ways. His confidence, the way he doesn't take shit from anyone...

Well, now's my chance.

For once, *I'm* going to be the drama. I'm going to make a scene... Flip tables, throw drinks. As Tate used to say, I'm gonna get *ratchet*.

For *him*.

It's my turn to be trouble... for him.

"Lance, are you sure that's a good idea??" Ellie asks while I'm grabbing clothes.

If I have any chance of making it there in time, I need to leave like right now.

"Fuck yea." I grin. "And you should come with me. It'll be even more impactful if we're both there." I glance at her. She looks worried. "But you don't have to. If you're not ready, or it's too much—"

"I'm in," my sister gasps, eyes alit with the enormity of this situation, from all angles.

We both look up as Marcus pops into the doorway. "I'll drive!"

Ellie and I smirk at each other.

Looks like we're crashing church.

I don't think I've ever been more nervous in my life.

Maybe losing my virginity... Or that night in Tate's dorm.

Our first kiss... Now *that* was nerve-racking. But in a good way. It was exhilarating; the way something you've wanted to do for so long mixes eagerness with fright until you're trembling from head to toe. In fact, all of my firsts with Tate have been like that.

He feels like skydiving. *Adrenaline personified.*

The last time I felt this nervous *here,* in this place, was probably the day of my first sermon I ever gave. Right inside this building... South Valley Pentecostal Church.

I was shaking like a leaf, swarmed with anxiety and doubt, insecurities telling me I wasn't good enough. *I'd never be like him...*

My father pulled me aside and said, "Let God speak through you, son. He'll do the talking... You just be His vessel."

Great advice, Dad.

That's exactly what I'm going to do.

We walk inside the church at ten-thirty, which means we're thirty minutes into the service. I can hear my father's voice booming from behind the closed doors.

Glancing at my sister one last time, I ask, "You good?"

Trouble

She nods fast, taking in a breath.

Marcus kisses her cheek. "I'm gonna hang back. This is a family thing..."

"You're family," I tell him firmly.

He shows me a smile. "Thanks, bro. I'll be waiting back here... Shoot me a nod whenever you're ready to dip and I'll pull the car around."

I squeeze his shoulder, grateful for his support. I'm really glad my sister found someone like him. He's going to make a great dad, and an even better partner. I'm sure of it.

Unlike that asshole in there.

Breathing steadily, I prepare myself for whatever might come. It's probably going to get tense up in here. And I'm sure there are better, more mature ways of doing this, honoring family privacy and whatnot. But I don't fucking care about any of that right now.

This is a long time coming.

This is for *Tate.*

Pushing open the doors, I'm hit with my father's words.

"In his letter to the Galatians, Paul says, 'Carry each other's burdens, and in this way you will fulfill the law of Christ.' What does this mean?" He pauses, and I'm shaking, heart racing in my chest at the words he's spoken... This *message.* "Paul is professing that we should be forever selfless, as God has been for us." My fist tightens at my side. "Carrying the burdens of our fellow man or woman, just as Jesus has done, carrying the sins of God's children..."

Oh, hell no.

I can't take it anymore.

"'He must manage *his own* family well and see that his children obey him...'" My voice echoes through the room, and every face turns.

All eyes land on me, the room having gone completely silent.

"Lance..." my father rumbles. He looks confused, maybe surprised. "It's good to see you... We were worried."

"'*And* he must do so in a manner worthy of *full respect.* If anyone does *not* know how to manage his own family, how can he take care of God's church?'" I stomp up the aisle. Every single set of wide eyes in the room is on me as I march toward the pulpit, spouting the words I've had memorized for years.

My father balks, watching me carefully with angst etching his face. "Lance, maybe we should talk after—"

"'But if someone doesn't provide for *their own family*, they have denied the faith. They are worse than those who have *no faith*," I bark. And when I reach him, a withering glare is aimed right at his face. "Have you provided for your family, Dad? *All* of them..."

"Son..."

"Tell us all the truth, Pastor..." I growl. "For if a man hath ears, let him *hear*."

"Lance, sweetie..." My mother stands, but I hold up a hand to her.

"Not now, Mom." My gaze slinks to hers. "But trust me, you'll want to hear this too."

My father's eyes shine, like he already knows why I'm here. It's as if he's been expecting this moment for thirty years.

"Whatever this is..." he says under his breath, to only me, "it can wait."

"No. It can't," I state, containing my aggression as best I can. "In fact, it cannot *possibly* wait one more second."

Glancing out over the crowd, everyone is stock still. I see Desiree and her parents in the front row, next to my mother, gaping up at me in horrified confusion.

Ellie is at the back of the room, visibly trembling.

My father mumbles, "Lance—"

"Tell us about your son, Gio," I hiss, limbs filling with rage. "The one you *abandoned* before he was even born!"

I hear a few gasps and collective murmurs from behind me. But I just keep staring my father down. Conveying my animosity with an unwavering stance.

His lips part, and for a moment, I think he might deny it.

But then he sighs, shoulders slouching a bit in defeat. "How did you find out?"

"I found your storage locker," I teem. His brows zip. "*Sixteen years ago.*"

That gets him.

He looks shocked. Disturbed. Eyes round, mouth agape. "Lance, please, just listen—"

"No more bullshit!" I roar. "You had an affair with Tate's mother, and when you found out she was pregnant, you... what? Just *vanished??* What kind of father... What kind of *man* does something like that?!"

"There's more to this than you think, Lance," he whispers to me frantically. "Let's just talk in private." Straightening, he speaks over me, to the crowd. "I'm sorry, everyone... These are personal matters that need to be dealt with between family."

Trouble

"Enough trying to smooth it over!" I snarl at him. "No more brushing it under the rug, carefully hiding your secrets away in a locked box! Air out your dirty laundry, *Father*. You knew Tate was important to me, and rather than saying anything, telling the *truth*, you went on like nothing happened. Like he wasn't your fucking son too!"

A gasping sob from my mother drowns out the murmurs of everyone else, and I turn. "Mom, I'm so sorry you had to find out this way. But your husband is not who he seems. He's a *liar*. A manipulative bigot, and worst of all, a fucking hypocrite!"

My mother says nothing. She just shakes her head over and over, covering her mouth while the whispers of the congregation grow around us. I'm momentarily paused by how unsurprised she looks right now.

But then I notice the ushers walking around, quietly instructing people to get up and leave.

"Lance, I'm so sorry," my father mutters.

I glare at him. "*Why?* Because you got caught?? Because you lied and cheated, fathered a son you turned your back on?? Or because you conspired with Desiree's parents to arrange our marriage, all so you didn't have to deal with the truth??" I'm fuming now, chest heaving, pain and fury weaving through my every muscle. "You were too much of a coward to come clean about who Tate was to you, so you shoved this girl in my lap?!"

My voice has raised, so that by the end, I'm shouting at him, my arm flying out to gesture to my soon to be *ex*-wife.

"That's quite enough!" Desiree's father jumps up. "You've made a mockery of my daughter, wasted years of her life while she could have been starting a family with someone else!"

An incredulous laugh gusts from my lips, and my eyes fall to Des, who's squirming awkwardly in her seat. "Oh yea... I'm sure *I'm* the one wasting everyone else's time. Look, I'm not going to blow up your daughter's spot, but let's just say she doesn't want kids. At least not with me."

"I don't blame her!" Clark shouts. "You're unhinged!"

I roll my eyes.

My father holds up a hand to shut Clark up, looking only at me. "Lance, we really need to talk—"

"We *will* talk." I nod. "But before these people sneak away, I have something to say." Spinning, I face the crowd once more as many of them are shuffling away, fleeing from this unbearable tension. "This isn't the way I wanted to do this, but I need to make a point..." I take a breath, and release the words, "I'm gay."

Many of them look stunned, a few mortified. Some are rushing out of the room like they might catch the plague, and a few others are staying right where they are, as if they're impressed.

But I don't care about any of that. This isn't for *them*.

Turning to my father once more, I get up in his face. "There you have it, Dad. You didn't stop it. You *can't*. It's not something you can pray away, or simply turn off by marrying me to some woman. I'm *gay*, and unlike you, *God* loves me exactly the way I am." Stepping in even closer, I whisper, "And I still love Tate. That didn't change either."

My father looks devastated, and I won't say it doesn't hurt my heart a lot... To see how disappointed he is by my truth and who I am.

But I don't give a fuck. I don't need his approval anymore, because it's not worth a damn.

"I would have loved him regardless..." My voice quivers. "But you could have stopped so much heartache... If you'd just told the truth."

He looks shattered. But then he rumbles, "As could you..."

"What the fuck did you just say to me?" I snarl, eye twitching.

"You say you knew for all these years..." His broken voice crawls. "But you never confronted me either, son. There must be a reason for that..."

I swallow a sour taste in my mouth. "Don't put this on me. I was trying to spare our family... Protect *him* from the pain of knowing you."

"Exactly. Because you knew the truth was better left hidden." He blinks. "Admit it. You're just like me, son..."

"I am nothing like you!" I roar, and he cringes. "You abandoned a child! And you know what, *Dad*? He's the best person I've ever known! He's *incredible*... Smart, and funny, and generous. He loves so hard, but so *broken* because of you! Because you were ashamed of your indiscretions, so you hid him like a dirty secret... I *almost* followed in your footsteps, and I *hate* myself for it."

Pausing to compose myself before I break the fuck down, I pull in oxygen. "I made a lot of mistakes. I should have confronted you when I found out. I should have told Tate the truth as soon as I knew it... Yes. That's on me. I fucked up too... Hell, I even left him myself, because I thought I had to... But it wasn't because I was being selfish, you asshole! It's because I've been in love with him the whole time, and you fucking *ruined* it!"

Tears are flowing from my eyes, but I'm hanging on as tight as I can. I refuse to let myself cry. Not in front of him.

Trouble

My father grabs my arm, but I yank it free. "Lance... It's... I'm *sorry*, but it's not—"

"Gio..." my mother calls out.

"No! I can't do this anymore," he gasps in visible pain. "Lance, it's not what you think... You and Tate... you *don't* know the whole story."

"Then fucking *tell* me!" I bellow. "Stop *hiding* and tell the fucking truth!"

"I'm not your father!"

His voice echoes for miles. Then the room goes quiet.

Silence stretches out over the entire church, amplifying the cries and sniffles and panting breaths, turning them all the more prominent. My head is ringing with nothing but sounds of devastation... and those *words*.

"What...?" I croak.

My father is shaking, losing his composure for the first time in my life as he breathes, "I'm not your... biological father." His face falls into his hands. "I raised you, Lance. You *are* my son. But we... we don't share blood."

My entire life flashing before my eyes. It feels like the sky is falling. *Everything* I thought was reality is floating away as if there's no more gravity.

But a familiar voice pulls me out of the depths of Hell. "Wait... what??"

My face whips. It's Tate.

Tate's *here*. Standing at the entryway of the church. Pale, like he's seen a ghost, eyes bugging, lips parted and shivering visibly even from here.

I'm so... *happy* to see him. I want to run to him, scoop him up in my arms and kiss him forever. But I'm rooted to the floor by the weight of all this.

He said... I'm not his son?

My father's hands fall slowly away from his face. His gaze locks on Tate at the end of the aisle. And he looks... stunned. Terrified. Captivated.

Amazed.

"Tate..." he whispers.

My heart is splintering in my chest.

Tate shifts, radiating unease, like part of him wants to turn around and run far away. But when I peek at my father, he appears the opposite. He looks like he wants to run to Tate as much as I do.

Tate glances at me. Our eyes lock, and I witness him swallow. His brows are knitted, face etched in so much confusion and fear. But he's staring at me like he wants to be with me right now. So we can deal with this *together*.

He starts walking, striding up the aisle and coming directly to me. Stopping when he's close enough that I can smell him, and it's easing so much of the pain I'm currently feeling.

"Trouble..." I whisper, wishing I could smile at him, but it's not working.

"Hi," he mutters to me, peeking at my dad.

Our dad...?

His dad...?

I have no fucking clue anymore.

"This is so awkward," Tate breathes. But he slips his fingers through mine.

In an instant, I feel two feet taller. His presence is bandaging up my gaping wounds; his touch, his warmth, the fact that he came here to figure this shit out because he *loves* me and will do anything to make us work... It's the strength he's always carried, and he's sharing it with me in this moment.

"Tate," my father says again, blinking at him. "Hello..."

Tate purses his lips and sniffs. "Sup..."

He's clearly having trouble making eye contact with Gio.

I squeeze his hand tighter in mine, taking in a deep breath. "You owe us an explanation," I demand hoarsely, eyes bouncing between my parents. "Both of you."

Gio is staring at Tate like he's mesmerized, and I don't necessarily want to think about it, because it's weird as shit, but when they're standing in front of one another, you can definitely see the resemblance. Looking to my mother, I finally notice it...

Tate's eyes are like my father's... And mine are lighter, like my mother's.

Am I not his child...?

Then who is my real father??

Finally, Gio snaps out of it, rumbling, "Let's... talk."

He and my mother share a look, and he takes her hand.

I hadn't even noticed that the church has fully cleared out. Everyone is gone...

Leaning into Tate's side, I whisper, "Please help me breathe, baby..."

"I'm right here," he says, though his voice is shaking. "We're in this together."

Ellie saunters up beside us, her gaze all over Tate. He glances at her.

"Tate, this is... Ellie," I mutter, robotically, because I'm sort of switched off right now.

I feel like I'm outside of myself, looking down over this whole scene.

Tate's mouth opens, but he's visibly speechless.

Trouble

"Hi," Ellie manages. "Th-thanks for... making my brother happy."

Tate appears more overwhelmed than I've ever seen him before, and I just focus on not collapsing onto the floor, using as much strength as I can muster to keep breathing.

Tate and I take a slow seat in the first row of pews. Sitting on the bench, I remember the deliciously sinful sex we had in this exact spot.

Simpler times, for sure, though it didn't seem like it then.

I catch Tate running his fingers along the wood, and I breathe something chuckle adjacent. He glances at me, eyes sparkling.

I love those eyes. As it turns out, they're not eyes we share. They're different.

But he's the son of the man I thought was my father... It's insane.

We all stare at Gio, collectively holding our breath for his long-awaited explanation.

"Oh... where to start..." He sighs, rubbing his eyes. "I am so very sorry that it came to this. I don't know that anything I could say will make this better... but here is the truth." His gaze slides to Tate. "Your mother was not the *other woman*, Tate. Freja was." He gestures to my mother. "I was in a relationship with Sloane when I met Freja, working at the church in Encino. She came to the church seeking guidance... After her husband, Lance, was killed in a tragic car accident." My mother squeaks beside him, covering her mouth as she cries. His eyes flick to mine. "She was pregnant with you at the time."

My head is spinning.

Breathe. Remember to...

Tate squeezes my hand.

Breathe.

"Understandably, your mother was devastated. Scared, and alone." I swallow a mouthful of nails, stiff as a board, watching Gio comfort my mother. "I was there for her as a friend, and it turned into... more." He gulps, a look of guilt passing over his features when he glances at Tate. "I found out your mother was pregnant with you just after I ended our relationship..."

"She said she told you, and *then* you ended it," Tate grunts.

Gio rubs the back of his neck. "The timeline is... iffy. But regardless, I was in the wrong. I *am*, I mean... I have been this whole time," he stammers. "I fell in love with Freja, and I was focusing on the wrong thing. Helping her through the birth of her son... But in the midst of it all, I turned my back on you and your mother, Tate, and it was... abhorrent. I've lived with this guilt every day since..."

Tate clears his throat, glancing at his lap. "Well... isn't that touching."

"I'm so sorry, Lance." My mother steps over to me. "I should have told you the truth, about your real father. I know that I should have. But Giovanni raised you. We were married when you were barely six months old, and he adopted you right away. He *is* your father, my love, regardless of the blood in your veins."

I'm so dizzy, I think I might pass out, or vomit. Or both.

I can't even process this...

My real father is dead...?

Who was he? Was he a good man? Would I have liked him?

Did he look like me...?

"Baby, say the word and I'll get you out of here," Tate whispers in my ear. "This is fucked up..."

Pressure builds behind my eyes, so strong I can't barely see. But I blink past it, peering up at Gio Hardy... my *father,* for all intents and purposes.

"So... Tate and I... aren't brothers?"

He rubs his eyes. "No. Not by blood."

For as completely shit-fucked as this situation is, a wave of relief crashes over me. Everything I thought I knew about my life has been flipped upside down... And some of it is shocking and seriously fucked up. But there's one brilliant light at the end of this tunnel of pain.

He's not my brother...

We're not related.

He can be mine, no sin, no fight... no trouble.

He's mine *to love.*

"But you s-still lied," my voice scrapes. "You could have told me all of this when you found out Tate was my friend. But you hid it, and it fucked up *so much.*" I yank at my hair. "You pushed Desiree into my life to keep me from falling in love with your son... But it was too late."

"I know..." Gio rumbles, regretfully, but it's not making me feel any better. "I've been beyond selfish for so long, Lance, and I need you to know that I regret so many things..."

"I was miserable without him..." I whisper, peeking at Tate. "And I didn't need to be." Taking his face in my hand, I gaze into his beautiful eyes, unable to stop the quiver of emotion in my voice. "Baby, we wasted so much time..."

"No." He shakes his head. "It happened the way it needed to. I believe that now, Lance, because *you* made me believe it. Maybe if we'd been together the whole time, it wouldn't have..." His voice trails, and he swallows.

"I'm just so sorry I did this to us..." I whimper, clearing past the emotion lodging in my throat.

Tate sniffles, holding me while I hold him, our foreheads together. "Hey... *you* got us here. You came back, baby. We're here, and I *love you*, and I promise I'm not going anywhere. We'll work through all of this together."

"I love you so much, Trouble," I gasp, kissing him softly.

"I love you, Sunshine," he murmurs on my lips. "No matter what, remember?"

I nod fast. "No matter what."

The agony in my heart subsides. Because I have him, this brilliant, stunning man, like my god of the sun. I have him, and it's *good*.

All of the other bullshit can fuck off. I have my Trouble. He's finally mine.

"Take me home," I whisper to my man, melting into him because he's the only thing that makes sense now.

It's crazy. He used to be the most confusing thing in my life. And now *he's* the simple, while everything else is falling apart.

Tate nods, turning to me and brushing my hair back with his fingers. I'm shivering, but I'm weightless as he presses a soft, way too brief kiss on my lips.

But we're *kissing*, in front of the people who held us apart.

All truths out in the open. We're not scared anymore.

I love him, and he loves me.

No matter what.

"I wouldn't have cared if we were," Tate whispers. "You know that, right?"

I nod. "Me neither.

Standing, Tate pulls me up with him. We both peer at our parents. I'm not sure what to make of the looks on their faces.

But I mumble, "Your sons kissing... in church. Bet you never expected that, huh?"

"Lance, I wasn't trying to keep you from being gay." Gio shakes his head.

"You were just trying to keep me from being gay with *Tate*... Right?" I huff despondently.

He's hovering a few feet from us, like he doesn't know what to do with himself. "I messed up. I was *wrong*. I just wanted you to have a full life, a family..."

"What makes you think we couldn't have that together?" Tate growls.

My heart thuds. And I peer to my mother.

"Did you know...?" I ask hoarsely. My mother balks. "Did you know he had a son with another woman?"

She looks like she could faint at any moment. My mother's clearly not used to this kind of openness. She manages to nod. "I knew... I didn't know it was Tate." Her glassy eyes flick to Tate. "I only found out a few years ago..."

Tate shakes his head while I gape at her. "And you said nothing?? You didn't care that he'd been lying to you for years??"

She simply goes on, crying quietly and covering her face.

"'Be tolerant with each other,'" Gio says quietly. "'Forgive each other, as the Lord forgave you.'"

Tate scoffs quietly. "By the way, we had sex right there too." He points at the pew. "Hope God can *forgive us* for that. Let's go, baby."

He tugs me along, and Ellie shoots up, most likely wanting to get far away from this bullshit herself.

"Lance..." my mother whimpers. "Elisa..."

"Mom, we just... need some t-time." I shiver.

"Tate, I... I'm sorry!" Gio calls out as we walk away. I feel Tate quaking, but he doesn't look back. He just holds me close while we stagger down the aisle. "It's... wonderful to finally see you."

And for all of the anger I still feel toward him, I can't deny that he sounds torn to pieces.

"Dude, I really can't..." Tate whimpers.

"Lance, you're still my son!" he continues yelling after us.

"Fuck me..." I whine.

"It's okay, baby," Tate whispers. "I have you."

Leaving the church, we pass Desiree and her parents, still lingering for some reason. We don't even glance their way. I just can't deal with all of that right now.

Divorce is pretty low on the list of my life's bullshit right now.

Outside, Marcus already has the car pulled up, which ghosts a smile on my lips.

"Ellie..." Tate rasps to my—*our*—sister, and she looks up with tears in her eyes. "I'm, um... going to bring him to my place." She nods, eyes wide as

Trouble

Tate gulps. "But I'd... like it if we could talk. One of these days... If that's alright with you, I mean."

Ellie's lips twist, and she nods again. "Sure. I'd like that too."

Tate smiles at her, and it opens my cowering heart right up.

I kiss Ellie on the cheek. "I love you, Elisa Doolittle."

She chuckles softly, "I love you too, Sir Lancelot," brushing my hair with her fingers. "I'm so proud of you."

Smiling timidly, I lift my wrist, showing her my pride wristband. We both laugh through our emotional damage as she hops into the car. Marcus cheers.

"I like them." Tate smirks and I chuckle, waving to them while we hobble to Tate's Maserati. He lifts a brow at my rainbow-clad wrist. "That new?"

I can't help but snort while he laughs softly, and it feels so good. Being back with him... Knowing everything will be okay, as long as we're together.

Once we're nestled inside his fancy car, I can breathe a bit easier. Really, *nothing* is easy right now... It's all pure chaos, things I've believed for years, my entire *life* even, turning out to be lies.

Turning to Tate, I grab his hand, and he glances at me. "Tate... I'm so s-sorry..." He looks confused, brows knitted. "I'm sorry that he... fucking left you for me." I scoff and sniff, shaking my head. "It's so fucked up, baby... That he stayed to raise me and not you..."

"Hey," he snaps, calmly, taking my face in his hand. "*Never* apologize for that asshole. None of this is your fault, Lance. *He* made shit decisions, and you were just a baby. We were both victims of his lies, okay?" He runs his thumb along my jaw while my head spins. "Tell me you understand, Sunshine."

"I... understand," I croak.

He leans across the center console, kissing me softly. "I don't want to hear you saying sorry for him ever again, okay?"

Nodding, I lean into his touch, and his warmth, absorbing it, because it's the only thing in my entire world that's steady right now.

I'm confused, and distraught. *I'm fucked the hell up.*

But as long as I have him, the rest is just background noise.

He's the simplest truth, clear and present.

My home, my *real* family.

Chapter Thirty

Tate

"Troy... Can you email the partners and tell them I'll be out for the week?"

My assistant is quiet for a second. "Uh, yea. Sure. Is everything okay...?"

Exhaling, I pinch the bridge of my nose. *Not really, but sort of?*

"Yea, I'm fine. Just tell them I'm sick."

"Are you sick?" he asks.

I glare at the wall. "Why would I say I'm sick if I'm not?"

"I don't know, you just said you were *fine*..."

"Goddamnit, Troy!" I bark. "You can be sick and fine at the same time, okay?? Just send the damn email. I'm forwarding my work phone."

"Hey, if you want, I can bring you some of my mom's famous chicken soup!" he chirps, as always, completely unaffected by my moods. "It's really good. Cures all ailments."

Does it cure Maury Povich-style family drama, Troy??

"No thanks, I'm good." But then I pause, watching Lance shuffle past me toward the fridge like a zombie. "Hang on." I pull my phone to my chest, eyes set on my poor, traumatized man. "Baby, you want some chicken soup?"

Lance grabs a beer out of the fridge, opening it and taking a large gulp.

I cock my head. "It's supposedly really good at... being delicious." I cringe at how stupid I sound. Lance blinks at me. Sighing, I bring my phone back to my ear. "Never mind with the soup. I'll talk to you later."

Trouble

Troy is still speaking, but I hang up on him, tossing my phone onto the counter.

"How are you feeling?" I inch closer to Lance.

He shrugs. "Was that Troy?"

"Yea." I nod, choosing not to fixate on him not answering my question. "I told him I'm staying home this week." *To be with you...*

Not that I told Troy that was the reason. Because doing so would mean I'd have to explain what's going on, and it's a bit of a head-trip.

"You don't have to do that, baby," Lance rumbles, drinking half the bottle of beer in one slug. "You should work. It's important to you."

"Not as important as you," I murmur, placing my hand over his heart whilst trying not to become distracted by the softness of his skin, or how lusciously *firm* his pectoral muscle is.

Finally, he cracks an almost-smile, pinching my chin between his fingers. "I love you, baby." He presses a kiss on my lips that has me melting. "But you should work. At least one of us needs to have a purpose in life, right?"

Spinning away, he saunters to the living room, crashing back onto the couch. He's been watching a marathon of *Impractical Jokers* since I woke up at six and found him out here, so who knows how long he's been up.

Not that I blame him. It was only yesterday that the grenade of his family's lies was tossed into his face and went *kaboom*. It's obviously going to take more than twenty-four hours to absorb this shit, which is why I can't even worry about work right now.

I mean, yes, I'm still dealing with my own stuff too. Meeting my father, and my half-sister, for the first time was crazy and overwhelming as fuck. But for whatever reason, I'm just able to process this a little easier than Lance. Maybe it's because I've had thirty-five years of practice not giving a fuck who my dad is.

Either way, I can brush this shit off well enough. I never knew my dad; therefore, I don't need to know him now. If anything, I feel like eight tons of uncertainty were lifted from my shoulders when I found out that Lance and I don't actually share blood.

It was the biggest relief ever, and despite how bonkers the experience was, I'm beyond glad I showed up in South Valley for that revelation.

Basically, here's how it went down.

I decided to pop in on Daddy Dearest at the church and confront him about his being a massive Grade-A dickwad. But when I arrived, I was

413

surprised and charmed as heck to find Lance already there, doing exactly that.

I snuck into the room right when Lance was coming out in front of everyone, and confessing that he loved me in the most amazing, Lance-like declaration he does so well. He's just such a passionate, loving, sexy giant, and when he stands up in front of people and tells them the truth, it's like you can *feel* how much it means to him in that moment. I know he lacks confidence in certain things, like his sexuality, but that's just something every queer person deals with. Coming out is different for everyone. Waiting for the right moment doesn't mean you're not self-assured. *Sanguine and such.* Whether you say the words when you're a kid, or in your sixties, it makes no difference. Each person's story is beautiful in their own way.

Walking up that aisle toward my father, I was struck with déjà vu, the memory of my mother bringing me to his church as a child rushing back with force. I remembered how angry he was at my mother for showing up, and how scary I found him, of course not knowing at the time that he was my father. He was just a large man with mean eyes who didn't want me near him.

But yesterday, when I saw him for only the second time in my thirty-five years of life... I wasn't afraid. He wasn't frightening or huge, like some foreboding monster.

He was just a man. A shitty man, but still, a man all the same. And he didn't look angry that I was there. In fact, he seemed glad. Nervous, remorseful, but... relieved.

He was *happy* to see me.

But the thing is, whether I eventually see Giovanni Hardy again, or keep him out of the rest of my life too, it doesn't matter anymore. I got the closure I needed by finding out the truth, and I got my own redemption when I showed up in that church with my head held high.

I already have a family, and they're fucking awesome. *The rest is just paperwork.*

Anyway, all other feelings took pause when I heard Gio say that Lance isn't technically his son... Like, *biologically.*

Oof. What a train wreck.

Honestly, the whole experience was like one long emotional mindfuck. And here I'd thought I was going to stroll in, tell off my bio-Dad, and then find Lance so we could kiss in the rain or something. I know it barely ever rains here, but still. He can't *always* be the romantic one. For once, I wanted to have my rom-com, *get-the-guy* moment.

I want to sweep *him* off his feet for once, since he's always sweeping me with his love confessions. *Maybe sweeping him is harder, since ya know... He's huge.*

Yesterday in the church was its own kind of moment, though. We broke down the last remaining barriers between us. And sure, it sucked, because Lance found out his real father died before he was born, and his parents lied to him about it for his whole life. Not to mention that he and I aren't even blood-related, so the whole secret reason he left in college was all for naught. It was a rough one for my Sunshine, regardless of the good news, and the fact that we kissed and declared our love in front of his parents.

But that's just life, as we know. Good balanced out with bad, and no conceivable way of knowing which one you're going to get at what time. The trick is learning to appreciate the good for how truly wonderful it is. Once you start doing that, you take away the power of the bad.

The moral of yesterday's story is that parents aren't superheroes. They're just people. And sometimes people are fucked up. They lie, and hide things from you, and it's always done to *protect* you from the pain of the truth.

When will parents learn that sheltering your kids isn't *protecting* them from shit? It does more harm than good, that's a given. And I swear, if I ever become a parent, I'll make it a habit to never lie to my kids about anything.

Well, maybe little white lies, like brushing your teeth makes you live longer. But deep, *foundational* lies are a terminal disease. They eat away at families from the inside, without us even realizing it.

Shaking off the fact that this now makes several times over the last couple of weeks when I've imagined myself objectively being a parent, I blink at my man over in the living room. I hope that him just being here with me, focusing on the good, will be enough to help ease the pain of his past.

My eyes shift to the fridge, and a bemused smile pulls at my lips when I see the magnet on it. It's the one I gave Lance in college, after my spring break trip to Nashville with Jake. Johnny Cash with his middle finger up.

I live like Johnny Cash... Somewhere between Jesus and jail.

I can't help chuckling to myself as my chest warms. *That's so Lance. My sinful preacher.*

Honestly, I'm not even surprised he still has the magnet. It's just like

415

him to save some dumb little trinket I gave to him when we were kids. He must have put it up after Ellie and Marcus brought his stuff over this morning. Not all of it, just some clothes and random toiletries. I want him to know I have no problem getting him new stuff, but I also don't want him to feel like I'm supporting him financially, because I know it's a bit of a pain point at the moment. He's on edge about not having a career or a home anymore, and I don't think me waving around the fact that I'm rich as shit and could totally support him for the rest of ever will help at all.

Lance has always had structure. For the first time in his life, he's staring at a giant question-mark, and regardless of how good I think this will be for him—finally swerving off-course from the rigid path he'd been guided down by his father, his wife, the church—I can also understand how scary it must be to have everything up in the air.

He finally gets to make his own choices for his future; follow his heart, his dreams and passions. I just hope he knows that where he's going to live should be the easiest question to answer.

Padding over to the couch, I put all of my swirling thoughts to rest for now and slither down next to him, resting my head on his shoulder.

If he needs more time to process his grief and everything that's happened, I'm more than happy to give him that. As long as he stays right here, so I can touch him, and kiss him, and love him as much as we both need. To make up for lost time.

I guess we end up falling asleep on the couch, because the next thing I know, I'm waking up groggy, glancing around the dark room. The clock reads nine-thirty, which means we definitely fell asleep for hours. It's fine. *Nothing going on, anyway.*

Just a lazy, quiet day in my condo with my new boyfriend and our entwined family issues.

Lifting myself up, I notice I'm actually lying on top of Lance, who's so wide he takes up most of the couch. He's still asleep, eyes cinched shut, mumbling as if maybe he's having a bad dream.

Pouting, I run my fingers along the curves and slopes in his chest. I don't want him to be sad, in real life or in his sleep.

I love him. He's the only man I've ever loved... *That makes him super special.*

He deserves a reward for being so amazing.

Fingertips trailing down his abs, I shiver at the sight of his massive erection pressing upward into the front of his sweatpants. *God*, his dick is so *big*, and thick, and generally wonderful. The fact that it's so hard right now is clearly a sign that it needs to be worshipped. *By me.*

Lowering to his chest, I trail kisses down his muscles, watching his face as I go, to see if what I'm doing is having any effect. His forehead is still creased, but when I slide my tongue along the waistband of his pants, he breathes out a hum that sounds much less pained, and much more pleasured.

Smirking to myself, I tug his pants down just enough for his big juicy crown to poke out. I flick it with my tongue, and it flinches, springing up toward my mouth. So I do it again, teasing the head, making his dick dance for me. I snicker and pull his pants down farther, giving me more inches to work with, my tongue sliding up and down to paint him with saliva.

Fuck, this is really hot. Toying with him while he's asleep... Definitely a perk to having a boyfriend who lives here. I can play with his massive love stick whenever I want.

My thoughts begin to wander while I lick and lick...

Would he like to live with me...?

We haven't discussed it yet... But I mean, it would make total sense. He doesn't technically have a home. Shouldn't this be his home?

I think I'd love to have him here all the time, walking around in these sexy sweats, or his boxers. Or nothing. Being all gorgeous and huge and adorable.

That's it. I've decided.

I want him to move in.

I'll tell him when he wakes up.

Grinding my own cock into the couch beneath me in excitement for my new roomie and his delicious body, I slope my lips over his tip, sucking him deep into my throat. His big body writhes, whatever bad stuff happening in his head having seemingly dissipated, replaced by the good sensations I'm giving him, because he deserves it.

He deserves excellent head whenever he wants. He deserves to have a mouth as talented as mine pulling him out of bad dreams, slurping and sucking out pulses of precum while his chest heaves.

He deserves the love and happiness he always wanted with me, but thought he couldn't have. And he deserves to know that it doesn't matter how fucked up things get outside of here, because inside this home we'll make together, it'll be all about *us*, loving each other.

"God, I love you, Lance Hardy," I whisper hoarsely, yanking his pants down to his thighs so I can kiss his balls. "Stay with me forever, baby."

Nuzzling all over his nuts, I lick and suck them, driving myself *crazy* with need. Lapping back up his cock, I suck him in once more, bobbing and groaning, getting lost in giving him head in his sleep like a total fiend.

He mumbles something that sounds like *fumble*, and I peer up at his face.

Oh, Trouble. He said *Trouble*, with his head tipping back, fingers digging into the couch.

Aww... He knows it's me!

I'm totally incepting him through his dick right now!

Moaning on his cock, I stuff him back deep while massaging his thighs with my fingers. My balls throb as my hand moves in between his legs, creeping toward the crack of his ass. I should probably wake him up before I do something like this, but I can't deny how hard my dick is at the thought of slipping a finger inside him while he's sleeping.

Reaching in between the couch cushion, I locate the bottle of lube I keep hidden in there—*always keep lube hidden in every room of the house. You never know when you'll need it.* All the while, I'm marveling at how engorged his cock is in my mouth; how thick and swollen and eager it is, sliding down my throat. I squirt some lube onto my fingers, but I end up stuffing my hand into the back of my own pants, teasing my hole from behind. Because I guess I'm just a selfish little buttslut right now.

"Mmmfff..." I groan with my mouth full, giving myself two at once because I'm fucking *dying*. So needy, I'm leaking everywhere, pushing my fingers into my ass with zero warm-up.

Like the song, I'm fucking *sailing* away.

"Tate..." Lance's grumbly sounds turn to actual words, my eyes springing open at the shout-out. His are still closed, but he gasps again, hands gliding onto my shoulders. "Fuck, *Tate*, I love you, baby..."

"Mm mmm mmm mm," I tell him I love him too, with his dick jamming down my throat, my eyes watering and trying to close as my hand pumps into my ass.

"You're so perfect, Tate." His abs clench, fingers toiling in my hair. "I don't even care that you're my brother, baby..."

My eyes shoot open once more, and my rampant sucking slows all the way down.

He said... what now?

Lance is barely conscious, squirming, whimpering, just loving the sleephead I'm giving him. But in his mind, apparently, we're still related...

And I'm beginning to wonder if maybe that's what's got him so rock-hard right now.

Trouble

My mouth twists into a wicked grin, as much as it can with a big dick in there, and I resume my sucking.

Listen, I'm no Boy Scout. *Clearly.* I'm glad Lance and I aren't *actually* brothers. But I'm also not opposed to a little incestuous role-play. I don't judge.

And truth be told, the fact that my dirty preacher man is imagining such things really *cranks my shaft*, if you know what I mean.

Tugging off of his wet cock, I grind my hips harder into the couch, fucking myself rough with my fingers. "*Fuck yea...* I'm your brother..."

"This is... so bad," he whines, bucking up to my mouth while I lick him all over. "We're being *so* bad..."

"Yea we are," I groan. "I shouldn't be sucking my brother's big cock..."

"Mmm... who gives a fuck about *should*..." he rasps, and I beam.

I remember saying that to him. *Twice.*

And now look at us... In love, fooling around while pretending we're related.

They grow up so fast.

"Hardy..." I grunt, feasting on his nuts, licking down his taint. "I'm gonna eat you out. Wake up now if you wanna be, like, not asleep for it."

Lance shudders when I flick my tongue along his crack. I really need two hands for this, but I don't want to stop fingering myself. *Just a few more pumps...*

"Holy... fuck..."

I peek up to find him blinking awake. His fingers trail my jawline as his Adam's apple bobs.

"This was really happening...?" he whimpers, eyes widening when he sees what I'm doing to my own ass. "Naughty Trouble."

I kiss his inner thighs. "You were dreaming that I was really your brother."

He scowls at me, cheeks flushing crimson. "No, I wasn't..."

"Yes. You were," I chuckle deviously. "It was hot."

He gulps again. "What kind of sinner do you think I am?"

"The best kind," I hum. "Now, open up wide so your *brother* can lick your little hole."

He shivers, biting his lip. But he doesn't protest, spreading his legs wider for me. My mouth sinks in between, using my free hand to hold him open. Then I feather my tongue over his rim, keeping our eyes locked the whole time.

"Ffuck..." he grunts, liquifying instantly. I rumble in salacious amusement, licking his hole slow, teasing it before going in for some sweet suction. "Oh... ohhh, Tate, that's... mmmm..."

"You like it?" I growl, lapping at him until he's soaked, mouth wedged between his cheeks while I slam my fingers into my ass.

"Fuck yesss..." He fists my hair, shoving my face in deeper. "Eat my ass, *bro*."

Purring, my dick pulses a hot shot of precum in my pants. I literally don't give a single fuck if this is weird or perverted... It's hot as hell, and I'm already winding up tight.

"Baby, I wanna suck you," he whimpers, yanking my face up by my hair.

It stings, but the pain turns me on even more, as does his aggressive, dominant reign over my body.

"You wanna suck your brother's cock?" I breathe ragged, finally tugging my fingers out of myself.

Lance's face has never blushed redder as he nods, chewing on his bottom lip. He looks like the hottest, most timid secret sex freak ever, and I'm *obsessed*.

"I fucking love you," I grunt, crawling up him and kissing his mouth fast and hard, because I can't not.

He's irresistible. I can't fucking *believe* I get to have him.

"I love you more," he whispers, pushing my pants down my thighs.

"Move in with me." I suck and nibble his lower lip, barely even aware of what I'm saying.

I think we all knew I wouldn't be very cool in my first relationship. It's just so new to me... Feeling this way for someone. It's like a desperate need I can only sate by touching and kissing him every moment I'm breathing. I have literally *zero* chill right now.

Whatever. I've spent my entire adult life being aloof. I'm alright giving it up for Lance Hardy.

I guess when it comes to him, obsession is officially my love language.

Lance's lips sweep into a massive smile. "Marry me."

My heart practically explodes in my chest. I think he can feel it because he's rumbling out these sexy, smug little laughs.

"Shut up," I growl. "Stop trying to top my proposal with your... shenanigans."

"I'm not kidding." He smirks, holding my face and kissing me silly. "You know you're gonna marry me, Tate. You might as well just say yes now..."

Trouble

"I'm ignoring you," I rub my cock on his, quaking at his words while pretending I'm not.

Moving in is one thing, but *marriage* is a whole other question... One the grabby hands in my heart seem to want to answer already.

But I refuse. *This is about cohabitation, not... matrimony.*

"If I answer your demand-like question, will you answer mine?" He grabs my ass hard and squeezes until I mewl.

"No," I hiss. "You're still married. So yours is irrelevant." Sitting back, I reposition so that my dick is right above his mouth. "Now—" I drag the leaking head over his lips, and his lashes flutter, "—are you gonna move in with me... or not?"

He nods fast, parting his lips for me to push the tip in, sucking hard enough that my toes curl and my head drops back. But then he bites me, and I flinch.

"Just know that as soon as my divorce is final, you're marrying me, Tate Eckhart." He's speaking with the head of my cock brushing his lips, cocking a brow as he flutters his tongue underneath. "It's gonna happen."

I purse my lips to contain my grin. "Do I get a say in the matter?"

"Of course you do." His hands glide up my hips. "What you're gonna *say* is 'I do.'"

"You're the fucking worst... *bro.*" I smirk, and he laughs.

Then he smacks my ass, grabbing me quick and flipping me around. He yanks my pants all the way off, kicking out of his own, positioning me so that I'm kneeling over his shoulders. And he wastes no time sucking me into his warm, wet, perfect mouth, guiding me possessively with his hands on my ass.

Being inside his mouth is a wonder, the confidence he displays giving me head now a *new* fantasy playing out before my eyes.

I used to like curious straight guys more than anything... But as it turns out, I *love* a man who found his sexual identity with *me* and me alone.

Resuming my devouring of his tight virgin hole, I open him up and lick him senseless, grinding my hips against his face to ride his mouth. At this position, my cock is really spearing down his throat, but he seems to have found his groove, ignoring the gag reflex, breathing through his nose at the right moments... *Jesus, the way he's blowing me is blowing my mind.*

"Sunshine... you're sucking the life outta my cock, baby," I purr into his ass, feeling his hands doing something... Pouring lube onto his fingers. "Mmm, nice. You read my mind."

He groans, vibrating my cock as his slick fingers play with my rim, one long digit probing me slow. I gasp, sticking my tongue into his hole as he adds a second. Then a third.

"Fuckin' stretch me, Hardy." My eyes roll back as he pets my prostate. "*Unnghh*, right there... Punish it. Show your brother who his ass belongs to."

Lance cries on my cock while I suck his hole until it's dripping, creeping my index finger up to it.

"You want it, sweet Sunshine?"

"Mmmm..." he whines.

I press my fingertip in. "Remember, if it gets too intense, our safeword is Antidisestablishmentarianism."

I can feel him laughing, but my cock is in his throat, so it's more like a choking gurgle. Rumbling a villainous chuckle with my tongue swirling on his rim, I stuff my finger into his ass, slowly, using the excessive pool of saliva to work it in and out. His toes are curling already. And when I push it in and aim for the good spot, his big dick flinches enough to tap me in the chest, dripping out a hefty throb of precum.

"Ohh, *baby*, that's it," I croon while he cries, fingering him and kissing his hole as I go. "Look at you... loving my finger in your sweet ass. You want more?"

He nods, groaning with my cock just lodged in his throat. His fingers aren't even moving in me anymore. In fact, he's pretty much just lying beneath me, trembling, while I play with his hole.

I give him another finger, and his entire body quakes. I can feel his balls twitching on my chin as I fuck him gently, his hips writhing into my hand, and my face. His legs are wide open, just *giving* me his ass while I chase his pleasure as if it's linked to mine.

Eventually, his movements pick back up, and he rides my hole with his three huge fingers, letting me hump his face, gazing at the way his asshole grips my two.

It's intoxicating. To think I get to have this every day has me racing right up to the edge of a stupefying climax.

"Lance... *fucking*... Hardy, I'm gonna come down your throat." My ass clenches.

But right before I erupt, he shudders and starts spraying me down. Hole clamping on my fingers, he's crying on my cock, shooting cum all over both of us.

"That's it. Come for me, baby," I gasp, kissing his balls, fucking his face. "I love how you come so sweet for only me..."

Trouble

His wet dick is sliding between us while his mouth goes to town on me at the same dedicated tempo as his hand. I'm stiffening all over, when he lifts my hips to pull me out of his mouth.

"Come on my ass," he croaks, shoving me forward. "Pour it all over my hole, baby, *please.*"

Don't have to ask me twice.

Lance reaches down, jerking my cock for me, for only a moment before I bust.

"*Fuuuck yeaa*, take it, Sunshine," I groan, shooting on his balls and between his cheeks.

His legs are spread-eagle while I hold him open, coming all over his ass. Using my fingers, I stuff my cum inside him, and he sobs.

"Uhhh, *Tate, fuck*, your cum is in me," he whimpers, his dick twinging. "Push it in more..."

"You like my hot cum in your hole, filthy boy?"

"Fuck yea... *Mmmf...* fuck me with it."

"Are you my gorgeous slut now?"

"Uh-huh..."

"Say it. Say *I'm your gorgeous slut.*"

"I'm your g-gorgeous s-slut..."

"Fuck me, I can't believe you're still coming..." I marvel at his dick, pulsing out more, and *more.*

"I'm... gonna... die..."

Raspy giggles pour from my lips as I finally come down from the longest orgasm high of my life. I collapse on my man, my heart damn-near exploding from the dazed look on his perfect face. Hair all mussed up, cheeks pink, lips shivering.

"You're a work of fucking art, Lance Hardy," I sigh, draping my body over his.

We're both covered in sweat and cum, but I don't even care. This is *amazing.*

"You're the best thing that's ever happened to me, Tate Eckhart," he breathes, bringing my lips to his.

We kiss for a while, slowly, deep and meaningful. Our lips are cherishing, tongues tangling devotion with breaths singing a song only we can hear.

Dozing, I come to with his fingers in my hair, his hooded gaze on my face.

"I could stare at you for the rest of my life..." He whispers.

Nyla K.

My heart is full. The organ in my chest that used to be empty is now overflowing thanks to this man.

And I can't believe I *ever* wanted *anything* but this.

"Is that another proposal?" I tease, and he chuckles.

"Not just yet." He grins. "We can live together first... Test the waters."

"Mmm, we'll need to do that. Because I've been living on my own for a long time, Hardy. I can't guarantee you won't be demanding a refund after a few weeks."

"Do I look scared?" His brow arches. "You don't intimidate me, hotshot. I can't wait to see you go from bachelor to boyfriend."

Laughing, I rest my chin on his chest, gazing up at him. "I'm serious. I know you're going through a lot right now..."

"We both are," he whispers.

I nod. "But when it comes to this, *us*, being a real couple, I'm gonna need you to be the strong one for me, baby. You have to always be the one who's sure... Because I don't know how to do this." Insecurity lines my tone as I purse my lips. "I'm gonna fuck up, Hardy... I know I am."

"You're not gonna fuck up," he says with certainty.

"How do you know that?" I grunt. "It's only been a couple weeks... What if a few years go by, and I start... acting like an idiot?" I shake my head. "I never want to hurt you, baby, but I'm just not used to this..."

"Tate... that's the exciting part. Don't you see?" He cups my jaw. "We're so *different*, baby... And I love that about us. I love that you're the wild one, the smirking, mischievous, dark side to my light. Your heart is every bit as huge as your personality, and you think it's not, but it *is*, baby. Just ask your friends... your *family*." He pauses to make sure his words are sinking in. I swallow as he rolls us onto our sides, sloping his leg over mine. "I don't need you to be the perfect boyfriend, or someone you're not. I want you just the way you are. I'm in love with your *trouble*, Trouble. You're every single thing I've been missing my whole life."

"Sunshine..." I whisper, flat-out astonished by his words, his beautiful illustrious feelings for me, and how unbelievably sure he is that he only wants me forever. It just makes me want to do the impossible for him... To be *me*, for him. "Falling in love with you is my biggest accomplishment."

He grins, kissing my lips. "That means a lot... coming from someone who's done so many amazing things."

"I can't believe we're finally here..." I hum.

"Thank God," he whispers, nestling me against his chest.

I can feel his heart beating into me... The love that's in there, and also the pain of recent events. It's miraculous to me that he can be so confident in us, even when he's not feeling that way about himself or his own life. But I guess that's how he's always been. Willing to carry the burden of pain so that the rest of us don't have to.

Lance Hardy has enough love inside him to support us both, but I want him to know he doesn't need to anymore.

Because I'm here now. Just as in love with him as he is with me. Ready to share any of his pain, help him carry his burdens. And we all know I don't half-ass things.

Only full ass from Tate Eckhart.

"Babe..." I whisper.

"Yea, love?"

I lift my chin to peek up at him. "It's okay to be fucked up over this... you know that, right?"

He lets out a breath. "Yea, I know."

"Good." I reposition. "Then you must also know how *incredible* this whole thing turned out..."

Lance shifts to make eye contact, looking a bit chagrined, but still sighing, "I do. I get it. We're not brothers, and that's a very fucking good thing." He takes my hands in his. "But it's going to take me some time to wrap my head around it all. Not even just that it turns out I never actually knew my real father, which is probably the biggest mindfuck since I found out we were *brothers*. But also just... accepting that we're not."

I lift my brows, only mildly confused by his words and waiting for him to elaborate.

"Look, I'm not some crazy pervert... I don't actually wish we *were* brothers." His lips twitch while I chuckle. "But the truth is... I spent a lot of years thinking we were. Losing that... that closeness I felt with you, the bond I thought was deeper than just regular love... it kind of hurts." He swallows, painful lines framing his face. "It's almost like I just found out I have no real family, you know? I mean, my dad isn't really my dad, my sister is only my half-sister, and you're... Well, you're Tate. Not *just*, because you're the love of my life, but you're not..." His voice trails, and he shakes his head. "I don't know what I'm trying to say. I think I'm just tired. I'm sorry, baby..."

"Don't do that," I grumble. "Don't diminish your feelings. It's all valid, babe, even if no one understands it but you."

He exhales slowly, nodding, though he still looks a bit distraught.

"Listen to me. If anyone knows about finding love and family in people who don't share your blood or your last name, it's me. The people I love most in this world, the people I would die for or kill for... They're not biologically related to me. But that doesn't matter, Hardy. Because family isn't DNA and chromosomes or whatever science-y bullshit. It's much more emotional than that. And I know you know what I'm talking about, because you're a man of *faith*."

"You haven't seen your higher power with your eyes, but you feel him in your chest." I tap my finger over his heart. "Your soul knows he's a part of you, spiritually, not tangibly. Family is the same way. It's more than words on a piece of paper, or some DNA test... Ellie is your *sister*. And say what you want about him, but Gio is your father. And as far as you and me are concerned... we've been blood since the moment I met you. You've always been my family, Lance Hardy, and this love runs through my veins. *You* do. You've gotta know you're ingrained in my soul, baby."

His lashes flutter, as if he's stunned speechless for a full five seconds before he grabs my jaw, and kisses me. Abruptly enough to pull out a gasp, but still slow and full. Needy, greedy, and overflowing with love.

"Are you saying that I'm... your *soulmate*?" He grins on my lips, and I grumble.

"I would never say something so corny," I gripe while he chuckles. "But... yes. That's exactly what I'm saying."

He laughs. "I love you beyond all rationale or reasoning, Tate Eckhart. Thank you for being my family."

"Well, you know what I always say." I smirk. "When you're here, you're family."

"That's Olive Garden," he chortles.

"Mhm, and you can eat my breadstick and toss my salad as much as you want."

He cackles, while I beam with pride. "Wait, why is your dick a breadstick?"

"Stop ruining my hilarious jokes!" I tease, rolling on top of him and pinning him to the couch.

It only works for a second before he's fighting me back for control, wrestling me into submission while we both laugh so hard we can barely breathe. We end up rolling off of the couch and crashing onto the floor, which only brings more raucous laughter.

And it leads to him between my legs, as it does, fucking me deep and slow for a long, *long* time. Until my toes are curling and my muscles are sore, and we're coming together... Bodies *and* souls.

Trouble

Falling in sin and divinity. A glorious descent of heavenly hosts... crashing into wicked, mortal soil.

Epilogue
Lance

6 months later...

"Did you know... that sunflowers can soak up high concentrations of radioactive isotopes and sequester them in stems and leaves?"

Tate's eyes shift from the road for a second.

"Because of this, they're often planted in contaminated sites following nuclear explosions or spills as a means to clean up radiation."

He squints at me, and I can tell he's trying really hard not to seem affected by my cool sunflower fact.

"Don't change the subject," he grunts, and I grin.

I love his grouchiness almost as much as I love his playfulness.

"I'm just saying..." I walk my fingers up his thigh. "It's pretty neat, huh?"

"I'm still mad at you, Hardy," he grumbles. "Spouting odd information about sunflowers, while adorable, won't get you off the hook this time."

"Sorry," I faux pout.

"No, you're not," he huffs, and I chuckle.

He's right. I'm not.

How could I be when the thing he's mad at me for is being too excited about our future??

Okay, maybe I shouldn't have brought everything up in front of Jake, but I couldn't help myself. I'm ecstatic at where things are going with us. I also assumed he'd already mentioned it to Jake, since they tell each other everything and swap secrets like high school girls. The fact that he hadn't is kind of throwing me for more of a loop than anything.

The last six months have been like a complete overhaul of my entire life, and if we're being honest, I'm loving every second of it, despite how monumentally overwhelming it was at first.

Naturally, it took me some time to deal with finding out that Giovanni Hardy wasn't my biological father. My real dad, a man named Lance Olsen, died tragically before I was born, and my mother quickly remarried Gio, turning me from Lance Olsen Jr. to Lance Hardy.

I'm not sure I'll ever get over it, but after I started seeing a therapist, and finally worked up the courage to see my mother again, I realized I'm not meant to.

Life is full of unexpected twists and turns. They're not all going to be as wonderful as falling in love and discovering your true identity. The trouble is in learning to love the bad as much as the good. Because without pain, could we ever truly appreciate pleasure?

Once you fully accept that God's plan isn't meant to be all sunshine and rainbows, you can begin to heal from your trauma, and bask in the knowledge that what doesn't kill us most definitely makes us fucking badass.

Battle scars are beautiful, inside and out.

A few months ago, I went home to South Valley. Just me.

Tate's dealing with his own feelings regarding our strange, interwoven family drama, and it's important for us to work on these things separately, while still leaning on one another for support.

I had dinner with my mom and dad, and Ellie. And it actually felt good to see them and spend time with them, all truths out in the open. My mother and I looked at pictures of my birth father, and she told me stories about him. I guess he wasn't perfect, and their marriage wasn't without its issues, but then, whose is?

Things between me and my adoptive father are still a bit strained. But we're working on it. I told him that I'll always consider him my father, and he cried, and hugged me harder than he ever has before. And when he told me that he's proud of me for coming out, and that he loves me for exactly who I am as a gay man, I might've cried a little myself. *Okay, I definitely did.*

I know he doesn't get the gay thing, but he's trying, and I have to give him credit for that. He also didn't give me shit about leaving the church, which was much appreciated.

Nyla K.

South Valley Pentecostal has a new pastor, Gary something. My parents say he's a good guy, but they've since started going to church elsewhere. After the drama that went down that day in front of the congregation, our little town was buzzing with so much gossip, it felt like a reality show. Thankfully, Ellie, Tate and I stayed far out of it. But my parents were caught in the crosshairs for a while there. I couldn't feel too bad about it, though. They'd made their mess. It was only fair that they stuck around to clean it up.

And the truth shall set you free, as they say.

I moved in with Tate the day after he asked me, and haven't looked back since. He still travels a lot for work, and is constantly bouncing back and forth between Corona and Santa Fe. Sometimes I go with him, sometimes I hang back, depending on work. But I make it a point to schedule my jobs around his trips out of state, mostly so we can be together, since being apart is insufferable for both of us. But also, I can't miss an opportunity to travel with him all over the place on his firm's dime.

For the last few months, I've been working as an independent contractor, specializing in elaborate gardens and landscape design. It's my dream job, and I'm *finally* doing it. I plant trees and flowers, using my extensive botanist knowledge, and create intricate designs for people's homes. Not to mention, I get to work with my hands, which is something I always missed in the church.

Basically, it's amazing, and I'm loving every second of it. And it would never have happened without Ben Lockwood.

He's a masonry contractor, and he owns one of the most successful companies in the state. So when I was looking for work, Jake suggested I hit him up, and see if he needed any laborers. Just for something to do, to get me out of the house, and help me feel like I was contributing. I know Tate is more than capable of supporting us both on his hefty investment banker salary, but I'm not interested in a free ride. Even if I only make a fraction of what he makes, it's still something.

As much as he likes to joke, I'm *not* his sugar baby.

I was working with Ben for a couple of weeks before we got to talking about some ideas I had for landscaping. He pitched it to a few of his clients, and they went crazy over it. And thus, Lance's Landscaping and Design was born.

Tate wanted me to call it Lance-scaping, because he's an adorable dweeb. So we conceded, and I made it my tagline on my business cards. I still laugh every time I look at them.

Trouble

Work has been going great, though it's slowing down now that it's winter. But I don't mind. It gives me more time to work on my side-hobby...

Preaching the word of God to people who need it.

The struggle with my faith after everything happened had nothing to do with my *faith* at all, and everything to do with the church, my father, and religion as a whole. That's always been the place where I stray from normal theological ideals.

I didn't leave the church because I stopped loving God, or stopped believing in Him. I left because that job never truly had my heart in the first place. Trying to be myself there was a constant battle I was always losing, and it enabled my denial for way too long.

As soon as I came out, I knew I needed to make a change, and speak to people of the LGBTQ+ community about God in a way that fights the hate and bigotry we've experienced for so many years.

So I started a social media account; Instagram and TikTok, mostly, just to get the word out about God not being the old white dude sitting up in the clouds judging everyone. Really, I was just doing it for myself, to satisfy my need to expel the bevy of religious knowledge from my brain and preach my interpretation of faith and spirituality. But much to my own surprise, it took off.

I've been called a lot of things, from "the hot preacher," to "the gay preacher," to "Preacher Daddy," and of course the standard "blasphemer", "heretic," and a ton of other hateful words I'm choosing not to repeat now, because the internet is an awful, treacherous place sometimes. But I don't let that deter me.

The sheer volume of messages I got after I told the story of me and Tate finding each other again, about how God brought us back together and we fell in love, made all the rest of the hurtful comments from strangers worth it. Trolls will always do their damndest to dampen your shine, but you have to let all the noise fade into the background and focus on who you are. People's opinions don't define you, especially not bored assholes on social media.

We are who we are. *Human beings*, each of us completely different, with different views and beliefs. I would never dream of pushing mine onto others, so I don't tolerate others projecting their bullshit onto me. I just want to make sure every person, especially the marginalized or the down-trodden or the fearful, knows that we are *all* worthy of love. Each and every one of us is worthy of the gifts of this life, granted to us in a great, cosmic expanse, the likes of which we'll never truly understand.

Whether you're gay, straight, bi, pan, Demi, ace, any and all pronouns, all races and colors and ethnicities, believers and nonbelievers, of all religions and spiritualities... We're all here, *together*, on this planet as one humanity. And we all deserve love and equality.

Life is too short to be spent hating and hurting one another. Faith is about the truest and most ethereal love in ourselves, not war between religions. As cohabitants of this world we call home, we should be able to see the commonality in us all, despite our differences.

It's a hard sell, I know, especially today. But I'll keep trying, no matter what. Because I'm a preacher of *love*. And as someone very important to me once said, "If you're pissing people off, that just means it's working."

And so there you have it. Thirty-six years old and my life has finally begun. *Better late than never, right?*

Tate and I just got back from Tokyo a few weeks ago, then we spent another magical week in New York. And now we're home, on our way to dinner with the family at Ben, Ryan, and Jessica's.

We were supposed to be going out to dinner with Jake and Laura, but their sitter fell through, and they decided at the last second to go to Ben's so the kids could play together while the adults hang out, which I guess is pretty common. Apparently, Ben, Ryan, and Jess just got back from some extravagant vacation in Tulum, and we haven't seen them in a while, so it'll be nice to get together as a group. I love Tate's friends. They're very much his found family, and there's never a dull moment when they're all together.

The only thing is that I guess Tate's been keeping the seriousness of our relationship under wraps a bit, and I'm not crystal clear on *why*. He says he's afraid that telling everyone about us will jinx it. And as much as I keep assuring him that won't, I have to tread lightly with his feelings, because it seems like this *jinx* excuse is just Tate-speak for *I'm still nervous*.

Look, if I could have married him already, I would have. But I'm trying to go at his pace. Still, for all the bachelor-isms he continues to display on a daily basis, *he's* the one who's constantly—*and not very subtly, I might add* —hinting that he's ready for more.

My divorce was finalized yesterday. It was nothing shy of miraculous how quickly and smoothly the whole process went. Desiree and I are on speaking terms, though we really only do it when completely necessary. We were able to agree on things easily enough, because I told her I didn't want

Trouble

anything. She kept the house, and Sunny, who I promised to visit on occasion, then I took my truck, and that was it. An amicable split.

Tate and I had dinner last night to celebrate. And I nearly died of swoon, because he just wouldn't stop pestering me about proposing.

"You don't really want to marry me, Hardy..."

"Proposing the same day your divorce finalizes is tacky, don't you think?"

"If you get down on one knee with anything less than twenty-four carats, I'm saying no. Beyonce's ring needs to be the starting point."

He's honestly so ridiculous, it just makes me love him infinitely more. *As if I can't tell he's totally Bugs Bunny-ing me right now.*

The guy is seriously a minefield of emotional issues, but I'd be lying if I said I wasn't already fully sold on it. After all, I knew what I was getting myself into with Tate. In a lot of ways, we're polar opposites, and because of that, I've always assumed trying to wife him up would be complicated. But what can I say? *I guess I love the chase.*

Even more so when he basically ties himself up and hops into my trunk, so to speak.

Maybe I fucked up by casually letting it slip to Jake and Laura that we'd be engaged by the end of the night. Because now he's all broody and pouting, which only makes him a million times sexier.

When we get to Ben's house, Tate's snark-level is at about a hundred, and I'm just along for the ride, as usual.

Right off the bat, it seems like Ryan is aware of something going on between us, because he's acting clingier than usual with Tate. I've managed to eradicate most of my jealousy regarding their history. Being in love with Tate Eckhart means being in love with someone with a very *rich* history of sexual partners. Usually, I can just pretend they don't exist, but Ryan is always around, more or less. And he and Tate have a rather close friendship for two people who have seen each other naked a bunch of times.

Regardless, I trust Tate. And Ryan is madly in love with his partners, so it's not really an issue. The jealousy will always be there, especially after Tate confided in me a few months back, and told me he might've had something feelings-adjacent for Ryan when they were sleeping together. It took a lot of effort not to react in my knee-jerk possessive, hulking-beast type way. But I had to remain calm, because Tate trusted me enough to tell me the truth about it, and he's done nothing but prove to me since we started sleeping together that he's not interested in anyone else.

I have to give him credit where credit is due. For someone who's never done more than casual hook-ups, Tate is slaying monogamy. I like to think he's so in love with me that it's a non-issue. But even if that's not the case, my job is to love and support him, and always give him the benefit of the doubt. No matter how loud the little green monster can be sometimes.

Adding to the already hefty tension we've seemingly brought with us, apparently Jacob and Laura failed to mention that we'd be tagging along for dinner until the last second, so there isn't enough food for us. And now I feel awful.

But Jessica is the sweetest, loveliest moonbeam ever, and she brings me into the dining room for some appetizers. I'm expecting Tate and the guys to follow, but then Ben pops out of nowhere and steals Tate, dragging him and Ryan down to the basement.

I'm confused, and nervous, but I'm trying not to let it show as I much on mini quiches, glancing up in surprise when Ben and Jess's daughter, Hailey, struts in with her boyfriend, Oliver, neither of whom I've seen since the day I showed up here looking for Tate.

So, yea. The awkwardness is climbing.

"Don't worry about the guys," Jess says to me. "Ryan's just super nosy when it comes to you and Tate's relationship."

Okay, that doesn't make me feel any better.

"Aren't we all," Hailey huffs, snagging an app for herself.

"Why?" I grunt, eyes flicking between all of them. "What's so exciting about our relationship?"

"Oh, come on!" Jake laughs, handing the twins an iPad, which they take excitedly and scamper off with. "What *isn't* exciting about it? You started out married to a woman, working in a church, cheating on your wife with Tate, which definitely tracks for Tate, by the way." He gives the ladies a look while they nod along. My brows furrow in offense. "But then you guys find out your dad is actually *not* your dad, but Tate's dad. And in an equally shocking turn of events, you got the terminal bachelor himself to stop whoring around, and now he's even more obsessed with you than he was in college. Is that it? Did I miss anything??"

That last bit about Tate being *obsessed* with me naturally makes my stomach flip. But I scowl over it and mutter, "Nope, I think you nailed it. Thanks for the recap."

Jessica's eyes widen, and she points at me. "Oh my God! You're even sarcastic and bitchy like him now!" she squeals. "You two are made for each other."

"Mhm..." Jake is grinning at me, which clearly catches Jess's and Hailey's attention.

Trouble

"What was that look?" Hailey gasps eagerly. "Is there more?? Tell us!"

"Man, Tate was right... You guys do love to pry," I chuckle, biting into another mini quiche.

"Let's just say coming into this family as an outsider is a bit jarring," Oliver mumbles to me, and I laugh softly.

I love his British accent.

"You know they've been living together, right?" Jake says to Jess.

She nods. "Well, yea. Ben told me when he needed an address to send you checks." She sneers, and I fake smile.

"Yea, but for six months," Jake smirks.

"Uh, no." She peers at me. "I didn't know it was that long..."

"Yea, no one did. They're very secretive about their adorable relationship," Jake croons.

"Why?" Jess asks. "What's there to be secretive about?"

"Are you still married?" Hailey asks.

"Hails, leave the poor bloke alone." Oliver shakes his head.

"No," I sigh, conceding to their interrogation. "My divorce finalized yesterday."

"Ooh, congrats." Hailey smirks.

"So what's the problem??" Jess squeaks.

"There is no problem... At least, not for me." I rub my eyes. "I'm not the one who needs the drama. That's all Tate. In fact..." My voice trails. Jake's eyes are bugging. "Never mind."

"Oh, come on! You can't just say that and then not tell us!" Hailey whines.

Jake makes a noise, shaking his head as he leaves the room, most likely going to join the guys in the basement.

"I just... I've been thinking about... the future." I'm staring at the appetizers. And when the room is silent, I look up.

Of course, they're all staring at me.

"Oh... my... God..." Hailey gapes.

"You're gonna propose!" Jess jumps, clasping her hands together in what can only be described as pure glee.

"Maybe," I correct, and they shriek in unison.

If all goes accordingly, this is the family I'll be marrying into... God, I might need to rethink this move.

"I'm gonna go play with Ethan," Oliver scoffs in amusement. But he pats my shoulder on the way out. "Congrats, mate. Or... good luck."

"Bold move with Tate Eckhart," Jess says. "Do you think he'll say yes?"

"I know he wants it." I can feel my face flushing, butterflies swarming my gut at the notion of proposing to him. Of actually marrying someone I've been in love with for over a decade. "I can read him like a book, but out of spite? He might say no. Begrudgingly, like the stubborn brat he is."

The girls laugh.

"He is known to be trouble." Jess beams, and I chuckle. She rubs my arm. "I'm sure he'll say yes. It's like Jake says, everyone can see how obsessed he is with you. It's cute as hell watching him squirm and act all moody, but when all is said and done, I can't see any scenario where he won't seal himself to you forever, because you make him *happy*, and that's what he wants."

I can't help the pout that tugs at my lips. "Jeez... will you propose to him for me?"

Jess laughs. "I already proposed to someone. And was proposed to!"

"Brag much?" Laura teases, sauntering into the room with baby Ethan resting in her arms.

Immediately, my attention is now zoned in on the adorable little boy.

"When I proposed to Desiree, it felt so forced," I tell them, playing with Ethan's toes. "I mean, I was happy because I felt like I should be, ya know? But it wasn't exciting. I wasn't nervous. I knew she was gonna say yes. There was no..."

"Drama?" Jess smirks, and I grin, shrugging. "Yea, well... if you want drama, you're proposing to the right man."

Laughing softly, I shake my head. And now I'm really thinking about it... I didn't go into tonight expecting to propose to Tate. And I think I love that fact. I've known I wanted to marry him for a long time. Long enough that I bought a ring... It's not Kardashian-level, but I know he'll love it. And I've just been carrying it around, waiting for the right time. Waiting for him to be ready, waiting for me to be ready.

The divorce finalizing is great, but I didn't *need* that to ask him. Truthfully, all I need is to see love when I look into his eyes, glistening amongst all the other things he carries in those vibrant irises the color of a decadent dessert.

"Go ask him now!" Hailey swoons.

"I'm not gonna ask him right *now*..." I grumble. But then I bite my lip. "What do you think, little man?" I ask Ethan, lifting his hand and waving it around. "Should I ask Uncle Trouble to marry me?"

"Pa-pa!" Ethan wails, and we all chuckle.

"Oh, so now all blonde men are Poppa??" Jess gasps playfully. She takes

Trouble

Ethan from Laura, standing him up on the floor while holding his hands to keep him upright. "Remember this night forever, baby boy. It'll live in infamy as the night your wild Uncle Tate got *engaged*."

Rolling my eyes, I want to protest their insistence. But I can't... because they're right.

Stubborn or not, I want to make Tate Eckhart mine, *officially*, forever. I've been breaking down his walls since I barged back into his life, and I have no intention of stopping now.

Stalking out of the room, I ignore the squeals and wails behind me that have my face flushing hot, heading downstairs to the basement. When I get there, everyone's faces fling in my direction, wide-guilty eyes like raccoons who just got caught in the garbage can.

"Am I... interrupting something?" I ask nervously.

Tate jumps up, waltzing over to me. "No, no. They're just berating me for details on our relationship like a bunch of high school girls." He rests his hand on my chest, meeting my gaze. I can see so many varying emotions in his beautiful eyes. But as much as he's trying to hide it in pretending to be mad at me, I can see the love brightest. He holds his glass of scotch up to my lips. "Drink?"

"You know I don't drink," I murmur, giving him a pointed look.

"Oh, right. I forgot..." He rolls his eyes. "You're allergic to fun."

God, I just want to kiss the sass out of that sweet mouth.

I fidget for a moment, knowing there are eyes all over me right now. "Well, I like you." I shoot Tate with a subtle smirk.

"You sure you're not allergic to me too?" He pouts, and I cock my head.

"Tate, give the poor guy a break," Ryan chuckles. "You're such a drama queen."

Tate glares at him. "Don't you start."

"Alright, why don't we give these two a minute," Ben says, ushering Ryan and Jake toward the stairs. "Dinner's ready anyway."

"But... I wanna know what's happening," Ryan mutters.

"I know you do, kid," Ben grumbles in amusement.

But they all leave. And now it's just me and my man... alone in the cave.

I gulp and clear my throat. "So... what did Ryan want?"

"A blowjob," Tate quips, and I narrow my gaze at him. He grins sheepishly. "Sorry. You set me up for that one."

Growling, I grab him by the waist. "Why are you giving me so much trouble, Trouble?" He makes a sulking face. "And why doesn't your family

437

seem to know how serious we are?" I slip my finger under his chin, lifting his gaze. "Are you ashamed of me?"

He scoffs. "No..."

"Then what?" I pull him closer to me so that our fronts are flush. "I thought you were happy..."

"Nothing makes me happier than you..." he whispers.

"Then how come you're mad at me for telling Jake I want to marry you?"

He's pouting in silence for a moment before he grumbles, "I thought you were kidding."

"Did that upset you?" I smirk.

His gaze narrows in a forcibly stubborn look. "No."

"So you don't want me on my knees...?" I cock my head, daring him for a moment before dropping to my knees, gazing up at him with only loving desire in my eyes.

"What are you doing down there, Hardy...?" His voice comes out breathy, barely audible.

"Whatever you want," I hum, playing with the button and zipper on his pants. I hear him purr, though he tries to cover it up. "So many things I could do with my mouth down here..."

"Like what?" He bites his lip.

"Well..." I open his pants, pushing them down just enough that the outline of his erection is visible through the jock underwear he apparently decided to wear tonight. A growl reverberates in my chest. "I could kiss you... here." I run my lips along his shape, and he shudders. "Or I could ask you a question..."

"*Ffuck*... what k-kind of... question?"

"Tate... Eckhart..." I whisper, dragging my lips up and down his clothed cock. "Will... you..." he's shivering, gazing down at me with eyes somehow wide and lidded at the same time, "bend over, please? I'm gonna fuck the brat outta you, since, you know... you seem to have forgotten who you belong to."

Tate whines and pouts. "I hate you..."

"You *love* me," I hiss, pulling out his long cock. "As is evident by how much of a pain in the ass you're being." I waste no time sliding him into my mouth.

"Mmmm... you're right. I do love you," he whispers, fingers threading in my hair as his head tips back. I hum while sucking up and down on his inches. "I'm sorry... I am a pain in the ass. But—*uhmff*—I *love* when you're a pain in *my* ass, baby..."

The next thirty minutes go by in a haze. I suck Tate's dick until he's crumbling, getting him up to the edge and stopping enough times that he's flushed and tight all over. Then I shove him onto his knees so he can suck me, just enough to make me nice and slippery wet, after which I bend him over the arm of the couch and lick his ass sloppy, purring how much I love him into his hole while his knees shake.

By the time my dick makes it inside him, we're both only a few pumps from exploding everywhere. Draping my chest over his back, I fuck into him hard, as deep as physically possible, fisting his hair and growling into his ear.

"You wanna be mine forever, don't you, baby?"

"Yes, *yes yes*, I do."

"You're gonna say *I do*, alright... When I marry the shit out of you because you *belong* to me."

"I will! I promise I will, baby," he whimpers. "I fucking love you, Hardy..."

"Why are you such a *gorgeous*, big-dicked nuisance?" I growl, thrusting in him roughly, working my cock deep, until he's in tears.

"You... knew—*ah, fuck, right there*—what you were getting... *into*, God, baby, I'm gonna come!"

"Are you saying this is my fault?" I chuckle breathlessly, grabbing him by the throat, holding his back to my chest while my hips buck. "You think I *love* the trouble?"

"I know you do," he grunts, tightening all around me. "Fuck, baby, come in me. Come in my ass and make me come for you..."

"I'll never get over this, baby." My head spins, ball drawing. "I love every messy inch of you and me." My forehead falls into his hair, and I kiss his neck. "I'm coming in you, love..."

"Good... Fuckin' breed me, baby."

"I'm breeding you..."

"You love coming in me?"

"I *love* coming in you, baby..."

"Am I yours?"

I growl, then groan. "You're gonna marry me so hard, you pretty little slut. That's how fucking *mine* you are."

And then I come. And he comes. And we come together, crying and clutching each other, trying to keep our voices down because I wouldn't be surprised if our friends had their ears to the door right now.

When we finally fizzle down from the heavens and clean ourselves up, I'm blissed out beyond belief, my dazzling love for this man more amplified than ever before. So clearly, there's only one thing left to do...

"Tate..." I rasp, watching him fix his clothes.

"Yes, baby Daddy?" He smirks, focused on a stain he's trying to rub off of his shirt.

Stepping over, I take his hand. He pauses, glancing at me.

I fall to my knees. Again.

"Baby... will you—"

"Cut the shit, you loon!" He rips his hand away.

I chuckle and shake my head from the floor. "What??"

"You're not doing this now..." He grunts, all flustered. "Let's go. I'm sure everyone's talking shit about us up there."

"They're not talking shit, Tate. Will you just stay still for a second!"

But he's already running toward the stairs. "Bye, Hardy! I'm leaving you here!"

Scoffing, I roll my eyes, standing up and following after him. We say a quick, pretty awkward goodbye to the Lockwood's, but I'm not even worried about them right now. I'm too busy chasing Tate down the walkway to his car.

I manage to throw my body in front of the driver's side door before he can whip it open.

"Move, bitch," he grunts.

"I wanna drive," I gasp.

"No way. You can't handle this fine Italian machine."

"Are you talking about the car... or you?" I bite my lip.

Just seeing how hard he's trying not to laugh has me cackling out myself.

"You're such a... fucking... gorgeous idiot," he murmurs, breathing raggedly, shaky and clearly a bit nervous. I can almost feel his heart pounding, because mine is too.

"Tate, I'm gonna fucking do this," I state firmly, giving him my most serious, love-filled gaze. "So just shut up and let me do it."

He looks part thrilled, part horrified as I drop onto one knee for the third time.

"Tate *Trouble* Eckhart..." I grin, and he snorts, eyes wide and shimmering. "From the moment we met, I felt like you could see right through me.

Trouble

Beneath the external layer and into the *real* me... and because of that, I know you know how much I've loved you since that moment. And you know how much I'll *always* love you, more than anyone or anything. You're my blessing, and my curse," I tease, and he whimpers. "My sweetness and my sin... my past and my future. You're every piece of my heart, baby. So please... come back down from the sky and *marry me*, Trouble."

He starts shaking his head, and I can tell he's trying not to cry.

A soft laugh shivers out of me. "Don't you fucking dare..." I rumble, with my heart in my throat.

He clears his, lashes fluttering. "Yes."

I'm falling apart.

"Really??"

"Uh-huh." He nods. "*Yes*, okay? You win, Hardy... I can't pretend I'm not about to melt all the fuck over the place for you, baby..."

Sniffling, I reach into my pocket and pull out the ring. "Now, it's not twenty-four carats..."

"Holy fucking shit," Tate gasps, falling onto his knees on the ground. "You actually got a ring?! Dude, I was kidding!"

I laugh. "Like I said, it's not Jackie O's or anything." I grab his trembling hand and slide the platinum ring onto his finger. "But it's for you, baby. Because I want you wearing my ring, and my last name, for real." I kiss him while he quakes and purrs, kneeling with me on the ground next to his Maserati.

He looks more beautiful than I could ever imagine in this moment. Beneath the moonlight, flushed and shaking, hair mussed up, fancy clothes rumpled... Lips puffy and waiting to be kissed for hours in celebration. Split open, his vulnerability exposed, and all manners of stubbornness evaporated.

He's still scared, I know that. Because I am too. You're *supposed* to be when it's something this big.

It just means it's worth hanging onto with all your might.

Tate lifts his hand, gawking at the ring. "Oh damn..." His sparkly eyes lift to mine. "It's so beautiful, baby." I grin, and he blinks. "Now I feel bad for being so annoying..."

Grasping his face, I chuckle while pulling his lips to mine. And I whisper, "I forgive you."

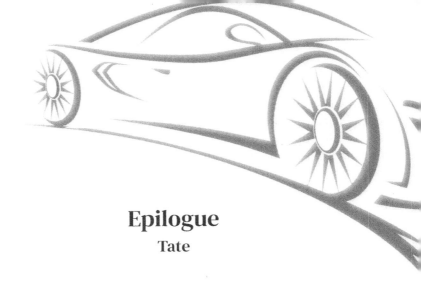

Epilogue
Tate

6 months later...

"Oohhh my God! Look at this amazing bakery," Troy gasps, flipping his phone around from across the table to show me. "They make the most gorgeous wedding cakes."

I lift my eyes from my own phone, peeking at the carousel of cake pictures on this bakery's website. They're definitely pretty, and they look delicious, which is a must. I'll never understand people who get wedding cakes based solely on their appearance, not caring whether they actually taste good or not.

My wedding cake will need to be beautiful *and* scrumptious. Not to mention huge, so we can save a bunch and eat it for days after.

I mean, come on. Sex and cake. The best things about a wedding.

I offer Troy a nod and a sound, because while the cakes do look nice, I can't even really think about wedding stuff right now. There are too many other huge things happening...

One of which is supposed to be happening in a few minutes, right here in this cafe.

"Oh, look. They did Bradley Cooper's wedding cake," Troy goes on, scrolling his phone screen. "Red velvet with pistachio buttercream and a blood orange meringue center. A little bold for a wedding, but still..."

"Where is Lance?" I drop my phone onto the table, rubbing my hands together nervously. "He said he was on his way like a zillion years ago..."

Trouble

"Or ten minutes ago," Troy snickers.

I glare at him, but he's still in the cake zone. "If they show up first, I'll die of awkwardness."

"It's okay, boss." Troy grins kindly. "I'll be your moral support."

"About that... Look, I'm gonna need you to hit the bricks when they get here," I tell him, fully serious.

He frowns. "I don't get to stay for lattes and uncomfortable family time?"

I roll my eyes. "No, fool. This is going to be weird enough as it is. I can't have my dippy little minion lurking around."

He grins and cocks his head. "You're so sweet. I love and value you too, Tatum."

"That's not my name, and I told you a million times, I hate when you say that you *love me*," I grumble while he chuckles. "We both know what we mean to one another... You're very important to me and I wouldn't be able to function without you..." He pouts. "And *I* am essentially your God. It's fine. There's no need to say it out loud all the time."

Troy is wiggling in his seat. "I love how nervous you are."

"I'm not that *nervous*..." I breathe, shaking out my sweaty hands.

"You are. You get extra mean when you're nervous." He smirks. "I am so incredibly bewitched by how far you've come in a year, boss. I mean, honestly... It's nothing shy of miraculous."

"God..." I scoff, rolling my eyes to the heavens and back.

"That hot preacher fiancé of yours really saved your wicked soul," he chuckles. "He deserves a Nobel Peace Prize or something."

My brows furrow. "He's plenty taken care of, don't you worry. Are you forgetting I took him to the Amalfi Coast for ten days for our anniversary?"

Troy keeps giving me that look he's been giving me for the last few weeks, since I told him the big news. Honestly, I should be familiar with it at this point, because it's the same look *everyone's* been giving me when I tell them. The same look they all gave me when Lance and I announced we were getting married.

It's like part *the sky is falling* befuddlement, part fawning pride. Like the look you give to your formerly troubled teen when he announces he's going to Harvard.

Really, I don't blame any of them. I'm a bit shocked myself at how my life is unfurling. I never used to think I would even *date* a man, let alone marry one, and...

"I'm here, I'm here." Lance swoops over to us, breathy like he ran here or something. "Sorry I'm late." He squeezes Troy's shoulder, sliding into the seat next to me and immediately grasping my chin to place a lush, adoring kiss on my lips that melts away my nerves. At least, for the moment. "I got held up at the job site. This new design I'm working on is *so* complex, I'm telling you. And the client keeps adding new extravagant aspects to it... Fountains, and birdbaths and hanging canopies. I have to keep reminding them, this is a home in Santa Fe, not a botanical garden in Tuscany."

Smiling at him, I can't resist taking his hand under the table. He's just so passionate about his job, it turns up the swoon factor exponentially. I could sit here and listen to him talk all day. In fact, that's kind of what I wish we were doing instead of what we *are* doing.

Also... *and this is going to make me sound really annoying and gross, but...* I missed him.

Is that weird? Being that we live together, and it's only been like seven hours since he left for work this morning?

Alright, no need to answer. I know I'm obsessed, bordering on codependent, and you're probably thinking, "What happened to you, Tate? How on earth did you go from a kween of the one-night stand, scotch-swilling, money-loving bachelor who rode dick like a seasoned pro and then sent 'em packing, to a fiancé planning a wedding and making ginormous future moves, walking around with Cupid's arrow in your ass?"

Well, the long and short of it is this: Lance fucking Hardy.

Lance Hardy happened.

He's the *one*. The *only* one who's ever made me want any of this.

And that's the craziest part... I *do* want it. I'm excited as hell to do these relationship things with him, because with him it doesn't feel forced or corny or *typical*. Together, we're our own unique version of a lovesick couple, and I'm here for all of it.

I haven't changed at all in the ways that count. I'm still Tate Eckhart, the rich, cocky troublemaker who wears fancy suits and drinks expensive scotch. But that's how I know this is the real deal. Because I haven't had to change who I am to be with Lance. He loves me, just like this. Emotionally stunted and all.

If anything, he's helped me grow up in a lot of ways. The difference in Tate Eckhart from last year to now is that *now* I'm trying. I feel my emotions and I share them with him, and he does the same. We're open and honest with each other, and we communicate. He doesn't hide things from me to protect me anymore, and I don't push him away by pretending I don't care.

Trouble

Okay, so I'm still stubborn and snarky, and I sometimes use sarcasm to deflect when I'm feeling overwhelmed. They're hard habits to break, after all. But he's showing me that I don't need to hide behind masks anymore. I don't need to be afraid of loving him, because he loves me deep, and he's not going anywhere. *No matter what.*

So together, we've progressed in our relationship, as we both decide we're ready. But we're still *us*, together and individually. Neither of us are running anymore.

We held hands and jumped into the deep-end *together*.

Lance's phone pings, and he checks it with his left hand, since I'm playing with his fingers on his right. He gets a crease in his forehead that tells me what the message said without him even having to voice it.

"Troy, go grab yourself whatever you want. On me," Lance says, fishing his card out of his wallet.

Troy smiles at him like he's smitten, a look I don't *love*, though I have to admit, it's entertaining watching my assistant go gaga over my fiancé.

I mean, he is *very* fucking fine.

He deserves the hype.

"That's not necessary," I grumble. "I'll buy him whatever he wants. It's a write-off."

Lance peeks at me. "I know that, baby, but I'm doing it as a gift, to show my appreciation..."

"Aww!" Troy swoons.

"Before we tell him to vamoose," he adds, showing Troy an apologetic smirk.

Troy sighs. "Fine. I know when I'm not wanted..."

"Do you?" I snort and smirk.

He shoots me a *faux-put-off* grin. "I'll just choose to interpret this as two men fighting over who gets to spoil me." He jumps up with Lance's card, scampering up to the counter, most likely to order way too many things, just because Lance offered.

"You don't need to spend your money on him, baby." I ease into Lance's side, kissing his jaw.

"Love, you pay for literally everything," he grunts, running his thumb over my engagement ring. "I'm stacking up cash insanely fast because I never spend it." He chuckles.

"How about this? Why don't you pay for our next getaway?" I hum by his ear. "I hear Ibiza is lovely at Christmas."

He laughs again, fingers slinking up my thigh. "That sounds great,

445

Trouble, but we might have to think of a more... kid-friendly vacation spot this time."

Our eyes meet, and he cocks a brow. I bite my lip, stomach getting all fluttery with dread *and* excitement.

"I love how nervous you are," he rumbles, giving me the sex eyes. "It makes me hard as fuck."

"And *you'll* have to stow your boners, Sunshine." I smirk. "Things are about to get all kinds of PG up in here."

He chuckles, kissing my bottom lip before he sits back with a sigh. "They'll be here in five minutes."

Would you look at that? My nerves are back. And they've multiplied.

Just as Troy is returning Lance's credit card and scuttling off with his coffee and bag of pastries, in strolls Gio and Freja Hardy.

Lance greets them first, kisses and pleasantries for his mom, and a mildly stiff hug for *our* dad. Not that I blame him for hugging without vigor. I still think it's more than Gio deserves after all the lying and meddling in Lance's life.

But my man is forever the disciple of peace and forgiveness.

So he forgave. And I forgave too, because what good comes from holding grudges? Forgiving is easy, but forgetting... *Now, that's another story.*

We've seen Gio a few times over the last year. Lance goes to the occasional Sunday dinner at his parents' house, and I've tagged along all of once. Three months ago, I got tired of dodging Gio's calls and brushing off his attempts at getting together, and agreed to have lunch with him.

It wasn't the worst experience in the world. Of course it was awkward as hell—that's a given—but it wasn't as bad as it could've been. He spent the first five minutes straight apologizing until I told him to stop because he was making me want to die. I think he caught on after that... My personality isn't like Lance's, whatsoever. And because he seems smart, I'm sure he realized he would have to approach me a lot differently than his adoptive son.

Really, the whole situation is enough for me to want to keep it at a full distance. The fact that Lance and I have the same father, though he's biologically related to me and not Lance, and *I'm* the one who wants nothing to do with him, but Lance still sort of does... It's definitely the kind of family nonsense they'd cover on a daytime talk show.

But I don't blame Lance at all for still wanting Gio in his life. He's his *father*. As we already know, blood doesn't mean family. And I don't

Trouble

mind having Gio around, but I prefer to think of him mostly as Lance's father.

That first time we got together, I told him I didn't want him asking about my *childhood*, or any crap like that.

"If you'd cared about me as a kid, you would've been there." My exact words.

And he agreed, because mainly I think he's just trying to smooth things over; he's trying to keep both me and Lance in his life without making things even weirder than they already are.

Naturally, my mother was upset when I first told her I'd had lunch with him. I get where she's coming from, too. She doesn't want him swooping in, charming me into letting my guard down, then hurting me in some way. But to that, I remind her that I'm a grown-ass man who's lived, and lived *awesomely*, for thirty-six years without a father. I don't *need* him for anything.

But my man does, and so for that reason, I play nice.

Let's not pretend my mother isn't concerned mostly because of her own ego, anyway. She's always been my only parent, and she doesn't want Gio replacing her, which is pure poppycock.

But parents are just people. Irrational, jealous, manipulative, emotional. They can be selfish at times. But then they can also be extremely *selfless*, giving up so much of their own happiness for their children.

I don't hold anything against my mother. I understand why she kept the details of her and Gio's relationship from me. At the time, I wouldn't have truly understood. But now I do. And I'd say everything worked out exactly as it was supposed to.

Lance and me getting together caused a ripple effect. None of this would have come to light if it weren't for me and him falling in love, and I find that pretty amazing. Sure, not all of it has been pretty, but we live out in the open now. Basking in the truth, and the sublime comfort that comes from not hiding shit.

It's that awakening that led us to where we are now...

Sitting in a cafe with our parents, preparing to break the good news.

"So good to see you, Tate." Gio smiles at me, as he does, like he's still overwhelmed and mystified by seeing me face to face. And he gives me one of those shoulder-pats, which is all I'll allow, contact wise.

"You look great, as usual, sweetie," Freja says to me, with one of her own kind smiles.

She's a nice woman. And *nothing* like my mother, which has me wondering about Gio's type. Because my mother would never let a man casually reveal an illegitimate child and just go about their life like nothing had happened.

Denial runs deep with some people, I suppose. But it's not my problem to worry about that. She's Lance's mother, and in terms of loving and supporting him, she's done alright. A bit vacant, shallow at times. But again... *It's none of my business.*

"Same to you, Freja," I tell her politely.

"Why don't I get us some coffees?" Lance stands, his hand resting on my back.

"I'll come with you." I peer up at him.

"Don't be silly, love." He gives me a look that's too smirky for my liking. "You stay. I'll be right back." He kisses my jaw, winking and sauntering off while I frown after him.

You transparent, sexy thing...

Taking a seat, I force a smile at Gio and Freja while they smile back. It's already awkward as shit, and I know it's only going to get worse. I guess I should just settle in and prepare for new levels of tension.

"So, Tate... how's work?" Gio asks, interested. He always seems fascinated by my career, which gives me some minute satisfaction that I choose not to dwell on.

"It's awesome," I answer, tapping my fingers on the table. "The market is hot right now, so there's a lot of buying and selling going on. Tons of new business."

"Any big work trips coming up?" Freja asks, illuminated. She's always more fascinated by the places I get to go for work, and the fact that her son gets to tag along most of the time.

But my muscles stiffen a bit at the question, and I gulp. "Uh, actually, I'll be staying in the New Mexico area for the next few months. Taking a little break from business trips..." My eyes lift and they're staring at me. "For the holidays."

They both make the *ah, I see* face, nodding along.

Oh boy, this is already weird.

I peek up at the counter to check on Lance. *How long does it take to get coffees?! Honestly...*

"When's the last time you guys saw Ellie?" I ask them, quickly shifting the conversation off of me.

Freja squeals. "Oh, we just had dinner at their house last weekend! My granddaughter is just the sweetest little cherub baby ever!"

Trouble

I grin while Gio pulls out his phone, no doubt to show me pictures. "Marcus and I spent almost the whole time putting together bouncy chairs and play pens and whatnot. The girl is spoiled rotten already."

Chuckling, I look at the pictures he's showing me of them with Ellie, Marcus and their baby daughter, Raelyn. She really is an adorable child.

Lance and I were in the hospital when she was born, and it was definitely a cool day. It reminded me of being in the hospital celebrating the births of my other nieces and nephews. That family experience I was always present for, as the bachelor uncle.

Something I never, *ever* thought I'd want for myself.

Shit, maybe I am growing up...

Lance finally returns with a drink tray of coffees, delivering them to us all before taking a seat at my side. His hand is immediately on my thigh while I'm sipping my cinnamon latte, knee bouncing rapidly beneath the table.

"How are things with you two?" Gio smiles at us. "Wedding plans coming along?"

"We got the save the date," Freja cheers.

"It's been a lot of fun," Lance sighs, peeking at me. The love and pure contentment on his face is enough to ease most of the tension I've been feeling for the last few weeks over this monumental impending change. "I don't know if I can wait until next year..." He gives me a teasing look, and I purse my lips. "But the reason we decided to hold off is because, well... We have some news."

God, this is probably the hundredth time we've announced this information and it's still just as nerve-racking as the first time we said it.

Gio and Freja are staring at us in suspension.

Lance lifts his brow at me like he's asking if I want to be the one to say it. But clearly, I'm frozen into the same befuddled statue I become every time we tell people.

"We're going to be parents," Lance croons, the smile on his perfect mouth simply enchanting. I swallow hard as he scoops up my hand, squeezing it. "Well, *temporary* parents to start."

Gio and Freja share a look.

Yea, that's the standard reaction. Pure, stupefied shock.

"We're fostering," I somehow manage to croak.

"And if it works out, then we'll be... adopting." Lance bites his lip, like he too is still stunned. *I'm glad I'm not the only one.*

"Oh, my goodness..." Freja gasps. "*Wow*... That's incredible!"

Nyla K.

"I did not expect that," Gio laughs softly, eyes wide.

"Yea, no one did," I grumble in amusement. "Not even us."

Lance chuckles, pulling out his phone for our own pictures. "His name is Charlie. He's six years old. His parents passed away when he was two and his aunt, who was his only available guardian, lost him to the state." He flashes some pained empathy. "It's really terrible. He's been bouncing around the system for a bit, so it might be tough at first, but he's such a sweet boy."

"You've met him?" Freja gapes, displaying her disbelief.

"We went for a sort of casual meeting type thing," I answer, remembering the day like it just happened minutes ago. "They don't tell the child anything until all the paperwork has gone through and they've done a bunch of home visits. It was kind of just like a, *here, meet these nice strangers* type vibe."

Gio appears blown away. "What's he like?"

"He's very quiet," Lance answers. "Nervous around new people, which is to be expected. But we got him talking after only a few minutes, which they said was a great sign."

He smiles at me, and I bite my lip.

"This is..." Freja's voice trails, and she shakes her head. "I'm so proud of you two. This is amazing. I'm sure he'll love living with you."

I hope so... I chew the inside of my cheek, still teetering on a tight rope over a massive vat of *what the fuck am I doing?!*

I've been going back and forth for the last two months, between jittery excitement and wanting to pull the dam ripcord on this whole thing.

I *never* saw myself as a parent. It was the last thing I ever thought I'd do... Raise a child. *I mean, I still feel like a child sometimes. How can I be expected to raise one??*

But then the more we talked about it, Lance and I, the more it started to make sense.

And I guess I kind of want to be what I never had growing up. Because I know what it's like to raise yourself, in a sense. Sure, I was lucky enough to have my mother, and she was great. But I did a lot of growing up on my own, so I know how difficult it can be.

If I could be even just a father-*figure* for a child who needs one... Well, I think that's something I might really love. As unlikely as it seems, and as out of my element as I know I'm going to be, I'm excited.

I mean, I'm freaking the fuck out, but then that's probably normal for any soon-to-be parent... Right?

Trouble

"You're really doing it," Gio says, starling me out of my thoughts. "You're starting a family... I'm just..." His voice cuts out in emotion, and he glances at the table to compose himself. "I'm so proud of you both. I'm happy for you, and I'm just so sorry that I ever thought it couldn't happen." He looks up at Lance. "I've never been more wrong about anything... To think that you needed to be with someone like Desiree to have a family."

"Dad..." Lance rasps, his voice husky with his own emotion as he shakes his head. "It's fine. We've moved on from that..."

"No, I know, but I can't believe what a fool I was," he goes on. "You and Tate are going to make amazing fathers. Better than I was, that's for sure." We try to wave him off, just being polite. *Because he has a bit of a point...* "You're doing this right. Being in love and taking in a child who needs that. Seriously... God bless you both."

Lance and I share a knowing look. It's the same stuff we've been talking about for the last few months...

How scared we are. How unsure, but also *sure*.

It's like despite the fear and uncertainty, it does feel right. Somehow, against all odds, it feels righter than anything.

Tate Eckhart... Adoptive father??

Am I in the bizarro world?!

Hours later, we're back at penthouse in Santa Fe, which we now own. The relief of everyone in our lives knowing about the fostering feels good. And now, all we have left to stress about is a six-year-old coming to live with us in a couple of weeks.

No big deal.

"How are you feeling, Trouble?" Lance asks while we sit out on the terrace, cuddled up on the chaise, legs tangled, hearts beating together in this love bubble we've been growing for the past year, which has expanded to places I'm not sure either of us expected.

"I'm cool as a cucumber, baby," I hum, and he chuckles.

"You're freaking your shit out, aren't you?" He grins down at me.

"And you're not??" I call him out. "You've gotta admit, this is huge, Hardy. Even for you."

He sighs. "It is huge. Planning a wedding and fostering a kid at the same time... I might need a hit of that weed pen of yours."

I laugh softly. "Get high while you still can, Sunshine. Once the kid gets here, it's bye bye booze, bye bye weed... Bye bye drawer full of easily accessible sex toys."

"Well, that's not true," he rumbles. "I know you didn't *actually* get rid of all that stuff..."

"Damn straight." I smirk. "I'm becoming a foster dad, I'm not *dying*."

"That's my fiancé," he chuckles, lifting my chin to kiss me softly.

"But seriously, though... It's locked up tight."

He grins. "I know, babe. You're going to be a good dad."

"Right..." I scoff, unable to hide my sarcasm. "*You're* going to be a good dad. I don't know shit about raising kids."

"What are you talking about?? Of course you do." He shoots me a pointed look. "You've been watching your best friends raise kids for years, and you're their favorite uncle."

"Because I ply them with toys and candy to make them like me," I huff.

"So? Do that with Charlie and you'll be golden." I shake my head, while he gazes at me, conveying the confidence he used to always think I had so much more of than him. But when it comes to things like this, being *sure* about love and responsibility, he's got me beat. "Look, we're just fostering for now. He knows we're not his *parents*, and chances are he'll be fine with that, as long as we show him that we care about him, and we're going to protect him, give him stability. And if we end up adopting him, he'll still know we're not his biological parents, because we'll have been honest about it... But we'll be his *family*. And who knows better than me and you how important that is?"

I nod, because I know he's right. But I'm still worried, and I know it's not something that'll go away with one of his pep talks.

"What if he hates me...?" I whisper, letting my vulnerability out for him, because he's the only person who takes it and holds it for me. He eases the burden of my insecurities by letting me be honest with him and never judging me. He's the best person I've ever met in my life, and I'm *so* damn blessed to be loved by him. "What if I'm too selfish and set in my ways?"

"You're *not* selfish, Tate," he says with certainty. "You haven't been selfish since you gave yourself to me. I know you're scared, baby, and trust me, I am too. I've told you that. I'm fucking petrified. But I also know that you and me together have so much love to give. And this boy deserves some." My throat closes with the tightness of all this heavy stuff. "The one thing I want you to remember is that we're doing this *together*, as *us*. You are going to stay you, no matter what, and he's going to love and appreciate you just the way you are. Like I do. Because you're awesome."

Grinning, I bite my lip, shifting my body so I can kiss his sweet, perfect mouth. Those lips that belong to me... The lips of a man who will be my husband one day.

And who knows? We might even become parents together.

In fact, I'm *sure* we will. Because even if it's something I never saw myself doing, I also never saw myself falling in love. I never saw myself being in a committed relationship, living with someone... getting married.

I never thought I would do any of the things I've *loved* doing with Lance Hardy. Because he's the exception to all my rules. The addendum to my bachelor code of detached superficiality.

He's the only one who's made me want more. Rays of sunshine cast over my dark doubts.

"We'll do this our way," I repeat his words back to him, with renewed confidence, and he nods. "Trouble and Sunshine... as badass parents."

He chuckles. "You know it, baby." He cups my butt hard while I purr.

"You'll be like the dorky dad," I hum, and he laughs. "The one who embarrasses him, because you're basically a hot landscaping nerd." He laughs. "And I'll be the cool dad who dresses him in Armani and buys him a sports car for his sixteenth birthday."

"We'll be the best of both worlds." He grins.

Kissing his bottom lip, I hum, "Thank you for dealing with me. Just know, I'm not gonna stop freaking out about this. I'm pretty much guaranteeing weekly panic attacks."

He rumbles. "Don't worry, Trouble. I've got you."

"Yea..." I blink at him. "You do."

"Fuck... fuckity fuck shit fuck."

"God help us," Lance chuckles, shaking his head. "This kid is gonna get suspended so many times."

"I told you..." I wring out my hands. "I'll tone down my cursing to fifty percent. But that's the best I can do."

He wraps his arms around my waist. "My sexy numbers man."

"Are we allowed to touch like this in front of him??" I shiver nervously. "It's not like... inappropriate or anything, right? Oh *God*, what if he's never seen gays before?! What if he's a little homophobe?!"

"I love how ridiculous you're being right now," he chuckles, kissing my neck.

Nyla K.

Yea, he says that a lot. Apparently, my fiancé is purely smitten with the things about me other's might find off-putting.

I guess that's how you know it's meant to be. When you not only tolerate your partner's bizarre, slightly obnoxious quirks, but love them.

The doorbell rings, and my heart flies up into my throat. It actually rocks my entire body to the point that Lance laughs.

"Relax, Daddy." He pats me on the ass, going for the security system by the door to buzz them in downstairs.

"Okay, I told you not to call me that," I hum. "It's turns me on way too much..."

He shoots me a wink. And the next two minutes go by in a haze. Before I know it, Lance is opening the door, and the social worker is coming inside, followed by a small, timid little boy with dark brown hair and wide blue eyes.

Our foster son.

The whole time, I'm just fluttering nervously, sweating all over, watching the kid while he looks around, and Lance does all of the talking to Lisa, our social worker. I follow them as they show Charlie around, getting him settled in his bedroom and dropping off his things, all the while quietly observant, as if there's an alien in our home.

Eventually, Lisa leaves. And it's just the three of us.

Me, Lance, and the extraterrestrial.

I've never been more out of my league. And I just need to keep reminding myself of Lance's words he's reassured me with over and over again.

You don't need to pretend to be anyone else.

Just be yourself. He'll love you the way you are... Like I do.

It was the only way I could wrap my head around being even a *potential* parent. Knowing I wouldn't have to morph into some strange new version of Tate just to be a dad.

I won't be buying a house in the suburbs with a picket fence. I'm not giving up my scotch, though I did quit smoking. And I still have my Maserati... But I bought a Mercedes sedan, so I could have a car with a back-seat just in case. It has a car seat in it, and so does Lance's truck... *It's wild.*

But I'm not changing my lifestyle just to be a parent, because who says parents need to behave a certain way? Who says you can't travel with your kids, live in a penthouse and eat sushi and drop the occasional F-bomb?

We're still going to be *us*, just with this boy in our lives. And it's scary, but I'm honestly eager to see how it works out.

I am excited to get to know this kid. And to be someone for him that I didn't have at his age.

"Are you hungry?" Lance asks Charlie, and he nods, peeking up at Lance.

Then he aims his deep blue eyes at me.

I stare back at him, lifting a brow.

Hello, strange creature.

"What would you like?" Lance asks. "Tate's pretty awesome at making Eggo waffles."

I glance at my fiancé and he smirks.

The room is silent for a few extended moments. "Do you like waffles?" I finally speak to the kid.

He just nods. Looking every bit as nervous and unsure of what to expect as I am.

"Okay, then," I breathe. "Waffle time."

"Waffle time..." he whispers, and I peer at him, a tiny grin twitching my lips.

The three of us go into the kitchen and I heat up an entire box of Eggo waffles while Lance makes humdrum chitchat with the boy. He's not speaking much, but that's to be expected.

They told us he's quiet as it is, and that it's pretty common for kids in the system to internalize and refrain from speaking. Charlie's been through a lot in his young life. I can barely even fathom what he's had to endure. So as nervous as I am having him here, I just want to make this a safe, comfortable space for him.

I want him to know that we're not just going to toss him out, turn our backs on him or anything. I'm sure it'll be difficult... We have a long road ahead of us, but the last thing I ever want him to think is that we're just going to dump him off when the going gets tough.

I would never do that. Fatherly or not, I'm no asshole.

When the waffles are done, we let him eat in the living room while watching TV. And the whole time, Lance and I are watching him, just staring at him like we have no earthly clue what to expect.

"I think this is going well," Lance says quietly.

"How can you tell?" I mutter. "Nothing's happened yet."

"I just mean he seems... comfortable." Lance chews his lower lip.

"Don't project, Sunshine." I shoot him a look. "If he's not comfortable right away, we have to be okay with it, remember?"

He narrows his gaze at me.

But then Charlie turns around, peeking at us over the back of the couch. He doesn't say anything, but I think he wants to...

"You good, bud?" Lance says.

And my heart fucking swells so large it nearly breaks my ribs, because he's already such a hot dad and I'm *dying*.

Charlie blinks at us.

Lance wanders over. "You need more juice?"

The kid looks at me. I stare back at him.

Slowly, I walk over to the couch. I don't know how I can tell, but I think he wants us to... sit with him.

So I slope down onto the couch. Lance gazes at me for a moment before taking a seat on his other side.

And Charlie lets a tiny grin out, going back to his waffles and the cartoon he's watching. I peer at Lance over his head, and Lance grins. He drapes his arm over the back of the couch, running his fingers along my shoulder.

With little Charlie in the middle.

Here's the thing...

I knew taking in a foster child would mean Lance and I probably wouldn't be having the amount of wild, loud, *voracious* sex we're used to. It's a sacrifice we just had to make, and maybe *slightly* begrudgingly, I was fine with it. *At first.*

But now it's been a week. Our first official week with Charlie in the house, and we haven't fucked not a once.

We've done *stuff. We're not dead.* The quiet blowies at night when we're sure he's asleep have been enrapturing, mainly because it's all we can get. But it just seems like we're afraid to actually fuck with him here.

I'm afraid of being too loud and scarring the poor kid for life, and Lance is terrified that he'll walk in while we're going at each other like wild animals, because we don't want to lock the bedroom door yet, since he's new here and still a bit reticent.

We got a baby monitor, just to be safe. His bedroom is down the hall, and we weren't sure if he has nightmares. He's woken up scared more than once since he got here, and Lance is always the one who ambles in there all *protective, comforting Daddy*, getting him a glass of water and calming him back to sleep.

Trouble

I'm still too nervous myself to go in. But I'm working up to it... *I think.*

So yea... I haven't been pounded into oblivion in one week, and it's making me a little grouchy and irritable. I don't want to take it out on the kid, so right now, I'm focusing on work.

In my office, I'm shuffling through some papers, scrolling spreadsheets on my laptop, when movement catches my eye. The door, which was open a crack, pushes open more and in shuffles the small being. He wanders around my office, poking at things, while I watch him, flabbergasted that this is my life right now.

Eventually, I just go back to work, because why not? He can come in here and look at stuff while I'm working. I'm sure it's fine. I'm not easily distracted.

"Um... Tate?" His little voice creeps up at me, and my eyes shift.

"Yea?"

"What are you doing?" He asks, stepping carefully over to my desk.

He's been opening up and speaking more and more, which is a great sign. But he talks to Lance a lot more often than he does to me. I guess we're still feeling each other out.

"Working," I rumble my answer, typing numbers on my keyboard.

"What kind of *working*?" His voice is small and inquisitive. It's really cute, I'll give him that.

Actually, the kid is adorable. With his messy strands of dark brown hair, tanned complexion and deep ocean blue eyes. We don't know too much about his parents, but Lisa mentioned that they were Latinx.

"Well," I sigh, "I'm inputting projections for investment growth." I point at the screen. "These are percentages of capital investment, to infer profits."

He blinks his wide eyes at my face, and I chuckle.

"Am I speaking gibberish to you right now?" I grin.

He blinks again.

I hand him my calculator. "Here. Play with this."

He presses the buttons, rather aggressively, while I go back to my work, smiling softly to myself. After only about five minutes, he gets bored and leaves. But to my surprise he returns with his dinosaurs and sits on the floor of my office, playing with them while I work.

It goes on for a bit, until my back is stiff. Stretching, I glance down at him. He seems perfectly content to play by himself, I guess because he's used to it. But I'm excited to get him back to school so he can be around kids again.

Nyla K.

He's due to start school here after the break. In the meantime, we're going to Ben, Ryan and Jess's for Thanksgiving, and it'll be everyone's first time meeting Charlie. It might be a little stressful for him, meeting the family. But at least there will be kids there he can play with, though not exactly his age. Still, it should be fun.

And fucking bizarre.

Lance had to run out to handle some crisis at one of his job sites. He was supposed to be off work for the next three weeks, to spend tons of time with Charlie while he's getting acclimated. After which we're going to rotate our work schedules so one of us is always with him. The plan is to do that for a few months, while we process the adoption paperwork. And once all of that is set, we'll consider a nanny, just for the times when we both have to work, which hopefully won't be that often.

It's nuts, but we're pretty much already onboard with adopting the kid. We're going to give it some more time, but the way Charlie has already settled into life with us, it just feels like a perfect fit.

And no, it hasn't been easy. But believe it or not, it's been much easier than we thought it'd be. So we're taking that as a sign.

At the same time, there is the possibility that his aunt could get her life together and come to take him back. Lisa said it's unlikely, but it *could* happen. And that presents us with a crossroads... Would we rather let him go back to his *family*, or should *we* be his family?

Together, we agreed that it should be us. Because blood *doesn't* always mean the best, most capable option for a child. Nothing against his aunt, but we're never going to let him come to any harm on our watch.

I can try to be a dad... And I know I'll be a damn good one, whether I seem like a typical one or not.

"Hey, kid..." I call, and he looks up. "You want a happy meal?"

His eyes light up, a big smile covering his lips as he nods animatedly.

See? I got this.

Hours later, we're back from McDonald's, settled on the couch watching *Toy Story*—the first one. One of the only kid movies I'll watch, because it's from when I was a kid, and it still holds up.

I'm chuckling at the tea party with Mrs. Nesbitt scene when Lance comes in, and his face splits in half at the sight of us. Charlie is dozing off, with his head resting on my arm. Stifling my own grin, I peek up at my fiancé and wink.

We're freaking doing it, man!

Lance gets Charlie to bed, and we head off ourselves. But of course, because it's only ten at night, I can't sleep. And I'm *hungry* as fuck for some of that thorough dicking that makes me come cross-eyed, which I haven't gotten from my man in *way* too long.

Kissing turns heated in an instant, and we're writhing around, rubbing our dicks together, trying to be quiet while he pins me to the bed and grinds into me, still reminding me of that night in my dorm all those years ago... When he was just my curious friend who thought he was my brother.

Good freaky hot times.

"Fuck me, baby..." I whisper into his mouth, and he growls. "Fuck me fuck me—"

A whimper freezes us both solid, our eyes flinging to the screen of the monitor. Charlie must have had a bad dream. He's up and crying.

"Fuck me..." I sigh, frustrated as hell and burning alive.

Lance drops his head onto my chest for a moment. "It won't be like this for much longer, baby. We just need to be there for him... while he gets used to this."

I nod and exhale. "I know."

He starts to sit up, crawling off the bed slowly, most likely waiting for his erection to die down before he goes to get the kid.

But I stop him, grabbing his arm. "Can I... go?"

Lance beams, nodding slowly, shooting me with so much love in his eyes. He takes my face in his hands and kisses me softly. "I love you so much, Trouble. I can't believe we're here... doing this together. And I can't *wait* to make you my husband."

"Ditto," I tease, and he smacks me in the chest. "I love you forever, Sunshine. No matter what."

"No matter what."

Getting up, I wander slowly up the hall, to Charlie's room. He's on the floor, looking underneath his bed.

My forehead creases. "What are you doing, kid?"

"Looking for monsters," he says, like it's the most normal thing ever.

"That's pretty ballsy." I kneel down next to him, peering under the bed with him. "You see anything?"

"No..." He sighs. "I guess I woke up for no reason." I chuckle. "I'm sorry, Tate."

"For what?"

"Waking you up," he whispers.

Sitting down on his bed, I pat the mattress next to me. And he gets in. "Don't apologize for that. You're allowed to be scared. We all are."

"You get scared?" He asks, intrigued.

I huff a soft laugh. "Oh yea. Big time."

"Of what?"

"Grown-up stuff," I tell him. "Failure... Change."

"Is Lance scared of that too?" He asks intently.

"Lance isn't scared of anything." I wink at him, peeking at the camera that feeds to the monitor. Getting him settled back in bed, I scoot in close. "I made up a song for him. You wanna hear it?"

Charlie nods.

"Now, admittedly, I'm not the best singer ever. But still... better than Johnny Cash." I smirk, knowing Lance is watching and listening right now.

"Who's *Johnny Cash*?" Charlie asks.

"Exactly," I chuckle. "Alright, here goes." And I start singing, softly, "You are my sunshine... my only sunshine. You make me happy when skies are gray. You'll never know, dear..." my eyes slide to the camera once more, "how much I love you. Please don't take... *my sunshine*... away."

"You didn't make up the song," Charlie yawns. "I've heard it before."

"You caught me, kid," I laugh, tucking him in. Then I get up. "Sleep tight, little trouble."

"Goodnight, big trouble," he murmurs sleepily.

And my heart is melting as I leave the room, going back to my man.

My man who attacks me with kisses the moment I return.

My man, who's given me everything I never thought I could have... Everything I never knew I *needed*.

My man who brought light back into my life, who makes me happy, when skies are gray.

My *only* Sunshine, my troubled pastor. I'm his tainted flock.

And nothing will *ever* feel as right as a life spent living out in the wide-open sky... with him.

The End.

If you, or anyone you know, is struggling with their sexuality, or coming out, please just know I'm always here to listen.

We are all worthy of love, and the gifts of this life.

This year, *Trouble* (the novella version) as part of *Worthy: A Pride Anthology*, helped to raise money for a wonderful organization called The Trevor Project, in support of LGBTQ+ youth. Check out their site for resources, and as an ally, consider supporting this great nonprofit.

Another great nonprofit organization with resources for empowering LGBTQ youth around the world is It Gets Better Project. Check them out here!

A new website established during the pandemic, Free 2 Luv, is a great place to find support. Check it out here!

Always be unapologetically *you*.

A note from Nyla

Why, hello there!

I see you've found your way to the end of this book! That's good. Hopefully, you've been thoroughly satisfied (giggity) with your reading experience!

How much *trouble* did this book get you into? Did your partner kick you out of the bed for being too frisky? Did your vibe burn out?? Hopefully you didn't lose your job or forget to pick up your kids from school because you were too busy reading.

LOL okay, stop fucking around, Nyla. Get to the point.

This is the part of my books where I do a nice lil recap of all the research, inspiration, motivation and revelation that went into writing the novel. Mostly it's just be ranting and raving. But believe you me, there was a ton to unpack in this book, being that I've known Tate Eckhart for about five years now, and all along, he's been every bit the sassy, ostentatious lover of *himself* you've hopefully grown to adore as much as I do.

So without further adieu, here we go! Let's talk *Trouble*, shall we?!

Push! (*She names another book lol*)

It all started there. For those of you who read *Push*, you were most likely intrigued by Tate. Maybe not... But how could you not be?? He's *fantastic*. And even though he was technically *the bad guy* in that book, I think we could all sense there was probably a little more to his character than met the eye, which must be why I got so many messages, comments, and questions about whether he'd get his own book someday!

463

A note from Nyla

Seriously, many of y'all were incessant, and frankly, I was very much here for it.

I can't say that I went into *Push* knowing I'd one day write a book for Tate, but as soon as I was done with it, I sure as shit wanted to. All it took was one message asking for it, and I jumped on board so fast, I practically capsized.

Naturally, it took a little while for me to figure out Tate's situation, *and* for his perfect opposite to start speaking up... In the form of a tall, shy introvert with a heart just *begging* to be shaken up by the likes of our Trouble.

And then last year, I wrote the *Push goes to Pride* bonus scene for *Pull*, and *bam!*

There was Lance Hardy. Tate's mysterious former friend he was caught blowing by Ben and Ryan. ;)

We'll get to Lance in a minute, but first I'm going to talk about Tate a little more, and his connection to the *Push* boys—*cool name, right??!*

As I'm sure is apparent, Tate Eckhart isn't without his flaws. I mean, *he* thinks he's perfect lol. But then he also clearly knows he isn't. Though, that's not the side of him we see in *Push*, which is why I was so *very* excited to tell his story.

In *Push*, it almost seems like Tate is just sleeping with Ryan to get a rise out of Ben, am I right? And whenever Tate and Ryan were together, it's reiterated time and again that Tate *doesn't do serious*. He's *Mr. Casual*.

But I'm here to tell you that I knew *right away* there was more to it than that!

I'm not saying Tate was in love with Ryan or anything, but he definitely had a stronger *like* for Ryan than with his other casual sexual partners, and I think that, mixed with seeing the repercussions of his actions on someone so hopelessly in love with Ryan as Ben, gave Tate a little nudge in the right direction—the *love* direction.

Listen, we all know I could talk about Ben and Ryan for the rest of my life, as could I write a zillion more pages of them being in love because they're my OG babies and they'll always hold an *extremely* special place in my heart. But this is Tate's book and I can *hear* him rolling his eyes right now, so I have to stop. Basically, for all of the *Push* lovers out there, I hope you had as much fun seeing Ben and Ryan (and Jess lol) again as I had writing them again.

Speaking of the side characters in this book, we also get to see that close-knit group of friends we met in *Push & Pull*. I know they're not the most memorable characters ever, and they have the most average of names, (*I'm looking at you, Bill and Greg, and your wives*), but still, they're just as much Tate's friends as they are Ben's. Not even mentioning Jacob Lockwood—the Beavis to Tate's Butthead.

I *loved* seeing Tate and Jake Lockwood's adorable bromance up close and personal.

The point is that Tate has a *type* when it comes to his friends. Most of them are straight, married with kids, and insanely different from him. And guess what? I'm *living* for that.

Like Tate does, I find it offensive to insinuate that gay guys can only hang out with gay guys or straight women, because I've never known that to be the case. So, I *personally* love the fact that Tate, a guy who came out as fully gay in high school, considers these *boring married dudes* to be his best friends in the world. *And* he hasn't hooked up with *not a one of them*!!

It's refreshing and awesome, as is how supportive everyone in his life is of his sexuality. It's almost as if his sexuality doesn't *define* him...

Because it doesn't.

Tate Eckhart is a lot of things, and *gay* is just one small section of the label.

However, there is one straight friend of Tate's who gave him more than a little grief for a while there...

It's our dirty-talkin preacher Sunshine himself, Lance Hardy.

From the moment we meet Lance (even in *Pull*) it's super obvious that he and Tate are basically polar opposites. We know that Tate likes to surround himself with friends who are fascinated by him, while Lance likes to surround himself with friends who are extroverted and can help break him out of his timid shell a bit.

They did have a great friendship, but it was also clear from the jump that there were pretty strong feelings beneath the surface, from both sides, which I think was a factor in Lance running out on Tate in college.

There was no hope of him sticking around just to be Tate's *friend*. The hooking up was inevitable, like three years of attraction bubbling to the surface, despite Lance having found out the *truth*.

Honestly, I won't beat a dead horse on the reason Lance didn't just tell Tate the truth about his father in *college*, right after he found out, as opposed to keeping quiet and leaving him, *or* why it took him sixteen years to finally spill the beans and confront Gio...

He pretty much summed it up himself.

Above all else, Lance wanted to protect Tate. That was the main reason.

Was there also a sliver of self-interest there? Of course. As is the case with most martyrs, you're content to carry the burden of pain, and sacrifice yourself for others... But it's still inherently selfish, in that it's your *choice* to do so.

Aha, philosophy!

A martyr is a martyr because they want to be a martyr. Simple as that.

When Lance first found out what Gio was hiding, I'm sure he wanted to believe he could hold the secret inside and remain *just friends* with Tate. But as we now know, the attraction was just too strong. And Lance's own inner guilt, shame, confusion anger prompted him to flee. It was the easiest option to ensure Tate was still protected from the truth.

And to be honest, Lance wasn't necessarily *wrong* to leave. I mean, look how well Tate turned out...How much of that do you think was in spite of the best friend/potential first love who left him?

Yes, he became a bit emotionally stunted as a result, but he *also* turned into a strong, successful man, who started from the damn bottom and rose to the top. That might never have happened if Lance had revealed the *bio-dad secret* while they were still in college. And if he had stayed, and they got together, maybe Tate wouldn't have honed his career and self-confidence the way he did.

While I'm sure it's the last thing he wants to recognize, there are great similarities between Lance and his adoptive father, Gio, in terms of their behaviors and instinctual reactions, though let's not pretend Gio didn't hold onto his own secrets mostly out of self-preservation. Still, I do believe a tiny bit of him had Lance's best interest at heart in some of the things he did... And as we see at the end, Gio was very much remorseful, and interested in knowing Tate *now*, even though we know it's too little too late for a father-son relationship.

Let me ask this... Prior to finding out the *truth* about why Lance left, how many of you were irritated by his behaviors with Tate?

Did you think he was acting selfishly? When it seemed like Lance left Tate because he was afraid to confront his sexuality, did you find him cowardly?

If you did, those feelings would be totally valid (to some degree, anyway).

I went into writing this book knowing some of it might frustrate some of you (*lol*), and that when you find out Tate and Lance are *blood-related*, it might gross out or disturb some of you... *And* also that when we find out they're *not* actually blood-related, it might disappoint some of you! (*Haha! Those of you who feel that way know what I'm talking about!*)

Really, I think the point is that regardless of how plot twists go down, not everyone will be satisfied (*story of my publishing career lol*).

No but seriously, it's true. This story is emotionally *messy*. But hopefully, a majority of you came away from it knowing one thing with certainty: that Tate and Lance's love shines as bright as the sun, and burns just as strong.

Maybe that sounds corny, but fuck it. I feel like these two are *made* for each other.

Lance is the perfect, adoring, stoic and generous piece to Tate's charming, snarky, troublemaker. Lance has forever more confidence in *everyone else* than himself, and Tate has enough confidence in *himself* to last a lifetime. So they lean on each other for support; a perfect ebb and flow.

This is why I'm just so GD obsessed with writing opposites attract. There's nothing quite like that sweet give and take, imo!

Speaking of Lance's martyrdom (*is that really a word??*), and his lack of confidence in his true identity, I'm sure you can tell it mostly stems from Gio, and his stifling religious upbringing.

Here's the thing... I don't *always* set out to write books with *religion versus faith* undertones, but sometimes it just happens. It's something I feel very strongly about—*clearly*—especially as it pertains to acceptance of love and equality in all forms in the church, the hypocrisy of organized religion, and the recognition that true faith in *God* comes mainly from faith in *ourselves*.

So much of Tate's independence and him referencing having to *raise himself*, in a sense, that was taken from my own life. I was fortunate enough to have my mother *and* father growing up—*and to still have them today*—but that doesn't mean, by any means, that my childhood was perfect. Because simply having parents around doesn't mean you're going to have a wonderful childhood, just like being raised by a single parent doesn't mean you'll have a poor childhood. It's all circumstantial.

Tate saying that parents are *just people, not superheroes*, is an important point. As kids, we see our parents (or guardians) as *gods* in a way. They make the sun rise for us. But as we grow older, and maybe become parents ourselves, we realize that our parents have always just been people trying to live their lives. *Some of us learn that lesson sooner than others.*

But anyway, let me reel myself back in. *Independence*, I feel, plays a big part in self-acceptance, which leads to true faith in oneself. And faith in *yourself* is faith in *God*, because *God* made us—*a similar notion to Lance's sermon in chapter sixteen I think.*

Just know that when I say *God*, in no way do I mean an old man with a beard sitting in the clouds, or even a man like Jesus. I mean the *spiritual God, Allah, Krishna*, the earth, the elements, the universe, the simulation, literally *whatever* you want to call it. To me, God is a *feeling*; an understanding that we're not meant to full understand...

There are no right or wrong answers to the questions of the universe, no black and white, truths or fictions. We must find peace in the chaos, and take solace in the reality that we're not meant to *know*.

Anyway, oh my GOD, I can't believe I'm already spouting this third-eye acid trip shit. LOL okay, back to the point once more...

Lance Hardy never really wanted to follow in his father's footsteps and become this strictly *Pentecostal* pastor, preaching the words of the *Holy Bible* as pure fact, not to be interpreted (*because that's ridiculous... The Bible is a* book. *Of course it's open to interpretation.*) But in disguising himself with the martyr's shroud, he stuffed down his own inner truths, because he thought it was best, to live comfortably drama-free rather than happy.

Listen, here's something else I could jump onto a soapbox and yell about for hours... You are *not meant to understand*, comprehend, or relate to the journey *someone else takes* toward coming out.

Can we say it again, louder, for those in the back that might not have heard?

Every person who comes out of the closet has *their own experience*; takes their own path. Some people, like Tate, have no issues coming out. They have confidence in their sexuality, and are blessed with a fantastic support system. Others are not so lucky.

Lance Hardy coming out was one of the more emotional journeys to a character discovering sexual identity I've ever written. If you know anything about living life as a queer person within the church, you'll know what I'm talking about.

It can be hell. Even when people smile in your face, their support often isn't genuine, and when that type of stuff comes from your own *family*, it can be very damaging... And it can set you back a lot of years.

In the club in New York, when Lance finally admitted to himself that he was gay... I'm telling you, I had a hard time editing that scene because I cried *every time. Happy tears*! But still.

It just felt so very powerful, and I really hope the emotions came through there, because I wrote that with my *soul*, as if Lance was speaking through me. And him having Tate there, to share that moment... Their do-over in the club listening to *Teenage Dream* lol... It was everything.

Moving on... I'm not going to get into how reviled the *"cheating trope"* is in romance. The fact that many readers will read straight up on-page sexual assault before they'll read infidelity blows my motherfucking mind-hole open. But hey... again... *Not gonna talk about it.*

Basically, one of the main similarities between *Push* and *Trouble* is the cheating on a spouse, the sneaking around and lying about it, and the ulti-mate dramatic confrontation.

The dinner scene with Lance's wife, is one of my faves. *Gahhh* the tension that cheating can bring to romantic fiction is unrivaled in my opin-ion. It makes me feel more things than some of the forced *darkness* or *taboo* factors even can. Throw cheating in there and I'm hooked, because the angst and emotional pain feels *so damn good* to overcome.

Before finding out about Desiree's dishonesty, Lance was more or less behaving like a selfish shitbag. I mean, cheating is *bad*. We *know* that. There is absolutely nothing wrong with getting a divorce! If you've grown apart, you've grown apart. Sure, it can be rough in a lot of ways, but the reason why so many people cheat in real life is because there's *still* a stigma to this day on divorce, and it's ridiculous.

There's also way too much unnecessary societal pressure to get married, but that's a whole other thing.

Nevertheless, here's the cold hard truth: cheating happens. It just does. And honestly, treating it like it's worse than rape in romance books gives me the major *icks*.

But like I said, I'm trying really hard not to lecture here lol.

So yes. Lance *cheats* on his wife. *Gasp!*

And *yes*, it kind of sucks. She does turn out to be not the best person, but she's not *evil*, and neither is he. It's just something that happened, all due to his lack of confidence in his true self as a gay man, which is why empowering people to come out as their true selves is *so damn important*.

In the grand scheme, Lance cheating on his wife for a few weeks is more than justified after years of stuffing down his identity and not being with the man he loved. *I said what I said.*

He showed contrition and told the truth, that's what matters most. (*This is from the mouth of the author, but you don't need to agree with me. Just know that if you* do*, you get it, and if you* don't*, maybe ask yourself why... What's your motivation for hating cheating so much it's worse than assault? Just curious lol*).

A note from Nyla

Okay, end rant!!!

Another quick point... I have to mention the juxtaposition between Tate's mother, Sloane's relationship with Gio Hardy, and Tate falling into a relationship with his son, who's also a pastor. There are some interesting ties to these two relationships, but I'm only going to mention one for now; their personalities—Tate is similar to his mother and Lance is similar to Gio, though I'm sure neither of them want to be.

There's a lot more I could say about Tate and Lance's entwined families, but I'm trying to refrain. The thing is that the truth of what *really* happened between Sloane and Gio lies somewhere in between their two sides of the story... But *this story* isn't theirs. And sometimes knowing all the facts doesn't help you move on any easier.

Tate and Lance are not brothers. Lance's real father died shortly before he was born, and Gio Hardy adopted and raised him. Sloane was so fixated on her hatred of her son's absent father, she almost became an absent mother.

Freja probably knew much more than she was letting on... She likely knew Gio was in a relationship when he started seeing her, she might've even known Gio was turning his back on another child to help raise hers. I think it's clear that she was probably also involved in shoving Desiree at Lance, in order to keep him from potentially going back to Tate.

Why did Gio wait to stop paying Tate's tuition until after the falling out happened between Tate and Lance? And how did he even know it was a falling out? Did he just see Lance moping around and assume, or was he watching his son more closely...?

These are questions that don't need concrete answers, because again, sometimes having more details prevents you from moving forward. The past *is* the past, and Tate and Lance have done an impeccable job of overcoming it. Falling in love so deep and hard (giggity), reigniting feelings that were buried for so many years...

I think Tate says it at one point, but they learn to stop resenting the pain they both experienced, from one another, their family issues and their sullied past, and see their relationship for what it is in the present...

Fate. Part of the plan. Written in the stars.

And it's this faith in their love that leads them both away from fear and toward a bright future... Getting married, and adopting a son.

Here's the real kicker, man... Never in a *million years* did I expect Tate to become a father.

I did *not* go into writing this story thinking I would *ever* end it with

A note from Nyla

Tate and Lance raising a little boy together. But as I was writing, it just started to feel more and more *right* for them.

If you've read my books, you know I'm usually pretty opposed to the addition of children (*sorry not sorry... I'm not a kid person*). I don't care for the notion that *everyone* needs to become a parent.

Of course, Ben, Ryan and Jess are my only characters who had a baby (after my debut trilogy), and for them it felt right too. But for Tate and Lance... Fostering just made *perfect sense*. And *nothing* made my heart melt like Velveeta faster than picturing Tate Eckhart holding the hand of an adorable little boy, bringing him shopping, or talking to him about numbers like the kid had the slightest clue what he was saying.

Seriously, I had to physically *force* myself to stop writing Tate's epilogue where I did, otherwise it could've gone on forever.

That said, there will *definitely* be more Tate and Lance. Most likely another continuation novella, because I just need to experience Tate as a nervous, *non-dad-like* dad. It's already the cutest thing I've ever seen in my mind.

So the moral of this story is even when Nyla thinks she can wrap something up quick... It still takes forever. *LOL!*

No, the real overarching message in this book is about found family. The family you choose versus the family you get.

Blood doesn't always equal what you *need*; the family that's good for you. Does that mean you simply write them off? Of course not. But it's good to recognize that your friends can be your family, and there's nothing wrong with that.

Just because you're raised by someone who doesn't share your blood, doesn't mean they're not your parent, and even if you're an independent badass, hustling your way through life, you still need supportive people to have in your corner.

And thus concludes one of the longest author's notes in history! *It might be coming close to Fragments!*

Quick honorable mention to some new side characters who were so fun to meet... Troy, Tate's assistant. I absolutely *love* Troy's bubbly personality and how it just seems to bring out Tate's inner grouchy bitch. Lance (*and Tate's lol*) sister, Ellie, and her awesome AF partner, Marcus (*yes, modeled after Daddy Marcus Parks from Last Podcast On The Left*). And how about Tate's fellow bankers at his firm?? They were interesting... Especially Josiah Pierce... *What's up with him?*

;-)

471

A note from Nyla

Honorable mentions to New York City, Toto Ramen and Hardware (the restaurant and club they went to, not mentioned by name, but that's what I was going for), Flaming Saddles and just Hell's Kitchen overall because it's the best, Papaya Dog, Tate's Maserati, Econ305 (from *How I Met Your Mother*), Johnny Cash, Jake's dog named AC Slater, vibrating/thrusting butt plugs, Element (which was a gay club in Providence me and my best friend used to go to *long* before we were 21), how disgusting sunflowers look in the middle, the great states of Arizona and New Mexico which I know absolutely nothing about, and... back bush.

Done.

Suffice it to say, if you made it to this point, you win the title of *Nyla K Rambles Fan*. But in all seriousness, hopefully you're just as satisfied as I am with our *Troublesome Tale*, four years in the making!

Nothing has made me happier than to carry Tate and Lance around with me for the last few months. And although it was stressful at times, I am just so very in love with the two of them. Their chemistry, their history, their deeply-rooted love... and of course, their EPIC, elaborate and frequent bouts of delicious sex!

If you want to see how I've grown as a writer over the last four years, read a *Push* sex scene, then read a *Trouble* sex scene. *LOL. Honestly.*

And that's no shade on *Push* at all. It's normal to grow and evolve in your craft. But I'm just sayin, these poundtown scenes have been glowed up times a hundred!

Another reason I'm so happy I get to revisit Ben, Ryan, and Jessica here in the future...

Because they were the beginning. My first.

Started in the basement, now we here ;)

And trust me, it's far from over.

Acknowledgments

I'm going to start by thanking, whilst simultaneously chastising, literally everyone who's been physically around me for the last three months.

Writing this book was like an experiment in how much shit can be thrown at Nyla while she attempts to write a book. Pretty much everything that could go wrong did, all of the drama in the world was dumped all over my head, and I've *never* been more distracted. The fact that I was even able to finish this book two months after I'd planned to release it is nothing shy of miraculous. So I'm going to thank my friends and family, and Patrick, for not commenting on how much of an under-the-bridge troll I became, but also say a sarcastic, *"thanks a lot,"* for the constant distractions. You made it so I didn't even think I liked this book until I was completely done... And then it turned out that I love it and I'm obsessed. So... thanks? I guess?

To Team Nyla, aka Amber & Karie... Now, *you guys* get a genuine thank you. Because I'm sure there were times when you thought I was dead... But you just kept on trucking, not bothering me, responding to comments and messages for me, being my rocks, checking to make sure I was eating, sleeping and drinking water... You know, the things I need to survive lol. I just love and adore you both and I'm so beyond grateful to have friends who are also my readers, who are also my squad, who are also my sisters... I could go on. Love you my babes. Fuheva.

To my editor, Kay... Bruh, I don't even know what to say. If I thought you were going to have me committed after *Double-edged*, or *Fragments*... Or writing that 40k antho story in 4 days... This one would've been the straitjacket that wrapped me up because I just... don't even know how we got this done. Seriously, how did we?? I'll go out on a limb and say your love for Tate is the *only* reason we actually accomplished this. And surprise surprise... It came out amazing. So, I'll buy you a GranTurismo for Christmas ;)

To Kenzie, of Nice Girl Naughty Edits... My proofreader, and someone

I can honestly call one of my best friends. Dude, I'm laughing while writing this because of how ridiculous this entire process was. I can't even believe this book is actually done and going to be released. It doesn't feel real. Thank you for dealing with delay after delay, change after change to your schedule... Honestly, how you didn't just block me I have no idea lol. But seriously, you're just incredible. Hooking you was the best thing I ever did. You can have Tate as a best friend. On me.

To Melissa, aka Mel D. Designs, who made this fabulous cover and graphics I used months before the book was even done LOL. Thank you for capturing the essence of Tate in this cover, but also giving it subtle *Push* vibes! You really nailed it. I'm so grateful to have you as a friend, an artist, and a fellow Mainer!

Thank you to Andi Jaxon... GORL... I can't even with how much I adore you. I'm so happy to have met you for five minutes in London and formed a lifelong bond based on how unorganized and anxiety-ridden we are LOL. Thank you for doing my formatting and making me beautiful graphics and just being a generally bomb-ass human being. Rock the fuck on, babe. I'll get you a Maserati too while I'm at it.

To Nisha from Passion Author Services... Thank you so so SO much for handling the PR on this release that's been delayed more times than planes coming out of JFK. I appreciate you staying patient with me and understanding that I can't force my genius (omg I'm totally just kidding lol. I'm sleep-deprived so I'm only twenty-percent sure I'm actually writing this right now. But if I am... you're amazing!)

To the Flipping Hot Fandom... I couldn't do *anything* I do without you guys. At this point, I'm totally reliant on you. You guys are always there for me, supporting me, hyping me up when I feel so low I'm practically underground. You always understand that when I go silent for a few days, it doesn't mean I'm ignoring you or slacking off... It's because I quite literally can't tear myself away from my control-freakish nature to work myself to the bone. I do it for you guys, and that's not to say I think you *expect* me to destroy myself, because I know you don't... But you make me want to be the best possible author/business I can be. I promise I'll keep hooking you guys up with extra goodies because if anyone deserves it...

And to the Flipping Hot Readers, the fans, the ARC readers of this book, and anyone's who's been patiently waiting for TATE MOFREAKING ECKHART... Thank you all so much for your love and understanding! I say this to my family and friends all the time, but I'm fully certain that I have the best readers in the whole damn world. You badasses don't harass me (maybe in a fun joking way lol but I like that), you don't attack me for delaying releases, or for closing my signed books shop for more than half the year... You understand that what I do can't be rushed, but also that I work myself hard af because it's who I am. And I think you're confident that if I'm ever late with something, it's because I'm putting my soul into it, and it'll be worth it in the end. Because you rock. You are all Tate... Unapologetically fucking awesome. Middle fingers up forever, fam!

Also by Nyla K.

Thank you for reading

Flipping Hot Fiction by Nyla K

Subscribe to my Patreon for bonus content, like *The Vacation* (PUSH/Alabaster Pen, etc. Crossover), and more!

The Midnight City Series:

Andrew & Tessa's Trilogy

(Forbidden/Age Gap, celebrity romance, suspense. Read in order)

Midnight City (TMCS #1)

Never Let Me Go (TMCS #2)

Always Yours (TMCS #3)

Alex & Noah

Seek Me (TMCS #4 – Standalone/Spin-off, Friends to lovers/Angst)

Unexpected Forbidden Romance:

PUSH (Standalone, Taboo/MMF)

PULL (Continuation novella!)

Trouble (Spinoff, MM, second chance)

(Stay tuned for audio news!)

To Burn In Brutal Rapture (Standalone, Taboo/Age Gap)

Double-edged (Standalone, MMM Age Gap, Twincest – **BANNED by Amazon!** Can be found on Nyla's website, Google Play, Lulu, & Eden Books.)

For The Fans (Standalone, MM, Stepbrothers) Also available is audio!

Alabaster Penitentiary:

Distorted, Volume 1 (MM, prisoner/prison guard, dub-con, mindf*ck) Audio available now!

Joyless, Volume 2 (MMF, the guards, second chance, forbidden) Also available in audio!

Brainwashed, Volume 3 (MM, doctor/patient, true crime) Audio coming early 2024!

Fragments, Volume 4 (MM, frenemies to lovers)

Shadowman, Volume 5 (MM, bi-awakening) – Coming in 2024!

Ivory, Volume 6 (The Finale)

The Control Room, a FREE Alabaster Pen short!

Twisted Tales Collection:

Serpent In White (A drug cult MMM poly retelling of *The White Snake*)

Standalone Novella:

Unwrap Him by Nyla K (An Age Gap, Taboo MM) – Available across all digital retailers, and Nyla's website!

Join my Facebook reader group for discussions, giveaways, and all the best Nyla K madness!

Don't forget to share and leave a review! It means the world!

About the Author

Hi, guys! I'm Nyla K... Author of Flipping Hot Fiction, which basically means all things unique & boundary-pushing! If you're looking for the same old story, you won't find it here. I'm the... *bad guy* ;)

I'm an awkward sailor-mouthed lover of all things romance, existing in the Dirty Lew, up in Maine, with my fiancé, who you c

an call PB, or Patty Banga if you're nasty. When I'm not writing and reading sexy books, I'm rocking out to my various awesome playlists, cooking yummy food and fussing over my kitten (and no, that's not a euphemism). Did I mention I have a dirtier mind than probably everyone you know?

I like to admire hot guys (don't we all?) and book boyfriends, cake and ice cream are my kryptonite. I can recite every word that was ever uttered on *Friends*, *Family Guy*, and *How I Met Your Mother*, red Gatorade is my lifeblood, and I love to sing, although I've been told I do it in a Cher voice for some reason. I'm very passionate about the things that matter to me, and art is probably the biggest one. If you tell me you like my books, I'll give you whatever you want. I consider my readers are my friends, and I welcome anyone to find me on social media any time you want to talk books or sexy dudes!

Get at me:

AuthorNylaK@gmail.com
    Visit AuthorNylaK.com for Banned books, Signed Books & Merch!

The Flipping Hot Newsletter!
    Patreon: Where you'll find Nyla K UNCENSORED!

Instagram:@AuthorNylaK

Facebook: AuthorNylaK

Tiktok: @NylaKAuthor

Twitter: @MissNylah
    (Misc uncensored content! NSFW!)

Goodreads: Nyla K

BookBub: @AuthorNylaK

Happy reading!

Made in the USA
Monee, IL
04 April 2025

15158194R00288